BRYCE COURTENAY is the bestselling author of *The Power of One*, *Tandia*, *The Potato Factory*, *Tommo & Hawk*, *Solomon's Song*, *Jessica*, *The Night Country*, *Smoky Joe's Cafe*, *Four Fires*, *Matthew Flinders' Cat*, *Brother Fish*, *Whitehorn*, *Sylvia*, *The Persimmon Tree*, and *Fishing for Stars*. *Jessica* has been made into an award-winning television miniseries. Bryce was born in South Africa, is an Australian and has lived in Sydney for the major part of his life.

Find out more about Bryce and his books at
www.brycecourtenay.com

BRYCE COURTENAY

THE PERSIMMON TREE

McArthur & Company
Toronto

First published in Canada in 2008 by
McArthur & Company
322 King Street West, Suite 402
Toronto, Ontario
M5V 1J2
www.mcarthur-co.com

This paperback edition published in 2009 by
McArthur & Company

Library and Archives Canada Cataloguing in Publication
Courtenay, Bryce, 1933
        The persimmon tree / Bryce Courtenay.

ISBN 978-1-55278-784-7

    I. Title.

PR9619.3.C598P47 2009   823'.914   C2009-903225-2

Design by Tony Palmer © Penguin Group (Australia)
Cover photographs: Front: Woman – Mel Yates / Getty Images;
Persimmon tree – Photolibrary

Printed in Canada by Webcom

10 9 8 7 6 5 4 3 2 1

For Lorraine and Greg Woon
Many thanks

PART ONE

———•———

Standing in the soft lamplight was the most
beautiful woman I had ever seen. I suppose at
sixteen you're not truly yet a woman, but Anna
Van Heerden couldn't possibly be described as
a young girl. I guess since I was just short of
eighteen I could still be seen as a young bloke,
but the extra two years of maturity I may have
gained on her were totally specious. I was the
callow youth and she was . . . well, I didn't
know how to describe her, in my inadequate
male vocabulary she was . . . she was a total
knockout! But certainly she was a woman and
not a girl.
Nick Duncan
Butterfly collector, Java 1942

CHAPTER ONE

'If you want a hard time as a kid,
decide to be a butterfly collector.'
Nicholas Duncan

THE CARLEY FLOAT APPROACHING the beach
through the pounding coral reef was making tough progress.
I counted nine, no, ten men – four in the water clinging to
the ropes on the sides of the cork and canvas float, while six
others, one of them lying face down, huddled on the raft. All
of them wore lifejackets, Mae Wests as the Yanks called them.
From what I could make out through the glasses they were all
black men.

The float was being pushed forward with each incoming
wave, but then, as the wave crashed into the coral heads it sent
plumes of spray into the air, drenching the men on board and
causing the float to spin and skip, dip and career, sending it
several yards backwards again. With all the turbulence I was
having difficulty framing them and holding focus long enough
for a closer examination.

The poor bastards clinging to the side of the float would be
copping heaps from the coral. Coral cuts untended are a nasty
business. They are full of live polyps and algae and invariably
fester and, unless treated carefully, cause a high fever and take

months to heal. The best treatment is first to squeeze the juice of fresh limes into them to kill the polyps and only after that apply an antiseptic. I didn't have any fresh limes, but if I cleaned the cuts thoroughly and got them early enough I could use diluted iodine. I had a bottle on board the *Vleermuis*, probably not sufficient for four blokes, but it was all there was.

What was becoming increasingly clear to me was that everything had suddenly changed and, using an unpleasant metaphor, I was up to my eyebrows in excrement. On my own, I reckoned I had a slightly better-than-even chance of avoiding the invading Japanese ships and aircraft and sailing the twenty-nine-foot cutter *Vleermuis* from the Spice Islands across the Indian Ocean to Australia. But now, with what was taking place below me, I would have ten additional men on board, one seemingly unconscious or badly wounded.

'You're dead in the water, son,' I said aloud to myself.

The shipwrecked men had obviously come off a warship, which don't carry lifeboats for a good reason: in the heat of battle they usually get blown apart by the incoming shells and become a liability. These guys were lucky. Most warships don't carry enough Carley floats. Going down with the ship is, after all, an established naval tradition.

Ten black men off a warship suggested an American cruiser had sunk, which explained the fierce gunfire that had wakened me with a start shortly before midnight yesterday.

I'd come ashore the previous evening, a night and a day's sailing out of Batavia. While I could see no fires or smoke rising as a sign of a native village on or beyond the long crescent beach, it made sense to attempt to remain unobserved. It was after sunset and gathering dusk when I slid through the reef passage into the narrow channel made by a muddy creek and into the mangroves beyond. By moonrise I was safely moored, my gaff rig mast protruding only a few feet above the mangroves. Varnished brown, in the daylight it would blend perfectly with the surroundings. The only way I reckoned I could be spotted was by someone coming upstream and passing me directly.

While the *Vleermuis* was a beautiful boat to sail, the thirty-four hours out to sea had been a steep learning curve for me and, frankly, I was exhausted. I was an experienced sailor and familiar with a boat this size, but no two yachts are the same and all have their own personalities. Like any woman, they take a fair bit of understanding. Besides, a cutter this length was getting close to the capacity of a lone yachtsman to handle. My muscles, grown unaccustomed to the task, aching bones and general weariness were also part of the reason I'd pulled into shore, delaying any attempt to sail through the strait that night, the last day of February.

Considering the complete chaos of the Dutch evacuation from Batavia and the imminent arrival of the Japanese invading force, getting through the strait a few days earlier would have been the more sensible thing to do. But doing the sensible thing is not the strongest drive in a young bloke and there was, I admit, yet another reason for delaying my escape.

Piet Van Heerden, the Dutchman from whom I had acquired the *Vleermuis*, had warned me that a growing section of the native population was becoming increasingly assertive. Gangs of Javanese youths were patrolling the streets of the capital at night. Several 'whites' had been attacked, making it unsafe to be out after dark. He'd indicated the Smith & Wesson in a khaki canvas holster strapped to his waist. 'Everything, she is up the pot!' he'd exclaimed. I guess he meant 'up the spout' or 'gone to pot'. 'The servants, even they are now cheeky.' He'd emphatically recommended I get a gun immediately.

However, I'd ignored his advice. In the two months I'd been in Batavia some of the local Javanese had seemed a bit off-hand. But, if they were not over-friendly, I'd certainly never felt threatened. There was most certainly an air of restless anticipation among the island people who, after two-and-a-half centuries under the Dutch colonial thumb, knew their lives were about to change. Many saw the new invaders as liberators and it was hardly surprising that the mood on the streets had darkened somewhat.

Unlike the Dutch colonials, I didn't expect the locals to adopt a servile manner towards me. In New Guinea I'd always resisted the prevailing notion of white supremacy and, as a result, had been rewarded with a great many cherished local friends. Besides, carrying a gun strapped to my hip simply wasn't the kind of gung-ho behaviour appropriate to an itinerant butterfly collector.

The Dutchman Van Heerden was a large big-bellied man with the sanguine complexion of a big drinker. He was also bald, but with the bushiest eyebrows I'd ever seen. It was as if the ginger hair he'd lost on top had somehow gathered over his brow to form two untidy thickets above a pair of piercing blue eyes.

In the month I'd come to know him I'd learned that he was didactic, opinionated, confident, in all matters thought himself correct and was loud in everything he said and did. I'd taken a job as the afternoon barman at a small restaurant, a task I was far from qualified to do. The regular barman, a Javanese man named Ishmael, of long and apparently faithful service, had suddenly gone amok late one afternoon and attacked two white patrons with the knife he used for slicing limes. Piet Van Heerden had helped restrain the diminutive Ishmael and afterwards rather proudly carried a rapidly healing and superficial cut from the barman's knife that ran the length of his arm from elbow to wrist. The attack was always described by him as unprovoked, an extreme example of the developing recalcitrance of the local Javanese. But when I got to know him better, he'd admitted that the two men had set about teasing Ishmael, a devout Muslim, and in the process mocking the prophet Mohammed and profaning the name of Allah.

'It was only for fun. *Ja*, these men are a little drunk, they do not mean what they say, you understand,' he'd explained.

'Yeah, but obviously that's not how the barman took it,' I replied.

'*Ach*, no, he is a servant! He cannot say anything. Now we are going, they are getting cheeky.' I had discovered he loved the word 'cheeky' and used it at every opportunity to describe the growing insubordination of the locals towards the white colonials.

The owners of the restaurant, *De Kost Kamer* (The Food Room), were a Dutch couple who were in the process of closing it down. Due to the growing unrest, white people stayed home at night so that now the restaurant only opened for lunch. They were reluctant to hire another Javanese barman and, while inexperienced, I was prepared to take the small wages they offered in return for a room in the restaurant compound and a meal at noon. I daresay if times had been normal I wouldn't have lasted five minutes. I didn't speak the Dutch language and knew very little about the working side of a bar.

I was given the afternoon shift, from 2 p.m. to when the restaurant closed, about 6 p.m., which was usually after the tropical rainstorm that arrived for half an hour or so around five, the rain pelting down so fiercely you'd swear each drop could drive a six-inch nail into a solid block of teak. The late-afternoon storm cooled everything down for an hour or two before the humidity returned later in the evening. The afternoon boozers would always claim that they had to wait until after the downpour to go home. I dare say I couldn't do too much harm. Well-oiled from luncheon, they were, generally speaking, a fairly affable lot. I opened an occasional bottle of wine, dispensed gin and tonics to the ladies and lager beer, scotch, brandy or rum to the men. If I was asked for something more exotic such as a Manhattan, I pleaded ignorance and flattered the customer by asking to be taught how to mix the requested cocktail. The job suited me ideally. I could spend the mornings hunting butterflies when they were at their most prolific, the tucker was plentiful and good and I had an iron cot and a lumpy coir mattress to sleep on, an outside toilet, tub and washroom shared with the live-in staff and a few guilders to keep me in necessities such as toothpaste, toilet paper and soap, commodities that were already only available on the black market.

Piet Van Heerden was a regular luncheon patron and also usually the last to leave at six o'clock. With his overweening personality he was not the kind of man with whom I would normally associate. He prided himself on his knowledge of English and, Broome being the first point of arrival for evacuees from the Dutch East Indies, he was determined to practise it on me.

As the barman I was trapped, forced to partake in those infamous obligatory conversations between barmen and lone patrons, or to use a different expression, bartenders and melancholy drunks of whom the afternoon session had a fair few. Most of the patrons were long-time colonials who stood to lose everything they'd built up, often over generations. They had become accustomed to a way of life they couldn't possibly replicate anywhere else in the world. Like Piet Van Heerden, they were as much islanders, white Javanese, as the darker-skinned locals. Whatever you do and wherever you go, there's always one, a person who gets up your nose. It was my misfortune to have the big Dutchman as my nemesis.

Although I must admit, while he was constantly whingeing about his loss, like many big men who are seasoned drinkers, Piet Van Heerden never appeared to be inebriated. But as the afternoon wore on and he held his eighth or ninth stein of lager clenched in his big fist he'd become increasingly morose and frown so fiercely that his wildly exaggerated ginger eyebrows would meet, become entangled and in the process completely cover his eyes. After one such late-afternoon verbal barrage I rashly admitted to having done a fair bit of sailing in New Britain. From that day on his boat, the *Vleermuis*, became the leading subject of his ranting. He became determined to show me his boat, insisting no finer sailing boat existed in Batavia than his twenty-nine-foot gaff-rigged cutter.

'First I love *mijn* daughter, Anna, after this only *Vleermuis!*' he'd explained to me late one afternoon.

'What about your wife?' I'd teased.

'*Ja*, also,' he'd growled. 'But she is not *goed*.' He didn't explain any further, dismissing any affection he may have held for her with a flip of his large hand.

Eventually after two weeks of one-way badgering I'd reluctantly agreed to accompany him to the yacht basin to inspect his boat.

The Dutchman was so loud and full of braggadocio that I had expected to be disappointed, but the *Vleermuis* was everything he'd said it was and more. The beautiful teak yacht with its solid bronze fittings and cabin walls panelled with rare amboyna wood was more than simply a rich man's indulgence. It was a boat that could sail anywhere under virtually any conditions. It was equipped with a full suit of sails, plenty of cordage and, as far as I could ascertain, in seagoing condition.

We'd come back from inspecting the cabin below and stood on the deck when he turned to face me, bottom lip trembling, eyes suddenly misty. He indicated the yacht with a wave of the hand. '*Ja, zo*, I leave this, I cannot take,' he said in what for him was a muted tone.

He'd never mentioned this possibility before, merely bragging about the cutter. 'Can't you load it onto a tramp steamer with the mast removed?' I asked.

He sighed heavily. '*Ja, ja*, no, the authorities will not allow.' He sighed again. 'It is too bad this.' Without warning he reached out and wrapped his arm around the mast and sank to his knees on the deck, where he commenced to sob.

The Dutchman was well over six feet tall and must have weighed at least twenty-two stone and now he was blubbing at my feet like a small child. 'Steady on, sir,' was all I could think to say. I was acutely embarrassed and at a complete loss how to go about comforting him. I was not yet eighteen and a grown man sobbing at my feet was beyond my limited experience. Patting him on the shoulder, I kept repeating, 'Steady on . . . steady on, sir.'

After a while, utilising the mast to haul himself up, he stood somewhat unsteadily, looking confused, as if not certain in the gathering dark where he was. I guess the melancholy of losing his beautiful yacht combined with the twelve steins of lager he'd consumed during and after lunch wasn't helping his equilibrium. Then I realised, for the first time, that he was very drunk.

Piet Van Heerden turned and gave me a bleary-eyed look, then stabbed a fat forefinger at me. 'You come to my house!' he demanded.

'No, not tonight, sir.' Quickly I added, 'I have things to do.'

'*Ja*, you come. We eat. You see Anna. She want to meet you.'

'I have eaten, sir. Some other time, perhaps.'

'*Ja*, again you eat. You meet *mijn* Anna,' he demanded belligerently, any trace of cordiality gone from his voice.

Just then a trishaw, known locally as a *becak*, came up to the mooring and the Dutchman yelled out, 'Boy!' even though the man pedalling it was clearly an adult. The *Vleermuis* was tied to the side of the dock, cushioned by a couple of motorcar tyres, and I allowed Van Heerden to take me by the upper arm so as to make the small step up onto the dock. He continued to grip my arm as we walked towards the *becak*. I helped him into the small two-seater cabin and then realised that he was attempting to pull me in beside him.

I jerked my arm free. 'No!' I protested.

His watery blue eyes were bloodshot and it was now obvious that he was pretty pissed. He looked at me, his expression a mixture of surprise and confusion. 'But . . . but Anna, she is waiting!'

I signalled to the driver to go. He nodded.

'Next time maybe, sir!' I said, not really promising.

'*Ja, fok jou!*' the Dutchman shouted, jerking backwards as the *becak* driver started to pedal furiously, anxious to get away in case his passenger changed his mind and robbed him of a fare.

'Goodbye, job,' I said aloud to myself. Not only was the Dutchman a good customer at *De Kost Kamer* but he was also related by marriage to one of the proprietors. I told myself it was probably a good thing; it was high time I left Java. Every day was becoming more chaotic with the docks piled two storeys high with large wooden packing cases waiting to be loaded. Many contained two centuries of the goods and chattels of colonials who, for ten generations, had known no other home but the Spice Islands. Shipping was at a premium and every rust bucket in the South Seas had gathered in the harbour to share in the chance to make an indecent profit from the fleeing colonials. Each daylight hour brought lorries carrying more packing cases to fill their holds.

I was hoping to work my passage home on one of the cargo vessels that were making a small fortune. Capitalising on the growing panic to get away before the Japs arrived, they were loading their holds with packing cases and then selling deck space to desperate passengers. If the holds could be cleaned up, electric lights rigged and air piped below, they were loaded the other way about. The current rate was fifty Dutch guilders or ten Australian pounds for a square the size of a large packing case marked out in chalk on the deck or within the hold. If I was unable to work my passage, I had the required ten pounds, two months' salary saved while working for W.R. Carpenter in New Guinea.

I arrived back at the darkened restaurant and made my way to the tiny room at the back I still occupied until, as seemed certain, I was summarily booted out on the morrow. Lighting the hurricane lamp, I attached it to a wire hook hanging from the ceiling and then, for want of something better to do, sat on my small iron cot and started to pack my knapsack. I could have read, I suppose. But of the four books I'd brought with me, three I'd read at least twice and, if asked, I could describe in detail, as well as recall the Latin names of every butterfly and moth in the fourth, a rare and cherished edition of a book taken from my father's large private library, its title a mouthful: *A List of Butterflies of Sumatra with Special Reference to the Species Occurring on the North-east of the Island*, printed in 1895 and written and compiled by L. De Niceville and L. Martin.

My absurd journey in pursuit of a single butterfly had proved a complete disaster. I was alone and rumours of the whereabouts of the Japanese were becoming increasingly bizarre. People had almost taken to checking for signs of the enemy under their beds. It was unlikely that I'd be able to get back to New Britain – Rabaul, to be more precise. As was the case with Java and Batavia, it was being referred to as a Japanese strategic priority, though this wasn't my greatest concern. I hoped my father, who was a missionary, and my expat friends would have already left for Australia and I could only trust that my local friends would be safe. In three weeks I would turn eighteen, whereupon, if I got safely back to Australia, I'd join up. The butterfly excursion to the Spice Islands had been intended as my last taste of freedom and, as it was turning out, a very sour-tasting one at that.

Deep in thought, I was startled and surprised to hear a knock on the door. The six Javanese kitchen staff who occupied the remaining rooms in the compound rarely spoke to me and certainly never when off-duty. There followed a second, slightly louder knock and a female voice called out, 'Mr Duncan?'

I opened the door into semi-darkness, the lamp hanging from a wire hook suspended from the ceiling only throwing sufficient light for me to make out a silhouette etched against the outside darkness. 'May I come in, please?' the voice asked, each word accompanied by the tiniest pause, as if it had been silently rehearsed and now was being tested out loud.

'Please,' I said, stepping aside. Then recovering slightly I added, 'Not much room, I'm afraid.'

I caught the smell of fresh lemons as she passed into the lamplight and then turned to face me. 'I am Anna,' she announced, the words again carefully phrased.

I confess that on the way back from the mooring I had imagined the Dutchman's daughter as being big-boned, blonde and clumsy, probably, like her father, overweight and almost certainly dull. I told myself his anxiety for me to meet his daughter was because of all these imagined characteristics. I'd grinned and given myself a mental pat on the back for refusing his invitation to dinner and thus avoiding an embarrassing evening.

Standing in the soft lamplight was the most beautiful woman I had ever seen. I suppose at sixteen you're not truly yet a woman, but Anna Van Heerden couldn't possibly be described as a young girl. I guess since I was just short of eighteen I could still be seen as a young bloke, but the extra two years of maturity I may have gained on her were totally specious. I was the callow youth and she was . . . well, I didn't know how to describe her, in my inadequate male vocabulary she was . . . she was a total knockout! But certainly she was a woman and not a girl.

Had I been forced to give a more formal description of the astonishing creature that stood within the soft light of the hurricane lamp it might go something like this. Anna was of mixed blood; I suppose you'd call her Eurasian, Javanese mother and, of course, a Dutch father. She was slim and fine-boned though taller than the women of her mother's nationality. She wore a simple, light-blue cotton dress worn off the shoulders, the sleeves slightly puffed and covering the top of her arms, which, like the rest of her skin, was the colour of honey in sunlight. Her hair fell just short of her shoulders and was jet black and framed a heart-shaped face. Her lips were full and generous and her cheekbones high – together with her arched eyebrows they seemed to emphasise her incredible eyes, only slightly almond-shaped and framed in rich dark lashes. In the prevailing lamplight they appeared to be a deep violet colour.

She smiled and my heart skipped yet another beat. 'I have heard much about you, Mr Nicholas Duncan.'

'Nick, please call me Nick,' I managed to say, first clearing my throat and with my voice sounding fully half an octave higher.

'Nick . . . Nicholas,' she said as if testing both on her tongue. '*Ja*, for me, I think, Nicholas. I shall call you Nicholas.'

I grinned, trying to look relaxed, again clearing my throat. 'As a kid, I only got called Nicholas when my father was angry,' I managed.

She looked concerned. 'No! It is a nice name. Nick, it is too hard . . . Nick, brick, stick . . . '

'Prick!' I added, then realised what I'd just said and blushed violently.

'No!' she exclaimed again, before giggling until we were both laughing. I was in love, head over heels, hopelessly, helplessly in love. It was the most painful feeling I had ever experienced and I felt I was going to cry.

'So, Nicholas, now you are wondering why I am here, *ja?*'

'Well, surprised,' I managed to say. Later when I replayed the moment in my mind I rewrote the script to add in an Errol Flynn-like voice, complete with the required slightly quizzical look: '*Well, surprised, my dear. Beautiful women don't make a habit of knocking on my door at night*', but knew, even if I'd thought of such a reply in the first place, I would have lacked the courage to carry it off.

A look of concern crossed her pretty face. '*Ja*, I am sorry if I disturb you.'

'"Disturb" is the right word but in the wrong context,' I said, grinning like a chimp.

Anna frowned. 'Pardon?'

I was being too clever for my own good and hastened to reassure her. 'No, no, you are very welcome!' I spread my hands. 'It's . . . it's just that, well . . . I was surprised, that's all.'

'You said "disturb" is the right word,' she accused, then pursed her lips and her right shoulder twitched in a barely discernible shrug. 'Maybe you like I go now.'

'No, please, Anna! Please stay,' I protested. Then using courage I didn't have, I pulled a forlorn face and added quickly, 'If you go it will break my heart.'

She laughed. 'Okay, so now you must ask why I am come here, Nicholas.'

I realised that we were still standing. Apart from the cot with its lumpy mattress there was a three-legged stool to sit on. I pointed to the stool. 'Would you like to sit, Anna?'

She sat, placing the basket she carried on the floor beside her, then adjusted her skirt, pulling it down to partially cover her knees, which she held together while her sandalled feet were splayed just as a small child might sit. Such had been my state of flummox that I hadn't even noticed the basket she carried until the moment she'd placed it down. I sat on the edge of the iron cot so as not to appear as if I was standing over her. 'Okay, so tell me, why have you come, Anna?' I asked dutifully.

She looked at me seriously. 'I have cooked a nice dinner and apple strudel, the apple is only from a tin, and you didn't come, Nicholas. My papa said you would come tonight,' she added accusingly.

'But . . . but he only invited me when we were on the boat and . . . well, he was a bit under the weather, so —'

'Under the weather?' she interrupted. 'I do not understand.'

'Sozzled.'

'Sozzled? It means maybe drunk?'

'Well, yeah,' I replied, nervously wiping my palms down the sides of my khaki shorts.

'*Ja*, he is very sad man. He is not always drunk. But now he is going away, after two hundred years. It makes *mijn* papa very sad and so . . . ' She didn't complete the sentence but shrugged instead, suddenly dropping her lovely eyes and then slowly raising them, looking up at me again, silently pleading with me to forgive her father's behaviour.

'Yeah . . . must be pretty hard after all that time, good reason to . . . yeah,' I agreed, finding no suitable words with which to continue.

Anna suddenly brightened. 'So I have now here dinner!'

'What, here?'

'Of course! I have come on *mijn* bicycle. It has a basket on the front. It is not so hard.'

'But it's dangerous! I mean to come out alone at night.'

Anna laughed, dismissing any thought of danger with a flip of her hand. '*Ach*, I do not look Dutch, only *mijn* eyes.' She lifted the basket to her knees and removed the tea towel covering it to reveal a neatly folded, bright-red chequered square of cloth. 'There is no table,' she said, needlessly looking around the tiny room as she unfolded the small tablecloth.

I pointed to the packing case that acted as a bedside table. It carried my books, a candle stuck in a chipped cup and a smallish wooden box containing my butterfly paraphernalia, the killing jar I used so as not to damage a specimen, and a small metal container of ethyl acetate. 'Only this, will it do? I can move my stuff.'

Anna shook her head and pointed to the worn linoleum. 'No, a picnic! We shall have a picnic,' she announced, placing the basket on the floor beside her, and without rising from the stool she spread the cloth on the floor at her feet. Thank God for the Dutch – even in these difficult times a maid washed the linoleum every day and the floor was spotless. Anna rose and from the basket produced two plates, cutlery, two freshly ironed damask table napkins and a cruet set with salt, pepper and mustard and a small jar of horseradish.

Dinner was cold roast beef and still warmish roast potatoes. My unexpected dinner hostess explained that there had also been beans and pumpkin, but she didn't think I'd like to eat them cold. 'I am not so good cook,' she apologised, adding, 'The cook from always since I was little girl, her name is Rasmina, she has gone back to her *kampong* near Malang.'

'You could have fooled me – this food is great, you're a natural,' I said, meaning it. After that she produced two fresh plates and a large apple strudel, and she once again apologised for using tinned apples. 'Before the war they are fresh from Australia, but now not, only tins and no more also those. I hope you will like, *ja?*'

After two slices of her delicious strudel and repeated compliments from me on the pie and the picnic, Anna wrapped the remainder of the strudel in the tea towel and placed it on the packing case. 'For tomorrow, Nicholas,' she said. 'Take when you go look for butterflies.'

So she knew about the butterflies. I had never mentioned it to the Dutchman. I glanced up to see if there was the usual half-concealed amusement mixed with scorn that appeared in people's eyes whenever I was introduced as a butterfly collector.

'This is Nick, he collects butterflies.'

'Oh really, how interesting!' Thinks: *Hmm, looks normal enough . . . never can tell, can you? Sort of thing that should have been stopped, discouraged early on by his parents. Never know where it might lead. Big strapping boy like him should be out there kicking a football with his mates. Butterflies, ferchrissake!*

But there wasn't a hint of irony in her voice when she asked, appealing to me with her eyes, 'Nicholas, can I come, please?'

'What, to collect butterflies?' I asked, surprised.

'*Ja,* I would like very much.' She frowned suddenly. 'But maybe you don't want?'

I laughed. 'Of course! But I must warn you, you can get pretty badly scratched chasing a butterfly.' I realised that my heart was beating faster. The idea of having this beautiful creature with me in broad daylight was beyond my wildest fantasy. But then I thought of the Dutchman. 'Your father, will he agree?'

She tilted her head towards her right shoulder and brought her forefinger up to touch her lips. She appeared to be considering her old man's reaction. 'No,' she said, then grinned, 'but I will come.'

'Anna, I . . . I don't want you to get into strife with your old man.'

'He is not so old, only forty years,' she protested.

'No, sorry, it's just what we, that is Australians, call our dad, our father, our "old man". It's just an expression, like you say "*mijn papa*", we say "my old man".' My grin was feeling tight and my explanation becoming more convoluted and confusing by the second. 'It's, you know —'

'*Ja*, I understand,' Anna cut in, saving me any further embarrassment. 'In Dutch we say *oude man*, it is nearly the same. My English to understand is not always so good. But, *ja*, it is true, *mijn papa* will not let me go with you for the butterflies, my stepmother, she also. But I have told them tomorrow morning I am going to visit my friend Heidi who is leaving Batavia the day after tomorrow.'

I looked at her, surprised. 'You mean to say you'd already decided? That is, about coming to hunt butterflies?' I was becoming more gauche by the minute.

Anna looked at me scornfully. 'Of course not! Maybe I don't like you, then I cannot go.' She took two paces so that our bodies almost touched. She had small breasts so that the whole of her body seemed equally close to mine. I was suddenly conscious of the growing and involuntary warmth between my thighs. *Oh, Jesus, no, not now! Please God, not now!* I begged silently. I had a sudden vision that the only part of me touching her was the one part that definitely shouldn't. The fresh lemon perfume was there again. I concentrated on lemons, anything to get my mind off the fire down below. It must have been the soap she used, for she wore no make-up and I'd never heard of a perfume that smelled of lemons. I was just over six foot and I judged her around five feet five so that it was easy for her to rise onto her toes and kiss me lightly on the cheek.

'I like you, Nicholas. I have never known another butterfly collector.'

She said this in a way that suggested that the two factors taken together were responsible for her decision and that one of them on its own might not have been sufficient to make up her mind to accompany me. She touched me lightly on the shoulder. *Don't look down, Anna. Please, God, don't let her look down!* 'Now I go home, it is very nice to meet you,' she said, taking a single step backwards. 'I am here again, seven o'clock tomorrow morning. Okay?'

'Yes . . . no, I will see you home. It's late and not safe to be out,' I protested.

'It is not necessary. I have *mijn* bicycle. You have a bicycle, Nicholas?'

'No. I'll run, I'll run beside you,' I said, quickly making up my mind.

Anna looked doubtful. *'Ja, nee.* It is three kilometres, maybe a little more.'

'Yeah, okay, I can manage that,' I said, not knowing if I could, but also prepared to die in the attempt.

'You are sure, Nicholas? We can walk also. There are some hills.'

She hadn't protested as I'd expected she might. Nor dismissed the notion of danger as she'd done when I'd first mentioned her venturing into the streets at night alone. *Maybe she likes me a little bit?* She'd just said she did and kissed me. More a peck, but in my mind it was already a full-blown kiss. *Do girls really mean it when they say they like you?* The idea filled me with such an intense joy that I felt myself decidedly light-headed. Giddy is a better word.

Trotting beside her bicycle was easier than I had supposed. I spent most mornings running and darting after butterflies and unbeknownst to myself I was pretty fit. I soon got my second wind and regretted the short distance when we reached Anna's home. We'd laughed and talked and got on like a house on fire.

As the *Vleermuis* had done as a yacht, the Van Heerden home surprised me equally. Even in the moonlight it was imposing. It was built, Anna explained, nearly two hundred years previously and added to by ensuing generations. It sat in large grounds and was reached through two ornate wrought-iron gates that rose ten feet into the air and opened onto an avenue of enormous dark oak trees that led up to the whitewashed stables, outhouses, servant quarters and a large covered gangway, then on to a low white wall that enclosed a formal rose garden and the home itself, a triple-gabled traditional Dutch colonial-style building, all of this seen in the bright moonlight. In the daylight the oaks must have looked equally grand and incongruous in the tropical setting. I was to learn they were nearly as old as the house itself.

I was too young to understand the power of a continuity imposed by ten generations of inheritance, each progenitor in the same home, in the same business, with the same overweening principles of superiority inculcated into them and never questioned by the next generation. I nevertheless began to realise what it would mean to Piet Van Heerden to be wrenched from a way of life he would have seen as his birthright and to know he might never return to it. It was hardly surprising that he was hitting the booze.

Unable to summon the courage to kiss her, I shook Anna's hand. 'See you tomorrow morning,' I said, trying to keep my voice sounding matter-of-fact.

Anna laughed softly, seemingly amused by the handshake and even more beautiful in the moonlight. 'Goodnight, Mr Butterfly.' The large gate swung open and I turned to go when she called out, 'Ja, Nicholas, I think it is much better name than Nick . . . brick . . . stick!'

'Prick!' I called back, this time laughing.

'No!' she protested once again. 'No, no, no!' Her laughter followed me down the street.

I was up well before seven when Anna tapped on my door. She wore a pair of faded khaki shorts that came down to her knees, a white shirt and the same sandals she'd worn the previous night. In the morning sunlight she appeared even more beautiful. I was suddenly overcome by shyness. It was as if daylight brought quite another person to my door and I panicked that we would have to start all over again and I didn't know where to make a beginning. So, with my usual tact I said, 'Sandals?' looking directly at her feet.

She looked at the boots I was wearing, then turned and pointed to her bicycle. Tied to the back carry-tray were a pair of Wellington boots. 'Ja, I have brought. Good morning, Nicholas,' she said, smiling, and then promptly kissed me on the cheek. I had no need to apologise for my abrupt manner, she could see all she needed to know from my grin.

The *dokar*, a small two-passenger cart pulled by a tiny Timor pony, which I'd hired for the morning, was waiting to take us to a marsh some distance out of the city on the edge of a rainforest. I'd visited the site previously and knew I was unlikely to find the Magpie Crow of the *Danaidae* family of butterflies there, but other species had been plentiful and we would catch them together. Anna was more beautiful than any butterfly I could ever collect. I didn't for one moment stop to think that, at best, I would know her and love her for no more than a few weeks and then I would lose her. I was in love and a few weeks seemed as if an eternity of being in love lay ahead of me.

Anna had brought breakfast – small bread rolls, cheese, hard-boiled eggs and a thermos of coffee – and we sat in the cool of a large banyan tree as we ate. She poured me a cup of coffee. '*Ja*, so Nicholas, I have confession,' she said, not looking up from the cup she handed me.

My heart skipped a beat. In my experience confessions seldom brought good news. 'Confession? You didn't clean your teeth this morning?' I chaffed.

'Of course,' she looked up, appealing to me. 'I have told my papa that I came to see you last night.'

I didn't know quite how I was expected to react. Piet Van Heerden obviously hadn't stopped her coming, or if he had, she'd disobeyed him. All I could think about was that Anna was with me and that's all that mattered. 'Was he angry?'

'*Ja*, a little bit, but I said he is drunk last night.' She shrugged her shoulders. 'How can I ask him, he knows I cannot.'

'And this morning he allowed you to come?'

'*Ja*, I am sixteen,' she said simply. 'He wants you should come tonight. He wants to talk to you. It is important, I think.'

'Important? Do you know why? What he wants to talk about?'

'*Ja*, maybe, but I cannot say. He will tell you.' She appealed to me with her eyes. 'You will come tonight, Nicholas?'

I sensed Anna wasn't going to tell me more and I didn't want to spoil the day by persisting. 'Only if you do the cooking.' I laughed.

Anna clapped her hands. 'I will make you a nice peaches

pie, but they are only from a tin.'

We spent the morning netting a variety of butterflies, nothing special, but Anna seemed interested in them all, big and small, plain and fancy, and also happy when I released them. It was almost the time the pony-cart driver had been asked to return when she netted a Clipper, a large and gorgeous butterfly and not one that is easy to find, its wing pattern resembling an old sailing ship in full sail, hence the name.

'You beauty!' I yelled. 'Congratulations!' The Clipper, also found in New Guinea, is a truly beautiful large butterfly. I took the net from her. 'Would you like to keep it?' I pointed out its likeness to a sailing ship and told her its name.

'Oh, yes, Nicholas, I will keep it always.'

'I'll prepare it and mount it for you. I'll bring it tonight.'

'Mr Butterfly, I like you very much,' she said and gave me an unexpected kiss. Not on the lips but much closer to them than the one last night and less of a peck. Another inch and I know I would have been reduced to a gibbering fool. As it was, I had to wait a few moments for my hands to stop shaking so that I could prepare the glass jar to contain the beautiful butterfly. This I did by placing a thick layer of tissue paper on the bottom that was impregnated with ethyl acetate. I then carefully removed the gorgeous specimen from the net and placed it in the jar to allow the fumes to kill it without a struggle, the humane way to do it and also to prevent damage to its wings.

We finished the rest of the strudel Anna had brought the evening before and the *dokar* arrived shortly afterwards to take us back to the city.

Anna had told me that her father would not be at *De Kost Kamer* for lunch and that I should come to dinner at around seven o'clock. It was a nice evening and I decided I'd walk to her home, taking with me in a small canvas bag the specimen I had mounted. The Clipper is a lovely butterfly and mounted in the small teak display box with a glass cover I must say it did look splendid.

A gardener was waiting at the gate to let me in when I arrived. Walking down the oak-lined avenue in the fading light I could see that a section of the house was covered by a brilliant scarlet bougainvillea. I passed through the walled rose garden and was about to knock on the impressive front door when it swung open. 'You are welcome, Nick!' Piet Van Heerden boomed. 'Welcome to *Grootehuis*. Welcome to the big house,' he translated. Moments later Anna appeared, wearing a sarong *kebaya* and an apron embroidered with tulips, wiping her hands as she walked towards me smiling. 'Anna already you know,' the Dutchman said. Then turning suddenly he swept his daughter into a great bear hug. '*Ja!* This is Anna. *Ja* blood, to mix in marriage, is no *goed, ja!*' he joked.

'Papa, *nee!*' she protested, laughing and slapping at his broad back.

'Not so bad, *ja*,' the Dutchman said, releasing Anna. It wasn't hard to see he adored her.

We walked through a small hallway into a very large room, huge dark beams crossing the ceiling where five elaborate brass candelabra, now converted to electricity, hung. All were lit, giving the impression of a small ballroom, for the room was empty of any furniture and where once there were pictures, possibly family portraits, there remained only white squares against the yellowing walls. The wide teak floorboards reflecting the light from the highly polished wood looked as if they carried the weight of generations of waxing. In the very centre of the room was a wheelchair in which sat a stern-faced woman who looked to be in her late thirties. Anna had told me when we'd been hunting butterflies that her stepmother had fallen off a horse while competing at a local gymkhana and had broken her back, then added, touching her head, 'Also, not always she is good in the *kop*,' then she touched her heart, 'Also sometimes her heart is getting very angry, maybe sad also, *ja*.' Anna's stepmother wore her hair parted at the centre and pulled back into a bun, giving her a severity that belied her still-firm features. It was a face grown bitter and frustrated long before its time.

The woman stabbed a finger at Anna. 'Marriage!' she shouted, '*Hoerkind!* Whore child!'

'This is Katerina, my stepmother,' Anna said gently. 'You must excuse. Today she is not feeling so well.'

'Marriage!' the woman shouted again, this time pointing at the Dutchman.

From the scornful look on his wife's face, she'd obviously overheard the conversation in the hallway and 'marriage' was probably not the word she would have chosen to describe the liaison that had produced the beautiful Anna, and to confirm this she shouted, '*Hoer!* Whore!'

'*Kom, Katerina, wij gaan nu eten,*' Piet Van Heerden said evenly, advancing towards the wheelchair.

'Whore!' his wife cried again, throwing up her hands. 'Whore! Whore! Whore!' Whereupon she spun the wheelchair around and, propelling it with considerable speed, sped through a door at the opposite end of the large room.

'I will take later her food,' Anna said, attempting to hide her sudden tears at the use of the ugly word and her dismay at her stepmother's behaviour in front of me.

We ate at the kitchen table sitting on a long wooden bench, the table, bench and an ancient rumbling Kelvinator fridge the only loose furniture in the room apart from a few necessary pots and pans and kitchen utensils that hung above the stove. The kitchen was another big room with a wood-fired stove from which Anna produced food, assisted by a diminutive thirteen-year-old Javanese kitchen maid named *Kleine* Kiki, Little Kiki, who Anna had previously told me was an orphan they'd adopted and who would be leaving Java with them. '*Mijn* stepmother she likes only Kiki,' she'd explained.

Dinner was a spicy Javanese rice and fish dish that was delicious, if a little too hot for a constitution still not fully accustomed to the more spicy local diet. The peach pie served with tinned cream was delicious.

At the conclusion of the meal Little Kiki cleared the table silently, having to kneel on the bench to reach the rice dish in the centre. She took the dishes into the scullery to wash up. Piet Van Heerden rose, scratching his massive belly, then lumbered like a huge bear over to the fridge. He opened it and withdrew two large bottles of lager. Anna fetched two rather battered pewter mugs from a cupboard and a bottle opener, apologising that the beer steins were already packed. Opening both bottles, the Dutchman placed one in front of me. '*Ja*, now we drink, eh, Nick?' he announced. I enjoyed a beer or two from time to time, a glass or two that is, but the bottles held at least two mugfuls and the over-large pewters at least two glasses. From the Dutchman's known consumption, a single bottle wasn't going to be the end of it. My sobriety was in question and two pewter mugs of lager was definitely my limit. If I attempted to keep up with my host, I'd soon enough end up under the table.

We filled the mugs, each from his own bottle. 'Australian and Dutch, they like to drink beer, *ja*!' Anna's old man pronounced in a jovial voice.

'I doubt I'll get through this bottle, sir,' I grinned. 'I'm not much of a drinker.'

'Nick, we drink, it is *goed*, vun bottle *piftt*! It is not enough, you are young man, strong, *ja*,' he announced, overriding my protest. Holding up his pewter mug, he waited until it was clinked by my own. 'Cheers!' he said in English.

'Cheers,' I replied, knowing that in the beer stakes the next hour was going to be a tricky one for me.

We both drank, the Dutchman taking a deep swig as opposed to my moderate sip, then withdrawing and smacking his lips. '*Goed!* Now we talk, hey, Nick?' he said.

I grinned, not knowing quite how to respond. Anna had said he wanted to talk to me, but I had no idea what about. She had placed a plate of food on a tray and had left the kitchen to take her stepmother's supper to her room or wherever she had fled in the wheelchair. I was alone with the Dutchman, his overbearing presence and the prospect of a night of drinking ahead inwardly disconcerting me. Two days ago I might have managed – then the arrogant Dutchman had meant almost nothing to me – but now there was Anna and I wanted badly to impress her old man. But he had me trapped with a gigantic bottle of lager on the table in front of me. My manhood was to be judged on my ability to hold my alcohol. *I wonder if he knows I collect butterflies?* The subject had never arisen in the afternoon bar, the Dutchman's loquacious diatribes essentially involved his loss of a privileged lifestyle he never once questioned as anything but his absolute birthright. Ours was essentially a one-way conversation, perhaps the single exception being when I'd foolishly mentioned having done some ocean sailing. In this regard he'd grilled me closely and incessantly, the final result being the previous evening's drunken visit to inspect his yacht.

'Nick, how you get back to Australia?' he asked suddenly.

'I have a working passage on the tramp steamer I arrived on,' I replied, then added, 'It's due into port at the end of February.' This wasn't strictly true. I'd worked my way over two months previously and the Greek captain had more or less promised that if he should need extra crew on his next trip, if there was one, he'd be happy to consider me. No firm promise had been made and as he said, he might not even turn up. I had begun to worry about this last possibility. With the Japs on the doorstep the Dutch people in Batavia were growing more panicky by the day. On January the 9th Japanese aircraft had bombed the harbour in a surprise attack and had continued to do so regularly since then. Several merchantmen now rested on the bottom of the harbour, their superstructures reaching out like arms from a watery grave. A large merchantman on her side almost blocked the entrance to the harbour. I doubted very much that my Greek master would return to Batavia.

'Maybe you take instead *Vleermuis*?' Van Heerden said, looking directly at me.

'What, sail her back?' I replied, astonished at the idea.

He shrugged. '*Ja*, why not, hey?'

I laughed. 'I've never sailed that far.'

'Not so far, down the archipelago, zen soon *vooosh*, New Guinea.'

'What about the Japanese?'

'*Ach*, no, man! They will not come. Before Singapore you will see they will stop.'

I hesitated. 'I don't know about that, sir. There's plenty of speculation, people, yourself, deciding to get away.'

'*Ja*, maybe they come. But by that time already you are long time in Australia.'

'I don't know, sir. It comes as a bit of . . . well, a bit of a surprise.' I glanced at him. 'This isn't meant to be a joke, is it? You don't even know how well I can sail.'

Piet Van Heerden spread his hands. 'I know. Some people always they try to bullshit. You, I think you can sail *Vleermuis*,' he said, flattering me.

'Thank you, sir, but I haven't even taken her out.'

'*Ja*, this is a problem.' On a previous occasion at the bar he'd lamented that in the emergency the Dutch navy had forbidden pleasure craft on the congested harbour, nor were they allowed out to sea if they intended coming back. 'I will take a chance you can do it,' the Dutchman said generously.

I laughed despite myself. 'I would have thought it was me who was taking the chance, sir.'

'*Ja*, but you are getting maybe *Vleermuis*.'

I straightened up with a jerk. 'You're kidding, sir. Are you *giving* me your boat?'

'*Ja*, and also no.' He pursed his lips, making several tiny popping sounds. 'We are making, how you say . . . ?'

'A proposition?'

'*Ja*, a proposition.'

I frowned. 'What sort of a proposition, sir?'

He pointed to my pewter mug. 'Drink, Nick, za beer, it gets otherwise hot.'

I took a sip. *What the hell was going on? A proposition.* A sudden wild thought crossed my mind. If he'd let Anna come I'd agree to anything he wanted. I remained silent, pretty sure this wasn't the sort of proposition he had in mind.

'Money? You have some money, Nick?'

It was my turn to grin. 'To buy the *Vleermuis*?' I shook my head slowly. 'Not that kind of money, sir.' What on earth was he going on about? He'd already told me he couldn't take the gaff-rigged cutter with him. It was worthless left on the mooring. Did he take me for some sort of fool?

'How much?' he demanded.

It was a bloody rude question. If it hadn't been for Anna I think I might have got up there and then and left. I didn't owe the bastard anything. 'As a matter of fact, ten pounds,' I said, an edge of resentment to my voice. The Dutchman was embarrassing me, forcing the information from me. But for a few Dutch guilders it was all the money I possessed in the world. It was my way out of Java should I not get a job on a ship. For me it was a considerable amount, two months' wages as a dispatch clerk at W.R. Carpenter and a small win at poker. I wasn't about to hand it over to him.

'Give to me,' he demanded, stretching out his enormous hand, a smug look on his fat, perspiring face.

'Hey, wait a minute, sir. May I ask what this is all about? You told me yourself you couldn't take the boat with you. Now you want me to sail it to Australia and you want to make me a proposition that begins with me giving you ten pounds for the privilege. Why would I do that?'

'*Ja*, I am glad to see you are not a fool, Nick. It is a *goed* question. For the papers zat ten pounds. If you have the papers then you will own *Vleermuis*.'

'Is that all, sir? You said a proposition?'

'You think ten pounds is too much, Nick?'

'No, sir, it is a ridiculous price. Providing, of course, that I get *Vleermuis* back to Australia without running into the Japanese navy or a reconnoitring Zero or two.'

'*Ach*, there is plenty of time, you will see.'

'Sure, they bomb the harbour every few days.' The Dutchman did not react to my aside, so I continued. 'So, that's it? Ten pounds and I get the *Vleermuis*?' I asked suspiciously, for once not addressing him as 'sir'. I was once warned never to do business with a Dutchman if I hoped to keep the shirt on my back.

Piet Van Heerden smiled and spread his arms. '*Ja*, okay, maybe never, also maybe one day, who knows, eh? After za war Anna comes to Australia. Then she give you ten pounds and you give her za papers for *Vleermuis*, *ja*?'

'Anna?'

'*Ja*, always, one day she has *Vleermuis*.' He shrugged, giving me an unctuous smile. 'But now we are leaving and I cannot give her *mijn* beautiful boat.'

'Sir, with the greatest respect, that sounds like bullshit. Isn't it just another way to get your boat back after the war?'

He laughed, lifting his pewter as if to salute me. '*Goed*! *Ja*, that is *goed*, Nick! Ha! Ha! *Ja*, *nee*, no, you are wrong! Anna, also . . . she loves this boat, already she can sail *Vleermuis* by herself, she is *goed*, better even zan me, *ja*.'

'Okay, then give it to Anna now. Sign it over to her and let her sail it with me to Australia?'

'*Ja*, papa, let me go with Nicholas. It will be a big adventure. We are going to Australia, we will meet you and Katerina and *Kleine* Kiki again there,' she said ingenuously. Neither of us had noticed her return to the kitchen, or how long she had been present and what part of our conversation she might have overheard.

I confess a disparate thought had begun to form in my mind: that this might be a conspiracy between father and daughter and that Anna had been playing me for a sucker all along. The supper, the butterfly hunt, was it simply all a come-on? If it was, it was more than I could bear to think about. She was so beautiful, so lovely; for her to turn out to be deceitful would have broken my heart. But now she obviously wasn't part of a conspiracy. She'd freely admitted that her family's destination was to be Australia. She couldn't possibly have been implicated or she would never have proferred this information and so exposed the Dutchman's motive. What's more, she wanted to accompany me. I couldn't believe my ears. There was no need for the Dutchman to con me. With Anna on board I'd happily accept the use of the cutter and give it back to him, to her, when we arrived. A month at sea alone with Anna was a wild and exhilarating thought.

I turned to look at the Dutchman for confirmation. His large head had turned almost purple, the veins on his neck stood out like fat worms and the capillaries that normally flushed his chubby cheeks looked as if they might burst at any moment. He was snorting like a rhino. Then his huge fist came crashing down on the table. '*Verdomme, nee! Nee! Nee!*' he bellowed.

'Papa! Papa!' Anna cried, rushing to her father's side. She kissed him several times on the forehead and then started to knead his shoulders.

'I think I'd better go,' I said, standing.

'No, please to stay, Nicholas,' Anna cried.

'I don't think I'm welcome,' I said in a whisper though conscious that the Dutchman could probably hear me.

Anna walked from behind her father to where he could see her. 'So, papa, for Nicholas it is okay to sail to Australia, *ja?*

For me, *nee*, no?'

The Dutchman ignored his daughter and looked directly at me. 'She is too young.'

'But, sir, you said it was safe, that she is a good sailor and knows how to sail the *Vleermuis*.'

'She must look after her stepmother!' he said, raising his voice.

'She has already *Kleine* Kiki, papa,' Anna protested. 'Katerina wants only she.'

'*Nee!* Too young!' Piet Van Heerden shouted. I could see he was coming close to losing his temper again.

Anna was not put off. She folded her arms across her chest and glared at her father, her eyes daring him. 'For what, Papa? Why I am too young?'

The Dutchman's fist smashed down on the table. '*Heere, man! Jy is te jong om te fok!*'

It was crude and direct and said in Dutch, but the one essential word needed no translation.

'Sir, you have my word of —'

'Sssh! Nicholas,' Anna interrupted. I looked at her, surprised. Tears formed in her lovely eyes, then escaped to run slowly down her cheeks. Her voice was steady as she spoke to her father in English. 'My mother was fifteen! *Mijn moeder was slechts vijftien!*' she repeated in Dutch.

The Dutchman brought his arm back to strike Anna as he rose from the bench. I saw the dark healing line of the superficial cut Ishmael, the barman I'd replaced, had made with the lime-slicing knife down the length of his massive forearm. I had the Dutchman in a headlock before he was halfway up, squeezing hard to cut off his air supply and pulling him backwards so that he was off balance and then forcing him back onto the bench.

He was a huge man, but still enormously strong as he pulled at my arms. But I was standing and he was seated, giving me the immediate advantage, and I knew he couldn't resist for long while I was choking him. Unable to pry my arms from his neck, his face near-purple from the constriction, he gave up and tapped the table with the butt of his hand to indicate that he'd had enough.

'First promise you won't hurt Anna, or punish her!' I demanded.

A croak followed and a slight movement of his head and shaking of his shoulders indicated to me that he agreed. He tapped the table a second time. I was happy to release him. I wasn't small and I guess I was fairly strong, but had he been a younger and fitter man he might well have been too much for me. As it was I was panting from the effort of holding him down.

Anna's frightened face looked first at me and then down at her father. 'Oh, Papa!' she howled and rushed to embrace him, kissing his scarlet and furiously perspiring face.

'Now I'd better go,' I said emphatically, still panting. 'Will you be okay, Anna?'

'*Ja*, thank you, Nicholas,' Anna said, glancing up, now wiping her father's face using her tulip apron. I noticed that a small trickle of blood ran from his nose and that a smudge of it stained her pretty sarong. 'Nicholas, please forgive *mijn* father,' Anna said, appealing to me through sudden tears.

The Dutchman looked up, but when he opened his mouth his voice, intended no doubt to sound as a fierce reprimand, came out as a gravelled rasp. 'Go! You will not see again Anna. If you do I shoot you! You understand?' In his newly acquired squeaky voice it didn't sound too dangerous.

But Anna screamed. '*Nee, nee!*' she shouted. 'Do not believe, Nicholas! He doesn't mean.' Then she began to sob, using the apron to cover her face.

'Whore! Whore! Whore!' It was Katerina, the stepmother, wheeling herself into the kitchen and shaking an accusing finger at the Dutchman. All that was needed was for Little Kiki to appear and to drop the dishes on the kitchen floor and we had a complete Mack Sennett scene, the full slapstick. But, of course, at the time I thought it far from funny.

I picked up my canvas bag and turned to go when I suddenly remembered that I hadn't given Anna the specimen I'd prepared of the Clipper. 'Oh, this is for you, Anna,' I said, removing the small display box from the bag and placing it on the table. 'With my love,' I said softly.

Walking home I was close to tears on several occasions. 'What a balls-up! What a total fucking balls-up!' I said aloud, looking at the sky and wondering how love could possibly hurt so much and how lost love hurt even more.

I lay awake for most of the night. Naturally I expected to be fired from the restaurant the following day. This meant losing my room and having to find alternative accommodation. It was high time to get out, to attempt to go home. I admit I felt thoroughly sorry for myself. I decided I would write a letter to Anna, telling her I loved her and giving her an address in Australia. But then I told myself confessing my love was a mawkish thing to do and she'd probably tear it up and laugh. In the two days we'd known each other, two pecks on the cheek, one quite close to my mouth, were the sum total of the affection she'd shown me. She'd admitted she liked me on two occasions, but this wasn't exactly a burning commitment or a meaningful love affair. No promises, no lingering sighs, no 'if only's, not even a kiss on the lips. In total, a shared meal on a worn linoleum floor and a morning spent hunting butterflies followed by the utter fiasco of tonight.

I packed my gear in anticipation of being given my marching orders in the morning. To my surprise there was no knock on the door first thing to tell me to hit the road. I spent the morning at the docks seeing if I could get a working passage out, but without any luck. I turned up at *De Kost Kamer* for the afternoon shift and nothing was said, nor was the Dutchman to be seen. I spent the early part of the evening visiting the dockside pubs questioning seamen about work on board, but again nothing. Crew were, for the most part, Malaccans or from Goa, and I didn't speak Dutch so the various ships' masters I talked to saw no point in my working as a third officer or a liaison officer on one of the tramps now hastily converted to take refugees.

At 9 p.m., somewhat depressed, I arrived back at the restaurant compound to see a light in my room and Anna's bicycle leaning against the wall. My heart started to beat rapidly and I felt a lump in my throat. Anna must have heard me coming because the door opened and with the soft lamplight behind her she stood, a slender silhouette, in the doorway.

'So now you are coming, Mr Butterfly.'

I grinned, so pleased to see her that I was momentarily lost for words. 'Anna, you came!' I managed at last.

'Of course, Nicholas, why not?'

'Well, last night . . . ?'

'*Ja*, I am sorry.' She stepped aside to let me in and the scent of lemons was back in my life.

'And your father? He knows you're here?' I asked tentatively.

She giggled. 'You are afraid, *ja*? He will not shoot you, Nicholas.'

'Afraid? Not for me, Anna . . . for you,' I said, hastily correcting her.

'Nooo! He is *mijn* papa! He will not hurt me.' She seated herself on the stool and adjusted her dress as she had done the first night we'd met. 'This morning he is coming to me, still he is talking' – she cleared her throat, touching her thorax – 'how you say?'

'Hoarsely? I'm sorry, I thought he was going to hit you, Anna,' I apologised.

'*Ja*, hoarse. Then he says, "Nick is *n regter man*, Anna. *Hy is n goede jange kerel.*"' She laughed. 'It means you are a *proper* man. A good young man,' she translated. She looked down at her feet, then slowly back up at me. 'Nicholas, myself I think also the same,' she said shyly.

I was suddenly choked, tears blurring my eyes. I swallowed hard, trying to find my voice. 'Oh, Anna . . . can't you see I'm crazy about you?'

Anna jumped to her feet and, throwing her arms around my neck, kissed me, this time on the mouth, holding the kiss with her lips soft and tender and ever so slightly apart. So much for my masculinity. My knees started to tremble as I put my arms around her slender back and I drew her to me. *Oh, God! Do I open my lips? Hers are slightly open. Do I put my tongue into her mouth? You're supposed to do that, aren't you? Oh shit! I should know all this! Will she know I've never kissed a girl before? Oh, Jesus, oh, oh, oh!* Then quite suddenly Anna pulled away, her arms still about my neck. 'Mr Butterfly!' she murmured softly, then sighed. We kissed and kissed and kissed again and I was getting better at it by the moment and our lips parted.

Oh, my God!

Now I can't say all this kissing and holding tightly didn't affect the nether parts, the fire down below, because it did. But those were different times to today and I didn't even have the courage to put my hand on Anna's breasts, even through the material of her cotton dress.

All good things must come to an end and Anna eventually pulled away from me. 'You must eat, Nicholas,' she said in a practical voice. 'I have some *ryst-tafel* but it is not hot; also coffee, it is hot from the thermos.'

I had been too miserable to eat the ample meal the restaurant provided before I went to work at the bar earlier and realised that I was positively starving. Whereas the misery of thwarted love left me without an appetite, love's sudden recognition had the opposite effect and I wolfed down the rice dish followed by what remained of the peach pie of the previous night. Anna poured two mugs of coffee, handing me one.

'Nicholas, *mijn* papa, he say you can have *Vleermuis* if you want,' she said suddenly. I remained silent, placing the mug of coffee on the packing case. Anna quickly added, 'The papers he will give, they are yours, you don't pay. When you are in Australia you can keep always that boat.'

'Anna, will he let you come?' I asked.

Anna shook her head slowly, then burst into tears. We were sitting on the edge of the iron cot and I took the mug from her shaking hands, placed it beside my own and took her into my arms as she began to sob, her head against my chest. 'I must stay!' she sobbed. '*Mijn* stepmother . . . *mijn* father . . . to look after them . . . *Kleine* Kiki, she cannot . . . she was only just turned thirteen . . . *Mijn* papa . . . he cannot . . . he is a man . . . I must . . . ' She looked up at me tearfully. 'Oh,

Nicholas!' Then she burst into fresh sobs.

'Anna, Anna, don't cry . . . it's okay! You're going to Australia. I'll see you there.' I put my hands on her shoulders and looked into her eyes. 'Anna, I don't want to lose you!' I cried.

I withdrew my arms and reached for my handkerchief to wipe her eyes. Her own was a wet ball clutched in her hand. 'Here, use this,' I said, handing her my handkerchief. 'Now listen to me,' I said, trying to sound practical. 'When I get back I'm going to join up – I turn eighteen in nine days.'

'Oh, Nicholas, we are going in seven days! I cannot be here for your birthday!' she cried, distressed.

'I'll be at sea, silly!' I joked. 'We'll celebrate it together in Australia.' I hesitated, then added tentatively, 'It can be sort of our engagement?' Then with my heart in my mouth I asked, 'After the war . . . will you . . . er . . . marry me, Anna?'

To my surprise she giggled and kissed me smack on the mouth. Like whack! Then pulled back. 'Of course! *Mijn* papa says after the war I must find a man just like you, Mr Butterfly,' Anna said, laughing.

I don't suppose I knew what her reaction might be, but her ingenuous response came as a surprise. I guess I still had a lot to learn about women. Still do, as a matter of fact. In an attempt to recover I said, 'Well then, it will have to be me. I don't suppose there are too many butterfly collectors in my age group.'

Anna clapped her hands, delighted. 'Then I can be Madam Butterfly!' she laughed, rising suddenly and plonking herself onto my lap, hands clasped around my neck as she kissed me all over my face. *Oh, Jesus, she's going to feel it!* Here I was at the happiest moment in my young life and I had a hard-on that could have demolished a brick wall. I could feel it pressed against her thin cotton dress. It was pressing right on the spot it shouldn't be! *Oh God, what if I come? I have to get her off my lap!*

I pushed gently at her shoulders. 'Anna, I . . . ' But suddenly her bottom started to press downwards and her lips closed over mine, her tongue inside my mouth. 'Oh, Jesus!' I cried. It was too late! I was gone! All over, red rover! I was no longer in control. It was simply marvellous! I had never, of course, done the real thing, but every young bloke 'took himself in hand' from time to time, yet this was different, quite different; if doing it was even better I couldn't imagine how. I had disgraced myself. The next few minutes were going to be hell. There would be a wet patch the size of a football at the front of my khaki shorts. *Oh shit! What do I do next?*

Anna withdrew her lips from mine and kissed me lightly on the forehead.

'Anna, I'm . . . '

'Sssh! Now you are feeling better, Nicholas. That is good, *ja*, I think so.' She rose from my lap, her hands placed on my shoulders, smiling down at me. 'I love you, Mr Butterfly,' she said softly.

'I'm sorry, Anna.' I looked down into my lap, shaking my head ruefully. I could feel the hot blush infusing my face. If the damp patch wasn't quite the size of a football, it certainly wasn't possible to conceal in the lamplight.

'You have some other?' Anna asked, her voice suddenly practical as she pointed to my shorts. 'I can wash, in the morning they are already dry.'

'Yes, no, I'll do it, wash them, excuse me,' I mumbled, panicking, then pointed in the direction of the door. 'The washroom, it's outside.' I reached to the end of the cot and took the towel hanging from the iron rail that made up part of the foot of the iron bedstead.

Anna touched me lightly on the shoulder and I turned to face her, the towel held to my front. She looked at me, her face serious. 'Nicholas, I want to make love to you very much. But we cannot. We must not make a baby.'

'Oh, Anna, of course, I understand. I never thought . . . I can wait . . . I . . . I *want* to wait!' I added with some emphasis, giving her a sincere look. I loved her and although I don't deny that I'd fantasised about making love to her from the first day, I was still a virgin. My father was an Anglican minister. I'd always known I'd have to do the right thing. *Wanted* in my heart to do the right thing. God says you must. It's just that nature is such a bastard sometimes. I took a fresh pair of shorts from my knapsack and prepared to go to the outside shower-cum-washroom and laundry.

'Nicholas, I must go home now,' Anna said, moving forward to embrace me.

'Anna, no, please, can you wait until I get back? I'll run home with you. But first there is something I need to say to you.'

I filled the three-feet-deep concrete tub that was set on the floor with water and washed my pants and underpants, then emptied it, refilled it, stepped in and ladled the water over me, the cold water refreshing in the humidity. I placed the offending garments over a line in the yard to dry. In all, I guess I couldn't have been gone much more than ten minutes. Anna was sitting on the three-legged stool as pretty as a picture, her basket packed. So much had happened between us, including my disgrace, that she seemed suddenly like a different person, a part of me, a loving, familiar part from which I felt I couldn't ever be separated.

I kissed her. That was a part of the new feeling. I could kiss her whenever I wanted. My mother had died when I was five when we'd lived in Japan. My father, always a pretty stern man, wasn't big on affection and had consequentially turned from being the headmaster of the International School in Tokyo to become an Anglican missionary in New Britain, where, at the age of eleven, I'd moved with him and then been sent to boarding school in Australia. He was a solitary man and I don't know whether it was the grief over my mother's death or what, but he never remarried. I guess I'd been short of my share of female kisses, even of the maternal kind. Women, even the feel of them, were a complete mystery to me.

'Anna, I've made a decision, I'll sail the *Vleermuis* to Australia. But I don't want your father to give it to me, only to sign the papers over to you. Put them in your name. If I get through the war, well, then it will be ours anyway. But I want him to grant me just one favour.'

'Nicholas, I don't want you to sail *Vleermuis* without me,' she said, alarmed. 'It is too dangerous! *Mijn* papa say, if you want, you can have that boat. It is only to say he is sorry. You know, what happens last night. It's okay. You do not have to take it!'

I took both her hands in mine, our faces close. 'No, listen, Anna, it's a good idea. I've been down to the harbour today. It's going to be difficult to get a working passage to Australia or home. Papua is expecting the Japanese to invade at any moment. It's a mad panic down at the docks, the cost of a deck space is now twenty-five pounds.'

'I will ask my father, he will lend —'

'No, no, I don't want that!' I cried in alarm, not wishing

under any circumstances to be in the Dutchman's debt. It hadn't yet occurred to me that he was to be my future father-in-law. On the last occasion we'd been together he'd threatened to shoot me. 'It's a good boat and rigged for the open sea.' I smiled. 'I'll enjoy the adventure.'

'What favour? If you sail *Vleermuis*, already that is doing *mijn* papa a favour.'

'No, this is different, when I get back to Australia I want to change the name of the boat.'

'You don't like *Vleermuis*? In English it hard to say, *ja*?'

'Yes, true, but that's not it. I want to call her *Madam Butterfly*. It's your boat and it will be a sort of . . . like a promise between us.'

'Oh, Nicholas!' She pulled her hands from mine and clapped them happily. 'Mr Butterfly and *Madam Butterfly*.'

'Yeah,' I said, a little embarrassed, suddenly conscious that to anyone else it might sound pretty corny, but nonetheless still liking the idea a whole lot.

'Wonderful! It is beautiful idea. We will do it, *ja*.' She suddenly gave a little squeal. 'It is a sign, that butterfly I caught!'

'The Clipper?'

'*Ja*, Nicholas, it's so beautiful! When I am catching it you say to me, "See, the wings they look like a sailing boat." It is a sign! A good sign!' she repeated emphatically.

'Your father may not like the name change,' I ventured.

Anna pouted prettily. 'So? Now it is *mijn* boat. He cannot say.'

'We'll do it when we get back to Australia and the boat is registered in your name. You can mention it to your father then.'

The Dutchman came to the restaurant the next day and expressed his delight, and even if he didn't offer his apologies for the insulting manner in which he'd propositioned me in his home, his manner indicated that he wanted things to remain cordial between us. His voice had recovered and was at its booming best so that the whole bar could hear him. 'After the war, when Anna is older, by me, I am happy she is with you, Nick. You will marry, *ja*!' It wasn't a question and he stuck out his huge paw. '*Ja*, also *mijn* boat, *Vleermuis*, now it is hers.' He laughed. 'A *goed* marriage present, *ja*, I think so!'

'Madam Butterfly,' I said under my breath, both your daughter and your boat.

I resigned from my afternoon job at *De Kost Kamer* and went to live on the *Vleermuis* as it needed a fair bit of maintenance. The gaff-rigged cutter hadn't been out sailing for nearly five months and I spent the next few days doing all I could to be sure she was seaworthy. The bilge pump wasn't working properly and I spent a fair bit of time getting it right. Anna spent as long as she could working beside me. The Dutchman was right, she certainly knew her way around a boat and didn't mind getting her hands dirty painting or using a caulking iron and pitch.

The Japanese invaded Sumatra on the 14th and the following day Singapore fell. I should have scarpered there and then, but there is a passage in the Bible my father quoted to me when I was fourteen and going through puberty. It was, I suppose, as close as he could get to the standard lecture one receives at this time of one's young life in regard to the birds and the bees. It's in Proverbs 30 and is known as the Sayings of Agur. 'There be three things which are too wonderful for me, yea, four which I know not: The way of an eagle in the air; the way of a serpent upon a rock; the way of a ship in the midst of the sea; and the way of a man with a maid.' Thoroughly mystified at the time he'd sonorously recited Agur's confession to me, I now finally understood what he'd been getting at. Anna was due to leave on the Dutch passenger steamer *Witvogel* sailing on the evening of the 26th of February and I wanted to be with her every possible minute until that time. She begged me to go when news of Singapore came through, but I refused and declared I would sail out on the evening tide of the day after they'd sailed, catching the offshore wind. I guess I should have left sooner, but there you go, 'the way of a man with a maid'.

By this time the locals were plundering the European shops and the Dutch were afraid to enter them. The Javanese shopkeepers and market people were charging extortionate prices for anything they were prepared to part with. Anna had brought whatever was left in the family pantry to the boat. There wasn't a great deal – several bottles of sauces, a small bag of sugar, coffee, some dried fish – but certainly, with the other provisions, there was sufficient to last the two and a bit weeks it should, with any luck, take me to sail to Australia.

My additional rations consisted of four-dozen cans of tinned fish, mostly mackerel, which is an oily fish and not much to my liking; a dozen tins of canned vegetables, mostly peas and carrots, neither a favourite of mine but beggars can't be choosers; a ten-kilo sack of rice (approximately twenty-two pounds); a canteen of tea; a jar of salt; and a small bag of curry powder. The last two items were a timely reminder of how bad things were in Batavia towards the end.

Curry powder may seem like a strange thing to single out for mention. I do so only to illustrate how in the last few days prior to our departure the local population had most certainly turned on the departing Dutch. Anna had given me everything she could from her larder but curiously they'd run out of salt, the most common commodity of all. I needed to get a tin of caulking pitch and some oakum, both easy enough to obtain even in these scarce times as it was always plentiful in the market. So I took the opportunity to get sufficient salt for the galley at the same time. Having purchased the pitch and a roll of oakum, I found a woman selling spices and attempted to buy a large screwtop jar of salt, offering her a generous denomination in the local Dutch currency. This she'd promptly refused. Then I proffered an Australian pound, an absurdly large amount for the jar of salt. This too was unsmilingly and with a sullen shake of her head rejected. I turned to go, resigned to a long voyage without salt, when she grabbed my arm, pointed to the silver signet ring on my finger, then reached down and held up the jar.

I'd won the ring of almost knuckleduster proportions at a game of poker in a pub in Port Moresby and it had no sentimental value. I would have given it to Anna but the motif was a human skull and so it would have been entirely inappropriate. I twisted it from my finger, handing it to the spice seller. She placed it between her teeth, tasting to see if it was genuine and, seemingly satisfied, handed over the jar of salt and then, with the mere flicker of a smile, tossed the small bag of curry powder in for good measure, curry having less value in local cooking than any other spice.

The 26th of February finally arrived, the day Anna and her family were due to depart on the evening tide. In the few weeks I'd known Anna, a great deal had changed for the Dutch in Java. Singapore, thought to be the one impregnable fortress, the place where the myopic Japanese moving down through Malaya on their absurd bicycles were certain to be halted by the mighty

British, had fallen with hardly a whimper.

The Japanese had already reached the islands of Bali and Ambon and landed on Sumatra. The next step was Java, in particular the port city of Batavia with its huge, safe harbour, and Surabaya for its magnificent naval facilities. Suddenly the Dutch in the East Indies, who'd assumed they had ample time to get out, were thrown into a blind panic. The Japanese were moving into the Pacific like an invasion of angry wasps and the Dutch forces and colonial citizens they were protecting had been caught with their proverbial pants down. The Javanese soldiers, many in sympathy with the Japanese, had no stomach for a fight and were deserting in large numbers, hastily discarding their boots, webbing and rifles and escaping into the jungle. Almost every afternoon now there were Jap air raids on the ships in harbour, their oil tanks on fire.

The carefully planned colonial exodus with the wharves piled high with wooden packing cases, many made out of finely worked teak planks intended for later use as wall panelling, was suddenly thrown into hopeless disarray. The white colonials scurried like ants aboard any ship available. Dirty tramp steamers accustomed to carrying bulk cargo were selling deck space at *Queen Mary* cabin prices and the space in the hold that would normally have housed their possessions was given over to accommodating people at an only slightly less exorbitant cost. Left behind on the loading docks were all their neatly packed and sorted crates for the locals to carry off.

The Dutchman and his family had their passage previously booked but instead of occupying two cabins they now shared one with another family of four, in all eight people, one of them being Anna's stepmother in her wheelchair. Piet Van Heerden was not a happy man and I begged him to let me take them all to

Australia in the *Vleermuis*. But he was one of the few passengers to get his packing cases loaded and he was adamant that they were staying put, whatever the inconvenience. I asked again if Anna could come with me and I thought he was going to have an apoplectic stroke on the spot. 'It is too dangerous!' he'd yelled – so much for his previous reassurances that my sailing to Australia would be duck soup, nothing to worry about.

Anna and I had said our tearful farewells during the day and then again on the crowded deck. When the ship's horn sounded and I had to go ashore she was crying and clutching the specimen box containing her butterfly. 'Nicholas, I love you!' she shouted almost hysterically above the noise of the passengers.

'I'll see you in three weeks, maybe a month, in Broome. Wait for me!' We kissed one final time, Anna clinging to me. Then she drew away and quickly handed me a square of white cloth. 'I'm sorry I did not have paper to wrap it, Nicholas. Please look, I have embroidered it myself.' She smiled through her tears. 'I have also one the same. You must keep it till when we meet again.' I unfolded the handkerchief and in the corner she had embroidered the beautiful Clipper, her personal butterfly.

I was completely choked. I had no idea I could love someone as much as I did this lovely creature. 'I will keep it always,' I stammered, barely able to hold back my tears. A final urgent blast from the ship's horn and I had to rush to get to the gangplank in time. As the steamer pulled away from the docks I lost sight of her but found myself foolishly waving the embroidered square, unexpected tears running down my cheeks. Women, I had discovered, were simply marvellous creatures.

Once back at the cutter alone I began to realise I had been a bit of a fool. No, more than a bit. Quite clearly I *was* a fool, a thoroughly frightened fool! It had been foolish to come to Java in the first instance. Foolish to hunt for a Magpie Crow, a rare species of butterfly that only I cared about. I reminded myself again what a stupid name it was for a butterfly! There were butterflies with names such as Dragontail, Jezebel, Peacock, Red Lacewing, and I had become obsessed with a black-and-white butterfly called a Magpie Crow! But I'd met Anna and fallen in love and now, still a fool, but the luckiest fool in the world, I was still a long way from home.

With everything changing as quickly as it had with the Japanese I now realised that the odds were heavily stacked against me. I'd volunteered to undertake an absurd sailing adventure with a battered school atlas as my only chart. I was sailing a 29-foot cutter I knew nothing about, on a voyage across the Indian Ocean in the middle of the monsoon season when the weather could dish up a cyclone that might last a week or more. The Japanese navy was suddenly everywhere and their aircraft owned the skies from Singapore to the Indonesian Archipelago, and God knows how far their dominance extended into the Indian Ocean. If I wasn't spotted and run down by a Japanese ship or shot out of the water by a Zero I could go down in a storm at sea. It was little wonder that the Dutchman had gone apeshit when I'd suggested, once again, that Anna accompany me.

I spent the following day making minor adjustments and waited until after dark when the land breeze carried me down the harbour and out to sea. From Batavia it is only about fifty nautical miles to Port Nicholas, the highest point on the island, where a left turn takes you into the Sunda Strait between Java and Sumatra. I fondly imagined I would enter the strait just before dawn. With a half-decent wind this wasn't a big ask for a cutter such as the *Vleermuis*.

However, I hadn't reckoned on the time of the year. In late February there can be calm periods that can often last all day until the next weather comes through. While I made some little progress, the land breeze soon petered out and the yacht was becalmed. My hope was that by dawn I would encounter a wind front, even if only a breeze, anything to get me out of the sun. A storm at sea is the stuff of drama, but with no wind to propel it, a sailing boat becalmed in the tropics is an altogether horrible experience. The yacht lurches from side to side as it wallows in the swell. The deck becomes too hot to stand on and below decks the heat is so suffocating as to be unbearable. What's more, there is nothing you can do to change the intolerable conditions. At least in a storm, even in a violent one, you're moving, there is something happening; crisis with the fear it carries is always stimulating. Sitting helpless in the remorseless heat and without movement except for the incessant wallowing can drive a sane sailor crazy.

Dawn came and with it no wind. I was a sitting duck for any Japanese aircraft or ship at sea that happened to spot me.

Not long out to sea from Batavia I had noted that the head blocks controlling the straight top of the sail were sticking and would need to be repaired before I got to the Sunda Strait. With the violent lurching from side to side in the swell there was no way I could make the repairs at sea. I would need to moor somewhere so I could safely climb the mast and grease the blocks. If I didn't get them working smoothly they could jam completely under load, preventing me from shortening sail in a blow, thus all but deliberately inviting a fatal result in heavy weather.

Mercifully, by late afternoon a light sea breeze sprang up

and I used it to get ashore. As far as I could make out going by the battered school atlas, if it was vaguely accurate I was moored slightly east of Bantem Bay.

This was the night of the 28th and, as it happened, my eighteenth birthday. It was the one birthday I had told myself I would *really* celebrate. I'd promised myself I was going to get myself gloriously pissed, absolutely blotto, smashed, blind, motherless, completely stonkered! Finally I was old enough to join the army.

What a joke! Now there was the distinct possibility that I could be celebrating my last birthday on earth while sitting in a mosquito-infested mangrove swamp. Even worse, I could be taken prisoner of war by the Japanese before I'd pulled on my first pair of army boots or once again kissed my darling Anna. The thought that she'd never know what had happened to me brought a fearful lump to my throat as I wallowed in self-pity.

I opened a tin of mackerel, mixed it with a handful of rice left over from breakfast and then sat with my legs dangling over the back of the boat, eating the cold concoction and feeling, I admit, lonely, homesick and decidedly sorry for myself. Too weary to go through the rigmarole of boiling water for a cup of tea, I toasted myself with a glass of water, drank half of it and used the remainder to clean my teeth. After dousing myself in citronella mosquito repellent I crawled into my bunk. I managed to sing, decidedly off-key, almost all of the words to 'Happy Birthday' and can remember reaching the penultimate line of 'Happy birthday, dear Nick' when I must have fallen asleep, to be wakened later by the guns of a naval battle.

With the first salvo in the sea battle waking me I'd come up from below and sat on deck listening to the booming gunfire and watching the flashes of the big guns like distant lightning on the horizon far out to sea. The sea battle came from the direction of the Sunda Strait and my heart sank knowing that I might have left my escape from the Dutch East Indies too late.

The sound of the big guns continued until shortly before daylight, and although greasing the head blocks, making one or two other repairs and mending a small rip in the flax sails wasn't going to take long, I now couldn't risk sailing in daylight. I could well sail right into the area where the naval battle had taken place and besides, the air over the strait would be alive with Jap Zeros.

Rather than remain on deck all day, I decided I'd take the first couple of hours of morning sunlight to hunt for butterflies and make the repairs in the afternoon. It couldn't do any harm and it would take my mind off the problems that undoubtedly lay ahead for me and, as well, remind me of the morning with my darling Anna on our single butterfly excursion, an occasion we'd never managed to repeat.

It was March the 1st and there's always something hopeful about the first day of a new month. Anna had presented me with a single egg, a real find, and I'd eaten it for breakfast, after which I packed my day knapsack with my binoculars and collector's field paraphernalia, filled the canvas-covered metal water bottle my father had given me for my fourteenth birthday, slung its strap around my neck and under my right arm so it rested on my hip, grabbed my butterfly net and slid over the side of the boat into the four feet or so of muddy stream and picked my way across a dozen yards of mangrove growth to firmer ground. From there I climbed up the small hill and into the coconut plantation to wait for the sun to rise.

I told myself it was extremely unlikely – I had one chance in God knows how many thousand that I'd happen upon a

Magpie Crow. But then again, hope springs eternal. I was on the right island at the correct time of the year, not too long after the pupae had hatched; maybe, perhaps, who knows, it was worth a try, wasn't it? My luck had changed meeting Anna, so why not with the ever-elusive trophy butterfly?

Now seated and waiting for sunrise when the morning dew would dry on butterfly wings, I saw the Carley float battling its way in on the tide.

The task must have appeared formidable to the men on the float as they reached the final barrier, the last line of coral before attaining the calmer water beyond. Two of the men crawled to the front of the float, each carrying a crude wooden paddle. Gripping the rope that looped around the outside circumference with one hand and lying on their stomachs, they attempted to reach out and push the float clear of the jutting coral heads. This was proving to be a fairly futile business as the float was carried fiercely inwards by an incoming wave, and bumping into a coral head, the men were immediately jerked backwards by the water smashing into the reef where the float spun and skidded every which way until the process was repeated by the next approaching wave.

Some fifty feet ahead of them I could see a clear channel leading all the way into shore and I silently willed them to find it. 'Left, go left,' I said stupidly to myself, knowing they had no possible say in the matter. 'Left!' I urged again. The float, caught in a sudden contrary current, moved to the right and away from the safety of the channel; then just as suddenly it was picked up broadside by an arching white line of surf to ride the wave back in the direction from which it had come. I winced as I watched the four men clinging to the ropes as they were swept over several outcrops of coral but then, mercifully, the wave broke and the float subsided into the channel where it spun briefly before calming in the waist-deep water. They'd made it through. The men in the water would be badly cut and bruised, but they'd made it. Moments later an incoming wave caught the float and carried it the thirty or so yards onto the beach.

They'd come into shore the hard way; half a mile further down was the lagoon where I had entered the creek the previous night. Had they found the same opening, life would have been a lot less tedious for the last part of their perilous voyage. I guess they couldn't be blamed. Exhausted, they'd come out of a dark night and a frightening experience and it was still not long after dawn. At first light they would have seen land directly ahead and with the incoming tide being sufficient to cover several of the lower parts of the outer reef, and perhaps not understanding the nature of coral construction, they'd thought what looked like clear water was a break in the line and they'd been swept forward to be trapped within the reef.

I watched as the black guys carrying the man I'd seen lying prone on the float stumbled up the beach. Four of them moved him like a sack of potatoes, one each gripping his ankles and the other two holding him by the wrists while his head lolled like a broken doll's. I guessed he was dead and to their credit they hadn't thrown him overboard but intended to give him a burial ashore. They carried him, often stumbling in the soft sand and almost falling, up the full length of the beach to place him in the shade of a line of low bushes that grew at the edge of the beach. One of the other men hastened up, kicking sand in little puffs as he ran, at the same time removing his shirt, pulling it over his head. While I couldn't see with the bush in the way he must have spread it under the foliage before they lowered the dead black sailor onto it. I remember thinking how it was a curiously gentle and touching thing for an exhausted man to do for a mate. After all, if he were dead, why would it matter if he lay directly in the sand? I focused on the naked torso of the man who'd removed his shirt and I saw him reach up to his chest and pull a broad strip of black tarlike substance from his skin. Underneath he was white. Their blackened skin, as I should have realised, was as a result of oil spilled over the surface of the water from the sinking cruiser. Crude oil is thick, almost glutinous, and when it spills from a ship it rides on the top of the water and sticks like tar to the skin. While some of it will strip off as it dries out a little, it requires a strong non-irritant solvent such as kerosene to get the tar out of the pores of the skin.

I had four 1-gallon tins of kero for the galley stove and decided I'd allow them to use a bit on their faces and hands and their crotches. A man has a right to piss clean. I'd also use kero to wash the immediate area around their coral cuts before using the precious iodine, but that would have to be the lot. As I've previously explained, the food Anna had given me for the voyage to Australia was heaps for one person even allowing that I might be blown off-course and lose a week or two. But as tucker for ten blokes it was a different matter entirely: one small meal, a handful of rice, a tablespoon of tinned fish and a dusting of the mild local curry powder a day if we were lucky. The rice was the one essential ingredient and without kero for the galley stove we'd starve.

I began to plan the rescue and our escape from the Japanese forces. I decided that the chances of being spotted were too great if we hugged the shore, going down the archipelago and veering off across the Indian Ocean from Timor. The *Vleermuis* was well found and capable of handling the open sea and so, depending on the monsoon winds, I intended to attempt the direct route across to Broome. This meant no stop-offs to gather coconuts or water – the yacht's freshwater tank was fairly big but not for a crew of ten at sea for perhaps a month. Two cups a day, I decided, then let's pray it rains.

With a bit of luck and a fair wind I could, with difficulty, carry the nine shipwrecked sailors back to Australia. If I succeeded they'd be dirty and we'd all be near starving, but safe. Alternatively, if what I'd heard of the Japanese conquest of Manchuria was anything to go by, being taken prisoner of war by the Imperial Army wasn't going to be a whole lot of fun. It was apparent that the Japs couldn't even spell the two words 'Geneva Convention'.

The sun had begun to rise and I stood in preparation to make my way down to the shipwrecked sailors when I saw a group of men, thirty or forty in number, coming up the far end of the beach, the opposite end to where the *Vleermuis* was concealed in the mangrove swamp. I watched them through my binoculars. They were not dressed in the remnants of the uniforms the native soldiers deserting from the Dutch army usually wore, retaining only the shorts, sometimes a shirt, but the remainder, boots, gaiters, webbing and caps discarded. Piet Van Heerden's warning had been not to trust them. He'd informed me they were useless, unenthusiastic recruits, most thought to be supporting the nascent independence movement. Singly they were cowards; in a mob, dangerous. But these men wore only the native sarong and were bare from the waist up. They appeared not to be carrying any weapons so I concluded they must be from a local village. I was surprised at such a large group in one gathering, presuming their women and children, chickens and the like would have indicated a fair-sized fishing village and I had seen no fires last night when I came into shore or fishing boats drawn up on the beach this morning.

The men were alone and that too was unusual. Perhaps they were *copra* workers, on their way to an outlying coconut plantation. I decided none the less to stay put and observe what happened when they reached the shipwrecked men. If they proved to be friendly we might be able to get further supplies for the voyage.

The men off the float seemed not to notice them until the islanders had drawn within hailing distance, although, of course, with the pounding of the surf they would have needed to be almost upon each other in order to be heard. I then saw the first greeting take place, the natives waving their arms in what seemed a friendly manner and the shipwrecked sailors waving back. I found myself smiling as the two groups merged. I fixed my glasses on one of the islanders to see that he wore a wide grin while extending his hand to greet one of the white blokes. Still half-smiling to myself, I watched the group of Javanese men as in one accord they reached behind their lap-laps and withdrew their *parangs*.

It was as if I was witnessing some ghastly pantomime, since the pounding surf made the cries of the attackers and those of the shipwrecked sailors impossible to hear. The morning sunlight glinted on the vicious blades as they arched high above the white men, who were surrounded too quickly to attempt to escape. The natives encircled them, moving forward and bunching them together. The shipwrecked men fell to their knees, holding their hands wide or above their shoulders, palms turned outwards in the universal gesture of surrender. Their attackers suddenly rushed forward and the hapless sailors brought their arms over their heads to protect themselves from the blows of the vicious blades. The *parangs* slashed downwards and then raised and slashed, raised and slashed again and again, in what soon became a killing frenzy, all of it coming to me in silence except for the booming background of the surf.

I heard myself whimpering, then felt myself sobbing and my hands holding the binoculars shook so furiously that I kept losing focus. The attack seemed to go on and on until at last the circle of attackers parted and I could see eight dead men sprawled in the sand in various grotesque attitudes, three face down, one curled into a foetal position while four others lay on their backs and stared up at the sky, their arms and legs flung wide. A lone victim was still seated with his legs tucked under him, his hands resting on the beach on either side, just as a child might do when building a sandcastle. He might have been dead seated like that. I watched as one of the attackers moved forward and, swinging his *parang* in a wide arc, lopped off his head. While there must have been a great deal of blood and plain enough to focus on through my binoculars, I wasn't conscious of seeing any of it until the sailor's head tumbled into the sand and a crimson jet rose into the air from his severed neck, drenching the man who'd performed the beheading. He ran to pick up the severed head and, holding it up by the hair to show the others, he then turned and, swinging it in an arc three times, he hurled it into the surf. I was shaking too violently to hold the glasses and I started to throw up, collapsing against a coconut palm, vomiting, snivelling and weeping like a small child.

I forced myself to recover, wiping my eyes and returning to watch through the binoculars. The attackers were searching the bodies of the dead men. I focused on one of them who'd recovered a wallet from a bloodied shirtfront. He opened it and appeared to withdraw what I took to be money, then flung the wallet aside. The others did the same, removing the watches from the wrists of the murdered sailors and then the boots, tying the laces together so the boots hung around their necks. They gathered around each other comparing the watches they'd stolen before placing them on their wrists.

The sudden thought occurred to me that if they continued down the beach to the river they might find the *Vleermuis* and that would be pretty well the end of me. Stranded and alone, I would have no means of escaping Java. I'd make for the jungle, I thought wildly. I told myself I could survive. In New Guinea I'd often enough gone into hidden valleys, the so-called impenetrable jungle, after butterflies, staying for two or three days at a time. As a kid my native friends had shown me what to eat, how to make a trap for small animals. But I knew in my heart that this was wishful thinking, utter bullshit; I didn't even have a box of matches in my knapsack.

I watched as the group removed the bloodied Mae West jackets, some of them cut and torn by the vicious swipes from their *parangs*. Six men lifted the Carley float above their heads, then started to return the way they'd come.

I guess self-preservation is a primal instinct. The tide was still coming in, though it had not yet reached the bodies sprawled on the beach. I waited almost an hour until eight o'clock when the attackers were well gone before making my way down to the beach. By this time the tide was in and spent waves were breaking over the dead men, white spume bubbles popping and water swirling in patterns around their inert bodies, the force of the water not sufficiently strong to wash them back into the surf. Some, lying on their backs, still had their eyes open and seemed to be staring at me accusingly. I avoided looking at the bloke with the missing head.

Several small wallets and pieces of paper were being carried in and out of the surf and I gathered these frantically into a pile. Not stopping to examine them, I shoved them into my knapsack. I was berating myself, telling myself to act calmly. I'd seen dead bodies before, even those that had been mutilated. My father was a missionary and was often called in after a tribal fight. Though most of the outlying New Britain villagers were 'heathen', as he called them, they nevertheless didn't mind having a spare whitefella god in attendance at burial ceremonies.

I began to drag the mutilated bodies above the high-tide mark. Some began to bleed again as I moved them, leaving traces of blood and oil in the sand. Several had their arms all but severed, blood and sinew, muscle and viscera scarlet against their shining oil-blackened bodies; others carried great gashes to their torsos with ribs protruding like bloodied and broken cages. The vicious *parang* blades had slashed willy-nilly at their bodies, cutting deeply wherever they landed.

I fought back the need to sit down and howl and on two occasions I threw up violently. I was also near crapping myself, I was so afraid the murderers would return and find me. I knew I should do the decent thing and bury the bodies. The sand was soft enough to scoop out a ditch for each. But it would take too long and I was too scared. All I could think was that I must somehow tidy things up. So I began placing them in a straight row, each about two feet from the next. I had left the headless bloke until last, unable to summon the courage to drag him up to the other bodies.

Then the thought entered my befuddled mind that I was the son of an Anglican missionary who was a clergyman and I had attended hundreds of funerals in the past. I knew the funeral litany by heart. I must do something. Say a prayer or recite a passage from the Bible. I started collecting driftwood from the beach and with a ball of twine I carried in my knapsack hurriedly fashioned nine crude crosses, every minute or so looking towards where the attackers had gone. I tried to tell myself that they had no reason to return, they'd taken everything they could find – the Carley float, Mae West jackets, watches, money; they'd even taken the boots, though they couldn't have any possible use for them as these men were all barefoot and had probably discarded the boots they'd once worn in the Dutch forces before deserting. These reassurances didn't work, I was still damn near messing in my pants, glancing every few moments in the direction they'd gone.

I placed a cross above the head of every corpse and then with one cross left I could delay the gruesome task no longer and forced myself to walk further down the beach. Not looking at the severed neck, I grabbed him by the boots and dragged his body up the beach, averting my head for as long as possible and finally placed him in line with his mates. There seemed something profane about a body lying with all the others but without a head. Then I saw it, the head. It was being pushed up onto the beach by an incoming wave and then dragged back again as the wave receded, in a manner I had seen so often with a coconut washed ashore.

I knew I mustn't stop to think about it and I dashed towards the water, not conscious that I was sobbing as I waded into the shallow waves that were breaking at my ankles. I reached down and grabbed the head in both hands, not looking, the wet hair soft to my touch. Stumbling and running up the beach, I deposited it above the dead man's shoulders and made myself look at the dead sailor's head, only to see that I had placed it sideways, his left ear resting on the top of his severed neck. I was forced to pick it up and look into the blackened face for the first time. The dead sailor's eyes were open, staring at me, a piercing blue colour almost identical to the colour of Anna's. I screamed, dropping the head, where it rolled away from the body and was covered in sand. Still sobbing, I retrieved it and placed it more or less correctly onto the neck. I didn't have the means or the courage to wipe the sand from his face. I sat on the beach, my hands resting on my knees and my head lowered between them, panting and whimpering, mucus running from my nose.

I was emotionally exhausted and, rising unsteadily, I placed the last of the crosses in place. In my confused and overwrought mind I was not sure if I could remember the words, or at least some of the words, to the Anglican burial service. I stood more or less at the centre of the nine men laid out in a row and with my palms held in front of me in the manner of an open prayer book began to recite as I had so often heard my father do at a native funeral. In my panicked state of mind I decided to choose only two small and very common passages I thought might be appropriate.

'"I am the resurrection, and the life", saith the Lord: "he that believeth in me, though he were dead, yet shall he live: and whosoever liveth and believeth in me shall never die . . ."'

I suddenly mistook the sharp cry of a gull for a human voice and glanced backwards, terrified, very nearly wetting my pants. It took several moments to regain my composure. With my knees trembling, and still breathless from the effects of the sudden rush of adrenalin brought on by fear, I pronounced the remaining words in a voice that seemed to alter pitch every few moments:

'neither death, nor life, nor angels, nor principalities, nor powers, nor things present, nor things to come, nor height, nor depth, nor any other creature, shall be able to separate us from the love of God, which is in Christ Jesus our Lord.

'Earth to earth; ashes to ashes; dust to dust; in the sure and certain hope of resurrection to eternal life.

'Amen.'

I ended by saying the Lord's prayer, adding in retrospect, 'May you rest in peace'.

The performance of the small, hastily improvised ceremony had a strangely calming effect on me. I felt as if I had brought some measure of decency into the horrific deaths the sailors had suffered. If, like many of the sons of ministers of religion, I wasn't religious myself, I nevertheless had a deep respect for the calming process of sacred words.

Despite trying to put him from my mind, my thoughts kept reverting to the poor guy with no head. His blue eyes, so reminiscent of Anna's, had shaken me badly, somehow his death seemed worse than that of the other men. Poor bugger didn't even possess a shirt as a shroud.

Oh God! He must have been the one who had removed his shirt for the dead man they'd placed under the bushes. The man under the bushes! I'd entirely forgotten about him. I began to shake. When was the horror going to end? I'd have to repeat everything! The thought filled me with terror.

I walked the small distance up the beach to where I thought

they'd placed the dead sailor under a line of bushes. I fell to my knees in the soft sand so I could peer under the low-hanging leaves. The first thing I saw was a naked foot, then it moved and I heard a groan.

CHAPTER TWO

*'Lissen, sonny boy, where I come from,
giving a sucker an even break is considered
a crime against humanity!'*
Kevin Judge

I RAISED THE LOWER branches of a bush from where I imagined the sound of the groan had come. It revealed a black head and torso lying face upwards. The sailor's eyes were closed and from his nostrils two small mucus bubbles rose and receded with each completed breath. He had a nasty cut above his right eye that showed as a bright-red open gash against his oil-blackened skin and extended in length to the centre of his forehead.

'Mate? You okay?' I asked, unable to think of any other way I might gain his attention. No reply came, not even an acknowledging groan, although I noted that his chest continued to rise and fall in what I imagined was a pretty even manner. I reached out and shook his shoulder but got no reaction.

The distance to the mangroves and the creek was about three-quarters of a mile. If I was going to get him on board the *Vleermuis* I would have to carry him. I wasn't prepared to wait until he came around; that is, *if* he came around. I'd heard of cases where people lay in a coma for days, even weeks. Fortunately he wasn't a big man, in fact he was smaller than average – in the parlance of Australians he was a bit of a runt. I could heft him into a fireman's lift, and with a stop or two along the beach I felt sure I could get him to the boat. What I needed like a hole in the head was a guy in a coma on a sailboat crossing the Indian Ocean. I didn't want to think about it.

I was on my knees and I pushed the lower branches aside with my left shoulder until I could position myself more or less behind him so as to get a grip under his armpits. It was awkward work; I had to shuffle sideways with the branches springing back and slapping the unconscious man across the face. Fortunately the sand under him was soft and smooth. His head and shoulders still rested on the headless sailor's shirt and this came away with him as I pulled him clear of the foliage.

It was then that I first saw his IDs, the two aluminium discs American sailors wear around their necks. I lifted one without removing it and rubbed the oil from its surface with the pad of my thumb. Stamped on the disc was his name and serial number and I would later learn the 'C' stood for Catholic and the 'B' was his blood type; USN, of course, stood for the US Navy.

Judge
K.
164834
C
B
USN

The little bloke was an American. I was surprised, having decided that the other sailors were, like myself, Australian. Then I noticed that his oil-stained clobber was different to the shirt and shorts the others had worn. He'd come off another warship. The last few inches of the tail of the shirt he'd rested on, the bit that tucks in, was still comparatively clean. I used it to wipe the mucus from his nose and to clean up around his eyes and mouth. I then attempted to give him water, pushing the neck of my water bottle into his swollen, cracked and partially open lips. But the contents simply dribbled from the corner of his mouth and down his neck.

The sun was now well above the horizon but there was some cloud; it would probably build later in the day and bring on a thunderstorm and it was already uncomfortably hot. At least K. Judge and I wouldn't be spending it becalmed, wallowing out at sea. I was anxious to be well clear of the killing beach as soon as possible and decided I'd wait until we got to the boat before attempting to clean up the little bloke any further.

But then I did a very strange thing – which goes to show I wasn't all that calm and in control. In truth, I was probably deep in shock. The little bloke, that is what I'd taken to calling him in my mind, was barefoot and I decided on the spot that he needed boots. *Must have boots. It was imperative that he had boots to wear.* This extraordinary notion may well have been prompted in my unconscious mind by thoughts of the deck which, the previous day, had been hot enough to fry the soles of one's feet. I cannot think how else this bizarre compulsion could have entered my head. The attackers had removed the boots from five of the six men who had been on board the Carley float, while the four who had been hanging onto its side had been barefoot. Only the headless sailor had retained his boots and I can remember clearly thinking with some alacrity: *Hey, without a head he's not going to need his boots.* I scrambled down the beach to where I'd laid him and quickly removed the boots, pleased with myself for my amazing perspicacity.

I returned to the still unconscious sailor and pushed the

boots, splattered with congealed blood mixed with beach sand, into my knapsack. I shouldered the knapsack, whereupon I hoisted the little bloke in a fireman's lift. It was at that moment that I remembered my butterfly net. With my arms fully occupied with the unconscious body across my shoulders I had no way of carrying it. I have already mentioned that stubbornness is not a pleasant part of my character and there was no way I was going to leave the net behind. If my mind had been functioning properly and I'd stopped to think for the briefest moment, I would have realised I had no further use for it. You don't catch butterflies in the middle of the Indian Ocean. It wasn't valuable and another would be easy to obtain. In fact, I could make one in less than an hour.

I lowered the sailor back onto the sand, picked up the net and placed it over his head, its long bamboo handle resting against his spine and extending to give his bum a bit of a tail. Then I lifted him onto my shoulders again. Silently congratulating myself for such clever thinking, I set out to carry him along the beach towards the distant mangroves.

What happened next was sufficient to stretch anyone's credulity and if I didn't still possess the evidence I would have put it down to a hallucinatory episode brought on by my heightened state of shock. I had moved to the top of the beach where the sand petered out and the ground was firmer. I'd gone about three hundred yards and was beginning to feel the strain from carrying the little bloke when I saw it resting on a low bush feeding on the nectar of one of the yellow star-shaped blossoms covering it. As it slowly opened and closed its wings the Magpie Crow was everything I'd imagined it to be, a truly beautiful butterfly.

May God forgive me! I swung the poor hapless sailor from

my shoulders and dumped him roughly onto the ground at my feet where he landed with an audible thump, his head jerking within the butterfly net. I hastily and not over-gently removed the net from his head and shoulders and flung the knapsack from my back just as the butterfly flew off into the air. Crashing through the scrub I took off after it. Half an hour later, scratched and bleeding, I had the beauty safely in my net.

It took me a good twenty minutes to return to where I'd summarily abandoned the little bloke. The knapsack was there, but the recently unconscious K. Judge was missing. I scanned the beach in the direction from which we'd come and forward to the soft green line of mangroves. The beach was pristine, empty except for a dozen resting gulls, their reflections caught in the wet sheen left by a retreated wave. He was nowhere to be seen. Vanished into thin air. Gone. Vamoosed!

I was faced with a terrible dilemma. Do I go after him or do I process the precious butterfly? In less than a minute I could infuse tissue paper placed in the jar with ethyl acetate and keep the beautiful specimen intact. After which I would have to find the newly resurrected seaman in no more than an hour or the Magpie Crow could start to spoil – condensation from the heat could cause bits of its wings to stick to the glass sides. *Shit! Shit! Shit!* I chose to process the butterfly and take the chance that I'd find the disappearing sailor in time. To my confused mind it seemed a fair division of priorities. After all, I'd waited two months for the elusive butterfly and I'd been aware of the American's existence for less than an hour.

My infusion of the Magpie Crow finally completed, I grabbed the bottle of water and slung it round my neck so that it rested on my hip. I soon found the sailor's tracks. He'd headed inland, into the scrub and towards the coconut plantation from which I'd earlier watched the tragedy on the beach unfold.

For a while his footprints were reasonably clear, zigzagging in the slightly softer soil. *Small feet – the headless bloke's boots would be miles too big!* But then the ground grew firmer and his progress was harder to follow. My heart began to beat faster. I found a freshly snapped twig and a place where the bushes had recently been parted, but soon I was beyond the waist-high coastal scrub and starting to climb towards the *copra* plantation. I knew that once within the coconut palms, he'd be almost impossible to spot. Multiple vertical shapes in a shady environment confuse the eye. Worse, once in the plantation there was a greater likelihood that he'd meet or be seen by a native.

I checked my watch. I had to find him within ten minutes or my specimen would be placed in jeopardy – ten minutes, then fifteen more to get back to the beach. Nearly half an hour! And I'd taken thirty minutes to catch the Magpie Crow and another twenty to get back to where I'd started the chase! If he'd regained consciousness shortly after I dumped him, he could have been gone almost an hour. I was beginning to panic on two fronts. I was going to lose both the little bloke and the Magpie Crow.

What was it about this fucking butterfly? Trying to find it had brought me nothing but bad luck. In medieval times both the magpie and the crow were considered to be bad omens. If either was seen as the first bird of the morning the day was certain to bring trouble.

I pushed my way through some tall scrub and there he stood, the ground rising behind him, his small black shape facing me. The lighter patches where I'd cleaned around his eyes, nose and mouth gave him a distinctly simian appearance. He stood facing me, adopting a threatening pose, his arms hanging, elbows bent and away from his body; in every sense he gave the appearance of a chimpanzee.

I was almost overwhelmed with relief. 'Thank God I've found you!' I cried, then hastily added, 'Gidday, Mr Judge,' as I took a step towards him.

'Don't move, sonny boy!' he growled.

Then I saw he carried a rock in his left hand. He must have picked it up when he heard me coming. He's left-handed, I thought to myself, apropos of nothing. 'Come now, sir,' I said, smiling and spreading my hands in a gesture of friendliness, 'we have to go.'

'I ain't goin' nowhere, punk!' he said. 'You ain't takin' me back. I ain't gonna go back.' He shook his head. 'No way, José! Ya hear? The judge says I hadda join the US Navy, then I'm clean. You hear that, sonny boy? Clean! They gonna wipe my record. I'm gonna be a cleanskin! I'm navy now. American navy! I ain't no dog you can push around no more! I'm Uncle Sam and I ain't on the lam! Navy, sonny boy! You hear? US fuckin' navy!'

He was talking in a rasp through cracked lips. It was the first time I'd seen anyone hallucinating and I didn't know what to do next. 'Here,' I said, holding out the bottle of water. 'I'm a friend; look, I've brought you water, Mr Judge.'

'Don't gimme that "I'm ya friend" bullshit, sonny boy! I know a fuckin' cop when I smell one.' He sniffed, drawing back mucus. 'Lousy fuckin' cop! You smell, you hear? Cop smell!' He couldn't take his eyes off the bottle of water I held out to him. 'Throw it here,' he commanded, nodding his head at the bottle.

I removed the water bottle from around my neck, at the same time taking a step nearer to him. He raised the rock above his shoulder. I held the bottle out to almost within his grasp. 'C'mon, you need to drink. I won't hurt you and I'm not a cop.

I'm a butterfly collector.'

Even to his fevered brain this must have seemed funny. He lowered the rock and I took another step forward. He appeared to be bemused. 'What kind of cockamamie . . . ? Did you say butterfly? Like wid the wings and the flowers?' he croaked.

I sighed. 'Yeah, don't give me a hard time, Mr Judge,' I said, grinning and taking a final step so that I now stood directly in front of him, holding out the bottle. He snatched it from my hand, but the metal-topped cork stopper remained on. He tried to pull it out with his teeth but was unsuccessful. Panting with rage and the urgent need to drink, he dropped the rock and withdrew the stopper. I made no move to grab him as he started to drink greedily, swallowing too quickly and choking, then bringing it up again. 'Jesus, Mary and Joseph!' he gasped.

'Take it easy, mate; sip at it slowly, that way you won't throw it up.'

He took a sip and then another, gasping, bent double, his hands resting on his knees after each sip. 'C'mon, sir, let's get going, you can drink on the way,' I said unreasonably, anxious to get back to the Magpie Crow. In my mind's eye I could see the condensation forming on the sides of the butterfly jar.

He brought the bottle down. 'You got a warrant?' he demanded.

I sighed again, somewhat showing my exasperation. Using language I thought might get through to him and affecting an American accent, something I'd learned as a child at the American School in Tokyo, I said, 'Listen up, sailor! We are surrounded by Japs. We're deep inside enemy territory! We gotta get the fuck outa here and back to the boat pronto or you and me, we're dead meat, sailor!'

To my surprise he sprang to attention and saluted me, the

water bottle held stiffly to his side. 'Yessir! Right away, sir!'

In his hallucinatory state I was no longer a cop but now a naval officer. He was no longer a tough guy but a sailor responding to an order.

'Let's go!' I said, turning away and starting to walk back in the direction of the beach, hoping he'd follow.

Understandably the poor bugger wasn't in great shape and we were forced to stop several times. On each occasion I made him sip from the water bottle. Not wanting to chance my luck and have him fall back into the cop-and-delinquent routine, except for my crisp command 'Drink!' each time we stopped, I remained silent until we'd regained the beach. 'Take a rest, sailor!' I said in the peremptory manner I'd adopted.

The little bloke collapsed gratefully onto the beach as I ran towards where I'd left the killing jar in the shade of a low-hanging bush. A merciful angel on duty in heaven must have decided that I'd had enough trouble for one day. The beautiful butterfly rested in the tissue paper in the centre of the jar, completely intact.

My field kit lay where I'd left it in the sun, the jar of ethyl acetate still open, the contents all but evaporated. It was careless in the extreme and I should have reprimanded myself – meticulous attention to detail makes a successful butterfly collector. But for once I didn't care. Game, set and match! I'd finally snared my quarry.

From my paraphernalia box I withdrew a small triangular envelope, one of several I'd prepared two months previously at the onset of my (*hooray!*) now not entirely disastrous expedition. Using a pair of tweezers I extracted the Magpie Crow from the jar and carefully placed it in the specially folded envelope and then into a sleeve in the box where it would be protected from being damaged. Now all I had to do was to get it home. Get *us* home! I can't say I felt ashamed or remorseful for my behaviour. I know I should have, but I didn't. The two things were separate, the butterfly and the sailor. As long as I can remember I've possessed the capacity to keeps things in separate compartments. My mother's death when I was five, my father's stoic and bewildering silence afterwards, the loneliness of a Caucasian child growing up in Japan, my father turning from a cold academic into an equally passionless missionary where God was always angry and redemption was more punishment than joy, the shock of going to school in Australia and the cruelty of the kids who referred to me as 'the Jap' or as 'Yellow Belly', the constant derision when they heard I collected butterflies. All these things, I had told myself as a child, must be kept separate, so they did not collectively overpower me. Now it had become a habit.

I turned to where I'd left the little bloke. We hadn't been formally introduced and so I still didn't know his Christian name. He now sat with his elbows resting on his knees and his head hanging forlornly, chin on his chest, his nose dripping. My water bottle rested on the sand beside him.

Deciding to abandon the superior officer routine and the phoney Yank accent I squatted down beside him. 'Mr Judge?' At the sound of my voice he glanced briefly up at me, then returned to looking down at the sand between his knees. 'My name is Nick . . . Nick Duncan. And yours is . . . ?' I asked softly. His fingers fumbled for one of the dog tags around his neck and, stretching the bootlace that attached it to its extremity, he held it out to me. 'No, no, Mr Judge,' I laughed. 'Your Christian name?'

'I ain't telling you nuthin', sonny boy!' he snarled, reverting back to being a hard arse.

I picked up the water bottle and shook it. It was empty. There was no choice, I decided. I had to revert to an American accent so he would understand me and go back to the peremptory manner I'd previously affected. 'Okay, Mr Judge, this is how I see our situation.' I picked up the water bottle and shook it. 'We're fresh out of water. If you remain here you'll die of dehydration. You may as well give me one of your dog tags so I can report you dead. Your ship has gone down. You've been shipwrecked. The Japs are coming to get you. If they don't get you, the savages will.' With the reference to savages he looked up quickly with a frightened expression. Seeing his sudden fear I added, 'You'll be soup by tonight: big black three-legged soup pot and you in it stewing and boiling, plop, plop, plop!' I was letting my imagination get carried away. The threat of being eaten would, I hoped, penetrate his confused mind. 'Now, listen, Mr Judge, I'm here to save your ass! Come with me and we may escape. Stay here and you are certain to die. Dehydration! Japs! Terrible torture! Or soup for savages! You choose, because I'm not hanging around any longer. I've got to try and save my own sweet ass!' I concluded, deliberately using the American 'ass' and not 'arse'.

K. Judge didn't react and kept staring, snot dripping, the cannibal threat – or any other – evidently not getting through to him. I sighed and got to my feet, slung the water bottle strap over my head and walked over to my knapsack and lifted it onto my back. 'Coming or not?' I said, as I started to walk away, not glancing back. The empty water bottle bounced on my hip, making a muffled tinny sound.

I hadn't gone more than ten yards when I heard him shout, 'Sir! Sir!' I waited without turning to look at him. I could hear the squeak his feet made in the dry beach sand as he stumbled towards me. When he reached me he fell onto his knees at my feet, gripping the top of my right boot in both hands and in a frightened child's voice implored me, 'Please, sir, don't let them turn me into savages' soup!' Then he started to bawl.

The experience of having grown men bawling at my feet was becoming all too familiar, although the little bloke was probably close to my own age but I couldn't really tell with all the oil covering him.

'What's your name?' I asked gently.

'Kevin, sir!' he sobbed.

'How old are you, Kevin?'

'Six, sir.'

'Righto, you get up now and take my hand.' I held out my hand for him; he took it and I helped him to his feet. 'Now don't let go of me. It's very important if we're going to escape.' I pointed to the strip of green, the mangroves at the far end of the beach. 'I've got a boat hidden in there. We've got to get there as fast as we can to escape the terrible human-flesh-eating savages,' I said, laying it on thick.

'Yes, sir,' he choked, still blubbing, his hand gripping even tighter around my own. I looked down at his legs and feet to see that they were scratched and bleeding from when he'd previously gone bush.

Poor little bastard; I wondered how much longer he could keep going. I had to get him onto the cutter and attend to his head wound. The water he'd swallowed would have helped a bit, but he would still be pretty dehydrated. I walked him down to the edge of the surf where the wet sand was harder and it would be easier going, while the salt water washing in from the spent waves would help the cuts. I reasoned our footprints would be washed away fairly quickly. I decided I'd have to carry him across the short stretch of mangrove forest when we got there. The creek hadn't been more than four feet deep when I'd previously waded across it. With the tide now fully in, it might be somewhat higher. The little bloke wouldn't have been much taller than five feet and couldn't swim.

'Okay, you can stop crying now, Kevin. I reckon we'll be just fine. You hang onto my hand – don't let go no matter what – and we'll be safe,' I cautioned. We continued at a fairly steady pace, mostly in silence as all the time I was trying to listen for any sound of native activity. I also didn't want to say too much lest I trigger a different Kevin Judge, a persona from the past who might be more difficult to handle than the compliant 'six-year-old' I was leading to the boat.

When we reached the mangroves the incoming tide had hidden the roots and, in particular, the smaller shoots that pierce the mud at low tide. These are hard, with sharp tips, and can cut badly if you step on them; the cuts not as bad as coral cuts but liable to fester and become quite nasty. I made Kevin shoulder my knapsack and then climb up to sit on my shoulders where I thought he'd be easier to carry than if I piggybacked him. We proceeded through the muddy waist-high water, stumbling once or twice against hidden roots but finally arriving unscathed at the edge of the creek.

'Now, Kevin, I want you to take off the knapsack from your back. Whatever you do, don't drop it.' The thought of the knapsack falling into the water and damaging my precious specimen was unimaginable.

Kevin didn't reply and I held my breath as I felt him trying to wriggle free, to get the straps over his arms. 'It's okay, I've got your legs, you won't fall, I promise.' I then castigated myself silently. I should have left the knapsack on the beach before we entered the mangroves, and returned for it when I had him safely on board. He eventually managed to get the knapsack off and held it out, with one arm still clutched around my forehead.

'Now, Kevin, I want you to hook it over a mangrove branch, this one next to us. Make sure it's secure, very secure!' I fought back the panic as he struggled to do as he was told. All I needed was for the knapsack to slip from his grasp and the Magpie Crow . . . I couldn't bring myself to complete the thought. I heard the rustle of leaves, then silence, then Kevin pushing away from the branch and all the while I hadn't taken a breath. 'Okay, Kevin, is it safe?'

'Yes, sir, I think so, sir.'

Oh God, please let it be! I thought to myself.

I still wasn't sure how far the incoming tide had managed to raise the level of the creek, but reckoned from the depth of the water in the mangroves I should be able to walk across to the boat with Kevin sitting on my shoulders.

'Can you swim, Kevin?' I asked, just in case I'd underestimated the depth.

'I ain't learned yet, sir. Only when we're eight,' he replied.

'Righto, you stay on my back; it's not deep – about five feet, perhaps a bit more – so hang on while I walk us through.' I stepped into the deeper water and I could feel him shaking, his hands clasped around my forehead as he hung on for dear life. At its deepest the water came to just under my chin. I made for the bronze mooring post on the starboard quarter of the deck and by the time I'd reached the cutter the creek level was just above my navel. 'Righto, Kevin, hop aboard,' I instructed.

'I'll fall, sir,' he said in a small voice.

'No you won't, I've got you. Just loosen your grip on my head and grab that post in front of you, then climb onto my shoulders. Here, I'll push you up.' His arms left my head and I let go of his legs as he wriggled frantically. Placing one foot on my shoulder he managed to scramble aboard, lying on the deck gasping furiously just as a young kid might. 'Well done!' I called and waited until he sat up and had pulled himself well clear of the edge of the deck. 'Now, Kevin, wait for me. I'm going back to get the knapsack. Just sit, don't move. Okay?'

'Yes, sir,' he replied meekly. Wherever the little bloke had been brought up as a child, it hadn't been easy. His tone of voice carried all the hallmarks of regularly enforced obedience.

I returned to my knapsack, then recrossed the creek, holding it well above my head and finally depositing it onto the deck. I heaved myself aboard and started to remove my clobber. 'Everything off, Kevin,' I called cheerily. 'Time to clean you up, mate,' I said, reverting to my normal accent.

I expected the little bloke at any moment to return to his 'Lissen, sonny boy' adult personality. We were safely on the boat and I told myself I could deal with a recalcitrant sailor when he had nowhere to go. If it came to a fight, I was too big for him to take on and hope to win. But he remained a small kid, anxious to cooperate for fear of the dreaded cooking pot.

I got out the kero and some of the cleaning rags Anna had stowed for the voyage together with a couple of worn towels. Kevin 'ouched' and 'aahed' and winced a fair bit, the kerosene stinging and uncomfortable on his skin. When it was all over I scooped a bucket of water from the creek and soaped him down, rinsing and repeating the soaping three times, each time making him do the same over his pubic area and bum. Finally, I reckoned he was almost good as new.

The cleaned-up version of Kevin Judge, aka 'the little bloke', was no metamorphosis from chimp to prince. His eyes, the whites still very bloodshot, were a tawny hazel colour. His crew-cut hair was mousy brown and his ears appeared too large for his sharp little face. His front teeth overlapped slightly and were somewhat crooked, the sign of early dental neglect. I wasn't sure how his nose had started out in life because it had been broken, perhaps more than once, and was flattened like a lump of dough pressed into his face. His legs were thin and bandy, an indication that rickets had probably been present in childhood. In appearance his type is often referred to derogatively as 'bog Irish', an undernourished look that was common enough among the working class in post-Depression Australia and that stamps itself indelibly on the adult who evolves from the neglected child. I guessed it was much the same in America.

Oh, yes – there was something else. On his right hand between the first and second knuckle of each finger was a crude and amateur attempt at tattooing, a single letter on each finger: the first an 'L' on his pinkie and, facing outwards, it was followed by the other three letters spelling the word LOVE. Identically, on the fingers of his left hand was the word HATE. He was left-handed so I had to assume that HATE assumed the greater importance.

The gash on his forehead needed stitching if it wasn't going to leave a bloody great scar, which wouldn't add to his good looks. I had no way of stitching it and my only treatment was cotton wool soaked in iodine and a bandage from the first aid kit. I also treated the cuts on his feet and legs with a solution of iodine, and fortunately they appeared fairly superficial.

'I'm hungry, sir,' the new, clean, white and very battered-looking version of Kevin cried in a plaintive voice.

I cooked him a bowl of rice and tinned fish and watched him eat it ravenously.

'I think you should lie down, mate, you look pretty whacked.' He'd copped a bit of sun, although it could have been worse – the cloud cover had increased as the morning wore on and it was now completely overcast, moreover the greasy oil would have effectively protected his fair skin. I gave him a couple of Aspro. Anna had given me three bottles, the only medicine I had in the medical kit except for Epsom salts and iodine. She'd insisted I take all three bottles even though I protested that I hadn't had a headache in two years. I recall how she'd laughed, '*Mijn* papa, he buys always a big box, twenty-four bottles, for the morning his head and *ja*, also at night.' It wasn't hard to see that the little bloke was completely done in. Still in the nuddy, I took him down below where I made him climb into the double bunk in the forward cabin. Despite the noonday heat, in a couple of minutes he was dead to the world.

I changed into a spare pair of shorts and climbed up the mast to fix the faulty blocks, greasing them and making a few small adjustments. Then I set about the task of washing his clobber as well as my own, his several times in an attempt to get rid of the oil. But each time they dried they remained stiff as a board. Fourth time around, while badly discoloured, I reckoned they could be worn. I rinsed the blood and sand off the headless bloke's boots and set them out to dry. They'd be miles too big for the little bloke but along with the wallets and scraps of paper would be further evidence of the atrocity if ever we made landfall in Australia. I gathered up all the wallets and paper and dried them on deck, only giving them a cursory examination. They confirmed that their murdered owners were Australians off HMAS *Perth*. I would read them more carefully at a later time, I decided.

My final task was to create a waterproof wallet out of a small square cut from the hem of my stormweather oilskin. Into it I put the triangular envelope containing my precious butterfly, then placed the wallet within the infusion jar and screwed the lid back on. If we sank it would float to eventually turn up on some golden beach fringed with coconut palms where a beautiful young woman, very reminiscent of Anna, would find it and treasure it forever. My imagination was working overtime, no doubt triggered earlier by my evocation of the little bloke turning into soup, simmering away in a huge three-legged cannibal pot. It occurred to me that had we been marooned on some remote beach in New Guinea instead of Java, the threat I'd used on Kevin would not have been an idle one, cannibalism being still practised among some of the more remote tribes.

Around five o'clock, with the clouds now low and dark with moisture and the air almost overbearingly humid, I gathered everything from the deck and stowed it below. The little bloke lay bathed in a lather of sweat and I had some trouble waking him. Eventually I got him to sit up and made him drink. In all he must have consumed half a gallon of water since the morning and had yet to take a piss. I gave him two more Aspro tablets and he collapsed wearily back into the bunk and in moments he was out to it again.

I removed my shorts to prevent them from getting wet in the threatening tropical storm and returned to the deck, where I rigged a canvas sheet fashioned into a trough to catch drinking water. Moments later the deluge arrived and I sat with my back against the mast, my face raised to the sky, where I let it all come at me, the hard pellets of rain pelting into my face and skin in a vain physical attempt to wash from my heart and mind some of the ugliness of the day.

I was dead weary, having been up half the night, but knew that I had to make for the Sunda Strait and be clear of it by morning. I would be forced to remain at the tiller throughout the night, hoping that under cover of dark I could avoid the Jap warships. I felt fairly certain they would have entered the strait prior to mounting the land invasion of Java.

It was comparatively cool after the storm and so I went down below and climbed into a bunk and fell asleep, to wake an hour or so later in the gathering dusk. Kevin was still completely out to it and I thought to wake him and give him more water but decided against it. I had a fair bit to do and the last thing I needed was a newly personified and recalcitrant K. Judge 'sonny-boying' me while I got us under way. I examined the chart and using the dividers and parallel rulers I worked out my position and wrote down the various compass bearings I'd need in pencil, stuffing the note into the back pocket of my shorts. I made myself a thermos of strong black coffee, reheated the rice and a tin of fish, and ate, knowing it would be my last meal for a while. Even though it was not yet dark I lit the kero lamp in the binnacle to illuminate the compass, fearful that even this dim pinprick of light might be seen. As a final touch, knowing I'd have to stay put all night, I brought a waterproof cushion up from the cabin and placed it on the grating at the bottom of the cockpit; seated on it and leaning against the back of the cockpit with my arm resting on the tiller, I would be comfortable enough for the long watch that lay ahead.

The tide was beginning to recede so I went forward, ran

out the jib on the bowsprit and hoisted the staysail, leaving the sheets loose as I was still sheltered by the mangrove trees on both sides of the creek. I'd hoist the mainsail once I was clear of the mangroves and the reef and when I was able to use the breeze that was just beginning to come off the shore.

The clouds hadn't cleared after the five o'clock downpour and still hung low and dark on the horizon, threatening further rain. This was a good omen. It would make it much harder to see the *Vleermuis* with its dark hull and brown sails in the rain-dimmed evening light. Later the clouds would mask the moon, making it even more difficult to spot a tiny boat out at sea.

I lashed the tiller and using the sweep poled my way downstream, the outgoing tide making it comparatively light work. Once clear of the mangroves I sheeted in the foresails, whereupon *Vleermuis* started to move gently across the small lagoon and into the passage dividing the reef. Soon enough I started to feel the slight lifting to the sea that told me I was away. I hoisted the mainsail to catch the offshore breeze and unlashed the tiller. Glancing at the threatening clouds I pulled my oilskin coat on. Being wet ashore is one thing, but with a breeze hitting you out at sea it can become bloody cold and miserable.

Half an hour later it started to rain again, not a thunderstorm but a steady downpour. The sea was starting to rise, the boat coming off the tops of the waves, steeper now, the fall into the troughs deeper, the bow one moment poking into thin air and the next seemingly buried in a trough. I set my course to sail the ten nautical miles to the point where I calculated I would enter the strait.

Conditions such as these take a fair bit of sailing, as the boat has a tendency to move in three directions: up and down, forward and back, left and right, then twists around its own centre of gravity. In such conditions, except for adjusting the sails, I was stuck to the tiller for the duration. The good thing was that I'd have to practically ram a Jap ship to be discovered and so we were reasonably safe. If the little bloke was to wake up with all the movement (*Jesus, he's almost certain to be seasick!*), there was precious little I could do to help him. I'd left a canvas waterbag hanging where he could reach it from his bunk. If he started to throw up at least he wouldn't dehydrate. He was bollocky so thankfully I wouldn't have to wash his clobber again. But it can become quite cool at sea in the tropics and I'd left a blanket hanging over the end of the bunk. Getting vomit off a blanket isn't a pleasant task. But one thing was certain – whatever persona emerged after his long kip, if he was sick as a dog K. Judge wouldn't be making too much trouble.

The cutter's shallow draft meant I could safely hug the coast about one mile offshore. With the coastline still dimly visible I set the course west-nor'-west, estimating it would take me three hours, maybe four, to clear St Nicholas Point, when I would set a course south-west through the strait; the wide course would avoid the risk of running into Java or Sumatra. My chart had shown several islands within the strait, and in the murky darkness I would have to rely on the strong current to carry me around them. Well, that was the theory anyway.

I crossed the mouth of Bantem Bay where the weather had turned blustery with frequent squalls hiding the shore. But when one such squall abated, to my consternation I saw my first Japanese warships – two troop carriers with their lights on close to shore, unloading troops and supplies. The moon was only just up, and coming from behind a cloud it suddenly brightened the shore and I could see their landing craft pulled into the shallow water beyond the beach. To show lights at night could only mean they were confident that they'd routed the American and Australian naval forces. I was grateful when a few minutes later another rain squall arrived. If I could see them, particularly when the moon showed through the cloud, then they might be able to see me, although with all their activity directed towards the shore they were probably too preoccupied to worry about watching the open sea. Whatever, I now knew the Japs were well and truly present. It was going to be a long night at sea.

After crossing the bay and clearing the land I felt the water smooth; the current running at about six knots through the strait was beginning to take effect. Together with the land breeze the two elements would speed me through the danger zone, effectively doubling my speed across the water. Feeling slightly more confident, by the light of the kero lamp in the binnacle I adjusted the compass to read slightly south of west-sou'-west, about 240 degrees. The offshore breeze was now abeam and I felt the vessel heel slightly and begin to cut through the water. The long straight keel of her traditional hull design made *Vleermuis* very stable directionally. I could see the bow with a slight chuckle of white water, but beyond it was a void.

If I hadn't been shitting myself, I should have been enjoying the fact that we were both in our preferred element. I loved to sail as much as I loved collecting butterflies. From the age of twelve, with the mission natives acting as my crew, I'd been responsible for sailing the clumsy old mission schooner along the coast of New Britain and over to New Guinea, both being an extension of my father's parish. He wasn't fond of sailing and had a tendency to become violently seasick in the slightest swell. The boat was yet another burden placed upon his stoic shoulders by an angry God.

To take the edge off my fear, I decided to begin in my mind to think of the splendid little sailing boat by her new name, *Madam Butterfly*. When and if Kevin eventually emerged from the cabin as his adult self, he would know her only by this name.

Vleermuis, pronounced 'Flay–mace', was a mouthful anyway and calling the lovely little gaff-cutter after a flying bat was yet another indication of the Dutchman's lack of sensitivity. Now every time I referred to her as *Madam Butterfly*, it would have the additional effect of recalling my darling Anna.

During the night I passed several dark shapes, their silhouettes too irregular in form to be ships, and I concluded they must be islands, the powerful current theory working and carrying me away from them. I kept myself preoccupied with holding my course, ensuring the sails were drawing well, but by 4 a.m. I was starting to feel pretty knackered. I realised I'd been running on strong black coffee and natural adrenalin all night, convinced that at any moment I would be spotted by a Japanese warship or patrol boat.

I had reached the stage where I was awake though not quite certain if I only imagined that I was, and began feeling the slight swell that might indicate I was heading into a wider area where the strait merged imperceptibly into the Indian Ocean. I decided to take the chance and swing into a course due south, the direction I would need to follow to take me away from the land. The wind began to pick up from over my shoulder from the north-west. Every mile I could make before dawn would be a mile further away from danger.

I thought about Anna and how it might have been had the Dutchman agreed to her sailing with me to Australia. She would have almost certainly accompanied me on the butterfly

hunt and witnessed the slaughter on the beach and then had
to cope with the resurrection of K. Judge. How would she have
reacted? I hadn't done too well myself. In addition I would have
been panicking that we'd be picked up and that she'd fall into
the hands of the Japanese. My already overwrought imagination
started to make pictures of such a catastrophe and I forced myself
to stop thinking. I had read about some of the things Japanese
soldiers had done to Chinese women in Nanking.

The Dutchman had made the correct decision. I wouldn't
have wanted anyone, male or female, to go through the
past nearly twenty-four hours, let alone someone I loved and
cherished with my whole heart. I could feel a lump in my throat
and a heaviness growing in my chest just from thinking about
the effect on her mind, had she been with me. It would be
something she would never forget; the stuff of nightmares for the
remainder of her life, as I fully expected it would be of mine.

Dawn, when it came, was a smudgy affair; low clouds scudded
across a dirty red horizon and the squalls continued. I snuffed
out the binnacle lantern as I could see the compass card
clearly by now. We were picking up speed to what I estimated
was about five knots. In a lighter craft I might have shortened
sail, but heading downwind in a sea flattened by the effect of
the landmasses Sumatra and Java behind me, I felt confident
she could carry the increased speed. *Madam Butterfly* (*hey, it's
working!*) was heeling less than I had expected, a tribute to her
solid displacement, although I'm not sure that the two words
'solid displacement' were ones that should be used when referring
to a beautiful woman. It was a bit like saying that Anna, the

future Madam Butterfly, was gorgeous except for her enormous bum. Which wasn't true. Anna had a simply lovely bottom, which had fitted perfectly into my lap when I'd so lamentably disgraced myself.

Madam Butterfly was tracking beautifully and had settled into a rhythm. Her low gaff rig meant the tiller needed almost no input from me. I experimented with lashing it and leaving it to see if the boat would hold her course and was pleased to see she kept cutting through the water. After experimenting with various positions I discovered that securing the tiller slightly to starboard kept her sailing on course.

It was time for breakfast and a chance to stretch my legs. The cockpit was small – about three feet deep and about as wide as two coffins – and even with the cushion I'd earlier placed on the grate my body felt stiff and my bones ached. I rose and opened the sliding hatch, placing the washboards on the companionway. I then slid the hatch forward, hopped over the washboards, onto the companionway ladder and went below and into the galley, lighting the little stove and placing the kettle on it. A cup of hot sweet tea, a bowl of rice with maybe half a teaspoon of curry powder added and a bit of fish and I knew I'd feel a whole heap better. I would have killed for a couple of hours' sleep but it was a luxury I couldn't yet afford. I'd have to be a lot further out into the Indian Ocean and beyond the possibility of a marauding Japanese warship before I'd dare to take a bit of shut-eye.

I turned from the stove to see the little bloke, wrapped in a blanket, standing at the entrance to the forward cabin staring at me.

I quickly examined the blanket for signs of seasickness but couldn't see any. 'Morning,' I said, trying to keep my voice casual, not sure what version of K. Judge was about to confront me.

'Who are you?' he demanded.

'You don't remember?' I asked.

'Nah.'

'Nick Duncan,' I said, once again introducing myself.

He looked around, confused. 'Where the fuck am I, sonny boy?' 'Sonny boy' was back, although I didn't know if this was a good or a bad thing.

'You call me Nick and I'll call you Kevin, okay?' The lack of sleep was beginning to show.

'How ya know my name?' he demanded, thankfully eliminating the 'sonny boy' epithet. Without waiting for a reply he stabbed his finger at me. 'So, I'm gonna ask you again, where the fuck am I?'

'Where are you? You're approximately fifteen nautical miles into the Indian Ocean, going south. What exactly do you remember, Mr Judge?'

He ignored my question and countered, 'Am I taken prisoner?' He touched the bandage on his head. 'You do this?'

'No to both questions,' I replied. 'Now, tell me what do you remember?'

'The *Houston*, we're takin' a poundin'. The Japs are giving us hell. I ain't no fuckin' hero, you unnerstan'?'

'Well, your ship went down. You don't remember that?'

'Nah.'

'And nothing since that time?'

'I jus tol' you, sonny boy!'

'Nick! It's Nick,' I said, growing increasingly impatient. I sighed and shrugged my shoulders and looked him in the eye. 'Kevin, mate, I'm the big bloke and you're the little one. What say I throw you overboard? Nobody will ever know and I'll be rid of a rude, aggressive little shit I'm doing my best to rescue from the Japs. Now, don't you *ever* call me sonny boy again!' I pointed to the seat opposite the galley, a small pin-cushioned leather settee. 'If you shut up and sit down, I'll make you a cup of tea and bring you up to date with your plight – *our* plight. Orright? How many sugars?'

'I ain't got no clothes,' he replied, sulky at the reproof but unwilling to challenge me.

'They're on the spare bunk,' I said, calming down. 'I've washed them but they're probably still a bit stiff from the oil.'

'Oil?'

'Get changed and I'll bring you up to date,' I said, attempting unsuccessfully to smile.

'I gotta take a piss! How I gonna do that?'

I pointed to the companionway. 'Up on deck, mate. And hang on tight, it's pretty squally. Leave the blanket, you don't want it to get wet.'

He unwrapped the blanket from his scrawny little body and to my surprise folded it neatly and placed it on the pilot berth and then scrambled up the companionway.

'Not into the wind!' I shouted after him. A version of K. Judge wearing the contents of his bladder was all I needed to further sour the day.

That was one problem solved. He was sufficiently hydrated to pass urine although I knew the first piss after so long would hurt like hell. A burning urinary tract might give him something else to think about. It seemed the little bloke, in adult form anyway, didn't know any other way to behave but be aggressive. The flat lump of dough that passed for his nose suggested he'd paid a fairly heavy price in the process of maintaining his bellicosity.

I'm usually fairly easygoing and slow to anger; butterfly collectors have to be or they find themselves too frequently in pointless scraps proving they're not poofters. I'd also been awake for thirty-two hours, my nerves were shot and I'd just about had enough 'sonny boy' bullshit together with the various manifestations of K. Judge. On any other day I might have been more tolerant. After all, he'd taken a bad knock to the head and was probably suffering a headache two Aspro every once in a while was not going to fix. Besides, he was most likely still concussed.

However, I didn't believe he was hallucinating any longer. He was seeing me crystal clear. What I was facing was a cantankerous little shit who'd just had the benefit of eighteen hours of sleep. It was my further misfortune that he didn't appear to suffer from seasickness, the effect of which would have kept him preoccupied and out of harm's way.

I placed two teaspoons of tea into the red anodised teapot and added sufficient water for just two cups, as little water as possible onto as little tea as possible in order to make the strongest possible brew for two, the cautionary habits of a long-distance sailor. I'd asked him how many sugars and he hadn't replied. By way of a silent apology for my returned rudeness, I added three teaspoons, a luxury I decided I could only afford to indulge him with the once.

He returned down the companionway wet from the rain and I pointed to a towel hanging from a hook. 'How's your wound?' I asked.

'Don't feel too bad,' he replied.

'Throbbing?'

'Nah.'

'Headache?' He nodded, starting to dry himself. 'I'll give you a couple of Aspro, it's all I've got, I'm afraid.' I reached up into the first-aid locker and retrieved the bottle.

'Gimme four,' he demanded, replacing the towel on its hook.

'No, two's enough. Four's too much.' I handed him two tablets and drew him half a mug of water. He swallowed the pills but didn't thank me. 'Your clobber is on the spare bunk.'

'Clobber?'

'Clothes.'

He returned a short while later just as I was pouring the tea. Now dressed in shirt and shorts he grinned at me. 'Say, Nick, I wanna apologise. I bin a regular asshole. Whaddya say we go back and start again, eh, buddy?'

'That's a fair way back to cordiality,' I replied, still a trifle miffed and in my mind not yet prepared to reconcile his sudden change in attitude. I wondered briefly if 'buddy' was going to be the new 'sonny boy' and thought to pull him up right away but decided to let it pass. It was an epithet common enough among Yank soldiers and didn't have the patronising ring to it of the other one. I handed him the cup of sweet tea. 'Here, get this into you. Three sugars, special treat.'

He took the mug, held it in his left hand and extended his right. 'Kevin Judge, US Navy, Chicago, Illinois.' He paused. 'Nah, let me repeat that. Kevin Judge, asshole, first class.'

I grinned and then took his hand, his grip surprisingly firm for a little bloke. 'Pleased to meet the real Kevin Judge at last,' I laughed.

'I guess I had that comin',' he chuckled in return, then looked suddenly serious. 'I wanna thank ya for takin' care o' me, Nick.'

'That's okay, mate. I reckon you were pretty badly concussed.' I pointed to the leather settee. 'Sit down and tell me how much you remember.'

He sat, holding his cup between his legs, and shook his head ruefully. 'What a bitch, man! I guess I been outa my sensibility. I don't remember nuttin' since them Japs opened up. There's smoke and shit flying every which way and me, I'm thinkin' I'm gonna die. Any moment now da Judge . . . he is gonna be dead, man!' He looked at me and, grinning, repeated, 'I ain't no fuckin' hero, you hear? Big fuckin' battleship, got steel reinforce six inches! But the *Houston* she's takin' a poundin' like we's a matchbox caught in a fuckin' storm drain! There're explosions and bodies flying everywhere – this leg, it ain't got no body attached, sonofabitch still got his boot on, and it lands right next ter me where I'm hiding behind a hatch cover! Then, boom! I don't remember nuttin' no more!'

'Okay, I'm going to dress your head wound and while I do so I'll try to fill in the gaps.' I undid the bandage and the cotton wool, using another piece soaked in water to remove the bits sticking to the ugly gash. The wound hadn't festered and appeared to be clean. 'It needs stitches. I'm afraid you're going to wear the scar it leaves as a badge of honour.'

The little bloke grinned. 'I ain't got no honour gettin' it, man. I was shittin' my britches behin' that there hatch cover.'

I laughed. 'Purple heart, mate, that's the least they can do.' I doused the wound with fresh iodine and applied a new bandage as the one he was wearing was wet from going out into the rain. I'd wash this one later, as I only possessed one other.

I started to tell him what had happened, first making the assumption that he was picked up by the nine survivors of HMAS *Perth*, and continuing from there. I completed the dressing and kept talking in some detail. I told him about seeing the Carley float battling through the reef and then how, once ashore, the Australians had carried him up the beach, one of them removing and laying down his shirt before they placed him under the shade of a bush.

'That's a mighty fine thing,' Kevin said, shaking his head. 'From now on, they're me brothers; I owe them big time, no mistake!' He looked at me curiously. 'Where're they now? Somebody else rescue them?'

I had more than a bit of trouble relating the massacre on the beach. It's funny how your subconscious sets about burying a traumatic event, swaddling it in a protective mental bandage and stuffing it into the nearest dark hole in your memory. Retrieving it and unwrapping its ghastliness is to repeat the initial experience, although this time you see it happen in slow motion: the slashing blades catching the morning sunlight, the spume of scarlet blood from the sailor with Anna's eyes, the awkward angular positions of the oil-dark bodies as they lay sprawled on the bone-white beach. Finally I came to the nine bodies in a row in the sand and the pathetic little driftwood crosses. I was pretty choked and had to wait a bit, sipping at my mug of tea.

Kevin rose and walked over and placed a scrawny arm around my shoulder. 'Take it easy, Nick. Steady on, buddy,' he said softly, then added, 'Later . . . you take it real easy now, you can tell me later, eh?'

I was bone weary and knew that if I had to, with half a gallon of coffee inside me, I could probably go another twelve hours. But now, with the little bloke not suffering seasickness and seemingly having emerged from his concussion, hallucinations – whatever – I decided I might be able to get him behind the tiller for a few hours. Just the thought of this possibility and the break it might afford me was causing an even greater sense of weariness. Any resolve must be held tightly within the mind – the slightest relaxation in commitment will bring it quickly undone. Not even thinking about resting is one of the basic rules of staying awake for a lone sailor in bad weather out at sea.

'Yeah, maybe we'll wait,' I said, struggling to recover from the memory of the slaughter and the collection of the bodies on the beach. 'The rest of the story is less important for you to know. You're on board and that's what matters. But what you'd better get to understand is that we're far from out of this bloody awful mess. If, while at sea, we should manage to avoid the Jap ships and aircraft – a bloody big 'if', if you ask me – and *if* we make it to Australia, we'll be at sea at least three weeks. I guess there's plenty of time to talk. In the meantime can you hold a compass bearing, Kevin? Have you ever done any sailing?'

The little American shrugged. 'Nah, I ain't never done no boy scout stuff.' He looked up. 'This is the first time I bin on a sailboat in my goddamn life. I sol' peanuts on the shore when I was an itty-bitty kid, that's the nearest I got to them rich folks in their cockamamie sailboats. Negative to both, friend.'

I guess he meant he sold peanuts on the shores of Lake Michigan. 'It's not hard,' I assured him. Then I looked at him appealingly. 'Think you could try? I've been up thirty-two . . . nearly thirty-three hours. I'm whacked, mate.'

'Sure. I ain't no Christopher Columbus, buddy, but I can try. Nobody never said the Judge ain't willin' to try.' He grinned. 'I try everythin' once, dat's the main reason I mess up my life, man!'

I made him put on an oilskin – fortunately there were two

on board – led him up the companionway into the cockpit, unlashed the tiller and checked the compass. *Madam Butterfly* was holding true south. 'Here, get the feel,' I said, handing him the tiller. 'It's not hard and needs very little input. Gentle, just a gentle touch.'

'Like k-ressin' a tit,' Kevin replied.

'Yeah, something like that,' I laughed, although I had never touched a bare female breast. I pointed to the compass card. 'See, we're going due south – all you have to do is hold the course. If anything happens just lash the tiller in place and come and fetch me.'

'Anything? What you mean, anything?' he asked anxiously.

I pointed to the sails. 'See, they're full. If they begin to flap and you feel the boat trying to change direction, going a bit jiggery-poo, you know, sloppy in the water,' I said, using the friendly sounding nonsense word to put him at ease, 'then come and call me, wake me up. If you see a ship it will probably be Japanese, so call me quick smart, but don't shout. If these squalls persist we could get lucky; the visibility is way down. If we can maintain five or six knots, by tonight we ought to be about sixty miles off Java, but that's far from safe. As the mouse we're only a twitch or so beyond the sleeping cat's paws. Let's hope to Christ the weather holds and it keeps pissing down. Japs can't see any better than we can in this murky weather.'

I was trying to make him feel complicit, a part of our escape. In these relatively easy sailing conditions, with the steady breeze, holding a true course ought not to be too difficult. I sat with him for a further twenty minutes, holding his hand on the tiller, guiding him, getting him to acquire the feel as well as the habit of checking the compass every once in a while. I showed him how to sit on the waterproof cushion and ease his back against the rear of the cockpit. 'Just take it easy. There's nothing to worry about. I'll make you some hot grub before I turn in, but if you can give me four hours' shut-eye, I'll love you like a brother, Kevin,' I told him.

'Sails flapping and boat doing jiggery-poo, then I call you?' he repeated anxiously.

'Yeah,' I laughed. Just then a wave broke over the bow, sending spray over the cockpit, drenching us and filling the cockpit up to our ankles.

'Fuck! Jiggery-poo!' Kevin yelled in a sudden panic.

'No jiggery-poo!' I laughed, beginning to regret my use of the word. 'That's normal – you'll get a wave like that every once in a while in this weather.'

I returned to the cabin and made the usual, rice and fish, the dreaded mackerel, flavoured with a bit of Indonesian *ketjap manis*, the sweet soy sauce I'd been introduced to by Anna and taken a liking to while on the island. I made a thermos of sweet black coffee for Kevin and took it up to him along with the meal. 'Chow time – get this down your laughing gear, mate,' I said, handing the bowl to him. He wolfed it down.

'Nice gravy.'

'It's soy sauce.'

'Chink stuff? You sure? I don't eat Chink! Dey lousy, sneaky, treacherous – watch out for dem.'

I pointed to his empty bowl. 'Yeah, I can see you hated it. We're on fish and rice for the duration of the voyage; we'll try you on a bit of curry powder next time.'

'That Chink?' he asked suspiciously.

'No, Indian.'

'From India?'

'Well, yeah, originally.'

'They got slit eyes?'

'No.'

'I'll try it,' he said, ending the ridiculous conversation that nevertheless served to confirm yet another aspect of the K. Judge character. I wondered how he felt about Negroes, but decided not to probe any further. 'Righto, I'm off – see if you can give me a few hours' kip. There's four cups of coffee in there,' I said, pointing at the thermos flask. 'No more than one an hour; when the last cup's poured wait an hour, then call me.'

'Aye, aye, skipper,' he said, touching the bandage on his head in a mock salute.

CHAPTER THREE

'Nevah you mind, sailor.
Put yoh money away now.
Take offa yoh pants.
Dis one foh Uncle Sam!'
Kevin's dream

'JIGGERY-POO! JIGGERY-POO!' I awakened with a start to find Kevin shaking my shoulder. I could immediately feel that the boat wasn't sailing correctly and was annoyed at myself for not having sensed this in my sleep and wakened. I guess we hadn't been at sea sufficiently long yet for the instinct to kick in and alert me when *Madam Butterfly* wasn't sailing true. I glanced at my watch to see that I'd been asleep six hours.

As I jumped from the bunk I touched Kevin briefly on the shoulder, 'Good work, Kevin.' I could hear the sails flapping. 'Wind change, still raining?' I asked.

He nodded. 'They tell me rich folks, they do this cockamamie shit for fun?'

I grinned. 'You obviously enjoyed it?'

'I done better things . . . Like attemptin' suicide.'

'You haven't been seasick, that's a sure sign that God meant you to go to sea.'

'Den He shoulda made me a fuckin' duck!'

I climbed into my oilskins and went on deck, laughing, grateful to the little bloke for the extra sleep. The sun, invisible behind the low cloud, shone dimly and the rain had turned to a soft drizzle. Visibility thankfully remained low.

I adjusted the sails and set a new course to sou'-sou'-east, around 160 degrees. This I hoped would take me east of Christmas Island. After leaving the archipelago, Christmas was the only island before Darwin on the Australian mainland and seemed to me a logical place for the Japs to build an airstrip.

In fact, I'd decided to give Darwin a miss, for while it was much the closer landing point, it also meant hugging the Dutch East Indies archipelago, already occupied by the enemy. 'Go south, young man,' I said to myself. Broome was tempting. I'd told Anna I'd meet her there but I now decided it was too close to the archipelago. That left the West Australian coast. But if I hit it too far north it was pretty well the equivalent of landing on the moon. Allowing for leeway I reckoned I could get to Shark Bay or a bit further south to Geraldton. Given half decent weather, Fremantle was only three days' sailing from there. Anna would have arrived in Broome long before me and I'd get a message to her if we made it to Fremantle. The big advantage of taking the longest route meant sailing on a broad reach all the way, which is the most efficient method when sailing a small boat.

If it all sounds fairly cut and dried, we had covered about 120 miles in twenty-four hours, but still had around 1200 miles to go! That is, if we didn't encounter a storm and get blown off course or an enemy plane didn't use us for strafing or bombing practice. The course I had in mind would be adding another few days to the voyage, but I reckoned that was a damn sight better than spending the rest of the war as prisoners of the Japanese. That is, if they bothered to take us prisoners. With the little bloke being wounded they were just as likely to shoot us on the spot. Before leaving Batavia the news had come in that the Jap navy was sinking merchant shipping carrying evacuees and then strafing the survivors in the water or simply leaving them to drown. My enormous concern was, of course, for Anna. What if the *Witvogel* went down? I couldn't bear to entertain the thought. Civilian prisoners were no use to the Japs, whose supply lines were already stretched. They were taking the easy way out with civilian survivors and ignoring the Geneva Convention, which they refused to sign.

Hopefully a warship wasn't going to stop or change course to apprehend a yacht the size of *Madam Butterfly* and in this respect we'd be safe enough once we got beyond the range of the smaller patrol boats guarding the coastline. Aircraft might see us, but even on a clear day we would be a very small target in a very large ocean and unlucky to be spotted. I told myself I'd be happy for the weather pattern to remain as it was; poor visibility from the air, the overcast conditions, frequent squalls and a good blow provide much better sailing conditions than a blazing sun, cloudless sky and little or no wind.

My first aim was to get about 400 miles clear of Java. We'd achieved this on the evening of the fourth day. Having the little bloke on board meant I could get some regular sleep. I took the night watch and while he manned the tiller for a few hours during the day I'd sleep. But I was discovering that having a comparative stranger aboard has its disadvantages. There is little or no privacy on a small yacht and I am by nature a bit of a loner; more precisely, since my childhood in Japan I had learned how to keep my own company. When I look back, it probably all began then, where I spoke Japanese but wasn't Japanese. I understood and lived within their culture, ate their food, played with Japanese kids, learned Japanese manners and mannerisms, yet went home each night to an English hearth and a cup of Ovaltine at bedtime. I now realise that throughout my early childhood I would have been considered an alien, a *gaijin*, and secretly been despised by the Japanese people.

This early pattern consolidated somewhat when my father took up his ministry in New Guinea and I was sent to boarding school at the Church of England Boys' Grammar School ('Churchie') in Brisbane. We'd arrived in Rabaul from Japan in April and it was the second term when I started boarding, so the other new chums had already been there a term. Here too I was forced to keep to myself. I was treated as an outcast and branded a surrogate Jap.

I recall on the second evening there, the housemaster, Mr Grimes, at the beginning of evening prep made me stand up and introduce myself in front of the whole house. 'Righto, lad, let's begin with your name. Say it loud and clear so everyone hears,' he announced. He had a habit of jiggling with both hands in his trouser pockets so that the area about his fly flapped like a ferret attempting to escape. Hence his nickname, 'Grimy Ferret'.

I stood and announced, 'Nicholas Duncan, sir.'

'And where are you from, Duncan?'

'New Guinea, sir, but before that Japan, sir.'

'Japan!'

'Yes, sir, I was born there, sir. We left last year.'

'Ah, that accounts for your peculiar accent,' he remarked, smiling and jiggling. This got the first laugh of the night.

I had never thought my accent was different to anyone else's, even though this must have been obvious. 'Yes, sir,' I said, not knowing how else to answer him.

'Japan and New Guinea; Rabaul is it?'

'Yes, sir.'

'And your parents?'

'My father, sir . . . he's an Anglican missionary, my mother, she died in Japan, sir.'

'Ah, I'm sorry to hear that,' he said, not sounding in the least sorry and immediately asking the next question.

'And in New Guinea, what does a young boy do?'

'Beg pardon, sir?'

'Hobbies, model aeroplanes, that sort of thing?'

'No, sir, I am a lepidopterist.'

This brought the second snigger from the boys, although plainly they didn't know the word. 'A what?' the housemaster exclaimed, the jiggling ceasing for a moment.

'A butterfly collector, sir.'

Grimy Ferret removed his hands from his pockets and turned to face the other boys. He bowed low, one arm across his stomach, the other sweeping forward in a theatrical gesture. 'Gentlemen, I give you our resident butterfly collector!' Grimes had been unable to resist the cheap laugh and he was duly rewarded with a great guffawing from the rest of the house. In one stroke my fate was sealed forever.

Without the training in games that comes naturally as a part of the outdoor environment enjoyed by Australian children, I lacked any ball skills, which added to my banishment from the company of the other boys. A big kid who didn't play sport and spoke a different kind of English was a natural target and I was subjected to a fair bit of derision and persecution. I didn't play cricket and, at first, lacked even the skills to be a prop forward in the lowest rugby team. In addition to all this, I suffered the disadvantage of having a reasonable apportionment of brains, having read more books by the age of eleven than my class combined and possibly the entire school. Finally, and perhaps not surprisingly for a lonely child, I was a butterfly collector, with a hobby and an obsession that attracted nothing but scorn among my peers. *Swot, poofter, sissy, yellow-belly, slit-eye, dickhead, Jap!* I'd been on the receiving end of every epithet in the schoolboy vocabulary except 'coward'.

I wasn't afraid to fight, but I hadn't ever learned to scrap, which is almost a birthright among Australian kids. I usually took a beating but accepted this with a fair amount of stoicism, accepting that I was learning to exist in a new culture and had to learn its many peculiar ways. In fact, later in life, it was a source of constant bewilderment to me that the Japanese children with whom I'd spent my early childhood and who had seldom quarrelled and never fought, had grown into adults capable of the most unmitigated cruelty, whereas adult Australians, taken overall, are a fairly peaceable and friendly bunch.

All in all, the earlier part of my Australian experience, until I'd mastered the colloquial language and could use my wit and have my wits about me, was a pretty bruising and lonely one. I felt unwanted, alienated and confused by being constantly reminded of my shortcomings. It's funny how sometimes the smallest hurts stick like a burr to your memory. I recall how on one occasion the gym instructor at school derisively remarked in front of the other boys, 'Duncan, you're a big, clumsy, useless bugger! You don't belong here. So why don't you just piss off and go and read a bloody book!' I laugh about it now, but at the time his derision hurt like hell. If I'm being entirely truthful it still sometimes stabs at my memory.

However, towards the end of my school career I'd mastered the game of rugby sufficiently to play in the front row for the seconds, a position where size and strength was thought to be the primary requirement. The rugby master once advised me, 'Duncan, we don't need your brains in the scrum, just your size, grunt and aggression.' I also played in the water polo team, again perhaps because of my bulk, and I daresay the size of the ball made it easier to catch.

I became the company commander of the school cadets without being in the slightest interested in becoming a leader of men. 'Tally-ho', 'Gung-ho' or 'Righto, let's go', the three 'o' injunctions used to spur action in others, were not for the likes of me. I put this elevation in military pursuits down to butterfly collecting. At cadet camp during jungle exercises, my platoon consistently ended up capturing the enemy while never losing a man. I also earned a bit of a reputation in the military classroom for organisation and tactics and what the regular army captain who conducted it called 'original tactical thinking', which earned me (along with the jungle stuff) a recommendation to the school from the permanent army that I be made a cadet officer.

All of which, in combination, entitled me, in senior schoolboy terms, to be finally accepted as a respected brain, head of the school debating team, a prefect, the guy who usually won at cards and to whom you went to settle an argument or to verify a fact. I had learned the peculiar ways of my new culture well enough to survive more or less unnoticed within it. However, aloneness, as opposed to loneliness, becomes an acquired habit and, in the end, a cherished one. I had learned from my school experience in Brisbane to create a niche for myself. Add to this a melancholic widower father, an academic turned Anglican missionary, a silent man who had very little to say to me that could be construed as parental guidance and who usually answered my questions by handing me a book from his vast and cherished library.

We invent our own ways to survive and mine was hardly earth-shattering in its ambition. I can now see that it all pointed to the need to create a place in my life where I felt safe: somewhere I could be someone and do something, without having to necessarily compete – hence the butterfly collecting, sailing, books and finally acquiring the ability to be alone without being lonely. I was known to have a stubborn streak and, moreover, my determination wasn't always seen as meaningful and was often enough interpreted as foolhardy in a young boy.

For example, to the consternation of my father's expatriate parishioners, during the school holidays in New Guinea I would spend several days seemingly alone deep in the jungle. The children of missionaries are always thought to be a bit peculiar, but my proclivity for collecting butterflies as a teenager and to undertake dangerous excursions into the unknown to do so, became a constant source of local gossip, most of it aimed at my poor hapless father's ineptitude as a parent. In truth, I was generally in the company of native village children, who taught me the ways of their vast and beautiful playground where I soon came to feel completely at home.

I guess you could say another example of my stubbornness, if it were to be seen through the eyes of others, would be my unreasonable and ill-considered search for the Magpie Crow. It would be possible to argue that it is a butterfly commonly found in Singapore and Malaya, and while both these countries were now occupied by the Japanese, I could as easily have acquired a specimen before this happened from a local collector. Any local collector would have happily mailed me a Magpie Crow in exchange for any number of rare New Guinea butterfly varieties not available to them.

But there you go. As I saw it, I had one great advantage – I was free to make my own mistakes and to accept the consequences. I was seventeen, I'd worked for a year at W.R. Carpenter as a clerk, a job that required neither brains nor initiative but allowed me to save sufficient funds to embark on my quest for the Magpie Crow in the time I had off before joining up to do my duty for King and country. Sailing *Madam Butterfly* alone to Australia across the Indian Ocean was just another so-called foolish decision and look what happened – I'd met Anna and fallen head over heels in love. Being headstrong is not always the disaster it is so often made out to be. Now, with the little bloke on board, things were suddenly different. I was no longer a free agent responsible only for myself and, furthermore, I was no longer alone.

Kevin did what he was told though he was instinctively wary of volunteering. But at dawn on the ninth morning out to sea he suddenly and unexpectedly appeared on deck. I'd left the cockpit after having lashed the tiller and was standing at the stern of the boat looking out to sea. The sky had cleared up somewhat during the night but the horizon was stained a deep red. My heart skipped a beat; this was an almost certain sign bad weather was on the way. To add to my misgivings there was a big underlying glassy swell with waves coming through on top.

It was the first time since leaving Java that we could clearly see the horizon and traditionally this is the time when all navigators wait for what is paradoxically known as 'nautical twilight' when, if you have a sextant and tables and know how to use both, you take star sights to establish your position. We didn't have a sextant on board and I didn't know how to use one even if we did. To find out approximately where we were I was forced to plot my estimated position based on the course steered and the distance we'd run. I was about to do this. The log, a long length of knotted rope, was at my feet and I was preparing to throw the line overboard when the little bloke's head poked above the hatch.

'Hey, man, we got us a horizon,' Kevin called cheerfully.

'Morning. Sleep well?' I called back.

Kevin shook his head ruefully, stepping on board and coming up close to me. 'I dreamed I was in this whorehouse in Bronzeville, Chicago. This pretty black mama, she's givin' me the house special. I only had two bucks and it's five bucks and she says, "Nevah you mind, sailor. Put yoh money away now. Take offa yoh pants. Dis one foh Uncle Sam!"' Kevin shook his head and gave a little laugh. 'Goddamn! It the first time in my life I've gotten laid for free!'

I grinned. 'I guess you meet a better class of whore in your dreams! I suppose a cuppa would be out of the question?'

He went below deck and returned a short while later with the steaming mug of sweet black tea just as I'd picked up the log again.

'What you doin'?' he asked. 'Fishin' for sharks?'

'The log is a measuring device used to calculate speed at sea. It's a small piece of wood, like this one, attached to a length of manila line with knots tied in it exactly twenty-four feet and four inches apart. The line's thrown overboard with a dragging float and the number of knots pulled through your hand in fifteen seconds, 240th of an hour, is your speed through the water. I'm measuring our speed through the water.'

'Hey, yeah, we learned about that when we was training in San Diego, but I didn't take too much notice. Whaddya doin' it for? We're in the middle of the fuckin' ocean and far as I can see, we ain't goin' nowhere, man.'

I grinned. 'Yeah, but we've got to know where nowhere is if we're going to get somewhere.'

'And you can do that with a piece of rope? You can find us Australia?'

'Probably without it because it's a bloody big target, but we don't want to hit it just anywhere. Once I know our speed I can work out how far we've travelled in a day. We do this twice every day, now and at dusk.' I pointed to his head. 'After I do your bandage and while you're still below deck, I do this; that's why you haven't seen it done before. I mark where we are approximately on the school atlas that has to serve as our chart. As a method it's not all that precise – the atlas is probably a bit dodgy. But I guess, if the log was good enough for Captain Bligh, then it's good enough for us.'

'Who's this Captain Blight?'

'Bligh, *Mutiny on the Bounty*. You don't know that story?'

'Hey, I seen that movie!' Kevin exclaimed. 'He was a real sonofabitch! It happened here, right here?' he asked, clearly impressed.

'Yeah, well, it was on the other side of Australia but in similar conditions. He covered well over 3000 miles and all he had was a compass, a log like this and his memory of some early charts. And he was in a small open boat half the size of this one with eighteen men aboard. Essentially we're following the old Dutch trade route in reverse.'

'Dutch? Them the same white folk escaping the Japs?'

'Yeah, they've been in Java and Sumatra and sailing these seas for over 300 years, almost before America was discovered.'

He shook his head. 'Goddamn! Now they gotta vamoose? Get the fuck out?' He pointed to the knotted rope in my hand.

'This Captain Bligh, he done the same as you, eh?'

'Why sure, let me show you how it's done. Come a little closer, mate. I've got over 200 feet of rope here, which should be ample. I wait until the second hand of my watch hits twelve o'clock and let the log go, then grab it exactly fifteen seconds later.' The thin line whipped through my fingers and after fifteen seconds I grabbed it, holding it tight and using my free hand to pull the log in, meanwhile counting the knots in the rope.

'Just over five knots,' I announced. 'We're doing around 120 miles every twenty-four hours.'

'Hey, that's clever, man. This Captain Bligh, he invent that rope trick?'

'Hell no, it happened way, way back, even before Sir Francis Drake, or the Dutch navigators.'

'I ain't never heard of him. They make a movie of this Sir Drake?'

'Probably, he was the first Englishman to sail around the world.'

'I ain't seen it,' he sniffed.

Not long after sunrise the weather started to close down again. The wind continued from the north-west, clouds obscured the sun and by the time I handed the tiller over to Kevin the intermittent squalls had returned. In the back of my mind was the red sky at dawn, but hope springs eternal. Once you're away from land, conditions usually don't change a lot, and I was confident that Kevin could manage with the slight increase in the wind to around twenty knots.

'Just keep her on course, she's sailing well,' I told him. In fact, *Madam Butterfly*, sailing with only a slight heel, burying her shoulder a little more as she slid into the troughs with the odd slop of spray over the bow, was revelling in the conditions. This was a time at sea I greatly loved, with the only sounds being the hiss of water down her sides, the creak of the rigging and a chuckle from her bow as she cut through the waves. If there was such a thing as a sailor's heaven, then this was surely it.

I recalled Joseph Conrad's writing about youth and the sea and repeated it to myself:

> *By all that is wonderful, it is the sea, I believe, the sea itself – or is it youth alone? Who can tell? But you here – you all had something out of life: money, love – whatever one gets on shore – and, tell me, wasn't that the best time, that time when we were young at sea; young and had nothing, on the sea that gives nothing, except hard knocks – and sometimes a chance to feel your strength.*

I contemplated staying awake to enjoy the conditions, but one of the more important rules at sea, one that even Conrad would have followed for a lone sailor, is to grab every safe opportunity you can for a bit of shut-eye. Kevin knew nothing about sailing and as far as handling the cutter was concerned, I considered myself the lone sailor at sea.

I cooked breakfast and took a bowl of the usual rice and fish out to him and a thermos of tea.

He sniffed at the bowl. 'No gravy?' He'd grown to love the sweet soy sauce.

'Only for dinner from now on, a special treat. The soy sauce bottle is half empty and I'm trying to make it last the voyage.' I grinned. 'You can have a pinch of curry.' He had, I knew, developed a deep aversion to curry.

'Nah! It sets me fuckin' ass on fire when I take a crap. I

figure that's why them Indian fuckers wear them diapers.'

'You mean *fakirs?*'

'Yeah, them with the flute and the snake. They got two reasons to shit themself, the curry and the rattlesnake!'

'It's usually a cobra,' I laughed.

With Kevin's take on the nappy-wearing Indians ringing in my ears, I crawled gratefully into my bunk.

I woke with a start and glanced at my watch. It was midafternoon, the wind had lessened and I could feel *Madam Butterfly* was moving sluggishly. I hastened on deck to find Kevin asleep at the tiller. As I entered the cockpit he woke with a start.

'Musta dozed off,' he said guiltily.

'Easy enough to do,' I replied in a distracted voice, checking the compass.

We were only slightly off course but a heavy swell seemed to be coming from the north-west. Moreover, the afternoon light had a strange brassy look to it and the oily appearance of the swells indicated a tropical depression, a sign that heavy weather was coming our way. I had been correct to feel a foreboding with the crimson morning sky. At this time of the year tropical cyclones can develop in the Indian Ocean and sweep along the Australian coast. We'd had nine good days' sailing and now our luck was about to run out. A cyclone would be a disaster and my earnest hope was that its path would miss us. I was aware that just being brushed by one of these revolving storms would be an extreme danger even for a boat as well found as *Madam Butterfly*.

I corrected our course. 'Spot of bad weather on the way,' I

said, keeping my voice casual.

'How bad, buddy?' Kevin, at once anxious, asked.

I shrugged. 'She'll be right. As to the weather, we'll just have to wait and see,' I said, still trying to sound noncommittal.

'I ain't no hero, you unnerstan', Nick.'

'You'll be right, mate,' I assured him, attempting to convince myself, adding, 'just follow my instructions.'

As the afternoon wore on, the wind started to increase and so I got rid of the jib. I pointed to the forecastle. 'Give us a hand, Kevin,' I shouted above the wind. 'Gotta get the storm staysail out, it's pretty bloody heavy.' I knew I could probably manage it myself, but thought to get him involved. Already he was looking doleful.

We'd completed the job when he said, 'Hey, buddy, whaddya say I get outa yoh way . . . go below?'

I didn't want to tell him that if the blow really got up I was going to need him. 'Hang around, stay on deck; it's early times yet, Kevin,' I advised. Then I changed my mind. I didn't need him yet; best to keep him busy and take his mind off the weather. 'On the other hand, why don't you cook chow? We'll eat early. Open a tin of peas and carrots and it's dinner, so you can use the "gravy", but not too much, eh?' In my mind's eye I could see the little bloke adding with a thumping great fist the sweet soy sauce that I'd decided to ration.

'No carrots!' he growled. Kevin disliked tinned carrots second only to curry.

He arrived a little while later with the chow as well as a thermos of coffee. I didn't tell him it might be the last time he ate for a considerable time. He'd brought my bowl of rice and fish mixed with tinned peas, flavoured with a teaspoon of curry, to the cockpit. In the interest, no doubt, of saving his precious soy sauce, the cunning bugger had left his own meal below so that he could get back and out of harm's way. London to a brick, he'd appropriated my share by doubling up his 'gravy' with a generous splash.

My meal completed, together with a cup of strong black coffee, I decided to get the staysail ready to hoist when it was needed. So I hanked it on, attached the spare halyard and secured it ready to hoist when I wanted it, then shifted my attention to the mainsail.

The mainsail has three lines of reefing points, so I decided to reef the main before the rapidly rising wind turned it truly into a job beyond my strength. In such a case I didn't want to have to rely on the little bloke as it can be a fairly tricky job, even without a big blow. I chose the middle line of reef points so that when I decided to rig it I had only the heavy staysail forward. With a greatly reduced mainsail area my speed immediately fell away, though I knew this wouldn't last. Almost as I watched, the wind and sea started to rise rapidly and I changed my mind, yelling for the little bloke to help me. Together we got the staysail up.

By nightfall the seas were roaring down on us from the north-west, their height climbing alarmingly. We were riding high and then falling, careening down into deep troughs. The tops of the waves, covered with white foam, rose above the mast. The wind was sending a deep thrum through the rigging, while, despite our reduced sail, our speed was climbing rapidly.

There was no way I could communicate with Kevin. An experienced sailor would have been useful to have with me, but the little bloke knew nothing and had never experienced conditions such as these in a small boat. Besides, he was rapidly becoming pop-eyed with fear. I knew I might need him at some time later as the worst of the storm still lay ahead of us. I considered securing him with a lifeline, knowing that if he got swept overboard there would be nothing I could do to rescue him, but decided to send him below instead. He'd be in for a bumpy ride but would be out of the rain, and provided we didn't sink, he'd be safe enough.

I moved over to him and stood with my mouth close to his ear, holding his left shoulder. 'Get down below!' I screamed against the howling wind, pointing to the hatch and starting to move toward it myself. Kevin nodded, pushing past me in his haste to be gone, a grateful expression showing on his wet face. I watched as he scuttled across the deck and disappeared like a rat down the hatchway.

I followed him below deck where the noise of the gale wasn't quite as bad. I pointed to the rope locker. 'Kevin, help me lay out the mooring lines. We've got to lay them out on the cabin floor, I may need them later.'

'It gonna get worse, Nick?' he asked in what wasn't too far from the apprehensive voice he'd used as a six-year-old on the beach in Java.

'You just stay down here, mate, it's going to be okay,' I said, trying to sound convincing. After we set out the mooring lines I went back on deck and into the cockpit to unlash the tiller. The white tops were beginning to slop over the windward gunwale and I was hugely grateful that we were taking the sea on the starboard quarter – the easiest point to weather what was almost certainly a big blow coming our way.

The sound of the wind in the rigging rose to a higher pitch, screaming. Each time *Madam Butterfly* lifted up the face of a giant wave, as we reached its peak, foam, sharp as flying tacks, blew over the weather rail, stinging like buggery. Sailing boats are much better in a heavy blow than even a large ship. This is because the sails tend to steady the craft, leaning away from the wind, so that surprisingly we held our course.

I put in the third reef, struggling with the heavy wet sail and silently blessing the sail maker who had set up a downhaul clew so I could more easily secure the outer edge of the sail. This little consideration is not mandatory and not all sail makers are so thoughtful; perhaps they are the ones who haven't found themselves at sea in a big storm.

As it turned out I got the sail reduced in the nick of time. Running off before the wind with less than a third of full sail, my greatest concern was that we might broach, although more and more I was coming to appreciate the design of *Madam Butterfly*. The gaff rigger was based on a Norwegian double-ended design, built originally for conditions in the North Sea and the Atlantic Ocean. With a long keel and deep forefoot she was able to keep tracking in bad weather.

The tiller had developed a tendency to pull to port, so I rigged a line to take the strain, using two turns around the tiller to take the load off my aching arms. This is where even Kevin might have proved useful. But, while he seemed normal enough, he had frequent lapses of concentration and I was fairly certain he was still suffering from concussion and, besides, he was over-fearful of the conditions. Not a safe bet at a time when a high degree of concentration is essential.

The moon occasionally appeared through the clouds, showing what appeared to be at least thirty-foot waves towering above us. As *Madam Butterfly* went over the crests I would ease the helm, pulling it back as she started to rise from the troughs. My task was simple enough: it was to prevent the huge waves from starting to curl and then slam directly into us. I was attempting to angle over the crests to allow them to pass under us. But it was impossible to prevent the odd one slamming into the stern quarter, drenching me and pouring foam and water over the entire deck. The big cockpit drains were working overtime, gurgling and moaning as they sucked the water from the cockpit.

The storm seemed to be intensifying and reaching a climax, carrying the overwhelming sense of something terrible and alive, an elemental and unstoppable force, bent on the destruction of everything in its way. Fifty-knot winds drove foam over the gigantic seas in huge white streaks like the horizontal swipe of vicious and malevolent blades. I could barely see as we plunged onwards with the full fury of what I estimated must be at least a force-ten storm on the Beaufort scale. I could only pray that the centre of the depression didn't come any closer.

I felt the boat was moving too fast. It was time to use the mooring lines I'd laid out with the little bloke on the cabin floor. I lashed the tiller and dived down below to find Kevin sitting with his legs drawn up against his chest, arms clasping his knees, blubbing and choking with fear, his eyes tightly shut. 'Mary, Mother of God, save us!' he was chanting over and over, oblivious of my presence in the dim glow from the cabin lamp. I touched him on the shoulder and he opened his eyes with a start. 'Are we dead yet?' he asked with a sob.

Despite myself, I grinned. Things were pretty desperate, but we were still riding the storm. 'No, mate, that's only tomorrow or the next day. Can't talk now,' I yelled. Picking up the mooring rope, I passed both ends into the cockpit. Turning to return up the hatchway, I shouted, 'Hang in there, mate! I promise I'll let you know when we're dead!'

'I ain't no hero,' he cried, arms outstretched in supplication.

'I ain't no fuckin' hero, Nick!'

I decided he deserved better. 'Kevin, we're in a spot of bother, mate. Stay where you are, but lash yourself to your bunk as things could get a bit tricky.'

Once in the cockpit I joined the ends of the rope with a sheet bend, then passed them through the stern fairlead and took them around the heavy bronze mooring post in the starboard quarter the six-year-old Kevin had used that first time to climb aboard *Madam Butterfly*. I began to feed the doubled length of three-inch manila out into the churning ocean. My hope was that the drag of 300 feet of rope in the water would stabilise *Madam Butterfly* and slow her headlong rush down the force of the waves.

The drag proved tremendous, two turns around the mooring post barely sufficient to hold the rope in place. Securing the two ends of the rope to a cleat, I immediately felt the effect of the restraining rope on the tiller. *Madam Butterfly* was riding easier, no longer attempting to turn up into the wind. Heaving to was simply out of the question in this fierce weather, so I decided that the only thing left was for me to take in the remaining sail area.

This was a bloody sight easier said than done. Tying on a lifeline by using a double bowline, I lashed the tiller amidships and struggled forward. Dropping the small staysail, I wrestled with it and while it is not a big sail, in the howling gale it was like wrestling an angry boa constrictor. I finally secured it and stuffed it down the fore hatch. That, despite taxing my immediate strength, was the easy part. Now for the deep-reefed mainsail. I rested a couple of minutes and thought briefly of hauling Kevin up on deck to help me, but decided this was no task for someone who was asking for help from the Mother of God. A sudden slap from the sail was likely to send him on his way to heaven and into the comforting arms of the Virgin.

Dropping the gaff unleashed pandemonium. The deck was heaving and bucking like a rodeo horse and I was the cowboy on its back. As well, the wildly flogging sail was bent on hurling me into the sea. Desperately securing the gaff at the tack and clew, I began working my way along the sail, tying it down with a series of hitches. When I'd finally subdued it, my fingers were bleeding and I was utterly exhausted, but, miraculously, I'd done what should have taken the two of us. It's not always easy being a big bloke but sometimes it's useful having a tad more strength.

My final task was to secure the bundled sail, gaff and boom to the deck, lashing it to the boom gallows midships. I returned to the cockpit having played my last card. I'd endured an hour of abject terror because I hadn't taken in all sail hours earlier. At sea there are always new lessons; that is, if you live to learn them.

Dawn brought more bad news. Huge dark seas grey as a whale's back marched behind us, driving *Madam Butterfly* remorselessly forward. The wind was still shrieking through the rigging and the low clouds racing above me seemed to be touching the tops of the monstrous waves. The eerie dawn light was just sufficient to tell me I'd done all I could and that, from now on, we were in the lap of the gods and the boatbuilders who had constructed the gaff-rigged cutter the Dutchman had boasted could go anywhere and sail any kind of sea.

There is a certain point you reach when the forces of nature simply overwhelm every possible endeavour and numb resignation sets in. I was exhausted, but even with all the will in the world, there was nothing more I could do. I lashed myself in place in the cockpit, hoping the little bloke had taken my advice and done the same. I was now a part of the boat and we would live or die together. So much for stubbornness as a virtue; this time I had truly come unstuck.

I stayed lashed to the tiller for the next thirty-six hours, no going down below to check on the little bloke and, of course, it was much too rough to cook. Under normal conditions there would have been sea biscuits to take the edge off our hunger but these were not available in Batavia towards the end and it was not the sort of grocery item that would have come out of Anna's depleted pantry. We'd have to do with water. I was worried about re-dressing Kevin's head wound, although I only had two bandages and both were soaked. Last time I'd looked it had been coming along nicely and was healing at the edges, the wound clean with no suppuration. Regular applications of iodine had worked, although without stitches he was going to have to wear a nasty scar for the rest of his life. That is, if there was going to be much more time left to live.

If I told you that I lived and died through several lifetimes in those thirty-six hours at the helm I wouldn't be exaggerating. Nobody brags about getting through a storm like this one. Every ocean-going sailor worth his salt knows survival has only partly to do with skill or knowledge. There is only so much you can do. On several occasions during the next two days and nights I was prepared to crawl down the hatchway to announce to the little bloke that we were now officially dead. I'd never been in anything as fierce at sea and trust that I never shall again. Many a large ocean-going merchantman or similar has simply disappeared without trace in a storm of this magnitude. But somehow, perhaps with the help of Kevin's Virgin Mother, we kept afloat, a tiny bobbing cork in the vast watery and angry firmament.

Dawn on the third day revealed that the crests of the

waves were not being blown off by the wind, although I was not prepared to speculate that it had started to abate. I was so bleary-eyed for lack of sleep, and my eyes were stinging constantly from the effect of the salt spray, that I wasn't sure I hadn't manufactured the lessening of the storm from a sense of sheer weariness.

By mid-morning there was no mistaking it. The wind had dropped to around twenty-five knots. The seas remained huge but not as steep, while the tumbling, breaking crests, so dangerous for a small boat, were rounding out. Our headlong dash to the south, a decision perhaps I can take credit for, meant that the storm had turned east towards the Australian coastline. Had we decided to sail to Broome we would have been caught in the centre of the storm, instead of being brushed by its southern edge. I was under no illusions; if we'd taken the shorter route we would not have survived.

I was simply too exhausted to raise sail and left *Madam Butterfly* to run trailing warps as if still within the storm. My weary body told me to wait until the wind had moderated further and the seas abated, but at least I could lash the tiller and leave the cockpit for a while. Then I could have a bit of a kip; that is, if the little bloke was in any condition to take over even for only a couple of precious hours. I'd been up for sixty hours. Fear can keep you awake and alert when under normal circumstances you'd be dead on your feet, the complete zombie. It is coming down, the process of returning to normal, that can be the horror trip.

In my mind I begged the little bloke to be in a reasonable frame of mind. On the other hand, if he'd been whimpering and 'Mother Marying' for three days he'd be in no condition to help. I reckoned *Madam Butterfly* was just about sailing steady enough for him to manage the tiller. It wasn't entirely his fault. Any storm in a small boat that's mildly severe, let alone a near-cyclone, will scare the bejesus out of a novice aboard. He will, if he was still with us, have learned that big-boat sailors of the type that go to sea for Uncle Sam live in a very different world.

I tried to summon the energy to attempt to stand and then to leave the cockpit and to drag my stiff, sore and exhausted body down the hatch to cook a meal for both of us. I decided if he hadn't died of fright in the meantime, Kevin could have the whole bloody bottle of sweet soy sauce if he was in a condition to do a two-hour watch. Just two hours, it wasn't asking for much. Frankly, I was on my last legs.

I stood painfully and turned towards the hatch. It was my time to hallucinate. The little bloke had his head protruding from it, his expression as tentative as a bunny emerging from a burrow knowing the local fox is out and about. His face lit up. 'Jesus, Mary and Joseph! You ain't dead. You still there!'

I attempted a grin. 'I can't be sure.'

'Say, buddy, ya wanna cup a java?'

I nodded and sat down again, suddenly too exhausted and pathetically grateful to move. Five minutes later I held a mug of steaming, heavily sugared black coffee in my trembling hands. That was the moment I knew we were going to make it. The little bloke cooked a meal and I ate silently, too tired to ask him about his own ordeal below deck. For once he seemed to sense this wasn't the moment to yak and he kept quiet.

After eating and drinking another cup of coffee, I felt sufficiently strong with his help to hoist the staysail and then, shaking out the reefs, the mainsail. The warps took another half-hour to haul out of the water and stow. By five o'clock the wind was below twenty knots and the sky clearing, as if the storm had sucked all the moisture from the air. *Madam Butterfly* was sailing well, seeming no worse off than before the storm, though I knew there'd be a host of minor repairs once we had the time to inspect and attend to them.

The little bloke had never done a night watch so I said to him, 'Mate, think you can take the tiller until eight, until moonrise?'

'What about jiggery-poo?' he asked.

'Unless we hit a whale, it's all plain sailing from now on.'

'Whale? You ain't said nuthin' 'bout a whale!'

'It's okay, by this time of the year they've usually migrated well beyond these parts.'

The sun was setting in a blaze of gold when Kevin took the tiller and I took to my bunk. I woke to his touch at dawn. 'Sorry, boss, I can't stay awake no more,' he said, apologising. He'd allowed me to sleep for a miraculous twelve hours.

I made breakfast and coffee for both of us and went on deck to see that he'd lashed the tiller in place, keeping *Madam Butterfly* on course. Something for the better has happened to the little bloke during the storm, I thought to myself. Maybe he'd never make a sailor, but he might yet turn out to be a useful deckhand.

The sun was rising to a beautiful day with moderate seas and a stiff breeze, perfect sailing conditions. I had no way of knowing what our speed had been during the storm, but making an educated guess based on my dead reckoning we'd covered 1200 nautical miles in the thirteen days we'd been at sea. The storm had really pushed us along. This would mean we would be abeam off Exmouth Gulf and about 150 miles, a little over a day's sailing, from the Australian coastline. Which, in terms of having escaped the Japs, was one thing; but landing on a harsh and uninhabited coast was quite another. We had a lot of sailing yet to do if we hoped to get to a friendly coast and back to people who didn't want to kill us, although I was fairly confident that we were now beyond the range of land-based Japanese aircraft.

Kevin came on deck about midafternoon carrying the usual brew. It was a glorious afternoon and we sat down to talk, the first opportunity to have a bit of a yak since the advent of the storm.

'Here, Kev, let me take the bandage off. Let's see if there's any storm damage.'

'It's the only place that don't feel broke,' he said, rubbing the tops of his arms.

'Well, storms don't get much worse and you remain alive to tell the tale.'

'Alive? We still alive? You sure now, Nick?' Kevin shook his head. 'I'm a Catholic —' he started to explain.

'Yeah, I noticed,' I interrupted. 'You seem to have a particular fondness for the Virgin Mary.'

Kevin looked at me sternly. 'She the Holy Mother! When the shit hit the fan, that where you gotta go, man!'

'Well, it seemed to work. The first time I went below decks you weren't in great shape. But I must say, you seem to have survived quite well.'

'That because I'm dead.'

'Dead?'

'Yeah, when we die we cross this river, it's called Styx, the River Styx, it's the way to purgatory. You know what is purgatory, Nick?'

'Sure, it's a sort of halfway house where you Catholics earn your way to heaven, sort of,' I said, not entirely certain my answer would please him.

'Yeah, somethin' like that. Anyhow, while we bin in that storm, when I'm shittin' myself and praying and sobbing and asking Mother Mary to get me outa this place, the Holy Mother, she appear right there in front of me and she say to me, "Sonny boy, you outa here! You dead. You are one dead Irishman!"' Kevin looked up at me and shrugged. 'So that official, see? Ain't nobody gonna contradik the Holy Mother. When she say you dead, you dead . . . ain't no resurrection gonna happen, man.'

'So, what then?' I asked, staring at the recently dead Kevin.

'Well, I reckon if I'm dead, then this the boat that's takin' me across the river.'

'The Styx?'

'Yeah, ain't no point in worryin' no more. Ain't nobody drowned in the river Styx 'cos they dead already.'

'So, from then on . . . you were okay?'

'Well, I got myself some shut-eye 'cos I'm dead but I'm also exhausted from prayin' and blubbin' and snottin' like a kid.' He glanced up at me and then, not for the first time, explained, 'I want you to know I ain't no fuckin' hero, you hear, Nick?' He shrugged, continuing, 'So, then I wake up. Hey, we must be close to the udder side! I think. We ain't rollin' and jumpin' like before. So I come up and I seen you sittin' there by the tiller. Hey, whaddya know! Nick don't tell me he is also Catholic. We both dead, I thinks. But, iffen he ain't, I mean ain't a Catholic, then we ain't on the River Styx and I ain't dead. So, to be sure, I ask if ya wanna cup a java? That when I'm sure, for sure, we ain't dead no more. They ain't got no coffee in purgatory.'

'Welcome back to the land of the living,' I laughed, while wondering how long concussion lasted and if the hallucinations were back. But I must say, back from the dead a second time, he seemed a different person and happily agreed to change the watch schedule so that I wasn't always on night watch. We'd do two hours on and two hours off, adopting a normal sailing procedure. I reckoned, with a bit of luck and a following wind, we had about two, maybe three days to go before we sighted land.

The following two days proved to be picture-book sailing, blue skies with only an occasional billowing mass of white cumulus on the horizon. It was during this time that Kevin began to tell me his story. We were sitting on deck having lunch, same old rice, same old fish, but without Kevin's gravy. Despite the four meals we'd missed in the storm it had finally run out. I should also add that, with the exception of curry, the little bloke had never complained about the monotonous diet and seemed to consume all his meals with evident relish, providing they contained no tinned carrot.

'I ain't never again gonna think, "Fish! It gotta be Friday,"' he said, looking down into his bowl of rice and tinned mackerel.

'Sorry, mate, it's not exactly *cordon bleu*.'

'Whazat? Gordon blur?' he asked, at once curious. The little bloke may have lacked a bit of polish but he was sharp as a tack and curious, not afraid to ask or to appear ignorant – not a bad start in anybody's book.

'*Cordon bleu*, it means "blue ribbon" in French. You know, high-class chow. Supposedly the best there is,' I explained.

'Haddock? You tasted it? Tastes like a whore's pussy. We kids could smell it in the air when we woke up. "Pussy! It's

Friday!" everybody shouts.'

Hoping, while eating my rice and mackerel, to avoid any further analogy describing Friday's haddock in Kevin's family, I asked, 'Come from a strict Catholic family, did you?'

He sniffed. 'Nah, no family. Not no more. The big strike in '21, we was kicked out of our place in Canaryville. That's like being kicked out o' hell, three floors up, cold water in the winter it freeze in the faucet pipes. Hot water is in the kettle boiled on a coal stove. There ain't no other place for the working Irish to go on the South Side, them two rooms in Canaryville, it the end of the fuckin' line. Nobody is working no more, 'cept the niggers.'

All this came in a rush, almost as if he was reciting it. 'What did your father do?' I asked.

'Meatworks on the South Side, from 39th to 47th and from Halsted Avenue to Ashland Avenue, just the one square mile. The smell it was like the sewage plant broke down, only all the time, but people said that smell meant work.' Kevin chuckled, recalling. 'They'd say they used everything in the animal except the squeal and they was working on that.

'Fifty thousand people worked there and they was all treated like dog shit. Irish, Poles, Germans, Lithuanians, Bohemians. The Irish lived east, in Canaryville, east of the stockyards. I gotta tell you I ain't never heard a canary singing in Canaryville. The Poles lived west, back o' the yards, they worked on the killing floors. The Lithuanians, north, in Bridgeport. The others, I don't rightly remember, we never mixed. The niggers, beyond Wentworth Avenue, it was called Bronzeville, they done the dirty work on the killing floors, the Poles done the skinning, cutting and slicing.

'Me daddy worked in the stockyards, me mother cleaned

the guts of the slaughtered animals for sausage skins. With the strike they both got the pink slip.'

'The strike? What was it over?' I asked.

'We, the workers, we was getting thirty cents an hour and they wanted two cents increase. Two lousy cents an hour! Armour & Co, they the bastards, they the biggest – they can slaughter 1200 hogs in an hour. They say to the union, "No rise, no union, no say, go away!" That's the slogan.'

'So everyone came out?'

'Only the whites, not the niggers, they stayed. They bin comin' up from the South, they the baddest off, but now they bringin' in more and more to break the strike. Before, everyone kept to themselves, we did our job in the stockyards and they did theirs on the killin' floor. It was a peaceable arrangement. No problems. But after the niggers blacklegged us and took our jobs there wasn't nuthin' we could do; they had us over a barrel. My father, he took no more interest. He vamoosed. California, someone says later.'

'Leaving you with your mother?'

'She says she can't take no more, her nerves. She brings me to Angel Guardian where the Sisters of the Poor who are the handmaidens of Jesus, and the brothers, who are the guards, look after kids that got no family. I'm four years old.'

I did a quick calculation. The little bloke must have been born in late 1917 or early 1918, which made him twenty-four or twenty-five, depending on the date of his birthday.

'There was over a thousand of us kids there, but not everybody's an orphan, unnerstan'. I'm legit, some other kids also. We got parents, only they couldn't look after us because of the strike and what the niggers did to us. My mother she began to visit Dr Bottle.'

'Dr Bottle? What, for her nerves?'

'Dr Bottle. Booze. She's hittin' the booze.'

'Ah, I see! Dr Bottle!' I hadn't heard the expression before.

'Sometimes she visits me. She says she's gonna go straight and she'll come and get me. Then after I'm six she don't come no more.'

'Kevin, where did you hear all this?' I protested. 'You were only four when that strike took place.'

The little bloke looked at me, plainly astonished at the stupidity of my question. 'It's the history of the Chicago Irish. Every kid in Angel Guardian knows it backwards. The brothers never stopped talkin' about it. Mr Kirk Bell, him who was the top honcho of Armour & Co, he's a Protestant, the devil incarnate and the number one bully in the US of A! That's why they call it "bully" beef! They named it after him.' Kevin paused, then said, 'The South Side Irish at the meatworks and what was done to us by Armour & Co and them niggers, according to the brothers and the nuns, that second only to what the Romans and Jews did to Jesus Christ on the cross.'

'I take it there were no black kids there?'

Kevin laughed. 'Hey, man, the Irish kids wudda killed 'em. The brothers they all sadists, they wudda flogged 'em to death and took the pleasure of it as a gift from the Lord.'

He was silent for a moment. 'But I gotta say this. Later at Pontiac, this big black kid, Joe . . . Joe Popkin, we were buddies. I met him the same day we at Audy Hall, that's where they hold kids waitin' to go to juvenile court. We sittin' there waitin', waitin', in those places waitin' is the name o' the game. Learnin' to wait, that the first sentence you get in Juvenile Justice. Joe, he is next to me, he falls asleep when the guard is talkin' to us, givin' us our instructions for the court procedure. So the guard hits him across the head. Whack! "Wake up, nigger!" he says.

'The guard is Irish like me. "Hey, leave him alone, he didn't do nothing to you!" I say to him when I shoulda known to keep my big Irish mouth shut because it only a nigger he's hit.

'So the guard, he gives me a great whack on the side of my head. I go flying off that bench onto the polished floor and when I look up it's Joe, he takes my hand and pulls me up. That the first time I touched black skin and later Joe says it's the same for him, only it's white.

'From that time Joe and me, we buddies. He's a big guy and he ain't scared of nuthin'. In Pontiac, the reformatory upstate where that juvenile judge send us, he always took care o' me. That where I stopped thinkin' like it ain't no coincidence niggers are the colour of shit. It woke me up. They folk like Joe Popkin, they good as us, almost.'

You had to laugh. Racism, black skin, wasn't only an issue in America. I'd seen my fair share of it in New Guinea and in Australia. But I didn't want him to jump ahead. 'Hey, Kev, we're still in the orphanage, don't jump ahead,' I said, eager to hear the story from the beginning.

At sea on a good sailing day, with the sails full, the wind at your back, time is not at a premium. It has always been a tradition that old sea dogs like to take in the breeze on deck and yarn when the weather is fair. We weren't quite in this category but it was a good time for yakking and an excellent place to be doing it. The Irish in Kevin was all it took to get on a roll. 'Tell us about, you know, what it was like at Angel Guardian.'

Kevin looked pleased at my obvious interest. But then his expression turned serious, rearranged to befit the mood of the story to come. There was a lot of theatre in our Kevin.

'We slept in these big dormitories, fifty kids, beds straight as coffins lined up after the St Valentine's Day massacre. In the winter just one blanket each, so thin you could blow holes through it whistling Dixie. I tell you, man – we froze our balls off. In the summer it was steamy, hot as hell, like one o' them Turkish baths. The dormitory windows were shut, nailed shut all the stinkin' summer, they had bars on them, but in that place the kids were so skinny the brothers didn't take no chances.'

I chuckled, in my mind's eye seeing a skinny kid slipping through a barred dormitory window and making his escape into the world. 'Food no good, eh?'

Kevin rolled his eyes. 'The chow was terrible, shit on a shingle! Creamed beef, scraping they musta got from the meatworks' killing floor! Served on stale mouldy bread the Polack baker give us rather than feed it to the hogs. Pea and potato soup so weak you could wash in it. That was the winter special. Mash potato, it so glassy you can see the pattern on the plate through the itty-bitty dollop they give you! It supposed to have peas in it, the ones that never got into the soup. If you found one you knew you must be the princess with the pea and the mattress. Every Friday, like I told you, it's stinkin' pussy. When it ain't potato it's boiled carrots, mashed. There was never enough to eat in that place. You was always hungry.' He paused, remembering, shaking his head. 'Shit! It was all shit, but still never enough.'

'There must have been *some* happy times?' I volunteered.

'Who ya kiddin', sonny boy, wit them cocksuckers?'

It was the first time he'd used the 'sonny boy' epithet in almost two weeks, although, in my mind, it had become somewhat ameliorated since being used by the Virgin Mother in her appearance during the storm to announce Kevin as officially dead.

'Nothing good ever happen to you? I mean, something must have?' I insisted.

'Yeah, the day I left at fourteen to go to Pontiac, to the reformatory. It was the middle of the Depression but we couldn't tell, it made no difference. Angel was in the middle o' the fuckin' Depression permanent! Leavin' – that the goodest moment! Lemme tell you something, Nick. There weren't no angels there. Nobody in that place was good. Nobody was holy – us kids, the Irish brothers or the nuns. In there, it was everyone for himself; to give a sucker an even break was considered a crime against humanity! No angels in Angel Guardian, but lots of guardian. Yeah . . . that part they done real good. They guarded us like we was criminals and they told us every goddamn day how they nurture us, how lucky we are to be in God's good care.

'Father Geraghty, he says every morning, "We, the Brothers and the Sisters in Christ Jesus, are here my children to be the moral guardians of your souls, the angels in cassocks and habits, charged by no other than His Holiness the Pope Himself to mind over your spiritual and temporal life."

'Ha! That the biggest joke, buddy, they beat up on us for anything. You got ya hand in ya pocket scratching your nuts. *Whack!* That lust! You use too much shit paper. *Whack!* That waste. You eat too fast. *Whack!* Gluttony. Caught fightin'. *Whack!* Intemperance. You answer back. *Whack!* Arrogance. Swearing. *Whack!* God's name in vain. Catechism incorrect! *Whack!* Ineptitude. Locker untidy. *Whack!* Sloth. Farting. *Whack!* Pollution. Smokin'. *Whack!* That theft, because how else you gonna get them fags. Every one of them *Whacks* I said real hard – that a regular floggin' from Father Geraghty.

'Okay, lemme take you through the floggin' routine, Nick. You standin' in Father Geraghty's office waitin' for him to come from this little room behind his desk, he calls it his sanctum sanctorum, it suppose to be holy, but it just a bed where the fat bastard can have a kip any time he likes. The office, it got shelves, bookshelves, lotsa holy missives, some other books also. On the walls there's pictures, ya know, photographs – baseball, the Chicago Cubs, Gaelic football players, they wear these little caps with tassels and they all got big moustaches and they clasp their arms over their chest, nobody smiling. There's one photo of Big Jack Dempsey, the American Irish heavyweight champion of the world, it's signed "Jack Dempsey, The Manassa Mauler – Knockout knowing ya, Father G!". There's one of the Pope doing a blessing in St Peter's Square, but it ain't signed. Then there's this big coloured picture of the Blessed Mother. It's a proper paintin', done with oil and it says, on a brass plate underneath, "To Father Geraghty, from Mother Superior and the nuns of Derry Abbey, Ireland".

'On his big desk, dark shiny wood with these carved legs, they's lion's claws grabbin' hold of a wooden ball at the ends. On the top, there's this big square glass bottle with a glass stopper and six little glasses on a silver tray; inside is Irish whiskey. There's photos in silver frames of Mayor Dever shakin' hands with Father Geraghty, another one of Monseigneur O'Hara doin' the same, then a photo of Father Geraghty's sister, Mary, who is a nun in the Holy See.' Kevin flicks me a quick look. 'Lemme tell ya, she ain't no Greta Garbo. He's even got one of Archbishop Mundelein, it's signed "With all good wishes, George".

'There's this big brown leather armchair to one side o' the

desk.' Kevin glances up and, pointing his finger at me, gives me a significant look. 'Remember that for later,' he instructs and then, taking a breath, continues. 'So, now the good father comes in from out his sanctum sanctorum, he's yawnin', scratchin' his fat ass and he points to the paintin' of the Blessed Virgin. "Will you look at that now, boy? Such a beautiful face at'al, at'al . . . will you not beg her forgiveness for what you've done?" He points a fat finger to the floor. "On your knees, boy! At once! Ten Hail Mary's for the likes of you! God is not mocked and neither am I! You have sinned grievously and the wages of sin are mine to deliver! Now, boy, make ready for the verity of Geraghty!"'

'He said that?' I exclaimed, repeating the phrase.

'Yeah, that's his slogan. It means he's about to beat the livin' crap outa ya. So, when you've kneeled in front of the Virgin's picture and asked her forgiveness, he says, "Stand up, boy! You've had the love of the Blessed Mother, now you shall have the wrath of the temporal Father. Take off your britches. There's a bad lad. Right off, hang them on the chair, bottom bare, lift your shirt, higher lad, higher, up round your neck. Tilt boy, tilt your bottom!" Then he'd remove his big, black leather belt. You'd hear the "click" of the unbuckle. That strap, it three inches wide and a quarter inch thick and you're bendin', shittin' yourself. He strikes the belt through the air – *Vhooosh!* – then it lands against the back of that big leather chair. *Whack!* "Let the lamentations begin!" he says. "Grab your ankles now, boy! Now think of Ireland, our beautiful emerald isle, nourished by the sacred waters of the Shannon."

'Then he commence to whack the bejesus outa ya. He whales away at ya ass, gruntin' and snortin' like some fat hog. When he's finished, he collapse in that big old leather chair. He's got his fat fingers inside his cassock. The boys who work in the laundry, they say it got no linin'. The pocket in his cassock, it got no fuckin' linin'! You can see his boner inside like a tent pole stickin' up, his eyes they closed. "God forgive me!" he moans. The front of his cassock, it moving every which way, like a rat got himself trapped in a burlap sack.'

I had been so absorbed in the little bloke's story and now, laughing uproariously at the burlap sack incident, at first, and unforgivably, I hadn't realised what was going on around us. But the sudden cry of a seabird penetrated my concentration. I looked up to see that we were surrounded by wheeling seabirds, some flying low, others diving for small fish. A school of dolphins appeared at our bow.

'Hooray! We've made it, we're near land!' I yelled, leaping to my feet and throwing my arms up above my head like an excited schoolboy. Kevin, suddenly aware of what I was saying, jumped up and we danced around the deck, yelling, laughing and yahooing, acting like idiots.

The little bloke suddenly stopped and looked at me, his expression serious. Then he grinned, looking down at the deck and shaking his head. 'I owe you big time, buddy,' he said. 'Twice! Twice you saved me.'

I didn't know what to say. I couldn't tell him it was a coincidence, the right time in the wrong place, and that I'd really been out chasing a butterfly. 'No, mate, afraid I can't take the credit. You got it arse about face. It was *Madam Butterfly*. She saved us. I only helped a bit with the navigation.' I grinned. 'I ain't no hero, you understand?'

CHAPTER FOUR

*'I like dis blacksmith work, man. I black, this mah
work, man.
It good, you pick up dat big ole hammer, you
sweatin' like a nigga,
de metal it red-hot from dat forge.
You hit it hard, you change da shape.
You keep hittin' 'til you ain't angry no more!'*
Joe 'Hammer-man' Popkin
Illinois State Reformatory

AT SIX O'CLOCK IN the evening we sighted a low island
I thought must be the northernmost islet of the Houtman
Abrolhos. If I was correct then we were about forty miles off the
coast of Western Australia, roughly 240 miles west of Fremantle.
With sunset almost upon us I hauled out to sea for two hours to
avoid the reefs and shoals I knew lay south of us and set our course
to the east of sou' south-east, 155 degrees allowing for leeway.

The following morning dawned bright and sunny. There
are mornings at sea where conditions are so perfect you think
you're sailing inside a crystal goblet. If the two days ahead were
like this, we'd be having a cooked breakfast in Fremantle the
day after tomorrow. Bacon, eggs, sausages, fried tomato, milk in
my tea. A second cup, more milk. I wondered briefly what the
little bloke would order.

He'd been quieter than usual at breakfast where we'd both

had a double helping of rice and the last tin of tuna. We still had six tins of mackerel and two tins of carrots, no more peas and still plenty of rice. Anna's supplies had lasted and then some.

'What's the matter, mate, cat got your tongue?'

He looked up and smiled. 'I like that word. Since Joe Popkin I ain't never had a mate.'

'You've got *me*, mate,' I said, stressing the word.

'Yeah, that what I bin thinkin'. I reckon Joe saved my life once or twice at Pontiac, now you the same.'

I avoided the compliment knowing I would have done the same for anyone. I was growing fond of the little bloke but because of my previous experiences and being the kind of person I was, forming a lasting friendship would be difficult. Anyway, we'd soon be forcibly parted by the exigencies of war – he'd be sent to the States for rehabilitation and I'd be in the army. It was simply and literally ships passing in the night.

'What happened after you left? Did you keep in touch with Joe?'

'Nah, he didn't get the four years' education you hadda have for the military so the judge don't give him no option. I went to Camp Paul Jones at San Diego and . . .' He paused. 'Man, he don't write good and I ain't the letter writin' type. I called him long distance twice then.' Kevin shrugged. 'His landlady she say he ain't there, he gone to Noo York.'

'Popkin. It's an unusual name; maybe when you get back to the States you can trace him?'

'Nah, sometime it's better let sleepin' dogs lie. That landlady, I can tell she ain't tellin' me the truth. Joe, he ain't gonna go to Noo York widout he tells me. He's done a heist and got himself caught. He ain't a juvenile no more, he's doin' penitentiary time. He knows I joined the navy. If he wants he can find me. I don't wanna put no shame on him.'

'You said yesterday that Pontiac was an improvement on Angel Guardian?'

'Yeah, man, it just a big jail for kids. What the hell, I bin in jail all my life. In Angel I got beat up every day; in Pontiac I had Joe to take care o' me. It the first time I ever got as much as I could eat. The others, they was always complainin' about the grub. Me? I thought I was in fuckin' paradise. Stews in gravy you can stan' your spoon up in, pieces of meat you can lift out wid a fork dey so big, corn-beef hash, vegetables, fill yer plate with spuds, boiled, mashed, baked, they got carrots but nobody makes you eat dem. Breakfast, you wudda not believed it: eggs, bacon, hash browns, hot cakes, flapjacks, maple syrup. I thought, I'm dead and gone to heaven.'

'Mate, I don't know about the flapjacks, hot cakes and hash browns, but I can guarantee you bacon and eggs when we get to Fremantle. Okay, you're in Pontiac. Why?'

'Why? Don't ask. I'm small. Small kids can climb in small windas. One thing I could never figure, every mart is the same, dey got security front and back, dey got the mart locked like it's Fort fuckin' Knox. Then dey go home and leave the winda in the washroom open. The little one above the toilet, it's always left half-open. Climb in the winda, step on the cistern, step on the toilet seat, step on the floor, step in the storeroom, load up, three cartons only, you don't be greedy and they don't even know you bin there. Cigarettes and booze, dey the two things you can sell on the street, outside any saloon. You do the heist and in ten minutes yer clean. Only one day I sell a carton of Luckies to a plainclothes cop. I got two more, Chesterfield and Camel, hid in the front o' my 'cheater.'

'They sent you to a reformatory for three cartons of cigarettes?'

'Nah, the asshole cop dat caught me, he tol' the desk sergeant he bin watchin' me, I on the way to being a habitual offender. There're three heists in other marts they got on der books, the cop who arrest me says he hears talk I done dem. It ain't true. I ain't stoopid. Them three heists, they got greedy and took too much and leave a mess behin'. But they put me down for them. Cops don't like unsolved when dey got some dumb kid to blame who ain't got a daddy.'

'What about the brothers, Father Geraghty?'

'Yeah, they know the system. Irish cops and priests, dey a brotherhood. Dey ain't gonna rock the boat. First it's Audy Hall, like I tol' you, it's this big buildin' where they hold the kids for processin' and assessment wid a social worker. That all bullshit. It's just another fuckin' jail. The social worker, Mr Smybert, ask me these questions. Did I sleep wid my mother? "Sure," I say, "I was four years old, there weren't no other bed." I'm just supposin', I can't remember, I'm four years old, ferchrissakes. Did I wet my bed? That the next question he ask me. "What now? Or when I slept wid my mother?" I say. He don't smile, he jes write all this crap on his yella pad. Do I play wid myself? That his next question, that his exact words, "play wid yourself". "Yeah, I ain't got no friends, I a lonely chile," I say, 'cos it a stupid question, I'm fourteen, nearly fifteen, it ain't possible I don't. "Masturbate?" he says, now he's smilin' and he's got one eyebrow cocked like he's suggestin' somethin'. "Nah," I says. "When the devil temptation come, I think o' Jesus."

'Next thing I know I'm in the Juvenile Court and the judge says, "Your social worker's report indicates that you were extremely uncooperative and recalcitrant." Later, at Pontiac dey tol' me, if I let Smiley Bert, dat the social worker's nickname, play wid my wienie I coulda got a good report.

'The judge says my intelligence test is good. I must learn me a trade. He gonna send me to a correction facility upstate, the Illinois State Reformatory at Pontiac, to Mr Googerty. He gimme three years. "Get some education, son," he says to me. "The best helping hands you are going to get in life are attached to the ends of your arms." He don't tell me that is because Mr Googerty, the superintendent at Pontiac, is a master blacksmith and every boy got to learn himself blacksmithin' skills. Workin' wit your hands, it suppose to break delinquent habits. Lemme tell you summin', it don't work – when we got outa that place we all got good blacksmithin' skills, and there ain't no place we can't break into, no safe we can't open.'

'So you're a blacksmith by trade?' I asked.

'Nah, they say'd I'm too small for the work. I got to do general duties. Joe, he was good.' Kevin laughed, recalling. 'One day he says to me, "Judgie, I like dis blacksmith work, man. I black, this mah work, man. It good, you pick up dat big ole hammer, you sweatin' like a nigga, de metal it red-hot from dat forge. You hit it hard, you change da shape. You keep hittin' 'til you ain't angry no more!"'

'You never know, maybe he went straight and he's a blacksmith somewhere?' I said.

Kevin looked doubtful. 'Yeah, maybe.'

'And you? What did general duties involve?'

'Library, laundry, sanatorium duties, but it mostly involve getting me an education, three years' high school. I already got one year when I at Angel, De La Salle Catholic High School. But I didn't take much notice in the classroom. I couldn't read so good, so the brother he ain't interested. Now they say

I must get me three more or no general duties. If I don't do no learnin' dey gonna send me back to the workshops wit the big hammer.' Kevin laughed. 'It's funny, when I ain't in juvenile detention I hate school, the brothers, they call me stoopid, useless, brain-dead, or dey jus' ignore me. Now in kids' jail I like it. They gimme special lessons for slow readers and in three months I'm readin' everythin' I can find in that library. They said I ain't stoopid no more. In fact, I suppose to become bright. So I learned me everythin' I could. At the end, graduation, dey said I was the best they ever had. I was college material. Mr Googerty say he disappointed I don't turn out to be no blacksmith but he gonna try an' get me wunna them state scholarships. It ain't easy cause it jes after the Depression, but he gonna try. But by den I done my time and I'm back on the street. I'm seventeen, I can make my own way, I don't have ter go back to Angel.'

'No college then? You didn't accept?'

'Hey, maybe I ain't so bright after all. But, man, all I want is freedom. One way or 'nother I bin in jail all my life. I seventeen years and not one day I get to do what I want – when I don' need permission to scratch my ass.'

I thought how, with the exception of boarding school, I'd lived my life largely unsupervised and at seventeen had been free to go butterfly hunting in Java and then, as we were doing at present, sail across the Indian Ocean. It was quite a contrast to the little bloke's first seventeen years.

'So what did you do with your first taste of freedom?' I asked.

'Ha! Freedom! That a big, big joke! Wit my record I can't even get a job stackin' groceries at the supermart.'

I laughed. 'I should think not!'

Kevin did a quick double-take, but then got the joke and chuckled. 'Yeah, maybe you right. I get dat job, hey, I doesn't need no toilet winda no more. Dat a whole lot o' temptation to put in front my two hands dat suppose to be the best help I gonna get in life.'

'What about Joe Popkin? Was he with you, released at the same time?'

'Nah, he was involved in this fight in the washroom. Three big wop kids, Latinos, they attack him, one wit a knife, they gonna cut him bad. It about cigarettes . . . the wops dey control the distribution o' smokes. They chargin' unfair and the black kids, they got to pay more dan the white kids. Joe says they ain't gonna pay no more, they gonna start their own supply, get deir own outside connection wit a guard.'

'So, what happened? Joe get hurt?'

'He got cut on the arm, but it ain't bad. He broke the arm o' the wop wit the knife. He broke the jaw of der second one and the last, he threw him against the shower wall and he got himself, that wop, he got fifty-two stitches in the head. Joe says to me, "You da cigarette man, Judgie. Why you not go talk to dat Irish guard wid da red head. We can do dis busy-ness, man. You got da distribution and I do da protection. What you say, man?"

'So I talk to the carrot-head, Mick O' Rourke, that the same as my mother's maiden name, Mary O' Rourke, and he got hair, freckles jus' like I remember hers. But he says he don't know her, he come from Detroit. I put the deal, the proposition, to him. He greedy, but he agree to give me three cartons' credit if we pay triple for the first order and after dat double above retail. It ain't good, but also it ain't bad. Soon we got ourself a good cigarette business wit the blacks and then wit the white guys. The wops, dey don't come near, because Joe, now he the man, black an' white, dey call him "Joe 'Hammer-man' Popkin"! "Hammer-man" fer short, like, "Watch out, here come the Hammer-man!"'

'Punishment? The fight?' I asked, feeling certain they couldn't have got away with the washroom brawl.

'Yeah, nobody grass, not even the wops, but der's too much blood and bones broke, the sanatorium, dey involved. Dat mean no cover-up. Joe got six months added on for assault and battery. Mr Googerty he put in a good word wit the judge 'cos Joe is the best blacksmith apprentice he got and he don't make no trouble before, otherwise he coulda got two years for A an' B. Dat wudda meant when he turn eighteen, he ain't no juvenile no more, he got to leave Pontiac and go to Joliet, the state prison. But now wit the six months added, Joe don't come out wit me.'

'That's tough,' I sympathised. 'I mean losing a good mate like that.' It occurred to me that I'd never had a Joe as a mate. Never had anyone like that. Aloneness has its drawbacks.

'I shoulda gone to college,' Kevin said, shaking his head ruefully. 'But I got dis one dumb idea. I want to find my mother, dat the first thing.'

'Oh? Hasn't she been gone a fair while, since you were six? How did you know where to start looking?'

Kevin gave a grim little laugh. 'Saloons. She's a lush. Irish. Mary O'Rourke. If she still pretty, it ain't too hard to figure.' Kevin looked up at me knowingly, expecting me to react. But I didn't, not sure what it was I was supposed to figure out. 'The game . . . she floggin' pussy,' he said quietly.

'You mean she's a prostitute?' I said, somewhat shocked at this assumption.

His voice grew suddenly angry. 'Stands to reason, don't it? Poor Irish, she's an alky, how else she gonna buy her booze?'

'But you couldn't be certain?' I protested.

'Nah, yer right, maybe she become a nun,' he said, still angry, but I could see, also hurting inside like hell.

'So you didn't find her?' I asked, almost hopefully. I tried to immediately dismiss the name Mary O' Rourke from my mind. When Kevin had mentioned his mother's name the lyrics to a song I'd heard sung in a Rabaul pub jumped into my mind. It had been sung by a drunken Irishman, a broken-down jockey named Tony Crosby, while he strummed a very indifferent guitar. I don't suppose it was much of a song but it brought the house down when Tony sang it and it had the virtue of earning him copious drinks. I learned the lyrics while playing poker in a room at the back. It was a story of four young Irish lads and their first attempt at seducing a girl in the pub, something I knew it was damn near impossible to do in Rabaul. To pick up a young white woman in the pub, that is.

You could get a mission girl for five shillings and a puk-puk girl for two and sixpence, but it wasn't the sort of thing the son of the local Anglican missionary could get away with. The funny thing was, hearing the diminutive little ex-jockey singing about a girl in a pub in Ireland made it all seem so wholesome, clean and romantic. You'd imagine this girl with shining titian hair and rosy cheeks with skin so fair it was almost translucent. Whereas imagining a similar scene in a pub in Rabaul seemed impossible. There were the odd hennaed or over-bleached blondes, beaten-up tarts in their fifties known locally as 'scrubbers', and the rest were native women, black as the ace of spades, with skin roughly the consistency of a croc's back.

Sweet Mary O'Rourke

We're four young jocks who have a thirst like a drain.
We've been out doing track work from the break of day.
So now it's down to the local to ease the day's strain.
Two pints of Guinness ought to wash the horseshit away.

There at the saloon bar stands Sweet Mary O'Rourke.
She's a long-legged young filly, pretty and frisky.
We'd welcome her company and a bit of small talk.
So we'll lash out and buy her a wee glass o' whiskey!

'Good day, Sweet Mary, how goes the pretty one?
We're four young lads who good company seek.
Would you fancy a whiskey and a rare bit o' fun?
It'll brighten yer eyes and add a blush to yer cheek.'

Now it's well known Sweet Mary is fond of a drop.
'Ta, lads, it's Irish, pray . . . how did you know?'
She's wiggling her bottom and she's straining on top.
We've all got this warm feeling of fire down below.

'Shall we have yet another, lads? What do you think?'
Mary's skirt has crept up near the top of her thighs.
We're laughin' and clinkin' with a nod and a wink,
All hoping we'll be first to win this delectable prize!

Then it's ice over a double Irish for Mary to gargle.
Her fingers are nimble and she's willing to please.
Her flick of a fly button is nothing short of a marvel.
Is she checking for size or is she simply a tease?

One last whiskey! It's clear we've won on this track.
She's home and she's hosed and she's willing to star.
It'll be a romp in the sandpit as she lies on her back.
Then it's 'Time please, gents! We're closing the bar!'

'Barman! A stall in the stable?' we boldly request.
'Rooms are paid in advance, lads, show us the brass.'
Alas, our pockets are empty; Mary drinks only the best.
We're flat broke and we're on the bones of our arse.

'Come, lads!' says Mary. 'There's no need to fret.
Such stabling fees would be my pleasure to pay.
But I've looked at the fare and it's with some regret,
The bangers are too small to put on the menu today!'

The filly had bolted when we thought she was tame.
But she left this message with quite clear directions.
'Lads, grow up just a wee bit, then we'll all dine again.
When I promise to sup well on your rampant erections!'

Tony had a voice not all that bad, perfect enunciation and he would sing with a sense of nostalgia that touched every expat, even Mustafa Malouf, the Lebanese cement contractor. He'd be bawling his eyes out at the end of it. That's the funny thing, it was a comic song, meant to get a bit of a laugh, but in Tony's hands it turned into pure nostalgia and always brought tears to the eyes of the drunks. Funny, that. I pushed the memory of the song to the back of my mind and brought my attention back to Kevin.

The little bloke was sitting cross-legged on the deck, elbows resting on his knees, hands hanging loose, staring at the deck between his legs. Finally he spoke. 'I found her. At first I ask they know a Mrs Mary Judge. Nobody heard of no woman got that name. Then I ask them if they know Mary O'Rourke? Then it not too hard. I check all the sleazy saloons in the docks near the Lake. Pretty soon I get the nod, drinkers, regulars, who know her. My mother gone changed back her name.' He shot me a wan smile. 'Ain't nobody like to sleep wit a Judge. "Son, you don't want to go there," they say; some they warn me she's a lush, a two-dollar whore who done blow jobs for drinks.' Kevin was close to tears. 'Some say, I should try the Bosun's Locker but leave my watch and wallet at home. I ain't got no watch and there ain't nothin' in my wallet anyhow.'

'Did you find her there?'

'Nah, it was too late, she were already in the hospice wit advance Vee Dee. I seen her there.'

'Did she know who you were?' I felt trapped into asking. Suddenly I was desperately anxious to find a way to abandon the subject of Kevin's mother.

Kevin glanced up at me, his expression somewhat impatient. 'Course not, but she start to scream when I come in the ward, "Patrick, ya bastard! You fuckin' dogshit! You left me!" She's sittin' up in her bed and she's shakin' her fist, her long red hair it flyin' from her head, it got all grey streaks like a witch. Den she get hold a glass of water and she throw it at me. Der's water and broken glass on the green polish floor and she's still screamin', "You left me with da fuckin' stoopid ugly brat! Go away, ya bastard! Ya fuckin' dog turd! Ya piece o' useless crud! Fuck off, ya Irish motherfucker!"

'The sisters dey is running every which-way, holding der hands against der face, shooin' me out the ward. Black cleaner-woman come runnin' wit a bucket and mop. Outside, the doctor, he says Mary O'Rourke she ain't right in the head no more. I tell him I'm her son, my name's Kevin, that Patrick, the name she's yellin' out, he my father, maybe he can explain to her?' Kevin glanced dolefully up at me, his voice uncertain. 'I jes want to see her once, Nick. Hold her hand, tell her it's okay, I unnerstan'. Tell her maybe I can go to college. Make her proud o' me. But he, dat doctor, he says it too late, she got third-stage syphilis, it the final stage, she crazy, she gonna die, I mus' leave her alone. No excitement allowed in dat place 'cos everybody dere, dey is busy dyin'.' Kevin was now sobbing softly, his little crew-cut head bowed and shaking, the bright morning sunlight shining crimson through his jug ears.

I moved and sat down beside him. Anna was the only person I had ever held in my arms. I knew I should do the same for the little bloke, hold his head against my chest, embrace him and comfort him. I tried to force myself, but I couldn't. I couldn't bring myself to do it. I'm no good at touching. So I put my arm around his shoulders. 'Steady on, mate, take it easy now.' It was the best I could do to comfort him. I felt ashamed. He deserved more from me.

Two days later in the midafternoon we were idly watching the sails respond to the variable wind. I spotted a tiny speck on the horizon that I took to be a lone bird, then realised its course was straight and steady. As it came closer the low throb of an engine could just be heard above the slop of the waves. I remembered how the Dutchman, teary-eyed, had presented me with the Dutch flag by way of a handing-over ceremony. With the flag hurriedly hoisted and the two of us waving like mad, the flying boat dipped its wings to tell us we'd been spotted and took a lazy right turn and soon became a slow-moving dot on the cloudless horizon.

'If I'm correct we ought to sight the coast sometime early tomorrow and with a bit of luck it should be Rottnest Island. They've seen us and know we're here so someone will be looking out for us.'

'We safe, huh? No more dirty, rotten, stinkin' Japs. That Captain Bligh, he sure know a thing or two wit the rope trick.' Kevin reached up, grinned and patted me on the back. 'You the best, Nick!'

'Safe?' I paused for a moment, trying to cover my embarrassment. 'Yeah, just about, maybe, *nearly* safe. A sailboat without an engine is only really safe once she's moored, and we've got almost a day's sailing ahead of us. Right now, with the Japs practically in our backyard, everyone would be a bit trigger-happy. I wouldn't be at all surprised if the patrol boat from port defences isn't a tad wary of us. Notice how the Catalina stayed up above two thousand feet and didn't come any lower to take a closer look?'

'Two thousand feet, that pretty damn low, ain't it?' Kevin asked, concerned. 'They seen us good, they said so wit der wings.'

'Ah, the Catalinas are strange birds, with only a top speed of ninety knots, they're sitting ducks for any fighter plane or anti-aircraft. I've spoken to the crews who occasionally used to fly into Rabaul. Bloody deathtraps they are, made of canvas with no self-sealing fuel tanks, so if they cop a machine-gun bullet in a tank they're history. They've got two machine-guns on board but seldom get to fire them in anger except perhaps at targets like us. On the other hand, we might carry a machine-gun and putting a couple of dozen bullets into their tanks wouldn't be that difficult. If we were the enemy it wouldn't be us who were the sitting ducks. That's why they're staying well clear. But they're ideal for reconnaissance and coastal guardwork as they can stay in the air for up to twenty-eight hours. They know we're here so their job is done. I'll take down the flag for now but remind me to hoist it again around daylight tomorrow, will you?'

Sitting on deck eating the usual gourmet meal from the paddy and the sea via the cannery, I couldn't help wondering if this would be our final evening meal together on board *Madam Butterfly*. I guessed I'd give rice and tinned mackerel a miss for a while. I was anxious to hear the remainder of the little bloke's story and knowing this might well be our last night together I started right out, hoping to somehow skirt around the subject of his mother.

'So, Kevin, you're out of Pontiac, you don't want to go to college and nobody seems too keen to give a reformatory kid a job. How'd you survive?'

'Spottin' pins.'

'Huh?'

'Tenpins?' Kevin could see from my expression that I didn't understand. 'Bowlin' alley, players knock down the pins, you gotta collect 'em and stan' dem up again. End o' the day, twelve hours, you can't lift yer arms and your back's broke, ten cents an hour so you got yourself a buck twenty. If you don't work fast and the customers complain you keepin' them waitin', they don't get their money-worth, that the end of you. There are plenty of kids outside, dey willin' to fight you for that shit job.' He looked up. 'But that don't last too long, my big mouth soon seen to that and yours truly is back on the streets where there ain't no jobs for a kid who bin to reform school, ain't no jobs anyhow comin' out of that Depression, ain't no welfare, ain't no jobs, ain't no hope. Ain't nothin' for it, I gotta turn back to crime to make me a crust, 'cos I'm starving, man.'

'What, back to toilet windows?'

Kevin grinned. 'Nah, numbers racket. That the funny thing, man, the wops gimme the chance, one of the wop kids from Pontiac who is out and he see me in the street. "Hey, Judgie, how ya doin', man?" he ask me. In the reformatory Irish kids don't talk to wops and visa-versa. I can bullshit, give him some good rap, but what the hell, I'm broke and I'm hungry and he the first friendly voice I heard in a while. "I'm on the bones, buddy," I tell him. He gives me his hand. "Mario . . . Mario Parissi." We shake hands, I never done that with a wop before. "You et?" he asks. I shake my head. He don't know I ain't eaten for two days. "Come. You eat pizza?"'

Kevin glanced at me and laughed. 'Everybody in the world got a best meal. You know, the best dey ever had. For me that day in the Italian quarter, Maxwell Street Market at Mario Parissi's uncle Franco's Pizza and Ice-Cream Parlour that the best, the number one, all-time, big league, home run, best. *Peperoni*, mozzarella cheese, smoked ham, salami, cabanossi, other things I don't even know you can get before, all sittin' bubblin' in this melted cheese that got a brown crust on top. I ate me that whole giant-size pizza. Man, I died and gone to heaven!'

'Sounds great, I've never eaten pizza. I've only seen them in films in the cinema.'

'Whatcha mean? You ain't got no wops in Australia?'

'Sure, in Sydney and Melbourne, and we had an Italian guy at school in Brisbane, good swimmer. Some Italian engineers I once met building a road through the jungle in New Britain, but no pizza parlours that I know of.'

'First chance you get, take my advice, Nick, Italian sausage, the hot chilli one, that the main ingredient you want to get. Remember now!'

'Yeah, okay, Italian sausage, the hot chilli one.'

'It called *peperoni*, don't forget, *peperoni*!'

I nodded, wondering how long it might be before I had to remember the *peperoni*. A pizza parlour springing up in Rabaul seemed improbable. With the imminent Japanese invasion a sushi bar was more likely. It had been a fair while since I had eaten Japanese, although occasionally my father would make tempura prawns and vegetables. He couldn't boil an egg but someone, somewhere in his Japanese past, had shown him how to make a tempura batter and very occasionally he'd exercise this single culinary skill and cook up a batch of prawns and vegies if the bishop was visiting. That is, if he could find a light cooking oil, which was pretty seldom. Most island cooking was done in coconut milk, pork fat or lard, and what passed for cooking oil, when available, had roughly the consistency of something you'd find in a diesel engine sump.

Without further prompting the little bloke continued. 'That's how I got into the numbers racket. Mario tells his uncle Franco how I am the top brain in the reformatory and how wit the Hammer-man we run cigarettes in the kids' jail, but we don't interfere wit the wogs. He don't say nothin' about the fight in the washroom. He say I reliable and trustworthy and I am organised and ain't no dog and I also a Catholic. His uncle say he'll talk to his brother Bruno, that if I can't be a wog then a Mick's the next best thing. Uncle Franco's brother Bruno is connected to someone who's connected to someone who's connected to someone that is a lieutenant in the Frank Nitti mafia family.'

Kevin paused, then explained, 'Frank Nitti he take over when Al Capone got his indictment, but he ain't no big talker like Capone, he don't rock the boat, everythin' is connections. So now I'm workin' for the mafia six times removed sellin' numbers tickets on the street, nickels and quarters, and I'm gettin' me a percentage. It ain't big but I'm making enough for a dosshouse and I can eat. But mostly it's pizza and sometimes Mrs Franco she say, "Come, boy, tonight you gonna eat pasta."' Kevin looked up. 'You know what is pasta, Nick?'

'Like noodles?' Then remembering I'd read the word somewhere, 'Spaghetti, isn't it?'

'Yeah and lots more, linguini marinara, lasagne, spaghetti con le vongole, gnocchi alla burro, fettuccine al burro,' Kevin reeled them off, ticking each dish off on his 'love' fingers, then his 'hate' ones. 'Wog food, buddy, it the best! I'm also learnin' dat wogs, like niggers, they ain't all bad. Mario is a good guy and soon all the other wogs runnin' numbers, they accept me and I'm hangin' out wit dem. I've got previous and they respect that. Maybe Mario told them, but they know about the washroom and the cigarettes. Some of the Hammer-man, it musta rubbed off on me, 'cos they think I don't take no shit. I'm doin' okay and I'm givin' Mario's cousin, Nico, who is a stonemason apprentice, fifty cents a week for the tombstone he's carvin' for my mother's grave. He's gonna carve me an angel wit wings for only five dollars more than one o' them square headstones. The inscription it read:

'Mary O'Rourke
1898–1935
Now only blue skies.
Life's stormy weather

gone forever!
R.I.P.'

'That's very nice,' I said. 'Did you compose it yourself?'

'Nah, dey the words on this embroid'ry picture in Father Geraghty's office. One of the nuns, she done it for him when his mother died in Ireland. It's also got a red rose wit leaves an' thorns in the corner of the picture, but Mario's cousin said he ain't learned yet how to do a rose in granite, he still learnin' to do the thorns on a Christ head.'

Carving a rose sounds a lot less complicated than carving an angel and I couldn't help wondering what the little bloke got for his money. 'Good job was it, the angel?'

'Yep, considerin' the wings.'

'Wings?'

'He couldn't get a piece a stone big 'nough so the angel's wings they can't spread out, so dey folded an' the angel arms dey ain't nowhere and he tell me dey suppose to be hid unner the wings so you don't see dem and he ain't learned to do feet yet.'

I couldn't contain myself and I started to laugh. Kevin started laughing as well and soon we were rolling around, hugging ourselves. 'The face, the angel . . . is it pretty?' I asked finally, still giggling.

'He ain't done faces yet. It more like an owl. It got a beak and two holes, no mouth. He ain't done faces yet. I got me an owl angel!' Kevin roared.

'But the wings, they're nice . . . folded, but nice . . . I take it he's done wings?'

Kevin thought for a moment. 'One wing, it okay, but the udder, it like the angel, she got a hunchback on the one side wit some feathers hangin' down.' Kevin started to laugh again. 'I got myself a hunchback owl angel wit no arms and the feet they ain't come out the rock yet!'

'All for an extra five bucks?'

'Nah, I don't pay him the five spot.' Kevin grinned. 'I give him some free advice 'bout what he can go do to his sister.' The little bloke pushed his forefinger into the soft flesh of his pug's nose and made a small circular motion, then grinned. 'Dat's when I find out dat apprentice wog Nico, he can do noses real good.'

I thought to myself that a battered and broken angel was probably a very good symbol for Sweet Mary O'Rourke, the little bloke's mother. I patted him on the back. 'Mate, it was a lovely thing to do for your mother. Sorry about your hooter . . . Jeez, I must say, he did a damn good job.'

'Nah, he only the secon' time, the first happen at Angel when I ten years old, dis big kid, he sixteen, he want me to suck him off, but I won't do it, so he whack me an' break my nose, dat the first time. Then the third is when we, Mario and my wog buddies, do dat cigarette van heist.'

'What's it with you and cigarettes, Kev?'

'Fags! It like stealin' money, Nick. You don't have no trouble wit unloadin' them, everybody in the world smokes and everybody want cheap fags and don't ask no questions. We sellin' numbers so it's easy to carry two cartons wit you. Sell a numbers ticket then you ask, "Want cigarettes, ma'am, sir?" Nobody gonna say no dey don't buy hot. Der some folk who dey never bought der fags no udder way.'

'You said a cigarette van. I take it this was rather more than a few cartons through the toilet window?'

'Hey, dis one professional. We got us a wog kid on the inside who work for the wholesaler. The vans dey loaded at night an' den dey locked in behin' dis big security fence. The guard he like to have him some shut-eye two, three in the morning in a shed where he got a bed. Dey don't have no dogs. So we cut the gate chain wit bolt cutters and we tie up the guard and we take ourself a van.

'We laughin', we rich, maybe a thousand cartons in dat van and we away and goin' down this highway tunnel when we burst us a tyre. There ain't no spare, it four o'clock in the mornin' an' we ain't goin' nowhere, man. It time to kick the dust, get outa der. But first we push the van into the side 'mergency tunnel so maybe nobody don't see it 'til the mornin'. Den we vamoose.

'We bin walkin' a while when this patrol car pulls up, the lights are flashin', the siren goin' and it stop and two cops get out. We heared it comin' and Mario says, "Judgie, if da cops, dey Irish, you talk, if dey wops, I talk." He turn to the udder four guys, "Allayas shurrup!"

'Both cops are Irish. One look and you can tell. They got der gut spillin' over der belt and one of dem hitch his trousers up before he speaks and everythin' upfront it wobbles. But he don't speak to me but to the other cop. "Fuckin' wops," he says, shakin' his head like he just opened a garbage can and come across a bag o' vermin. Mario looks at me and gimme the nod I must talk.

'"Mornin', officer, we got ourself a predicament, thank gawd you've come," I say.

'"Sonny boy, you got yourself a predicament orright, you in the middle of a goddamn traffic tunnel!' the trouser-hitch cop says.

'"Yessir, officer, we from outa town, Pontiac, junior baseball team, Hawks, Illinois State Junior semi-finals, we got ourself lost and we don't know dis tunnel it only for traffic." I shrugged my shoulders. "Den suddenly it too late, we don't know iffen we near the end or we shoulda turned back. We scared, officer! We shittin' ourself!" I say and give him a bug-eyed look.

'The second cop he looks at me, then he looks down at his boots, then back at me. "Dat van," his head nods towards where we come from, "dat cigarette van back dere, you know summin' about that?"

'"Van? We ain't seen no van," I say, lookin' him in the eye, then lookin' at the others who is noddin' they don't see no van.

'"Yeah, yeah," he points to my 'cheater. "Zip!" I pull down the zip o' my windcheater and he see there ain't nuttin' hidden dere. He looks at Mario. "Zip!" then to all o' us, "Zip!" Now there's cartons of Lucky, Camel, Chesterfield, Winston, every bran' you can name fallin' down, clatterin' on the road. It's now near five in the mornin' and the tunnel traffic is buildin', zoom . . . zoom . . . zooooom, early trucks and some autos buildin' the noise in the tunnel.

'"Temptation!" I spread my hands and give him a sheepish grin. "All dem cigarettes in dat broken-down van. We only hoomen, officer," I try to explain.

'Wham! Hitch-trousers, he hit me on the nose. "Wops ain't hoomen!" he says. "Dey greasy filth!"

'"I ain't no wop, I'm Irish," I say. I got my head bowed and the blood it drippin' from my nose like a leakin' faucet.

'Whack! Uppercut. He hits me again on the nose, what bones ain't broke before dey broke now. "Irish consortin' with wops, dat ain't natural, that disgustin', sonny boy!"

'"I ain't took no cigarettes," I say, pleadin', snot and blood sniffin', trying to save my own ass, then ashamed I said it, the whiny Angel Guardian child comin' out in me. What you made to do as a kid always comes back when you scared.

'"Irish consortin' with wops *and* also stoopid!" he says and hits me one more time, now I only got mash left, bloody mash, bitsa bone.'

Kevin looked up at me and grinned, his hooter spread across the centre of his face. 'Our fingerprints dey all over dat cigarette van where we pushed it into the safety tunnel, there ain't no pleadin' petty theft, a few cartons took outa temptation. The judge he gonna throw the book. That when he offer me the military, or else. "Join up or Joliet," he says. Joliet, dat the state prison and where, witout Joe Popkin to protect me, I ain't got no protection and I'm gonna be someone's butt-bitch.'

'So you chose the navy?'

'Yeah, I ain't much for marchin', I done 'nough marchin' at Angel and den Pontiac, swingin' yer arms, knobbly knees touchin'.'

Two hours at the helm and two hours below sounds difficult, but at sea it's the ideal watch, even at night. At dawn the next day when my time was almost up I saw what I took to be Rottnest Island. We'd made it. It wasn't something you said with an exclamation mark. No dancing on the deck. Luck had played a huge part. I suppose a bit of seamanship had helped as well, but mostly the sailing part, anyway, was due to *Madam Butterfly*. A yacht is essentially a woman – you really know very little about her until you mutually experience a crisis and that's when you witness her hidden depths. What's more, you can never tell by just looking, measuring, checking the design; it's something that happens beyond the theory, beyond the maths. I suppose you call it character. Men carry it like a badge, cultivate it, flaunt it, call it names – leadership, guts, steadfastness, will, drive, bravery, commonsense, charisma – we wear it like a bright uniform, pin medals to it to attract other men and the admiration and adulation of women. But women never think about it; it's simply there when the crisis comes or it ain't, bright tears or shining steel, rock or shifting sands. Boats are like that.

But, of course, at the time I knew a great deal more about boats than I did about women and probably wasn't capable of such an analogy. I hadn't even undergone the apprenticeship of a mother. My experience of the female gender had been limited to the starched and veiled, over-powdered, un-lipsticked school matron or the pre-lunch or afternoon-gin-and-tonic-lubricated expat wives at the Rabaul Country Club in white tennis dresses. Except perhaps for the mixed Easter services in the Anglican church, where the native women sang with a full heart and the white women stared, thin-lipped and hostile, mouthing the hymns, both sets of female worshippers uncomfortable and diminished in the presence of the other. I was no expert on women, that was for sure. Anna was separated in my mind as someone unique, a loveliness born of a mixture of white and dark in unknown proportions, a secret of genetic pigments and therefore not to be compared or included; mine alone.

I went over to the hatchway and called down to Kevin, 'Wakey, wakey, mate, this is the moment, we've made it. Rottnest Island! Next stop Fremantle! Bacon and eggs, easy over!' I had learned the expression from American movies.

All his life in institutions had made the little bloke an instant waker-upperer and he leapt from his bunk and hurried on deck, standing in the nuddy, feet apart, shielding his eyes from the rising sun as he examined the dark shape of the island.

'Dey got folk dere?' he asked.

'Yeah, probably.' I turned to him. 'Get your strides on and bring up the flag, we should see a naval launch heading our way pretty soon.'

I had barely spoken when a grey launch headed towards us and as it drew nearer I saw that two sailors were manning a machine-gun in the bow with two other machine-guns on both sides of the bridge. Kevin appeared carrying the Dutch flag and I lost no time hoisting it, whereupon we stood in the cockpit waving frantically to show we were friendly.

'Fuckers ain't gonna shoot, are they?' Kevin, eyeing the machine-guns, said fearfully. 'Them sailors . . . dey don't look too friendly.'

'Hope not, keep waving, you can't shoot a man who's waving at you. Smile, look happy, both hands in the air, show them we're unarmed.' I confess I was using a confident tone I didn't feel.

A sailor carrying a megaphone hailed us, 'What vessel and where bound?'

I cupped my hands to my mouth. '*Vleermuis* bound for Fremantle!' Then added gratuitously, 'Out of Batavia!'

'Nationality? Are you Dutch?' the megaphone asked.

'Australian and American!' I shouted in reply.

'Welcome home, sailor . . . welcome to Australia, Yank! We're coming aboard, please cooperate!'

The launch drew aside as Kevin and I lowered the mainsail and a sailor from the naval launch threw us a rope, then a petty officer and an ordinary seaman jumped on board. 'Jesus, look what the cat brought in!' the petty officer exclaimed, stepping on board *Madam Butterfly*.

The sailor looked around, then shook his head in wonderment. 'You blokes come from Java in this ocean-going bathtub?'

I grinned. 'It's a gaff-rigged cutter, solid teak, you couldn't ask for better,' then sticking my hand out to the petty officer, 'Nick Duncan.' I turned to the little bloke. 'This is my offsider, Ordinary Seaman Kevin Judge, US Navy.'

'Howdy,' Kevin said, using a greeting I'd never heard him adopt before.

'Gidday, I'm Kim . . . Kim Rabbits.' He indicated the sailor beside him with a nod of his head. 'Dave Tompkins.'

'Pleased ta meetcha,' Dave said. 'You two blokes *really* sailed this old crate across the Indian Ocean? Fuckin' astonishing if you ask me.'

Kevin seemed pleased with Dave's use of the expletive he himself so dearly loved. He grinned, then jabbed a thumb in my direction. 'Him, he done it. I jes come along for the ride. Mostly I just shit myself. I want you to know I ain't no fuckin' hero.'

Having introduced ourselves I suddenly realised how scruffy we must look to the two shaved, scrubbed and smartly turned-out naval men, their white canvas belts and polished brass and boots belonging to a world half-forgotten. Kevin was in grease-stained shorts and shirt and mine were not quite as stained but faded and only in a slightly better condition. We'd both not shaved for the duration, the little bloke's scar now almost healed, though badly, a great broad crimson worm across his forehead. Kevin's navy crew cut still retained a semblance of order while my hair, already in need of the clippers before I left Batavia, now fell in curls at the nape of my neck and almost to my shoulders, a sun-damaged straw-coloured mop that would wreck a horse comb. We'd both lost at least a stone in weight, our eyes were sunken and my skin burned a deep nut-brown, while the little bloke's was veering more towards the lobster. All we had going for us was that we weren't dirty, having stripped and washed every day of the voyage.

'Got any papers?' Rabbits asked me, his tone almost apologetic.

I produced my passport and the papers for the *Vleermuis* (*Madam Butterfly*) and Kevin indicated his aluminium discs. Then he cleared his throat. 'Wouldn't have a smoke, buddy?' he asked Tompkins.

The sailor hesitated momentarily. 'I can roll yer one, mate.'

The little bloke glanced up at me, confused. 'He'll tailor-make you one, Kevin,' I explained, and nodded at Dave Tompkins. 'Make it big and fat, please. It's been a long time between smokes.' In truth it had not until that moment occurred to me that the little bloke, whose entire criminal career was based on nicking cigarettes, probably smoked like a chimney. He would have suffered horribly from withdrawal, but had never once expressed a craving for tobacco.

Kevin watched fascinated as the sailor produced tobacco and papers and rolled a decent-sized fag. 'Jesus, dis the wild west, man!' Kevin laughed, gratefully accepting the neatly rolled homemade cigarette, turning it around in his fingers, then holding it up to examine it. Rabbits produced a box of matches and cupping his hands to protect the flame from the breeze allowed Kevin to light up.

'We'll have to tow you into Fremantle, it'll be a bit choppy, but with the *Durban Castle* in the harbour and the WA boys from the sixth and seventh Divisions disembarked, the whole place has gone apeshit!' Rabbits said.

This was news to me. 'But aren't the sixth and seventh Divs supposed to be in the Middle East fighting against Hitler?'

'No, mate, it's in all the papers this morning. Curtin's ordered them home to defend Australia against the Japs.'

'That's great news, looks like we're going to need them.'

'Yeah, mate, we're with the Yanks now!' Leading Seaman Tompkins growled. 'Bloody good thing if you ask me, after what the Poms did to us in Singapore!'

'Who's Curtin and who's da Poms?' Kevin asked.

'Curtin's our Prime Minister and the Poms are the English,' I said, having no time to explain properly.

'Limeys?' Kevin asked, his expression indicating distinct disapproval.

'Yeah, we call them Poms or Pommies here,' I said, then asked the two sailors, 'When was this? When did you know the troops were coming back?' thinking that was why the Catalina had been out, looking for the fleet.

'That's the whole point, mate, we didn't. National secret. I reckon to keep the Japs from knowing the convoy's whereabouts. Nobody here knew until a few hours before they arrived. One moment the harbour's a sleepy pond and the next there's the *Durban Castle* and a Dutch ship and we hear it on the wireless and everyone's goin' crazy, you can hardly see the water for the small craft.' Then he spoke more slowly. 'That's why it's a good idea to tow yez, we could easily lose you in the harbour traffic.' He laughed. 'Nobody's takin' no notice of the water police.'

Kim Rabbits stayed on board with us until we reached Fremantle and I was to learn that the Dutch East Indies had surrendered while we'd been at sea.

We were towed into the customs wharf, though not without ceremony. You'd have thought that after the *Durban Castle* we'd be very small fish, but waiting for us was a group of uniforms wearing expressionless faces, police masks, customs masks and navy masks, each, it seemed to me, practising their *gravitas*. I felt at once let down; after all, we'd completed an ocean-going journey not without distance and danger, and the odd welcome smile would not have gone astray. In their own understated way Rabbits and Tompkins had been generous in their admiration, but this mob in braid, blue and khaki, standing at semi-attention in their spit 'n' polish boots, wore a collective downturned mouth that made me feel as though we'd done something criminal. I was also discovering that being towed into port was humiliating, a form of captivity and capitulation. *Madam Butterfly* looked disconsolate with her sails collapsed on deck, a pretty lady caught wearing dirty underwear.

'Don't like the look of dem fuckers,' Kevin said out of the corner of his mouth.

'Stay here, I'll talk to them,' I said, my voice rising just above the hollow throb of the launch engine and the swish of water from the bilge as the yacht was manoeuvred into the dockside. I stepped onto the steel ladder leading up to the wharf and had barely gained the top when a policeman stepped forward. 'Identification, please,' he demanded, omitting, no doubt due to my scruffy appearance, the appendage 'sir'. I handed him my passport. He examined it, checking the photograph of a beardless me with short back and sides, then flicked through several pages and handed it to the customs officer. 'Seems orright,' he said, adding, probably for the benefit of the others, 'He's Australian, Nicholas Duncan.' He nodded with his chin towards Kevin, who was standing in the cockpit.

'American! I'm an American!' Kevin shouted up before I could reply, his voice tetchy.

'Kevin Judge, he's an American sailor off the USS *Houston*, sunk off Java on the twenty-eighth of February,' I said, then added, though I don't know quite why, 'Wounded in battle.'

A naval officer stepped forward. 'The *Houston* went down the same night as the *Perth*.' He turned to me. 'You were there? The *Perth*? Crew?' he asked.

'No, sir.' I pointed to *Madam Butterfly*. 'I picked Seaman Judge up on an isolated beach the following morning; he was the sole survivor of a massacre by the local natives that killed nine Australians off the *Perth*. I've got their papers with me,' I concluded.

Well, that sure as hell put the cat among the pigeons, there was no more playing high and mighty and competing among the braid and brass to be officious. There was mumbling all round and then the policeman said it was best to come with him, that there was a boarding house opposite the station where we could stay, have a shower, shave and get into fresh clobber.

Standing next to the policeman, I called down to the little bloke, 'We have to go, mate, are you ready?'

I hadn't realised the effect the police uniform would have on him. 'We under arrest?' he asked somewhat tremulously. This clearly wasn't the kind of welcome he'd anticipated.

I grinned, attempting to put him at ease. 'Nah, bacon and eggs.' I turned to the cop. 'Sausages?'

The policeman grinned. 'Yeah, I reckon a couple of snags are not beyond the station's petty cash.' Suddenly there were grins all round. I climbed down back on board to grab my knapsack with the papers of the murdered men from the *Perth*,

Anna's handkerchief and the oilskin package containing the Magpie Crow plus my spare shorts and shirt, clean but in poor repair and no longer streetworthy.

With Kevin climbing the ladder ahead of me we returned to the wharf to find the naval Lieutenant Commander standing near the head of the ladder. He smiled and said, 'Nick, my name is Rigby . . . Roger Rigby, I'm from Naval Intelligence. I'm afraid you'll have to give me your passport and any personal papers, also the wallets or anything else you kept that belonged to the men from the *Perth*. Don't worry, it's just that we need to check one or two things, we'll return your personal stuff as soon as we can. Oh, and by the way, well done and welcome home.'

'Thank you, sir,' I grinned. 'It's bloody nice to be home.'

He pointed to the policeman. 'Senior Sergeant Hamill is in charge, you're a civilian matter for the time being, but I'll be in touch.'

'Sir, captain, can you tell me whether the Japanese are in total control of New Britain yet?'

'Yes, there wasn't much we could do to stop them.'

'The expats? Did they get off the island?'

'I'm afraid I can't answer that, Nick. All I can say is that it was a nasty business. Why do you ask?'

'My father, sir, he was a missionary on New Britain.'

He sighed. 'Wish I had more to tell you, we can only hope, son.'

Before we left I sought the assurance of Lieutenant Commander Rigby that *Madam Butterfly* would be properly berthed. He called over to Petty Officer Rabbits and gave him the appropriate instructions. 'She'll be well cared for, Nick,' he promised. 'She's a beauty.'

Showered, shaved, clothed in army shorts and shirts and

each issued with a pair of brown Dunlop tennis shoes at the police station, we were then fed handsomely with eggs, bacon, snags, chops, tomato and lashings of toast and tea at the café across the road. Then we were told that a room had been booked at Mrs Beswick's boarding house for me and that the Yanks would be calling for the little bloke after we'd eaten. We were beginning to feel decidedly human but for the fact that two plain-clothes policemen never left our side and that my personal papers along with the wallets and passports of the dead men on the beach had not been returned to me. When I queried the non-return of my passport and other details one of them explained to me that I had an interview at noon with some government bigwig who was driving down from Perth. A little later the Americans, two white-capped and belted provost army personnel, arrived in a jeep to escort Kevin to the Americans. I must say it seemed strange parting from him. Sometimes a whole lifetime takes place in a few days and I couldn't imagine life without the little bloke at my elbow. Of course, we promised to keep in touch. Kevin's last words as he was being led away were, 'I owe you big time, Nick, don't ever think I don't know dat!' Then as he was getting into the jeep he grinned, 'I ain't no fuckin' hero, you unnerstan', but you the biggest and I'm gonna tell 'em personal from K. Judge!'

I wondered just how important the arrival of two scruffy kids who'd crossed the Indian Ocean in a sailboat might seem to the top military and naval brass, American or our own. Not very, I should think. But in this respect I was to be proved wrong. Shortly before noon, accompanied by my two plain-clothes minders, I was taken in a police car to a building several blocks back from the harbour side. I knew it was pointless asking the men, one on either side of me in the back seat, where we were going or who the bigwig coming from Perth might be. Even if they knew, which was unlikely, they'd been chosen because they understood that silence is far more threatening than chat or any answers they might supply. They both had identical army haircuts and Errol Flynn moustaches, wore similar-looking tweed sports jackets, mid-brown pants and nondescript ties knotted beyond their normal life expectancy that hung limp and worn, less a tie than the official requirement to have something attached to a buttoned collar. Their shirts were standard white. They were the kind of men who would be invisible in a crowd but who obeyed orders without thinking where they might lead.

The building we drew up to sat right on the pavement, squat, blunt, three-storey, red brick, designed by a government architect seemingly at the height of the Great Depression, for it gave off a sense of ugliness and austerity that would cause anyone entering it to despair of a visit that might lead to a positive outcome. It was, in appearance, the kind of building where documents are stamped and licences issued for all the dull and ordinary pursuits in life. But miraculously, from a circle cut into the cement pavement not ten feet from the entrance, its perimeter fitted with heavy steel ribs and banded hoops that rose about five feet to protect its mottled trunk, grew a Western Australian flowering gum, ablaze with outrageous stems of pink blossom, each flamboyant stem humming with bees gathering nectar. I automatically scanned the blossoms for a butterfly, a Monarch perhaps, a peripatetic species that seems at home in almost any environment, but on this particular day only the bees were in possession, hogging the pollen.

I was taken along a dark wood-panelled corridor and up a set of wooden steps to the first floor, where the downstairs linoleum floor had been replaced by dark-brown carpet, and then up another set of carpeted stairs and along a green-carpeted corridor, into a large office that contained a large old-fashioned desk and behind it a chair and another chair in front of it. A steel filing cabinet stood against the left-hand wall. The floor was polished wood and from the window behind the desk hung a lopsided Venetian blind, one end of which fell below the windowsill and the other rose above it to reveal a small triangle of light through the bottom pane of glass. The walls were newly painted and bare. I was told to sit on the chair facing the slightly bigger one at the opposite side of the desk, whereupon my two minders left the room, closing the door behind them.

If the atmosphere in the room was intended to intimidate me it was succeeding very well. I began to feel vaguely guilty, though I wasn't quite sure what it was I should feel guilty about. The trouble with finding yourself isolated in a room like this is that you immediately assume you've lost even before you've opened your mouth. I began to think what my interrogator might use against me. Was it the nine men I'd left unburied on the beach in Java? But surely they'd understand that I would have been deeply fearful that the murderers might return? I would explain that, to the best of my ability, I'd given them a Christian burial.

Or did they think I might be a Japanese spy? It would be difficult to explain why I was in Java looking for a butterfly when any sensible person, knowing war in the Pacific was imminent, would have kept well away. But they could soon enough check on Kevin and they'd know he was fair dinkum.

Maybe they thought I'd stolen *Madam Butterfly*, but her papers were in order; besides, in the context of the panicked evacuation of Batavia, even if I had, it could hardly be considered a war crime.

I decided it must be the Japanese connection. My passport showed that I had been born in Japan and among my papers was a British embassy document to say that though I had resided in Tokyo until the age of eleven, I was entitled to Australian citizenship by virtue of my father's nationality. It had never occurred to me to ask whether my birthplace entitled me to Japanese citizenship. The citizens of Nippon so deeply despised Westerners that I couldn't imagine them granting me automatic citizenship by virtue of birth. As a child in the company of the adult Japanese I, or any other child of foreign blood, was never referred to by name, but simply and contemptuously as 'It'.

The door opened and turning around to see if it was my interrogator I was met by a thin woman in her fifties wheeling a tea trolley. Judging from her lined face she'd seen a fair bit of life, a working-class lady to the last sinew in her body. Her over-powdered face had no other make-up and the tiny vertical lines engraved around her mouth, some of them caked with talc, indicated she was a heavy smoker. She wore a black, somewhat down-at-the-heel shoe on her left foot and on her right a navy-blue felt bedroom slipper with the area around the big toe cut out. Her hair was covered with a hairnet and she wore a cotton uniform, dark green with large white buttons down the front.

'You've hurt your toe,' I remarked needlessly.

'Nah, it's me bunions, love,' she said, pointing to the slipper. 'This one's playing up. It's the weather, must be rain comin', can always tell.' She looked down at the slipper, shaking her head. 'Perfectly good pair of slippers me daughter gave me for Christmas, seems a shame havin' ter mutilate 'em like this. Cuppa, love?'

Without waiting for me to reply she began to pour from a large aluminium teapot into a white cup, then added a splash of milk. 'No sugar. Sorry about that, it's wartime. Yer have ter bring yer own or go without.' She paused, handing me the unsugared tea. 'Now, what I want to know is this. All them lads fightin' and gettin' our sugar, which I don't resent, not for one moment . . . but they ain't usin' no more sugar than they did when they was back home, are they? They're not takin' four teaspoons at the front when before they only took two at home. So, answer me this. What's happened to all our sugar?'

I laughed. 'I really don't mind my tea either way,' I replied, not knowing the answer to the great sugar mystery.

'That's not the point, is it? If you ask me, it's them government blokes in Canberra, the buggers are hoardin' it.'

I rose from my chair to take the cup from her. 'I'm Nick Duncan,' I said.

'Dorothy, love. Bickie? Only Arnott's digestives.' She laughed. 'The war. Only the generals get chocolate bickies.' She stirred the tea and put a plain brown biscuit on the saucer before placing it beside me on the desk. 'Better do one for his nibs. He never drinks it, but gets grumpy if he thinks he's been neglected.' She poured a second cup, added no sugar and placed a chocolate biscuit in a separate saucer beside the cup. 'It's so the chocolate won't melt against the side of the cup,' she explained.

'Er . . . who . . . whose office is this, Dorothy?'

'Nobody's,' she replied. 'His nibs uses it when he comes down from Perth.'

I pointed to the chocolate biscuit. 'Is he a general?'

She laughed. 'I don't think so, love, he put himself on the chocolate bickie list.'

She left and it seemed only moments later that a small bald and greying man, with what remained of his hair combed over and stuck to his scalp, and wearing steel-rimmed glasses, entered. He propped at the door, holding it open, and I rose and turned towards him. He seemed oblivious of my presence. He wore a navy woollen suit, the jacket of which was shiny from wear at the back, and I could see had no chance of buttoning around a pumpkin-sized paunch. Everything about him was small except his stomach, which looked as if it belonged to someone else and he'd simply borrowed it for the day. White shirt, nondescript dark-blue tie and a returned soldier's badge in his lapel. He held the door open, allowing a woman to enter. She carried a bentwood chair and a notepad and he made no attempt to take the chair from her. She was taller than him, about five foot nine, with a slim figure in a plain, light-blue cotton dress and appeared to be in her mid-thirties. Her nice chestnut hair was swept up into a bun behind her head and she wore no discernible expression. At first you thought she was plain but when you looked twice you could see, with her hair allowed to fall loose and a bit of make-up such as lipstick and stuff, she would be quite pretty. I rushed forward and took the chair from her and waited for them both to pass me. The little guy still chose to ignore my presence and went straight to the chair behind the desk, hefting a briefcase onto the desk and sitting down. Then he poked a finger into the tea to see if it was still hot. The lady walked to the side of the desk and waited for me to place the chair down. 'Thank you,' she said in a pleasant voice. 'I'm Marg Hamilton, I work here. I'll be taking notes.'

'Nick Duncan,' I said, smiling.

I was beginning to feel decidedly awkward, standing in khaki shorts and shirt and brown sandshoes, waiting for the old bloke behind the desk who was reading from a single piece of paper to pay me some attention. I wasn't game to simply sit down, not even sure if I wasn't under some sort of arrest.

'Hurrumph!' he growled, clearing his throat, then reached for his cup, took an absent-minded swallow, replaced it on the desk, missing the saucer by several inches, but somehow managed to find the chocolate biscuit, which he held suspended in one hand while he continued to read from what I assumed was some sort of briefing paper that had been left for him on the desk.

I glanced over at Marg Hamilton, who was seated with her legs crossed at the ankles. Nice long legs. She grinned at me and then glanced quickly at the man, then back at me, lifting one eyebrow almost imperceptibly. She was plainly in sympathy with me and I told myself I liked her.

I'd been back in civilisation only a few hours and was already growing weary of the self-importance people seemed to place on the roles they played in the business known as 'the war effort'. The old bloke now opened his mouth, giving me a glimpse of silver and gold fillings, and swallowed the entire biscuit, licking his fingers where the chocolate had melted. Then, still ignoring me, he unclasped the straps of his worn briefcase and withdrew my passport, some of the additional papers I'd handed to the Lieutenant Commander on the wharf and, to my surprise, Anna's embroidered handkerchief of the Clipper butterfly, and finally the oilskin wallet I'd made to protect the Magpie Crow. He looked up at last and seemed to notice for the first time that I was still standing. 'Sit, please,' he said crisply, and when I was finally seated he reached over the desk to shake my hand. 'Henry Customs,' he said, barely touching my fingers in a handshake as firm as a dead squid.

'How do you do, Mr Customs?' I said, smiling and then withdrawing my hand, adding, 'Nick . . . Nick Duncan.' I wasn't at all pleased that they'd been through my knapsack, probably when we'd been at breakfast.

'No, no, it's Henry . . . Mr Henry, Commonwealth Customs and Immigration,' he said irritably, glancing at the secretary.

'Oh, I'm sorry, sir,' I said, blushing and then looking rather sheepishly at the secretary myself. She returned my glance with a secret little smile.

Henry reached out and picked up my passport, then leaned back in his chair and allowed it to fall back onto the desk. 'Japan.'

'Japan?' I was still rattled from the introduction and didn't catch on immediately.

'You lived in Japan,' he accused.

'Yes, sir, I was born in Tokyo.'

'Why was that?' he asked. I was reminded of Kevin's description of the social worker who had asked him if he slept with his mother. This question seemed equally stupid.

'I don't think I had much choice; my parents conceived me there, sir.'

He jerked his head towards Marg Hamilton. 'I must remind you that this is an official interview, Mr Duncan,' he said. 'Every word is being taken down in shorthand.'

To my surprise Marg Hamilton, using a deliberately didactic tone, read from the pad, repeating the words, 'Japan?' spoken by me, then Henry's 'You lived in Japan,' then my 'Yes, sir, I was born in Tokyo,' followed by his 'Why was that?' and concluding with my somewhat facetious reply. 'Do you *really* want it put down just like that, Mr Henry?' she asked, looking directly at him.

'No, no, girlie, expunge,' Henry blustered, then turned to me. 'Do you speak Japanese, Mr Duncan?'

'Yes, sir, my father and I left when I was eleven, by which

time I was bilingual.'

'And your mother? She Japanese?'

'No, sir, French, she died when I was five.'

'You speak French?'

'No, sir, I was too young.'

'Your father, why was he in Japan?'

'He taught English and was the headmaster of the International School in Tokyo. It was run by the American Embassy.'

'Where is he now? Have you contacted him?'

'He's an Anglican missionary in New Britain, hopefully escaped before the Japanese invaded, and no I haven't; we only arrived this morning and I have no news.'

'Then how do you know the Japanese have invaded New Guinea?' he shot back, head cocked to one side, one eye half-closed.

'Lieutenant Commander Rigby of Naval Intelligence told me, sir.'

'Write that down, girlie,' Henry shot out.

Marg Hamilton looked up and while she didn't exactly sigh you just knew she was doing so inwardly. 'It was on the wireless, Mr Henry.'

'Write it down . . . write it down, Rigby, Naval Intelligence. Loose talk costs lives,' Henry insisted. He reached out and picked up Anna's carefully folded handkerchief and placed it in front of him, opening each fold carefully as if it might contain something. It was finally spread out showing the embroidered butterfly in the bottom right-hand corner facing me. 'What is this?' he demanded.

'A handkerchief,' I replied.

'A woman's handkerchief?'

'Yes, sir, it's a keepsake.'

He stabbed a finger at the square of linen. 'The butterfly? That mean something, some sort of code?'

I laughed. 'No, sir, it's an embroidery of a Clipper butterfly.' I was damned if I was going to tell him any more. If I should do so, the next thing would be that he had turned Anna into the Mata Hari of the Dutch East Indies.

He reached for the oilskin wallet and tossed it in front of me. 'Open it,' he instructed.

I opened the wallet, fearful that my precious Magpie Crow might have been damaged by a recent clumsy inspection. But when I withdrew the triangular envelope and carefully opened it I discovered my specimen was in perfect condition. I sighed, grateful to someone unknown.

'Another butterfly, eh?' he said suspiciously. 'Would you like to explain, Mr Duncan?'

'It's a Magpie Crow, sir. Only found in Java, Sumatra, Malaya and Singapore,' I explained, then added, 'I collect butterflies, sir.'

'Write that down, girlie, Java, Sumatra, Malaya and Singapore, all under Japanese occupation, oh, and add that the subject asked about New Britain, *also* now under the Japanese occupation! Ha! Butterfly collector, pull the other one!' he added gratuitously.

Marg Hamilton glanced up quickly, her eyes grown large. 'Shall I write that too?' she asked.

'No, of course not, use your head, girlie,' Henry said impatiently. Then, shaking his head and clicking his tongue, 'Butterfly collector, what next?'

I had always been taught to be polite to people older than myself and to those I should respect, and Pumpkin Paunch was obviously my superior in this situation. But I'd had enough of this buffoon with the three strands of greying hair glued across the top of his small, bald pink head. 'My father is a personal friend of the Archbishop of Perth, Henry Le Fanu, who is my godfather, perhaps someone might call him?' I said, my voice sufficiently loud for Henry to peer over the top of his steel-rimmed glasses, a look of surprise on his face. Marg Hamilton giggled, then quickly brought her shorthand pad up to her mouth to cover her grin.

Henry rose from his chair. 'You will remain here, please, Mr Duncan.' He turned to Marg Hamilton. 'You too, girlie.' Then leaving my things on the desk he crossed and left the room, closing the door behind him.

Marg waited a few moments. 'He's getting worse!' she giggled. 'Thank God he retires next month, when Australia will be a safer place for all.'

I grinned. 'He's certainly different,' I said cautiously. 'How long have you been his secretary?'

'Oh, I'm not his secretary, he thinks I'm from the typing pool.'

'And you're not?'

'No, I cover him when he comes down from Perth,' she said, and then without explaining any further she reached for the phone and dialled a number, then waited for the other end to respond. 'Sir, it's Marg, it's probably time for you to come in.' She listened while the other end said something. 'No, he's left the room to call the Anglican Archbishop,' she said, smiling into the phone. 'Have someone bring in a chair for you.' She replaced the receiver. 'Do you really know the Archbishop?' she asked.

'Yeah, fair dinkum, he's my godfather.'

'Good, that should be sufficient to send Customs and

Immigration scuttling back to Perth. Horrid little man!' She moved over to look at Anna's embroidered handkerchief and then at the Magpie Crow specimen. 'They're very pretty, you must tell me about them sometime. Do you really collect butterflies?'

I nodded, grinning. 'I'm afraid so.'

'That's nice, I like that – an intrepid ocean-going sailor who collects butterflies,' she said, smiling.

'No, it's stupid.' I pointed to the Magpie Crow. 'That little black-and-white specimen damn nearly cost me my life.'

She gave me a serious look. 'You don't strike me as stupid, Nick,' she said.

CHAPTER FIVE

'That's nice, dear, but you must appreciate there is a war on.
Please don't ask me again, we ration everyone to one
shower a day.'
She pursed her lips in disapproval. 'You may choose
morning or night, but not both.'
Mrs Beswick
Boarding-house keeper

SEVERAL MINUTES PASSED BEFORE the door opened and Lieutenant Commander Rigby stepped into the room alone, not carrying a chair. 'We meet again, Nick,' he said pleasantly, then turning to Marg Hamilton, 'I take it you've met Chief Petty Officer Hamilton, Naval Intelligence?'

'Well yes, sort of,' I ventured, smiling at Marg. 'I've met the amanuensis version anyway,' I said, using a word my father preferred to 'secretary', a rogue word that he was fond of pointing out had a number of other meanings in the English language.

'Sorry about Bert Henry, we're obliged to give Customs and Immigration first crack at anyone coming ashore; they need to check your passport, papers, that sort of thing, which is fair enough. But Bert's a conspiracy theorist who sees the enemy everywhere, that's why Marg here acts as a stenographer. Thankfully up to this moment he hasn't caught on that she's Intelligence.' He laughed. 'A week ago we had a group of escaping English soldiers, who, like you, sailed from the East

Indies but in a *prahu*, a sixty-foot Malayan outrigger canoe. Like your own escape, it was a remarkable effort and, in addition, at one stage they'd endured a machine-gun attack by a Japanese Zero. We should rightfully have treated them like the heroes they undoubtedly were. But Bert Henry became convinced they were fifth columnists and wanted to clap them into jail on the strength that he didn't believe anyone could sail an outrigger that far, least of all a bunch of Pommie soldiers. The men were all from the north of England with broad Sheffield and Liverpool accents, and our Bert couldn't understand most of what they were saying. This he took to be further evidence that they were deeply suspect and he declared them to be Germans masquerading as English. Marg's notes, if they had been submitted to Bert Henry's superiors, would have said more about Bert Henry's mental condition than that of the half-starved English soldiers.'

'What do you do with the . . . er . . . notes?' I said, pointing to the shorthand notepad.

'Type them up, delouse them when necessary, then post them on with a copy to Bert's immediate superior. Like us, they're anxiously waiting for his retirement next month.'

'Mr Henry, will he be coming back?' I asked.

'No, having called the Archbishop's palace and received confirmation of your relationship leaves him with nowhere to go. He's a stickler for God, king and country and with God confirmed as being on your side I guess he decided his temporal duties were over. He's agreed your passport is authentic and your papers in order. That's about it for his department, anyway. We thanked him for his help and ordered a navy car to take him back to Perth. He usually comes by train, so he'll enjoy the prestige associated with the ride and see it as confirmation of his importance in the scheme of things. Besides, he's done his bit;

he won a military cross at Passchendaele in the last war and we should respect his contribution.'

Lieutenant Commander Rigby took the seat behind the desk and Marg Hamilton sat down again with her notepad. Rigby pointed to my passport, papers, Anna's handkerchief and the Magpie Crow envelope that was still open. 'I regret we had to go through your things, Nick, although I can't apologise, it's standard procedure. You may have them back, but I confess I'm curious to know about the butterflies.'

His manner as a contrast to Pumpkin Paunch was so easy and relaxed that I found myself totally disarmed as I told him why I'd ridiculously gone to Java in the first place, my meeting with Piet Van Heerden and his desire that I take his yacht to Australia, and the butterfly-catching excursion with his daughter Anna, who had embroidered the butterfly she'd caught onto the hanky as a keepsake. I didn't dwell on Anna and made it sound as if our relationship had been casual; good friends only. This was partly because I lacked the vocabulary to deal with how I felt about her and also the fear that, as an older man, he would simply see it as puppy love, the first real-person sexual arousal in a young bloke, the transition between randy images conjured up in the toilet and under early-morning sheets and the shock and delight of the real thing, even if it was the unconsummated real thing. It never seems to occur to adults that one of the greatest love affairs in literature took place between a fourteen-year-old Juliet and a sixteen-year-old Romeo.

I went on to talk about my escape and of being awakened at around midnight a night out from Batavia by the noise of big guns coming from the direction of the Sunda Strait. I told of the tragedy witnessed on the beach the following morning. But now I decided to come clean. I confessed to Lieutenant Commander

Rigby that I hadn't had the courage to bury the dead men, afraid the natives would return and find me. I explained the indecent compromise I'd reached by laying them out in line and placing a small, hastily made wooden cross above the head of each one and then, from memory, conducting a funeral service. 'I'm ashamed to say I was afraid, sir,' I confessed, Kevin's immortal words '*I ain't no fuckin' hero*' jumping into my head.

I guess I'd become pretty overwrought by this stage because Lieutenant Commander Rigby raised a hand. 'That's enough for the time being, Nick. Although allow me to say that few men would have had the courage to do what you did and the navy thanks you. It was a ghastly business, one of the small and darker moments for mankind, but with your actions, civilised man prevails.' He sounded a bit like my father.

Marg stood up. 'May I be excused, sir? You will recall we have a luncheon meeting with the Americans and I ought to get changed. Where will I meet you?'

'Come back here, Marg. Nick and I will be a while yet, but you have no further need to take notes,' Rigby said, then added, 'Oh, when you return, bring in 14 P. We'll both witness it.'

Marg left and Lieutenant Commander Rigby asked, 'Nick, who else knows about the massacre on the beach? Have you told anyone else here in Fremantle?'

'Only Sergeant Hamill, sir. I neglected to give you the boots belonging to one of the *Perth* sailors and when we got to the police station I handed them to him. You'd mentioned the *Perth* on the docks and he questioned me further; it seems he had a cousin serving on it.'

'Was there anyone with him, with you, at the time?'

'No, I don't believe so. The two plain-clothes men were there, but they'd left the room at the time.'

'Did he write it down?'

'No. He made me sign for the boots. It wasn't, if you know what I mean, an interrogation.'

Lieutenant Commander Rigby snatched up the phone. 'Switch, get me Sergeant Hamill at Harbourside Police Station.' He replaced the receiver and turned to me. 'Nick, we're going to have to inform Canberra of the massacre in Java. My gut feeling is that the information will be classified. You know what that means, don't you?'

'Better let the Americans know, sir. Kevin Judge knows the whole story,' I replied, anxious to cooperate.

'It could mean it's given top-secret status, in fact that's almost certain. I'm afraid you're going to have to sign a form forbidding you to talk about what you witnessed to anyone. As far as you're concerned, it never happened.' He gave me a deadly serious look. 'I must ask you to cooperate in this, Nick.'

'What about their next of kin, sir?'

'We're at war, son. We don't know the casualty figures for the *Perth*, how many dead, how many captured by the Japanese. We may never know and certainly not before the end of the war. The Japanese are not signatories to the Geneva Convention. As far as Seaman Judge goes, awaiting Canberra's instructions, we've alerted the Americans to take his evidence in camera and I'm meeting my American counterpart at lunch today.'

He hadn't answered my question. But then again, the known and awful end of the nine men on the *Perth* and the unknown outcome for the huge number of other personnel on board wasn't exactly heartening news. I could understand why a wartime government would want to conceal the facts from the public and, in particular, the next of kin of the nine dead men. What I wasn't to know at the time was that Rigby had anticipated Canberra's reaction correctly and the beach massacre in Java would remain buried within the secret files of the government in Canberra for the next fifty years.

The phone rang and Lieutenant Commander Rigby picked up the receiver, listened for a moment, then said, 'Put him on.' Then, 'Afternoon, Sergeant, Rigby here, have you got a moment? Are you alone? Good. I have young Duncan with me and he's just told me about the . . .' – he paused, not wanting to spell the details out on the telephone – 'the Java beach incident.' He listened for a moment. 'Yes, that's right, we've classified the information awaiting a reply from Canberra.' Pause. 'No, of course, but you'll have to sign a 14 P, a formality,' he laughed, 'they'll have my guts for garters otherwise.' Pause. 'Thank you, I appreciate you cooperation; Chief Petty Officer Hamilton will bring it over this afternoon, she can witness it initially. Cheerio and thanks.' He replaced the receiver. 'Nice bloke, salt of the earth,' he said. Lieutenant Commander Rigby was, I decided, a man accustomed to getting his own way. He leaned back in his chair, clasping his hands and resting them on his lap. 'What are your plans, Nick?' he asked.

'Well, sir, I guess to join up. I turned eighteen last month.'

'Have you considered the navy?'

'No, sir, I just automatically thought it would be the army.'

'Would you consider the navy?'

I thought for a minute. 'Right at this moment I've had my fill of the sea – a bit of square bashing on solid land seems like a good idea. But first I hope to contact my father. Sergeant Hamill says that some people may have got out of Rabaul and be on their way to Cairns. I'm hoping he's amongst them.'

'You mentioned that on the wharf. Marg is already onto it; leave it with us and we'll get back to you.'

'Thank you, sir. He's a stubborn old bugger and speaks Japanese fluently; my fear is that he'll think it's his duty to remain with his flock and negotiate on their behalf with the enemy.' I clicked my tongue and shook my head. 'He's just silly enough to think that as a man of God he'll be respected. The Japanese my father knew in Japan were a highly sophisticated and civilised people, but he hasn't yet met up with Tojo's murderous mob.'

'Nick, you left Japan at the age of eleven; that was seven years ago. How is your Japanese? A bit rusty?'

I smiled. 'I shouldn't think so, sir. My father is a classical Japanese scholar and insists we speak Japanese whenever I'm home. He's a stickler for grammar and correct usage. Japanese is very much a language of intonation – the ear is as important as the mouth. It's not only what you say, but also how you say it.'

'Oh, so would you say you've advanced from, say, the grammar and vocabulary of an eleven-year-old?'

'I would think so, my father is a perfectionist. I know he expects me by now to speak and write at a pretty sophisticated level.'

'Good. That's good, so you write, read Japanese . . . excellent.'

'It's a bit more than that,' I explained. 'Your status is decided by the way you use language, a bit like the English upper class and cockney. I guess if they didn't despise Caucasians as they do, we, certainly my father, would be considered well-educated upper middleclass.'

'Butterflies!' Rigby said suddenly, changing the subject. 'Tell me about collecting butterflies.'

I thought for a moment, not sure how to answer him. 'There isn't a lot to tell, sir. People collect things, I collect butterflies. There are about eighteen thousand different species in the world, many of them in New Guinea.' I shrugged. 'For a lepidopterist the Pacific is paradise.'

Lieutenant Commander Rigby smiled. 'And you'd venture into a war zone to capture just one of them?'

I looked down at my knees and shook my head, glanced sideways at him and said, 'Yeah, I know, it must sound pretty bloody naïve.'

'Intrepid,' he replied. 'Determined. I guess butterflies aren't all found around the backyard daisy patch. Do you ever need to venture into really difficult terrain?'

I smiled, happy not to dwell on the Java incident. 'That's a big part of the fascination, going into the unknown, disappearing for a week at a time, sometimes more, determined to find a particular specimen.'

'On your own in the jungle?'

I laughed. 'Not too many people care to be rained on twice a day and bitten by every insect known to man and some species not yet identified. But fortunately I don't mind my own company and have come over the years to feel pretty at home in the jungle. It looks formidable, but really if you know what you're doing you can avoid dysentery, and citronella keeps the mossies away . . .' I trailed off, thinking I was becoming too garrulous and perhaps big-noting myself.

'So you could survive for a week at a time, perhaps more, and live off the land, so to speak?'

'Well, no, not exactly, a billy, a pound or two of rice, tea, a tin of condensed milk, citronella and salt tablets, that's about it, the rest is hunter–gatherer stuff. Fruit bats, for instance, are excellent eating, easy to catch in a net and good protein on a spit.'

He thought for a moment, tapping the edge of the desk

with a forefinger. 'Good!' He hesitated momentarily. 'And you'd consider joining the navy, Nick?'

I grinned, reminding myself that Lieutenant Commander Rigby was a man who liked to get his own way. 'I didn't say that, sir. There aren't a whole heap of butterflies on the ocean, nor for that matter is it covered in jungle.'

He laughed. 'You're a very surprising eighteen-year-old, Nick Duncan.' I think it was meant as a compliment, because he went on to say, 'The navy isn't all about battleships and keeping things shipshape. That's about enough for today, though. I want you to meet one or two people over the next day or two; maybe we can convince you?'

Moments later there was a knock on the door and without waiting for a reply Chief Petty Officer Marg Hamilton entered. I must say I was surprised. She wore a WRANS uniform that emphasised her slim figure and long legs. Her rich chestnut hair, formerly in a severe bun, was now loosely tied up. She wore eye make-up that emphasised her green eyes, and a brilliant scarlet lipstick. When I'd first seen her I thought she must be in her thirties, but now I revised her age to somewhere in her twenties. How do women do that? Transform, as if by magic, brush, smear, pat, dab, and a different woman, just like that? Lieutenant Commander Rigby's assistant was the whole delicious eyeful as well as obviously being nobody's fool.

I signed the 14 P form that bound me to the Official Secrets Act and both the Lieutenant Commander and Marg witnessed it. Marg then said, 'His Grace the Archbishop phoned, and he'd like Nick to come for lunch tomorrow.' She smiled, looking at Rigby. 'We're both included.' She paused. 'Rupert Basil Michael Long will be there as well.' The way she stressed all the names suggested that whoever he was, he was not the kind of man you'd happily invite home for dinner.

Lieutenant Commander Rigby gave a low whistle, then glanced at me. 'You command powerful friends, Nick.'

I blushed, embarrassed by the invitation. Henry Le Fanu was a nice enough old codger and though he was my godfather, I'd met him on only two occasions (except of course at the christening) when he'd visited my father in New Britain. As I recall, he was an expert on Chaucer, as was my dad, and on the two visits they'd spent most of the time in the library arguing and drinking tea in the afternoon and what my father referred to as sharing one or two bottles of excellent libation during and after dinner. These were a self-consumed though generously shared gift from the Archbishop. An Anglican missionary's salary doesn't extend to wine or brandy of such excellence and my godfather wasn't prepared to settle for the excruciating Tolley's brandy or cheap Portuguese sherry my father served to his more sophisticated guests. Afterwards my father would claim he always won the afternoon debate but, lacking the Archbishop's tolerance for alcohol, invariably lost the evening one. As for the other bloke with the three Christian names, I'd never heard of him, nor did it seem my place to ask who he might be.

Marg now turned to Lieutenant Commander Rigby. 'We really ought to be going, sir. The car will be waiting downstairs.' She turned to me. 'Nick, I've arranged for you to have lunch at the canteen on the ground floor. It's not the greatest but the corned beef and the shepherd's pie are usually excellent.' She handed me a ticket. 'Just hand this in to the staff, then tuck in for all you're worth, there's no limit on seconds. The bread and butter pudding's not bad either.' Then she held out a folded sheet of paper. 'It's a map showing you how to get back to your boarding house in case you get lost.' She reached out and tucked it into the top pocket of my khaki shirt. It seemed the kind of thing a mother might do to her small boy charged with delivering a note to his teacher, although, I must say, I liked the sense of familiarity.

I collected my passport and papers, Anna's handkerchief and refolded the Magpie Crow back into its triangular envelope and then the oilskin wallet. Again Marg Hamilton anticipated me and promptly produced a large brown manila envelope. On the way out they directed me to the canteen. Lieutenant Commander Rigby shook my hand and thanked me for my cooperation. 'It's been a pleasure, Nick,' he said. 'See you tomorrow.'

Marg smiled. 'Nick, we'll pick you up outside your boarding house at eleven tomorrow for the ride to Perth. Oh, and Peter Keeble from our signals department will call around about nine, he's roughly your size and fancies himself as a bit of a natty dresser. He's volunteered to lend you the clothes you'll need for the lunch. I don't suppose you'd wear a bow tie? Peter is particularly fond of bow ties.' I grimaced and she laughed. 'I'll tell him a normal tie. What size shoe do you take?'

'Eleven, broad fitting,' I replied.

'You'll have to settle for navy officer issue. I'll see a pair is sent around. Cheerio, Nick.'

Gosh she was pretty.

'Thank you,' I said. She'd solved a problem that was already secretly concerning me, but one I hadn't the courage to bring up. Lunch with the Archbishop in khaki shirt and shorts wearing cacky brown sandshoes without socks seemed a tad underdressed. There was also something else I wanted to say so I took the plunge. 'Miss Hamilton, Lieutenant Commander Rigby, sir,' I said, addressing them both, 'concerning your lunch with . . . er, the Americans? You said it was with your intelligence counterparts. If you get the chance, will you ask them to take good care of Seaman Judge? Kevin has been through a fair bit; I'm fairly sure he was concussed for the first week or so we were at sea and has a nasty head wound that's not entirely healed. If you get the opportunity, can you tell them he conducted himself with exceptional courage and I couldn't have completed the voyage without him.' I smiled, inwardly hearing the little bloke's voice clearly in my head: 'Lissen, I want ya ter unnerstan, I ain't no fuckin' hero!'

Commander Long, the fourth guest at lunch, which was a cold collation served in a gazebo in the Archbishop's glorious garden, turned out to be the head of Australian Naval Intelligence who was on a visit to the west from Melbourne. He didn't say much, and on the way Lieutenant Commander Rigby described him as having a steel-trap mind. The two Intelligence officers were clearly a bit nervous and I'm not sure they were all that keen about attending the lunch. As an eighteen-year-old surrounded by these bigwigs, I felt decidedly out of place and wasn't about to add my twopence-worth to the general conversation.

I was nervous and afraid I'd be out of my depth. Lunch with Henry Le Fanu alone would have been a difficult and awkward process without having to cope with other influential guests. I consoled myself with the thought that I'd keep my mouth tightly shut, mind my manners, speak only when spoken to and that at least I looked okay. Peter Keeble had proved to be almost exactly my size and his clobber – light-grey flannels and

a brown sports coat, grey socks, white shirt and scarlet woollen tie – and from Marg a pair of navy officer's dress uniform shoes that pinched a bit but would wear in nicely, gave me a sense of being presentable and at the same time commonplace enough to be almost invisible. That is, if a six feet three inch, fourteen stone, clumsy-looking eighteen-year-old can ever look like he isn't present. Size among small and powerful men is always a problem and the more you hunch your shoulders the bigger you seem.

Oh, I forgot to say that the folded note Marg Hamilton had tucked into my shirt pocket intended supposedly to give me directions back to the boarding house contained a ten-shilling note and the words: *Dinner money and perhaps a haircut?* I wondered if the incomparable Marg ever missed anything. So there I was in the Archbishop's garden politely sipping a beer, with short back and sides, tie knot correct, neat as can be. The barber, a Greek or Italian, had run his fingers through my hair. 'Where you been, mister? You gonna be shipwreck maybe?' he'd asked. Afterwards I'd felt obliged to give him a sixpenny tip for the extra work involved.

There was some small talk about the speed of the Japanese Pacific invasion and the somewhat hasty capitulation of the Netherlands East Indies on the 8th of March. Apparently rather more had been expected from the Dutch forces in the Pacific. Though I wouldn't have dreamed of venturing an opinion in such company, I had seen nothing in Batavia that suggested they would offer any real resistance to the Japanese. The white Dutch officers who had come into *De Kost Kamer* had all been pretty pessimistic and, as I've mentioned previously, the native troops were at best ambivalent and most were secretly happy to welcome the Japs as liberators who were more or less of the same colour and, like them, Asians. Dying for the Dutch wasn't an option. Three hundred years of Dutch colonial rule had failed to impress the locals.

What came as a surprise was the antipathy during the pre-lunch conversation towards Winston Churchill, who, it appeared, had attempted to dismiss us as a bunch of redneck colonials and to ride roughshod over Australia's desire to bring our troops home from the Middle East, insisting we send them to Burma. It seems our new prime minister, Mr Curtin, had told him to go to buggery, or used the diplomatic words to that effect. This, taken along with the inept and disgraceful capitulation by the English in Singapore, where a further sixteen thousand well-drilled and combat-hardened Australian troops had been taken out of play, left Australia totally disenchanted, unprotected and somewhat gobsmacked at Churchill's blatant disregard for our welfare. With Churchill deciding Australia, along with the remainder of the western Pacific, was expendable, we were now looking to General MacArthur and the Americans as our logical partners in the war that was taking place in our own backyard.

While I don't suppose all this was exactly top secret, being privy, a fly on the wall, to the conversation of three men and one woman who were fairly important in the scheme of things was exhilarating for someone just turned eighteen and about to become the lowest form of life in the Australian army. It became clear that Archbishop Henry Le Fanu wasn't simply high up in the Anglican synod, but that God's man in Western Australia was also extremely knowledgeable on matters of the war. Later I was to learn that he was a personal friend of Mr Curtin and, until recently, Vicar-General for all the armed forces and so would be as well informed as anyone in the country outside the war cabinet.

We hadn't yet entered the gazebo for lunch and were

standing in the garden with our drinks, an elderly butler hovering half hidden and out of earshot behind a stand of bright-red canna lilies with a tray, anxious to immediately replenish any empty glass, when Lieutenant Commander Rigby pulled me aside. 'Nick, the Commander wants you to tell the story of your escape all over again. He's read Marg's notes but says he wants it from the horse's mouth, so to speak. He also wants to know more about the American, how he survived and the others didn't. He's pretty sharp, so don't leave anything out – the smallest detail may be important. He'll be reporting to Canberra and he'll want to know *everything*. You said yesterday the American knew the story. We must know as much, if not more than the Yanks about the incident on the beach. After all, you are the prime witness. Marg will be taking notes. I'm afraid this isn't a casual lunch with your godfather, you're centre stage, son. The only consolation is that it will probably be the last time you need to tell anyone what you witnessed on that dreadful morning.'

'Thank you, sir, I'll certainly do my best,' I said, filled with sudden trepidation.

'Oh, by the way, Nick,' Rigby then said, 'at lunch yesterday I brought up the matter of Mr Judge with my American colleague. He said it was just the sort of example of courage in the face of the enemy they were looking for. They may need a statement from you, but I wouldn't be surprised if he isn't in for the full box and dice in commendations.'

I grinned, imagining the little bloke, sun shining scarlet through his Mickey Mouse ears, being medal-pinned by an admiral or maybe even MacArthur. Sometimes you've got to believe there is a God in heaven. But then a thought struck me. 'But, sir, if the Americans talk about it and it's classified top secret here, isn't there a chance it will all come out?'

Lieutenant Commander Rigby smiled. 'Good point, Nick. Marg and I had to do a fair bit of tap-dancing at lunch yesterday, anticipating Canberra's response while at the same time accommodating the needs of the Yanks. You've heard the old adage, "Truth is the first casualty of war"? Right now the Americans need a hero, but on the other hand we don't want the full-blown incident on the beach to come out. That's the problem in a nutshell. So, there's the inevitable compromise. The story changes just a little, not in truthfulness, but by omission. Mr Judge is wounded during the sinking of the *Houston* and, clinging to a life raft, is washed up onto a lonely beach in Java where he lies unconscious. That's when you find him, rescue him and effect a remarkable escape avoiding the Japanese and crossing the Indian Ocean in a small sailing boat. It's not untrue. It's merely a simplified version of the truth in order to accommodate our needs as well as those of the Americans. They have a hero and we have one who deserves a commendation but won't, I'm afraid, be getting one.'

'I see,' I said, not at all sure that I did, but vastly relieved that I wasn't going to be classified as a hero. My abject terror that the villagers would return, which left me too afraid to give the nine men a decent burial was not only affecting my dreams but also often enough penetrating my waking thoughts. To be named a hero would simply add further to my secret shame.

We were all called to lunch, a serve-yourself affair of cold meats – pork, lamb and beef – potato salad, various other salads, canned pineapple, cold beetroot, raw onion, sliced white bread and butter and a large jug of orange juice. During the voyage on *Madam Butterfly* I had lacked the imagination to dream about such a variety of food. There were no staff on hand to help serve lunch and it was obvious that this was deliberate. I was there for four sets of ears only, with poor Marg having no time to eat as she took down my every word in shorthand.

One good thing about being a loner, a listener and an observer is that you absorb detail. You remember the bits others forget or don't notice, as well as every gesture used in a conversation. Our hands are often more articulate than our speech. Over the years close observation of people had turned me into a competent mimic and I'd also been told often enough that I had a good ear for accents as well as languages, not only Japanese, but also several of the native languages spoken by the various tribes in my father's parish, though, of course, by no means all of them. In New Guinea there are over eight hundred distinct languages. I knew about five of them and could probably bumble my way through another five. If this sounds impressive, it isn't; primitive languages have quite small vocabularies, about the same as those a seven-year-old might have in English. Moreover, Kevin had been a natural raconteur and I was equally a natural listener; after a month on board alone with the little bloke I could speak Chicago English better than he could. I'd scrubbed every word he'd spoken until it was squeaky clean, and if I haven't always put it down exactly as he enunciated it, that's because some of it simply wouldn't make any sense on paper. But I decided if Commander Long wanted the full bottle, I'd tell it that way. It would be my last telling of the massacre on the beach and somewhere inside me I felt that if I told it precisely, as if in confession, exactly how it had all happened, blow by blow, I might overcome the nightmares that were already occurring. In this respect, I was to be proved entirely wrong. The Official Secrets Act was to have a profound effect on the remainder of my life.

For the next two hours, give or take a dozen hastily chewed

mouthfuls, I told the story from the beginning to the end, omitting nothing. For the most part the lunch guests seemed totally absorbed. The incident where I'd dropped the little bloke to catch the Magpie Crow brought the house down and even Marg stopped taking notes to laugh. They seemed to enjoy it when I changed to Kevin's accent, and the story of his mother's headstone had the Archbishop practically pissing his pants.

When I finally came to the end it was three-thirty in the afternoon and I was exhausted. I'm not a naturally garrulous person but I guess on that occasion I could be accused of a liberal dose of verbal diarrhoea. But it failed to act, as I'd hoped, as some sort of catharsis. Commander Long, who had stopped me on several occasions to ask questions, was clearly no fool, a stocky, tight-lipped man who snapped out rather than phrased his questions, expecting immediate answers – although in the actual lips department he possessed a set of lips that belonged to the opposite gender, for they were as perfectly formed as a cupid's bow and would have done Greta Garbo credit. As a kid he must have had a hard time at school. To my surprise, at the conclusion he congratulated me and confessed that it was one of the more memorable afternoons he'd spent lately. He'd made it sound like some sort of entertainment, although I hadn't meant it to be. The Archbishop said it was an astonishing exhibition of total recall and Lieutenant Commander Rigby smiled and said, 'We're hoping Nick will consider joining Navy Intelligence.' Only Marg Hamilton remained silent and when I glanced at her she had tears in her eyes. I wondered if, as I did, she felt that I'd said too much and in the plethora of words that accumulated during the telling had unintentionally diminished the massacre. The escape story of our voyage, the storm at sea and the many details of Kevin's unfortunate childhood seemed to have overridden the tragedy on the beach. I felt secretly ashamed to be receiving their accolades.

As for myself, I can't ever recall speaking as much at any one time in my life. At the conclusion, all I wanted to do was to find a corner to hide in. If this was to be the last time I ever talked about the incident, then I'd done my very best. Having done so, I promised myself, come what may, I would never repeat the performance. I strongly felt as if, in this final telling of the massacre, I'd betrayed the memory of the men on the beach. Ever present in my mind's eye was the huge excitement of the nine sailors making it safely back onto land; then their care to place the unconscious little bloke under a bush out of the sun, a shirt forfeited and placed behind his head, even though he wasn't one of them, simply someone, an unknown American sailor they'd hauled onto their raft in the middle of the night. I'd witnessed nine compassionate men slaughtered in front of my eyes, each losing his life to a vicious flashing blade that caught and held the soft morning sunlight.

Afterwards, the Archbishop drew me aside. 'Chief Petty Officer Hamilton has already initiated enquiries about your father, Nicholas. But, as his friend and Bishop, I've taken the liberty to exert a little further influence in the process of trying to locate him. We'll check any boat that docks carrying civilians from Rabaul. We think one may arrive soon but as far as we know your father isn't on board. But Commander Long has promised that when his men interview each of the passengers, as they will do, they'll be instructed to enquire if anyone knows anything about his circumstances.'

I thanked him and asked if he would grant me a personal favour, to which he readily agreed. 'Your Grace, a ship named the *Witvogel* left Batavia the day before I did on the twenty-seventh of February, bound for Broome. It would have arrived roughly a week later. Is there any possibility we could trace the whereabouts of a particular family on board? I speak of the Van Heerdens, whose yacht I sailed to get here.'

'Shouldn't be too difficult, I imagine. I'll have a word to Commander Long. By the way, he's very impressed with you, Nick, and wants to talk to you. I've told him you're about to join up and I think that's what it's all about. He's a pretty brusque sort of chappie as you will have gathered, but you can trust him – fine mind, good man. You'd do well to listen to what he has to say to you.' He touched me on the shoulder. 'Well done this afternoon, I know it can't have been easy for you.' Then he handed me a cheque for twenty pounds. 'Nothing worse than not being able to pay your own way.'

'Thank you, Your Grace, I'll pay you back,' I said, knowing that he had solved yet another of my problems.

'It's a gift, rather overdue, from your godfather,' he laughed. 'I'm afraid ecclesiastics make lousy godfathers, Nick.'

It was time to leave and to my surprise Marg came up and said, 'Nick, I'll call you at your boarding house around six tonight; perhaps you'd like to come home for supper?' She grinned. 'I don't think either of us had our fair share of the splendid lunch. What about bangers and mash, fried onions, gravy on the top of the potato volcano – what do you say?'

'Whacko!' I accepted with alacrity, of course. It was the meal that most frequently possessed my imagination while on *Madam Butterfly* but I was rather surprised that she'd think to mention it to me out on the lawn of the Archbishop's palace and not in the car or when we arrived back in Fremantle. Then she added, 'Good luck, mate, you're travelling back in an official staff car with Rupert Basil Michael Long, our esteemed boss, who you will have by now gathered sits if not on the right hand of God, then pretty close to Him.'

We drove off, Commander Long and myself sitting in the back of a brown '39 Chevrolet with white-wall tyres and driven by a sailor called Barnsey, although I wasn't sure whether Barnsey was his nickname or legitimate surname, as Commander Long barked it out along with his instructions as if it was a military command. Barnsey, in return, made no sign that he'd heard him and throughout the journey to Fremantle never said a word. We were driving along the banks of the Swan River past the brewery when Commander Long turned, well, half-turned, to me. 'Plans!' he barked.

'What, mine?' I asked, surprised.

He shot me a withering look. 'Of course! Joining up, I hear. Army?'

'Yessir.'

'Nonsense. Can't use you.'

'I beg your pardon, sir?' I asked, confused.

'Sergeants calling you names on the parade ground, poppycock! Free spirit! Damned hard to find. Don't want that drummed out of you, lad.' There seemed no answer to this, so I remained silent. 'Japanese. Jungle. Too young but sensible enough.' He glanced at me. 'Shoot? Handle a rifle?'

'Yes, sir, in the cadets a 303, then a 22 at home in New Britain. It's a good jungle weapon – light, accurate, you don't need distance in the bush,' I over-explained in an attempt to regain my composure.

'Marksman?' he barked.

In fact I had been regarded as an excellent shot at school. It had been one of the reasons I'd been made battalion commander. The permanent training officer at cadet camp had written

'Good tactician, bushcraft exceptional, can shoot the eye out of a coconut at a hundred yards. Excellent Duntroon material.' It had been this report that had impressed the headmaster and inclined me towards the army without my having really considered any other branch of the service. 'I guess I'm okay, sir,' I replied.

'Free spirit, Japanese, jungle, excellent shot . . . are you stubborn?'

'Yeah, I guess so,' I confessed with a slight grin.

'Excellent, everything the military dislikes.'

'How's that, sir?' I asked, growing a little bolder.

'Free spirit, soon crush that, very bad for general discipline! They think the Japanese are for shooting, not for conversation. Jungle, leave that to the fuzzy wuzzies and dengue fever. Good shot? Snipers have not been needed since the First World War. Stubborn? Don't tolerate independent thinking. Do-as-you're-told-or-else philosophy.' He shook his head. 'No, lad, you're quite unsuitable for the army,' he concluded.

Despite my trepidation at being seated beside the Commander in the confines of the big Chevy, I laughed. He wasn't the humorous type and his highly specious remarks about the army were, I guess, the closest he ever got to being funny.

'Sir, I would imagine, put like that, those are all the characteristics that would alienate any branch of the armed forces.'

It was as if he'd anticipated my answer. 'Ha! All but one!'

I waited, not asking which one as undoubtedly he thought I would. My father would often build his arguments in this manner, forcing you to ask the critical question and then be saddled with the prepared answer, his form of argument game, set and match. I was an old hand at the technique of dumb silence that forced him to finally reveal his hand. Commander Long's voice changed suddenly. 'Nick, I can't tell you too much, but we are going to need people with your skills. You are, I'm told, fluent in Japanese, you're familiar with the jungle, you can handle a small boat, defend yourself and if your voyage across the Indian Ocean is any indication, you are prepared to make decisions and if necessary change them quickly. Son, I'm not the type to piss in your pocket, but we have a shortage of your kind of chap.' He turned sideways to face me. 'Now listen to me seriously for a moment. Australia is in real danger from the Japanese. If we don't halt them in the islands . . . well, Australia, the top end anyway, is a goner. The Japs may never be able to get across the continent, come down south. But that's what they said about Singapore, that the Japanese couldn't cross Thailand and come down the Malayan peninsula and they did it on bicycles using jungle paths and crept up and kicked us up the arse while our British generals were gazing out to sea with our big guns primed and pointed at the imperial horizon! Rule Britannia, Britannia rules the waves!'

He was treating me as an adult and I must admit I was impressed. The head of Naval Intelligence in Australia was taking the time off to talk to some snotty-nosed kid about war tactics. 'I saw how quickly they, the Japanese, can move in Java, sir. The Dutch were caught napping,' I said, rather pointlessly, adding my tuppence worth so that I didn't seem to be the complete ignoramus.

'We all were. The Japanese have brought a new meaning to speedy land and sea invasion. What we suspect they're attempting to do is to form an arch above Australia, a series of airfields, Guadalcanal, Rabaul, the Shortland Islands; they already have adequate landing strips on Buku Island and Kavieng on the northern tip of New Ireland. They possess long-range four-engine Kawanishi flying boats that make the Sunderland look like an airborne jalopy. Flying from Rabaul and Tulagi they could direct land-based aircraft from these airfields and make sea transport between Australia and the rest of the Pacific, in particular the west coast of America, very dangerous, if not bloody impossible.' He jabbed a finger into my shoulder. 'Nick, this is not top-secret stuff, but it isn't for general consumption. It's also where *you* come in.'

'Me?' I said, genuinely surprised.

'You're a bit young, but in every other respect you comply. We desperately need coastwatchers, men who can go behind enemy lines and survive; we also need people who can speak Japanese, who can tune into their field frequencies, watch their operations and get back to us. The Japs are directing their land invasion from on board ships, there's a constant jabbering going on and we're not getting any of the local ship-to-shore stuff. We don't have the two things in combination, someone who not only understands Japanese – which, in itself, is hard enough to find – but who is also equipped to do the jungle duty. I admit you're a bit young for such an assignment, but after listening to you today I think you can do it. I will admit, if it works, it will be a real feather in our cap with the Americans. You know the islands, speak some of the native languages, have proved you can survive in this terrain.' He paused. 'What do you think, lad?'

I was silent for a moment, a bit overwhelmed to say the least. It was the last thing I could have contemplated or imagined doing as a member of the regular army. On the other hand, I'd always preferred to be alone and to make my own decisions. I didn't see this as a particular virtue, but a necessity brought about by my childhood in Japan, being the son of a missionary in New Britain and my somewhat discombobulated career at school in Brisbane. In fact, one of the attractions of being in the regular army was that it was high time I learned to mix with other blokes. I was a big bugger, just on six foot three inches. I could defend myself, but, because of my size, seldom needed to. I thought the barrack-room life and the army might teach me a little more about the world around me. I'd decided that the army would in some strange way bring me out of myself. It would serve as Nick Duncan's personal rehabilitation course. Now I was being asked to go back into the jungle, a loner once more. On the other hand, how the hell could I refuse? When someone asks you to do something important for king and country you can't simply turn around and say, 'Sorry, it doesn't suit my personal plans, sir.' Moreover, there was Anna – there would be regular leave in the army and I'd be able to see her. This wouldn't be the case if I should be stuck in the bloody jungle on some mosquito-ridden island to the north. I wouldn't even be able to write to her or receive letters from her: *Nicholas Duncan, Poste Restante, Scratching his insect bites behind enemy lines somewhere.* Eighteen-year-olds are bullet-proof and it never occurred to me to add to the picture the possibility that I might be captured and lose my head to a Japanese officer's samurai sword.

'And I'd have to join the navy?' I asked rather stupidly. 'Be land-based, but in the navy?'

'Well, initially, it's the quickest way. We'd arrange a short-term commission for you in the Royal Australian Navy Volunteer Reserve; this would last for the duration of hostilities, until the end of the war. Then you'd be seconded to the Allied Intelligence Bureau, which is inter-service. They control the coastwatchers and one or two other bits and pieces I can't talk about.'

'But I'd be trained where?' I asked, thinking of Anna.

'There's a short course starting in two weeks' time, it takes place at HMAS *Cerberus*, which is near Melbourne. I feel sure I can get you on it.' He turned to me. 'Then you'd have to do a training course in the use and maintenance of a long- and short-range field radio as well as a course in codebreaking. You'd do that elsewhere, but I'm not at liberty to tell you where that is.'

I was silent for a while, looking out of the car window. We were passing a row of flowering gums that stretched to the horizon on both sides of the road, large sprays of brilliant pinks and orange and red, indigenous to Western Australia and, in terms of their blossom, the most brilliant of all the many varieties of eucalypt. It all seemed so normal from the window of the travelling car, so settled and forever and not to be disturbed. The landscape had the same peaceful appearance of a child sitting in the branches of a tree, lost in a book, oblivious to the dangerous world around him. It would be two weeks before I started the course; I had the Archbishop's twenty pounds and I still had five quid left of the money I had originally intended to use to buy my passage in a tramp steamer from Java. If I could fix up some transport (Lieutenant Commander Rigby, I felt sure, would help, or the inimitable Marg), wherever Anna was I might be able to get to see her for a few days at least before reporting to HMAS *Cerberus*.

I took a deep breath and turned to Commander Long. 'Yes, okay, thank you, sir,' I said, and in those five words completely changed my life.

'Good man' was all he replied, and he stuck out his hand and we shook. The clasp wasn't as firm as I'd expected. 'I must say you've added a new dimension to butterfly collecting, Nick,' he said. Then leaning slightly forward he tapped Barnsey on the shoulder. 'Don't spare the horses, we have to get back to Perth to catch the night train.' Barnsey nodded, putting his foot down, and the big car began to gather speed.

I knew I hadn't been the reason Rupert Basil Michael Long had come across to Perth, but was simply a small complication he found himself incidentally involved in: a random, single-colour piece in the jigsaw puzzle he supervised. Now with my unimportant destiny decided it was time, as Kevin would say, 'Ter kick the dust. Vamoose', and to get on with the job of winning the Intelligence war.

Back at Mrs Beswick's boarding house I asked if I might take a shower. 'Didn't you have one this morning?' she enquired.

'Yes, but I'm going out tonight.' On a sudden inspiration I added, 'I've got a date.'

She gave me a small asinine smile. 'That's nice, dear, but you *must* appreciate there is a war on. Please don't ask me again, we ration everyone to one shower a day.' She pursed her lips in disapproval. 'You may choose morning or night, but not both.' Then she handed me the key to the shower block, tied with a piece of string to a large wooden toggle. 'We're all expected to do our bit,' she proclaimed. Cold-water showers were evidently another generous concession she'd made to the war effort.

Peter Keeble had left me a second shirt and so I washed the one I'd worn during the day under the shower and, finding a hanger in the rickety wardrobe, I hung it from the window clasp of my first-storey bedroom, making sure the hook was firmly round the clasp and buttoning the wet shirt up to the collar so that a sudden gust of wind wouldn't carry it away. With a bit of luck it might be dry in the morning, whereupon, I felt sure, I would discover a whole new set of war-effort rules imposed upon the use of the communal iron and ironing board. After weeks of wearing what had eventually become a ragged pair of khaki shorts and a torn shirt, dressing up to go out was a nice feeling and the idea of having dinner with Marg Hamilton was brilliant. Normally I would have been overcome with shyness; she was pretty and even in her uniform she looked glamorous. But she was also quite a bit older than me so she probably thought of me as a big kid in need of a good feed. She was dead right about this last aspect. I'd dropped a lot of weight on the voyage and, besides, had eaten almost nothing at lunch with all the talking I was expected to do. But even in the two days I'd known her – and, of course, Lieutenant Commander Rigby – I'd overcome my shyness and knew that she was not only a pretty lady but also a very nice one. She couldn't have been more different in appearance to Anna: while her chestnut hair was also dark it gave off a different sheen, she had lovely green eyes and quite a prominent nose, not big, but not the little button that was part of the oriental look Anna inherited from her mother. Marg was also really nice in front, not at all flat. Even under the WRANS uniform you could see she had a terrific figure that tapered to a small waist, and she had firm buttocks. I think I've already talked about her long legs. I admit I wasn't much of an expert at these things, but a man's got a pair of eyes and anyway, that's what I saw when I looked at Marg Hamilton.

I was waiting at the front gate of the boarding house at half-past six when a little chocolate brown Austin 7 came to a halt in front of me and beeped and there was Marg smiling at me. I laughed. She'd said she'd pick me up and I thought . . . well,

I don't know what I thought – perhaps that we'd probably go to her place by bus, so the little Austin was a big surprise. I got into the passenger side where my head bumped up against the inside of the roof, so I sort of hunched down a bit and brought my knees up to my chest. Marg laughed. 'There's a thinga-me-bob under the seat that lets you slide it back a bit and gives you more room. I forget how big you are, Nick.'

'This is nice,' I said, patting the dashboard of the Austin 7 and activating the lever under the seat that yielded another three or four inches so that I could remove my knees from the base of my nostrils.

Marg changed into gear and pulled away from the kerb. 'It was my brother's,' she replied.

'Was?' I enquired, not thinking.

'He was killed in Greece last April.'

'Oh, Marg, I'm so sorry,' I said, reaching out and touching her lightly on the arm. My father would have pointed out the trap that lay in the word 'was' and chided me for not spotting it. 'Language is full of road signs,' he'd say. 'Each sentence is the precursor of the next and carries its paraphrase. We build argument and meaning with words and you must always be aware of the cornerstone, of the "was".' But I'd clumsily missed it. I thought of my father, anxious for him but all the while knowing that his fine mind was far from being a practical one, that he almost certainly would have helped everyone to board the boat to escape the Japanese and then remained behind himself, convinced that his knowledge of their language and their peculiar ways meant that he would be able to make some sense of the invader and in so doing make it easier for those who were forced to stay behind.

Marg looked at me, her big brown eyes suddenly glistening.

'It's all right, we've come to terms with it. You have to, or life simply treads water.' This time the cornerstone was the 'we've' and I avoided taking it further. The meaning of the sentence would, I knew, eventually be revealed. Marg hadn't spoken of her family or mentioned a mother or father or any siblings. 'It's a joyous little car,' she said at last. 'It runs on the smell of an oil rag.'

We arrived at a block of red-brick flats, typical of the ugly buildings that seemed to have sprung up everywhere in the thirties, and Marg stopped outside one of the garages built on either side. I peeled myself out of the little car and opened the garage door to allow her to drive in. I noticed blue smoke coming from the exhaust when she'd stopped and I'd opened the car door for her. 'You probably need an oil change,' I said, knowing that it was a sign it was needed urgently.

'Oh, do I? Thank you, Nick. My brother, John, would be furious if he thought I was neglecting his precious car.'

'If you've got a jack I'll do it for you. The tappets also need adjusting.'

'Tappets? Thank you. Wherever did you learn about motorcars, Nick?'

I laughed. 'On the mission station you learn to do a bit of everything, jack-of-all-trades and master of none,' I quipped nervously, quoting the old cliché. I'd always been at home around machinery; it was logical stuff and you could usually work out what was wrong. I was happy that I could do something useful for Marg, as thus far it had been a one-way street. I would use some of the Archbishop's money to buy the oil and grease. The car probably needed the spark plugs changed and timing and points adjusted too. Although the tyres seemed in good condition, returning from opening the garage door I saw that both front tyres were beginning to wear on the outside edge, so the steering probably needed realignment. It was all stuff I knew how to do on an Austin 7. As a motorcar, mechanically it wasn't a great deal more complex than a Singer sewing machine. It would give me an excuse to come back, although I wondered briefly at this thought. But after weeks on board with the little bloke as my sole companion, just the presence of a pretty female was an exhilarating if somewhat nervous-making experience.

Marg's flat was on the ground floor at the back of the building, with a bit of a yard where I think I met the cornerstone I'd deliberately avoided – the 'we've' turned out to be a dog of indeterminate breed named Timmy and a Burmese cat of aristocratic lineage, every inch a princess, with the improbable but entirely appropriate name of Cardamon. Timmy was a bitser without a bad bone in his black, white and mottle-eared body, appended with a perpetually wagging tail. He was the kind of dog more likely to welcome an intruder than chase one away. The cat . . . well, what is it they say about the difference between dogs and cats as pets? Dogs have masters and cats have servants. Marg explained that, like the Austin, she had inherited the cat and the dog from her brother. 'I'm not sure how I would have coped without the two of them at my side when the telegram came. We've survived together.' She smiled a little sadly, patting the lolling-tongued Timmy and stooping to pick up Cardamon, who placed her elegant paws over Marg's shoulders and snuggled her pretty head into her neck, purring like a tractor in a most unregal manner. 'I guess they're my family now,' Marg commented.

Carrying the cat indoors, Marg led me into the tiny though pleasant lounge room and invited me to sit down in a comfortable old leather chair, placing Cardamon on my lap. The cat stood up for a moment, arched her back, turned about and then settled happily into my lap, accepting as her due my stroking her sleek, lavender-coloured neck and back.

I was probably just an overgrown kid to Marg, but that doesn't mean I wasn't nervous in her civilian presence. She was attractive in her WRANS uniform but now she wore a green cotton summer dress (I would later learn it was known as a 'shirtmaker') that buttoned down the entire front and was belted at the waist. With this she wore sandals, her arms and legs bare and tanned, though not as dark as my own where the tropical sun had burned my skin almost black. It was as if sunlight had brushed her skin lightly in passing to give it a soft, almost translucent sheen that was very, very attractive. Well, actually a bit more than that. This added to the sum of her assets in no small way. What can I say? I'd be lying if I denied there were no stirrings going on below. This immediately made me feel guilty about Anna, although I wasn't really being unfaithful in my mind. It was just that the part of my body doing the stirring seemed to be a quite independent part of me and possessed of a mind of its own. But as I felt sure Marg was playing more mother than lover, I was grateful that Cardamon's purring presence was seated over the offending area.

In the food department Marg proved true to her word – three whopping great beef sausages, a mountain of mashed potato, the full volcano, with brown gravy filling the crater, fried onions smothering the snags and three green beans. 'Must have something green on your plate, Nick,' she chided, smiling. I rather wolfed down the meal, not pausing for too much polite conversation. Marg, for her part, had one sausage and a big pile of beans and no potato and did most of the talking. 'Poor darling, you must be starving. All that talk and not a bite for either of us, never mind if the narrator or the amanuensis starve!' she said, cleverly teasing me with the word I'd used the previous day. Then she added, 'Men simply don't think and men in uniform are the worst of the lot!' She paused, stabbing her fork into a bean, then lifting it from the plate and holding it suspended. 'Commander Rupert Basil Michael Long is like a bull in a china shop, about as subtle as a kick up the backside,' she accused, mixing her metaphors as my father might have pointed out.

'Well, he certainly doesn't beat around the bush,' I said, adding yet another metaphor for good measure.

Marg looked at me, her expression suddenly serious. 'Nick, you don't have to do it, you know.'

'Do what?' I asked.

'Become a coastwatcher. With your brains and knowledge of Japanese, there are lots of other opportunities in Intelligence. Codebreaking, for instance.'

'Yeah, he said something about doing a course.'

'No, some of us have done it, but it's basic stuff. With a good command of Japanese you are different. We're going to need interrogators, translators, as well as codebreakers who can operate at a sophisticated level. Commander Long has become obsessed with having men behind enemy lines.' She looked suddenly angry. 'The war in the Pacific has hardly begun and already we've lost two coastwatchers, one to the enemy and one to dengue fever.'

'Who's "we"? Commander Long hinted at some other organisation.'

'Nick, you're trying to deflect our conversation. Just remember I'm an Intelligence officer, I shouldn't even have mentioned codebreaking, a taboo word in Intelligence. You also know I'm not going to tell you who the "we" is. Can we stick to the subject?'

I was being thoroughly reprimanded and at the same time was witnessing yet another quality of the remarkable Marg Hamilton. She didn't put up with bullshit! I was an expert at changing the subject in a conversation; it's part of being a loner, when you don't want to give away too much about yourself. I thought to apologise, then decided not to. It had been worth a try, anyway. I shrugged. 'It's stuff I know how to do. I mean the jungle, boats, living off the land and from the sea. I've been doing it since the age of twelve.'

She must have noticed that I'd finished my meal because she returned her fork with an impaled bean to her plate. She'd also all but completed her own dinner, only three more beans survived, not counting the one on the fork. She rose from the table, dabbing her pretty mouth with her napkin. 'Come and sit down,' she instructed, pointing to a small couch covered in a material patterned with hibiscus blossoms in pink and red. It was the brightest object in the room and I rather liked it, as it reminded me of the manse garden in Rabaul. All it needed was hummingbirds feeding on the nectar.

I sat down and Marg sat beside me, half turned to face me, her slender legs crossed. She was wearing a perfume that triggered a yearning in me, something in my long-ago past – maybe my mother had worn a similar one. 'Nick, you're only eighteen but already you're more of a man than anyone I've ever met,' she began. If she saw me blush she ignored it, and continued. 'You have a gentleness that is going to drive women crazy and a toughness they are going to be unable to resist. You have brains and beauty.' I guess by this stage I must have been roughly the colour of beetroot because she laughed. 'Men can also be beautiful, but if you prefer I'll change that to "looks"; looks along with brains and a tough inner core that women will beat down doors to get to. The butterfly collector and the young man – it's an irresistible combination.'

It was all a bit much and for a moment I thought she might be gently sending me up. But then I saw that she wasn't. 'You could have fooled me!' I mumbled, trying to grin but feeling my mouth go strangely lopsided. In a sense, I suppose, Anna had beaten down my door in the compound of *De Kost Kamer* when she'd brought me dinner, but then, I reminded myself, at that stage she wouldn't have known if I was a two-headed monster with crocodile teeth.

'Don't throw it all away, Nick. Don't do what Rupert Basil Michael Long wants,' she said, pressing her hand upon my knee.

'Why do you always refer to him like that, using all his names?' I asked, again deliberately evading an answer to her plea.

She threw back her head, her chestnut hair swinging and for a brief moment covering her pretty face before settling, at the same time withdrawing her hand and making me immediately wish she'd return it to my knee. She wore a look of impatience. 'He doesn't see men. He *only* sees solutions. He doesn't see a beautiful and exceptional eighteen-year-old with a lust for life. He just sees a radio operator behind enemy lines. For him it's a jigsaw puzzle . . .'

'Funny you should say that,' I interrupted. 'That's exactly what I thought. I was a one-colour component, one of those pieces you know must belong to either the sky or the open piece of ground in front of the giant's castle. When we shook hands and

I agreed to go to HMAS *Cerberus* he tapped the driver on the shoulder and told him not to spare the horsepower. I doubt if we said a dozen more words on the rest of the way to Fremantle.'

Marg leaned forward and replaced her hand on my knee, the closeness of her breasts made it difficult for me to breathe and that part of me below the waist with its singular mind was in all sorts of trouble. 'It's the Rupert and Basil and the cherub lips. In combination they've destroyed him; the Michael never had a chance. What do some parents think they're doing when they so carelessly saddle a child with names of past family? It must have been hell at school when he was growing up.'

I grinned. 'Try being a butterfly collector some time!'

Marg laughed. 'At least you were big enough to defend yourself. Rupert Basil Michael Long is very short and must have been a pathetic little bundle of misery as a child.' She was leaning very close, her beautiful breasts almost touching my shirt, her hand on my knee, lips wet and slightly parted. Her perfume sent me dizzy with desire. If I hadn't been sitting already I feel sure I would have gone weak at the knees. Her hand slid down into my crotch and at the same time our lips met. I'd like to think this last bit was due to my assertiveness, but I don't think it was. Anna and I had swapped tongues a fair bit so I wasn't the complete novice, but now it was below the waist that I was coming apart big time. Marg's clever fingers had the buttons of my fly undone and the rest acted like a jack-in-the-box.

Marg ceased kissing me. 'My goodness, Jumpin' Jack!' she exclaimed. She gave me a wicked grin. 'Nick, I'm sorry, there's a fire down below that needs my urgent attention or it might get out of hand.' I was surprised that she was also breathing heavily. Next thing you know, she'd slid from the couch and onto her knees on the carpet in front of me, then put her mouth on Jumpin' Jack, her lips sliding down to his base, then slowly back. It was the most exquisite feeling I'd ever experienced.

Now, I know every adult male in the world has probably experienced what Marg was doing to me. It hardly qualified as an aberration and every pimply schoolboy includes this in his fantasy agenda, imagining the soapy pads of his fingers as a pair of luscious female lips. I'd even taken D.H. Lawrence's *Lady Chatterley's Lover*, where such a moment is described, to the masturbatory peace and quiet of the outdoor toilet on the mission station when my father, in yet another of his birds-and-the-bees moments, had handed me the book at the age of fourteen and said gruffly, 'Instruction for the use of essential gender knowledge.'

There is a first for everything, for laughter and pain, for certainty and uncertainty, for joy and sorrow, and mostly we forget to inscribe these firsts in our book of memories. Often our first intimate sexual encounter is awkward, conducted between two inexperienced would-be lovers, as might have been the case between Anna and me, had she consented. We let the moment escape, thinking perhaps that this initial sexual fumble must improve, that eventually we'd acquire a desirable memory of the moment, one as we imagined it should be. All I can tell you is that I felt no sudden stab of guilt concerning darling Anna. If conscience plays a part in these things, then mine had gone walkabout. Marg stroking me expertly with her lips was for me akin to dying from pure pleasure, but instead of dying I felt as if I would explode from within with sheer joy. Crying out, I knew I was unable to contain myself. It was then that Marg, as if by magic, unbuttoned the front of her dress. I don't know how she'd managed to snap open the hooks and eyes that held her brassiere, but her beautiful breasts were bared in front of me, and at the moment I could no longer contain myself, her mouth withdrew and she moved forward and cupped her breasts about a now thoroughly jumping Jumpin' Jack, enfolding me so that I came against her softness. Then she rose and straddled my knees and allowed me to clasp her glistening breasts. 'Rub them, darling,' she said. 'Gently, this part of me is for you.' It was the first time I had experienced the true generosity of a woman giving herself to a man. 'That was the entrée, Nick. Into the shower and then the bedroom for the main course,' she instructed.

'Yes, ma'am,' I sighed. 'Anything you say.'

Together in the shower, gloriously hot, Jumpin' Jack recovered quickly. Towelled and glowing, Marg led me by the hand to the bedroom, to a double bed with crisp white sheets and what eventuated as the hardest-working night I had ever enjoyed.

'First a small ritual we need to go through, Nick. In case you're unfamiliar with their use, let me begin by explaining that I'm in Naval Intelligence not just for the duration of the war but as a permanent career. I am also a big girl now and a very careful one. Intelligence teaches you that,' she said, using a clever double entendre.

I started to blush. Was she going to ask me if I'd brought any French letters? 'Marg, I'm sorry,' I stammered. 'I never thought . . . er, anticipated.'

'No, of course you didn't, darling boy,' she interrupted. 'The nicest surprises are the unexpected ones. As long as you remain rigid I shall be at rigid attention,' she said, again cleverly while neatly removing my embarrassment. She produced a small square package, tearing it open. 'Naval issue. Kindly lie back and think of England,' she laughed.

'I've never been to England, or even to where I think you're taking me,' I said, trying to break the news of my virginity to her and in the process being too clever by half.

'Oh!' She grinned. 'Am I not the lucky one then! I shouldn't be surprised if in one night we enjoy several journeys to the nicest places, Nick.'

The trouble with writing about making love – I don't want to call it sex because to me it was much more – is that all the words are worn out. In Marg's arms and experiencing her lovely body I had come alive. Something dormant in me had emerged and making love was as much about the experience of being held closely, intimately, as it was about mutual gratification.

From the age of five I had been denied even the simplest physical comfort a child might expect from a mother. The Japanese woman who thereafter took care of my daily needs seldom touched me; to her culture I was an 'it', a Western child and certainly not worthy of a spontaneous or any other show of affection. Anna was the loveliest thing I could imagine, but Marg was a woman. I don't know how to describe the difference, but a young bloke, particularly a virgin, needs to be taken by the hand and led into the wonderful mystery of the female body while, at the same time, being shown how he must please his partner as well. Marg was a willing teacher who made no bones about her own demands and in me she had new clay to mould in any way she wished. I had more than discovered sex. I had discovered the wonderful mystery of womankind.

By morning I was utterly exhausted. Marg brought me breakfast in bed: scrambled eggs, toast, orange juice and a pot of tea. She was wearing a pretty, oyster-coloured dressing-gown and sat on the edge of the bed. 'Nick, that was lovely. More than lovely. I hope you enjoyed yourself as much as I did?'

'Marg, I don't know what to say except – thank you.'

She smiled and bent and kissed me lightly on the cheek. 'It's my call, you do understand that, Nick, don't you?'

'Your call?' I wasn't sure what she meant.

'My bed, my body, both belong to me alone. You must understand, Jumpin' Jack doesn't have proprietorial rights.'

I blushed furiously. It hadn't occurred to me to expect such rights. In childhood I hadn't ever enjoyed the proximity to the opposite gender that establishes the roles of the male and allows young blokes to make assumptions so that they think of a woman as a lesser being in the pecking order or in the bedchamber.

'Marg, if what happened last night was all that happens to me until I die I shall be eternally grateful to you.' I think she must have seen that this wasn't simply morning-after grateful boy-speak. I had grown up a whole heap in one single night, but that didn't make me feel as if I was entitled to an encore; to any more than she had already so very generously given to me.

Virginity in a male is a much overrated possession that has nothing to do with inner purity but is simply evidence of a lack of opportunity. I knew that I had been especially privileged in the manner in which I had experienced the second birth of the male, his delivery into manhood by a good woman. Now I tried inadequately to put this into words. 'If you're lucky, *really* lucky, you get a Marg Hamilton to terminate your virginity with an exquisite experience such as last night,' I said, hoping I didn't sound over-sentimental or sloppy or even pompous, knowing there was an element of my father's pedantic syntax involved.

Marg brought her hand to her brow, drew back her chestnut mane and laughed. 'Nick, you really are a thoroughgoing rascal! But I think that may be the nicest compliment I have ever been paid. Darling, don't let them bury you in the jungle. Please!'

I spent the morning in town buying a can of engine oil and a pot of grease. Examination of the spark plugs indicated that they were just about on their last legs. I paid a motor mechanic two shillings to lend me the equipment to adjust the tappets and timing, and a set of spanners to fix the wheel alignment, as well as a jack to lift the Austin sufficiently off the ground for a big bloke to crawl under the chassis. It took me most of the morning to source all the stuff I needed but then, of course, I realised that under wartime conditions taxis were unavailable. Finally I paid four Aboriginal kids who were hanging around a sixpence each to carry the jack while I humped the other stuff back to Marg's flat. I was sweaty and tired as I paid the kids. 'No fags, you hear . . . lollies only!' They laughed, running off.

I found a pair of overalls in the garage that had obviously belonged to Marg's brother. I undressed, conscious that I only had Peter Keeble's clothes and the clean, unironed shirt hanging from the boarding-house window. The overalls fitted more or less, with the legs about six inches short and a fair bit of my chest showing where the metal buttons couldn't meet the buttonholes. I worked on the Austin 7 all afternoon and into the early evening. It was obvious that under Marg's stewardship it had been badly neglected, but it was still a bonzer little car and there were careful touches everywhere indicating that her brother John must have kept it in tip-top condition.

It was nearly six o'clock in the evening when I'd completed the mechanics, returned the tools, and washed and polished

the Austin to within an inch of its life. I must say it scrubbed up really well. Underneath all the grime the duco was perfectly even and didn't have a scratch on it. Marg arrived back just as the sun was setting, the soft red glow of sunset reflecting on the little chocolate-coloured car, making it look brand-new. In a peculiar sense, I had tried to do for Marg's car what Marg had done for me the previous night. The strange thing was that I was still in love with Anna, but I knew that in an entirely different way I loved Marg Hamilton. Or do you think that's just Jumpin' Jack's influence?

'Goodness, Nick. I can't believe it!' she exclaimed. 'It looks simply wonderful!'

I wiped my hands on the polishing cloth even though they were dry and didn't need wiping. Wiping your hands on a bit of rag when customers approach is an essential prerequisite for the serious mechanic. 'I hope it goes better than it looks,' I said rather pompously. I must admit I was just a tad pleased with myself.

'Come in, you need a shower. Have you eaten?'

'Scrambled eggs in bed this morning,' I replied. In fact I had entirely forgotten to eat lunch. I indicated the shiny little car. 'Want to take her for a spin?' I offered.

'Nick, I'd love to, but petrol is much too scarce for a joyride. It's only meant to be used for official business. So later, when I take you back to the boarding house, you're still official business and that's permitted within the laws of petrol rationing. Now go and have a shower and we'll have something to eat. I have some news.'

'Good or bad?' I asked.

'I don't know, but you probably won't like it,' she replied.

I had a quick shower, not enjoying the hot water as much as I should have. I was anxious to hear Marg's news, knowing it might be about Anna or my dad, but first she made me sit at the table and eat the remains of a cold leg of lamb, a salad, and bread with a thin scraping of butter. After pouring me a cup of tea and placing it beside me, she sat opposite me at the kitchen table. 'Nick, there's no news of the *Witvogel* arriving in Broome. We've also checked Darwin.' She spread her hands. 'Nothing.'

My heart sank and I brought my hands up to hold my head, my elbows leaning on the table. Marg had no way of knowing how I felt about Anna. In the tell-everything at the Archbishop's luncheon, I'd played up Piet Van Heerden, and Anna had simply been his daughter who'd gone butterfly hunting with me and embroidered the handkerchief in the form of a keepsake. Loving-hands-at-home stuff you might expect from a teenager.

'It's Anna, isn't it?' Marg asked, and I knew from the way she asked the question that she hadn't been fooled for a moment. 'Oh, Nick, I'm so sorry,' she said, reaching over and touching my arm. 'Look, it doesn't mean too much, a number of ships were diverted to Colombo – we're trying to check there. It may take a few days. Going through a ship's manifest is asking a lot from the busy port officials, especially with a harbour packed with merchant and passenger ships carrying refugees.'

'Or it may have been sunk by the Japanese,' I said despondently. There had been frequent reports that the Japs had sunk merchant ships carrying civilian passengers.

'Yes, that's a possibility,' Marg said, not evading the issue. 'Nick, we can only live in hope.'

Marg drove me back to the boarding house, the little car purring like Cardamon the cat, but I felt too down-in-the-dumps to take any pleasure from its newfound power and quietness. Marg kissed me at the gate. 'Can you meet me at the office about lunchtime tomorrow? We should have some news by then,' she said.

I waited until she'd pulled away, the little car trapping the reflection from a street lamp. I confess I was close to tears as I opened the front door to be confronted by Mrs Beswick in slippers, hairnet and curlers, holding up my shirt. 'Can you explain this, please?' she demanded, prim-lipped.

'Yes, it's my shirt.'

'It was hanging from the window?'

'Yes, I know. I washed it and hung it out to dry.'

'We do not tolerate garments hanging from windows, Mr Duncan. Don't you know there's a war going on?'

Despite my extreme annoyance and the fact that the last thing in the world I desired was Mrs Beswick's coathanger mouth and pale grey accusing eyes confronting me, I felt compelled to ask, 'What has my shirt hanging from the window got to do with the war?'

'Ha! Signals! Enemy signals. Shirts in windows are well-known signals. It's the fifth column, they're everywhere!'

I grabbed the shirt from her startled grasp. 'Mrs Beswick, get stuffed!' I said, marching past her and proceeding up the stairs. I'd never in my life insulted a woman.

'I'll be calling the police!' she yelled after me. 'We can't have spies. This is a respectable boarding house!'

I turned on the landing. 'You wouldn't be related to Bert Henry, would you?' I asked.

'Bert who?'

'Never mind! I'll pay you what I owe you in the morning and be gone from this bloody fleapit before breakfast.'

'Breakfast is included!' she shouted back.

Sometimes you've just got to laugh or you end up crying.

PART TWO

'*You must tell my story, Nicholas,*
because I am too ashamed.'
Anna Van Heerden
a.k.a. Madam Butterfly

CHAPTER SIX

'Feathers can fly and so can I!'
Katerina Van Heerden

ANNA WATCHED AS THE *Witvogel* moved out of the harbour, trying to keep her eye on my rapidly receding form as I waved from the docks. She was surprised how quickly an image disappears. In only a couple of minutes the people on the wharf had become a blur of noise, for the sound of the people left behind seemed to endure longer than the focus on any one person. I had become a dot, then part of a smudge.

Already she was regretting the decision to stay with her family and not sail with me in *Madam Butterfly* to Australia. She knew she was in love, but love was an entirely new experience she had no way of evaluating. She had resisted making love to me, giving me her body, because at the time she'd felt it wasn't right, that she should wait, maybe even until we were married.

But now she wasn't so certain. She was afraid that I'd somehow disappear, that had she made love with me I'd be forever a part of her. No matter what happened I would have been her virgin lover, her introduction to coming into true womanhood. Now I might become no more than a memory that would fade in time, a boy that had quickened her blood and made her feel different, wanted and loved.

Her most ardent wish was that our romance should continue when the *Witvogel* arrived in Broome. But this too depended on so much: my arrival, her arrival, my joining the army. And then there was her father, who was not necessarily willing to settle in Australia, where there were no servants and where the lifestyle he'd taken for granted since childhood did not exist. 'New Zealand,' he'd declared. 'The Maori, they are servants to the white people. We will sit out the war in New Zealand. Ja, then we'll return to Java, to our rightful home.' It hadn't occurred to him that the Japanese might win the war, and when this was suggested he would loudly proclaim, 'They lost it at Pearl Harbor when they were stupid enough to attack the Americans.'

Anna could recall that he'd been drinking excessively for nearly a year. He'd always been a big drinker, most of the men in the families they knew were very active with their elbows, but he'd always been affable, a happy drunk, a big man who prided himself on his capacity to drink beer and brandy and be the last man still standing at the end of the evening. But in the last year, first with the uncertainty and then the certainty of invasion, and the loss of everything he and his family had stood for throughout ten generations, she'd witnessed him slowly come apart. He'd grown morose, moody, resentful and, above all else, self-pitying and unable to hold his alcohol as he had once done.

He'd come on board already somewhat drunk, retired immediately to their overcrowded cabin and opened a bottle of brandy from the case he'd brought with him, refusing to come on deck with her to farewell me or even his homeland. He'd merely paused at the top of the gangplank when they'd boarded and turned to look down at the wharf. 'We gave them everything and look at the bastards shouting at us. Underneath they're still savages,' he'd said of the small contingent of Javanese people who were openly jeering as they boarded the *Witvogel*. 'They were primitives when we Dutch arrived here, headhunters! It wouldn't surprise me if they go back to their old habits now that we've left. So much for three hundred years of teaching them decency and clean living.'

Anna, though more Dutch than Javanese in her upbringing, wondered what her mother might have said to this, when at the age of fifteen she'd had the privilege of being seduced by the big Dutchman who'd accepted that, as a native, she was fair game for his every carnal desire.

Anna had often speculated whether she would have been allowed to stay within the family had Katerina, her stepmother, not been barren and a cripple and if there had been 'pure blood' children in the family. She loved Piet Van Heerden, who had never made her feel like a half-caste, chiding his bitter-tongued wife whenever he heard her disparaging her. But right from the beginning, as early as she could remember, she'd had to sing for her supper. Be his little darling. His *skatterbol*, meaning 'ball of fluff'. Her status in the family depended on his love and protection.

She could remember as a five-year-old, when her back was turned, her stepmother crossing the polished wooden floors silently in her wheelchair and taking vicious delight in slapping her across the head with the flat of her hand, while yelling out, 'Bastard! Whore's child!' Her only refuge had been her papa, and as she'd grown older, she'd seen to it that more and more he depended on her love and reassurance. She had finally reached the stage when she could actually influence him, or perhaps a better way of putting it was that she could talk him into doing what she wanted.

Anna was only sixteen and thought of herself as no different to other girls of her age, but nevertheless sensed that she possessed an almost instinctive knowledge of males. She'd always felt beholden to her father's moods and was, she admitted, over-anxious to please him and to anticipate his needs. It hadn't been difficult, we men are simple creatures, and she had come to know that the males who cast furtive looks at her, even when she was a young child, were seeking something from her, though at the time she did not know what this might be.

It had come as an enormous surprise to her that she felt so wonderfully free and loved when we were together; no longer vulnerable, not finding it necessary to manipulate my affections. I was, after all, a big, clumsy butterfly collector who asked nothing more of her than that she be herself, the nicest and prettiest girl I had ever seen. I appeared to love her without any complication or demands, though she was perfectly aware of my desire for her and she'd secretly laughed at the thought of the 'accident' that had caused me to hurry to the outside washroom. She claimed our love showed through the way I looked at her, as if I couldn't believe my own good fortune – which was perfectly true.

She'd blossomed, grown into womanhood, earlier than the other girls at school, those whose parents were both Dutch. At first she was ashamed, thinking this an indictment of her Javanese blood. Her stepmother had voiced this once when she'd said accusingly after her periods had arrived, 'It's disgusting, you natives are on heat at the age of twelve!' But she'd soon noted the sly, hungry looks of the teenage boys belonging to family friends and the brothers of her schoolmates. Even older men, those of her father's adult male friends, when they'd consumed too much brandy, dared to attempt to grope her if they found themselves suddenly left alone with her.

Anna had been a survivor all her life and so she hadn't

reported the wayward hands of her father's male friends, knowing that Piet Van Heerden would respond violently. He was a big man with a violent temper and saw her as exclusively his personal property. Moreover, with her father on the warpath over her, Anna knew this would infuriate her viciously resentful and jealous stepmother, who would find a way to punish or taunt her.

The notion that she had a power over men, she secretly admitted to herself, was exhilarating. She was careful to hide this from her father and his friends; it was the first time in her life that she was not dependent on the goodwill of the male gender. It made her feel in control; she understood instinctively that she possessed a special kind of attraction that males lusted after and which amounted to a female's power over the opposite sex.

Though careful not to be thought of as a flirt, she was aware that her lithe body had a way of moving naturally that produced a hungry look in men's eyes. Anna countered this by averting her eyes when men looked at her and was careful never to flirt, but she didn't attempt to change the way she walked or moved. She'd seen tall Dutch girls round their shoulders and keep their heads bowed in an attempt to appear shorter, pretty girls who lost their femininity attempting to hide their stature. She determined to always hold her head high, chin forward, open her shoulders and allow her body to maintain its naturally feline movements.

I had once remarked that her every move, her every gesture, appeared elegant. I recalled saying, 'You seem to perform a beautifully articulated mime simply by moving, Anna.' Whereas her stepmother had stabbed an angry finger at her when she was just thirteen and sneered, '*Swartz!* You move like a black woman. Show some modesty, you little slut!'

Now, standing forlornly at the ship's rails, desperately trying to locate me among the smudge of people lining the docks and thinking me perhaps lost to her forever, she deeply regretted choosing her unravelling family and their voyage to safety in a grog-fumed cabin filled with snoring adults, where eight people were expected to share just four bunks.

She and the maid, *Kleine* Kiki, would have to sleep on the floor or perhaps on the deck. No, she realised that was impossible; the deck space had been chalked into squares that were now rapidly filling with desperate, quarrelling families who were aggressively policing their chalk lines. Their cabin also needed to accommodate Katerina's wheelchair, their trunk and the baggage of the four strangers who shared the cabin. The baggage hold had been turned into people space and, despite paying the full fare three months in advance, they had been refused stowage for their on-board trunk.

When Piet Van Heerden had pointed out that they'd paid for two cabins that included below-deck trunk stowage, the first mate had laughed. 'Count yourself lucky, sir. You have a cabin with only four extra people; we're selling single chalked squares in the hold to large families for more than you paid for both cabins.' He then suggested they might like to return to shore, where he was sure the owners would engage to fully refund their money.

'What about my refund for the money I paid for the second cabin?' Piet Van Heerden, already half-inebriated, asked belligerently.

The first mate delicately scratched the side of his nose with his forefinger, looking down in order to hide his grin. 'Ah, we have no authority to refund bookings. You'll have to write to the owners in Amsterdam, sir,' he replied.

'I ought to smash your teeth in!' Anna's papa had yelled at the man.

'That would be a big mistake, sir,' came the first mate's sanguine reply. 'Just say the word. It would give me enormous pleasure to escort a drunk and his family back to shore.'

'Come, Papa,' Anna cried, grabbing him by the arm. She shot an angry look at the first mate and then said, as if to her father, 'Papa, you know how it is – some men are born bastards, while others become bastards when they're given a little power.'

And so it had all started badly, and in addition she'd broken down in front of me, clasping her Clipper butterfly in its box to her chest as she said a tearful farewell. She'd been determined to remain dry-eyed and brave, but suddenly she didn't feel in the least powerful or in control of her womanhood. Instead, the farewell, saying goodbye to me, filled her with uncertainty and even dread. She was back to being the little girl afraid of the future, who wanted too much to be loved.

As the *Witvogel* passed the two wrecks at the entrance to Tanjong Priok harbour she thought of *Madam Butterfly*, its sails catching the breeze and the sound of the wind in the rigging, of being alone with me on the open ocean and watching the flying fish jumping ahead of the bow, two young lovers attempting to escape the pain of their suddenly topsy-turvy, brutal and unpredictable world.

She told herself she'd stayed out of loyalty to her father who needed her, although more and more Katerina despised her and all Piet Van Heerden needed was the oblivion of a brandy bottle. So what if I had taken her virginity? She told herself she'd rather I performed the ultimate introduction to her womanhood than anyone else in the world. A lovely compliment and one I would always treasure.

As they left the surrounds of Batavia and passed out into the open sea, Anna started once more to weep. She felt a tap on her shoulder and turned to see a fat woman with an incipient moustache. The angry-looking woman was wearing a floral dress printed with pink rosebuds and forget-me-nots that stretched over her enormous bosom, her mammaries using up so much of the fabric that the front hemline rose twenty-five centimetres above the back to reveal her fat, pink, dimpled knees. She appeared to be in her mid-forties. 'Excuse me, but you're standing in our square.' She pointed to the chalkline on the deck. '*Mijn* husband works hard and he paid good money for this space. You cannot stay here. Can't you see they've marked corridors for people to walk?'

The next two days at sea proved to be difficult ones for Anna; she slept hardly at all. Piet Van Heerden was perpetually drunk, Katerina more shrewish than ever, so that *Kleine* Kiki, also lacking sleep, was constantly in tears. The four other passengers – a bank clerk appropriately named de Klerk, his wife and his two thin-lipped, disapproving maiden sisters – were immediately hostile. Not that she blamed them, for her papa and stepmother were behaving appallingly. Her father was shouting out drunkenly, shaking his fist, angry at nobody in particular, and her stepmother was yelling at him to behave himself and then, in turn, taking her vexation out on *Kleine* Kiki.

But there was worse, much worse, to come. Thirty hours after leaving Tanjong Priok, when about one hundred and fifty nautical miles out at sea, the passengers heard a deep knocking sound coming from below and reverberating through the ship. The *Witvogel* suddenly stopped and was soon wallowing helplessly in the swell, the heat on board the impossibly overcrowded ship soon becoming unbearable.

At noon the captain announced over the ship's loudspeaker that they'd developed engine trouble and the ship's engineers were trying to rectify the problem. For the next three hours they heard constant hammering and eventually the shaft began to turn. Then to everyone's dismay the ship began to turn in a wide arc to the north-east. The captain came on the loudspeaker once again and announced that they were returning to Java, to the port of Tjilatjap, where repairs would take place. He left the worst for last – that the ship's speed, normally around eight knots, was severely reduced and it would take several days to get back to the coast and sail upriver to the port. He assured the passengers that the Japanese had not yet invaded and that hopefully the *Witvogel* would be on its way again and well out to sea before they did arrive.

It was also my birthday, and Anna told me how she had searched the ship for an empty corner and finally found it in one of the women's lavatories that was closed for repairs. She sat on the toilet seat and cried her heart out. 'Oh, Nicholas, I missed you so much! You were somewhere out there, close. I could feel it in my heart!' she told me, tears running down her cheeks when she was recounting her story. She was stuck on a broken-down ship that was wallowing in the tropical heat, knowing I couldn't be very far away, having left Batavia only a day earlier.

Finally she'd left the disused toilet and made her way on deck, where she found a chalked corridor that led to half a metre or so of railing that didn't trespass onto someone's square. Looking across the horizon towards where she thought the Sunda Strait might be, she shouted at the horizon, 'Happy birthday, Nicholas! I love you!', not caring about the startled looks of passengers in the adjacent squares.

And so began what Anna thought at the time were the worst four days of her life. At first the intruders, as she thought of the four members of the de Klerk family, made sly remarks amongst themselves about the drunken Piet Van Heerden. But seeing how pathetic and helpless he'd become, they were soon bawling insults openly at him. This, in turn, caused her stepmother to bare her teeth and scream back at them like a fishwife. The cabin had become a battleground. Every waking hour, internecine warfare raged between the two families, with the fetid air often blue with invective.

There was no space to move in the cabin and Anna spent most of her time standing or seated in the passageway, out of earshot of the caterwauling women and the self-important and hectoring bank clerk. He was a small man with black wavy hair that glistened with pomade; combed backward from his brow and flattened over his skull, it more closely resembled a nasty-looking toupee than it did his own God-given hair. Anna instinctively knew de Klerk was the kind of snivelling rodent who would slink away and hide rather than face up to a confrontation.

Not that Piet Van Heerden was interested in putting him in his place. After the incident with the first mate, and realising their fate was no longer in his hands, he'd taken seriously to the brandy bottle and lay all day in the top bunk in an alcohol-induced stupor. On several occasions, too drunk to go to the toilet or to ask for the brandy bottle he'd taken to using, he'd ended up pissing while still wearing his pants, groping at his fly to remove his penis and sending an arc of piss splashing against the cabin ceiling directly above him for it to return in a shower over his bunk, face, chest and already-stained trousers. This to the outraged howls from the de Klerks and silent disgust of Anna, who found herself forced to try to clean him up, though she avoided touching his penis, which he'd tucked back into his trousers, leaving a wet stain at the front. Despite all her efforts, the sharp tang of urine was soon added to the smell of stale grog, sweat and vomit in the overcrowded cabin.

The communal toilets were soon blocked and the ship below-decks smelled of seasickness and shit. They had to queue for two hours to receive a single small meal a day from the ship's kitchen. This consisted mostly of a handful of rice, tinned vegetables and a few stingy bits of pink bully beef coated in watery, grey gravy.

The water in the cabin had been cut off and Anna had to wait for an hour to clean her teeth in the women's communal bathroom, where the tap handles for the showers had been removed and she was obliged to share a basin of water with *Kleine* Kiki. Having washed as best they might, the little maid would return to the cabin with a wet towel to dutifully wipe her mistress down. Anna did the same for her drunken, mumbling and often pathetically weeping father.

The journey to the coast took four days and nights of sweltering heat. The ship's fans were no longer working, adding to the misery on board. It was rumoured that three elderly passengers had died of heat exhaustion.

When at last the *Witvogel* reached the mouth of the long, winding river that led to the port of Tjilatjap, some eleven kilometres inland, the despondent mood on board changed despite the fear of the sudden appearance of the Japanese. At least the passengers would be able to go ashore. They speculated that they'd be able to purchase food to bring back on board, as well as have a good wash, a general clean-up and get their laundry done.

In the shared cabin there was a general mood of renewed hope for the first time since they had left Batavia. The de Klerks, pusillanimous male and three females, and the Van Heerdens, drunken and self-pitying male and three females, ceased their bickering for the duration of the journey upriver. The three de Klerk women commenced brushing, rouging, powdering and lipsticking, a process that took all their attention as they primped and tarted themselves up for the visit ashore.

Katerina, with the help of Anna and *Kleine* Kiki, attempted to do the same. Anna even dug up a chocolate-brown linen suit from the trunk for her stepmother to wear. To this she added white gloves and a small brown straw hat sporting the grandiose tail feather of a golden pheasant. Finally, standing back – or as far back as she could in the crowded cabin – she pronounced her stepmother the prettiest of all the women. Which, it should be said, was not a major achievement and earned sour looks from the three other adult women.

Only Piet Van Heerden, who had somehow sobered up sufficiently to be aware of the events around him, seemed indifferent to the prospect of going ashore. Handing Anna a fat roll of high-denomination guilder notes, he instructed her to purchase as much brandy or Scotch whiskey or both as she and *Kleine* Kiki could carry and load into the canvas bag that hung from the back of Katerina's wheelchair.

'Find a Chink, you hear? A Chinaman always has contraband and black-market goods. Don't pay him what he asks, but pay what you have to.' His bloodshot eyes looked directly at her, imploring. 'Please, *lieveling*, don't come back empty-handed.' Anna noted for the first time that his huge hands shook uncontrollably.

'Papa, you must stop drinking like this!' she begged, as she had done every day since they'd come on board.

'Ja, ja, soon, when we get to New Zealand.' She noted for the first time the coin-sized patches of grey that had appeared amongst the ginger growth on his unshaven face. 'Don't forget, all the bottles you can carry, *mijn lieveling*!'

The *Witvogel* struggled up the turgid river, passing two ships that had attempted to carry escaping Dutch citizens to safety but had run aground, the rusty vessels now stranded on the brown mudflats. When at last the ship reached Tjilatjap at about three in the afternoon, the port was littered with sunken and abandoned ships. From its initial appearance, it seemed an unpropitious place to make any kind of repairs. An hour later, at about four o'clock on the afternoon of the 4th of March, the dirty, hungry and generally exhausted passengers from the *Witvogel* were allowed to go ashore.

The local population seemed less hostile than they'd been in the capital. The Javanese are natural traders and the unexpected arrival of a ship was an opportunity, perhaps their last, to charge exorbitant prices for goods and services to passengers who, they soon discovered, were desperate for any tinned fish, meat, vegetables, coffee, tea and condensed milk – in fact anything edible that wouldn't spoil. Fruit-sellers, especially those with fruit that might keep for a few days, such as oranges and mangoes, were asking and getting unheard-of prices, and the locals were soon scurrying back to outlying orchards to replenish supplies. People swarmed to local native restaurants and the marketplace; the three hotels in the river-port town were overrun with passengers wanting to eat and bathe or take a shower. The owners promptly trebled their room and dining prices and then closed their doors for fear of being overwhelmed.

The local Javanese, many of whom had appropriated the homes of the Dutch who had earlier left the town, were charging twenty guilders for a twenty-minute use of the washhouse. Many passengers, desperate for a wash, simply stripped and jumped into the river, unabashedly shedding their clothes down to their underpants or, in the case of the females, bloomers and bras, soaping themselves willy-nilly, their hands within their undies to get to their private parts. Smaller kids, male and female, ran joyfully into the water in the nude.

The Muslim locals were scandalised. While they were happy to capitalise on the misfortunes of the fleeing Dutch and take the exorbitant profits on offer, the public display of raw flesh by Dutch women confirmed their view of the perfidy of the infidel. These pink-skinned females, who had maintained their superiority and dominated their lives for many generations, confirmed the local mullah's assertion that they were as vile as pig meat and lower than village dogs. '*Haram!* Unclean!'

Anna left her stepmother in the care of *Kleine* Kiki at what was obviously once the private home of a Dutch family but was now occupied by an unsmiling native woman and her family who demanded twenty guilders for a small bar of soap and an hour's use of the outside washhouse. She paid the sum happily, leaving *Kleine* Kiki with more than sufficient money to go shopping afterwards for any supplies she might be fortunate enough to find, arranging to meet them in the town's square at eight o'clock that night. She departed to the sound of Katerina screaming at *Kleine* Kiki for not rinsing her hair correctly. *One day* Kleine *Kiki will have had enough and she'll walk out*, Anna thought to herself. Then she'd gone looking for Piet Van Heerden's proverbial Chinaman.

She found him after approaching the third Chinese merchant in the town. His name was Lo Wok and he claimed to possess four bottles of Scotch whiskey and three of Australian brandy, stock that had obviously once been the possession of a departed Dutch shopkeeper. Speaking in the local language, Anna enquired the price. His eyes narrowed and he demanded two hundred guilders, an outrageous sum that was ten times the usual value of the Scotch and brandy. Anna threw back her head and laughed. 'You insult me and my family by thinking of us as fools,' she declared, and named a price a quarter of what he suggested, knowing it was still an extortionate amount to pay.

Lo Wok wrung his hands. 'These are hard times. I too have a family I must feed.' He shook his head vigorously, naming a sum two-thirds of the original. Anna clicked her tongue several times, shaking her head in denial. 'I respect your worthy lineage, Lo Wok. Your esteemed ancestors are watching and what would they think of your lack of commonsense?' she chided him gently.

Lo Wok smiled, happy that this young girl standing in front of him was not going to be a pushover. All Chinese love the process of striking a bargain. 'Ahee! The Japanese are coming, they do not like the Chinese, I will not be allowed to run a shop, they will persecute me, anything could happen, there are hard times ahead,' he whined, looping the sentences together.

'Ha, precisely! Hard times! For you and for me, Lo Wok! So, it is time you showed some commonsense. The Japanese drink sake and if they want your Scotch and brandy they will not pay for it, they will simply confiscate it. The Muslims do not drink. The Dutch, those who can afford to drink Scotch and brandy, have all fled this town. I am your last customer and it is your good fortune that I am here at all. Now, tell me, Lo Wok, to whom do you intend to sell this Scotch and brandy for fifty-five guilders?' Anna said, slightly upping her previous offer to him.

'It is not enough. I have ten children and an extravagant wife. We must escape.'

Anna observed to herself that the Chinaman could not have been much more than in his mid-twenties. 'And at sixteen years old I am already the mother of five.' She shrugged. 'See? I exaggerate as well and as pointlessly as you do, Lo Wok,' Anna said, in this way telling the Chinese merchant that she knew he was lying while, at the same time, careful to ensure he didn't lose face.

'Sixty, I cannot accept less.'

Anna nodded though it was still three times above the usual retail price. 'Let me see the merchandise,' she asked.

Lo Wok left and shortly afterwards emerged with a wooden case containing the Scotch and brandy. She examined the sealed tops of each of the seven bottles to see that they hadn't been broken. The red wax on one of them, a bottle of Scotch, had a slightly pinkish colour and as they were all the same brand Anna pushed her fingernail into the seal to discover that it was soft, the consistency of candle wax. In fact, it *was* candle wax. She twisted the seal and it came away immediately without resistance. Pulling the cork from the bottle she brought it to her nose and her nostrils were suddenly assailed by the sharp tang of stale urine.

'Do you have a glass?' she asked the Chinaman.

'No glass!' Lo Wok said hastily.

'Would you like a drink from the bottle, then? A toast to

escaping our mutual danger?' Anna smiled sweetly, proffering him
the bottle of urine.

'No drinkie from bottle!' Lo Wok said, shaking his head
vigorously.

Anna retested the seals of each of the remaining six bottles
with a fingernail, then calculated the sum minus the bottle of
piss and, peeling off the correct amount from the bundle her
father had given her, handed it to him. Lo Wok accepted the
money, and smiling and shaking his head said ruefully, 'If you
were Chinese I would make you my number-one wife.'

'Ha! If you cheat like this in business then you would cheat
on me also. I would refuse,' she said haughtily, stooping and
lifting the wooden crate to her shoulders.

Lo Wok turned and shouted a name in the direction of the
back of the small shop. Moments later a Javanese lad of perhaps
thirteen appeared. 'Carry the box for the missee,' he instructed
the boy.

The lad, whose name was Budi, asked Anna where she
was going and she told him the main town square to meet
her stepmother and her maid. 'It's a big square, Miss,' he said
doubtfully.

'It shouldn't be too difficult. My stepmother is in a
wheelchair. She is wearing a brown straw hat with a long
golden feather; we should find her easily enough.' She turned
to face the teenage boy. 'Have you eaten your dinner?' Anna
asked.

'No,' he said. 'I only finish at Lo Wok's at nine o'clock
tonight.'

She had an hour to wait before meeting Katerina and *Kleine
Kiki* in the square and Anna suddenly realised she was starving.
'Come, I'll buy you dinner, Budi. Do you know a good place?'

'Yes, Miss, the very best – my mother works there,' he said ingenuously.

He led Anna to an eatery close by, a small place like hundreds of similar ones in the towns and cities of Java. The place must have had a good reputation because it was heavily patronised by the local Javanese. Budi pointed out a group of about a dozen men drinking from bottles of the local beer. 'Truck drivers,' he said. Anna took this to mean that the eatery was of good repute, truck drivers always knowing the best places to eat. Budi's mother was the cook and she fed them royally; at the end of the meal she called her son over and spoke to him. He returned to where Anna sat. 'My mother wants to know how come your eyes are so blue. Javanese women do not have blue eyes.'

Anna laughed. 'I am only half Javanese, my father is Dutch.'

Budi returned to his mother and then back to Anna. He grinned. 'She wants to know which half is Javanese.'

Anna laughed. 'That's easy, my heart. My heart is Javanese.' In fact, this is what Anna had always privately felt. Her mind was Dutch but her heart belonged to her mother's people.

Budi dutifully returned to the open wood fire where his mother was cooking vegetables in a wok, the smell of spices and frying shallots pervading the air. He soon returned. 'My mother says her son does not have to pay for food in her kitchen and the Javanese half of you is free.' He shrugged, spreading his hands, very proud of his mother. 'So, Miss, there is nothing to pay.'

'What about the Dutch part?' Anna teased. 'Should it not pay its half?'

'No!' Budi declared, but then seemed unsure. 'I will ask,' he said, trotting off once more.

He returned, his face serious. 'My mother says the Dutch half already has too many troubles. Next time, when you come back, the Dutch half can pay.'

Anna thanked the woman, feeling cheerful for the first time since they'd left Batavia, laughing as they left, knowing that Budi, once they'd reached the town square, would receive a generous tip, more than the meal would have cost her.

The boy had been right; it was a big square filled with hawkers and people strolling, an area where a couple, even with one of them in a wheelchair, could easily be swallowed in the crowd. It was almost eight o'clock and Katerina was a stickler for being on time. It was almost a passion with her. Because she was incapacitated it had become important to be punctual. Amongst her worst tantrums were those when she thought someone in the family was dawdling and they'd be late for an appointment.

Budi put down the wooden crate beside a bench. 'Sit, Miss, I will go and look. A wheelchair with a woman and a maid, you say?' He set off immediately at a trot.

'Her name, the maid's, is *Kleine* Kiki,' Anna shouted at his departing form.

'*Kleine* Kiki, a feather in a straw hat!' he called back, not looking, but raising his arm.

Anna sat on the bench for a good hour. It was almost dark and the street lamps and those in the square had come on. A blur of bats passed squeaking overhead. If anything, there seemed to be even more people strolling in the square and she felt safe enough, although she was becoming increasingly concerned about the whereabouts of Katerina and *Kleine* Kiki. It simply wasn't like her stepmother. Moreover, while it was a big square, it wasn't *that* big and the boy should have long since found them.

Two slightly inebriated American pilots walked up to the bench and propositioned her, but prepared to leave politely when they realised she was not for hire.

'Perhaps you should not be here, the Japanese, they are soon coming,' Anna said, carefully phrasing the English words.

'We're outa here in the morning, ma'am,' one of them replied. Then touching his cap he said, 'Sorry to – er . . .'

'That's alright,' Anna said, dismissing them with a quick smile.

It was shortly after the Yanks had left that Budi emerged out of the dimness beyond the nearest lamplight. Behind him were four barefooted urchins pushing a wheelchair.

'I found it, the wheelchair!' Budi called out. He turned and looked at the wheelchair and shrugged. 'But it is empty, Miss!' Drawing closer he said, 'I promised these boys ten cents each if they brought it to show you. They say it is theirs,' he added. 'They will sell it to you for four guilders.' The wheelchair unmistakably belonged to Katerina, the canvas bag was still attached to the back of the handlebars. 'They were racing it in the square,' Budi explained.

Anna felt her heart pounding. 'They have stolen it! They have taken it from my stepmother and *Kleine* Kiki!' she accused. 'We must call the police!' she shouted, almost hysterical.

'No, Miss, I asked them. They found it by the river. There was no one there, it was empty,' Budi explained again. Then he added in a reasoned manner, 'If they had stolen it and done what you say, they would have hidden it and would not be racing it in the town square.'

'Oh, my God!' Anna exclaimed. 'Where? Where did they find it exactly?'

'On the old oil jetty,' one of the urchins volunteered. From behind his back he produced Katerina's now rather battered little brown straw hat with the golden pheasant feather. 'There was also this, it was caught in the planks,' the urchin explained.

Anna was battling to make sense of what she was hearing. 'A guilder each if they take me there, to the jetty,' she cried urgently, snatching the hat with its ridiculous feather from the boy's grasp and clasping it to her breast.

One of the urchins moved up to Budi and spoke to him quietly, cupping his mouth so his voice wouldn't carry. Budi turned to face Anna. 'Is that on top of the guilder each for the sale of the wheelchair and the ten cents each for showing you?' Budi, not wishing to be seen to take sides, indicated the urchin asking the question with a backwards nod of his head.

'Yes, yes! Just take me there!' Anna was close to weeping, not caring about the money.

'It is dark, you won't see nothing,' one of the smaller urchins volunteered.

'Shurrup, stupid!' another cried, elbowing him in the ribs.

Budi loaded the wooden crate onto the seat of the wheelchair and the urchins set off followed by Anna and Budi. They crossed to the far side of the square in the direction of the river and soon entered the docks area where only an occasional electric light shone from the high doorway of a *godown*. Anna made out the shape of a crane against the darkening sky and somewhere a night bird called out. Then she found herself walking along an unlit section of the docks and could hear the sharp slap of the river against the harbour wall. Finally they arrived at the oil jetty. Water lapped softly around the dark pylons, its wooden decking extending out into the river that was now in total darkness. There was no way of gauging the length of the jetty. Anna saw immediately that a search was pointless, but she nevertheless began to walk along it and into the dark. 'Careful, Miss!' one of the urchins shouted. 'It is not safe, there are some planks missing!'

The walk to the oil jetty had calmed her a little. She turned to Budi. 'Where is the nearest police station?'

'In de Kaap *Straat*,' Budi said. 'It is not the main one, but my mother knows the sergeant there.'

Anna pointed to the four urchins. 'They must come with us,' she said.

Although she spoke in the local language so that the four boys were perfectly capable of understanding her demand that they accompany her, they nevertheless waited for Budi to address them. Anna was unable to see their reactions to her reiterated request, but when he returned the short distance to where she stood, he said, 'No, Miss, they will not go, they do not like the police.'

Anna sighed, knowing she would need them to make a statement. 'Two guilders!' she called into the dark, knowing it was a sum they simply couldn't refuse but also knowing that their presence as witnesses was essential. They agreed at once; it was not every day four street kids came across a walking goldmine. In all, Anna now owed each of them four guilders and ten cents, a month's wages for a dockworker and clearly downright robbery.

A lone Javanese policeman reading a newspaper, with his feet on the desk, was on duty at the police station as they entered the single room, which had three fly-blown shaded light bulbs hanging from the ceiling that made the interior seem almost dim and tinged it a yellowish colour. The floor consisted of bare boards, the only furniture being a desk and a chair together with a battered filing cabinet against the back wall. Anyone coming into the room would be forced to stand. There was a picture of Queen Wilhelmina on the wall above the filing cabinet, and a corkboard with multiple small pieces of paper overlapping each other covering its surface. On the wall directly facing the desk was a pendulum clock in a cracked glass case.

The policeman glanced up briefly as they entered to determine that they were not Dutch, then returned to reading his newspaper. The room seemed crowded after they'd all entered; the wheelchair, its seat now containing the crate of grog, would have appeared to the policeman – that is, if he'd been looking – as some kind of evidence.

'Good evening, Corporal,' Budi said, granting the policeman an immediate promotion. Ignoring the salutation, the cop took his time lowering the newspaper. No doubt he intended to make them feel ill at ease in his presence.

'Yes, what do you want?' he asked brusquely.

'Sergeant Khamdani,' Budi answered confidently. Anna was gaining an increasing admiration for the teenager.

'He is off duty. You must deal with me,' the policeman said self-importantly, his boots remaining on the desk.

'A policeman with his dirty boots on the desk is not usually ready to conduct a murder investigation,' Anna snapped, her voice somewhat imperious.

'Murder? You wish to report a murder?' the man said, hastily removing his feet from the desk.

'Yes – or possibly a drowning,' Anna replied.

'A murder or a drowning, which is it?' the policeman asked, somewhat regaining his composure. 'Do you have the body?'

'No,' Anna said.

The cop's face brightened. 'Ah, I see, a missing person. These days we have hundreds of missing persons.' He laughed, enjoying himself. 'Dutch missing persons running away from the Japanese! All the Europeans, they want now to be missing persons.' He giggled. 'We cannot take seriously a report on missing persons.'

'A cripple in a wheelchair,' Budi said. Then pointing he added, 'We have the wheelchair. These boys found it on the old oil jetty.'

Anna was growing impatient. 'I want someone to investigate. My stepmother, a Dutch woman, who is a cripple, has disappeared and so has her maid. We have found her wheelchair on a jetty by the river. I am reporting it and wish a search to commence immediately.'

The policeman seemed impervious to Anna's strident demands, knowing she was a woman and mistaking her for a local Javanese. He shrugged. 'It is night. Dark!' he pointed out, as if she was patently stupid.

'Her body may be in the river. Is there not a police boat with searchlights?'

The policeman leaned forward, squinting slightly as he examined the station clock. Anna realised that he was short-sighted. 'No, the engine is broken.' He sat back again and spread his hands. 'But the body, it is now one kilometre down the river.' He pointed to the clock. 'It is now ten o'clock, eight o'clock the tide goes out. The body is long gone, it will be tomorrow's fish food.'

'You must take down a statement from us,' Anna insisted.

The policeman leaned forward, squinting again, looking directly at her. 'Why have you got blue eyes?' he asked.

'Because I am half Dutch and it is my stepmother who is missing and I wish to make a statement. These kids are potential witnesses, you must have their names on record – they found the wheelchair.' She was still clutching Katerina's hat. 'And this hat, it was hers, my stepmother's. It is evidence.'

'That is a very long feather,' the policeman said infuriatingly. 'Very beautiful feather, what bird is that?'

'Statement!' Anna shouted.

The police officer was suddenly bored. 'Come back tomorrow,' he said, picking up the newspaper, then leaning back in his chair and replacing his boots on the desk. 'Go!' he shouted from behind the newspaper, sending the street kids scurrying out of the little police post.

Outside Budi tried to comfort Anna. 'I will tell my mother, who will tell Sergeant Khamdani.'

'Fish food!' Anna exclaimed, still furious. 'How *dare* he?'

'We must pay these street kids,' Budi reminded her. 'It is four guilders and ten cents each.'

Anna peeled off a twenty-guilder note, absent-mindedly handing it to Budi. 'Tell them to keep the change,' she said, not caring. 'Ask them to come back tomorrow at twelve o'clock.'

Budi looked doubtful. 'I don't think they will come, Miss.' Then he added, 'They are now very rich.' The four kids thanked Anna and scampered off. She could hear their joyful shouts long after she could no longer see them.

Anna took a ten-guilder note from Piet Van Heerden's roll, which she casually observed had grown a fair bit thinner. *It's only going to go on Scotch and brandy*, she decided. 'Here, Budi,' she said, handing the boy the note. 'Lo Wok will be angry that you have spent so much time with me.'

Budi seemed overwhelmed; it was more than his mother earned in two months while cooking twelve hours a day. He'd seen Anna's generosity to the street kids but had realised that she had no alternative but to pay them. He knew he could have successfully bribed them with a lot less, maybe one guilder and fifty cents maximum for everything.

'It is too much,' he said to Anna, hanging his head.

'No, no – you have earned it, every cent,' Anna replied. 'But now you must return to Lo Wok. You must tell him it is my fault you are late.'

'Then let me first push this wheelchair to the boat, Miss.'

'No, Budi, I need time to think. I can manage it. Can you ask Lo Wok to let you come to the police station at noon tomorrow?'

'I will be there, my mother also,' he assured her, reluctantly making his departure.

Anna glanced at her watch, a gift from her papa on her fifteenth birthday. She remembered Katerina's remark at breakfast when Anna was unable to stop glancing at her wrist, pleased as punch with her birthday gift. 'It's cheap rubbish, not even gold-plated!' her stepmother had remarked.

Anna began to push the wheelchair with the crate of grog in the direction of the ship, trying to make sense of what she knew. *Kleine* Kiki, Anna decided, had finally reached her breaking point. Anna was too confused in her own mind to know how she felt or, for that matter, if she felt anything at all. She'd always been dutiful to her stepmother while secretly hating her, and had often enough wished her dead. But wishing and actually doing are not the same thing. It was *Kleine* Kiki who, from childhood, had borne the real brunt of Katerina's bitterness and resentment. The little maid was an orphan and had never received a salary; only her clothes and food were supplied. Anna, ashamed that she had never thought about it until that moment, realised that *Kleine* Kiki was utterly powerless and had nowhere to go. Today she'd handed her sufficient guilders to purchase tinned food on the black market. It was enough to keep the little maid going, if she was careful, for several months. Perhaps she'd seen her opportunity and taken it. Anna wasn't sure that she blamed her. She was half Javanese herself and she'd often noted that the Dutch treated her mother's people as if they didn't quite exist on the same human plane. Somehow, in a subtle way – and this included even her – the dark-skinned population was regarded as a lower order, one with less intelligence and feelings, not capable of the same emotional reactions as the Dutch.

The scenario for the murder seemed obvious to her. *Kleine* Kiki had ritually wheeled her stepmother around the *Grootehuis* estate every evening before drinks on the front lawn. Having been bathed and shampooed in the washroom of the Javanese woman's recently appropriated home, and after being cooped up for nearly six days in their vile cabin, Katerina would have demanded an outing along the river. She hated crowds, thinking the people were staring at her. So despite its dreary *godowns* and unkempt riverbank with rusty winches, cables and machinery half-hidden amongst the coarse overgrown grass, she would have preferred the lonely towpath to the chatter of the town square. They would have eventually reached the jetty and, with nobody to observe them, *Kleine* Kiki, with a pocketful of money for the first time in her life, had tipped her mistress into the water.

Anna asked herself why the little maid would not have simply pushed her stepmother into the river, chair and all, but then thought of the years of persecution the diminutive little girl had suffered at the hands of Katerina. Anna thought *Kleine* Kiki would have felt her chance had come at last and she would have actively and angrily pushed Katerina out of the chair. The street kids had been emphatic that they'd found the wheelchair intact and abandoned on the jetty, the straw hat stuck between two boards, the golden pheasant tail feather announcing its presence. A girl who had just turned thirteen, she reasoned, would hardly be capable of a premeditated murder. It would have been a sudden, irresistible impulse. Katerina would have said something cruel and the little teenager, hardly aware of what she was about to do, would have given her a violent push, possibly grabbing her by both shoulders and shaking her violently, then catapulted her out of the chair and over the edge of the pier.

Anna was amazed at her own dispassion and ability to think in a crisis, particularly this crisis. She readily admitted to herself that grieving for her stepmother was hypocritical nonsense. Yet nobody had the right, no matter what the circumstances, to take another life. As Anna pushed the wheelchair with its cargo of whiskey and brandy towards the *Witvogel* she tried to think how she would break the news of her stepmother's death to her father. If he was drunk, as was almost certain, would he be capable of registering the news or even showing regret? She'd never quite understood the relationship between the two of them. She didn't even know if they still made love, although they shared the same bed and he would dutifully, and even sometimes laughingly, carry Katerina into the bedroom. He must have carried her to the bathroom as well. It was, she decided, one of those inexplicable bitter–sweet relationships people endure rather than part from each other.

Apart from her own illegitimate birth, she'd never heard a breath of scandal involving her father. And she was sure she would have done so if there had been any. Servants inevitably talked, the rumour mill in Batavia was widespread and ground exceedingly fine. A big city, as far as gossip and scandal were concerned Batavia was like a small village. If he'd visited a prostitute or kept a mistress, she believed the gossips within the *kampong* would have known soon enough. A wagging tongue was often the only revenge at a servant's disposal.

Besides, Anna recognised that Piet Van Heerden was not a circumspect man. He was clumsy both in appearance and by nature, a forthright, some said foolish, man. Anna knew that one way or another he would have inadvertently spilled the beans. He was sometimes shrewd, but it was not in his nature to do anything clandestine. Some said Piet Van Heerden was his own worst enemy and, to extend the metaphor, almost always ended up shooting himself in the foot.

She'd reached the top of the gangplank to be met by the first mate, whose name she had since learned was Van der Westhuisen, Gert Van der Westhuisen. '*Goed avend, mijnheer,*' she said politely, wishing him good evening. She'd learned, along with the other passengers, that the confrontation her father had had with him over the allocation and appropriation of their cabins the first evening they'd come on board was not an isolated incident. The first mate seemed to actively enjoy being disliked by the passengers and had been duly nicknamed 'Hitler's willing helper'. Now he planted himself directly in front of her at the top of the gangplank, his legs parted, intent on blocking her passage. 'And what have we got here, Miss Van Heerden?' he asked, looking into the crate. Then he added, 'I say! You got a bargain!'

'I beg your pardon?' Anna asked.

'In exchange for the old sow!' His smile reminded Anna of a reptile. 'Three bottles of Scotch, three of brandy, not bad, not bad at all!'

'When you were born your mother must have thrown away her baby and kept the afterbirth!' Anna spat. It was an insult she'd once heard when two labourers had been quarrelling in the *godown* at *Grootehuis*.

Pushing downwards on the handles of the wheelchair, the wheels lifted and she manoeuvred it around his parted legs. 'Excuse me,' she said, her heart pumping furiously as she wheeled the chair past the left side of him, the back of her right hand inadvertently brushing against his blue serge trousers. Then she continued down the main chalked corridor towards the entrance to below-deck.

'I could get you a cabin to yourself, Miss Van Heerden. All you'd have to do is be nice to all the ship's officers!' he called after her.

Anna stopped and turned to face him. She was furious, and despite an inner voice cautioning her to ignore him, she sneered, 'And you'd be my pimp, no doubt?'

Anna reached their cabin door, hoping like hell that the de Klerks were still ashore. The captain had encouraged passengers to remain ashore as the repairs would take several days. He'd even promised they'd clean up the ship. The three de Klerk women had talked excitedly about finding a hotel. As Anna slid back the cabin door, to her utter amazement and confusion she was confronted by the distraught and tear-stained face of *Kleine* Kiki. The maid saw the wheelchair and burst into fresh tears and began to howl, clasping her hands to her chest as if in prayer. Anna wheeled the chair into the cabin, then moved past it to where *Kleine* Kiki sat on the bottom bunk. 'What happened, *Kleine* Kiki?' she demanded, standing over the diminutive servant. Anna was too wrung out and confused to show any emotion. On the top bunk her father snored.

'She's dead!' *Kleine* Kiki howled.

'Yes, I know she's dead! How did she die? Did you push her?'

Kleine Kiki shook her head furiously in denial, but could only manage fresh howls of despair.

Anna realised that she was being too harsh and sat beside her and took her in her arms. 'Come now, *Kleine* Kiki, tell me what happened. Tell Anna what happened, darling.'

But *Kleine* Kiki, burying her head further into Anna's bosom, continued to sob. Anna held her, stroking the back of her hair. 'There, there, try to calm down. Tell me what happened. Slowly, there's no hurry,' she said soothingly. *Kleine* Kiki's reactions were sufficient to convince Anna that she'd possibly made a wrong assumption.

Kleine Kiki suddenly pulled her head away from Anna's breast and looked directly up at her, choking back her grief. 'She said she wanted to fly!'

'Fly? She was a cripple!' Anna exclaimed, almost laughing.

'Just once! She said she wanted to fly just once,' the little maid sobbed.

Anna waited for *Kleine* Kiki to continue but the thirteen-year-old was silent, sniffing and sobbing intermittently. They were sitting on the bottom bunk and now Anna released her and, standing up, found a glass. She reached out and broke the seal and opened one of the bottles of brandy she'd pushed aboard. Then she splashed a thimbleful of the liquid into the bottom of the glass. 'Here, drink this,' she instructed, holding out the glass to *Kleine* Kiki. 'All in one gulp.'

The little maidservant took the glass in both hands and brought it obediently up to her lips, throwing back her head and swallowing. The shock of the fiery liquid hitting her throat suddenly widened her eyes, an expression of shock and repulsion on her small tear-stained face. Then she began to cough and splutter, dropping the glass to the cabin floor. Anna grabbed her and drew her into an embrace, patting her firmly on the back several times. After a while the little maid grew calmer and then, at last, was silent. Piet Van Heerden continued to snore in a drunken stupor on the top bunk.

'Now,' Anna said gently, 'from the beginning, tell me everything. Everything that happened from the time I left you and my stepmother at that woman's washhouse. She, my stepmother, was shouting at you about her hair, about not rinsing it properly. Start from there.'

Kleine Kiki, benefiting from the effects of the brandy, sniffed and gathered herself together. She began slowly, concentrating, wanting to get it exactly right. 'After I'd dressed *Mevrouw* Van Heerden she said we must go for a walk. I must push her along beside the river. She didn't want to see any more people. She hated people, she said, and wasn't going back to that stinking cabin and those vile de Klerk women.

'"It's only a few more days on the ocean and then they'll be gone and we'll have lots of fresh air in Australia," I replied.

'"He wants to go to New Zealand," she said.

'"New Zealand is also nice," I replied.

'"What would you know?" she scolded me.'

Kleine Kiki looked up at Anna. 'Is New Zealand a nice place?' she asked.

'Very nice, they have lots of sheep,' Anna answered.

Kleine Kiki continued. 'Then *mevrouw* was silent and we had reached the river. It smelled bad and the water was dirty, and one place we passed smelled of rotten eggs, but she said we must go on. Then she started to talk, but it was not to me, it was to *Mijnheer* Piet. "Piet, I can take this jump. It will win me the blue ribbon.

I know I can!" Then her voice grew angry. "You have never believed in me, Piet Van Heerden! With this horse I can fly. You will see for yourself, I will fly over that jump and you can't stop me! You always want to stop me because you know in your heart I am better than you!"' *Kleine* Kiki drew breath. 'Then she was silent for a long while and we reached the path leading to the jetty. Then she started to weep. I stopped pushing and put my hand on her shoulder. "What is it, *mevrouw?*" I asked. She shrugged my hand away. "Go away, you little shit! You think you can do anything just because you can walk!" she yelled.'

Kleine Kiki paused, then went on. 'We had reached the jetty and I pushed her onto it. "Leave me!" she shouted. "Wait for me here!" I stood and watched as she wheeled herself along the jetty. She stopped once and took off her hat. I started to walk towards her to take it from her. She must have heard my footsteps and she turned. "Stay away!" she shouted. Then she dropped the hat between two boards so the feather stuck up in the air. "Feathers can fly and so can I!" she yelled and scooted off in the wheelchair, stopping just short of the end of the jetty. It was a long pier and stretched out quite far into the river. Tall old tree trunks held it up at the end and it was a big drop to the water. "Be careful, *mevrouw!*" I shouted, because by now she was right up to the end, to the edge. I couldn't help myself and I started to run towards her. Then, when I'd nearly reached her, she shouted out, "Look, Piet, I am flying!" and she pushed herself out of the chair and then spread her arms like wings and crashed into the water below.' *Kleine* Kiki brought her hands up to cover her face, her brow touching her knees. 'She only came up once,' she sobbed in a small voice. After a while she looked up at Anna. 'It's not my fault, Anna. I can't swim. I just ran back here.'

'Come, *Kleine* Kiki,' Anna said, taking the terribly

distressed little maid into her arms once again, stroking her dark hair. 'Come now, it's nobody's fault, you hear? She was a bitter, broken and frustrated woman and she decided she'd finally had enough.' They were the kindest words she could think to say about her deceased stepmother.

'I always did my best, Anna. Honest!' *Kleine* Kiki cried. 'Are you going to throw me out onto the street?'

Despite herself, Anna laughed. 'You are as much our family as I am, *Kleine* Kiki. Not that it's much of a family, mind you. Wherever I go you can come also. We will be together until one day you meet a handsome boy with rich parents, then I shall be your bridesmaid.'

'No, no, I will never leave you, Anna. I will be your maid always.'

'I think, perhaps, my friend, hey? I don't think I need a maid. We will be together, you and me, *Kleine* Kiki. We will take care of each other.'

In the bunk above them Piet Van Heerden continued to snore.

CHAPTER SEVEN

*'If you find this woman and she is floating in the river
and you fish her out, you can see she is dead.
Even some places the crabs have eaten her.
Anyone can see! If I cook a chicken I can see if it is dead.
I don't need a certificate to say this chicken is dead!'*
Mother Ratih
Kampong cook, Tjilatjap

IT WAS CLOSE TO midnight when Anna managed to get *Kleine* Kiki to crawl into Katerina's bunk. The little maid soon fell into an exhausted sleep. Anna then climbed to the top bunk and proceeded to slap and shake her papa until he came around sufficiently to help with the removal of his stained and stinking clothes. She placed a towel over his dirty underpants so that he could remove them himself. 'Papa, take off your underpants,' Anna shouted. He grunted, then managed to push them no further than his knees, from where she removed them. With the towel protecting his modesty, she then handed him a wet flannel so that he could attempt to wash himself around the crotch, turning away from him so that he could perform the task privately. He grunted again and she turned back to see that he was holding out the washcloth, which she gingerly accepted, dropping it to the floor as she had done with his underpants. She handed him a fresh pair, pulling them over his ankles and up to his knees so he could do the rest himself, then she

removed the towel that covered his midriff and washed the rest
of his body with the wet towel. He smelled vile, of stale urine
and sick. But at least, she thought, his willingness to remove
his own underpants and wash his private parts indicated that he
still retained a little self-respect. Finally, and with a great deal
of difficulty, Anna managed to dress him in a pair of long khaki
pants and a white singlet she'd found in the trunk. Washed and
in clean clothes, Piet Van Heerden collapsed back into his bunk.
'In New Zealand – in New Zealand,' he mumbled over and over,
the words becoming a drunken mantra in his grog-addled mind.
Anna climbed down from the bunk realising that in his present
state of befuddlement, it would be pointless telling her father
the news of Katerina's death.

While most people were ashore, the laundry had been
cleaned and disinfected and the ship had taken on fresh water.
Anna was too numb and distraught from the events of the
evening to cry or even attempt to sleep. As a penance that she
would have been unable to explain, even to herself, she took
the disgusting bundle of her father's accumulated soiled linen
to the laundry. She could as easily have taken it ashore in the
morning. Perhaps it was out of some innate sense of pride,
some feeling that by handing the foul-smelling clothes to a
local washerwoman and paying her extra, even double, to clean
them would prove to be a further degradation of her family. A
moment's thought would have told her that there was no need
to try to preserve the good standing of the family, and that there
would be no further humiliation perpetrated by her drunken
father that she hadn't already endured over the past days.

Despite the late hour all the tubs were being used by women
who were seizing the time as an opportunity to do their laundry.
They were, perhaps, too poor or mistrustful to place their clothes

in the hands of a native woman. Her father's clothes smelled to high heaven, a mixture of stale brandy, piss, vomit and on one pair of underpants the dried and crusted evidence where he'd shat. The women standing in the queue with Anna soon located the source of the smell pervading their nostrils. Disgusted, they sniffed pointedly, sighed and clucked their tongues, one of them demanding she go elsewhere. 'Where?' Anna snapped back at her. 'This is the laundry, isn't it? My father is sick.'

'Ha, your father is a drunk!' the woman exclaimed, loud enough for everyone to hear. 'Those poor women who must share your cabin, it's disgusting.' The de Klerks had, unsurprisingly, been tattling to others.

Anna held her place in the queue, enduring several more insults before she was able to appropriate a tub for sufficient time to hastily wash and rinse the soiled clothes. But she was now faced with a different problem. Every inch of drying space had been taken up in the laundry and when she had gone into the women's bathroom thinking she might hang them in a disused shower recess, these too had been utilised by others.

'For three guilders you can hang them on my deck railing,' a woman's voice behind her said. Then she added, 'They will soon dry in the morning sun.'

Anna turned to see the large, moustachioed woman who had chastised her for trespassing on her square of deck when she'd farewelled me. This time she was wearing a pink smock, although it had the same hemline disparity as her other dress.

'Three guilders is a lot of money, *mevrouw*,' Anna said, knowing it was daylight robbery. She'd been generous with Piet Van Heerden's stash earlier when she'd been ashore, but this was different – this was blatant exploitation and pure greed.

'Suit yourself,' the woman sniffed. 'It's what we're charging.

We paid good money for our square! We're entitled. You people with your fancy cabins think you're superior,' she declared self-righteously.

'I will pay it,' Anna said resignedly, knowing her father would soon enough need the fresh clothes.

'Bring it up in the morning, ours is the railing where you stood saying goodbye to your boyfriend.' Anna realised that the woman must have been watching her on the departure afternoon. She confirmed this by adding, 'You will soon learn that men are not worth a woman's tears.'

'Except when they work hard for their money like your husband,' Anna said, her voice tinged with irony, reminding the woman that she had not forgotten their unpleasant confrontation.

'Ja, maybe,' the woman said, ignoring Anna's rebuttal and offering her further advice. 'Give them half a chance and they'll spend it on getting drunk and on whores, and the children wear rags and go barefoot!'

'I wouldn't know, mevrouw,' Anna replied, turning away in an attempt to terminate the conversation.

But the woman wouldn't let her go. 'You wouldn't know, hey? Ha! And your father is now suddenly a teetotaller?'

Anna turned to face her. 'How dare you!' she shouted angrily.

The woman shrugged, her expression phlegmatic. 'Everybody knows, my dear. Don't waste your tears on a drunk. Take it from me, they will get you nowhere. Making excuses for them is a waste of time. Take my advice, walk out on the useless bastard and get on with your life.' Then almost in the same breath her voice changed to a harder tone. 'Three guilders, I must have it tonight or I will sell the railing space to someone else – there are plenty of takers, I assure you.' Then her tone changed once again and she declared piously, 'Laundry dried in God's good sunlight is one of His real blessings.'

Anna was too exhausted to follow her conversational pyrotechnics and handed her three single guilder notes. '*Dank U, mevrouw*,' she said, thinking the misery of this day and night was never going to end.

'Be there sharp, seven o'clock. Hans, *mijn* husband, and I are going ashore. Don't be late! Bring your own pegs.'

It was 2 a.m. when Anna finally returned to the cabin. Piet Van Heerden was perched on the edge of the top bunk, both hands gripping the edge to steady himself, his long legs dangling in the air, big feet almost reaching *Kleine* Kiki's sleeping form on the bunk below. His chin rested on his chest so that all Anna could see was his hedgerow of fiercely tangled eyebrows and his shiny bald cranium. He looked up as Anna entered, his eyes bloodshot. A yellow stream of mucus had collected under his nose. 'Piss bottle!' he managed to say before his head sank back onto his chest with a grunt.

Anna dumped the pile of wet washing she was carrying into the defunct cabin basin and grabbed one of the two empty brandy bottles kept for this purpose and reached up to hand it to him. He released his hand from the edge of the bunk in an attempt to take the bottle, which caused him to suddenly sway forward dangerously.

'Careful, Papa!' Anna called out. 'Hold on!' She rushed forward, dropping the bottle to the floor, and with both hands held him by the waist to steady him until he managed to regain his grip on the bunk's edge.

'Piss!' he cried plaintively.

She'd changed her father's soiled trousers and underpants

on several occasions over the past few days, always taking care to place a towel over his midriff so he could, if he was capable, remove his underpants himself and wash his own scrotum. If he wasn't capable, she was forced to let his urine-soaked underpants dry on him until he was sober enough to remove them himself. Nevertheless, on several occasions when he'd been completely unable to manipulate his fingers, she'd been forced to tuck his penis back into his trousers and button up his fly. She was surprised then at the small size of his penis – not that she had any comparisons. Hitherto she'd never seen a male organ in the flesh, but her father was such a big man that she was surprised to see the little circumcised acorn peeping out of his unbuttoned fly. She'd even wondered to herself why men make such an enormous fuss over such a small and unattractive totem. But then, she remembered, judging from the feel when I had pressed against her body when we held each other and kissed, it was an organ that, when suitably aroused, was capable of surprising and spontaneous growth.

Anna was past caring. The thought of another pair of piss-stained trousers to launder was simply too much to bear. She reached down and retrieved the bottle from the floor and placed it on the bunk beside him, then quickly undid his fly buttons and found his flaccid appendage. Pulling it out, she picked up the brandy bottle in one hand and with the other she inserted the purple-tipped penis into the neck of the bottle, grateful that its smallness meant she didn't have to hold it in place while he emptied his bladder.

Piet Van Heerden released his stream with a grateful sigh, filling half the large brandy bottle. Anna unplugged his penis, restoring his modesty but leaving his fly buttons undone in anticipation of a future emergency.

With his bladder emptied her father seemed to recover somewhat, for he peered over the edge of the bunk to the one below. 'Where's your stepmother? Where's Katerina?' he asked lethargically, but then seemed to lose interest in his own question. 'Did you find a Chinaman?' he now enquired.

Anna wasn't sure which question to answer or whether to address either. 'Papa, it is past two o'clock in the morning. Go to sleep. I will talk to you tomorrow.' To her surprise Piet Van Heerden withdrew his legs back onto the bunk and lay down. '*Mijn lieveling,*' he croaked, 'in the morning we are going to New Zealand.'

'Yes, Papa, now go to sleep,' Anna said, though she knew she would find it impossible to sleep. In the morning she must force her father to eat something. He hadn't eaten in two days, not a mouthful. She glanced over at *Kleine* Kiki, her small face innocent in slumber. Then she wearily changed into her pyjamas and forced herself to go through the motions of folding her clothes neatly. She switched off the cabin light and climbed into the bottom bunk that was the de Klerks'.

Lying in the dark Anna felt utterly miserable and alone, but still was unable to cry. She was sticky from the tropical heat and itched under her arms and in her crotch. She reminded herself that she must stink and hadn't bathed or even washed herself from the neck down for the past twenty-four hours. She wondered if she had come out in a heat rash. She'd earlier cleaned her teeth and washed her face in the women's bathroom, but the impatient press of women behind her had made her afraid to complete any further ablutions.

Anna now realised, and felt immediately guilty, that she hadn't thought of her stepmother's suicide since returning to the cabin, except fleetingly when her father had mentioned

Katerina's name. She was far more concerned about getting on deck by 7 a.m. to hang out his laundry, afraid she'd be late and the fat woman and her husband, Hans, would have departed. Anna tried to assuage her guilt by attempting to recreate in her mind *Kleine* Kiki's telling of the bizarre and altogether ghastly incident at the old oil jetty. But all she could think of was the pheasant's golden tail feather absurdly sticking out of a crack in the boards. The next thing she knew it was 7.15 a.m.

Anna dressed in a blind panic, pulling on her knickers, jumping from one leg to another in her haste. *Kleine* Kiki was awake and dressed. 'Come quickly, grab the washing,' Anna shouted almost hysterically. The little maid moved over and took up the bundle of wet washing from the basin, holding it up to her chest, wide-eyed and confused. 'Upstairs! Fat woman! No, wait, I'll come!' Anna shouted, slipping her cotton dress over her head. 'Come quickly, *Kleine* Kiki!' she said urgently, moving in her bare feet to the cabin door and sliding it open. Then exclaiming, 'Pegs!' she turned and rushed back, pushing past the little maid as she reached for the cotton bag containing the clothes pegs.

They arrived to find the fat woman, who still hadn't offered her name or surname, positively bristling. 'You are late! We are late! Seven o'clock! I said, seven o'clock, you hear? You are lucky that I am a decent woman or we would be gone by now. *Mijn* husband Hans likes to get going before the heat is coming.'

Anna glanced over to where Hans, the fat woman's husband, stood nervously holding a basket and a folded paper parasol. The picture was the full comic skit of big woman and small downtrodden man. Anna had learned the nursery rhyme at school when she'd been young and taking her first English lessons. Now despite her embarrassment at being late and her private relief at finding the woman still waiting in her chalked square, the words leapt into her mind:

> Jack Sprat could eat no fat,
> His wife could eat no lean.
> And so, between the two of them,
> They licked the platter clean!

'I am very sorry, *mevrouw*, I overslept,' she apologised.

'In your nice comfortable cabin without the sun in your eyes at six o'clock in the morning!' She stabbed a fat finger at *Kleine* Kiki. 'And who is this? You have your own maid already? My goodness, some people with their airs and graces think they are better than others!'

'She is my little sister,' Anna lied.

'Umph! Maybe your father is not too particular, hey?'

Anna had had enough. 'Look, I'm sorry we've kept you. I've paid my three guilders. Can we hang out our washing or will I call *Mijnheer* Van der Westhuisen? He is a friend of mine.' It was Anna's second lie for the morning.

The threat of the odious first mate seemed to work. The woman nodded. 'We haven't got all day. It is not *me* who was late.'

'You may go at any time you wish, we know perfectly well how to hang out washing,' Anna said tartly.

'We must stay until it is done,' the woman insisted.

Anna looked about her. The chalked square was spotless

and contained a single large tin trunk secured by a heavy brass padlock. Painted on its lid in large white letters was the name H.J. Swanepoel. They'd obviously locked away their worldly goods for the day. Anna pointed to the trunk. 'It's okay, we won't steal it.'

The Dutch woman sniffed. '*Kom*, Hans,' she instructed. '*Wij gaan nu!*' She turned to Anna. 'We are coming in the afternoon back. The clothes, they must also be gone, you hear?'

'*Nee, Mevrouw* Swanepoel, we too have to go ashore!' Anna protested, knowing they would be at the police station at noon. 'We may not be back in time.'

The woman stuck out her palm. 'One guilder!'

Anna shook her head. 'Only if we get back after you do.'

'Fair enough,' Hans replied, nodding his head in agreement.

His wife cast him a dirty look. '*Kom*,' she huffed and moved off, leaving Jack Sprat to follow her with the basket and parasol.

Anna and *Kleine* Kiki arrived back at the cabin to find Anna's father seated on the edge of the bottom bunk. He'd somehow managed to climb down from the top one, the sleep having sobered him up sufficiently to make the attempt, although he'd bumped his nose and a trickle of blood, now stemmed, still glistened at the base of his nostrils. Several drops had landed on his knees and dried. He'd found the brandy bottle Anna had opened to give *Kleine* Kiki a nip and he was already bleary-eyed, hugging the bottle to his chest.

Anna found a facecloth still damp from the night before and wiped his nose clean of blood and mucus. 'Where's everybody?' Piet Van Heerden asked, looking around, his expression dazed.

Anna placed the facecloth in the basin and came to sit

beside him. 'Papa, it is not good news. Katerina committed suicide yesterday.'

He seemed to be thinking for several moments. 'Then she is not coming to New Zealand?' he asked in a querulous voice.

'Papa, listen, your wife, Katerina, is dead!' Anna said, raising her voice. *Kleine* Kiki started to whimper. Anna cast an impatient look at the little maid. 'It's over, pull yourself together, *Kleine* Kiki,' she said in a loud whisper.

'Pull together!' Piet Van Heerden mumbled. 'Pull together!' He looked up and giggled. 'Bitch! She was – bitch!' He shook his head several times, then slurred, 'Not nice – person.'

'Papa, please give me the brandy bottle!' Anna held out her hand for the bottle. 'You must stop this drinking!'

Her father pulled backwards, clutching the bottle even tighter to his chest. 'No! Mine!' he said, as if he was a small boy refusing to share a bag of lollies.

Anna sighed. 'Please, Papa, listen to me! Katerina is dead! We have to go ashore, you must pull yourself together.'

'Listen? Must listen! *Ja!* Dead – we must have tomb – stone. Bury with tomb – stone!' He seemed to find this exceedingly funny and started to cackle. 'Katerina – not coming to New – Zealand. *Goed! Ja*, that is *goed, lieveling!*' He raised the bottle and took a long swig, then shook his head. 'Dead – it is *goed* to be dead now! This is *goed* time to be dead.' He then commenced to weep, clutching the bottle. Anna put her arms around him. 'It's okay, Papa, I will stay with you.' Deep inside she knew she despised her father for his weakness.

The breakfast session wasn't crowded for a change because the wealthier passengers had stayed ashore for the night. Moreover, the ship had ordered in fresh supplies and there were hard-boiled eggs, fresh bread and two common types of cheese; no butter – but that was to be expected, the cheese was surprise enough. Anna took bread, cheese and two eggs down to the cabin, but Piet Van Heerden was back into his drinking routine and refused to eat. Anna tried to persuade him to get back into the top bunk, where he was out of the way if the de Klerks should return, but he refused. She managed to get him to pee into the second empty brandy bottle. Then covering the two bottles of urine with a towel she sent *Kleine* Kiki out to the women's toilet to empty and rinse them.

They packed clean undies and sarongs into a cotton bag, *Kleine* Kiki remembering to return the money Anna had given her for supplies the previous day. Anna still had her father's roll of banknotes, a considerable amount even after Lo Wok's unabashed greed and her own generosity to Budi and the street kids the previous evening. They took the wheelchair with them, thinking the police might require it as evidence.

Together they headed towards the house in which Katerina had been washed the previous day, even though several of the locals were touting the washrooms of their newly acquired residences. The prices, Anna noted, had fallen considerably overnight. The woman greeted them and demanded the same fee as the previous day. To Anna's surprise, *Kleine* Kiki piped up, quoting a Javanese proverb. 'Yesterday is a distant land. We will pay one guilder, already too much, and not a cent more.'

The woman thought for several moments, then reluctantly agreed. 'That is one guilder for each of you, yes?'

Kleine Kiki's expression was scornful. 'Do you take us for fools? That is for both of us *and* the soap. Yesterday you cheated us!'

The woman laughed, quoting yet another local proverb. 'She who leaves a golden egg while searching for hen eggs is a

fool,' she said. Then she agreed to the new sum and left to fetch
a bar of coarse homemade soap.

Anna grinned. 'I must take you shopping more often, *Kleine*
Kiki.'

Bathed and wearing fresh sarongs, a style of local dress Anna
enjoyed, they went shopping. As they'd expected, there wasn't
a tin of anything to be had in the entire town, the *Witvogel*'s
passengers having the previous day bought anything that
required a can-opener. However, the fruit and vegetable prices
had been reduced considerably as the locals had stocked up in
anticipation of a repeat of the previous day's demand. There now
appeared to be a glut. The hawkers and market women looked
sullen; they'd found their golden egg, but were now beginning to
realise that there wasn't going to be another. *Kleine* Kiki proved
again that she was a frugal and canny shopper.

The wheelchair was an ideal shopping cart and they
arrived at the police station ten minutes before midday with
a full load. 'Do you think the police will think it disrespectful
loading the wheelchair with shopping like this?' Anna asked the
little maid.

'*Titch!* They are men,' *Kleine* Kiki replied, dismissing the
notion with the wave of a hand. Freed of the presence of her
tyrannical mistress, the little maid was turning out to be a
delightful companion.

Budi and his mother were waiting outside the police station
when they arrived and they both greeted Anna with broad
smiles, seeming genuinely happy to see her. Anna introduced
Kleine Kiki and explained why she had come with her. Then
Budi's mother, who said her name was Ratih, offered her
condolences to Anna.

'Thank you, Mother Ratih,' Anna said, paying her respect

but averting her eyes so the cook couldn't read anything into them. It was not yet noon and so they waited. Anna, anxious not to appear aloof, asked Budi, 'Was Lo Wok happy for you to come?'

'Who has ever seen a happy Chinaman?' Ratih snorted, replying for her son. 'That one, he is only happy making a profit.'

'He said to tell you his offer still stands,' Budi said. Then he added, 'He didn't explain.'

'He wants me for his number-one wife, but first I must turn Chinese,' Anna laughed. 'By the way, how many children does he have? He is still a young man!'

'Just one, a girl. He is not happy and says his wife is cursed, what use is a girl?' Budi replied.

It was precisely noon and Anna, having for years been conditioned by her stepmother's fanatical punctuality, now said, 'Shall we go in?'

Sergeant Khamdani stood up from behind his desk immediately as they entered. He was a big man for a Javanese and also a little overweight, not yet fat but well on the way to being described as such. Anna suspected Budi's mother's cooking was to blame. Her failure to greet him with the usual respect as they entered, as might have been expected from a local woman to a police sergeant, made it readily apparent that the two of them were more than just professional friends. Budi too seemed comfortable in his presence, although he was quick to greet the policeman formally and then to introduce Anna and thereafter *Kleine Kiki*. He impressed Anna by remembering the maid's name, pronouncing the Dutch adjective perfectly. They all shook hands with the policeman.

Three teak and rattan chairs had been placed on the

interviewing side of the desk. Whoever had thought to bring them, probably Budi, hadn't anticipated the presence of *Kleine* Kiki.

'Sit, please,' the sergeant said, indicating the chairs.

'I will stand,' Budi said quickly, knowing that in the local pecking order, his male status overrode that of the maid. Anna, aware of this and of the pride of Javanese men, admired his manners. But *Kleine* Kiki, anxious to preserve the rightful order of things, would have none of it. 'No, it is my place to stand. It is an honour to be here,' she protested, showing that she too was not without manners.

The sergeant sat down. 'We must make a statement.' He glanced at Anna. 'I am sorry for last night, my colleague – his wife is sick with the malaria.' It was about as close as he, a male, could come to an apology to a woman.

They spent the next hour writing down the statement, Anna repeating the story she had told the policeman the previous evening, with Budi adding the details of his search in the square for the wheelchair. *Kleine* Kiki, who burst into frequent tears in the process, then told of the suicide incident.

Sergeant Khamdani wrote ponderously in longhand, frequently stopping to ask a question and once or twice how to spell a word. He was thorough and serious throughout. 'There is a problem,' he said when he'd finally completed the task. 'We have no body.'

'Yes, I was hoping we could get the police boat to do a search of the river,' Anna replied. She was anxious to give her stepmother a proper funeral and, as her father had insisted in his drunken raving, a headstone.

'Ah, it is broken,' the sergeant said, confirming the night policeman's assertion.

Ratih, who had hitherto remained silent, now leaned forward. 'They are all good-for-nothings, those water policemen! They drink beer all night at the *kampong* and say they are Muslims and order food when it is time to go home! Now their Dutch captain has left they no longer go on the river.'

The sergeant shrugged. 'What can I do?' he asked. 'They are not *Pak Polisi*. Water is a different precinct.'

'Tell me,' Ratih asked, 'how much will it take to make repairs to this boat? Ten guilders? Fifteen guilders?' She glanced at Anna, who nodded. 'Not a cent more, Ajun, you understand?'

Anna memorised his name, Ajun Khamdani. The policeman seemed like a decent, honest type.

'I will try,' he said, sighing, picking up the telephone and dialling what must have been the central police switchboard. 'Get me the Water Police,' he requested. He waited thirty seconds or so before he spoke into the receiver. 'Water Police, this is Sergeant Ajun Khamdani from Central Town District. We need to search the river for a Dutch national, a woman, who is believed to have committed suicide.' There was silence, then 'Yes, I know it is broken, but how much to fix it? When do we want it? Yes, this afternoon, of course! Yes, to the estuary, a thorough search.' Silence. 'That is too much, I can offer you fifteen guilders?' Silence. 'Wait, I will ask.' He cupped the receiver with his hand, turning to look at Anna. 'Twenty-five, the repairs are difficult and there is the fuel.' Anna nodded agreement. 'Okay, twenty-five!' The sergeant nodded his head, taking further instructions. 'Good! Excellent! Yes, I must be on board, also someone who can identify her body if you find it. Two o'clock, we will be there. Yes, twenty-five guilders.' He put down the receiver, then turned to Anna. 'We must be there at two o'clock. With the incoming tide, it will wash anything upriver again if it hasn't already reached the sea.'

'What about the beaches near the estuary? When the boat came in I saw a long beach close by, a body could wash onto the beach,' Anna said, anxious that the Water Police be made to understand that she wanted a thorough search.

'I will tell them,' the sergeant promised. 'But now we have another problem. But only a *maybe* problem.'

'No more money!' Ratih cried. 'Twenty-five guilders! They are robbers!'

Sergeant Khamdani ignored her. 'If we find the body there is no coroner. He is Dr Van Tool and he left on the twenty-sixth, on the last boat.'

'What does that mean?' Anna asked.

'This is a Dutch woman, she cannot be officially dead, you understand. You must have a coroner's investigation, a verdict, then a certificate. Death by drowning, death by misadventure, death by violent means, murder, manslaughter, suicide,' he ticked them all off on his fingers. 'Only sickness when there is a doctor who can verify and write a certificate. Otherwise she is not dead until the coroner says so.' He paused and shrugged his shoulders. 'And we have no coroner!'

'Nonsense, Ajun! If you find this woman and she is floating in the river and you fish her out, you can see she is dead. Even some places the crabs have eaten her. Anyone can see! If I cook a chicken I can see if it is dead. I don't need a certificate to say this chicken is dead! What is this certificate? You are *Pak Polisi*! You can say she is dead. What is this nonsense? Who will argue?' Ratih declared with vehemence.

'It is the law,' the police sergeant shrugged. 'The law will argue. The law *must* have a certificate. You can't have people going around, even the police, saying so-and-so is dead. "Dead" is official. A doctor or the coroner must say it, put on a stamp, "Deceased", no more argument!'

'What if she is not found – the body?' Anna asked.

'Magistrate,' the sergeant said.

'Oh my, what is this now? Magistrate? He must now say she is dead if they can't find the body?' Ratih said scornfully.

'If we have a witness, a reliable witness, he can give a certificate.' The police sergeant glanced over at *Kleine* Kiki. 'How old are you?' he asked.

'Just thirteen, sir.'

The sergeant shook his head. 'No good. Thirteen is not a reliable witness.'

'So if we find her, she is not dead, even if she *is* dead, unless the coroner says she is dead and gives a certificate? If someone sees her dying, but isn't old enough to officially see her dying, then she is not dead and the magistrate will *not* give us a certificate? Is that right?' Budi asked. Anna grinned to herself – the boy wasn't stupid by any measure.

Sergeant Khamdani sighed. 'I know it is difficult, that is why we have to go to the police academy. Even then, it takes time. But after a while you understand how it all makes sense. A police enquiry is a serious matter and we must have rules of conduct.'

'And if there is no reliable witness who saw the person who is dead actually die, then the person is not officially dead. If this not-officially-dead person is not found, what then?' Anna asked.

The police sergeant smiled. 'This is precisely what I have been trying to say all along. That is easy! Missing persons! Dead, maybe, but not officially, no reliable witness, that is a correct definition for a missing person.' He spread his hands in a gesture of goodwill. 'I can issue a Missing Person's Certificate, easy. That is now a police matter and I am the police.'

Anna realised that it would be far better, all things considered, if her stepmother was never found. But she also knew it would prey on her father's conscience forever. Even in a drunken haze he'd insisted on a tombstone. Besides, in a funny way, you are not dead in the heart and mind until there is a place where your bones or ashes reside, until the *dominee*, the minister, has said the proper words and people have departed from the grave site with long faces and serious expressions. Commonsense, which is what the police sergeant was subtly advising, indicated that she should save the twenty-five guilders and allow him to give her a Missing Person's Certificate.

'How far away is the police launch? Can we walk?' Anna asked.

'*Ja*, we can walk, it is only ten minutes,' Sergeant Khamdani replied.

'It is just after one o'clock. May I buy you all lunch?' Anna smiled and turned to Ratih. 'The Dutch half will pay.'

At two o'clock precisely Anna and the sergeant arrived at the docks to find the police launch waiting. Budi had returned to Lo Wok and his mother had left for the markets to prepare for the evening meal at the *kampong*. Anna sent *Kleine* Kiki back to the ship with the wheelchair and shopping, with instructions to remove the washing from *Mevrouw* Swanepoel's portion of the ship's railing. She gave her a one-guilder coin in case the fat frump and Jack Sprat had already arrived back on board.

The sergeant in charge of the launch asked her, 'When did the body fall into the river?' A curious way of putting it, Anna thought, although it avoided talking about her stepmother in the first person.

'Yesterday, about five in the evening, maybe half-past five, no later.' *Kleine* Kiki did not possess a watch.

He thought for a moment, then drew Sergeant Khamdani aside and they chatted for a while, the land police sergeant frequently nodding to the other. Eventually he came over to Anna. 'It is not worthwhile searching this area by the docks. Last night the tide would have taken the body down the river, perhaps already out to sea. But it is possible that it landed on the mudflats downriver by the two recent wrecks. That is where we will go first.'

'And after that?' Anna asked.

Sergeant Khamdani addressed the other water police sergeant who answered directly, 'There is no "after that".'

'Can't we search the river?' Anna asked.

The policeman shook his head. 'The body will be there or nowhere else. The bodies are always there, if they have not already floated out to sea.' He made it sound as if the bodies as a group made up their own minds where they wanted to go. 'We never find them washed up on a beach, they never go there,' he concluded.

The launch took off downriver and against the tide. The water policeman explained that the incoming tide would cover the mudflats and the narrow draught of the boat meant they could get right up to the mangroves. 'There are special places to look, places they like to hide.' Again he made it sound as if the bodies, like elephants going to die, had a predestination, but cunning as they might be at hiding, he wasn't all that easily fooled.

However, despite nearly two hours of searching in all the special places, the certain-to-find places, Katerina, as usual, was contrary and difficult and refused to be found. It was nearly five in the afternoon when they landed back at the docks in

Tjilatjap.

Sergeant Khamdani seemed delighted with the result. 'Now I can give you your very own Certificate of Missing Persons. If you like I can also put on it "Presumed dead". The police can say that because it isn't a worry to the magistrate or the coroner, because there is no certainty, you understand?'

'Yes, thank you, Sergeant,' Anna replied. She couldn't fault him. He'd done all he could. It was a paradox: all the people who had been pleasant to her were Javanese and all the unpleasant ones had been Dutch.

Anna had one more task to complete before returning to the ship and so made her way to the *kampong* where Ratih cooked. She found her with a cleaver, standing at an enormous wooden chopping block and cutting chickens into bits to fry. Ratih looked up as she approached. 'I have no coroner's certificate, but they are dead,' she laughed, pointing to the chicken pieces.

'Ratih, can you give me a moment? It's about Budi.'

'Budi? He has misbehaved?'

'On the contrary, he is a fine boy; you should be proud.'

'What do you think, Anna, must I marry that *Pak Polisi*? The boy needs a father.'

Anna laughed. 'He seems very nice, very honest.'

'For a policeman, yes.' She sniffed. 'Budi's father was a good-for-nothing. I sent him back to his *kampong* in Sumatra. Those people do not know how to work! They scratch their bums and want to be paid for the effort!'

Anna laughed. 'There are Dutch like that also.' She paused, her expression suddenly serious. 'Ratih, Budi tells me he has left school?'

Ratih shook her head. 'I am on my own. We cannot afford

high school.'

'What does it cost?' Anna asked, knowing that one year of high school would entitle a Javanese boy to be apprenticed as a junior clerk.

'Ten guilders a year, but then also with the Chinaman he earns thirty cents a week, that is another fifteen guilders, that is less than you paid those good-for-nothing water *polisi*! It is a crime!'

'Ratih, I don't know what will happen to me, but if I get to Australia I will pay for Budi's education. You must let me know your address. I will give you the money for one year at high school now. Will you promise to send him back to school?'

Ratih brought her hands up to cover her face and was silent for some time, then teary-eyed she said, 'I promise, Anna.' Then she added, 'I think both halves are good, the Dutch and the Javanese.' Anna peeled off twenty-five guilders from her father's pile, now considerably smaller than it had been on the previous afternoon. Anna offered the money in both hands and it was accepted in the same way. 'I think you have made up my mind, Anna. I will marry that *Pak Polisi*.'

Anna laughed. 'You must feed him less, Ratih. You know what they say about a fat policeman!'

'I will remember, Anna. Maybe I will tell him that the fried chicken he likes to eat must first have a certificate from the magistrate, hey?'

Anna thought, with a mother like Ratih, Budi couldn't help but be intelligent.

Leaving Ratih and returning to the *Witvogel*, she found

everything in chaos. People were running around on deck like headless chickens and there was panic everywhere. The captain had, only half an hour before, announced that he regretted the ship could not be repaired, that for the benefit of the men on board, it was a big-end bearing failure and crankshaft seizure involving the Duxford engine. The 600 passengers and crew were stranded in Tjilatjap. With the Japanese thought to be no more than a few days away – and, some said, possibly a few hours – there could be no escape from Java. He had advised that the ship's crew would be on duty for only another twenty-four hours, then the ship would no longer be serviced and thereafter everyone would have to take care of themselves as the company had no further responsibility for their welfare. They must arrange to hire porters from the town to move their baggage at their own cost. There were lots of out-of-work dockworkers available, he'd added helpfully. Finally, he regretted the inconvenience.

Anna made her way back to the cabin to find the de Klerk women already packing while the bank clerk sat on the end of the bunk, slumped forward with his elbows resting on his knees, staring into space like a stunned mullet. Her father was snoring in the bottom bunk, oblivious to the goings-on, while *Kleine* Kiki sat in the top bunk with his laundry neatly folded on her lap. 'What will we do, Anna?' she cried anxiously as Anna entered. The de Klerk women looked up expectantly as if they too hoped for an answer.

'I don't know,' Anna said. All she could think was that she must find a way to send me a letter to tell me she was not coming to Australia. 'I must write a letter,' she said softly, hoping the three women didn't hear. But their ears were long since tuned to a level above her father's snoring and the bank clerk's wife laughed. 'Yesterday we tried already to send a postcard to the Netherlands; there is no aeroplane going to Batavia and the railway is finished, the Japanese have the trains. There are no letters going out.' All three women smiled, pleased that they could share this further bad news with Anna.

'How is your stepmother?' one of the maiden sisters asked.

'They have asked me already,' *Kleine* Kiki said quickly. 'I said she was sick and you had taken her ashore.'

The de Klerk sister pointed to the wheelchair. 'Then why is that here?'

'She does not need it at the moment,' Anna replied. '*Kleine* Kiki brought it back on my instructions.' It was, Anna thought, at least the technical truth; her stepmother certainly had no need of any further earthly transport. She didn't like the way she was becoming accustomed to fibbing almost at the drop of a hat.

'Good riddance!' the second de Klerk maiden sister sniffed, looking down at Piet Van Heerden on the opposite bunk. 'His drunken snoring is enough without her shouting.'

'Is that all?' Anna asked pointedly. Then she added, 'As a matter of fact she is very ill and may die. Now, do you have any more questions?'

This failed to get a sympathetic reaction from the three women other than a despairing sigh from the other spinster sister and with it, 'We may all soon be dead.'

'And how will you move *him*?' the bank clerk's wife asked, indicating Piet Van Heerden with a jerk of her chin.

'With the wheelchair, of course,' Anna replied. 'Any more questions?' She looked directly at the one fat and the two scrawny old hens. 'Now if you will excuse me?' She went to the trunk and withdrew a leather folder holding a writing pad with a fountain pen inserted into a small loop at the side of the pad. Then she climbed up onto the top bunk beside the little maid and sat with her knees folded, legs tucked under. Balancing the writing pad on her lap, she commenced to write:

Tjilatjap, Java
5th March 1942
My dearest Nicholas,

This was struck through and directly below it Anna wrote:

My darling Nicholas,
I do not know if you are alive and have come in the Vleermuis already to Australia. But I think it is so, or I would feel it in mijn heart.

I have some very bad news. We are not coming to Australia! I am so sad I am wanting to cry, but I must be brave, ja. We are in a town in Java. Its name is Tjilatjap. It is eleven kilometres on a river. The boat, it is here, but it is broken and they cannot fix, we cannot go with it any more. Tomorrow we must all go from this boat – I don't know where!

But there is more bad news. My stepmother commit suicide in the river, she is jumped in the river and Kleine Kiki she cannot rescue her because she cannot swim. They have not found the body. Mijn father he is also drunk since Batavia.

Nicholas, I don't know if this letter gets to you. The post office have no aeroplane for letters any more, the Japanese they have the trains. They are not here, but coming soon. Maybe even tomorrow! I am very frightened!

Nicholas, I love you. I am very sorry I did not let you make love to me. Maybe I will die and not know how it would be to make love to you!

I love you, my darling Nicholas. Forever!

Anna – Madam Butterfly X X X X

P.S. I have always the Clipper butterfly. I will keep it till I die.

I love you!

A

I must pause here for a moment in telling Anna's story because this letter, despite my having read it a thousand times, always brings me close to tears. Today I possess one of the world's great butterfly collections, certainly the best originating from the Pacific region. Collectors are, by nature, hoarders and in the span of my life I have gathered together many beautiful things. But this despairing and infinitely sad single-page letter is without doubt my most precious possession. It is faded and the creases where it was folded have finally parted. I have now placed it in a frame behind tinted glass along with Anna's embroidered butterfly handkerchief in an attempt to preserve them from further damage. Both are enormously precious to me, though I admit the letter is the more so. While I can recite every word by heart, I carry a copy in my wallet and read it almost daily. These bittersweet memories are the ghosts that come to haunt old men who have lived too long.

Anna completed the letter, sealed it in an envelope and then, showing amazing initiative, addressed it to:

Mr Nicholas Duncan
C/o The Archbishop of the Anglican Church

Perth
Australia

I had once told her that when we eventually married, my godfather, Henry Le Fanu, the Anglican Archbishop of Perth, would conduct the ceremony and she had remembered my silly and somewhat vainglorious boast. But it was in her next action that she showed she wasn't someone who is easily deterred.

Anna climbed down and went to the trunk and selected a pretty summer dress and her best Sunday sandals. *Kleine* Kiki watched, anxious and curious, from the top bunk as Anna rummaged through Katerina's make-up and then slipped a tube of lipstick into the bag that carried her toothbrush. 'I'll be back in a few minutes,' she said, carrying the dress over her arm and holding the sandals and toilet bag.

She changed in the women's washroom, brushed her teeth and hair and carefully worked her late stepmother's scarlet lipstick onto her lips before returning to the cabin. 'Come, *Kleine* Kiki, we are going ashore!' she instructed. She waited for the little maid to climb down from the top bunk and slip on her sandals. Moments later they left the cabin, to the curious stares of the de Klerk women. Anna noted that the bank clerk had stopped staring into space and was now reading from a small Bible, muttering the words of a psalm. The snivelling little coward was already in the process of giving up.

'Where are we going?' *Kleine* Kiki asked once they were ashore. 'You are all dressed up with Sunday shoes and lipstick.'

Anna thought how the child was really starting to blossom; previously she would have been too timid to ask or make such a comment. 'I'm not sure. It's just an idea. We are going to look for the Americans.'

'Americans?'

'Pilots!' Anna answered. 'The two I met were leaving today. Maybe there are still some here.' She paused. 'But first I must make a quick visit to Mother Ratih in her *kampong*.'

They hailed a *becak*. 'The airport where the Americans are, do you know it?' Anna asked.

The driver nodded, then said, 'But it is six kilometres.'

'Can you pedal that far, father?' Anna asked him. He was an older man, his hair turned grey, almost white, perhaps in his early fifties, thin as a twig and his skinny brown legs roped with muscle.

The *becak* man looked scornful. 'Of course! One guilder?' he asked hopefully.

Kleine Kiki started to protest but Anna cut her short. 'There and back one guilder?' The *becak* driver readily agreed; it was probably more than he earned in two days of pedalling the double-seated three-wheeler.

Anna directed the *becak* to Ratih's *kampong* kitchen and told *Kleine* Kiki to wait with the driver while she went in to see Budi's mother on a business matter. She returned about ten minutes later and they set off for the American airfield.

It was nearly ten o'clock when they pedalled up to the guardpost at the airport gates, to be met by a military policeman wearing a white helmet and belt. 'Halt! Who goes there?' he commanded, stepping into the road, rifle at the ready.

Anna got down from the *becak* into the spotlight that shone on the guardhouse and surrounds, concentrating hard to stop her knees shaking. 'Please, sir, I must see a pilot,' she said, having rehearsed the English sentence half a hundred times on their way to the airport. 'I must give him this letter.' She held the letter up for the American military policeman to see.

The guard relaxed; a strikingly beautiful girl was looking directly at him, appealing for his help. 'What pilot, ma'am? What is his name?' he asked.

'A pilot,' Anna answered.

'Any pilot?'

'Yes, sir. I want him to take my letter when he flies away and to post it to Australia.' She still held the letter up. 'The post office, they are not sending letters any more. It is to my fiancé in Australia. I have also two guilders for postage.' She held up the money in her free hand.

The military policeman shook his head. 'Ma'am, I'm sorry, I do not have that authority.'

Suddenly the guard shouldered his rifle and jumped to attention. Anna turned to see the lights of an automobile approaching, and moved to the side of the road. As the big American car drew up she burst into tears. The officer seated in the back looked out of the rear side window. He appeared to be a man in his forties and was obviously very senior, though Anna had no way of telling, not knowing how to read his rank.

'What is it, provost? Why is this young woman crying?' he called out.

The guard still stood at attention. 'She wants a pilot to take a letter out, Colonel, sir!' he said at the top of his voice.

'Steady on, provost, I am not your drill sergeant,' the officer chided, then glanced at Anna. 'Letter?'

Anna, stifling a sob, took the three steps to the car window. 'Please, sir, our boat it is broken and we cannot leave Java. I cannot go to Australia to *mijn* fiancé. Please, sir.' Anna held out the letter, her expression pleading. 'It is to tell him maybe I don't die and I will see him after the war!' Anna let go another heart-rending sob.

The officer reached out and took the letter. Glancing at it he read the address. 'Archbishop?'

'Yes, sir, he is *mijn* fiancé's godfather in Perth.'

'And you want it posted?'

'I have here two guilders for the postage,' Anna said, holding up the notes.

The colonel waved the money aside and smiled. 'Leave it to me, miss. What is your name?'

'Anna Van Heerden, sir.'

'You are Dutch, Anna?'

'My father is Dutch, sir, my mother Javanese.'

'That accounts for your eyes,' the officer observed, obviously admiring her. 'I am Colonel Gregory Woon. I hope some day we meet again, but even more, that you come through this safely and marry your young man from Australia.'

'Thank you, sir,' Anna said, replacing the tears of a moment before with a brilliant smile.

Anna's smile as a young woman was the kind that could make old men grieve for what might have been. It could melt a glacier or turn a young bloke's knees to putty and make his heart pound like a Haitian voodoo drum. 'I will personally see that it is posted safely, Anna,' the colonel said. 'Such a shame, the five Catalinas left last night for Australia, but we have six B-17's leaving for Colombo tonight.' He held Anna's letter up. 'Rest assured, I will do my very best to see it gets to Australia. I wish you luck, young lady.' Colonel Woon paused, then added smilingly, 'Those violet blue eyes, absolutely stunning! I shall not easily forget them.' With that he told the corporal behind the wheel to proceed and the military policeman lifted the boom gate. Anna watched as the car moved on into the airport and disappeared down the road to the base, its rear brakelights twin crimson eyes in the dark.

Anna had one more task to complete before returning to the ship, though it was not one she looked forward to. She had always been fond of *Kleine* Kiki and had become especially so since they'd shared the cabin. Waiting until the *becak* had reached the outskirts of town, she turned to the little maid. '*Kleine* Kiki, now I want you to listen to me very carefully, promise?' The teenager nodded. 'You know the Japanese soldiers are coming soon. They will be here any day now, perhaps even tomorrow. We don't know what will happen but it will not be good for the Dutch. I think we will be put in a camp for prisoners, *mijn* papa and me also.' Anna paused, turning and taking both *Kleine* Kiki's hands in her own and looking into her soft brown eyes. 'You are Javanese, a pure-blood. I don't think they will harm you. I have spoken to Mother Ratih, that is why we stopped at her *kampong*. She is an honest woman and, if you agree, I will pay her to take you into her house and train you as a cook, an apprentice, you understand? You already know lots about cooking, stuff you learned in the *Grootehuis*, but she is a professional. She will train you well and you will also be safe.'

Kleine Kiki burst into tears. 'Anna, please, please, let me stay with you!' she begged. 'I will be good, a very good girl! I will eat very little and do nothing to make you angry! I will look after you and *Mijnheer* Piet. Please, Anna!' she sobbed, broken-hearted at the notion of leaving Anna.

Anna took her into her arms and they both started to cry. After a short time Anna, still somewhat tearful, spoke once again to the sobbing teenager. '*Kleine* Kiki, listen to me. I know that I told you we would always be together and we would take care of each other. But when the Japanese come they will take *mijn* father and me also because I am a half-blood, and I cannot leave him. They will put us in a concentration camp, but they will not let you come. You will be left on your own with nobody to help you. I cannot allow this to happen. You are our family now. You are my little sister!' She took the diminutive maid by the shoulders and gently pushed her away so she could look directly into her face. 'Look at me, *Kleine* Kiki,' Anna said softly. The *becak* had reached the river and they were not far from the docks where so much had happened recently. 'If I am still alive after the war, then I will come for you, we will be together again.'

'Promise?' *Kleine* Kiki choked, then started to sob once more.

Anna attempted to smile through her own tears. 'Cross my heart! But maybe by that time you will have met a fine young man and have a restaurant of your own and so you won't want to come?'

'Noooo!' *Kleine* Kiki howled. 'I will never leave you! I will always be your maid, Anna.'

'My little sister,' Anna said. 'No more maid! That time is over. My little sister the famous cook, *ja*? You are clever, you will learn well from Mother Ratih and I will be very proud of you, darling.'

'When must I go?' *Kleine* Kiki asked tremulously, both hands attempting to knuckle the tears from her eyes, her little chest heaving from the effort of crying and her bottom lip trembling.

'Tomorrow, when we all have to leave the ship,' Anna said. 'Mother Ratih will meet us and take you to her *kampong*. She lives quite close to the kitchen. But first thing in the morning you must help me to get *mijn* father dressed and in the wheelchair.' Anna sighed. 'It will not be an easy task, I assure you. Then you must go ashore and hire two dockworkers to carry the big trunk.'

'And where will you go, Anna? What will happen to you? The Japanese will hurt you!' *Kleine* Kiki's expression was deeply concerned and her eyes were once again brimming.

'I don't know yet.' Anna tried to smile. 'But I do know it will be some place where there is no whiskey or brandy.'

They had arrived back at the ship and Anna added another fifty cents to the driver's fee. 'For putting up with our tears,' she said to him.

'*Ahee!*' he said, gratefully accepting the money. 'It is a natural thing to cry if you are a woman. The prophet tells us that Allah gave men courage and women tears, the one to fight and the other to mourn for what men do to each other.' He turned his *becak* to go, but then glanced back over his shoulder. 'With the Japanese coming, I think there will be many more tears for women to shed.'

CHAPTER SEVEN

*'If you find this woman and she is floating in the river and
you fish her out,
you can see she is dead.
Even some places the crabs have eaten her.
Anyone can see! If I cook a chicken I can see if it is dead.
I don't need a certificate to say this chicken is dead!'*
Mother Ratih
Kampong cook, Tjilatjap

IN ORDER TO CONTINUE to tell Anna's story it is
probably a good idea for me to outline the immediate future she
and Piet Van Heerden and all the other Dutch nationals who
had been unable to escape from Java and Sumatra were about
to face. It was now the 6th of March 1942, two days before the
Japanese arrived in the river town of Tjilatjap.

Although the Dutch forces in the East Indies hadn't
yet surrendered to the Japanese, the gossip was that the
Netherlands East Indies administration was about to capitulate
and the Dutch army would tamely surrender. The Dutch
army, which showed a great reluctance to fight, wore dark-
green uniforms and became known as Pawpaws – green on
the outside and yellow on the inside. In Tjilatjap, as in all the
towns and two major cities on the island, the more important
civil servants and the wealthy had departed and the town
administration, now in the hands of jumped-up local clerks

and municipal workers, was teetering on the brink of collapse.

Every remaining Dutch family was suddenly having to learn new ways to survive on an island where they now met great antipathy from the Javanese population. No safe place existed for any Dutch citizen to go, nor was there any place where they could earn a living wage and they were heavily dependent on what money they had accumulated in a bank account.

The great majority of the *Witvogel's* passengers were middle-class and unaccustomed to the exiguous requirements of a refugee. They had been unable to sell their homes or properties and were ultimately forced to abandon them. Furthermore, the passage to attempted freedom had not been cheap, with the result that once they found themselves abandoned, very few had the financial means to survive for very long.

The worm had finally turned and the locals could now openly show their antipathy towards their previous conquerors, the master race who, they maintained, had kept their people in servitude for a period of three centuries. The Japanese propaganda had been prodigious and, anyway, the locals were inclined to believe it, mistakenly anticipating that, as an Asian race, the soldiers of the Emperor would prove a more benign and sympathetic invader.

And so, to return to Anna's story . . .

A most immediate problem for the passengers on the stricken ship proved to be the custom of taking a cabin trunk on board when embarking on an ocean voyage, even one as traumatic as the business of leaving your homeland forever. Many a square on deck or in the hold was dominated by one of these large objects, which were often plated with tin sheeting and fitted with heavy brass corner-brackets. Similarly, the passageways outside the cabins were lined with trunks too big to be contained within. One trunk or two large portmanteaus was the maximum luggage that had been allowed on board and most people had opted for the more commodious trunk, often procuring the biggest one they could find.

Now, with the passengers becoming refugees, they were saddled with these great cumbersome boxes. They couldn't store them in a *godown* on the docks, as they might have done in a time of peace, while they waited for another ship to take them off the island. The breakdown in authority and the imminent arrival of the Japanese almost certainly meant that the locals would take to looting, appropriating anything they could lay their hands on. Nor could they expect to manhandle these large objects on their own.

That morning, the last day on board, chaos reigned. Passengers who had gone ashore the previous day and attempted to recruit dockworkers as porters had been largely unsuccessful. After one or two trunks had been transported the locals caught on to what was happening and withdrew their labour, knowing that the Dutch passengers would be helpless with these large and cumbersome trunks and they had only to wait for the rich pickings soon to become available.

It was for this reason that the *Witvogel*'s passengers were now engaged in reducing their possessions so that a husband-and-wife team would be capable of carrying a trunk. People had spent most of the night packing and then repacking, discarding what they felt they couldn't take into an uncertain future and keeping what they believed was absolutely essential to their physical and emotional wellbeing. These 'keep or discard' choices often proved curious, to say the least: for instance, a whalebone corset was kept and an extra pair of stout shoes was discarded. Frames were removed from photographs and thrown aside, photos from albums were arranged in various piles of importance, the least nostalgic cast aside while the important memories were rearranged in a single slim album or leafed into a family Bible. Mountains of dishtowels, crocheted doilies, antimacassars, embroidered table napkins and cloths and other niceties of homemaking were given up with a regretful cluck or sigh or even a tear, each object a tiny rip in the fabric of their lives. Soon the deck space, ship's hold and cabins were littered with this detritus of their past as well as their present despair.

This on-board mayhem was a situation where Anna was to learn a valuable lesson in survival. Like the owners of the ill-equipped, poorly maintained boats rusting for lack of maintenance or confined to coastal duties in every port in the Pacific that had scurried to Batavia to make a quick dollar, she was to learn that the advent of misfortune often favours the bold and that opportunities exist in the most unexpected circumstances.

Identifying a need and then finding some way to serve it is the very essence of survival. Anna also observed that you may learn as well from your enemy as you can from someone you trust. Both lessons came via the redoubtable *Mevrouw* Swanepoel of the nascent moustache and dress-gobbling breasts and her Jack Sprat of a husband, Hans the Obedient.

Anna first observed Hans scurrying down the passageway below decks shouting, 'Five cents for dishtowels!', repeating the call every few moments. He already carried a large number of these common squares of cotton cloth hugged to his chest. Anna knew enough about Mrs Fat and Mr Lean to know that

Hans wasn't simply using idle time to parade down the corridors collecting dishcloths. She followed him on deck to discover that a queue had already formed that stretched from the rescue square the couple occupied to the opposite side of the deck, filling all the chalked corridors in between.

Mevrouw Swanepoel was seated behind a manual Singer sewing machine that was resting on the H.R. Swanepoel-initialled trunk, sewing for all she was worth. She was joining four dishtowels together to make one side of a giant knapsack and then four more to make the flip side, cheerfully calling 'Nearly done!' as she stitched the two sections together for a grateful customer. To this she added shoulder straps of white rope, no doubt purloined from some part of the ship by Hans. The whole became a bag of considerable volume that could be carried on the back by a refugee. In the process she was making money hand over fist, unashamedly demanding five guilders for each of these hastily sewn sacks, items that in the market in Batavia would have cost no more than fifty cents and been made of a superior material. Opportunity, opportunity, opportunity! The dishtowel sacks were the answer to the prayers of many of the passengers and Jack Sprat's wife had successfully identified the need and exploited it. A husband and wife carrying their belongings on their unaccustomed and reluctant backs was greatly preferable to lugging a clumsy tin or leather trunk around between them.

Anna was forced to admire the gross woman for her initiative. To exploit the prevailing circumstances made perfect sense and it was a lesson she would remember at a later time. As *Kleine* Kiki had said to the woman hiring her bathhouse to them the previous day, 'Yesterday is a distant land'! We adapt or we die – *Mevrouw* Swanepoel had seen the opportunity and grasped the moment to turn it to her advantage. Morals, if there were any under such circumstances, have little to do with the immediate business of survival.

However, Anna couldn't bring herself to stand in the queue and be forced to eat humble pie and ask the fat *vrou* to make her a bag, so she sent *Kleine* Kiki with ten dishtowels she purchased at the going price of five cents to the native market where a Javanese seamstress made up a bag, using the extra two towels to fashion a set of comfortable shoulder straps, whereupon the little maid paid the grateful woman fifty cents for her time and labour.

I've seen one of these colourful dishtowel bags in the War Museum in Canberra. The exhibited one had been made up with towels of various stripes and patterns, with two towels in particular gaining my attention because one depicted a map of the Dutch East Indies that proclaimed the tricentenary of Dutch occupation and the other bore a picture of an unsmiling Queen Wilhelmina. One would have thought that whoever possessed this particular bag would have been a potential walking disaster in the prevailing anti-Dutch atmosphere. Anna claims that for her own bag she was careful to select dishtowels with floral designs that could be seen when the bag was on her back; one in particular was a single large sunflower.

It was almost noon by the time *Kleine* Kiki returned and Anna packed what she believed she and her father would need once they were living ashore. Most of what the trunk contained had belonged to Katerina, who had had expensive taste in clothes, fondly believing that if other women admired her fashion sense it would distract their attention from her physical condition. She had also possessed some valuable jewellery, and though she had been wearing her wedding band and a large diamond engagement ring (the solitaire diamond had been useful in disconcerting the three sour-faced de Klerk women) when she'd plunged into the water, there remained a second diamond ring, a ruby ring as well as a large sapphire ring, the latter bought for her by Piet Van Heerden when they had been on a short holiday to Colombo. There was also a double strand of pearls with matching pendant pearl earrings, six heavy gold bracelets, and an antique Dutch brooch of a pewter clog with silver sails so that the traditional folk shoe was turned into a little boat. The brooch had belonged to Katerina's mother and Anna had loved it as a child, but now she handed it to *Kleine* Kiki along with two of the six gold bracelets and the silver-backed hairbrush the little maid had used most of her life to brush her mistress's hair. 'Here, *Kleine* Kiki, when the time comes this will buy your wedding dowry. Keep the brush for your own hair and to remind yourself that you are no longer a servant.'

Kleine Kiki immediately protested, not wanting to take Anna's gift. 'I'm not going to marry. After the war I'm going to look after you!'

'Take them, darling. The brooch you can wear, it is not valuable; the bracelets you must keep in a safe place – they are much too big for your tiny wrists. Gold is always something you can turn into cash in an emergency. See, the brush is monogrammed with the initial "K", now that stands for Kiki!'

Anna kept the remainder of the jewellery and two pairs of Katerina's sunglasses, knowing that the sunglasses would conceal her blue eyes when she was in public. She reminded herself that from now on she would always dress in traditional native costume, as she had often done at home in Batavia. She was exceptionally tall for a Javanese woman, yet small-boned.

The only items Anna packed for herself and her father,

other than personal clothes and two towels, were a dozen handkerchief-sized cotton squares, the Clipper butterfly in its teak box, her embroidery silks and needles, an album of family photographs and a long, narrow, locked black tin of the kind usually deposited in a bank vault. The key to open it, she reasoned, must be the one that hung on a chain around her father's neck. Anna placed the tin in her dishtowel bag, knowing that it must contain items of value.

She then selected two elegant silk outfits that had belonged to her stepmother, two pairs of kid gloves and a pair of white high-heeled shoes her stepmother had worn in the wheelchair simply for appearance, the soles still unscratched. While not fat, Katerina had nevertheless been a tall, big-boned Dutch woman and Mother Ratih was a small Javanese one, but Anna reasoned she might be able to have the two *haute couture* outfits altered and so she put these along with the other items into the shopping basket that contained *Kleine* Kiki's few clothes and personal items. 'For Mother Ratih from you,' she instructed. The rest of her stepmother's extensive wardrobe she left in the soon-to-be abandoned trunk.

Getting Piet Van Heerden into the wheelchair proved easier than Anna had anticipated. He had woken early and found the last but one of the bottles of whiskey. He'd consumed half the bottle by mid-morning and had collapsed back into a drunken stupor, whereupon she had rescued the remaining half. Now, packed and ready to leave, Anna shook and slapped his cheeks until he came around sufficiently to demand his bottle. Anna held it up. 'We are going ashore, Papa, and you may have it when we've left the ship,' she said.

'Gimme! Not going!' he growled, his trembling hand stretching out to take the bottle.

'Get into the wheelchair, Papa, or no more Scotch!' Anna scolded. 'Come, we'll help you!' To her surprise Piet Van Heerden made an effort to sit up, then he allowed himself to be helped into the wheelchair. With the dishtowel bag on her back and with *Kleine* Kiki carrying her basket, manoeuvring the wheelchair with the canvas bag hanging from its handles and loaded with the slumped and heavy form of Piet Van Heerden down the ship's passageway between its many abandoned trunks proved a frightful task. By the time they reached the deck Anna was almost in tears. On deck they were met by a scene of complete chaos, with hundreds of people milling about, discarded trunks and personal belongings scattered everywhere so that there seemed no way they could reach the gangplank. Then, to her consternation, the first mate suddenly appeared and stood in front of them. Anna was exhausted and felt unable to cope with a confrontation and she simply burst into tears.

'Stay there, Miss Van Heerden!' the mate commanded. 'Don't move, I'll get some help.' Several minutes later he arrived back with two dark-skinned lascars, one of whom relieved Anna of her dishtowel bag, slinging it onto his back and then taking *Kleine* Kiki's basket as well, while the other took the handles of the wheelchair. 'Step aside! Step aside!' the first mate called out as he preceded them, parting the milling throng until they reached the gangplank. 'They can only take you as far as the dock, then they must come back,' the first mate instructed.

'Thank you, *Mijnheer* Van der Westhuisen,' Anna said, forcing herself to look directly at the ship's officer. 'We are very grateful to you.'

'*Ach!* Now we are all in the same boat,' he quipped. 'With the Japs coming any time now, who knows what will happen to us all, hey? Tonight I go ashore as helpless to save my own skin as anyone else.' He pointed to Piet Van Heerden. 'Good luck to you all!'

'And you too, good luck,' Anna said, thinking she almost meant it.

Smiling, the first mate then said, 'I suppose a little goodbye kiss would be out of the question?'

Anna stuck out her hand, forcing him to take it. 'A handshake is all I can manage,' she said crisply, not smiling. 'Thank you again for your help.' With this, she directed *Kleine* Kiki to follow the lascars down the gangplank to the dock below, walking behind her without looking back, her heartbeat steady as a metronome. Anna's innate sense of power over men was back with her.

Arriving on the dock Anna tipped the lascars a guilder each, then found that she and *Kleine* Kiki were being welcomed ashore by a smiling Ratih and Budi, the latter having taken a day off from Lo Wok's store. Budi thanked Anna profusely for allowing him to return to school, which he said would take place the next term. When Anna said it was a pity he'd missed the first term he shrugged. 'I will catch up easily.'

Ratih nodded her head, confident in her son's ability. 'In school he was always in first place. He will soon catch up, you will see.' Then she turned, waving to someone in the distance. 'I have a *becak* for the bags,' she announced.

The *becak* driver moved through the throng ringing his bell furiously for people to part. To Anna's surprise it was the same old man who had taken *Kleine* Kiki and her to the airport. There must have been hundreds of *becaks* in Tjilatjap and she wondered if getting the wise old man who had quoted the prophet's saying about women and tears was a good omen. Unlike most Javanese, he hadn't credited the arrival of the Japanese as liberators, but knew there were many more tears in store for the nation's women. 'This is my uncle, Til,' Ratih said. 'He will help us.'

Anna smiled at the *becak* driver. 'Ah! It is good, we meet again.'

The old man smiled, immediately recognising Anna. 'Airport. B-17 letter! Colombo!' he said, laughing. Then he added, 'Your tears were very good!'

Anna threw back her head and laughed; the driver had overheard every tear-jerked word between herself and the colonel in the big American automobile. 'That old one has ears like a jackass!' Ratih laughed. 'Some of the stories he brings back to the *kampong*, you wouldn't believe it, you never heard such stuff before!'

Piet Van Heerden, sitting in the wheelchair with his chin resting on his chest, started to grunt. 'This is *mijn* father,' Anna said to the little Javanese woman and her son. The driver had his back to them and was busy loading the bag and basket onto the three-wheeler and so wasn't involved in the introduction. Anna had not hitherto mentioned her father's drinking to Ratih. As their own men do not drink alcohol, to a Muslim woman the effects of alcohol on a man would be scarcely understood. Ratih smiled down at the huge man in the wheelchair and putting her palms together she bowed, greeting him formally and respectfully in the Javanese manner, while Budi said 'Good morning, sir' to him in accent-less Dutch.

Piet Van Heerden looked up, ignoring them both. 'Anna, *waar* is *mijn* Scotch?' he demanded in a petulant voice. '*Waar*? *Waar*? I must have it at once!'

'Papa, you cannot drink in public, this is a Muslim country,' Anna replied firmly. 'Wait a little longer until we find a place to stay,' she said, having no idea if they would find such a place or how long it might take.

'Ha! It still belongs to the Netherlands!' Piet Van Heerden objected. 'We are in charge here! I can drink *anywhere* I want to, these monkeys can't stop me!'

Ratih, not understanding the language, saw how he was unable to control the shakes. 'I think he is sick. Is it malaria?' she asked sympathetically. 'We must take him to the hospital.'

'He is drunk, which is another type of sickness,' Anna said quietly to the concerned cook. 'If we can find somewhere to stay, where he can dry out, he will be all right in a couple of days.' She knew this to be unlikely, for when Piet Van Heerden finally realised they were trapped in Java he would be much worse, trying desperately to drown his despair with the contents of a bottle.

'But he is not wet!' Ratih exclaimed, not understanding.

'It is an expression,' Anna explained. 'It means if he stops drinking.'

'Anna, we have a house! The sergeant has found one. I think it will be okay,' Budi said, trying to contain his excitement.

'It was the house for the police lieutenant who was in charge of the Central Town District Station,' Ratih volunteered. 'Now he has gone people have not taken it, because it is the house for the *polisi*. It is not big, only a house for a lieutenant. But we have cleaned it and that lieutenant, his name is Lieutenant Joost de Villiers, his wife she grows potatoes and so they have the money for the boat. He has left some furniture there and Budi has chopped wood for the stove.'

Anna could scarcely believe her ears. 'Oh, Ratih, that is wonderful!' She hugged the little woman and gave her a kiss. 'Thank you, thank you!' Then she did the same to Budi, who smiled and rubbed the spot on his cheek with the fingertips of his right hand where her lips had touched him. Anna couldn't tell whether his expression was one of bemusement or if he seemed pleased. 'Did you hear that, Papa? We have a house to go to.'

'Scotch!' Piet Van Heerden yelled out.

'*Ja*, Papa, soon!' Anna promised. 'When we get to this lovely house.'

Ratih was a cook accustomed to dealing with truck drivers who smoked hashish that, they claimed, kept them awake and relaxed on long trips and so she wasn't put out by the Dutchman's sudden outburst. 'I have cooked for you some food,' she said. 'Tomorrow morning Kiki will come over and help you to shop in the markets, she will only start with me to help in the *kampong* kitchen in the afternoon. She will stay with us, I have a spare mattress in my bedroom.'

'And what will happen when you marry Sergeant Khamdani?' Anna asked, laughing.

Ratih giggled. '*Ahee!* In his *kampong* he has a house bigger than mine, Kiki will have her own space I think.' It was the second time Ratih had used *Kleine* Kiki's name without the Dutch diminutive. This was a smart woman – the Japanese were coming; anything, particularly a Dutch expression, might lead to questions, whereas a cook's assistant named Kiki in a local Javanese eating house wouldn't raise the slightest interest.

'Do you hear that, Kiki? I think Mother Ratih is saying it is best we dropped the "*kleine*" from your name.'

Kiki nodded. 'It is alright, Anna,' she said shyly. 'I understand.' Anna knew instinctively that she longed to ask if she could stay with her and still work as Ratih's apprentice, but was too shy to ask. Much as she would have loved to have Kiki with her, Anna decided not to ask the cook. The sooner

Kleine Kiki started her new life the better. There was no point in delaying it with the Japanese perhaps only hours away.

'Scotch!' Piet Van Heerden demanded, thumping the arm of the wheelchair. He was slowly becoming more sober and with it more irritable and anxious.

'Can we walk to the lieutenant's house?' Anna, ignoring him, asked Ratih.

'It is ten minutes along the river. Budi will push your father,' Ratih said, then called to Til, who nodded and set off, his skinny, muscle-roped legs pedalling furiously. 'He knows that house for the Lieutenant Joost,' she said.

When they arrived Anna wheeled her father into the kitchen, leaving him alone and accompanying Ratih, Budi and Kiki to conduct an inspection of the house. It was a task that didn't take them long. It had two bedrooms, a kitchen and small pantry, a bathroom and outside toilet, and a *balkon* ran the length of the front to shade the house from the sun. It was, to all intents and purposes, a very plain little house like hundreds of others, a basic design a builder's foreman would knock up in his sleep. The house had been stripped of linen and anything the police lieutenant and his wife could conveniently pack, but the furniture remained. There was a large marital bed with mattress in the master bedroom and a single, also with mattress and an old batik cover, in the second smaller one. Anna momentarily regretted discarding the several sets of heavy monogrammed sheets her stepmother had insisted on packing, but then realised that the native market would be filled with discarded linen that she could purchase when she went shopping with Kiki in the morning.

When they'd returned to the kitchen Anna noted that Ratih had left her two pots, plates, some forks and spoons, tin

mugs and a cleaver from her *kampong* kitchen. She glanced
tentatively at her father, and saw that he was still in the
wheelchair parked in the centre of the kitchen and had become
incoherent with rage. 'Scotch!' he finally managed to burst out.

Budi said, 'There is one more thing, Anna.' He pointed to
an unobtrusive trapdoor beside the stove and then pulled the
heavy bolt and lifted it, using the neatly cut handgrip. Anna
felt compelled to move over and look. A set of wooden steps
led downwards. 'See, it is a cellar!' Budi announced, anxious to
show her this architectural aberration in the plain little house.
He began to descend the short flight of wooden steps. Anna
felt trapped; she knew she must tend to her father but, at the
same time, didn't want to delay Ratih and Budi or to have them
witness her humiliation at her father's cantankerous behaviour.
She elected to follow him into the cellar, knowing that she
would have the remainder of the day to administer to her
furious father, whose drunken behaviour was absorbing almost
every moment of her life, and she felt a tiny sting of resentment
deep inside her. 'Soon, Papa,' she called, trying to stay calm in
the presence of the other three and then following Budi down
the steps. Ratih and Kiki came too, not wishing to be left alone
with the enormous apoplectic Dutchman.

The cellar could barely contain the four of them, and the
ceiling was only just above Anna's head. A tiny window set
directly under the line of the ceiling created by the kitchen
floor let in a soft light and could be opened if necessary to let
in fresh air. Curiously, a tiny pair of neat canvas curtains hung
from either side of the window and below that a shelf had been
built to hold equipment so that it could be easily seen in the
light coming from the window.

'The cellar, it is for the potatoes. To store in the dark

so they don't start to grow,' Budi informed Anna in a serious voice, proud that he knew something extraordinary about the mysterious habits of potatoes spontaneously sending out shoots if left in the light. 'They have eyes,' he said. 'They grow from the eyes.'

'Lieutenant Joost, his wife, she sold her potatoes to the other Dutch who do not always like to eat only rice,' Ratih said. Then she added, 'The sergeant he is getting some potatoes from Lieutenant Joost and I have tried to cook, but I do not like.'

Anna only half-listened, for above them in the kitchen her father was shouting. He must have managed to rise from the wheelchair and was stamping his feet on the kitchen floor. 'Scotch! *Waar? Waar?* You *fokin'* little cow!'

The four of them emerged from the basement to find Piet Van Heerden standing, holding onto the edge of the kitchen table, his huge frame swaying dangerously. '*Fok* off, you black bastards!' he shouted, pointing unsteadily at Ratih and Budi. Anna, in abject tears, hastily led them to the front door, all the while apologising profusely for her father.

'It is all right, Anna. It is hard for him, he is sick,' Ratih said, while Budi remained silent, his expression indicating that he was not as easily mollified. *Kleine* Kiki said a tearful goodbye, her eyes pleading to be asked to stay on to help Anna with Piet Van Heerden. But Anna knew she had to face her father alone. From this moment on he was her sole responsibility. 'Don't forget to give Mother Ratih your gifts,' she called to *Kleine* Kiki, wiping her eyes on her sleeve. '*Not* from me, from *you*, Kiki!' She watched as they all turned and waved from the street, then she turned in the direction of the interior where her father was bellowing like an angry bull. 'Oh, shut up!' she shouted, knowing he would not hear her but vexed beyond her patience level.

Then covering her ears with her hands she yelled, 'Shut up! Shut up! You horrible, horrible man!'

She returned to the kitchen, shocked at what she'd just shouted. For the first time in many days she was alone with her father. It was readily apparent he was suffering from a great deal more than a bad hangover, for his entire body trembled. He had become a large, dangerous, incoherent bear that was rapidly getting beyond her control. Anna knew she would have to give him the half-bottle of Scotch, then after that the one remaining bottle. The frustrated giant had located the dishtowel bag and was frantically tearing at the contents, pulling them out onto the kitchen floor. 'Papa, it is not in there! If you go to the bedroom and lie down I will bring you the bottle,' Anna said, again close to tears, but determined not to cry.

'The *fokin'* Scotch! *Waar? Waar?* You slut! *Waar* is *mijn* bottle?' he roared furiously. He turned suddenly to face his daughter. 'Bedroom? You want a bedroom? You whore!' Then he pointed an accusing finger at Anna. 'You are not – you are not –' he stammered, 'com – ing – to New – Zealand, you hear? Slut! Slut! Whore!'

Anna walked over to the wheelchair and withdrew the half-full bottle from the canvas bag that hung from the back. She had made no attempt to hide it and it had been within his reach all the while. But in his confused mind, Piet Van Heerden hadn't remembered this obvious compartment. Anna held up the bottle and started to move towards the main bedroom with her shambling papa following, his bare feet dragging, a trembling arm stretched out in anticipation, smacking his dry lips.

Anna stopped at the bed. Two large down pillows, without slips, were arranged neatly against the bedhead, a final sad and tidy touch, perhaps from the lieutenant's wife. 'Sit!' she commanded, stepping quickly aside as he lunged at the bottle in her hand. The effort to grab the Scotch bottle caused him to lose his balance and career sideways, then crash face down onto the bed. 'Sit, Papa!' Anna commanded, not knowing where the strength and resolve within her voice was coming from.

Piet Van Heerden, using his arms against the sagging mattress, somehow managed to push himself up and roll onto his back with his head supported by one of the large pillows. 'Slut! Scotch!' he bellowed.

Anna removed the cork and handed the bottle to him. He grabbed it in both trembling hands and brought it to his mouth, so intent on swallowing that Scotch spilled from his juddering, anxious lips. He started to cough violently, spraying whiskey over the mattress, his bloodshot eyes bulging almost out of their sockets. Anna grabbed him behind his neck and forced him to lean forward, thumping his back while he clung frantically to the bottle. Finally his coughing fit ceased and he lay, his head against the large down pillow, sucking at the whiskey bottle like an infant, reaching for the personal oblivion it would bring him.

Despite everything, Anna loved her papa, but she was too young to understand what was going on in his mind. His was the tenth generation of his family in this hitherto halcyon land. He was not a Dutchman; his heart and mind and every fibre of his body proclaimed him as indigenous to Java. Now he was being thrown out of the land he loved as if he were a piece of garbage, even worse, a piece of shit, a dog turd.

Anna despised his weakness. He was the one who had always voiced an opinion on everything, loudly proclaiming right from wrong, the local expert on just about everything, especially regional politics. Yet he had collapsed like a house of cards when resolve truly mattered. A small example of this was that they could have escaped from Java and gone to Australia, as most of the wealthy had done, weeks earlier by flying boat, but his fear of flying had stopped this happening. He could have elected to fly his family to safety, but had been too selfish to contemplate such a solution. His needs were paramount and always had been. Anna now realised that her stepmother had seen the same weakness in him much earlier. The words *Kleine Kiki* said Katerina had shouted at the old oil jetty prior to her suicide, admonishing her young husband when, so long ago, she'd been determined to take the jump on her horse that had crippled her, must have sprung from only one of a thousand such put-downs she'd endured from him.

There had been too much unearned importance allotted to him all his life. The Van Heerden prestige had been a frame of reference he'd always worn as if he rightfully belonged to a higher order. His character had been weakened by privilege. When a portion of courage and determination was required he'd always gone missing so that now, when he was forced to face the total destruction of everything he had been brought up to believe in, he was incapable of grasping the prevailing tenor of the times. Now it was Anna's job to rescue what might still be contained within the epidermis that seemed to have become the outer shell encasing the hollow substance of her father.

At almost seventeen years of age, Anna could not have described her father's character or the influences that shaped it. All she knew was that her precious papa, the man she had always tried so hard to please, was falling apart. She had always seen him as her protector, especially against the vicious tongue of her stepmother, but now he was unable to cope with the crisis they all faced, drowning his fear and apprehension in a bottle.

Having settled her drunken papa, and hoping that half a bottle of Scotch would keep him quiet until the morning, Anna knew not only that they faced an uncertain future, but also that her problems with her father were immediate. She sat at the kitchen table and admitted to herself that she was unlikely to find outside help. Furthermore, if her father desired to drink himself to certain death – as seemed increasingly probable – there were no more supplies of Scotch, brandy or any other alcohol available that she knew of in Tjilatjap. Or, at least, no more that Lo Wok knew about, or the rapacious Chinaman would have procured it and Budi would have alerted her to the fact that the Chinaman was ready to open negotiations, though this time Lo Wok would have the upper hand, knowing that she had little choice but to pay what he asked. She could ask the Chinaman to scrounge around, to see what he could find in Dutch homes that had been appropriated by the Muslim population. After all, open bottles of liquor were not the kind of baggage departing colonials would bother to take with them.

Ratih had left a pot for boiling water and another containing rice and heavily spiced fish on the table and all Anna had to do was light a fire in the stove, already set, to heat it up. But although she had not eaten all day, she lacked the energy to cook. She reached for one of the two spoons the cook had left and ate absent-mindedly from the cold pot. Having eaten a few mouthfuls of the richly spiced fish and rice she tried to think what she might do. Rising from the table she gathered up the contents of the dishtowel bag her father had spilled on the floor, including the locked safety deposit box. She placed the box on the table before restoring the remaining contents to the bag.

She decided to more carefully explore the house and back garden. To her surprise the backyard was extensive and stretched down to the bank of the river. It had been carefully tilled and a crop of potatoes was being grown in the raised rows of soil. Pulling up a plant, she saw that the small white tubers were just beginning to form and were not yet sufficiently mature. She came across a small vegetable patch with a tomato vine with several ripe fruit, six plump cabbages, the outside leaves badly eaten but with the centres well formed, and a patch of mint. She opened the door to the outside dunny which, while dusty with a spider web in one corner, seemed clean enough, although a strong disinfectant down the hole would not go amiss. She made a mental note to add this to her shopping list. At the rear of the house was the only non-functional aspect of the backyard – against the back wall stood several flowering red hibiscus bushes.

Returning to the inside of the house, Anna sat on a cheap batik-covered couch and attempted to think of some way to solve what was obviously becoming her major preoccupation. She was aware that the Japanese were due to arrive at any moment, but so great had her concern for her father become that she'd pushed this frightening prospect to the back of her mind.

She had once read a story about a hopeless alcoholic in one of the backwater Pacific ports who had been discovered unconscious under a pier by a native dockworker. The native had carried him to his canoe and taken him to his distant island home. Here the native islander (Anna couldn't remember his name) tended to the drunk, feeding him and nursing him back to health. During his long rehabilitation the other villagers seemed to pay the white man great obeisance and brought him the best of what they had to eat. After a period when he had endured the shakes and cried out as he experienced the delirium tremens, having been plied with good food, drunk nothing but clean water and received tender care, the once-skinny drunk was restored to shining good health. He declared that he felt wonderful and as healthy as a newborn babe.

One day he turned to his native friend, thanking him for his solicitous care and suggesting that it might be time to return to the main island, to the port where his compassionate friend had rescued him. He promised that he would never again touch a drop of grog and that he would somehow find a way to reward him.

'Oh, no,' said his dark friend, shaking his head, 'the village people are already rewarded by your presence. Now we plan a great feast in your honour.'

'That is very kind of you,' the white man replied. 'But after that, I would be most obliged if you would kindly take me back to the port, to my own people.'

'Ah, I do not think so,' said his native friend, smiling benignly. 'I did not bring you back to my island to fatten you up so that you could return to the white man's world. We have made you nice and plump so we can eat you at our feast!'

It was a story Anna enjoyed, because the writer had told it so cleverly. It wasn't until the final sentence that you discovered that the kind and caring native had rescued the white man in order to eat him. But now she recalled the story with the idea that, if she could isolate her father completely, keep him from any possibility of obtaining alcohol, she might be able to bring him back from the brink of almost certain destruction.

Even though there would be no alcohol available for purchase in the town, she reasoned that those Dutch who had been left behind would almost certainly have whiskey, gin and brandy left over from better times. Piet Van Heerden was a rich man and also possessed the cunning of an alcoholic, so this notion would not escape him. The tin box on the kitchen table would almost certainly contain money and once these desperate colonials with half and full bottles in their cupboards discovered her father's need they would make the Chinaman's efforts at bargaining seem like schoolground play.

Mevrouw Swanepoel and her obedient Hans were by no means unique. Desperate times breed desperate people. Despite her misery Anna smiled inwardly, thinking that if the Jack Sprat duo had got even a sniff of her papa's need for the dwindling supplies of alcohol, Hans would have found a horse cart and driver and would be knocking on the doors of the stay-behind Dutch clutching a bundle of guilder notes, the money they'd earned from the manufacture of their dishtowel bags, and buying whatever bottle supplies were available. In her mind she could hear him now: '*One-third, half, full bottle, the best prices offered for your leftover brandy, gin, schnapps and whiskey! Hurry! This offer will not last!*'

Anna waited until she heard her father snoring in the bedroom, then she entered the room and crept to his bedside. The Scotch bottle lay empty beside him on the mattress, and a few dregs had spilled, leaving a small brown stain on the ticking. She removed the bottle, placing it on the floor. Then she lifted his shoulders from the cushion with her right hand and with her left delicately removed from around his neck the chain from which hung the key that she presumed would open the tin box. She allowed his head to sink gently back onto the pillow, where, to her relief, moments later he resumed snoring. She was breathing heavily, not only from holding up his enormous frame with one hand placed in the small of his back, but also from the rush of adrenalin caused by a fear that he might suddenly awaken and discover her theft.

She returned to the kitchen and inserted the key in the lock on the tin box: she had been correct, it opened with a single turn. Anna lifted the lid, to be confounded by the contents. The box contained five-hundred-guilder notes in six ten-centimetre stacks, each note worth about fifty pounds sterling, more than the average Javanese family earned in a year. Like most of the older Dutch colonial families in the Spice Islands the Van Heerden family had never outwardly boasted of its enormous wealth, and while they had maintained a big house, an out-of-town estate, several *copra* plantations and *godowns* along the docks, this had always been done unostentatiously as befitted one of the oldest white dynasties on the island.

Piet Van Heerden, the only direct descendant of the clan, was no different. Bombastic and superior in nature, he'd nevertheless taken great care to play down the extent of his true wealth. Although not exactly a tightwad, nevertheless, like many rich men, he knew the value of a guilder and was slow to part with his money.

Anna had never experienced the extremes of great wealth, and thought that perhaps her stepmother, conscious of her husband having spawned a bastard child, had seen to this. She had not been spoiled or given anything more than any of her schoolmates would have taken for granted. Katerina's personal collection of jewellery, while valuable, didn't testify to more than the expected indulgences of a woman who was the matriarch of a moderately wealthy family.

Piet Van Heerden was fond of crying poor and would often tell the story of his eccentric father, Koos Van Heerden. He would relate how, on the brink of the First World War, his father had sold off a good part of his vast estates, his reason being that he believed the Germans would win and, since they were already a colonial power in New Guinea, they would then take over the Netherlands East Indies. So his father had invested the proceeds of the sale in Germany, believing that proof of these investments would stand the Van Heerden family in good stead when the German annexation of the Spice Islands took place.

The old man's reasoning had been based on a simple premise and one that was paradoxically influenced by the number of Jews in Germany. Koos Van Heerden reasoned that the bulk of Europe's wealthy Jews lived in Germany and controlled much of the industrial landscape. They would naturally be financing the impending war with the single motive of making a large profit, particularly in the manufacture of munitions and armaments, which is where he elected to place the bulk of his money. His father's favourite quote, which in turn amounted to the reasons for his choice, was 'When you deal with a Gentile you deal with one man's ambition. When you deal with a Jew you deal with the knowledge of two thousand years of persecution and how to survive and prosper despite the ambition of the Gentile!' Piet Van Heerden would sometimes use this quote as a cautionary tale, suggesting it was the reason why the family was no longer as wealthy as it ought to be and should be prudent with what money was left. He would end with a quote of his own: 'Have nothing to do with what you know nothing about.'

The cash in the tin, if all the notes were of five-hundred-guilder denomination, was a king's ransom and more. The box also contained her father's last will and testament as well as a beautiful gold pocket watch attached to a heavy gold fob chain, the cover bearing the Van Heerden coat of arms. She had seen it on one or two occasions and knew it had belonged to her grandfather. With the watch was a seal that had the same crest used, no doubt, for important legal documents. A stick of unused red sealing wax lay beside it. Finally, the box contained two tiny white envelopes each with a waxed seal that spelled 'Amsterdam' in relief. She broke the seals to discover that each envelope held six fairly large diamonds.

Anna then opened and read her father's will, to discover that in the event of his death neither his wife, Katerina, nor his daughter, Anna, were benefactors. The will assumed the Allies would win the war and the Dutch would return to the Spice Islands. All the property in Java – farms, estate, plantations, *godowns* and urban investment property – had been bequeathed to various second cousins and distant relations who were now living overseas, some of them never having lived in Java. A thick sheaf of deeds to the numerous properties was attached to the back of the will. He'd also bequeathed various amounts of money to these assorted relatives, some Anna had never heard of. This bequeathed money must be, Anna decided, the money in the deposit box.

Anna sat, more numbed than sad or even angry. She had never thought of her inheritance and it was not this aspect of the will that overwhelmed her. It was the sudden sense of being worthless as a human. Slow tears ran down her cheeks. Papa's *lieveling*, his *skatterbol*, his precious darling, his love child, in the end had become his bastard daughter to be disowned for her native blood! She had loved her papa and so had tolerated the constant abuse and insults from her stepmother. As she grew older, she began to understand Katerina's bitterness at being crippled and unable to have children of her own. But now she thought all the attention her father had lavished on her had been in order to taunt and frustrate his wife. They had been conducting a kind of marital warfare and Anna had been his most effective weapon, his big gun. His occasional admonishments to Katerina in her presence about the way her stepmother treated her were all a part of the hateful game they played, intended to make Anna love him even more for coming to her defence. When she'd informed him of the suicide of his wife, she now realised, his immediate reaction was not simply the stupid outburst of a besotted drunk but revealed a deep and bitter hatred for her stepmother. Had she outlived Piet Van Heerden, her crippled stepmother would have been left helpless with no visible means of support. It was a cruel and heartless gesture, but if you hated someone sufficiently it was also the ultimate revenge. But why had he rejected her? What sort of man was this? Why would he hate his daughter? All she'd ever done was love him. Why then was she also a part of this bitter revenge?

As Anna sat quietly at the kitchen table she grew angry. Her father had treated her as being of no worth whereas he was, to put it mildly, the weak and worthless one, an alcoholic who, but for her care, would probably soon be dead. Anna told herself she could have her revenge right here and now. She could take the tin box with its contents and simply leave him. She could do it while he was snoring in a drunken sleep. Ratih and the sergeant would help her get away and, in turn, be handsomely rewarded. Or she could put into action her imagined alcohol collection. She'd get Budi or Til to find her a man with a horse-drawn cart, gather all the partially used and full bottles still in the possession of the Dutch stay-behinds and allow her father to drink himself to death. No, she decided, that might take too long! In his comatose state she could smother him with one of the large cushions and declare he had died of a sudden heart attack. There was, after all, no coroner to prove otherwise. She had money, much, much more than she needed to get someone to murder him. The promise of a single five-hundred-guilder note would bring a queue of would-be assassins to the front gate. Or she could get Sergeant Khamdani to report him to the Japanese as a spy; she would testify against him and they'd execute him, maybe chop off his head with a samurai sword in the public square. His great balding head with his ridiculous tangled ginger eyebrows would roll in the dust. The local population would be cheering their own heads off and waving Japanese flags. Or she could buy poison in the market, rat poison, and put it in the last remaining bottle of Scotch, then watch him die in agony – another neat solution!

By this time Anna's immediate need for revenge had subsided and she realised that she lacked the resolve and the hatred to harm her father. We love people despite and not because. He must, she decided, be given a chance to explain himself. There may have been a reason, though what it was she couldn't imagine. She'd always tried to be a dutiful and loving daughter to him.

However, if he simply detested her, she would need to hear his scorn for her from his own lips. She didn't want his inheritance. She was going to marry me and we'd live happily ever after, collecting butterflies. She simply wanted to know why he despised her. Moreover, she didn't want to hear it from the mouth of a snivelling drunkard, but from her papa when he was stone-cold sober and possessed of all the reasoning faculties he must have had when he wrote the will.

Anna decided she must evolve a plan to sober him up as

quickly as possible. The Japanese could well decide to shoot the old and the useless, which would almost certainly include the drunks. Or they might place all the local refugees in camps where she might be separated from her father. Then she would never know the truth or have the opportunity to confront him. She simply couldn't bear the thought of having to carry his scorn as long as she lived.

She decided she had no time to lose. She must do as the savage had done with the drunk and create a metaphorical island where there was no alcohol. This was more or less the prevailing situation in Tjilatjap anyway. She couldn't think what might happen beyond the time when her papa was sufficiently sober to be questioned, other than that they would almost certainly be declared prisoners of war and interned in a prison camp to face an uncertain future and perhaps neither of them would survive. But she knew she couldn't allow her father to escape and go looking for brandy or whisky, for fear of what might happen to him. This was no time for any Dutch person to be alone on the streets, let alone a helpless, shambling Dutchman looking for alcohol.

Then, what should have appeared at once obvious but wasn't occurred to her. The potato cellar was the perfect place to dry him out! She rose from her chair and walked over to the side of the stove to examine the trapdoor. It had a stout iron bolt and was made from the same heavy teak as the floorboards. The wooden steps were too steep for her large father, despite his still enormous strength, to climb and obtain the leverage to force it open once the bolt was shot in place.

Anna hurried out of the house and into the backyard to locate the whereabouts of the small window, eventually finding it behind a hibiscus bush. It was sufficiently large to accept a chamber-pot, a plate of food or jug of water, and the wide wooden shelf directly under it would enable her to leave these and any other essentials her father might need, and to remove his slops. She could talk to him through the window without placing herself in danger from his anger. She would also need to get the single-bed mattress down the steps, as well as an enamel basin, which she would need to buy, and also towels, a washcloth, a couple of chamber-pots (commonly used in *kampong* homes) and a blanket. She had learned in Red Cross classes at school that people suffering from trauma needed to be kept warm.

Anna, after a fair bit of effort, managed to get the mattress from the smaller bedroom down the wooden steps. It took up almost half the dark cellar. She had no idea how long it would take to get her father sufficiently sober to allow him out into the light from the twilight world (both metaphorically and physically) in which she was placing him. She started to weep softly, just thinking about what he was about to go through if she could somehow entice him into the cellar. She knew she wouldn't dream of incarcerating an animal under such conditions, yet she was planning to treat her papa worse than she would a mongrel dog.

She started to have doubts about what she was going to do. She was not quite seventeen years old and had no experience in treating someone suffering from alcohol withdrawal. She decided she would attempt to find a Dutch doctor or nurse, one who had been foolish enough or was sufficiently committed to remain behind. She would ask Ratih. But she already suspected such people would be very difficult to find in Tjilatjap. Besides, she told herself, treating an alcoholic would not be high on their list of priorities. She wasn't even sure if they would know how to go about it, or if there was a cure. She'd never heard of drunks being admitted to hospital or of doctors treating them. In their circle, people always talked about others who had a drinking problem in hushed tones if he was male, usually adding sympathy for his poor wife. If the person with the drinking problem was female, people, in particular other women, loudly proclaimed their scorn for her. She'd never heard of anyone undergoing rehabilitation. All she had to go on was the story of a drunk white man and a cannibal, written by an author whose name she couldn't remember.

Anna crept into her father's bedroom to see that he was still completely out to it. She removed the empty bottle of Scotch and took it through to the kitchen, where she poured half of the last remaining bottle into it, then took the one bottle and placed it beside the bed together with the extra pot Ratih had left. Her father, she knew, would probably sleep until the morning but when he woke he'd use the pot to pee in and then he'd seek immediate oblivion in the half-bottle of Scotch.

She returned to the kitchen, opened the trapdoor, descended into the cellar and left the other half-bottle of Scotch on the shelf under the window. This was how she planned to get him into the cellar. Finally she removed the two packets of diamonds and a single wad of five-hundred-guilder notes and placed them in her bag. The denomination of the notes was too large for her to use them without attracting attention, but she took them so that if the tin box was discovered by someone entering the house while she was absent she would not be without considerable funds. She still had a substantial amount from the original money her father had given her with the orders to find a Chinaman.

She then had second thoughts about leaving the safety deposit box behind and so, covering it with a towel as you might a chamber-pot, she took it to the outside toilet. The dunny contained the usual broad boxed seat stretching the full width to the side walls and standing half a metre or so high, with a hole in the centre over the drop. To the left and right of the seat and directly under it there was a dark space stretching to where either side of the box seat was attached to the wall. She placed the deposit box into the left-hand space and covered it with several old newspapers left there for the usual purpose. Even with the door open it was too dark to see into the cavity that now hid a vast fortune.

This done, she knew she could safely go to the markets in the morning with *Kleine* Kiki. If, though it seemed unlikely, her papa woke from the effects of the half-bottle she'd left beside the bed, he would find neither the remaining half-bottle of Scotch nor money to take and leave the house in an attempt to buy alcohol. Back seated in the kitchen, Anna made a list of the things she'd need: cutlery, crockery, plates, cups, sheets, and the items already mentioned, all the immediate paraphernalia required to set up a rudimentary household. It was all beginning to seem rather bizarre. The Japanese might round them up in the next day or two to march them off to a concentration camp, and here she was setting up house as if they'd come to stay.

Anna was dog-tired and collapsed on the lumpy couch, to be woken seemingly moments later by Kiki's knocking on the front door and to find that the sun was up. It was almost 5 o'clock. She let Kiki inside and then went to check on the condition of her father. He had done as she'd supposed he would, pissed in the pot and reached for the bottle. He was once again comatose on the bed.

She hurried to the bathroom, where she'd earlier placed the towels and flannel she'd brought from the boat, filled the washbasin and undressed quickly, calling to Kiki to find a sarong and top and fresh undies in the dishtowel bag for her to wear. Anna washed as best she could, combed her hair and changed into native dress. Her final act was to wear a pair of Katerina's sunglasses to hide her blue eyes. Although tall for a Javanese, she knew she could, as she so often had in Batavia when wearing sunglasses, pass for a native in the street.

Outside the front gate Anna was surprised to find Til waiting. Kiki explained that Mother Ratih had insisted he come along to help carry their purchases in his *becak*. The old man now also insisted he pedal them to the markets. 'I must make sure you are safe,' he said. 'There is a rumour that today the Japanese will come.' Then from a canvas bag slung across his neck and under his left arm he withdrew two small Japanese flags, each attached to a piece of split bamboo.

Anna's heart skipped a beat and she instinctively drew back. 'Mother Ratih says we must carry these. It is safer,' Kiki explained.

'It is – er – difficult for me,' Anna stammered.

'In the lion's den it is best to roar like a lion,' Til quoted, smiling.

They crossed the main town square and Anna remembered the two American pilots. She thought of her letter to me, wondering where I was on the Indian Ocean with *Madam Butterfly* and saying a silent little prayer that I'd make it safely across to Australia.

The native market was in uproar when they arrived, long queues of locals waited to buy for three cents a small

Japanese flag. The Japanese, when they came, were to be given a tumultuous welcome by the population of Tjilatjap. It was, after all, the liberation for which they had waited three hundred years.

While Anna didn't feel inclined to bargain with the sharp-eyed market women and men, Kiki and Til insisted. 'It will seem strange to them and they will remember,' Til cautioned quietly.

The native market was flooded with the household goods and linen discarded by the fleeing Dutch. With the Japanese possibly arriving that very day, Anna couldn't help wondering whether what she was doing was pointless. Moreover, the bargaining process added to their time and she was anxious to return home in case her father woke and wandered off into the neighbourhood, begging the Dutch stay-at-homes for alcohol.

Til and Kiki carried her purchases to the shop of a friend of Til, a man who sold pots and pans and cutlery, and who had personally done very well from what Anna had bought there with the minimum of bargaining. He promised to store their goods, as it was going to take the little *becak* rider several trips, pushing his skinny, rotating legs, to deliver everything to the house.

It was still just after nine o'clock when people started jabbering excitedly in the market. Til left to see what the fuss was about and returned shortly to say that the banks were not opening and that people were being denied access to their accounts. 'For us, maybe it is not so bad, the street people they do not trust the bank. But for the Dutch who must stay, maybe it is *very* bad.'

Anna could not have put it into words at the time, but she knew that Til, with his way of looking at every side of a question and not making hasty judgments, was a rare exception.

Ratih had also shown a similar propensity to be fair-minded and non-judgmental. But Anna knew them to be very much in the minority. The Japanese invasion had begun in a climate ripe for revenge and after their propaganda machine had completed its work, the Javanese people were clamouring for retribution. The vast majority of the common people would have relished the fact that the Dutch who remained behind would be stripped of their bank accounts and most would have agreed that, in the first place, the money had been earned with the blood, sweat and tears of the Javanese people. Any money remaining, they would have maintained, should be returned to the people whom the Dutch had exploited for three hundred years. In fact, all the bank deposits were lost since their Japanese liberators 'liberated' the funds by transferring them to Japan.

They continued to shop, this time for food of the kind her father might be persuaded to eat, although Anna wasn't sure what this might be, mostly opting for ingredients with which she could make various soups, knowing they were nutritious and easy to digest. They were just about to depart the market when a roar, like an approaching wave, rose in the crowded marketplace. Anna would later tell me that it was unlike any sound she'd heard before and she didn't have to be told that the Japanese had arrived. People were beginning to run to the nearest entrance to the town square. In their haste the mob knocked over several of the open-air stalls where the owners had already departed. The crowd was yelling, laughing and shouting joyously as it surged towards the town square or to the main road that led into Tjilatjap.

'What happens now?' Anna asked, when the bulk of the mob had passed. She was standing with her back to a wall next to a frightened Kiki, but there was no sign of Til. Moments later he emerged from his friend's pots-and-pans shop. 'I have put my *becak* in my friend's shop. Come, we must go to the town square!' he said urgently.

Anna baulked at this suggestion. 'Why can't we just remain here, Til? You go, Kiki and I will remain.'

Til looked at her, then down at his sandalled feet, shaking his head slowly, then he pointed to three old toothless crones seated at the counters of separate market shops. 'They cannot go because they are too old, but they are not too old to remember who remained behind when the Japanese came.'

Anna still hesitated, and said reasonably, 'Tush! They will not remember us.'

'Aha, you do not notice how people look at you.' Til held his hands up indicating a gap between them of approximately fifteen centimetres. 'You are the tallest Javanese woman in the markets. They will remember it was the tall one with the black-glass eyes.' His expression grew suddenly resolute, like an impatient father who had suffered enough nonsense from a child. 'We *must* go and you *must* wave your flag at the soldiers.' He looked sternly at them both. 'And we will smile and cheer. Come!' he demanded, moving ahead, his skinny brown legs bandy from years of pedalling.

Led by Til, they arrived at the town square to see it was packed to capacity though there were no Japanese soldiers to be seen. Even if there had been, from where the three of them stood at the rear, they would have been obscured by the crowd. At the centre of the square stood a massively tall flagpole that could be seen from most parts of the town. In fact, it was about the only thing they could see in the square, apart from the bronze head and shoulders of a statue of the Dutch Governor-General, Jan Pieterszoon Coen, which made Anna automatically recite in her head '1617 to 1629'. To her surprise the Netherlands flag still flew from the flagpole; catching a breeze from the river, it showed the full splendour of the red, white and blue tricolour.

Anna was not to know it, but this was to be the last flutter of the flag in the colony that had added so much wealth and history to the Netherlands. At that very moment the Dutch Government was suing for peace with the Japanese and would surrender the next day. The Government administration in Batavia had ordered its troops to remain calm and stay in their barracks to be meekly taken as prisoners of war. Later it would be claimed that the Dutch soldiers lay in their barracks reading magazines while those Allies who had been sent to help them, Australian, British and American, fought for their lives in an attempt to escape to freedom and so live to fight another day.

And then in the distance a sound of cheering reached the people in the square. It was coming from the main street that led into the town square and suddenly a buzz of excitement arose from the people who stood around her. The cheering grew louder and while the three of them couldn't see, it was obvious the Japanese soldiers were close. People around them started to move backwards and Til said, 'Put your backs together,' and then he quickly added his own so that they stood solidly as the people moved backwards. Despite the noise of the crowd, Anna could hear the throb of a motorcycle engine and the explosion of a weapon being fired intermittently. Then an American Harley-Davidson motorcycle with sidecar suddenly emerged about twenty metres from where they stood. It was being driven by a Japanese sergeant and seated in the sidecar was a Japanese officer who held a pistol that he was firing into the air to warn the mob to part and to allow passage for a small and ragged band of Japanese soldiers on bicycles. There were no more than thirty bicycle riders following, some riding, others pushing their bicycles because of flat tyres. Their uniforms were ragged and dirty and in all they were no more than a single ragtag platoon. They appeared to be half-starved and looked exhausted, barely aware of the cheering, ecstatic crowd frantically waving Japanese flags.

The motorcycle was coming directly towards Anna. The lieutenant in the sidecar fired yet another shot into the air and then cleared the chamber of his pistol, a spent casing landed at Anna's feet where she quickly covered it with the sole of her sandal, then bent and recovered it, placing it into her shoulder bag. It was an almost unconscious gesture and in the excitement of the moment she would forget it was there until she found it some days later when rummaging through the bag. The officer's captured American motorcycle passed within a metre of where she stood, and because she was taller than the people around her she was able to look directly at the officer seated in the sidecar.

'Smile!' Til hissed beside her. 'Wave your flag!'

The officer, in appearance, seemed no less weary than his troops. His uniform was almost as ragged. He wore a fixed expression, neither fierce nor passive, not even determined. For a triumphant conqueror he simply looked war-weary and uninterested in putting on any sort of show for the locals. He appeared to be looking directly at Anna as she attempted to smile and wave her flag, although his expression remained unchanged as he passed. The throb of the Harley and the oily smell of its exhaust fumes filled the air around her.

She felt Til take her hand. 'Come!' he said as soon as the weary soldiers had passed. He held Kiki's hand as well and they merged behind the ragged group of soldier cyclists to finally arrive at the flagpole at the centre of the square, where the motorcyclist halted and switched off the engine. The Japanese soldiers, to the command of the sergeant who had climbed from the motorcycle, formed into three ragged, unsmiling, in fact expressionless lines, holding up their bicycles.

Quite how he had achieved it Anna couldn't imagine, but the redoubtable Til had brought them to the very front row of cheering Javanese people, to witness the Japanese takeover of the town of Tjilatjap.

The flagpole was set into a wide, raised stone plinth with six steps leading up to it. Standing on the top was a very small, slightly bandy, middle-aged man dressed in an immaculately fitting dark suit and around his right biceps was a white band with round red orb at its centre. He wore a white shirt with a high, celluloid, detachable Eton collar and red tie; the toecaps of his shoes shone in the noonday sun, the top part of his shoes being concealed by a pair of white spats. To crown it all, on his head he wore a black silk top hat.

'Who is that?' Anna asked, surprised.

'He is the Japanese tailor, Onishi Tokuma. He has lived in Tjilatjap already twenty years,' the *becak* owner answered. Then he added gratuitously, 'The Dutch, always for them, he makes their wedding suit. He is the number-one for tailoring!'

'Ah! I see. He is to be the official translator?'

'I think now he will be the boss of this town!' Til observed with a wry grin.

The Japanese lieutenant climbed wearily from the sidecar and then, making a conscious effort, straightened his uniform and adjusted his cap. Then reaching down into the sidecar he withdrew what appeared to be a canvas-covered writing pad and a folded Japanese flag. The flag he gave to the sergeant. Then he mounted the steps, nodded briefly in the direction of Onishi Tokuma and, without shaking his hand, stood several paces from him. Opening the canvas folder, he cleared his throat and, head bowed, commenced to read in Japanese in a low mumble that Anna could barely hear. It was only a short passage and when he had finished he handed the folder to the town's number-one tailor, who bowed so deeply that his top hat fell from his head and rolled a metre or so from where he was standing. The tailor accepted the folder and, ignoring the accident with his top hat, which he left lying on the plinth, he opened the folder and studied it briefly. Then, taking a deep anticipatory breath and filled with self-importance and pride, he launched into a magniloquent and loudly proclaimed translation of the Japanese announcement into Javanese.

'To the people of Tjilatjap the Japanese Imperial Army and Navy bids you welcome! We come as liberators to join you in glorious coexistence with the Greater East Asia Co-Prosperity Sphere! You have all seen how the forces of the European colonial oppressors have been made to bow down to the Imperial Armed Forces of Nippon. For the peaceful transition from your unworthy oppressors to your humble liberators we require that you obey all orders without question! There can be no disobedience!' Here he was forced to pause as the crowd pressing around the plinth cheered wildly and those who were packed into the square beyond, unable to hear him, responded in turn to the cheering they heard coming from the flagpole. When silence had finally been restored the tailor-turned-translator continued: 'The Japanese Imperial Army under the local command of Lieutenant Mori will be in charge and I will be your new mayor!' He paused to let this important information sink in. Then he looked skywards and pointed, shaking his finger accusingly at the Dutch flag still fluttering from the effect of the breeze blowing from the river. 'We will now forever lower the flag of your hated oppressors and raise the glorious flag of Japan in the name of our sacred Majesty, the God King, the Emperor Hirohito!' He made a lopsided attempt at standing to attention. '*Banzai!*' he shouted so fiercely that a fine spray of spittle issued from his mouth.

Lieutenant Mori, somewhat taken aback by this unexpected solitary hail to the Emperor, drew to desultory attention and then, turning to the sergeant, indicated that the Dutch flag be lowered. For the first time everyone in the square and beyond could see what was happening and a tremendous roar rose as ten thousand or more tiny Japanese flags were raised and waved above each individual head, like a myriad red-and-white striped butterflies.

The roar increased to an even greater crescendo when the flag carrying the emblem of the rising sun was seen to slowly move up the post and suddenly, to the watching people, three hundred years of oppression ended. The Japanese flag reached its zenith, catching the same river breeze that remained impervious to the change in the colour of bunting it caused to flutter against a cloudless sky.

The Japanese sergeant tied the hoisting rope to its cleat, then turned smartly and called the thirty weary cyclists to attention. Lieutenant Mori, himself at attention, then raised his arm. 'Long live His Imperial Majesty!' '*Banzai! Banzai! Banzai!*' the soldiers all called out in unison. The crowd around the flagpole started to yell '*Banzai! Banzai! Banzai!*' until the entire population gathered in the square and streets beyond were shouting the traditional hail to the Keeper of the Chrysanthemum Throne, His Majesty, the Emperor Hirohito, henceforth to be their glorious leader as well.

Anna even had a brief though silent laugh when the

sergeant, at the conclusion of the flag-raising ceremony, turned to salute his officer and in the process took a smart step backwards and, raising his right boot, brought it down to a resounding stamp, stepping squarely on the mayoral top hat and crushing it beyond repair. The newly appointed titular head of the non-existent town council had already lost his crown.

'Now he has no hat to conceal his empty head,' Til said quietly.

The Japanese Imperial Army, in all its ragged, hungry, weary, two-wheeled and punctured-tyre glory, had arrived in Tjilatjap.

CHAPTER NINE

*'Allah created sleep so we can lay down our sadness for a
little while each night,
otherwise we humans would find the burden of sorrow we
carry too heavy to bear.'*
Til
Becak driver, Tjilatjap

THE SMALL, RAGGED TROOP of weary Japanese
soldiers moved to set up a temporary camp in an open area that
was sandwiched between the town square and the river, where
they asked that they be brought food and drinking water, these
requests being their only attempt to assert themselves. They
had come the breadth of the island, a six-day ordeal through
jungle and mosquito-infested swamps, bypassing the scattered,
ineffectual resistance that they encountered. They had arrived
in Tjilatjap hungry and suffering from total exhaustion. The
Japanese lines had been stretched almost beyond endurance
and these soldiers had been pushed too hard for weeks; they
needed rest above anything else and in their present condition
weren't the least bit interested in playing the role of triumphant
conqueror.

However, as if by some sort of osmosis, various Javanese
functionaries, petty clerks and general factotums to the Dutch
administration, and including some of the more self-important
townsfolk, suddenly appeared everywhere wearing the white

armband with the blood-red dot emblazoned upon it. Ratih was to name them 'Broken Eggs', Til's explanation being that when you cracked the egg's outside shell the contents within were messy and usually rotten. The expression soon caught on, for although they followed the letter of the law as laid down by the Japanese Imperial Forces, the local population appeared to be quite willing to be scornful of the shortcomings of these opportunists who, for the most part, proved alarmingly incompetent and officious, the officiousness usually applied in liberal helpings to cover up ignorance.

Directly after the flag-changing ceremony, the Broken Eggs were chasing people from the town square, advising anyone who asked – and several who didn't – that they were henceforth the town committee under the inestimable new mayor, Onishi Tokuma. The mayor, by the way, could wear a different suit to his office every day for a month and still have one to spare, while nobody else on the committee even possessed a jacket. This was not a sign of poverty but a sensible omission in a tropical climate. A little later people would also ask where the ubiquitous armbands had come from in the first instance. Nobody had seen them being made in the marketplace and all the evidence pointed to the Japanese tailor's shop. The little tailor had secretly sewn the armbands and then appointed himself the mayor, handpicked his cronies and issued them with their Broken Egg identification in anticipation of the arrival of his fellow countrymen and liberators. The first edict delivered by the Mayor of the Squashed Hat, as he soon became known, was that the Japanese soldiers were to be given the benefit of peace and quiet and nobody was to disturb them or enter the square for two days. As the town square was central to all the streets and businesses, this virtually closed down everything in Tjilatjap and brought the town to a near standstill. This first edict was to set the example for many others to come that often left the local people scratching their heads in bewilderment.

Although Onishi Tokuma was Japanese he had lived in Tjilatjap for twenty years and people remembered him not for his nationality but as the obsequious tailor who fawned over the Dutch, fussing over a wedding suit with much bowing and scraping, spraying them with unnecessary and extravagant compliments. He even supplied the boutonnières of a small orchid and lacy fern, their stems wrapped in tight silver foil that was tied in a certain Japanese manner, one each for the bridegroom, his best man, father of the bride and groomsman.

He now explained his fawning manner by saying he was all the while spying for the Japanese, that a tailor hears things that others don't. It was he who had prepared the soldiers of the Emperor for the ultimate liberation of the town. Furthermore, he maintained that the people of Tjilatjap ought to pay him due homage as a local hero and that his self-appointment as mayor was a logical outcome and just reward for his past covert efforts.

But few people were fooled by his vainglorious justification. If he had indeed played a part, then thirty weary cyclists and a disinterested officer and sergeant on a motorbike with sidecar weren't exactly the triumphant and glorious liberation the population had expected. In retrospect, despite the fervent flag-waving, street-lining and the cheering the soldiers had received, thirty exhausted soldiers almost amounted to an insult. The people of Tjilatjap felt they deserved a better parade to celebrate the joyous occasion of their liberation from the hated colonials. As far as they were concerned, Onishi Tokuma had been a toady to the Dutch and now he was one to the Japanese.

Sergeant Khamdani, while not refusing, simply neglected to

wear the Broken Egg insignia, although most of the Javanese *pak polisi* added them to their uniforms as a matter of course. As the months wore on, people, fed up with the general incompetence of local officials, would point to him in the *kampong* and say, 'See, there are still some good policemen around. He will give you an opinion that is correct for a change.'

Til returned to the markets to start the delivery of Anna's household shopping. Kiki accompanied her on the walk home, helping to carry the basket of fruit and vegetables and other ingredients for her papa's soup. Anna dearly wanted Kiki to enter the house with her but resisted the impulse to ask and when they reached the front gate she turned and kissed her on the cheek. 'Good luck, Kiki, you had better be off now, you don't want Mother Ratih scolding you for being late on your first day.' Kiki left with some reluctance, pleading that she could help make the soup and still be on time at the *kampong* kitchen, but Anna entered the house alone with her heart thumping, not knowing what she might find.

'Papa?' she called and waited. But there was no response. She crept as silently as possible across the teak floorboards to the main bedroom where she'd closed the door when she'd left the house earlier. It now stood slightly ajar. Peeping in she could see the vacated bed and the dent in the pillow her father's head had made. 'Papa, I'm home!' she called again. But no response came. She opened the door fully to see he wasn't there. The pot she'd left for him to piss in rested on the floor beside the bed. She walked in to examine it and observed that it had been used, the sharp smell and deep-brown colour of the urine indicating that he was badly dehydrated – another snippet of knowledge from the Red Cross lessons she'd undertaken at school about the treatment of survivors. 'Papa!' she now shouted out boldly. Still no reply came.

Anna brought her hand up to cover her wildly beating heart. What if he'd left the house? Maybe he'd wandered down to the river and fallen in? Or been robbed and beaten up? *For what?* she asked herself, since he had no money. *His pride and joy, his gold Baume and Mercier Swiss wristwatch! (Which would have remained unwound since we left Batavia)*, she irrelevantly thought. He was obvious prey, a stumbling, incoherent Dutchman with a valuable gold watch on his wrist that would act as a magnet to a thief or a gang of street kids, such as the ones who'd found Katerina's wheelchair.

Anna walked into the second bedroom searching, and then into the kitchen. At first glance he didn't appear to be there either until she saw that the trapdoor was open. She walked quickly over to it and peered down the wooden steps. It was too dark to see much beyond the bottom step but she could hear her father's heavy breathing. He'd taken the bait – she had him incarcerated in the cellar! The drying-out process was about to begin. She closed the trapdoor and shot the bolt, then lit the stove and set about preparing a vegetable broth in the hope that he might accept some sustenance when he eventually came around. But for a few crusts of dry bread and a little boiled rice on the boat, he'd eaten nothing since they'd come ashore.

Til arrived an hour later, apologising profusely, and explained that the town square had been closed by that Japanese idiot, him of the crushed top hat, Onishi Tokuma, forcing Til to go the long way around, at least another two kilometres of pedalling along rutted back streets and alleys with squawking chickens scattering in sudden fright, waddling ducks and mangy dogs snapping at his ankles.

Along with other cooking and household utensils the first load contained two enamel chamber-pots, an enamel jug and basin that Anna judged would pass through the small cellar window, and several plates, dishes and mugs of the same material that her father couldn't break or use as a weapon on himself.

While at the market she'd requested that one of the seamstresses make up six pairs of khaki shorts and flannel singlets and underpants. It had proved impossible to buy anything in her father's size off the rack. Anna hadn't the slightest notion how she might go about persuading her father to change his clothes, and was simply hoping that as he sobered up he might feel the need to wash and stay clean. She had no idea what to expect from him and was trying to prepare for every eventuality.

She'd tried to buy aspirin and cough mixture and was told that it wasn't available even on the Chinese black market. She made a mental note to talk to Budi and see if Lo Wok could help, knowing that if he could, there would be no bargaining and she would be at his mercy. She'd been fortunate enough to procure two large bottles of citronella oil, as the mosquitoes came in swarms from the river at sundown and in the dark cellar they would drive her papa insane. Whether she could make him use it or whether he would try to drink it she didn't know. She'd also found three jars of sulphur ointment, a bottle of iodine and some salt tablets, though she had no idea whether she would need them.

When she'd been at school, with the impending war they'd all been through a hastily contrived course in treating victims of bombings or survivors brought in from ships that had sunk. It had all been fairly superficial, the idea of the headmistress, Miss de Kok, who was also on the social committee of the local Red Cross. The course had been meant to spice up the curriculum and make her scatty teenage girls more aware of the war. Nobody really believed that the existing medical facilities would break down or medical personnel would go missing or, for that matter, that the Japanese would actually land. After all, Singapore was the impregnable fortress. Java would always be safe from an invasion, even in the unlikely scenario where Singapore fell to the Japanese. The Japanese lines would be stretched too far for them to get an army as far as the Spice Islands. Hence the terms used for the course: 'Treating victims of bombing or survivors of ships sinking'. It had a nice brave feel to it without being frightening. This never-to-be-taken-too-seriously trauma training was the total extent of Anna's knowledge and had nothing whatsoever to do with the rehabilitation of an alcoholic.

Piet Van Heerden started to bellow at two in the afternoon and Anna rushed to the back of the house and crept down between the hibiscus bushes to the small window. 'Papa, I'm here!' she called.

'Where am I? What is this? Where are you? It's dark!' he shouted.

'Here by the little window. I've made you some nice soup. You must eat, Papa.'

'Damn you, where am I? Have you put me in prison? Get me out at once!' Piet Van Heerden shouted, shuffling towards the window. Anna drew back so he couldn't reach out and grab her. As he emerged out of the dark into the light thrown from the window she could see his ginger-stubbled face was purple with rage.

'Papa, there is no more alcohol and I can't buy any, there's none available.'

'Get me out! Slut! Whore! Get me out!'

'No, Papa, only when you're better; you are safe down there and I will look after you,' Anna said, trying to pacify her enraged father. Then almost as an afterthought, she added, 'The Japanese are here and they are taking all the Dutch men into captivity. They are shooting some of them. I must hide you or you will die, Papa!' Anna spoke in a despairing voice, hoping this hastily contrived lie would control his anger.

Piet Van Heerden had to stoop to look through the window. 'Japanese? They are here? Where are our troops?'

'They are not here, Papa. They say we will surrender very soon, even perhaps today. The Japanese flag is flying from the town square, I saw it happen myself.' Anna was delighted to have thought of this seemingly real excuse to keep her father in the cellar.

Piet Van Heerden's expression turned from fury to disbelief and then he appeared somewhat contrite. 'I'm sorry I called you names, bad names, my *lieveling*,' he said. 'I was confused, you understand?'

'*Ja*, Papa, I understand,' she said, relieved that he appeared to believe her.

'Anna, you must find me something to drink or I will perish.'

'Soup, Papa, I have made some nice soup.'

'A bottle, brandy, Scotch, anything,' he called plaintively.

'Papa, I have tried, there is nothing. Even the Chinese, they have nothing, not even a bottle of sherry or schnapps.'

'Gin!' he cried. 'I will drink gin!' he yelled, as if by omitting it, Anna was saying it was still available.

'*Nee*, Papa. Gin also, there is none. There is nothing, no alcohol.'

'The homes, the Dutch, go to the homes, knock on the door, you hear! Offer them anything they want, ten guilders, more!'

Anna sighed, knowing she would do no such thing. 'I will try, but the imam has commanded that all alcohol be abolished. Everyone is scared, Papa, this is now a Muslim country – we have to obey their rules.' Anna wondered at her newfound capacity to turn into a consummate liar when it seemed necessary. 'But if you will drink some soup, I promise I will do another search.'

'Bring it,' Piet Van Heerden said in a sulky voice. 'I will try. I am not hungry.'

'Papa, we have sealed the trapdoor so the Japanese won't find you. Everything must come through this window. I will bring you food and water, a chamber-pot and a dish so you can wash. Please, Papa! I don't want them to find you!' Anna said in a pleading voice, hoping to convince her father.

Piet Van Heerden pushed his arm through the window, pleading. '*Lieveling, skatterbol*, you must find me some drink or your papa, who loves you, will die!' he begged, his voice choking. Anna saw that his hand was shaking violently; it would be impossible for him to use a spoon. She would have to bring his soup in a mug and strain the liquid first.

Anna left and soon returned with an enamel mug of soup and the other things, placing the mug on the ledge below the window. 'Papa, here is nice soup!' she called. 'You must drink it while it is hot.'

Her father must have been lying down because now he returned to the window, clutching the blanket around him. He managed to drink some of the soup, spilling some over the blanket. He returned the mug still half full. 'I have had enough. Now go and find me a bottle, Anna! Anything! Pay what you must! In the tin there is money.' He reached around his neck to discover the key was missing. 'The key! Where is the *foking* key?'

Anna hesitated, not sure what to say. If she admitted to possessing the key to the tin box he might suspect she had read his will.

'The key around your neck? I found it in your bed, the chain is broken. Is it for the tin box?'

'*Ja*, go quickly,' he pleaded. 'Open it, there is money.'

'Papa, it will not be possible to find alcohol,' Anna replied as gently as she could.

'Open the *foking* box!' her father shouted. 'Get the money and go! Pay anything, you hear? Anything! I *must* have a bottle!' His mood suddenly changed and a whine came into his voice. 'Please, *lieveling* – I am dying.'

Anna put the chamber-pot, a jug of water and a tin mug on the shelf, being careful to wait until her father's hand was out of reach. 'I am going now, Papa, try to sleep.'

'Go! Hurry! I am desperate.' His teeth were beginning to chatter and his body trembled despite the blanket that he had wrapped around him.

Anna has asked me not to write about the next few days in her father's life; she describes them as a time of terror, exhaustion and panic. At times she was certain her father was not going to live and, in truth, he might well have died since thirty per cent of alcoholics who are denied access to alcohol, if not properly medicated, do not survive. Many are diabetics and others develop bronchial problems and pneumonia; others perish of dehydration and yet others die of heart attacks. They will undergo exaggerated degrees of spontaneous shaking, then perspire until their garments are completely soaked, then feel intensely cold. Nausea will occur frequently, heart palpitations, acute diarrhoea and bad headaches. Anna was not to know that though alcoholics may die from alcohol poisoning, liver or kidney malfunction, the cause of death is often something else they've neglected to attend to. Piet Van Heerden had come aboard the *Witvogel* in fairly good health, a well-cared-for alcoholic with no symptoms other than his addiction, and so was likely to survive the ordeal. But this state of good physical health would not have helped the experience of withdrawal. When alcohol is withdrawn from the system the alcoholic begins to experience sensory overload. Everything becomes hugely exaggerated, sometimes by a hundred times. The light from the small cellar window would have seemed to Piet Van Heerden as if he was standing in the centre of a brilliant spotlight with his eyes being forced to remain open. Anna's footsteps on the kitchen floor would have sounded as if a herd of buffalo was above him. His trembling, even if slight, would have felt as if a goods train was passing over his body, ripping muscle and sinew to shreds, crushing his internal organs in the process. And then the hallucinations began.

The delirium tremens can take many fantastical forms. The sufferer may believe lice are crawling, centimetres thick, all over his body so he scratches frantically and screams out for help. He may have the same vivid experience with spiders or snakes, and no amount of reassurance will convince him that he is imagining this terrifying experience. He will also suffer insomnia and believe strange creatures are attacking him, devils with two heads, every type of horrible phantasmagoria. Piet Van Heerden would have lost all sense of time. He would have become consumed with fear, going into a full-blown panic attack, eyes bulging from his head, gasping for air, his body soaked with perspiration. This would happen over the next seventy hours – the begging, screaming, choking horror of it all – while once the withdrawal had started there was nothing Anna could have done.

On the morning of the fourth day a weak and exhausted Piet Van Heerden started to come out of withdrawal. Although Anna had placed fresh water on the shelf every hour, he had seldom reached for it. Now he was badly dehydrated but sufficiently conscious to start drinking water and then taking food. From the cellar the stink of vomit and shit reached her, but she persisted two more days before she opened the trapdoor and descended into the hell below.

The smell was overpowering; she had thought to wrap a handkerchief around her nose and face and then decided she couldn't appear in front of her father masked. She struggled not to throw up and the sight of her father lying on the mattress in the semi-dark was appalling. He was covered in excrement, having smeared his arms, legs and face with his diarrhoea, possibly thinking that it might ward off the effect of the imagined lice that he thought crawled like a grey blanket over his flesh.

Gasping and weeping at the same time she helped him to sit up, the crusted shit covering her hands. 'You are going to be well again, Papa,' she said, squatting down in front of him.

Piet Van Heerden could barely whisper, but Anna heard him plainly enough. 'I am going to kill you, *abangan*, she devil!' He raised his hands and tried to grab her around the neck, but the effort was so slow that she easily enough moved away, jumping to her feet. He was too weak to hold his hands up and they fell limply on his lap. Anna realised that her giant papa would have lacked the strength to throttle her.

Over the three days of his acute withdrawal she had escaped the house whenever she had a reasonable excuse, buying more tin mugs, managing to find a large tin of disinfectant, getting his khaki shorts and singlets from the seamstress. She had also learned that the local Muslim clerics were enforcing their order that all alcohol found in appropriated infidel houses be destroyed immediately and the same had occurred to the three liquor shops in town. The Dutch stay-behinds were also ordered to get rid of any alcohol they had in their homes. Tjilatjap was as dry as the Sahara Desert and even the production of beer had ceased. Whatever stocks had existed had been poured down the sewerage system in one grand day of decontamination. It was to cause a hundred-metre island of foam where the sewage emptied out into the river.

On the day after the arrival of the Japanese, Budi had arrived at the house to say that the Dutch had surrendered and every citizen was to attend the official ceremony in the town square, despite the Mayor of the Crushed Hat's directions to stay away. They hurried along with the rest of the townspeople to where Ratih, Kiki and the sergeant waited to meet them. Once again Til, who had gone ahead, had somehow contrived to find them space close to the front where they could witness the proceedings. Here they officially heard the news that the

Dutch had surrendered to the Japanese.

Now, as they watched, a somewhat refreshed liberator hauled down the Japanese flag and once again hoisted the Dutch one to the jeers of the population, and then Lieutenant Mori read a long speech in Japanese that sounded as if it was not dissimilar to the one of the previous day. It was followed by his first edict. In the light of the usual behaviour of an invading army, it was a curious one. Translated by the Mayor of the Crushed Hat, Lieutenant Mori began reading from a book of instructions: 'Edict Number One. In the name of the Greater East Asia Co-Prosperity Sphere and in harmony with the goodwill of the Japanese Imperial Army, fraternisation between Javanese women and Japanese soldiers is strictly forbidden. All such incidents must be reported. If a soldier of the Japanese Imperial Army has raped or sexually abused a local woman, even a prostitute, he will be severely punished and in some cases may be executed. If the woman is proved to be the provocateur, she will be summarily shot.'

After all this, the Dutch flag was unceremoniously hauled down and thrown into the crowd, where it was set alight to much cheering. Then, in a re-enactment of the day before, the Japanese flag was hoisted accompanied by many cries of *banzai* and shouts of loyalty to the Emperor. The people happily waved their little paper flags and cheered as they had done previously. Anna learned later from Kiki that there had been a great deal of feasting that night to celebrate the official freedom from the Dutch and she and Ratih had been up until dawn cooking for happy people who wanted to be with others to celebrate.

If these excursions away from home seemed callous under the circumstances, Anna believed that she would go mad from her father's despairing cries – cries of horror, abuse, fear, torment and sobbing that seemed to never cease. She herself could cry no more and as much as anything it was panic and despair and a sense of her own survival that drove her from the house. Throughout this long and traumatic vigil, when she often felt her father must surely die and she would be proclaimed his murderer, she told herself she must persevere, convincing herself that he would die anyway or be killed. For one so young it was an astonishingly brave decision and now, miraculously, it appeared to have worked. The worst was over.

Anna returned to the kitchen, leaving the trapdoor open, knowing her father was too weak to climb the wooden steps, though preferring that he should do so. It would be a lot easier to clean him in the bathroom than in the stinking little cellar. She took a basin and a large jug of hot water back down with her, as well as his new clothes, underpants and a pair of scissors. She cut the shit-stained singlet from him and commenced to wash his face, neck, arms and torso. She returned to the kitchen for more hot water, then cut away his trousers, leaving him wearing only his underpants, which were brown with dried excrement. 'I must cut off your underpants, Papa. I will try not to look.'

'No, let me turn my back,' he moaned. He turned slowly, like an old man does, uncertain of his balance. She cut the garment at the back, pulling it where the shit had caused it to stick to the skin and hair on his bum. Then she cleaned his backside, rinsed the cloth and handed it to him. 'Clean only your private parts, then cup them with your hands,' Anna instructed, by now well past any sensitivities. Piet Van Heerden did as he was told, then turned, his huge hands cupping himself between the legs while Anna cleaned the inside of his thighs. She could only wipe him down rather than use soap as she intended to do when he was sufficiently strong to climb the steps and get to the bathroom. He still smelled to high heaven.

She returned with another jug of hot water and washed his hair, making him somewhat less smelly. Then she made him step into the legs of his fresh underpants before hauling them up to his thighs, whereupon he turned his back on her and adjusted them properly.

She cleaned the stained mattress as best she could, wiping disinfectant over the surface, turning it over and covering it with a fresh sheet. When her father was lying down again she commenced to scrub the floor and shit-covered walls, constantly gagging during the whole process, her hands stinging and red raw from the strong disinfectant. The task took most of the afternoon and she made countless trips up the stairs to the kitchen for hot water.

Almost too tired to walk, Anna fed her father a bowl of broth, or at least all he could manage to keep down. 'Drink water, Papa, all you can, and tomorrow you can come upstairs.'

'What about the Japanese?' he asked, surprisingly remembering her invented story.

'They are not always around. Now that you are better, we will be careful and hide you if they come near.'

'Where are our soldiers?'

'The Netherlands has surrendered, Papa. The Japanese are in charge now.'

'Oh?' he said, looking bewildered. 'The Queen? She has surrendered to those yellow bastards?' There was no vehemence behind this statement, rather it sounded like a man declaring he had been abandoned and there was little point in carrying on.

'No, Papa. She is in London. It happened some days ago in Batavia. I think it was her generals who didn't want to fight, who surrendered. There was a ceremony here in the town square, and they burnt the Dutch flag.' If there had ever been any fight in her father, Anna decided it was now gone.

'Monkeys!' he replied.

'Papa, you must be very careful and *never* leave the house. You understand, *never*!' Anna cautioned, hoping this would strike fear into her father's breast.

Leaving Piet Van Heerden in the cellar, she climbed the steps and left the trapdoor open. Then, remembering his earlier threat to kill her, she thought better of it and, returning, closed it and shot the bolt. Anna drank a little of the broth, too weary to even sob. Then, utterly exhausted, she collapsed on the bumpy settee and then, moments before she fell into a troubled sleep, she remembered it was her seventeenth birthday.

The following morning Piet Van Heerden was still too weak to negotiate the steps but by late that afternoon, with rice and chicken in his belly and with a great deal of help from Anna, he finally made it into the kitchen, although once there he lay on the floor panting for half an hour. He still smelled atrocious but finally, by sundown, she managed to get him under the shower, where he was sufficiently recovered to refuse her help to soap him down, waiting until she had left and closed the door before he undressed.

It was two weeks before Piet Van Heerden had regained most of his strength and, knowing nothing about alcoholism, Anna thought him cured, not knowing that alcoholics are never cured. In fact, as there was no alcohol available he was eventually effectively restored to health and with good food and plenty of rest would soon be in better shape than he had been in several years. While Anna cooked some of the meals for herself and her father, most arrived via Kiki and as a result of the generosity of Ratih. There was rice, of course, and stir-fried vegetables, dried salted fish, spiced chicken, tofu, *krupuk* (fish and shrimp crackers), and most of the cooked ingredients were flavoured with *sambal* sauce. Piet Van Heerden was accustomed to Javanese food and enjoyed it, so his strength was quickly restored.

During this period a battalion of Japanese troops arrived by ship under the command of Major Masahiro Eiji, who took over the control of the town. Again, despite the fears of the Dutch stay-behinds, this was done in a surprisingly low-key manner. Major Masahiro Eiji was an engineer and set his troops to the task of fully restoring the harbour facilities and getting the dredges going again. Tjilatjap was the only port on the southern side of the island and the nearest to New Guinea, the Solomons and then Australia, and so was of vital importance to the Japanese.

As a consequence, things continued much the same as previously, the Dutch keeping to themselves and out of the way, only venturing out when forced to buy food or other necessities. The locals carried on with their lives as always, but now this was done under the incompetent administration of their Japanese mayor and his abysmal town committee. Much to his own surprise, Sergeant Khamdani was elevated to the rank of lieutenant and officially placed in charge of the central town precinct, one of the few decisions by the jumped-up Japanese tailor and his town-hall cronies that the people living in the nearby *kampongs* agreed was both intelligent and merited. The downside to this, although not of great consequence, was that he had to wear the Broken Egg armband.

As Til, who was always ready to supply a quote, explained, 'It is not what is around a man's arm but what is in his head that matters.' Budi had pointed out that when he'd alluded to the Broken Egg committee he'd said that when you cracked the shell all you found was a mess. Til, not to be beaten by the boy's smart-alec logic, replied, 'Ah, yes! It takes experience to break an egg and cook it properly, whereupon it becomes a useful dish. The sergeant has this experience, while the Broken Eggs appointed by the Japanese tailor lack it, and so they end up in a dreadful mess and he is a useful dish.' Til was indeed a man for all reasons!

Anna waited a month after her father's recovery. She had long since retrieved the tin box from the outside toilet and replaced the envelopes that contained the diamonds in anticipation that he might ask her for the box. Strangely, he hadn't requested the return of the key. Finally, one night when they were sitting at the kitchen table after the evening meal, she confronted him. She had earlier taken the will from the box and now had it beside her.

'Papa, you have suffered a great deal because of what I did to you in the cellar. Do you still wish to kill me?'

Piet Van Heerden was taken aback by his daughter's direct question. 'Anna! *Lieveling!* You are my most precious daughter. Why, your papa loves you! I was in a bad state, and sometimes we say things we don't mean! Of course I do not want to kill you!'

'You said it first, then you tried to throttle me!' Anna

accused, without raising her voice, her eyes downcast.

'*Skatterbol!* You are my life!'

'I did it to *save* your life, Papa. You were drinking yourself to death. I did it because I loved you!' Anna was close to tears.

'*Aag*, it was the withdrawal! I cannot tell you the stress, the suffering, the terrible hallucinations. Lice crawled all over my body, thick as a blanket, devils tormented me, snakes buried their fangs in my neck and deadly spiders, tarantulas, bit me. I was not myself, Anna. What I said was not me, it was someone else, you must understand.'

'Then you do not resent what I did?'

Piet Van Heerden thought for a moment before replying. 'Then, yes, of course. Now, no! You are right, I was trying to kill myself at the bottom of a bottle. You saved my life, *lieveling*. Whatever happens with the Japanese, even if we are parted, I will always know I was loved and that you cared for me.' Anna's father smiled. 'What more can a father ask of a loving daughter, eh?'

Anna switched tack. 'Papa, why did you stay with my stepmother when you hated her so?'

'Hated her? No, you have me wrong, she was often a spiteful woman, but she suffered a great deal, it was my duty to look after her. I couldn't leave her, I am not that kind of man.'

'When I told you of her suicide you said you were glad to be rid of her.'

'Anna, *lieveling*! It was a drunk talking! You mustn't take any notice, a drunk says things . . .' His voice trailed off.

'So, if she had lived you would always have looked after her?'

'Of course!'

'And if you had died from drinking and she had lived?'

Piet Van Heerden spread his hands wide. 'It is a husband's

duty,' he said simply. 'She would have been well off.' He paused, then added, 'You also, *lieveling*. Everything is provided for.'

Anna produced the will from behind her back. 'This is your will, Father.' It was the first time in her life she hadn't addressed him as 'Papa'. 'Your last will and testament, it was made a month before we left Batavia.'

Anna saw a look of sudden fear cross her father's eyes and then he was silent. After a few moments he rose and began to pace and Anna got ready to run if he should turn on her suddenly. As a precaution she had selected the chair closest to the kitchen door. While she was cautious, watching him closely, strangely she wasn't afraid; instinctively she knew she was his match. He was weak and she was strong. While he might have harmed her when he was drunk, when sober her father lacked the guts to kill her. Finally he sat down again, placing his elbows on the table, his hands cupping his chin. Then after a while he began to sob. Anna remained silent, offering him no sympathy. She didn't want his inheritance. She merely waited for an explanation. She had always loved him and had never done anything to harm him and had always tried hard to please him and to make him proud of her. Now she wanted to know why he appeared to hate her so. She sensed that her father was waiting for her sympathy, for some word of forgiveness. She had always calmed him, always taken his side. Now she could no longer do so.

Finally Piet Van Heerden looked up, his eyes glazed with self-pity. 'I – you will have seen that I am very small, a very big man with a very small pee-pee. If I had gone with a white girl before I was married she would have laughed.' He looked up. 'I raped her and she ruined my life,' he said finally.

'Who? Who did you rape? My stepmother? Katerina?' Anna tried to conceal her shock.

Her father shook his head slowly, looking down so that all Anna could see was the ginger and grey tangle of his eyebrows. 'No, Katerina was a virgin when we married. I did not tell her. When she saw it she laughed. "Your *slang* is only a fat little worm!" she cried.'

'Then who?' Anna asked again.

'Your mother – I raped your mother.' He let go another pitiful sob.

'You raped my mother?' Anna said, not quite believing her own ears.

'I was young. Besotted. I couldn't have her. I was the *white* man!' he protested. Anna didn't respond at first and they were both silent with her father sniffing, his head down.

After a while he looked up and Anna said, 'And I was the result.'

Piet Van Heerden nodded. 'I paid for it very dearly.'

'Because you were saddled with me?' Anna asked quietly.

'No, no, no!' he said hastily. 'It was not like that.'

'Oh?'

'They abducted me.' He sniffed again.

'They?'

'Your mother's people – the *alurwaris*!'

'That was her – my mother's name, Alurwaris?'

'No, that is the name of the kinship group. They are animists before they are Muslims.'

'And they harmed you?'

Piet Van Heerden looked directly at Anna and then broke down sobbing, gulping for air. 'They, the *alurwaris*, called in the medicine men, the *abangan*. They – they – cut off my balls!' He now commenced to wail in earnest.

Anna was too shocked to react and simply sat silently,

completely stunned. When in the cellar he'd threatened to kill her he'd used that word '*abangan*'. After a few moments she began to collect her thoughts. Her father's castration explained a great deal she would address in her mind later. The past weeks had been enormously harrowing, but they had also taught her to face up to some of the more unpleasant aspects of life.

She had coped with Katerina's suicide, her father's drunken behaviour and the horror of his withdrawal, the unexpected role of being a refugee with an uncertain future. Then had come the knowledge that she was not loved by her father, that, but for me (if I was still alive), there was nobody who cared about her and that under her present circumstances she was completely alone. Now Anna held back her tears, believing she deserved, indeed must have, a full explanation from her distraught and broken father.

She allowed him to continue to sob, resisting the temptation to go to him, to comfort and forgive him. She must, she told herself, hear the full story of her mother, who had always been a shadowy figure, cruelly alluded to often by her stepmother in terms that suggested she had been a prostitute, but never openly discussed. Anna had been strictly forbidden at an early age to ask about her, and so in her thoughts her mother was as insubstantial as if she were a ghost. There had always been a hollow part, a place that needed to be filled, an incomplete half of her that needed to know who it was that had given her the gift of life. Now she was determined to find out, to have the full story. And so Anna waited until her father's self-pitying sobs grew less frequent, then she handed him a dishtowel to dry his tears.

'Why, Father? Why did they castrate you? Because you raped her – raped my mother?' Anna's tone suggested that a white man raping a native woman was a terrible crime, but that castration was an extraordinary consequence and punishment.

Piet Van Heerden wiped his eyes and blew his nose into the corner of the dishtowel. 'She was highborn,' he replied.

'I don't understand. Highborn? What does that mean?'

'From a good family, an old family, one with property and water rights, a woman in such a family would have an arranged marriage with a man of the same social standing and must have the permission from the male guardian, who will arrange the *slametan*, the marriage feast.' Piet Van Heerden paused, then explained. 'I violated this custom and brought great shame on her family and loss of face to her formal guardian. He called on the kinship group, the *alurwaris*.'

'But why didn't you marry her?' Anna asked ingenuously.

Her father pulled back, alarmed at the thought. 'Impossible!' Then he added quickly, 'I was already married to Katerina six months.'

Anna recognised that his vehemence at the suggestion that he marry her mother had nothing to do with the rejoinder that he was already married to her stepmother. 'So what happened to her?'

Piet Van Heerden shrugged. 'If she married me or not, she would have been disgraced.'

'But it was *not* her fault!' Anna protested.

'They are not like us,' he replied simply. 'They are primitives.'

'Primitives! *You* raped her! Who is the primitive here?' It was the first time in her life that Anna had shouted at her father, showing her disgust, not only at his morality but also at the white supremacist she'd always known him to be.

Piet Van Heerden looked suddenly bemused, taken by surprise at his daughter's unexpected reaction. 'What about *my* disgrace? Do you know what they did to me? Let me tell you, my girl!' he shouted. 'Are you ready? Now *you* just listen to me, you hear?' He banged his fist down on the kitchen table. 'They overpowered me at the *copra* plantation we had at that time near Malang and they abducted me. Blindfolded me and took me away, strapped to a wooden stretcher. These people, the *abangan*, they are like witchdoctors.

'They took me to a large clearing in the jungle and removed my blindfold and then they tied me to a wooden frame with my arms and legs spread out to form an X. There was a fire in the centre of the clearance but it had burned down to the hot coals. In the middle were two flat stones and on the stones, so the curved blade was over the fire, they had placed a *kris*!'

Anna's father was becoming increasingly angry, verging on incoherent, as if he was relating the incident for the first time aloud, but had nevertheless rehearsed it silently in his head a thousand times, so that now the words that had lain dormant for so long rushed to get out, stumbling over each other in a stuttered delivery. 'Then these animals, a-a-a, these *abangan*, went through a-a-a *barong* performance, a d-d-dance where they go into some kind of trance and allow the spirits of their ancestors to e-e-e-enter their bodies!'

Her father paused to gain control of himself, his entire body now shaking with rage and humiliation. But when he resumed his voice was steady, cold, precise. 'Then one of these evil devils took a length of fine coir cord and tied it around the top of my scrotum, pulling it tight and knotting it so that my testicles hung in their sac from the corded flesh. The pain, it was unbearable, and I screamed and sobbed and pleaded, thinking I would die of this dreadful agony. They let me suffer, blubbing, begging, crying, for what must have been an hour until I was ready to pass out.' Piet Van Heerden looked directly at Anna and, imitating the lifting of an object and slicing with it through the air, said, 'Then they took up the red-hot blade and cut off my balls!', his hand once again making a slicing motion. Piet Van Heerden brought his arms onto the table and placed his head between them and started to weep afresh.

Anna, despite her feeling of revulsion and shock, rose quickly and went to him, putting her arm across his huge back and her head against his shoulder. 'Oh, Papa! Oh, Papa!' she repeated, unable to think of anything else to say.

After some time her father lifted his head from the table. 'Sit!' he instructed, pointing to a chair. 'There is more!' His anger had returned.

'Father, there is no need,' Anna protested.

'No, there is!' he insisted. 'You must know. You must know.' He pointed to the document lying on the table. 'You must know why your name is not on that piece of paper.'

'And Katerina's?'

'Later. I will tell you later about her,' he said with a dismissive wave of his hand, interested only in continuing the story. 'They took me back to the plantation, like before, blindfolded and tied to the wooden stretcher. They left me near the house, the place where we threw out the garbage.' He paused to let the relevance sink in. 'Rasmina, the cook, she found me there!'

Anna now remembered that Rasmina came from a *kampong* near Malang. Maybe she knew her mother? Or knew how to find her? 'Father, you could have bled to death,' she now said.

'Yes, maybe, but the red-hot blade, it cauterised me. Those evil bastards knew what they were doing.'

'Did you call, did Katerina call the police and the doctor?'

'No, not the police, the doctor, yes, old Dr Dupree. He was indebted to our family, a loan from my father once when he got into a gambling debt. He knew to keep his mouth shut. He said where they tied me high up, I must keep the cord. If he took it off I could bleed to death.'

'So nobody knew? Just Katerina and the doctor – and Rasmina?'

'The cook? No, they had replaced my trousers. But your stepmother never forgave me.' He shrugged. 'She wanted a child, of course. We were trying, hoping for a son to carry the family name. Every generation there has always been a son or sons,' he added gratuitously. 'She'd blamed me and said it was because I was too small, it couldn't go deep enough!'

'Why didn't she leave you, get a divorce?' Anna asked. 'She had every right.'

'Ja, perhaps, but she was from a poor family. I could give her everything she wanted and she wanted lots, that I can assure you. Then just two months later came the horseback accident that put her in the wheelchair. Now it was me who could never leave her! She had the power over me now, over the Van Heerden name, she could disgrace me, our good name from two hundred years, never a single blemish. She could bring us down whenever she liked. She never let me forget it, I can tell you! Never! Every day, every possible moment! That woman was nothing but malice!' He pointed to the will. 'That is why she is not in that.' He grinned maliciously. 'It was my only revenge.'

'You said you would explain why my name is also missing,' Anna said softly. Then she added, 'I don't want your money, I just wanted . . .' She didn't complete the sentence.

'As if I had not suffered enough, for six months we were trying to have a child but nothing and she was blaming me because of what I told you. If we had had a child it would have all been different. An heir, that is all I hoped for, but nothing, no male child, nothing! When this happened, when they cut me, all hope was lost.'

Anna, described by her father as 'nothing', winced inwardly, maintaining a brave face. 'Was my stepmother barren?'

'Who knows, sometimes it just takes a long time when someone is a virgin. But then, at that time we both thought it was me, I was too small. It turned out it wasn't. But this made things worse because one day in a cardboard box you were left at the back door. Rasmina, coming from the servants' quarters early in the morning to make our coffee, heard you crying. Around your neck was hanging a small leather bag.' Piet Van Heerden parted his thumb and forefinger, denoting the size of the bag. 'Inside was you know what, like two walnuts. You looked Javanese, brown skin, black hair, but your eyes were blue. Six months I tried with your stepmother, once with that other one and look what happened!'

'Father!' Anna cried out. 'She is *not* "that other one", she was my mother, she had a *name*!'

'*Ja*, I'm sorry, if she had one then I have forgotten it.' He thought for a moment. 'Rena, I think it was. *Ja*, Rena.' Anna's father, still consumed with self-pity, seemed oblivious to Anna's pain. 'She was beautiful, very beautiful, the most beautiful woman I have ever seen, but she cursed me. That woman with her *abangan* devils and spirits cursed me.' He looked directly at Anna. 'You are taller and you have blue eyes, but otherwise you are the same woman.' He choked back a sob. 'Every time I look at you, every day, for sixteen years, I see that bag hanging around your neck, I see my stolen manhood!' He pointed at her accusingly. 'Your *abangan* spirits have stolen my manhood!'

Anna was too astounded to answer, even to think of a reply. 'That is why your name is not on that will. Those devils, the *abangan*, they have put the spirit, the spirit of your dead mother's soul, into you! I cannot allow you to be a part of my family, to be a Van Heerden. You are possessed!'

What Anna heard above all else were the words 'dead mother'. 'My mother is dead? How do you know this?'

'Rasmina told me. She died in childbirth, you were too big.' He smiled, triumphant. 'What they did to me, I could have bled to death. But there is some justice. Now it was she who did.'

'You said Rasmina didn't know, that you wore trousers?'

'*Acht*, I lied, she found out, she belongs to the same *alurwaris*, the same kinship, but distant, you understand. Don't worry, she has been well paid to keep quiet. She has a nice house in her *kampong*, the best one, better even than the headman's.'

The implications of her father's accusations were just beginning to sink in. Anna was finding it too much to absorb all at once. 'I have the evil spirit of my mother within me? I am a she-devil? Is that what you think, Father?'

Piet Van Heerden tried to adopt a disarming tone, but instead it came out as overweening. 'No, *lieveling*! Not any more. Trust me, your papa loves you now. You are my loving daughter.' He spread his hands. 'You have proved yourself worthy to carry my name. I have decided.' He pointed to the will. 'You will inherit everything.'

Anna was astonished at her father's arrogance. She wanted to cry but knew she mustn't; that she must remain dry-eyed or he would think he had won her over. But quite suddenly she could contain her fury no longer. 'You can stick your money up your fat arse! I don't want it! I don't want *you*, I don't want you to be my father, you cruel, wicked bastard!' She had no idea where these words came from. She hadn't even thought to use such language previously to anyone, not even to Van der Westhuisen, the first mate on the *Witvogel*. 'Fuckwit!' she spat. 'Dirty, rotten shit! Arsehole!' It was then that she finally started to wail.

If Piet Van Heerden was shocked at Anna's vituperative language he concealed it well and didn't react other than to say, 'Shush, Anna, you don't mean it! It has been hard for you. But now that we are together and I am not drinking we must be partners, father and daughter. What I have told you is water under the bridge. We do not know what the Japanese will do. But I don't think it will be good for us in the end. We must be together, plan together. You have seen what is in the tin box, the money, lots of money and the diamonds, six in each packet, did you find them? They are good cuts, Amsterdam diamonds, worth a lot of money. Diamonds are easy to hide.' He paused. 'Stop crying, this is important. The money can buy our escape. Our lives may depend on it!'

'Who gives a shit!' Anna spat, but she stopped sobbing and started to hiccup.

Piet Van Heerden rose from the table and went to the pantry, where he filled a mug with water and returned, handing it to her. 'Here, drink – hold your nose, head back.' Anna, despite her anguish, did as she was told and her hiccuping ceased. 'See how well we work together? There are always hiccups, but if we work together they can be overcome,' he joked. For a moment he sounded like his old self. 'The diamonds, they are yours. Your inheritance,' he said smugly. 'What is past is past.'

'I do not want your diamonds,' she said, sniffing, addressing him neither as 'Father' nor as 'Papa'.

Piet Van Heerden made light of her rejection, cackling,

seemingly amused. 'When a gentleman gives a lady diamonds she is foolish not to accept, because when he has left her for another woman, she can always cash them in.' Anna wondered at his duplicity, his chameleon-like ability to change: one moment a snivelling, sobbing, self-pitying wreck, the next a conceited shit, and now, as if nothing had happened, making little jokes, her old papa again, the man she once loved but now realised she had never truly known, a man who had found her repugnant, believing her to be evil and possessed.

'You used me against my stepmother. You didn't love me; I was a weapon, a way to get back at her. Pretending to love me, you hated me all the while.'

'Anna! Anna!' he protested. 'We often say things we don't always mean. I admit, sometimes, yes, I used you. She was a harridan. She never let up. A witch. Day and night, I never went to bed that she didn't wish me evil. Her last words to me before she slept every night, they never changed: "Where is my child, you fat, disgusting eunuch?" You were all I could use to taunt her. But *skatterbol*, your papa loves you now. She is dead. We have each other. That is *goed*!' He reached out to touch her shoulder but she pulled away from him. 'You *must* have the diamonds, I insist,' he said.

Anna rose unsteadily, gripping the edge of the table. 'Go to hell! I am going to bed,' she said, fighting back her need to cry again.

Piet Van Heerden smiled and spread his hands in a gesture of reconciliation. 'Anna! Anna! *Lieveling!* That is no way to speak. Come now, will you not kiss your papa goodnight?'

Anna did not reply but instead turned and walked away. She wanted to have a shower, to wash away the hurt, the pain, from her soul. To gasp under a cold shower, use a hard scrubbing brush on her skin, to wash her hair, her dark-as-a-raven's hair, the hair her mother had given her. Her mother, who had died in a pool of blood, the child she had conceived from the giant who had raped her forcing, tearing, ripping her open. Anna was utterly exhausted, but knew she would not be able to sleep, the sorrow in her was too intense.

She had purchased a mattress at the markets that morning from another of Til's merchant friends. It would replace the one she had taken down to the cellar. Til had delivered it in a great roll tied with coir rope that he had somehow balanced high on his *becak*. 'Ratih's sergeant, who is now a lieutenant, has told her the *kempeitai* are coming,' Til warned her. 'Anna, they are not good. They are the Japanese soldier police, very fierce, very cruel. You must not let your father go out on the street and you must not forget to wear your black glass eyes when you go to the markets.' Then smiling, Til had added, pointing to the mattress, 'Allah created sleep so we can lay down our sadness for a little while each night, otherwise we humans would find the burden of sorrow we carry too heavy to bear.' He pushed at the mattress with his long bony fingers, laughing. 'You can enjoy it, this mattress, Anna. It is number-one. First class. Guarantee one year. It has little springs in it for soft dreams.'

CHAPTER TEN

*'But the cleansing of your society is not yet complete.
In the community of Asian people there lurks a mutual
enemywho has robbed you and exploited you! An
enemy who does not belong in the Greater East Asia
Co-Prosperity Sphere, who is like an army of fleas on a
dog's back, sucking its blood while contributing nothing
but disease. I speak, of course, of the loathsome Chinese,
who have forced you into onerous debt and demanded
crippling interest so that you are enslaved to them!'*
Konoe Akira
Colonel, Japanese Imperial Army,
5th Resettlement Battalian, Tjilatjap, 1942

ANNA, DESPITE THINKING SHE could not sleep,
nevertheless slept the sleep of the dead, too exhausted to
remain awake. It is, perhaps, the gift of being seventeen
years old, when the body and the brain decide that enough is
enough, that despite everything, they will cooperate to shut
down for a few healing hours. Young soldiers in the trenches
in France during the First World War were said to be able to
sleep through a bombardment, their exhaustion masking the
fear and quelling the rush of adrenalin brought on by the shells
exploding around them.

Anna wakened with a start to an urgent thumping and
knocking. Glancing at her wristwatch she saw it was some time

after nine, well past the time she usually rose. Bleary-eyed, she made her way to the front door, on the way passing her father's bedroom, where he continued to snore. After his withdrawal he now slept until a later hour, seldom rising before 10 a.m., another way to cope with depression. She opened the door to find Budi standing on the doorstep.

'Budi? What is it? Has something happened?' she asked, observing the worried face of the thirteen-year-old.

'Anna, there are two boats, a Japanese destroyer and a troopship. They came up the river very early this morning. They brought a battalion of Japanese soldiers and a detachment of *kempeitai*. At five o'clock this morning the band from the battalion played when they came ashore. The lieutenant says from now on the *kempeitai* will take charge and already they are rounding up all the Chinese merchants.'

'Lo Wok?'

'They have not yet found him. He is hiding in our *kampong* with my mother. But we cannot keep him, the others will soon inform the *kempeitai*.'

'And his wife and child?'

'No, only the men, the shopkeepers, the important ones, the triads and the communists, they want their money. Lo Wok sent his wife and the little girl to the mountains last week. He is not important. But the lieutenant says when they have their money they will kill them. Then they will kill all the other Chinese men. The Japanese, they hate the Chinese. Mother says I must ask you.'

'Ask me? Ask me what?'

'Will you hide Lo Wok in your cellar?' Budi saw the look of hesitation in Anna's eyes and quickly added, 'He has saved my mother's life once. He paid the ambulance and the doctor and hospital when she burst her – her stomach.' He touched his right side close to his groin.

'Appendix?'

'Yes, otherwise she would die. The doctor said so. The lieutenant says this house, it is in the police compound, the Japan police, the *kempeitai*, they will not look here,' Budi urged.

'The mattress down there, it smells awful!' Anna cried, unable to think, then added, 'Where is he now?'

Budi turned to look at the gate. 'Til, he has him.'

'Here? In his *becak*?'

'It has a curtain,' Budi replied. Anna remembered the *becak* had a curtain that unrolled from the canvas sunhood to offer protection from the rain or privacy if a passenger wished not to be seen. Til called it his 'brothel curtain'. A rich and important man travelling to see his mistress would draw less attention if he arrived in a *becak*. Til was known to keep his mouth shut and this method of transporting mistresses or a married lover was a lucrative part of his business.

Without waiting for Anna to say any more, Budi brought two fingers to his lips and whistled sharply. Moments later Til drove up to the gate with the canvas curtain concealing the top half of Lo Wok. Budi ran to open the gate that was only just wide enough to allow the *becak* to enter.

Til, grinning, pedalled up the short garden path to the door. 'Ratih and our family, we are very grateful, Anna. We know it is asking very much. But a debt of life can only be paid with a debt of life – anything less is not full payment. Ratih says Kiki will bring all the food and maybe, after a while, we can find a way for him to escape to Malaya if he has enough money. The Chinese have fled into the jungle to fight with some British who could not escape when the Japanese came.'

The curtains parted and Lo Wok's frightened face appeared. '*Ahee!* Ten thousand thanks, Missy Anna. I must pay! It is your turn now,' he said, anxiously reaching into his trouser pocket.

Anna took this to mean that the Chinaman saw that he was in no position to bargain and that she held the advantage and would naturally expect him to pay through the nose for his concealment. Anna shook her head, refusing. 'I do not want your money, Lo Wok. But if you give Til sufficient to buy you a mattress at the markets you will benefit greatly.' She grinned. 'The mattress in the cellar smells like a latrine.' Then she cautioned, 'Better come inside, there are always eyes.' Despite her acquiescence she knew instinctively that she was making a dangerous decision, one that could greatly jeopardise the position of her father and herself.

Lo Wok stepped quickly from the *becak* into the sunlight and then as quickly into the comparative shadow of the enclosed verandah, Budi and Til immediately following. Anna then led the way to the kitchen, where Til informed the Chinaman of the price of a mattress if he bought it from his good friend, assuring Lo Wok he would be getting the best possible deal combined with the highest quality. 'Guarantee one year. The springs so soft like a massage woman.' Lo Wok peeled off the notes needed from a bundle. Anna saw that it was not very thick and seemed not to contain any notes of a large denomination. The Chinaman added two guilders as a tip. Til thanked him for his generosity, but handed back the two single-guilder notes, protesting that it was unnecessary. 'Allah smiles when a good turn is returned by men who take pleasure in the act of returning,' he said in one of his more convoluted observations. Lo Wok looked bemused, as if he had never experienced anyone unnecessarily returning money.

'While you are here do you think we can remove the old mattress from the cellar?' Anna asked and then turned to Til. 'It smells pretty bad. Will you take it and throw it away somewhere?'

Budi opened the trapdoor and she asked him to bring down one of the kitchen chairs while she quickly gathered a packet of candles and a box of matches, a fork and spoon and a towel. She pointed to a basin and jug and asked Lo Wok to bring them down with him. To Til, she indicated a chamber-pot; it was no embarrassment for a Javanese to carry and as common a household object as any other. With the chamber-pot she handed him a dishtowel. They descended the stairs and Lo Wok was introduced to his semi-dark new home. Anna opened the little window to let in fresh air, meanwhile explaining to him that if danger existed, she would bring his food and water to the window. 'At night, when you light a candle, make sure the curtain is drawn,' she cautioned.

'It is much better I think if we move the stove over the trapdoor, Anna?' Budi said. 'If the Japanese police come they won't see it. The chimney pipe needs only to be moved a little sideways,' he explained. Anna thought again that for a boy of thirteen he was remarkably clear-headed and observant.

Lo Wok immediately agreed that she mustn't take any chances and he would remain concealed. 'I stay here, Missy Anna. I will not come out. Maybe you use that window for everything. To put the stove there, that is *good* idea,' he added emphatically.

'You will go crazy down here alone, Lo Wok,' Anna warned.

Lo Wok shrugged. 'It is better to be alone in a dark cell

than dead in the light. I am grateful.'

They proceeded to roll up the mattress and, not without some difficulty, got it up the wooden steps. It still carried a pretty powerful scent mixed with the strong smell of disinfectant where Anna had wiped it down, soaking the worst parts. Once upstairs, Til declared, 'It is a good mattress for a poor person to have, they will clean it. It has many dreams left in it yet.'

Anna wondered to herself how many more dreams Lo Wok and, for that matter, she and her father, might have before the *kempeitai* discovered them. They had been left alone by Lieutenant Mori's pathetic platoon of lethargic cyclists, for many of his soldiers were suffering from various tropical infections contracted over the weeks of moving down the Malayan peninsula and then across to Java. The engineer, Major Masahiro Eiji, was only interested in getting the port facility working properly and had made no effort to find the Dutch refugees and, to the surprise of the locals, had purchased rather than simply demanded all the food he needed for his battalion. But now, if the *kempeitai* were as Til and Lieutenant Khamdani had described them, and if the raid on the Chinese merchants was any indication, the days of the Dutch waiting for something to happen were over.

Lo Wok was safely hidden, the stove moved over the trapdoor and Budi and Til had departed when Piet Van Heerden finally emerged from his bedroom carrying the tin box. He grunted a cursory 'Good morning', his eyebrows a thicket of concern as he frowned and then sat down at the table while Anna brought him a cup of coffee. He brought the cup to his lips, sipped briefly and then put it down. Anna reached into her shoulder bag that was hanging on the back of a chair and silently handed him the key. He unlocked the tin and withdrew the two little packets containing the diamonds. 'Here, I don't want any further nonsense, I want you to have these,' he said, placing the tiny packets on the table. 'I can see the wax seals are broken, so you've already seen them,' he added in an attempt to exert his authority.

'I told you, I don't want them,' Anna said, not raising her voice.

Piet Van Heerden brought his fist down hard against the surface of the table. 'Stupid! Until now I did not take you for a bloody fool!'

'Father, in a few days we may both be dead or interned. The *kempeitai* are here, they arrived early this morning. They are already rounding up the Chinese merchants and taking their money. The lieutenant says after they have it, they will kill them all.' Anna pointed to the two envelopes. 'What do you think they would do to me, to us, if they found those?'

Her father seemed to take the news of the *kempeitai* in his stride. 'Sooner or later they had to come,' he said. 'Money is one thing, you can bury it, but you can't conceal it on your person.' He paused, looking directly at Anna, then gave a little shrug. 'Diamonds are quite another.'

'Oh? And why is that?' Anna asked, not understanding.

'Because God gave a man only one hole and it's full of you know what, but to a woman he gave two, one at the back and the other at her front, the one at the back is only the next-best pouch.'

Anna blushed furiously. 'Father! You don't mean . . .? Yes, you do!'

'You must think of a way, it is an excellent hiding place.' He picked up the two small packets and handed them to her.

This time Anna didn't refuse them. 'Thank you, father,' she said, accepting, her cheeks still flushed with embarrassment.

'It is a matter of survival,' Piet Van Heerden said simply.

'Yes, I understand,' Anna replied softly.

Her father abruptly changed the subject and said, smiling, 'The Chinese, hey? They are the first. The merchants, they have all the money. The locals will not object if they are killed. Many of the natives will owe money, now they will have no debt, no interest to pay. The day of retribution has arrived.' He grinned. 'About time too, they're all bloodsuckers!' Without looking up to see the expression of disapproval on Anna's face, he reached over and took a wad of notes from the tin. 'Keep this, but you must only carry sufficient money on you for our needs. In case you are searched,' he added.

'These notes are five hundred guilders each. Who will cash one?' Anna sniffed.

'The Chine— Oh – yes, of course,' he retracted.

Anna sat down, holding the two small envelopes in her hand. 'Father, we have another Chinese problem.'

'What? What Chinese problem? If they're all dead it doesn't matter. China has millions more.'

Anna told him about Lo Wok, stressing that he was the Chinese merchant who had supplied the Scotch and the brandy, but not telling him the real reason for offering him shelter – that the Chinaman had saved Ratih's life when her appendix had burst. Anna knew her racist father would think this unrelated act of kindness was even less reason to place them in jeopardy.

'Are you out of your mind, you stupid girl?' Piet Van

Heerden asked. Then he started to shout, 'He must go! Out! You hear? Out! Now!'

'No,' Anna said without raising her voice. She was aware that his concern was probably well-founded. Lo Wok's presence placed them in a perilous situation. She knew that it was foolish, even weak, to have agreed to hide him in the cellar. The first rule of survival is to avoid unnecessary danger. Her action in concealing him was asking for trouble, even courting disaster. Her first loyalty was to her family and not a Chinaman to whom she owed nothing, who'd filled a whisky bottle with piss. She could tell him to go, throw him onto the street to be killed. She would tell Ratih her father had demanded it. Ratih would understand. Absolute obedience to the head male in the family was the Javanese way. The cook would eventually convince herself that she'd tried to save Lo Wok, that Anna had also tried and that the father was the villain.

'He's in the cellar? I will personally throw the yellow bastard out! I don't want a *foking* Chink in my house, you hear!' Piet Van Heerden brought his fist down onto the table so hard that coffee spilled from the mug.

'It is not your decision, Father. Nor is it your house.' Anna felt the strength of her refusal, the heavy lumping of stubbornness within her. The time had arrived to assert herself. 'He stays. That is the end of it.'

'The end of it! We'll be the *foking* end of it, you hear? You're mad, I knew it! You're possessed! *Abangan!* Witch! Heathen! Saving a Chinaman and risking our lives? A white man's life! A white man's life for a Chinaman, ferchrissakes! A lying, cheating, rotten, stinking Chink!'

'Father, you may leave my house any time you like, but he's staying,' Anna said quietly.

'What? Are you fucking him? Is that it? My daughter is fucking a *foking* Chink!'

Anna rose, then placing the two envelopes in front of him said, 'Here, take these and stick them up your arse. I'm told it makes the next-best pouch!' She knew she had gone too far and moved beyond her father's reach, ready to run if she needed to.

Realising what she'd just said, Piet Van Heerden's expression suffused with renewed anger, then his face grew apoplectic with rage, his pale blue eyes bulging, his ears scarlet. He was trying to speak, his cheeks puffed out like a toad's, but no sound would come, strangled by the agitation and fury contained within him. He rose from the table, taking a step towards Anna, his fist drawn back ready to strike her, to break her jaw, cheekbone, nose, destroy her pretty face, her beauty, smash it to pulp.

Anna knew instinctively that the next few moments were critical to her life. Strength, seemingly from nowhere, rose within her and she stood her ground. It was a feeling well beyond the desire to survive; it was a thing of the will, of muscle and sinew and sharp white teeth. The next few moments would decide the remainder of her life. Her eyes, which never left his, held steady. Despite the knowledge that he might kill her, she was not afraid. She would not run. Nothing in this world would make her run.

She saw a look of fear, a flicker of uncertainty, enter her father's eyes, then immediately change to confusion and, as quickly, to defeat. It was as if the heat was sucked out of him and he seemed to grow smaller in front of her eyes. His fist opened and his arm fell to his side, his cheeks returned to normal and he ran his tongue across his lips as if afraid and preparing for what might happen next. Finally he dropped his eyes and took a step backwards, collapsing heavily into the chair, where he sat chin-cupped and silent. Then looking up, he pushed the tin, with the key still in the lock, across the table so it was close to where she stood and followed this with the two envelopes. 'You must do as you wish, Anna. From now on you are in charge.' He sighed and looked up at her, his eyes rheumy, close to tears. 'I am afraid, Anna. I don't want to die,' he said in a small voice.

Anna felt deeply saddened, her sorrow a deep pit plummeting so far within her that it seemed endless. Her past had withered to be insignificant, almost meaningless. Nothing had prepared her for this. She knew that she now controlled him as he had once controlled her. But previously she had thought herself controlled by his happiness, whereas her present control was born out of her sorrow. The sadness she had felt the previous evening, when she'd realised that if he could save his life by betraying her own, he would do so, was not nearly as overpowering as the sadness she was experiencing now. That he believed her contaminated half-caste blood was of a lesser human value than the pure Aryan blood that coursed through his own veins was not difficult to comprehend when viewed against the background of his life. But she had endured a mangled, misunderstood childhood that now amounted to nothing. She had defeated her father. She knew now that henceforth her fate was dependent on her own efforts. She was abandoned by him.

While she had in every possible sense been in control, in charge, from the moment they'd left Batavia, first as a servant to her father's drunkenness and then nursing him through his horrific withdrawal, she had hitherto seen herself as a dutiful daughter ministering to a deeply depressed and sick parent.

Now she knew there was nothing left, no filial duty and no past or present affection to ameliorate the task of survival that lay ahead. His act of relinquishing control contained no love, no loyalty, no feeling other than his own self-pity and fear of dying.

If blood may be said to be thicker than water, then Anna knew that the blood she shared with her father had been almost completely diluted. She had known that she had to look after him, care for him as long as they were together. A terrible sadness rose in her as she realised she would not now sacrifice her life for him as she might once have done, that the emotional cord that binds a daughter to her father had been forever cut. Anna was utterly and completely alone, although it never occurred to her to dwell morbidly on her predicament. She had a natural revulsion for her father's self-pity, unconsciously seeing it as a weakness she found she despised.

In fact, Anna now accepted that her young years were over and with this knowledge she shook her head with a wry, inward grin. She had a tin box full of money she couldn't spend, twelve diamonds about to go into hiding in a very private place, a depressed, helpless and fearful giant Dutchman on her hands and a terrified Chinaman locked in her cellar. Outside the bloodthirsty *kempeitai* ranged everywhere: ruthless killers who would most certainly cut her throat if they were to hear about the money, slit her open if they knew about the diamonds, or summarily execute her for hiding the Chinaman. Other than this, she was now in complete control of everything. That is, if nothing may be said to be everything.

'I will protect you, Father,' she said. 'We will try to get through this. One day you will be in New Zealand.' At these comforting but somewhat futile words, Piet Van Heerden began to cry softly. *God! What a weak, gormless, lump of lard he is,* Anna thought to herself. She felt a growing sympathy for her dead stepmother. 'A strong woman may be difficult to endure, but a weak man is beyond tolerating,' Til had once said to her. But the more prosaic matters of everyday life intruded into her mind and she said, 'Father, I think you should go to your room and rest. I have several things to do, but first, will you help me to move the stove away from the trapdoor? I have a mattress arriving this afternoon.'

Together they moved the cast-iron stove; it was no easy task but Piet Van Heerden, despite everything, was still a strong man. 'I will need you later to help with its return; now go to your room and rest,' she said brusquely. Her father immediately turned and left the kitchen, going directly to his bedroom like an obedient child.

Anna was suddenly overcome with her vulnerability. If there was an unexpected knock on the door by the Japanese police she would be caught on every front. She decided to put the tin box back in the recess under the outside toilet until she could think of a better plan, for it now appeared to her to be an obvious place of concealment. She reasoned that if it had occurred to her as a safe hiding place, an experienced thief or a Japanese policeman accustomed to making searches would think it an obvious one. She withdrew a wad of banknotes and the stick of red wax, locked the tin and, covering it with a dishtowel as she had done before, went outside and placed it in the recess under the wooden seat of the outside lavatory. She would give the wad she'd taken from the tin box to Ratih for safekeeping. It would be a returned favour for hiding Lo Wok. If she was killed or taken into a concentration camp she would instruct her to use it for Budi's education at the university in the capital. There was also sufficient to build a house and to purchase a *kampong* restaurant. Anna knew this single bundle of five-hundred-guilder notes was more than the cook and her lieutenant would earn in their lifetimes. She would ask Ratih if she could find a way to break a single five-hundred-guilder note into smaller denominations for her to use for current expenses. If she couldn't help, then Til, she felt sure, would find a way.

This left the diamonds and the gold watch. She wasn't too concerned about her grandfather's fob watch. It was the kind of thing the *kempeitai* would expect to find in a Dutch refugee family, a last heirloom only to be sold in an absolute emergency. She knew where the diamonds were supposed to be deposited but had no idea how she might go about doing this. It was then that she remembered the bullet casing that had landed at her feet when it had been ejected from Lieutenant Mori's revolver on the day the platoon of weary Japanese cyclists had arrived.

Anna retrieved the small brass casing from the shoulder bag and studied it. It was no longer than the top joint of her forefinger though somewhat wider. She shook the twelve diamonds into it and they fitted almost to the rim. If she sealed the aperture with sealing wax they would be safe in their human pouch and not difficult to retrieve, she concluded. She first sterilised the casing in boiling water, cooled it down, placed the diamonds within it and sealed the top with the melted scarlet wax. When it had cooled sufficiently she filed the rough edges around the lip with a nailfile. Somewhat nervously she inserted it. It slipped in easily enough and, if initially a little uncomfortable, after an hour she realised she hadn't thought about it for a good ten minutes. She then decided to remove it and after washing it placed the sealed casing in her bag knowing that given a few moments, if it were necessary to conceal the diamonds she could quickly insert it again.

Anna then cooked some rice and dried salted fish for Lo Wok. She lifted the trapdoor and called so as not to alarm him. Then she took the hot meal down to him together with a mug of green tea which she'd purchased for herself at the markets.

Lo Wok dropped to his knees, his head touching the cement floor as if he were a Muslim in prayer, then he looked up. 'You have saved my life once again, Missy Anna. Your honourable father does not want me here. I give you ten thousand thanks.'

The row between herself and her father had been in the Dutch language and Anna had stupidly concluded that Lo Wok wouldn't have understood. But, of course, most of the Chinese merchants spoke Dutch as well as Javanese. 'I'm sorry you had to overhear it, Lo Wok,' Anna said, placing the enamel plate of hot food on the chair.

'You are a very strong woman, Missy Anna. I will never forget you.' He looked up and without smiling said, 'I ask most humble forgiveness for the piss in the Scotch bottle.'

Anna laughed, pointing to the chamber-pot. 'I think you still win. It is me who must now empty it out. There is no need to thank me, Lo Wok. We are both far from over this calamity.'

'But you have acted with great honour, that is the first step,' the Chinaman said. He was beginning to sound like Til.

'It is Ratih and her family, young Budi, who have acted with honour, not me.'

'Were the gods to grant me a son like Budi, I would be content and burn incense at the temple one year.'

'If the gods grant you your life, Lo Wok, would that not be contentment enough?'

'*Ahee!* Missy Anna. With the Chinese it is always family and the good rice, a son, *that* is life.'

'Will your wife and daughter be safe where they are?'

'They have gold and money. They can buy their survival in the mountains. I have heard the Javanese there are not so bad. They can be bribed.' He hesitated and Anna realised he wanted to say more.

'What is it, Lo Wok?'

'Missy Anna, I have some books, Chinese books. If the Japan soldier police have not burned them, can Budi give them to Til to bring?'

'No!' Anna cried. 'There will be eyes and spies everywhere! The *kempeitai* will have issued orders to the locals to find you, to find all the Chinese. Budi *must* not go to the Chinese quarter or anywhere near your shop! If he is caught they will torture him to find out where you are!'

Lo Wok looked distraught, hanging his head. 'I am ashamed, I did not think. You are a very wise woman, Missy Anna.'

'That is enough compliments for one day, Lo Wok. Now eat your food. I must go upstairs. Til should arrive soon,' she added with a grin, 'bringing your one-year-guarantee mattress!' She pointed to the window. 'I shall come three times a day to see you and bring you food and tea, also water to wash and to drink. In the morning leave your plate and the chamber-pot on that little shelf, there is a dishtowel to cover it.'

Lo Wok shook his head sadly. 'I am ashamed. You will lose face, Missy Anna. I am very sorry.'

Anna wondered briefly what her father would think of her removing and disposing of a Chinaman's shit. In her mind she used the four-letter word, knowing it was the one he would himself have used. 'I must go,' she said. 'See you again when Til arrives.'

Anna climbed the steps up into the kitchen, then went to her father's room to see if he wished to come out for lunch. To her surprise he was asleep, his grey and ginger speckled beard now just down to his chest and looking decidedly bedraggled. He had not shaved since boarding the boat and she decided she would need to trim it. How dearly she would have loved to take the scissors to the messy tangle above his eyes, but she knew the bramble hedge of hair was (goodness knows why) his supreme vanity. When she'd been young she'd felt sure it were inhabited by small creatures who spent their entire lives hidden there, only venturing out at the dead of night to slippery-dip down his bald head.

Til arrived just after two o'clock, apologising profusely. 'No springs,' he said. 'The Japanese Major, at the docks, he bought the last springs. I am sorry, this one is coir only.'

'Has it got a one-year guarantee?' Anna asked, teasing the little *becak* owner.

'More! What can go wrong with coir? Maybe five years. I will ask my friend.'

Anna sighed. 'In five years who knows? There is no guarantee these days.'

'Allah says a man who lives without hope is already dead,' Til quoted. Anna suspected that most of the quotes attributed to God by Til were his own work. Allah simply gave them added authority. After all, one could hardly begin a serious quote with 'Til, the *becak* driver says . . .'

She helped him bring the mattress indoors and then, with it still rolled and tied, slid it down the wooden steps to Lo Wok, who was waiting at the bottom. 'Sorry, no massage woman!'

Til called. 'Only coir. But there is change,' he announced happily. He dug into his shorts for the money he'd saved before proceeding down the stairs. 'No tip needed,' he said cheerfully, handing the change to Lo Wok.

Back in the kitchen the two of them struggled but eventually got the stove repositioned over the trapdoor and the chimney adjusted. Til pointed to a brown, heat-blistered square on the whitewashed wall that clearly showed where the stove had previously stood. 'Tomorrow I will send Budi to paint this wall,' he said.

'Til, do you think you could find someone to change a five-hundred-guilder note?' Anna asked, deciding to use the opportunity to raise the problem directly with him.

The *becak* driver looked astonished. 'There is such a note?' he asked. She handed it to him. 'I have never before seen this,' he marvelled. 'With this I can build a house, maybe also buy a motorcar taxi!'

'Do you know anyone who might change it, Til?'

'Only the Chinese, and they are no more,' he said, shaking his head. Then he asked, 'Have you tried Lo Wok?'

'When he gave you the money for the mattress he didn't have a lot over, it was a very small bundle.'

'Ha! Old Chinese trick! Always an empty wallet and a full safe.'

'Besides,' Anna said, 'if he had the money, he may think he must give it to me. He has already offered to pay.'

Til looked incredulous. 'He is a Chinaman! If you have refused, he has saved face sufficiently.'

'But a good Chinaman. He saved Ratih's life.'

'But still a Chinaman,' Til asserted. 'Anna, I will ask him. Then he can save face. I will tell him you do not want his money, only smaller notes.'

Anna led him to the back of the house and together they crawled through the hibiscus bushes. Anna, first calling softly to Lo Wok, left Til at the window and returned indoors. Til returned a good fifteen minutes later with a large bundle of fifty-guilder notes. 'He lit a candle and held your five-hundred guilder to the light to make sure it wasn't counterfeit. Ah, he is a good man, but once a Chinaman always a Chinaman!' he sighed.

'That's great, Til! Thank you, a fifty isn't too bad.'

'A fifty everyone has seen,' Til said. 'It is a lot of money but it isn't a house and a taxi car.'

'Til, have you eaten, would you like some tea?'

'No, I must go. I have to make a living. But first, Anna, I have something to ask.'

'No more Chinese!' Anna cried.

'Yes, it is about the Chinese,' Til answered, his expression grave. 'The lieutenant says the *kempeitai* want all the people in the town square at four o'clock, when they will punish four of the Chinese, four of the biggest offenders. He says we must be seen there, Ratih and me and you, Budi also, because he worked for a Chinese merchant. In this way people will see us and so they will not be suspicious later. They will think, like everyone else, we hate the Chinese. He says we must be right at the front and he will make a place for us. You must wear your black glass eyes.'

'No!' Anna cried. 'I do not wish to go! I can't stand violence! Please, please, Til!' she begged.

Til was silent for a while, head bowed, looking down at his sandalled feet, his left big toe pointing sharply to the right where he must have broken it at some earlier time and never had it straightened. Then he raised his eyes and squinted up at Anna. 'It is the lieutenant that made this house available to you and your father. If the Japanese find out about Lo Wok, not just you, we will all die, even the lieutenant. They will call him a traitor and shoot him.' His gaze was steady as he looked at her. 'I will be here at half-past three o'clock to take you to the square. I will bring a Japanese flag for you to wave. There will be cheering and we must all cheer.'

Anna had a cold shower, washed her hair, dressed and made a cup of green tea to steady her nerves while she waited for Til to arrive. It was nearly a quarter to four when his *becak* drew up in front. 'There is a very big crowd, I was delayed,' he apologised. 'Come, Ratih and Budi will be waiting with the lieutenant, who will take us to the front.'

'What about Kiki?' Anna asked.

'She must mind the kitchen at the *kampong*. Ratih is very pleased with her. She will make a very good cook. Already she can do some of the difficult dishes.'

'Til, I will not be able to look. What will they, the *kempeitai*, do to the Chinese?'

Til shrugged. 'The lieutenant, he says they will use them to set an example. These people, these Japan soldier policemen, they control with fear. Even the Japan soldiers, they are terrified of them.'

'Will they kill them?' Anna asked fearfully. 'How can I stand and look and not cry out?'

'You have the black glass eyes, you can close your eyes and no one will see you are not looking. The people will be cheering. They will not be looking at you.'

While in Batavia I had told Anna about the atrocities committed on the Chinese by the Japanese when they'd captured Nanking, slaughtering 300 000 people – men, women and children – in ten days. Tens of thousands of male Chinese had been tied to posts and used for live bayonet practice to blood young Japanese recruits and give them *bushido*, the fighting spirit, to prepare them for war. I told her how General Tojo, then the chief of the Imperial Japanese Army and now the Prime Minister, had officially declared that the Chinese were not human, that killing one was no different to cutting out the entrails of a pig. A standard army joke was contained in the rejoinder, 'No, there is a big difference! When you gut a pig you can still eat it.'

They arrived at the square to be joined by Ratih, her lieutenant and Budi, and made their way through the crowd, the popular policeman greeting people, stopping to have a quick word with some, making sure they were seen as he moved them to the flagpole.

Surprisingly, the Japanese battalion band was playing German-sounding marching music, while the entire battalion ranged in three straight lines behind the flagpole. A rostrum had been set up with a microphone on the plinth, five steps up from the square. The large cone-shaped loudspeakers were a new experience for the people of Tjilatjap. Three of these cones, each pointed in a different direction, now replaced the headless statue of the early Dutch Governor-General, Jan Pieterszoon Coen. Elsewhere convenient lampposts carried the cones that blared the oompah-pah music to the very edges of the square. The German-sounding band would remind anyone who knew that the Japanese Imperial Army was based on the German

Army and its harsh Prussian traditions. Like most things the Japanese chose to adopt, its procedures were faithfully followed. To Anna it sounded similar to the military bands she had heard when they'd attended receptions at Government House in Batavia, although in every other respect this parade was an unfamiliar and frightening scene.

The square was jammed with excited people carrying Japanese flags. On the large cement platform at the base of the flagpole to either side of the microphone were four Chinese on their knees with their hands bound behind their backs with wire. Behind them stood twelve *kempeitai* at rigid attention, their uniforms immaculate, jackboots brought to a high sheen. The average Japanese soldier wore a nondescript uniform, khaki puttees wound around short thick legs, the entire turnout usually somewhat the worse for wear. However, the *kempeitai* were stone-cold killers with impassive expressions, always smart in appearance. Til nudged Anna. 'Death wears shiny boots,' he observed in a whisper.

'Those four kneeling are the most important examples,' Lieutenant Khamdani explained. 'Three are members of anti-Japanese organisations and the last one, Wang Lee, is the biggest merchant in town and has the largest department store. The townspeople are especially happy for him to die. Their debts, a lot of guilders, thousands, perhaps much more, will now be cancelled.'

Anna would later ask Til how the Japanese knew the political or criminal affiliations of the four men, indeed of the life histories of the numerous Chinese in the town, including Lo Wok. 'There are some Japanese like Onishi Tokuma, the tailor who is now mayor, who have been here a long time. They too are merchants, but small, not so rich as the Chinese. They are spies for Nippon, they have told the *kempeitai* who among the Chinese are the most important,' he replied, then added 'but there are also some Chinese who have informed against their own race. They wear hoods and attend line-ups organised by the Japanese and point to the communists and the members of the Kuomintang. They are helping the Japanese to decide who will live and who will die. Not all the Chinese have been put in jail, but the lieutenant says it will not be long before those in prison are dead. The Japanese do not want to waste food to feed worthless Chinese prisoners.'

'They will also behead them?' Anna asked.

'Of course not, public execution is done as an example to the people. The rest of the prisoners will just get a bullet in the head – already there are local Javanese men digging their grave down by the river, one big hole for them all – but only after they have been tortured to locate their money. The Japanese know the Chinese always have gold hidden away.'

'How do you and the lieutenant know all this?' Anna asked.

Til shrugged. 'It is *alurwaris*, the kinship of the family. When something happens in any town in Java or even Sumatra, if it is important, we will know it. We have known about this Chinese business ever since the *kempeitai* came to Sumatra. What they did there, they will also do here. A goose does not turn into a duck.'

'But wouldn't the Chinese also know and try to escape?' Anna asked, surprised.

'Some, but *we* would not tell them.' He shrugged. 'Some Chinese families have been here three hundred years, most many generations. Where would they go? Australia will not take them. All the other places in Asia and the islands, the

Japanese they are already there. They can only hope that maybe they can buy their lives with gold. That is the Chinese way. The *kempeitai* will agree. "Give us your gold and you will be freed," they will say. Then when they have the gold they will kill the Chinese anyway. There is no code of honour between the Japanese and the Chinese.'

Now, as they watched, the band stopped playing and the battalion was called to attention. A Japanese colonel in jackboots and tight-fitting army pantaloons stepped forward, his samurai sword held by his belt on his left, his revolver holster attached on the opposite side. He was tall with a lean though strong-looking build, except that he had a decided limp. He was followed by a much shorter *kempeitai* captain, similarly uniformed, the only difference being that the colonel's uniform was expensively tailored. Walking a respectable distance behind them came the Mayor of the Squashed Hat.

The mayor was dressed to the nines in tailcoat and striped trousers. A starched wing collar and black bow tie were attached to the neck of his white shirt. A titter ran through the crowd as they noticed he wore a brand new top hat that was somewhat too large for him, so that it rested just above his eyes. No one in the crowd had ever seen a comical get-up quite like this but, except for the top-hat titter, the townspeople remained respectfully silent in the presence of the Japanese. No doubt it would cause a great deal of mirth back in the *kampongs* later that night. The Mayor of the Squashed Hat was obviously there to interpret.

The colonel approached the microphone and the mayor hastened to stand on his left, the ends of his snowy white spats peeping from his cuffless striped trousers, highlighting the shine on his black patent-leather shoes. The *kempeitai* captain took two steps backwards, ignoring the four Chinese prisoners who knelt directly behind him, the nearest so close that he could have licked the heels of his jackboots.

The mayor leaned forward, and as the microphone stand had been set for the taller Japanese colonel, the mayor was forced to stand on tiptoe in front of the unfamiliar contraption, appearing as if he would lose his balance at any moment. Now he yelled at the top of his voice so that the speakers crackled alarmingly. 'People of Tjilatjap, it is with great honour that I introduce to you the esteemed Colonel Konoe, Commander of the Japanese Imperial Army Battalion, wounded valiantly in battle, a former Captain in the Imperial Guards Regiment!' He then stepped to the side so that the Japanese colonel could speak directly into the microphone and he could interpret.

'People of Tjilatjap, we come as your liberators and friends in the spirit of cooperation and in the name of the Greater Asia Co-Prosperity Sphere. We bring you salutations and now greet you as a free Asian people in the name of His Imperial Majesty, the Showa Emperor Hirohito.'

Shouts of 'Banzai! Banzai! Banzai!' came from the battalion and the assembled kempeitai, while several people standing near the front shouted out as well.

'The yoke of the colonial forces of the Netherlands has been lifted from your necks!' Colonel Konoe's voice rose to an emphatic level, though not quite a shout. 'They stole your land and your riches and enslaved you for more than three hundred years! Now they have scurried like rats from a sinking ship! However, this is no sinking ship, it will sail again as a vessel, as a freedom-loving and independent State, a partner in the war against the white colonial oppressors.'

He waited until the cheering from the large crowd died

down before continuing. 'But the cleansing of your society is not yet complete. In the community of Asian people there lurks a mutual enemy who has robbed you and exploited you! An enemy who does not belong in the Greater East Asia Co-Prosperity Sphere, who is like an army of fleas on a dog's back, sucking its blood while contributing nothing but disease. I speak, of course, of the loathsome Chinese, who have forced you into onerous debt and demanded crippling interest so that you are enslaved to them!'

The cheering from the crowd in response to this last remark rose to a roar that continued for at least a minute. Colonel Konoe was striking exactly the right chord and the crowd was ecstatic. When at last he could continue, he went on to say, 'While we will rid you of this pestilence, this evil presence, so that it no longer exists in your town, we have brought these four before you today as an example of our swift and honourable justice system. Others of their kind will be dealt with very soon. These four degenerates are typical of the evil influence that pervades yours and the other Asian societies we have liberated.'

He turned to glance at the four kneeling Chinese, then returned to the microphone. 'The first is a supporter and agent of the Kuomintang, the rapacious and evil-intentioned Chinese Government! The second is a murderous communist – no lower and more ill-conceived doctrine exists! The third is a Triad, a ruthless criminal in a brotherhood of evil! Finally, worst of all, the greedy and merciless merchant,' he glanced quickly at his notes, 'who entices and then cripples you with debt! The Emperor, His Benevolent Majesty, has particularly charged the Japanese Imperial Forces to rid you of this vermin, this pestilence, who are the lackeys of colonialism and grow fat and rich on the people's misery.'

'*Banzai! Banzai! Banzai!*' followed from the battalion and the huge crowd now took up and echoed the traditional cry, waving Japanese flags and, where there was sufficient room, hugging each other and breaking into joyous and spontaneous dance. If it were possible, they showed that their hatred for the Chinese matched that of the way they'd felt about the Dutch.

The tall Japanese officer waited until the cheering died down and finally came to the conclusion of his speech. 'I will now command Captain Takahashi to behead these four criminals in the name of His Imperial Majesty.' He paused only a second. 'Long live His Imperial Majesty! May he rule ten thousand years!'

'*Banzai! Banzai! Banzai!*' came the response as the people gathered in the square went wild with joy. They would tell their children later in the *kampongs* that they had waited a long time, but now the power of their two great tormentors was finished. Their Dutch oppressors were the first. Now the insidious Chinese usurers had finally been brought to justice.

Captain Takahashi came to attention and saluted, then rapped out a command. Four of the *kempeitai* soldiers immediately came to attention and took three paces forward, one behind each of the prisoners. To a second command from the officer, in unison, as if it were a practised drill, they removed from the right-hand pockets of their putteed trousers a blindfold, stepped another two paces forward and quickly and simultaneously blindfolded the hapless Chinese. Then they returned to the ranks by stepping four paces backwards. Another command and four more *kempeitai* stepped forward, first reaching down and picking up a small container of water placed on the dais behind them. They merely took a single step forward and remained standing, the dish held in both hands in front of them at chest height as if it was an offering.

The people who were able to observe what was happening grew quiet and the ominous silence seemed to ripple through the crowd so that the entire square appeared to hold its collective breath. The emotionless face of the *kempeitai* captain terrified Anna even before he drew the long, slightly curved *katana*. The only sound was the soft 'shrup' of the sword as it left its sheath. The colonel and the mayor retreated to the rear right-hand side of the flag platform facing Anna and the others so that only Takahashi stood slightly angled behind the first victim. In the accustomed practice of a beheading, this was so his shadow wouldn't fall on the bound, blindfolded Chinaman kneeling in front of him and cause him to flinch. Ancient tradition has it that in such circumstances awareness in the victim is so acute in the moments before death that even blindfolded he will feel the shadow of the master swordsman. Honour forbade the shadow of the executioner falling over the victim, causing a less than perfect decapitation.

Glancing quickly at the colonel, who nodded almost imperceptibly, the captain swung the curved blade up and over his right shoulder. The sword flashed down so quickly that Anna caught the entire beheading before she had completely closed her eyes. She did not see the Chinaman's head hit the surface nor the jet of blood that shot into the air from the neck stump and landed a metre away to splash down the steps of the flag platform. She felt Ratih gripping the top of her arm as a collective sigh, an expulsion of air, could be heard coming from those who witnessed the beheading. 'Try to look, Anna, so you can prove you came,' the cook whispered. She had seen from the side of the sunglasses that Anna had her eyes tightly shut. Anna opened them to see one of the *kempeitai* soldiers who was holding a dish step forward. The captain removed a small wet towel from the dish and wiped the blood from the blade of the sword, then stepped behind the next victim, again ensuring that his shadow didn't fall over him. This time Anna wasn't caught by surprise and her eyes remained shut while the captain beheaded the remaining three Chinese, each time wiping the blade of his sword with a fresh damp towel from a different dish. The *kempeitai* captain then turned to the colonel with a deep bow, his boots and army pantaloons splattered with the blood of the Chinamen. Konoe nodded his head, bowing almost imperceptibly in return.

Ratih still held onto Anna's arm. 'It is over, Anna,' she said. 'We can go now.' Anna opened her eyes and turned her face away but not before she saw the four heads that lay directly below the severed necks as if they'd been previously carefully arranged. Captain Takahashi's work had been precise. Anna fainted and Ratih's desperate attempt to prevent her falling knocked the sunglasses from her head as, too heavy for the cook to hold, she collapsed to the gravelled surface of the square.

Few, if any, people would have noticed Anna's collapse. The crowd was too busy yelling 'Banzai! Banzai! Banzai!', shouting and cheering, jostling, craning their necks for a look at the severed heads. The four remaining *kempeitai* now stepped forward and grasped the heads by the hair, holding them high in front of them, careful to avoid blood splashing onto their polished boots. However, the Japanese colonel chose that moment to leave the platform and, careful to avoid the blood on the steps, took a different route to the one by which he'd arrived and now moved directly towards Anna. He paused momentarily beside her prostrate form just as she opened her eyes. Anna, still dazed, saw the face of the Japanese officer staring down at her and screamed. A quizzical and slightly startled look momentarily crossed Colonel Konoe's face before he grunted and moved on. Budi and Ratih helped her to her feet and Budi retrieved her sunglasses, which had now been trampled underfoot, the lenses smashed and one arm missing. But they could not leave in the crush as people craned and pushed to see the four decapitated heads being impaled on long bamboo poles and secured, one at each corner of the flag platform, so they could now be seen from every part of the square – a grisly reminder that, with the Japanese military, retribution was swift and final. With mother and son on either side supporting Anna, Lieutenant Khamdani led them away, pushing his way through the jostling people, shouting 'Pak Polisi! Pak Polisi!' so the crowd would part to let them through.

I should pause here to explain what undoubtedly happened to the remaining two hundred Chinese who were captured in Tjilatjap. All Anna can recall of the massacre is that the four heads were prominently displayed together with those of some local criminals, remaining on the posts in the town square for all to be warned that the Japanese would tolerate no disobedience from citizens and, also, that for several days the air was filled with the stench of benzine, acrid smoke and the smell of roasted human flesh. Captain Takahashi had ordered that the Chinese prisoners be tortured, shot, burned and buried in the single grave the locals had dug for them.

The Chinese prisoners did not first dig their own graves, which would have been another form of psychological torture.

The reason for this was ghastly but practical. For the most part, the prisoners would have been unable to walk. Most would have received, among other forms of torture, the final and most painful of all. They would have been made to sit on a small wooden block about half a metre high, with their legs stretched straight out, heels resting on another block of similar size and height. Their hands would have been bound behind their backs and the torso suspended in a sitting position by shoulder straps attached to the ceiling. This done, the shinbones of each leg were shattered by a wooden club, not unlike a baseball bat, and thereafter the same was done to their kneecaps. There is said to be no greater pain that can suddenly be inflicted on the human body without causing it to go into total shock and cause a heart seizure or death.

Other forms of getting the Chinese to confess the whereabouts of hidden gold were the traditional water drip onto the forehead (by Japanese standards fairly tame), the application of electric shocks to the genitals, the ripping out of fingernails, or being tied up in the blazing sun for several days until they were literally sunbaked to death. As it required little imagination, whipping was the most common form of torture. They were simply beaten with various instruments: bamboo canes, leather whips and blunt metal instruments, until the flesh peeled from their bones. Another method was to place a prisoner in a vat and slowly bring it to the boil. It is claimed that these methods, used in Java and elsewhere, were child's play compared to what the Japanese did to the Chinese elsewhere.

My father spoke often of the poetry and refinement of the Japanese intellect. It had been one of the reasons he had taken a teaching position in Japan. He loved the Japanese aesthetes, their capacity to reduce a complex scene to the glorious simplicity of a *haiku* poem; how, with a few simple brush strokes, a Japanese artist could capture a wild and savage landscape, leaving scope for your imagination to supply the unseen detail. I was too young when I left Japan to appreciate much of this, but even at a young age I knew these people to be concerned with beauty, purity and simplicity. I have always found it difficult to accept that the same refined intellect can change into a remorseless and merciless killer, whose torture is blunt and brutal.

For ten days Lo Wok remained in the cellar, his fortitude and even humour remarkable, for he never showed himself as being depressed, never complained and never failed to thank Anna for his food, delivered most days by Kiki and sometimes Til, and for the less pleasant chores she performed.

Then one day Ratih and Til visited together to say that the lieutenant had visited a *Bugis' pinisi* schooner that was in the port to check the contents of the hold, only to discover that it was captained by an old Macassar acquaintance, Ahmed Nur-make, who had been arrested by the lieutenant some years ago and had served some time in a Dutch prison for piracy.

In my early childhood in Japan my father would threaten me with the sudden arrival of the dreaded bogeyman if I misbehaved. Later I would learn that William Makepeace Thackeray devised the term 'bogeyman' after learning about these *Bugis* sailors. The *Bugis* were criminals and always dangerous; sometimes they were pirates though they were also opportunists and genuine traders. During lean times other vessels were never quite safe when at sea. Boarding the *pinisi* schooner to look for stolen goods or contraband was, the lieutenant knew, a pointless exercise. The *Bugis* would have long since disposed of any illegal cargo before tying up at the wharf. It was a cat-and-mouse game where the mouse was usually smarter than the cat, but nevertheless the cat had to remind the mouse that it was still in the hunt.

The upshot was that the *Bugis* captain agreed to smuggle Lo Wok to Malaya for the extortionate sum of one thousand guilders, an unthinkable sum of money and far more than the schooner captain could hope to make in several years of ruthless boarding and pillaging and then selling the stolen cargo. It was simply his way of refusing. The lieutenant had protested, whereupon Ahmed Nur-make had shrugged. 'What can I do? He is a Chinaman, his life is worthless, but mine and my crew's, who are also my family, are not. *Allah akbar*,' he'd stated simply.

The lieutenant knew as well as he did that if caught smuggling a Chinaman to safety Ahmed and his entire crew would forfeit their lives. The usual price of smuggling a common criminal offshore was known to be fifty guilders. He'd left giving the *Bugis* captain's schooner a clean bill of health, knowing that under the Japanese the Macassar would consider themselves no better off than under the Dutch; a pirate is a criminal under any jurisprudence.

Lieutenant Khamdani reported the fee Ahmed Nur-make was demanding to Ratih, certain that it amounted to an impossible demand.

'We know he has five hundred guilders,' Til said to Anna. 'He changed the taxi-car-and-house note for you, but does he have more?' He gave a soft whistle, thinking about the demanded fee. 'It is twice as much as that, two taxi cars and two houses!'

'Why don't you ask him?' Anna said. 'Coming from you he will lose less face, rather than if Ratih or I – if a woman – asks him.'

Til went around to the back of the house and returned ten minutes later. 'He has only six hundred guilders. He says his wife has five hundred more and a little gold, but he has sent her and the girl to the mountains and does not know their whereabouts. They were told only to find somewhere they could buy their safety.' Til shrugged. 'To find them will take too long, the *Bugis' pinisi* will sail in two days.'

'I will give them, the captain, the remainder,' Anna said quietly.

'No! No, it is too much! More than a cook will earn in ten years!' Ratih protested.

'He saved your life!' Anna reminded her, then smiled. 'That is enough, Ratih. What's more, as long as he is here *all* our lives are in danger. You and Budi and the lieutenant,' she grimaced, 'as well as my father and me. We will all be killed.'

Ratih's eyes brimmed. 'Thank you, Anna, we will not forget,' she said quietly.

The following morning Til arrived with a cheap sarong and a tattered black cotton shirt, the uniform of a *Bugis* sailor. 'He cannot wear shoes or sandals, this *Bugis* they do not wear, they must climb up many ropes,' he explained needlessly.

An hour after sundown at eight o'clock that night, two of the *Bugis* pirates appeared with Til, and Lo Wok was taken in tow. Any acute observer would almost immediately have noticed the 'ouch and ooh' manner in which the Chinaman hobbled towards the river port, the soft soles of his bare feet unable to bear the uneven and rocky surface of the road. Watching him depart, Anna asked why the *Bugis* wouldn't simply throw Lo Wok overboard as soon as they were out to sea since they now had the money.

'It is a good question,' Til replied. 'But they are strict Muslims. The Prophet Mohammed says that honour must be repaid with honour. Two men both acting honourably are one man in their thoughts. The Lieutenant Khamdani has known Ahmed Nur-make since he arrested the captain and while he spent time in prison for piracy. They are old friends. It is true he is a thief and a scoundrel, but he is also an honourable thief and a reliable scoundrel, a man to be trusted in such circumstances. But, if the Japanese board the *pinisi* schooner, it is also true they will throw Lo Wok overboard to the sharks.' He paused, spreading his hands. 'That is only natural and the Prophet would understand.'

Lo Wok had been profuse and tearful in his gratitude. 'A hundred generations, those who are my progeny, will be in the debt of your progeny. I owe you my life twice over. If I live I will not forget, Anna.'

Anna smiled at this thought. 'If we live long enough to have progeny I will remind yours of this debt,' she said playfully. 'You must thank Ratih. It is she who saved you, Lo Wok.'

'That is a life for life and I will honour it,' Lo Wok said seriously. 'But you gave me my life twice over when you owed me nothing. It was me who pissed in the Scotch bottle!'

Anna threw back her head and laughed. 'I hope the gods send you good rice and you are blessed with a son, Lo Wok.'

And so the little Chinaman disappeared from Anna's life. For two days he had asked for extra water to bathe and she had supplied it. When, after his departure, she returned to the cellar she discovered that he had used the water to scrub the floor. The cellar was spotless, the mattress leaning against a wall, the kitchen chair now stood close to the window, the clothes Lo Wok had worn prior to changing into the old shirt and sarong had been washed and rinsed and hung damp from the back and the seat of the chair.

Three days passed and during this time Anna, visiting the markets wearing her stepmother's second pair of sunglasses, met a Dutch woman who was bargaining fiercely for a tiny portion of offal, a part of a beast that no Dutch woman would have previously known existed. She approached the woman, to be told that many of the Dutch families had run out of money and were close to starving.

That evening she visited Ratih and offered to buy her a restaurant of her own that would, in addition, act as a soup kitchen for Dutch families on the edge of starvation. 'Ratih, we will soon be interned, then you will have your own business. In the meantime, if anyone asks, the Dutch who eat here are paying you. Say that it is good business for you to serve them. It must not be known that I am paying for everything, not even by the Dutch. Do you understand? And perhaps you should discuss this with your lieutenant. If there is any danger to you then you must not do it! Promise?'

For Anna it was a way to use up some of the money in the tin, if only a fraction, her fear being that sooner or later the *kempeitai* would come calling and it would all be confiscated.

The following day an excited Ratih arrived to say that the lieutenant had agreed and had issued a licence for a business, but that as the kitchen and eatery where she worked was for sale, it would be cheaper and quicker to use that rather than trying to create a new one, even though she felt confident that the locals would come wherever she cooked because her food was good. 'I have asked Til also,' she said, 'and he says, "Ratih, the stomach is not racist. Your old customers will tolerate the Dutch if the food is good enough."'

Within twenty-four hours Ratih became a restaurant owner with no debts, plenty of working capital and Kiki now elevated to rice cook. In return, the poorer Dutch families got the best soup kitchen in Java without ever knowing the name of their benefactor. It soon became apparent that Til had been right – the locals continued their patronage, declaring the food, if anything, even better. In fact, this was correct since Ratih was free to choose the best of everything at the markets, no longer restricted by the previous owner's noted parsimony.

Anna, of course, talked to her father. 'Talked' was the operative word, as she had no intention of asking his permission but hoped instead for his advice. But the big Dutchman was increasingly depressed, nearly crippled by his own anxiety. He simply grunted, 'It is finished here for the Dutch anyway. We will all die; maybe starving would be better. Do what you damn well like.'

Anna had made the first decision that hadn't been forced upon her by circumstances or a sense of obligation, and it felt very good.

A week or so after Ratih had assumed control of her own eatery, at about four o'clock in the afternoon, Budi arrived at the house, the face of the thirteen-year-old deeply troubled. 'What is it, Budi?' Anna asked, immediately concerned.

'Mother Ratih sent me, Anna. The *kempeitai* have come

to the restaurant and are looking for the tall Javanese girl with the blue eyes who fainted at the beheading in the town square. The Japanese colonel Konoe, he has demanded that you be found and brought to him. The lieutenant thinks they must know – that somebody has told them – that Mother Ratih knows where you are.'

CHAPTER ELEVEN

'To the Japanese this is the symbol of life, a heartwood that will outlast everything man can make, a core within that, come what may, cannot be broken and represents our inner strength and divine spirit.'

Konoe Akira
Colonel, Japanese Imperial Army
5th Resettlement Battalion, Tjilatjap

ANNA SAT DOWN AFTER Budi left. They'd talked beneath a tree in the front garden where they had sat cross-legged on the grass, for she'd been anxious that her father would not overhear the details of their conversation.

'Anna, Ratih says you must escape to the mountains. Til has friends there who will hide you and you will be safe. They, the Japanese *polisi*, will not find you,' Budi said urgently, deeply concerned that the message entrusted to him be accepted.

Anna frowned. 'But you will not be safe! The *kempeitai* will find you. If Til is caught taking me to the mountains, or even if he is not, there are wagging tongues. They will know, they *already* know that we are friends. People see that Ratih now owns the *kampong* restaurant, someone has guessed where the money came from. The Japanese *polisi* are like dogs, their noses to the ground, only they are sniffing for money. If you fail to find me for them, they will soon persuade you to look harder.'

'Mother Ratih is an honourable woman. My mother will

never tell them, even if they torture her!' Budi protested loyally.

'Not just her. There is Til, you, the lieutenant. This house is in the police compound. How can he tell them he does not know how to find me? He will lose his job and you will all be tortured, beaten.' Anna sighed. 'And in the end they will find me anyway.'

The thirteen-year-old looked totally distraught. 'We have honour, Anna,' he insisted. 'You have done everything for us. I will be educated, the restaurant, Lo Wok. Now we must repay you.'

'With your lives?' Anna shook her head vigorously. 'No, I will not have it!' It was at that moment that the idea first struck her. She would go voluntarily to the Japanese colonel. She would avoid the *kempeitai* search for her and simply present herself to him at his home.

'Anna, Mother Ratih says Kiki will look after your father, we will honour him as our own. We are Javanese, the *kempeitai* will not treat us like the Chinese.'

'Ha! What about the heads of the Javanese criminals they have placed on bamboo poles around the town? They will treat you just the same if they think you are aiding the enemy to escape!' She grabbed Budi by the shoulders. 'Listen to me, Budi,' Anna said urgently. 'Tell Til he must find out where Colonel Konoe lives, his house, not his military headquarters – do you understand?' Budi nodded. 'Then Til must come and get me at 11.30 tomorrow morning. Tell him not to be late. No, don't, he is never late,' she corrected herself. 'Send Kiki over at eleven o'clock.' Anna was amazed at how clearly she saw the situation. Not for the first time, she'd managed to avoid panic when in a crisis. She didn't think of it as an inner strength, only that it had happened previously. 'Does Kiki know that the Japanese *polisi* are looking for me?' she now asked.

'No, Anna. We have not told her.'

'But with tongues wagging, surely she will hear?'

'She is in the kitchen, the rice cook. Mother Ratih will not let her serve at tables tonight. But, Anna —?' Budi questioned.

Anna cut him short. 'Do not argue, Budi, there is no time. If the *kempeitai* come to the restaurant tonight, tell Mother Ratih she must say that she expects to be able to report my whereabouts very soon. Do not resist them. Do not lie to them. Promise me, Budi!'

A thoroughly disconsolate Budi left shortly afterwards.

Now back in the house, Anna was suddenly terrified. The idea of the *kempeitai* finding her, manhandling her, possibly even torturing her, led her imagination to run riot. If they found out about the tin box, that she had a large amount of money, they would come and then treat her as they had the Chinese merchants. She had cautioned Ratih not to disclose where the money had come from to buy the restaurant. But people talk, they see and they speculate. Being a cook in a *kampong* restaurant isn't a highly paid profession. After all, every woman can cook. If the lieutenant accepted bribes these would certainly not be sufficient to buy a restaurant. Budi returning to school was another reason for speculation. Anna was known to be a friend of the *kampong* cook and, moreover, had been seen at the market buying pots and pans, towels, sheets and assorted household goods when the other Dutch were selling everything they possessed so as not to starve. People observed these things, the tall Javanese girl with the slightly lighter skin and the black glass over her eyes.

Ratih's sudden change of fortune would have set the *kampong* tongues wagging and, as Til had recently told her, reporting old enemies to the *kempeitai* was becoming a local sport. Ratih was a forthright woman. She would have made her fair share of enemies. As Til again had once said to her, envy is a close cousin to malice, and both are dangerous human characteristics. She wasn't sure whether this had been one of the Prophet's maxims. Anna had been desperately sorry for the half-starved Dutch woman buying a scrap of offal and for others like her, and had acted impulsively and foolishly to start the soup kitchen. She should have heeded her father's scorn at the idea.

Her very first concern was to conceal the whereabouts of the tin box. Hiding it under the outside lavatory seat now seemed downright careless – anyone knowing there was money hidden would find it in minutes. It must be taken off the premises. She would ask Til to hide it and if she was murdered by the *kempeitai* to use some of it to take care of her father, give Kiki her wedding dowry and her own house, put Budi through university, build Ratih and the lieutenant a new home and buy himself a fleet of taxi cars. In the meantime Kiki would take care of her father until the Japanese decided what to do with the Dutch stay-behinds. Even then, if Til could find a way to buy her father freedom with a bribe, he was to use some of the money for this purpose. Anna was trying to stay calm while preparing for her own death.

At dinner that night Piet Van Heerden, as he had increasingly been doing, complained about her cooking, pushed his plate away and declared the meal inedible. It was a sentiment that Anna, in her preoccupation, was willing to concede. She had never much liked cooking anyway and though she had once or twice cooked for me in Batavia, it was boy's food, meat and potatoes with gravy, with the one veg she insisted I must endure.

'Well, you'll be happy to know Kiki will be here to cook your food tomorrow,' Anna announced, placing a cup of coffee down in front of him. He hadn't noticed her preoccupation or anxiety.

'Kiki?'

'*Kleine* Kiki,' Anna said, remembering. 'She is now practically a qualified restaurant cook.'

'Why?' her father grunted.

'Why what? Why is she coming?' Anna said. Then taking a deep breath she announced, 'Father, there is trouble with the *kempeitai*, they are looking for me.'

Piet Van Heerden glanced up at his daughter, surprised. His face suddenly clouded. 'Police? Looking for you? The *foking* police are looking for you! Why? What have you gone and done?'

'Nothing, Father, it is the Japanese police, they are like hungry dogs, always sniffing around.'

'Dogs sniff where there is a bad smell! What is this about, hey? Tell me, Anna!'

'I can't say, I think it may be the soup kitchen.' Anna was reluctant to explain any further. Her father hardly knew Ratih, who hadn't been to the house since he'd emerged from the cellar.

'I *foking* told you don't do it! A few starving Dutch. Who gives a shit. I *foking* told you, Anna!' he repeated, stabbing a finger at her. 'Now look what you've done, you've endangered *my* life!' Anna saw his angry expression change to one of fear as this new thought struck him. 'They will find me and torture me! They will kill me! It is your fault,' he whined. Then, 'Pay them, give them money, lots of money, they can be bribed, all policemen can be bribed.' He looked desperately at his daughter. 'Anna, I don't want to die!' he wailed.

'Nor do I, Father,' Anna said softly, aware that the more likely prospect of her own death hadn't occurred to him.

'Money! There is lots of it in the tin box! Give them some!' he sobbed.

'Then they will want more. They *must* not know we have money,' Anna said. 'I will hide the box.'

'What about the soup kitchen? Have they found out you paid for that *foking* stupid idea?'

'It was not a lot of money. Just sufficient to run the soup kitchen from a small restaurant in the *kampong*.' Anna didn't mention that in addition she'd bought the restaurant for Ratih. Her father wouldn't understand.

'Listen, Father, I have an idea. I will go directly to the colonel.'

'What colonel? Who is this colonel? Is he the police?'

'No, Father. He is in command of everything.'

'He is not the police? You said the police, the *kempeitai*, want you?'

Anna could have kicked herself. She hadn't mentioned the execution of the Chinese to her father or the fainting incident in the square. The beheading of the four Chinese, she reasoned, would have caused him severe panic, even a heart attack. The terrible fear he had of being tortured or of dying in a brutal way now totally absorbed his every thought. Apart from going to the outside toilet, which he did furtively, he never left the house and was afraid to venture beyond the front gate.

'It is better than being picked up by the *kempeitai*,' Anna said, trying to recover. Then she had a sudden thought. 'If I go myself to the colonel, then the *kempeitai* won't know where we live and you will be safe. *Kleine* Kiki will take care of you until I return.'

Piet Van Heerden grunted, though Anna thought he was somewhat mollified. He rose from the kitchen table. '*Foking* stupid,' he said, moving through the doorway towards his bedroom. He paused at the bedroom door. 'Do not tell that Japanese colonel you have a father, you hear?' he said, entering and closing the door behind him. Then he opened it a moment later. 'Leave enough money for me for six months,' he shouted. 'Also the diamonds – I want them back!'

Anna, who no longer was afraid of, or even respected, her father, had no intention of returning the diamonds. Besides, she'd already made plans for his survival and welfare. She wrote a list of things for Kiki to do, topmost among them being to check his bed sheets each morning. While her father rose regularly during the night and the chamber-pot was always almost full, every once in a while he'd wet the sheets. He was gaining weight and seemed constantly thirsty, while during the day he made numerous covert trips to the outside lavatory. Anna was not to know that Piet Van Heerden had developed diabetes.

Kiki arrived as she had been instructed, just before 11 a.m., after Anna had served her late-rising father breakfast. She didn't want a tearful Kiki on her hands and had asked Ratih to tell her that Anna was going into the countryside to look for a possible house where her father would be able to go outside for walks and not be fearful of being caught. She knew Kiki was aware of her father's paranoia and would immediately understand, and so Kiki arrived at the house unconcerned and cheerful, anticipating the household chores as being a pleasant change from the grinding routine of working as rice cook in Ratih's kitchen.

'I will clean *everything*, Anna,' she promised happily. Entering the kitchen she pointed to the stove. 'I have brought stoveblack – it will be shining when you return from the country.'

Anna had previously told her father to say nothing about her visit to confront the colonel. '*Kleine* Kiki is a maid and she will talk. So, please, tell her nothing, Father!' she'd said to him, speaking sternly for added emphasis. Not that she needed to be concerned. Piet Van Heerden's fear of being discovered and tortured far exceeded any desire to gossip with a servant.

Til arrived at precisely 11.30 a.m. Anna, as usual, marvelled at his sense of time, especially as he carried no watch. To most of the population, half an hour here or there wasn't of great concern; it was tropical time, only the school was bewilderingly strict about its pupils being on time. She'd once queried his punctuality and how he achieved it. 'Allah gives us all the best watch. Hold your hand to your heart, you will feel the ticking of perfect time. That is how,' he'd said to her, perfectly straight-faced.

'Til, that is complete bullshit!' Anna had cried.

Til laughed and hung his head. 'I can see the clock on the church tower from most places. I cannot admit this because it is the infidel church, but when I see it, I know how far it is to my destination.'

'Well, I'm just glad Allah isn't involved for a change,' Anna replied, laughing.

'*Ahee!* Anna, that is not right. Allah made mankind and only man can invent a clock, a donkey can't, a heron that lands on water but doesn't sink can't. *Allah akbar!*'

Anna had removed her paternal grandfather's gold watch and fob chain from the tin box and placed it in her dishtowel bag. She reasoned that the colonel might not accept money and that attempting to bribe him might have serious consequences, but he might accept the gift of Koos Van Heerden's beautiful monogrammed watch. This, if he should hand her over to the *kempeitai*, possessed the added advantage of not suggesting that there was money to be gained. An antique gold fob watch was just the kind of heirloom a Dutch family would hang on to as long as possible, using its value only in a desperate situation.

As she approached the waiting *becak* she could see that Til was anything but his usual cheerful self. She was accustomed to being met with an ebullient welcome. Til had made the art of greeting his speciality, but now he stood with his toes wiggling in the dust and his head silently bowed.

'What is it, Til? Have I done something to hurt you?' Anna asked, her tone concerned.

Til looked up slowly. 'Anna, we are not fools. I got Budi's message and I know where is that house. We know what you are going to do. It is not right. Let me take you to the mountains. I have friends who will protect you and only for a small bribe that I will pay myself. Kiki will take care of your father and we will honour him and look after him. You will be safe.'

Anna was deeply touched, but stood her ground. 'Til, you *are* fools, all of you. Tongues have wagged, you said yourself people are reporting others to the Japan *polisi* to settle old scores. There is bound to be envy over Ratih buying the restaurant. It is my fault entirely. I was clumsy with the arrangements. Now, if the *kempeitai* don't find me soon, they will persuade you in their own ways to tell them where I am. You, Ratih, Budi, even the lieutenant will be made to suffer.'

'Allah says . . .'

'Stop right there, Til! I don't want to hear what Allah says. I just want you to take me to the Japanese colonel's house.'

But Til persisted. 'It is not right, Anna. You have made us rich. With Lo Wok, you preserved our honour. Budi will be educated. Now you ask us to stand by, to protect our own arses, when you are in great danger?' He looked up. 'How can we do this?'

Anna glanced at her watch, appearing to ignore his protests. 'We must get going. I will tell you what you can do to preserve your honour on the way.' Anna looked at the *becak*. 'Ah, thank you, you have attached the brothel curtain.'

'It is me who is the whore!' Til said, climbing unhappily into the tricycle saddle.

On the way Anna outlined what she wanted, pledging Til to take care of the tin box. He seemed delighted with the trust placed in him and Anna felt from his tone of voice that he believed the family honour, in some part, was restored. By the time she had completed talking, Anna heard the crunch of the tyres on gravel. 'We are here, Anna,' Til said. 'It is the old house for the owner of the brewery. He was very rich, the Dutch they like much the beer.'

Anna parted the curtain. In the weeks she had been in Tjilatjap she had seen the neglect of the big houses, especially the grand gardens. The locals who had moved into the larger homes, often three or four families at a time, had no eye or desire or even time for clipped lawns, trimmed hedges, pruned shrubs and neatly planted flowerbeds. Already the stronger plants, creepers and hibiscus hedges, bamboo and bougainvillea, were flexing their muscles, these bullies of the tropical gardens elbowing their way into space they had previously been denied. Small, more delicate exotic plants quickly abandoned the struggle to exist and withered or crept surreptitiously into dark, damp corners of foliage to hide. Strangler vines stretched over arbours, and pumpkins, feasting on the sun, imbibed its gold and grew rotund, the big, hairy-leafed vines sprawled over driveways and the edges of neglected paths. Hastily constructed henhouses sat on previously immaculate lawns, the fowls permitted to scratch for worms since their eggs were far more important to the new occupants than the pointless plants they uprooted. Circular gardens cut into large lawns, previously featuring exotic blooms imported from all over the world, were summarily ripped out and vegetables planted – bok choy, spinach, garlic, chillies, cabbage, tomatoes, curry leaf and shallots, all the common tumble and sizzle that went into the family wok.

But not so at the ex-brewer's mansion, now commandeered by the military. Two guards by the entrance of the wrought-iron gates, seeing a woman in a *becak*, waved them in. Gardeners seemed to be scurrying everywhere, pushing wheelbarrows, mowing lawns, trimming hedges, digging, turning compost and raking the leaves from under a large poinciana tree, its umbrella shape partially shading the driveway. They were short, thickset, shirtless men, their boots and socks discarded, and wearing only khaki trousers. That their solid slightly bandy legs were swathed below the knees in dirty puttees was the only testimony to the fact that they were Japanese soldiers. Even their ubiquitous forage caps had been replaced with wide-brimmed local straw hats.

Despite the humble *becak* in which she arrived, they bowed respectfully as she passed. Anna had never seen happier Japanese soldiers. When Til asked in Javanese how he might get to the back door they obviously didn't understand, though one of them who was on his knees clipping the edge of the lawn grinned and pointed to the front door and then with a bent forefinger made an imaginary knocking gesture in the air.

Anna asked Til to wait for her outside the gates, instructing him to leave if she hadn't returned in two hours, then handing him a few coins so that any of the soldier gardeners observing would think he was simply a *becak* driver dropping off a passenger.

Til nodded, his face showing concern. 'I will wait longer, until sunset,' he announced.

Anna, standing in the driveway near the front steps of the mansion, faced an immediate dilemma. If she walked to the rear of the house and knocked politely this would immediately indicate her subservience. While she had come as a supplicant she wasn't a servant and she instinctively realised that the manner of her arrival and the first few moments of being admitted were critical. On the other hand, if she pressed the polished brass bell on the front door announcing her arrival with a ringing that filled the interior of the mansion, it might be taken as a sign of arrogance, even of defiance.

The Japanese, she knew, did not take easily to defiance, and arrogance was a characteristic they reserved for themselves. After all, it was Colonel Konoe who had authorised the execution of the four Chinese and had stood calmly by as Captain Takahashi had severed their heads. This did not promise a man of sensitivity, and instead suggested one possessed of a coldness and arrogance of manner. Anna knew he was unlikely to answer the doorbell himself. Under the circumstances she didn't know what to expect, perhaps a servant or a sergeant.

Gathering all her courage she climbed the steps. To her

right grew a frangipani tree and impulsively she reached out and plucked one of the delicately perfumed yellow and white blossoms and tucked it into her hair above her ear. With her hand trembling slightly she took a deep breath and pushed the bell, a moment later hearing its sharp ring through the interior of the house.

Anna seemed to be waiting ages and was about to press the bell once again when she heard the slap of slippers on a wooden floor. One half of the impressive teak front door opened to reveal a Japanese woman of indeterminate age, anything between forty-five and fifty-five. She wore a working kimono and soft black cotton slippers. She smiled but did not speak.

Anna was surprised to be confronted by a Japanese woman and, knowing no Japanese, spoke in the native language. 'Good afternoon, Mother,' she began respectfully in the Javanese manner. 'I have come to see Colonel Konoe.'

'Oh, the Colonel *Konoe-san* is not yet here, he will arrive shortly. Will you wait for him?' she answered in perfect Javanese.

Anna smiled, anxious not to admit she lacked an appointment to see him. 'You speak Javanese very well, Mother.'

The woman laughed. 'I was born in Tjilatjap. My honourable parents came here in 1895 and I was born a year later. My husband, Onishi Tokuma, he is now the mayor, has granted me the honour of being *mama-san* for the *colonel-san*. Come, you can wait on the back verandah, that is where he will take his lunch.'

'No, I can wait outside,' Anna said quickly, wondering to what lengths the snivelling little sycophant, the Mayor of the Squashed Hat, would go to ingratiate himself with the military command. What kind of man would lend his wife to the colonel as a servant, doubtless unpaid?

'No, no, come inside,' the mayor's wife-turned-housemaid insisted, nodding her head towards the interior of the house while opening the door a little wider.

Anna followed her into the mansion that proved to be in the Dutch style in every respect – highly polished teak floors; expensive Turkish and Persian carpets; clumsy, carved massive wooden furniture; over-upholstered maroon velvet lounges and chairs; a huge breakfront sideboard, now empty, that would have originally displayed expensive china *objets d'art* such as figurines and antique Delft crockery. Picture hooks remained where family portraits and other paintings had once hung. The heavy silk-lined drapes were in the cold-climate European style, bunched and knotted at the centre by a gold tasselled rope, the whole effect making no concession to the tropical climate but simply intended to impress.

The only acknowledgement that the house was situated within the tropics was the large, wooden-paddled ceiling fans that hung in every room. Anna had been in dozens of similar big houses belonging to wealthy school and family friends. *Grootehuis* hadn't been very different. Anna wondered at the expensive oriental carpets – surely the brewery owner would have taken them with him when he fled Java?

The Japanese housekeeper led her to the rear of the house and onto the stone-flagged verandah. Here the climate was finally acknowledged, with large rattan and bamboo armchairs cushioned in light, coloured cottons. There was a low bamboo coffee table, its surface a sheet of clear polished glass, while several small side tables made up the remainder of the casual furniture.

On the coffee table stood a glass vase filled with a meticulous arrangement of yellow and white dahlias. It was precise to the extent that the stalk of each bloom had been cut to a prescribed length at exactly the same slanted angle, the leaves that would normally have been immersed in water had been carefully removed so as not to damage the stems, and those beyond the waterline had been culled so that what remained became a part of the carefully created formal arrangement.

Dahlias are by nature colourful and exuberant flowers, more jazz than ballet, and while the display was beautiful, the white and yellow blooms seemed to have been severely reprimanded and made to behave themselves.

'I will bring tea,' the *mama-san* said, scurrying away.

Anna sat alone and afraid, aware of the chance she was taking, knowing she was intruding, an uninvited guest in the home of a man who could with a snap of his fingers condemn her to death or, perhaps worse, hand her over to be tortured by the *kempeitai*. In her mind she saw the blood-splashed jackboots again. She was unaccustomed to wearing make-up, but when discarding possessions as they left the *Witvogel* she had kept a single tube of lipstick, the lightest shade among the many colours her late stepmother had possessed. Anna's thickly lashed violet eyes needed no mascara and her skin was flawless. She had worn the lipstick in an attempt to look more grown-up but now, in the process of containing her anxiety, she repeatedly ran her tongue over her lips and unbeknown to her, no trace of applied colour remained. Her attempt at worldly sophistication had been eliminated.

The tea arrived. 'It is Dutch tea,' the *mama-san* announced proudly. 'There was some left. We Japanese, we drink only green tea.'

'Thank you, Mother,' Anna said, not telling her that she would have much preferred the other. The locally born Japanese woman poured Anna's tea and Anna commented, 'The flowers are beautiful. I love dahlias, so many colours, they always look as though they're dressed and going off to a dance.'

'I cut two pink ones yesterday and put them in the vase and the *colonel-san* was very angry. He threw out the pink. "Do not touch the arrangement again!" he shouted.' The housekeeper looked serious. 'Japanese women who do not grow up in Japan cannot know these things. I must be careful and obedient and know my place. It is good for me to learn from the honourable *Konoe-san*, who is from a noble family and very wise.' She pointed at the vase. 'Every morning he removes the flowers and places them in a row with a number beside them, here on this table, then I must wash and polish the vase and bring him a jug of clean water. Then he will arrange them again, always the same as the last time, even the leaves the same,' she said, obviously awed and deeply respectful of the precise discipline involved.

'You do not find this strange?' Anna asked, confused and trying in her mind to decide what kind of man could become so obsessed with a single vase of flowers.

'Oh, no! It is culture. It is Japanese. It is the power of perfection! I must learn and respect this honourable vase of flowers.' At that moment the short stab of a car horn sounded. The Japanese woman visibly drew to attention. A frightened look crossed her face and then settled into one of concern. 'He has come. I must go to the door!' She turned and half-ran to the back door, then stopped. '*Ahee!* Your name, Miss?'

'Anna. Anna Van Heerden.'

'Anna,' the woman said, repeating, 'Anna, Anna.'

Anna had not introduced herself, waiting in the conventional Javanese way to have the older person make the first introduction and so signalling that they wished to know you. The locally born Japanese woman would have known this convention and, unsure of her master's reception of the beautiful young woman, would have refrained from introducing herself other than to mention that she was the wife of the mayor. This apparent lack of good manners was seemingly intentional, lest her familiarity with Anna cause her master, the colonel, displeasure.

Anna had rehearsed in her mind how she would manage the introduction to the Japanese colonel. She would rise from her chair unhurriedly and smile in her most engaging manner, as any politely brought-up young girl would do if they found themselves suddenly in the presence of an older stranger. *Keep calm. Keep calm*, she constantly repeated to herself. But suddenly he was there, a tall, good-looking Japanese man in shiny jackboots and an immaculate uniform, moving with a pronounced limp. Anna jumped to her feet, her hands clasped behind her back in the manner of an errant schoolgirl suddenly caught out. 'Oh!' she exclaimed.

It was only at that moment that it occurred to her that they had no means of communicating. He undoubtedly spoke no Javanese, was unlikely to be conversant in Dutch, and she knew almost no Japanese. The *mama-san* would need to translate, which was precisely what Anna did not wish to happen, but then again, she would be a better option than her husband, the mayor. That is, of course, if wordlessly he didn't have her arrested and handed to the *kempeitai*.

Colonel Konoe smiled and motioned for her to resume her seat. 'Anna, do you speak English, French or German?' he asked in almost flawless English.

Anna backed into her chair, her legs unexpectedly meeting the cushioned seat so that she sat down with an undignified thump. 'English, sir – and French a little, but only school French, no German,' she said, recovering.

The Japanese officer seemed pleased. 'English. Good. We shall speak to each other in English. I am Konoe Akira.' He came to attention and bowed his head slightly, no more than a formal jerk, followed by a sharp grunt, 'Ho!' He'd placed his surname before his particular name in the Japanese way.

'Anna Van Heerden. How do you do, sir?'

The Japanese colonel did not reply to her greeting but proceeded to seat himself opposite her, his body slightly twisted, awkward as he adjusted his bad leg. Finally settled, he leaned back against the large chair. He reached into the brass-buttoned breast pocket of his uniform and produced a slim silver cigarette case; withdrawing a cigarette he closed the case and tapped the end of the cigarette against the lid. He turned his head towards the door. '*Mama-san!*' he called and then added something in Japanese.

Moments later the housekeeper appeared with a silver cigarette lighter and a glass ashtray. With her hands shaking slightly, she lit the colonel's cigarette, then placed the ashtray in front of him. Anna noted that this was not a man accustomed to lighting his own cigarette, or perhaps not in the company of someone else. She wondered which of the two options it was, thinking there was a difference. The ashtray, she observed, was beautiful, and moulded into the bottom was a butterfly. Later she would tell me that this singular detail almost brought her undone. She also admitted it was at that moment she realised that so much had happened since we'd said a tearful farewell on the *Witvogel* that she wondered if I could possibly love the person she had become. She would later discover that the ashtray was French and signed by an artist named Lalique.

Colonel Konoe threw his head back and exhaled the cigarette smoke toward the verandah ceiling. 'Van Heerden? You are Dutch?' he asked at last.

'Half, sir. *Mijn* father is Dutch and my mother, she is dead, was Javanese.'

He frowned. 'Mixed colour? I do not approve of mixing races, the result is always inferior.' He announced this calmly as though it was a commonly known and proven fact and smiled as if this was a perfectly normal thing to say. 'But in your case I will make an exception. Ah, your eyes,' he said admiringly.

Anna did not know how she should reply – angrily to the insult or smiling at the compliment – and so she remained silent.

He pointed to the vase of flowers. 'Purity of selection is like those dahlias, one perfect colour.'

'But there are two colours, sir.'

'One!' he said sharply. 'Yellow. White is not a colour. It is simply there to highlight the perfection of the yellow.'

'Ah, then you must approve of such as me? I am yellow highlighted by white.' Anna held her breath, thinking she had gone too far. She smiled, though it was more an attempt at a quizzical grin, her beautiful violet eyes held wide.

Konoe Akira brought the cigarette to his lips, inhaled and then exhaled, and carefully placed it so that it balanced on the lip of the butterfly ashtray. 'Not only a beautiful woman but also a clever one,' he observed, bringing his hands together in a small token clap. But then he added, 'You should be careful, you play dangerously, young woman'.

Anna was becoming confused, unable to define the Japanese officer in her mind. He was rapidly becoming an enigma. Was he a potentially cold-eyed killer and racist who liked to arrange flowers and sought in them perfection? Or a sophisticated, urbane, almost likeable cultured and aesthetic man? Or both? Could one person be both? She supposed this was possible, but knew she was out of her depth and also that she should remain silent. But his racial antipathy and singular scorn and dismissal of someone of mixed blood burned within her. She had always seen herself as different, but never as lesser, never as inferior.

She pointed at the vase. 'Sir, you have chosen yellow as perfection, but the dahlia has many colours: pink, red, orange, magenta and, of course, yellow and white. Yet every colour is still a dahlia, still perfection. Is it not the same with the human race? We are still all dahlias but is it not our differences that are interesting?' she added.

At that moment the housekeeper came through the door carrying a tray. She placed it down on a small wicker side table and carefully removed the vase, the teapot and untouched cup of tea that was before Anna. Then, using both hands, she placed a small, exquisite yellow porcelain bowl in front of Anna and another in front of the Japanese officer. Then came a larger rice dish, a chicken dish and one containing tempura vegetables. This dish was also of the same, almost opaque, porcelain, only this time it was white. The *mama-san* set down each dish in a tiny silent ceremony. Then she laid a pair of beautifully proportioned, highly burnished black chopsticks beside Anna, carefully separating them so they were slightly apart but still somehow together; a tiny aesthetic touch, two lovers temporarily separated after making love. She did the same with those she placed in front of the colonel. Her final touches were to add a white porcelain rice spoon beside the rice and a pale green pot containing tea accompanied by two small yellow porcelain oriental cups. She had, in just a few moments, created a setting which, while simple, when reflected in the polished glass surface of the table, was exquisite. In its own way it replicated the vase of dahlias, the yellow and white of the blossoms and finally the pale leaf-green of the teapot. Anna thought it near to being faultless.

Konoe Akira picked up a chopstick and balanced it in his hand. 'In the heartwood of the sacred persimmon tree is ebony, the hardest, most beautiful of all woods. It is created by nature and will last longer than the *katana*, the layered and folded steel of the everlasting samurai sword.' He dipped and lifted his palm in the air as if weighing the chopstick. 'To the Japanese this is the symbol of life, a heartwood that will outlast everything man can make, a core within that, come what may, cannot be broken and represents our inner strength and divine spirit.' He paused, looking at Anna, his expression serious. 'Perhaps at another time you will permit me to recite the soldier's poem about the persimmon tree by the most venerable Taneda Santoka, *haiku* master. He was the last Japanese priest–poet. He passed away just two years ago. I will try to translate it into English.' He placed the chopstick down and indicated the food. 'You are permitted to eat. Please, some chicken?' He indicated the small squares of chicken on skewer sticks.

Immediately as the *mama-san* had placed the chicken dish down, Anna's acute sense of smell picked up a sharp sourness to the sauce. It was not the tartness of a freshly squeezed lemon. Instead an altogether different astringency assailed her nostrils. It was sharp, perhaps too sharp for her taste, although she could detect the smell of the soy sauce that had been added to render it less sour. She had decided to start with the tempura; the light batter and the vegetable oil used for frying smelled simply wonderful. She wondered if the whiteness of the rice was meant to highlight the gold of the tempura, but left this observation unremarked. But now that the colonel had suggested she start with the chicken she felt compelled to obey him.

'Thank you, *Colonel-san*,' she said, borrowing the respectful nomenclature from the mayor's wife as a change from her constantly repeated 'sir'. She added a little rice to her bowl and then removed the chicken from the small wooden skewer with her chopstick, allowing it to fall into the rice. Then she picked up a single square of chicken and popped it into her mouth. It tasted horrible. At home she would have covered her mouth with a napkin and left the table to hurry somewhere private to spit it out. Now she swallowed it bravely, adding rice in an attempt to ameliorate the taste.

In the meantime the colonel had helped himself to the rice and vegetable tempura, silent as he attended to the food in front of him. Anna waited for him to reach for a chicken skewer. If he ate it with equanimity then she would accept that what pleased the Japanese palate was chicken that had been allowed to go slightly off. He poured himself green tea from the pot, the steam rising from the small tea bowl, and then took another piece of the tempura. Finally he reached for the chicken, removed the pieces from the skewer into his bowl and brought a single piece to his mouth. Anna observed his face contort and twist in dismay. Without ceremony he spat the contents of his mouth into his rice bowl, repeating the spitting process several times to remove the last of the contaminated chicken on his lips. '*Mama-san!*' he yelled in a furious voice.

The Japanese housekeeper must have been standing

attentively just beyond the door for she appeared almost immediately. Konoe Akira lifted the dish containing four more skewers and emptied the contents over her feet. His rebuke was in Japanese so that Anna could only observe her dismay and with it her changing facial expressions. At first she brought both hands up to her face, then she began to sob, stooping to brush some of the mess from her slippers. The Japanese colonel proceeded to empty the bowl of rice over her head, followed by what was left of the tempura. Now she cowered at his feet, gabbling words of apology, attempting to scrape together the debris on the floor with her hands. Then he reached over, took up the teapot and poured the hot green tea over her neck and back, scalding her. His face had grown apoplectic with rage as he continued to rebuke the hapless, howling woman in Japanese.

Anna jumped to her feet, the act of pouring the hot tea finally too much. 'Stop, you cruel bastard!' she screamed. 'Stop at once! Let her alone, you piece of crippled shit!' Anna knew instantly with these final five words she had lost her life, the sight of the blood-splashed jackboots, her own blood, flashing through her mind.

The Japanese colonel stopped abruptly and with a dismissive hand told the distraught and injured woman to leave. But by this time Anna was kneeling by her side, trying to comfort the crouched and weeping *mama-san*, at the same time attempting to lift her to her feet. The Japanese officer rose from the chair and Anna, with her arms around the cowering housekeeper, glared up at him. 'Fuck off, you bastard!' she spat.

Konoe Akira stood over her and broke into a broad smile, then brought his hands together and clapped softly. 'I knew it! I knew it the moment I saw you in the town square where you fainted. I knew you were the one. You will be perfect!' He brought his heels together and jerked his head forward in the same semblance of a bow as previously, followed with a similar grunt of 'Ho!' Then, not as an invitation or as a request, but as a clearly issued order, he demanded, 'Tomorrow at twelve o'clock you will be present for lunch. A thousand apologies, the food, it will be better than today. We will talk about dahlias and differences. I will tell the *kempeitai* I have found you. My staff sergeant will now drive you home.'

Anna was, to say the least, surprised at his sudden and complete change of temper and his reaction to her vulgar language. She had deeply insulted him and yet seemingly he had been delighted. 'Thank you, that is unnecessary. I have a *becak* waiting,' she said quietly.

'As you wish.' With this Colonel Konoe turned. His back rigid, chin slightly jutted, he walked towards the door leading to the interior of the house, despite his pronounced limp every inch an officer of the Japanese Imperial Army.

Til was waiting outside the gate and looked overjoyed to see her. 'Anna, are you okay? You have rice on your shoes!'

Anna grinned, then burst into sudden tears, then grinned again through tear-brightened eyes. 'Til, I am here and still in one piece!' she joked.

'Allah be praised!' he said, helping Anna into the *becak*. 'Let us be gone, too many soldiers turned into gardeners or maybe the other way around. This place, it does not feel right, Anna.'

'Til, I am starving and I have a sour taste in my mouth; take me to Ratih's restaurant. I need fried rice and chicken, her special recipe.'

CHAPTER TWELVE

*'Konoe-san, my face is brown and I do not wish it
to be white or my cheeks to be stained with blush
and my lips the colour of fresh cow's liver.
My hair falls naturally to my shoulders,
I do not want to lift it to the sky or to
decorate it with chopsticks.'*
Anna Van Heerden

ANNA RETURNED HOME TOTALLY confused. As
well, she was disconcerted that she was immediately forced to
fib to Kiki, telling her she had been unsuccessful at finding a
place out of town and requesting her to return the following day
at the same time. Anna spoke to Kiki in the kitchen and failed
to notice the polished and gleaming black stove. Later she made
a mental note to apologise to her in the morning. The house
was spotlessly clean and the laundry done. What the little rice
cook had managed to do in less than four hours was remarkable;
she'd even prepared their dinner – a stew she knew to be one of
her father's favourites.

Piet Van Heerden was his usual depressed self. Anna had
managed to find a box of books in Dutch at the markets, but apart
from lifting them out and sniffing at each rather than opening
them, he'd returned them to the box where they remained
untouched. She knew that by asserting her independence she

had reduced him to someone of no consequence in her life, nevertheless she was unrepentant. If he asked again for the diamonds she would openly refuse to return them. They had been a gift and she had accepted them reluctantly, but now they were hers. If she had broken his spirit, then perhaps it had been too fragile in the first place. Anna resolved that there was little or nothing she could do to solve his morbidity or allay his fear of dying.

'She cooks better than you. Lunch was a decent meal for a change,' her father growled, not looking up.

'That's good. She has cooked your dinner, your favourite, meat stew with potatoes from the garden.'

'Humph! It is not much to look forward to,' he said self-pityingly.

'And you'll be glad to hear she'll be back tomorrow,' Anna said, trying to sound cheerful. 'I have to return to see that Japanese colonel.'

Piet Van Heerden was silent, seemingly not responding to this news. When eventually he spoke he asked, 'Did he take money?'

'No, I didn't offer him any.'

'Did he fuck you?'

'No!' Anna cried, shocked but at the same time indignant. 'He did *not*!'

The Dutchman rose from his chair, his rheumy blue eyes meeting hers directly. 'Then he will tomorrow,' he said in a flat, disinterested voice. Turning, he shuffled from the kitchen, his bladder alerting him to go to the lavatory.

Anna heard the screen door bang. Once again she felt completely alone and in her mind's eye she saw the wash of blood that had given her life while it had taken her mother's. Colonel

Konoe was wrong. It was the white that had been stronger than the brown. She thought of the beautiful opaque butterfly etched into the base of his ashtray. What had happened to her? She was no longer the sweet sixteen-year-old who had fallen in love with a big bear of a boy who collected butterflies. She didn't really know who she was. What had she become? What would happen to her? The last thing she had done before going to sleep each night since leaving Batavia was to kiss the glass lid of the box containing the Clipper butterfly and to wish me goodnight. 'I love you, Nicholas' were the final words she would utter before falling asleep. It was a love that remained innocent and pure. Now she had been reduced to using words, invective that except for one previous occasion had never crossed her lips, and even as silent, unspoken adjectives had never entered her head. Where had they come from? Was there a small dark room in the mind that contained foul language and was jerked open to release ugly words when under duress?

The Japanese officer clearly wanted her for something, some task, but what? He'd laughed when she had insulted him, even seeming pleased when she'd lost her temper. It was as if her foul language was connected with the task he had in mind. His mistress? Surely not. But this was the only thing that seemed plausible. This notion appalled Anna and she knew she would resist him. She knew nothing about making love, nothing about pleasing a man in that way. In fact, she knew very little about employing foul language for effect, if that was what he wanted. The sum of her experience of an aroused man was the hardness, the sudden swelling she'd felt when I'd pressed against her thighs while kissing her. But she didn't know if she would have the courage to resist him and, by doing so, risk her own death and the possible torture that might occur before she was killed.

She was terribly afraid but also knew she must never let him see her fear. She had observed how the *kempeitai* depended on fear as their strongest weapon. It seemed to be the Japanese way and there was no reason, despite his notion and desire for perfection, to think of Konoe Akira as being any different.

Anna had seen his reaction over the chicken pieces and the brutality he had shown to the mayor's wife. Had he possessed a dagger or pistol at the time, she felt certain that at the height of his fury he would have used it on the housekeeper. He had also warned Anna on one occasion that she was courting danger when there had only been a little clever repartee between them, a metaphor concerning flowers. It was said without threat, but now she wasn't so sure that the warning had been lighthearted.

How would he react when she refused to share his couch, to make love to him? If she told him she was a virgin, would this whet his appetite or would it restrain him? Would he take pride in peeling open the petals or leave the bud to open naturally? This was no simple man to be disarmed and turned away in a playful face-saving way, his pride intact. He was an enigma. Anna had never known a male like him – instantly brought to destructive fury, an east wind howling and out of control, then as quickly calm again. An urbane aesthete, a lover of beauty but anxious to tame it, control it, bring it to his own idea of perfection. Anna saw that there was tension in everything he did. The vase of dahlias was a perfect example of an attempt to restrain the underlying fury that roared within him. She was frightened, and it was a fear beyond anything she had previously faced for this was a fear where she was no longer in control. Is that what he would do with her? Pluck each leaf so as not to damage the slender stem, present the blossom rearranged precisely each morning in a polished clear-glass bowl?

Manipulate, snip, reduce, so that she would become the white, the non-colour, to highlight the glorious yellow of his alter ego?

Kiki arrived the following morning and Anna praised her warmly for the black burnished stove so that she beamed with pleasure. Til arrived precisely on time, again far from happy. 'That place, it is dangerous, Anna. I have been to the mosque and asked Allah to watch over you. You must be very careful.'

She thanked him and they set off, Anna telling him that the deal with the tin box remained the same as the previous day.

'I have found a place to hide it that nobody can ever find except me,' he boasted gently.

'And if a motorcar hits you today and you go to paradise and are given your allotment of seventy-two virgins, what then?' Anna asked, smiling.

Til stopped his *becak* in mid-pedal, shocked that he hadn't thought of such a possibility. '*Ahee!* Anna, I did not think of this,' he admitted, shamefaced.

'The virgins or the box?' Anna joked.

Til, for once, had no answer to the dilemma of the tin box and wrung his hands. 'The Prophet says only one person can know a secret; if there are two, it is no longer a secret, it may as well be in all the newspapers.'

'There were newspapers when the Prophet said that?' Anna asked, still joking with the little *becak* owner.

'What must I do?' Til asked, frowning.

'You must write a letter to Budi, then seal it and place it among your most private possessions. In it you must tell him the whereabouts, but don't tell him it is the tin or what it contains, just that you have left him something useful and where to find it.' It was the only idea Anna could think of at that moment.

Til remained silent; he'd dismounted and now looked down at the surface of the road, rubbing his big toe sideways, making circles in the dust. 'Anna, I do not know how to write a letter,' he said slowly.

Illiteracy was not unusual in Javanese men of Til's age. Anna said quickly, 'Turn back – there are shops not far from here, we can buy paper and a pencil and an envelope. Come, Til, quick, I mustn't be late!' Her haste and hubbub were more to cover the shamefaced admission of the wisest man she had ever known than because of the prospect that she might be late for the Japanese colonel. She had allowed more than sufficient time to reach the brewer's mansion.

Til's skinny brown legs quite possibly broke the world speed record for a *becak* with passenger. Arriving outside the first general merchant they came across, Anna handed Til some loose change to buy the writing materials. Using the broad saddle of the *becak* she wrote the letter, carefully describing the exact location of Budi's so-called inheritance, which turned out to be a small cave behind a permanently flowing waterfall that Til was certain only he knew about. He'd buried the tin box in the cave and then covered the spot with a rock. Anna handed the sheet of paper to Til, who folded it carefully and placed it in the envelope on which Anna had written in capital letters 'BUDI'. 'I will guard this letter with my life, I swear it, Anna. *Ahee!* One day, when I have the time, I will learn to write and to read the Koran.'

'If we ever get out of this mess, I will teach you how to read and write Javanese, but reading the Koran, that is different.' Anna climbed back into the *becak* and they set off. Once again she pulled the brothel curtain down to conceal her presence. After a while Til called, 'We are here, Anna.'

Anna parted the curtain and they passed the disinterested guards who were, quite possibly, the same two who had been on duty at the gate the previous day. All Japanese soldiers looked alike to Anna. The guards waved them on without stopping them. It occurred to her that they wouldn't speak Javanese, so how would they decide who was to be allowed in and who not?

Within the gates the gardener soldiers seemed as happily busy as before, but now each one they passed bowed politely to her. They may well have been ruthless killers but at the heart of things they were still peasants, and the soil, even the fecund tropical soil, they instinctively understood and so they were cheerful.

Anna left Til with the same instructions to wait for her, then climbed the steps to the front door, pausing once again to pluck a frangipani blossom and arrange it behind her ear. She had come to no harm on the previous day and somehow the small, perfumed blossom now became a tiny, serendipitous protection, like always touching some pretty object for luck when passing by. The blossom had not been remarked on the previous day, but now she consciously noted that it was yellow and white, with the broader part of the petals white and narrowing down to a bright yellow centre.

Anna pressed the doorbell and soon heard the slap of slippers approaching. The door opened and the mayor's wife, smiling, bowed deeply. 'Welcome, Anna, I am to take you to the back, to the verandah again, those are the instructions of the *colonel-san*.'

Anna smiled, greeting her in turn. The housekeeper did

not refer to the incident of the previous day as she led the way through the house to the back. She paused briefly before they passed through the door. 'There is a surprise!' she giggled, both hands to her mouth, then stood aside for Anna to pass onto the verandah.

All was as before, with the exception of the vase – now it was filled with dahlias of every colour, as carefully cut and arranged as the yellow and white blooms had been, not a leaf out of place. 'Oh, my!' Anna exclaimed.

The *mama-san* beamed. '*Konoe-san* went out into the garden early this morning, before he had even taken his tea, to cut them. I think he is pleased with your honourable presence, *Anna-san*.' She bowed. 'I will bring tea, Japanese tea,' she said, turning towards the door.

'*Mama-san*, tell me, how must I bow when the *colonel-san* comes?'

The housekeeper turned and demonstrated a low formal bow, her eyes downcast. 'You are a woman, so your bow must be lower than his, if possible twice as low. It is the proper way,' she said. 'You must never look at him. It is immodest and unbecoming for a woman to do so. The honourable *Konoe-san* is of nobility, he may not reply when you bow. You are tall, he is also tall, you must be careful. How tall are you, *Anna-san*?' she asked shyly.

'Thank you, *Mama-san*, I will remember. How tall? Too tall!' Anna laughed. 'I am one hundred and seventy-three centimetres.'

The cheerful *mama-san* seemed to have completely recovered from the humiliation of the previous day. She then said, 'Your waist, it is so slim. May I see?'

It seemed a surprising request but Anna turned so the little woman could place her hands about her waist, her fingers not quite meeting. 'I never had a waist so slim, even when I was your age, *Anna-san*,' she cried. 'You are very beautiful.'

'Thank you, *Mama-san*,' Anna said, smiling. It hadn't occurred to her that the Japanese woman might see her in this way. She'd seen pictures of geishas and often wondered why the Japanese converted a woman's face into such an elaborately made-up and formal mask as their idea of perfection. Now, left on her own on the verandah, she didn't feel very beautiful, simply confused and scared: confused by the multi-coloured dahlias in the vase in front of her. After Konoe Akira's didactic lecture on purity, the aesthetic perfection of one colour highlighted by the non-colour white, why had he changed his mind? If he *had* indeed changed it, which Anna very much doubted.

What was he trying to say to her? She could immediately see the different effect of the two equally precise arrangements: the quiet singularity of the first replaced now by the ebullience of the multi-coloured blossoms.

To the confused Anna this proved her point. The second arrangement was a joyous thing and despite the colonel's attempt to restrain it by means of its careful manipulation, the flowers resisted, fought back and selfishly insisted on being themselves. In contrast, yesterday's vase had been a group of handmaidens practising to be perfect in service, to be silently, rigidly present but never to be heard to laugh, joke or tease.

The *mama-san* brought green tea and placed it in front of Anna with an eggshell-white porcelain teacup, adding a second where the colonel would sit, and placing the beautiful butterfly ashtray down beside it. Then backing off slightly and bowing she said, 'I am Yasuko,' introducing herself at last. She brought both hands together, fingertips touching, and bowed. 'Yesterday you were very brave and honourable. I thank you, *Anna-san*. To be a woman is never an easy task.' Anna smiled, nodding her head in agreement. 'I must go now to prepare lunch.' The *mama-san* giggled suddenly, bringing her hands up to cover her mouth. 'No bad chicken today!' Then she hurried off, still giggling, accompanied by the slip-slap of her black slippers against the sandstone floor.

As Anna sipped the green tea her apprehension seemed to increase. Should she mention the flowers or ignore them? Pretend she hadn't noticed, play dumb, act like a silly seventeen-year-old who remembers nothing, like some of her school friends? The flowers were clearly a message, but not one she fully understood. She heard the sharp note of a car horn – his car horn. Bracing herself at the sound she glanced down at her wristwatch. It was precisely noon.

This time Anna rose quietly from her chair as the colonel came through the door. As he drew closer she bowed deeply. 'Good afternoon, sir,' she said, smiling.

The Japanese officer stopped momentarily and gave her his now familiar minimum jerk of his head. 'Ho!' he said, then continued to move towards the bamboo seats. He indicated her chair. 'Please.'

Anna turned, lifting a small batik cushion and moving it, giving him time to complete the awkward motions to adjust his bad leg before he was seated. Finally she sat with her eyes downcast, her heart beating furiously.

Konoe Akira went through the same motions with his cigarette case as he had done on the previous day, this time not calling out to the *mama-san*, but instead using a slim silver lighter he carried in the breast pocket of his uniform. He lit the cigarette and leaned back, drawing deeply on it, then exhaling towards the ceiling. 'So, Anna, we are together again to talk about differences.'

'Yes, sir, if you wish, sir,' Anna said quietly.

'I would prefer it if you used the suffix "san" rather than "sir". It has a more friendly intonation.' As always with him, it sounded more like an instruction than a preference.

Anna was reminded once again that the English he spoke was far better than her own. 'As you wish, *Konoe-san*,' she repeated a little more boldly, adding a quick, uncertain smile.

He smiled. 'The dahlias, you have seen them?'

'Yes, *Konoe-san*.' She didn't look at the vase but kept her eyes downcast.

'Are they vulgar or are they perfection?' he asked pointedly.

Anna looked up, surprised; in her mind both words were badly chosen. 'Neither —' She was about to add 'sir' but corrected herself in time. '*Konoe-san*.'

'Oh? Please explain.'

Anna was by nature honest and forthright as well, accustomed to having and offering an opinion when asked. 'They are trapped,' she said.

'Trapped?' The colonel was surprised by this answer but his tone was curious, not indignant.

'The arrangement is too formal, too perfect. These flowers, they want to dance and you are making them stand to attention. They are not an orchestra, they are a jazz group. Like people, flowers can be cut down and controlled, but that doesn't mean it is their . . . their personality.' Anna was aware that she could have expressed this better in Dutch or Javanese. 'We are all different,' she added lamely.

'You do not believe in discipline?' the colonel asked, stubbing his half-smoked cigarette into the pristine thorax of the beautiful glass butterfly.

'Only if it is to teach me right from wrong or to keep me from temptation,' Anna said, knowing the question was too hard for her to answer in the abstract. 'It is not the only thing, the purpose in my life,' she concluded.

On some past occasion Anna had questioned me about my life as a child in Japan and I had spoken about the discipline required to live in such a society, borrowing my sentiments and explanations liberally from my father. I had been too young to regard the experience as unique and to understand or make observations myself. This is what I more or less remember saying to her: 'It is all a matter of the space available,' I had explained. 'In fact, there is very little to go around in Japan and it must be carefully shared and even more carefully used. If the Japanese have the luxury of a garden, it is, at most, three or four metres in size, often much smaller. It will contain a single moss- or lichen-covered rock, seated in carefully patterned and raked white pebbles or sand. A lone blossom may have been carefully nurtured from a seedling. A perfect yellow chrysanthemum, for instance, or there might be a hundred-year-old bonsai tree, an exact miniature of a glorious forest giant. Tranquillity to the Japanese comes in tiny proportions and requires a rigid personal discipline. Cherry blossom outside a temple will bring visitors from afar to gawk at such singular beauty. Their homes are small, the interior walls of framed, opaque paper. The floors have *tatami* grass matting, the objects within the rooms are formal and minimal and always precisely placed – maybe a perfect vase or an elegant bowl. Beauty, to the well-born Japanese, is as much about discipline as it is about space. In fact, the two things cannot be separated in their minds.'

I probably rabbited on a bit more at the time, attempting to show off with my borrowed knowledge. If I remember correctly, I then went on to make the comparison with New Britain's outrageous fecundity. Its waste of space, sprawl of creepers and blossom, plethora of trees festooned with orchids growing at the juncture or clinging to the branches, exotic coloured birds with exaggerated plumage, and abundance of fierce forest life. I think I commented how, while New Britain's was an environment not without hardship, it conspired to create an entirely different view of life.

Anna, whose memory I was to learn was phenomenal, had obviously remembered all or some of this explanation, for now she said, 'You are Japanese, Konoe-san. In your country space is regarded differently and the arrangement of life itself is formal, requiring great discipline. I have always lived on a tropical island. While you may have a small garden of raked sand or pebbles, containing a single rock and flower or maybe a bonsai tree, I have had two hectares of garden to play in. While you learned to treasure a visit to the cherry blossom trees flowering outside the temple, I learned how not to be lost in the hugeness of a forest, where giant trees are festooned with orchids. The discipline is different and leads to differences in all of us.' Anna was more or less paraphrasing my words, sentiments which I, in turn, had borrowed from my constantly over-intellectualising father. But then she added an observation of her own. 'Our differences are what make us interesting. Not just races, but individual people as well.'

'That is very observant of you, Anna, very clever. How do you know about Japan?'

'I heard it once,' Anna explained modestly, 'from a butterfly collector.'

Konoe Akira smiled. 'What, then, do you think it is that makes you interesting, Anna? Interesting to someone like me, for instance?'

Anna wanted to admit that she had no idea, but knew this wouldn't satisfy him. She thought for a few moments, then decided to answer in the abstract. 'Well, at first it is the things we see in another person. Simply observation. I am tall for a Javanese. I have blue eyes, brown skin. I think someone could think this interesting. They would want to know a bit more perhaps, no? If they were Dutch they would think about my skin colour. If they were Javanese they would want to know about my eyes. Both would want to know how this came to be, how this happened.' Anna looked at him, then said rather tamely with a shrug, 'That sort of thing, Konoe-san?'

The Japanese colonel chuckled. 'No, Anna, in your case, let me hasten to assure you, all they will see is a very beautiful young woman. You are perfection.'

Anna dropped her eyes. While she was not unaccustomed to compliments about her appearance, she hadn't expected one from the conservative and disciplined Japanese officer. Nor had she expected a statement to be so openly made. 'Thank you, Konoe-san,' Anna said. 'Do you mind if I ask you a question?'

'Ask – please,' Konoe Akira said with a casual wave of the hand.

'Which of the arrangements am I? Yesterday's,' Anna pointed at the vase, 'or today's?'

Colonel Konoe was silent for some time, then, nodding his head, slowly said, 'I think you have taught me something, Anna. The answer is neither.'

Anna felt suddenly compelled to make a further point but to do so was to go where she had never been before. 'Konoe-san, may I tell you something? Then ask you a second question?'

Konoe Akira looked quizzical. 'Last time you sought permission to ask a question I think I was, as the English say, "put in my place". Now you want to pose another?' he sighed, enjoying himself. 'Permission granted.'

'Well, you know already that I am of racially mixed parentage but not of the circumstances of my birth. *Mijn* father was, is, a very big man. In his family they are all big, giants. *Mijn* mother was Javanese and the women they are all small. *Mijn* father brutally raped my mother and then he has discarded her, thrown her away like a piece of worthless rubbish. I was born, of course, nine months later, in a *kampong* where there was no doctor and I was too big and she has bled to death giving birth to me.' Anna paused, taking a deep breath. '*Ja*, now comes the question. To a Japanese like you – the *mama-san* says you are of noble lineage – how, if you are correct about perfection, how comes perfection from this?'

Konoe Akira was silent for even longer this time, then finally and somewhat anticlimactically announced, 'Now we will have lunch,' and turning his head towards the door called out, '*Mama-san*' and then a Japanese word Anna assumed meant food or lunch. Turning back to her he said, 'I will answer your question at some time.'

Lunch, with the beautiful porcelain dishes of yesterday back on display and with others added, was simple and delicious and eaten with barely a word spoken. To Anna's taste there was only one culinary misfortune, a rice ball with a sour plum within it. But she watched as Konoe Akira consumed the small vile-tasting dish with obvious relish. The mayor's wife, Yasuko, had not failed the colonel this time. Anna's distaste for the rice ball went unnoticed by her host, who continued to eat noisily in the Japanese way.

Anna poured tea for Konoe Akira from a fresh pot brought to the table. He leaned back. 'You have been very honest with me about our differences. I am Japanese. It is difficult for me to understand. With us, it is all about tradition, about discipline. We have a total sense of failure if we do not take the right path, if we do not uphold and cherish the traditions of those who have gone before, if we fail in our duty to our Emperor. You are too young to understand this, Anna. But failure cannot be tolerated.'

He reached for his cigarette case and took some time lighting up. Anna was aware that this pause was a space in which he would make a decision whether he would continue. Finally he said, 'I have never talked about what was required of me as a soldier and how I have failed. It is not permitted to show the weakness of confession like the Christian Catholics. Now I must ask you a question. You must be honest. In Japan we mask the truth in a thousand ways, because to speak from the heart is not permitted. Words are often as important to conceal what we mean as they are to speak directly. Simplicity of words is only allowed in the *haiku* poem and that is about nature and seldom about people. Politeness most often supersedes the truth.'

He drew at the cigarette, then said, 'You asked, is it not our individual differences that make us interesting? Not only our racial differences, but also the differences found in common people? We Japanese do not praise the character of ordinary people, only those who are to be venerated for their achievement. Sometimes it is a poet and sometimes a soldier, sometimes an artist, a potter perhaps, and sometimes a politician or a priest, but never a street sweeper or a housekeeper. In everything we seek perfection, wisdom and courage, but always in the name of tradition.'

Anna was beginning to lose the thread of what he was saying, deciding that with all this discipline it couldn't be much fun to be a seventeen-year-old growing up in Japan.

'Here now is my question,' Konoe Akira said at last. Yet he paused again, drawing on his cigarette, then turning and exhaling towards the outside edge of the verandah as if he was clearing his head. 'If when I saw you for the first time I saw perfection, what then did you see when you first saw me? Was it my limp?'

Anna looked at him, genuinely astonished. 'Limp? Of course I saw your limp. But how could it be of any importance? My heart was filled with fear. It still is. All I saw when you approached was that you had the power to destroy me. That you had absolute power and had commanded that four humans who were in front of me on their knees with their hands tied behind their backs were to have their heads removed. It was you who commanded the whole town to witness their execution. I knew that you could snap your fingers and I too would disappear. That you carried a limp was not my concern.'

Konoe Akira commenced to laugh. 'It is in the occupation force's manual. Imposing discipline is the first task of an occupying force. The beheading of four Chinese and then the exhibiting of the heads of local criminals on bamboo poles was to keep the population placid and grateful because their unpaid debts were absolved – a favour granted and at the same time a reprisal. Those criminals they most feared were eliminated. You came to the town square to witness both the generosity of the Japanese people and the consequences of not possessing moral discipline.'

Anna, even at seventeen, knew hyperbole when she heard it. She knew that fear is demoralising and cruelty is just cruelty, and neither can be justified when used as a weapon. But she did not possess the sophistication to argue with him.

'Colonel *Konoe-san*, how then did you get this limp?' Anna now asked ingenuously.

'My limp?' he repeated, surprised. She'd previously dismissed his limp as irrelevant. But he was now being asked about it in a simple and genuinely curious way by this beautiful young woman seated opposite him. 'I have never been asked this question by a stranger. Only my superiors know, only my family have been informed. The limp?' he asked, trying again, as if he had never previously been required to explain it as an incident without describing the consequences that had led from it. In fact, by the manner he kept shaking his head in denial, Anna concluded that he seemed to find the task of relating the plain facts nearly impossible.

He began in a halting fashion. 'As a wound it is tiresome to my body. But as a destruction of the spirit it is – unbearable. I am *Bushido*. My family is of the nobility. For a thousand years we have been samurai. To be a captain in the Imperial Guard is my birthright. It is what I was always meant to be. I studied to be an officer, a soldier, at the Military Academy, the Army War College, then went abroad. In England I went to Army Command and the Staff College at Camberley, and in Germany, to the Berlin War Academy at Potsdam. All to make myself the best possible soldier. This is the most glorious and noble fulfilment of my duty to the Emperor and to my honourable family. To be a samurai, a Japanese warrior, it is everything.' He paused and Anna could see that he was momentarily overcome. He glanced up at her, then, with head bowed again, continued.

'A bullet, a filthy Chinese bullet, not even straight to my heart where I would have been happy to receive it, to die honourably in battle, but a ricochet, a spent bullet, smashed my kneecap!'

The Japanese officer remained silent long enough for Anna to think she should say something, but she couldn't think of anything appropriate and instinctively knew that to offer her sympathy would be patronising and deeply insulting.

'Now I am a colonel, not even in charge of a regiment but of a battalion of street sweepers, of peasants who have no *bushido*! Gardeners and rice planters! Bicycle riders! I am to be a nursemaid to refugees, a policeman to submissive and grateful natives and cowering Chinese trash!' He looked at Anna and she could see the fury in his eyes, the quick blazing anger she had witnessed yesterday. And then it was as suddenly gone and he said slowly, 'My head has no limp! My heart has no limp! Only one cursed knee has a limp and with it . . .' He sighed, then in a voice barely above a whisper, said, 'I am reduced to nothing and my guilt overwhelms me. I *must* be punished.'

Anna remained silent, confused. Here was yet another part of a man whose several parts she had barely understood, a human too complex for the limited experience her years had gathered. She had worked out her father, which had been a painful enough lesson, but once she understood that self-pity consumed his life and had been the motivation for his drinking, and lately to this had been added his fear of dying, she knew what to expect from him.

Anna asked herself, was Konoe Akira also consumed by self-pity? Was this the key to understanding him? She thought not. Perhaps it was guilt? But why would he feel guilty? He had not deliberately brought about the wound to his knee. Anna had heard of soldiers who shot themselves in the big toe to avoid going into battle or to be removed from the fighting. But she felt sure this was not the case with Konoe Akira. He was too proud, too disciplined, his personality much too rigid. She had never met a man consumed by guilt. Her father had felt no guilt for what he had done to her mother, only self-pity for the consequences to himself. But then, the Japanese colonel felt no guilt over the Chinese he had beheaded. Was guilt personal, individual, seemingly absolved when following military orders? Was the guilt transferred to the institution from the individual perpetrator? Emotional personal responsibility lifted as an exigency of war? Did this mean that the young Japanese soldiers in Manchuria I had once told her about were not guilty when, for bayonet practice and in order to gain *bushido*, fighting spirit, they disembowelled living Chinese men?

Why then was Konoe Akira, wounded in the knee by an almost spent stray Chinese bullet, consumed by personal guilt? Why did he desire to be punished? Did it have something to do with his search for perfection? Anna knew that while she could ask the questions she could not begin to know the answers. Moreover, his admission of guilt served to increase her fear. She was reminded of what he had said the previous day, '*I knew it! I knew it the moment I saw you in the town square where you fainted. I knew you were the one. You will be perfect!*'

The colonel stood up awkwardly, his hands gripping the arms of the bamboo chair and bracing himself in order to come to his feet. Anna rose and he clicked heels, then bowing in his usual abrupt manner said, 'Ho!'

Anna bowed, making sure she did as Yasuko had shown her. '*Konoe-san*,' she said softly, 'thank you for lunch.'

'You will be here tomorrow at eleven o'clock.'

'*Colonel-san*, I must ask to be excused, I —'

But he cut her short. 'Tomorrow. At eleven o'clock. We have some work.' Then he turned and limped away, back held stiff, chin jutted in the manner, Anna imagined, of the Imperial Army.

The following day when Til arrived to pick her up she handed him an envelope. 'Inside is my will, it is no more than I have already told you of my instructions. Put it with your Budi letter.' She indicated the envelope. 'See? It has his name and also Ratih's on the outside.' Anna smiled. 'It is only in case you are in the arms of one of your virgins while another feeds you honeyed figs.'

Til placed the envelope in a small leather bag that was suspended from the crossbar of the *becak*. He wore a concerned expression. 'Why are we going earlier? Also, you have handed me that envelope, Anna. Will they harm you today?' He began to pedal.

'I hope not, Til. The Japanese colonel says he has some work I must do, but I don't know what it is. I still don't even know why he wishes me to attend lunch every day.'

'It is not my place to ask, but has he made any . . . suggestions?' Til asked without turning to glance back at her.

'No, nothing, he has not placed a hand on me.'

'The Japan man, they do not touch,' Til said.

Anna wondered how he knew this. Local prostitutes were forbidden to Japanese soldiers and she remembered Lieutenant Mori of the bicycle squad warning the town's women, on pain of death, against prostitution with the military.

Til, reading her thoughts, said, 'The Japanese, they have now chosen some women for the soldiers. There is a place they can go. I know one of these women,' he explained. Then realising what Anna might think, 'I take her to this Japan place. She is always behind the brothel curtain,' he added hurriedly, then added further, 'They are all very happy, because they are making a lot of money, much more than before.'

'Easy money for them, hey? You said the Japan soldiers don't touch them?' Anna teased.

'*Ahee!* Anna, you are very bad with a clever tongue!' Til said, laughing.

Anna was met by *Yasuko-san* at the door, the *mama-san* unable to stifle her giggles as she bade her enter. '*Anna-san*, today is a big, big surprise,' she announced.

'Bigger than yesterday, *Mama-san*?'

'Much bigger! If you please, will you follow me?'

The housekeeper led Anna down the passageway, across the lounge room and started to climb the stairs. 'Where are we going, *Yasuko-san*?' Anna asked, concerned, pausing at the bottom of the elaborately carved circular stairway. The mansion was so typical of the local wealthy Dutch that she could have found her way around it blindfolded, but it didn't take her knowledge of colonial architecture to know that the bedrooms were upstairs.

Yasuko, almost at the top of the circular stairs, her face only just visible when she leaned over a curved banister, saw Anna's cautious expression and hearing her anxious question brought her hands up to cover her lips, concerned. Then dropping them to grip the banister, she called down, 'No, *Anna-san*, it is quite safe to come. The *colonel-san*, he has not arrived, not until twelve o'clock for lunch. Please?' she added. 'It is nobody here to be concerned. It is only a nice surprise.'

Anna climbed the stairs slowly, prepared to retreat if needed. She arrived at the top where Yasuko was waiting for her. 'Anna, Anna,' she cried, 'do not be frightened.' The *mama-san* led her to a small room Anna knew to be common to every large Dutch house, the sewing room. Yasuko held the door open for Anna to enter. There standing in the centre of the small room beside a Singer sewing machine was the Mayor of the Squashed Hat. The little *mama-san* bowed to her husband. '*Anna-san*, this is my honourable husband, *Tokuma Onishi-san*.'

Anna managed to conceal her surprise with a quick smile at the surrogate mayor, who bowed stiffly but greeted her in Javanese. Anna dutifully bowed lower and returned his greeting, wondering what this sudden confrontation with the self-styled mayor was all about.

The little Japanese tailor then said, 'I will leave the room.' He bowed once again to Anna, who returned the gesture, and then said something to Yasuko in Japanese. She nodded and then bowed as he left the room.

Anna was becoming accustomed to the fact that the Japanese do a lot of bowing. Somewhat bemused, she asked the Japanese woman perhaps a little clumsily, 'Is your husband, the mayor, my surprise?'

Yasuko laughed. 'Of course not, a tailor is not a surprise!' She walked the three steps to a small wardrobe and opened the door and withdrew what Anna saw was an unfamiliar silk garment of extraordinary beauty. She didn't exactly say 'Da-*da*-da-dah!', but as she held up the garment for Anna to see, her triumphant expression suggested she wanted to say the equivalent in Japanese. 'It is your kimono, *Anna-san*, it is silk. The most beautiful I have ever seen.'

'Mine?' Anna asked, confused. 'It is beautiful, *Yasuko-san*, but . . . but I am not Japanese.'

'*Tokuma-san* has worked two days and two nights, he has not visited the mayor's office once and has slept every night only four hours.' She stepped forward and held the garment against Anna's body. 'We have made it for your size, one hundred and seventy-three centimetres.' She giggled and held her hands, fingers slightly bent to indicate a circle. 'And for your waist I have to guess with my hands. Now you must try it on. My honourable husband will make the necessary alterations, he is waiting to do a fitting.' She paused. 'You must be ready when the honourable *colonel-san* returns for lunch.'

Anna knew that there would come a time when she would have to resist Konoe Akira, but as quickly realised that if she refused to wear the kimono it would be the little Japanese housekeeper who would be blamed and punished, not herself.

'I am not sure, *Yasuko-san*. It is very beautiful – but it is for a Japanese woman.'

Yasuko had been too excited to sense her reluctance and now looked utterly crestfallen. 'But *Anna-san*, it is *silk*, even in Japan a silk kimono, only the highborn, the very rich, can have one! I myself cannot ever hope to own such a kimono. It is the highest compliment. The colonel *Konoe-san* is showing you great honour with this gift of silk!' It was clear that the *mama-san* found it impossible to comprehend Anna's reluctance to wear the beautiful gown.

Anna decided she would wear the kimono to protect the little Japanese housekeeper, but did so with a great sense of foreboding. Konoe Akira was, she realised, beginning to shape her, to do what he had done with the dahlias. Even if he admitted to himself that she was not the yellow and white vase, he had made the multi-coloured one stand to attention in the same way, leaves and stems and blossoms. She was to be that combination of discipline and perfection he strove so hard to attain as an aesthete – a beautiful thing, tamed and under his control, his ultimate achievement.

Anna slipped off her blouse and sarong, and Yasuko, fussing and happy, helped her into the silk garment. The kimono fitted surprisingly well and Yasuko informed her that the cut was the one used by young women for it had longer sleeves and the waistband, about nine centimetres wide and known as an *obi*, was tied in the *fukura suzume* way (the sparrow style) so that it resembled a sparrow and was suitable for an unmarried woman. The silk that was used for a young woman's kimono is traditionally more colourful, and this one was a design of cherry blossom against a blue sky, the blue almost, but not quite, matching the deep violet of her eyes. Anna, looking into the full-length mirror, could see that it was simply stunning. The mayor entered and nipped and tucked and left again for Anna to slip out of the gown so that he could complete it.

'Now we must do the make-up and hair. In the bedroom there is a make-up mirror,' Yasuko said.

'No!' Anna cried. 'No make-up. I am sorry, *Yasuko-san*, but the appearance of my face and hair is my own decision. I will wear the kimono out of respect for you and your husband *Tokuma-san* – it is only a garment – but no make-up, no hair-do; my face is my own.'

'But . . . but . . . he will be very angry, *Anna-san*!' Yasuko persisted. 'Those were his instructions.'

'With me, perhaps, but not angry with you. I will explain it myself to the *colonel-san* so that you do not get into trouble.' Anna's heart was beating fiercely as she spoke. Why had her life become all defiance? All about men who expected, as if they possessed a natural right, to exert their will over her and to dominate and override her own self? Konoe Akira, she knew, held ultimate power over her. He could kill her if he wished, but she instinctively knew that to do so would be an admission to himself that he had failed. Anna was aware that in his mind he would not have completed the task he intended to perform and, in turn, had not received what he desired from her. She was beginning to understand the mind of the Japanese noble.

Yasuko, relieved that Anna would take the responsibility for refusing any make-up, now said pleadingly, 'I have *geta* sandals and *tabi* socks, will you wear them, *Anna-san*?'

'May I see them?' Anna asked.

Hesitating at her reply, Yasuko said, 'There is one more thing.'

'What is it?' Anna, at once suspicious, enquired.

'I must show you how to hold your hands when you bow.' The mayor's wife demonstrated the height the arms are held and the width the elbows are apart so that only the tips of the fingers touch with the thumbs resting parallel to the forefingers. 'You will be wearing a formal kimono that is usually worn when remaining in the geisha house to entertain an honourable male or when going out. It is the one the *colonel-san* requested. When you hold your hands and bow as I have shown you, it is to show off your kimono, so the shorter and wider sleeves fall correctly and the silk appears in perfect repose.'

The Mayor of the Squashed Hat, now turned back into a very weary tailor, called out impatiently to his wife and they returned to the sewing room. He waited outside the door while Anna undressed, conscious of her simple cotton knickers and bra.

Yasuko brought her a long slip that she termed a *juban*,

followed by the single-layered silk kimono together with a wide *obi* of the same silk, which she tied in the sparrow style so that it was just below the bosom. While her husband may have been an indifferent town official, he proved to be an excellent tailor and this time the kimono fitted perfectly.

The *mama-san* produced the *tabi* socks and Anna laughed. 'I wore socks like this when I was a little girl,' she said as the housekeeper, now acting as a personal maid, knelt and fitted the white socks onto Anna's feet, then followed with heeled wooden thongs. Anna attempted to walk in them and was forced to take small steps, keeping her back rigid, if she hoped to keep them on. They clacked loudly as she walked. 'They make an awful clack-clack sound. Am I walking incorrectly?' she asked Yasuko.

'No, that is correct. A Japanese woman, she must not approach a man so he does not hear her coming; the clack-clack is out of respect so that she doesn't appear suddenly and he can call out to her if he does not wish her presence.'

Anna was beginning to understand my explanation that the Japanese have a rule or a convention for everything; that this was not a society where spontaneity was tolerated or originality and individuality were thought to be important.

She endured a final inspection by the tailor-turned-mayor-turned-tailor again. He seemed pleased with his work and, now that she had assumed an importance in his mind, bowed obsequiously and thanked her for the privilege of allowing him to create the garment.

It was five minutes to twelve o'clock and there was just sufficient time for Anna to assume her customary place at the bamboo setting. At precisely noon the horn of the big American car announced the arrival of the senior Japanese officer. But Anna was forced to wait a further twenty minutes before Konoe

Akira came through the door onto the verandah. She was surprised to see that he no longer wore his uniform but instead a black cotton robe of a crosshatch design that fell to the floor and was belted at the waist. She would later learn that it was a summer kimono called a *yukata* that originated from the dress of a travelling samurai warrior. It was a costume once worn by the fiercest of warriors, but Konoe Akira, approaching her with his pronounced limp in the middle of the day, reminded Anna of someone convalescing on a hospital verandah after an accident.

She rose to the rustle of silk and bowed deeply, trying to remember just how she should hold her arms: elbows slightly outwards, fingers only just touching, thumbs parallel to her forefingers. The Japanese officer's return bow was too ingrained to change and ended with the customary 'Ho!' Konoe Akira remained standing, then looking directly at Anna he brought his hand up and dabbed at both her cheeks and grunted.

Anna took a deep breath. '*Konoe-san*, my face is brown and I do not wish it to be white or my cheeks to be stained with blush and my lips the colour of fresh cow's liver. My hair falls naturally to my shoulders, I do not want to lift it to the sky or decorate it with chopsticks.' About her hair she wanted to add 'or turn it into a nest for eagles' but she lacked the courage, as they had never shared a joke and he might well consider the stark geisha make-up yet another form of perfection. But what she did add was, 'I will try to please you, but at best I will be a bloom in the second vase and not the first.'

Konoe Akira glared at her momentarily and then, as suddenly, threw back his head and laughed. 'You would not make a good *maiko*,' he said.

'*Maiko, Konoe-san?*'

The Japanese officer, having gone through the awkward

motions of being seated, thought for a moment. 'A neophyte, a trainee geisha. But if you could be trained, you would become a good *okami*, that is an older geisha who trains the *maiko* and when they become fully trained geishas she organises the patrons,' he explained and then added, 'Sit, please.'

Anna sat down carefully, unaccustomed to the kimono as a garment or how to arrange it when seated. It seemed to be a gown that was not styled for sitting in a chair but rather to be on one's knees in service to a male. 'I do not wish to be a geisha, *Konoe-san*,' she said quietly, then glanced up at him and he saw that while her voice had remained soft, her eyes were defiant.

The Japanese colonel looked surprised. 'It is not possible, *Anna-san*. You are not Japanese.' It was the first time he had referred to her as *Anna-san*. Konoe Akira lit a cigarette in the now-familiar manner. Finally he exhaled, sending the usual cloud of smoke towards the roof of the verandah. 'There is a philosophy that belongs to the geisha tradition but is, I think, instinctive to all truly beautiful women. Would you like to hear it?'

'As you wish, *Colonel-san*,' she said, though again her thoughts immediately strayed; it was probably some ponderous rationale the Japanese had evolved to cope with what the seventeen-year-old Anna saw as their restricted and over-particularised lifestyle. Besides, they viewed women differently, as objects or – she could think of no better description – inferior beings to be used for whatever purpose suited them. Anna was not vain, she knew she was pretty, beautiful if you like, but she was not overly concerned with this aspect of her person. Instead, she refused to be compliant or to be possessed, although her fear of death at the hands of the Japanese colonel had caused her, on more than one occasion, to compromise and to restrain her wilful nature and sense of independence. For sixteen years her stepmother had tried to destroy her confidence and to crush her personality and had not been successful. This was different – the threat overhanging her was much more severe. Anna knew she wouldn't openly challenge Konoe Akira's theory about women.

'There is the philosophy of the patron,' the Japanese colonel began.

'Patron? I do not understand, *Konoe-san*.'

'The man – that is, the male who is in a position to acquire a geisha or a woman.'

'Acquire? You mean a man who loves a woman and she him?' Anna asked, clearly confused.

'No. Love is not necessary. What use is love? Duty, discipline, service, dedication and occasional pleasure and offspring, is that not the natural role of a wife?' Before Anna could answer, if she was even capable of thinking of a reply, he continued. 'But a truly beautiful woman or a truly great geisha is different. She is already a potential work of art. She is her own art in the making, the creator *and* the canvas onto which the male's fantasies and desires are painted. Such a woman when acquired may become a wonderful artist and also powerful, because she holds the key to the male's innermost desires; he cannot be without her in his life. Do you understand, *Anna-san*?'

'She is his mistress, then?' Anna asked.

'No, it is more, much more, than that.'

'But you said he acquires her – he owns her?' Anna frowned. 'I would not like to be owned, *Konoe-san*.'

'Acquired does not mean owned. If a woman is her own art and canvas I cannot own her, I can only acquire the skill and, with her consent, the right to influence the artist. I can be her teacher. She must be brought willingly to express herself, to be different, to grow. A pupil needs instruction but she may possess a talent well beyond that possessed by the teacher. Then, if he demands that she change her art and alter the canvas simply to imitate him, he will destroy what he wishes to acquire. There is no point in acquiring what you already own. Whatever happens between us must be an experience heightened by the inspiration of the artist.'

Anna thought for several moments. 'Have you acquired *me*, *Konoe-san*?' she asked, looking directly at the Japanese man.

Konoe Akira stubbed his cigarette, this time obliterating a part of the butterfly's wing. He looked directly into her eyes. 'Yes,' he said simply. 'Yes, I have.'

Anna fought to contain her fury, valiantly attempting to choke back her indignation. 'And I have no choice?' She jumped to her feet, knowing it was the wrong thing to do but suddenly too angry to care. 'I am not a geisha!' She plucked at the sleeve of her kimono. 'I do not want to wear this – this Japanese dress!'

'Ah, but it is my wish that you wear a kimono,' he said calmly, amused at her outburst. 'That snivelling little tailor has been told to make three more; you will require them all. Sit please, *Anna-san*.' Konoe Akira spread his hands, smiling. '*Of course* you have a choice,' he said in a voice intended to mollify.

'What?' Anna replied rudely, still standing. 'Death or I am *acquired* by you?'

Colonel Konoe laughed. 'Possibly, but it is not me who will be the cause of your death.' He pointed to the chair. 'You have been directed by me to sit and you have not obeyed. Please sit at once and I will explain,' he barked.

Anna sat as he'd instructed, but she folded her arms across her chest, her mouth drawn into a disapproving pout. Having openly lost her temper to no avail, silent disapproval was the only defiance she could now openly demonstrate. Konoe Akira carried an innate authority, not only of a military officer of high rank but also one born of generations of noble lineage, of privilege combined with discipline. Piet Van Heerden had a similar background, ten generations of privilege, but he lacked the discipline that went with it and, in the end, the authority. The Japanese officer was the persimmon tree, the ebony heartwood at the core, while her father was pulpwood through and through.

The colonel began speaking slowly. 'We have in Tjilatjap two battalions, the one under Major Masahiro working at the port and the docks, and the one to govern the town, that is 1800 men and non-commissioned officers and sixty officers. These men have needs, physical needs, but are forbidden to fraternise with the local woman. But these needs must be met.' He paused, spreading his hands. 'Do you understand what I am saying, *Anna-san*?'

'Yes, but you have already used local women prostitutes for this purpose, *Colonel-san*.' The Japanese officer looked surprised that she should be aware of this, so Anna quickly added, 'The *becak* owner told me about the brothel for soldiers.'

'Ah, a small establishment with local women who are professional prostitutes organised with my permission for the *kempeitai*. They are different, a small military police unit who do not normally mix with the ordinary soldiers. You must understand, we are the liberators of the local people from colonial oppression, and do not wish to force respectable Javanese women into becoming whores. So you see, we have a problem. This still leaves 1800 soldiers and sixty officers we have to look after – to accommodate.'

'Dutch women!' Anna cried out, alarmed.

'Ho! You are very perceptive, *Anna-san*,' Konoe Akira said, pleased with her. 'Yes, exactly! Some, the younger attractive ones, will become comfort women for the officers. Others, the younger mothers and experienced women, for the men. Captain Takahashi will organise these facilities, one for the officers and a much bigger one for the men. The *okami-san*, the women who will run these houses, are on a ship coming from Japan and will be here in a month.'

Anna shuddered. 'Takahashi the executioner?' Her eyes filled with fear and she visibly trembled at the terrible implications of the colonel's words.

'Ah, Takahashi! He is very proficient with the *katana* and of a moderately good family,' the colonel observed. 'He is also an excellent organiser.' He was silent for a few moments, then said evenly, 'So, you see, *Anna-san*, you do have a choice. You may choose to be acquired, or forcibly recruited by Captain Takahashi to serve in "The Nest of the Swallows", the officers' house.' He paused, tapping the arm of his chair. 'I had previously decided that you are too precious a piece of art to allow him to have you, but now, as the second vase, I will allow you to choose your own immediate future.'

Anna's eyes suddenly welled so that she was forced to close them, whereupon from each a tear escaped to run down her cheeks. She opened her eyes and looked directly at Konoe Akira; his face, seen through her tears, was blurred. 'That is very cruel!' she sobbed, not appending the formal politeness of his name.

'No, that is life. Be grateful to the gods that they have

made you a work of art. Are you a virgin, *Anna-san?*' he asked suddenly.

Anna, sobbing softly, taken by surprise at his unexpected question, nodded, her eyes streaming.

'I am greatly privileged to know that the pearl nestled in the oyster remains perfect,' Konoe Akira said in a low voice. Using the arms of the bamboo chair, he braced himself and rose awkwardly to his feet. He stood silently, looking down at the distraught and tearful Anna. Then, as if he were issuing a casual order to a subaltern or sergeant, he said, 'You will now go upstairs and change, and tell the *mama-san* to bring lunch. I will see you back here in fifteen minutes.' He bowed stiffly, then turned and limped away, a proud, if physically crippled, samurai warrior. Konoe Akira halted and turned at the doorway to the interior of the house to once again face Anna. 'Then, "Second Vase", you will inform me of your decision,' he instructed.

Anna, having changed back into her sarong, returned to the verandah to see that the table was set for lunch. Yasuko, who had helped her remove the kimono, must have raced downstairs to set the table in time for the colonel's return from his rooms. Anna reached out and touched the glass butterfly. 'Nick, I have been acquired, will you forgive me?' she cried in despair.

Colonel Konoe, now back in uniform, joined her. Anna paid him due respect by rising and bowing low, while keeping her eyes averted. Within she burned with anger and humiliation but she knew there was nothing she could do, except attempt to salvage what self-respect she could.

Konoe Akira sat and went through his cigarette routine, then asked, 'Well, what have you decided, Second Vase?'

Anna realised that she had been renamed in the Japanese manner, her real name discarded when she was with him. It was, she supposed, a part of the anonymity required for whatever role he intended her to play in his life.

'Acquired!' She spat the single word out defiantly.

The Japanese officer threw back his head and laughed. 'You will never make a geisha, but perhaps within you I will find the samurai spirit? We will see when the lessons begin. At first, while you learn and receive instruction there will be complete obedience. After that we will see what is painted on the canvas. Do you have any questions?'

'Yes, am I to live here with you, Konoe-san?'

'No. You will be told when to come. You must be prepared at all times for my call. I will send a car for you. Except for the period while you take lessons, it will be mostly at night and you will be returned home. You will have your own room upstairs where you can change into a kimono and keep whatever you wish. No one will enter without your permission.'

'Konoe-san, I have *mijn* father; he is not well. Will he be protected from the *kempeitai?*'

'Of course, I will give instructions. What is his sickness?'

Anna decided that there was little point in hiding her father's condition and thought that the colonel might allow a military doctor to see him. 'He's an alcoholic who has come through an enforced withdrawal and is now very depressed. If you will allow a doctor to see him, we will pay.'

'I will attend to it. It will not be necessary to pay the doctor,' Colonel Konoe said with a dismissive flick of the hand. 'Now, returning to what is required of you, Second Vase, you will learn Japanese in the mornings for three hours. You will be here at nine o'clock every weekday morning to be tutored by your instructor and then we will have lunch together when I arrive at noon. I will send a driver.'

'That will not be necessary, *Konoe-san*. I have a regular *becak* driver who will bring me here. It is what I would prefer.'

'As you wish. Tell him to go to the *mama-san* to be paid.'

'I will pay him myself, *Konoe-san*. I am acquired, but not dependent on your generosity.'

The Japanese officer laughed. 'As you wish.'

'Are these the lessons you mentioned?' Anna now asked, relieved that she would not be seen leaving home each morning in a staff car. She knew her memory was good and was confident she wouldn't have too great a struggle learning a new language.

'No! But you cannot perfect your art without knowing Japanese. You must learn fast; in one month we must begin to converse. In two you will grasp more clearly Japanese meanings – there is much that is unspoken yet relevant. In three you will be able to start your instruction. Your English is good but your Japanese must be better!' He said all this as if it were a simple order and, notwithstanding any linguistic limitations she might have, one that *must* be obeyed. Konoe Akira then turned in his chair towards the verandah door and called to the *mama-san* for lunch to be served.

Anna recalls little about the few mouthfuls she managed to eat, the exception being a dish of eel and the fact that Colonel Konoe drank a small container of sake. 'This is a special occasion, Second Vase. I ordered eel in anticipation of our mutual success,' he declared happily. 'It is a very special Japanese dish.'

The eel had a flavour not greatly to her liking, but Konoe

Akira pressed the delicacy on her and ate his own with relish. He seemed extremely pleased with himself. It was almost as if he believed Anna had arrived, of her own accord, at the decision to become 'acquired'.

At the conclusion of lunch, rather than rise as he normally did, Konoe Akira said almost shyly, 'Second Vase, I promised I would translate the beautiful and forbidden persimmon poem by the venerable *haiku* master and poet–priest, Taneda Santoka. It is, alas, my poor translation of a great work and I regret I can never do justice to it in English, but you will, I hope, forgive my humble attempt.'

Anna was surprised at the obvious humility and even nervousness he displayed. She immediately understood that in Konoe Akira's mind, this was no simple poem to be recited as if an entertainment. Instead, she sensed every word was equally important. This man, who was all-powerful in his own immediate environment, became humble in the presence of the words of the poet–priest he was about to recite.

'Why is it forbidden, *Konoe-san*?' she asked.

'It is a poem for soldiers, a cry of pain! It suggests that the soldiers of Japan are not invincible, that we suffer the same fates and fears of all soldiers since the dawn of time. Prime Minister Tojo thinks it is bad for morale.' He began speaking, slowly enunciating each word.

Marching together
on the ground
they will never step on again

Winter rain clouds
thinking going to China

to be torn to pieces

Leaving hands and feet
behind in China
the soldiers return to Japan

Will the town
throw a festival
for those brought back as bones?

The bones
silently this time
returned across the ocean

The air raid alarm
screaming, screaming
red persimmons.

Konoe Akira was silent for a moment, then braced himself in the usual way and rose awkwardly. He bowed to Anna. 'Thank you, Second Vase. I will see you tomorrow at noon.' He turned abruptly and left.

CHAPTER THIRTEEN

*'Ah, that is up to you, Anna-san. If you do not
please him in this art, then he will crush the pearl.
The honourable Konoe Akira is a man of unlimited
power and his power over life and death requires as its
counterbalance an equal arbitrary and capricious
submission by him. He has chosen you and only
you to know this secret, to assuage his guilt.'*
The seventh okami-san
The Nest of the Swallows, Tjilatjap

THE THREE MONTHS OF language lessons and lunches
passed quickly and Colonel Konoe pronounced himself happy
with Anna's progress in Japanese. In fact, she was glad to be
using her mind again and proved to be an outstanding student
who took great pleasure in the teaching given to her by a
military instructor, 2nd Lieutenant Ando, a shy bespectacled
young scholar who had been a junior lecturer in linguistics at
Tokyo University before being called up into the army.

Ando was an unlikely soldier and had become disenchanted
with the thankless task of trying to teach Japanese to the Korean
conscripts, both male and female. The males did the dirty
outside work for the Japanese army, while the females worked
in the kitchens or as cleaners in the officers' accommodation
and the brothels. While they had the constitution of a mule the
lieutenant felt they also shared the animal's intelligence; most

of them were illiterate slum kids grabbed from the streets of Seoul and Pyongyang or from the impoverished rice paddies in the surrounding countryside.

Inspired once more, *Ando-san* delighted in the opportunity and challenge of teaching Anna. It was a case of a diligent teacher and a willing student and the results surpassed even Konoe Akira's ambitious demands.

If I make Anna's achievement seem effortless, that would not be correct. She studied deep into each evening and most nights went to bed exhausted, her head spinning with phrases and the inflections cast upon words in a language where what is said is seldom what is meant.

Dutch is a Teutonic and often pedantic language. Javanese, when well spoken, is a gentle and sometimes lyrical one. English, borrowed from everywhere and everyone, is perhaps the most difficult. But Japanese was by far the most introverted, subtle and formal language Anna had ever tackled. It is a language where what is left unspoken is often the more meaningful statement.

Nonetheless, the three months Anna spent with 2nd Lieutenant Ando before Colonel Konoe deemed her ready to enter the second phase of her Japanese initiation were the happiest she'd had since leaving Batavia. The shy lieutenant would continue to teach her for another two years, by which time Anna spoke Japanese with more proficiency than she spoke English.

The daily lunches over the first three months with Konoe Akira continued and with them a strange bond began to develop between Anna and her captor. The Japanese colonel, while appearing urbane, sophisticated and a patient mentor, nevertheless kept a tight hold on her behaviour. In numerous subtle ways, usually preceded or followed by small acts of kindness, he made sure she understood that without his patronage she was in mortal danger.

At no stage did he touch her or make any sexual advances; his preoccupation was with her mind combined with physical perfection, and she could only conclude (with immense gratitude) that this meant, given the manner in which he had referred to her chastity, the pearl that nestled in the heart of the oyster was to remain intact.

Anna's deep resentment at having been acquired by him gradually began to lessen, and as her knowledge of Japanese increased he delighted in testing her with more difficult precepts, and her naturally competitive nature rose to the challenge these presented.

During this same period Captain Takahashi, the commander of the *kempeitai*, had taken with enthusiasm to the task of conscripting young Dutch women for the two designated brothels. Girls from the age of fifteen, chosen for their looks and purity, were set aside to work in the Nest of the Swallows, the officers' house of pleasure. The older women, mostly in their late twenties or early thirties, usually married, sexually mature and robust, were chosen for the establishment created for the common soldiers and non-commissioned officers.

Seven *okami-san*, geishas too old for active service, arrived by ship from Japan to set up the two brothels. Six of them were required to work as keepers of an *okiya*, the Japanese name for a geisha house, running the establishments and disciplining the comfort women, while the seventh, also a retired geisha, was a woman skilled in every imaginable way of sexually pleasing a male. Her task as the supreme *okami-san* was to instruct the young Dutch women at the Nest of the Swallows in any sexual proclivity an officer patron might desire.

Both establishments remained open for sixteen hours every day and each comfort woman was required to work an eight-hour shift under the supervision of an *okami-san*.

While enforced prostitution is degrading, humiliating and psychologically deeply damaging, in many respects the more experienced women in the enlisted men's brothel were somewhat better off than the young inexperienced girls in the Nest of the Swallows. The older women were required to service thirty patrons a day and while this may seem physically inhuman, it was a carefully calculated figure. Most young soldiers arrive at a brothel with their testosterone at a very high level and their anticipation of things to come even higher. What has been imagined prior to sexual congress is much more important than the actual act of penetration. The cladding of a condom and the entrance to the tunnel of bliss were simply the final physical acts in the mental drama. Most experienced prostitutes, if they are being honest, do not feel unduly sexually abused by the quick and explosive orgasm of an over-excited young male. Thirty soldier customers a day was blatant and systemised rape, but the number and conduct of the customers was nevertheless carefully supervised. No self-respecting *okami-san* would dream of over-utilising her charges. This may have had little to do with her feeling any compassion since it was, quite simply, bad for business and the *okami-san* would be punished as a result.

Every once in a while Konoe Akira would make an oblique reference to the Nest of the Swallows, so that Anna was constantly aware that the captive relationship she had with the Japanese officer was a very privileged one. Also, his occasional veiled remarks were a reminder that her required presence for tutorials and lunch was a situation much to be preferred to the alternative choice of work under the overall supervision of the *kempeitai* and the dreaded executioner, Captain Takahashi.

Anna was also subtly reminded that the demands of Japanese officers were often peculiar and specific, and that virginity and the innocence of a neophyte was a much sought-after prize, particularly when the carefully inculcated skills of the seventh *okami-san* were added to their regime. In addition, the more sophisticated officer patrons seldom suffered from the spontaneous combustion of the young soldiers, and often required more complex gratification. While Anna couldn't begin to imagine what any of their sexual proclivities might be, she was nevertheless inordinately grateful to Konoe Akira for rescuing her from being recruited to the Nest of the Swallows.

Colonel Konoe would also ameliorate this underlying threat by rewarding Anna with small specific acts of kindness. As an example, Til lamented to her one morning that the tyres of his *becak* were worn down to the lining and were close to the point where they could no longer be mended, and the inner tubes had so many puncture patches that they too would soon be worthless. Since tyres or inner tubes couldn't be purchased, even on the black market, he explained that he would soon be unable to fetch her or, for that matter, earn a living. Anna had spoken to the colonel, who had seen to it that the little *becak* owner received six sets of new bicycle tyres and inner tubes and instructed that he was simply to go to the ordnance depot when he required more.

Kindness of a larger nature was shown in his command that a military doctor was to pay a visit to Piet Van Heerden twice a week to monitor his condition. The doctor had been unable to diagnose Anna's father's sickness – not surprising, as the medical profession at the time was unaware of the type 2 diabetes that caused his constant thirst and frequent need to urinate. The doctor probed at the discolouration of skin that Anna had first noticed at the back of her father's neck and which soon spread to his elbows, knees, knuckles and armpits, but could draw no medical conclusions. His patient also suffered from high blood pressure and hypertension, while at the same time he gained weight and became hugely obese without any increase in appetite. There was very little the Japanese doctor could do to help Piet Van Heerden and so he supplied him with a bottle of tablets, while cautioning that they were only to be taken when he felt particularly ill, as they would invariably lead to acute constipation. Anna came to call them his 'magic pills' as they quickly calmed her father. Unbeknown to her the prescribed tablets were pure morphine and Piet Van Heerden soon became addicted, as well as adding constipation to his list of woes.

As an aside, Java at the time was awash with heroin and amphetamines, the latter a Japanese invention while the former came from Japanese-occupied China. The Japanese military used them to subdue the more recalcitrant elements in a local society or to encourage collaborators, while at the same time a great many of the senior Japanese officers were addicted to a combination of the two drugs. When injected together they produced a sense of euphoria and a heightened since of awareness – the perfect fix.

Soldiers coming down the Malayan peninsula where they were forced to endure long marches through difficult conditions were issued with amphetamine-infused cigarettes to keep them awake and alert. At the conclusion of the war one warehouse in

Japan was found to contain 18 000 kilograms of amphetamine crystal. While it has never been officially confirmed, it is claimed that large amounts of heroin were found throughout the Greater East Asia Co-prosperity Sphere.

In August 1942 all Dutch men from fourteen years onwards were finally rounded up and placed in concentration camps; the youngest boys and the old men, the sick and disabled were to remain in Java, while the able-bodied were sent to Burma to work in the Japanese labour camps, where many died of starvation, dysentery, malaria and ill treatment. Piet Van Heerden was given a dispensation by the Japanese commander and was permitted to remain with Anna.

And so, with these and similar acts of kindness combined with occasional threats, Anna began to lose her fear of Konoe Akira. She had always been subject to patriarchy and so was accustomed to the dominance of a male in her daily life. With her increasing fluency in the Japanese language, taken with the fact that he'd never touched her or made a direct reference to a personal sexual need, it wasn't too difficult to regard the Japanese officer as being the father figure Anna would have hoped for, rather than the pathetic, incontinent and increasingly obese, fearful and self-absorbed one to whom she returned home each afternoon.

However, if these first months could be regarded as the halcyon days of Anna's benign captivity, they were to end all too abruptly. Exactly to the day when the three months Konoe

Akira designated for her initial language lessons had passed, Yasuko served eel once more. As on the previous occasion, a small container of sake was placed in front of the colonel.

At the conclusion of the lunch, Konoe Akira, first lighting a cigarette, leaned back in his chair. He now only spoke to her in Japanese.

'You have done well, Second Vase, and I am pleased with you. Now the time has come for the next part of your journey to become an artist and, at the same time, your own canvas. I am pleased with how you have advanced with the first learning. You have been quick to progress with the Japanese language. This afternoon you will not go home but retire to your room upstairs, where you will receive a visitor, a woman, who will begin your second instruction.'

Anna smiled. 'What is it to be, *Konoe-san*?' she asked.

'A second instruction only an *okami-san* can teach,' he replied, looking unsmilingly at her.

Anna laughed. 'You have said yourself that I would never make a geisha, *Konoe-san*.'

He got up from his chair in the usual awkward manner while Anna rose to return the customary bow that signified his departure.

She had grown accustomed to wearing a kimono, knowing how to prevent the silk from creasing when she sat, and she now adopted the wide-elbowed, fingertipped, reclining-thumb posture bow that Yasuko had taught her without having to think about it. She was wearing the prettiest of the four kimonos she possessed. This had come about when, having completed her language lessons with 2nd Lieutenant Ando, she had gone to her room upstairs to change for lunch only to discover Yasuko standing at the door holding the garment she was now wearing. 'Today this one, *Anna-san*,' she'd laughed. 'We are having eel and the honourable *Konoe-san* will drink sake.'

Now, to Anna's surprise, Colonel Konoe addressed her while standing and without bowing. 'I will see you tomorrow at lunch, but from now on you will be here in the afternoon as well. You will go home at five o'clock.'

'As you wish, *Konoe-san*,' Anna said quietly. 'I will do my best to learn this second instruction.'

'Yes, it would be best if you did, Second Vase.' He paused and, looking directly at her, said, 'It is why you are here.' He bowed, 'Ho!'; then, without waiting for Anna to return this gesture, Konoe Akira turned on his heels and limped away.

Anna bowed to his stiff neck and rigid, retreating back. She was suddenly very afraid.

She waited until she heard the sound of his car departing and made her way into the kitchen to find Yasuko. The *mama-san* was making rice noodles and greeted her with a serious expression. '*Anna-san*, there is a visitor for you, she is waiting in your room,' she said.

'Yes, thank you, *Konoe-san* has informed me of her presence. Who is she, *Yasuko-san*? The colonel just said a woman was coming to instruct me but did not explain any further.'

The housekeeper looked unhappily at Anna, then down at her feet. 'She is *okami-san*,' she said in a soft voice.

The title wasn't new to Anna; the *okami-san* were the seven women who had been sent from Japan to Java and, on more than one occasion, if only obliquely and with a twinge of threat in his voice, Konoe Akira had referred to them.

Anna's immediate fear was that her second instruction was going to take place in the Nest of the Swallows and the *okami-san* had been summoned to accompany her there. But then she realised it didn't make sense. If this was what Konoe Akira intended, then why had he gone to the extent of tutoring her in Japanese or required her constant attendance at lunch, where his satisfaction at her progress in the Japanese language was readily apparent? Why would she be permitted to go home at five o'clock if all along she'd been intended for the officers' whorehouse?

Anna, somewhat calmer in her thoughts, now asked, 'Has she, the *okami-san*, come to fetch me? To take me somewhere, *Yasuko-san*?'

The housekeeper had been instructed over the past three months to only speak to Anna in Japanese. But now, in case the *okami-san* came downstairs and was within earshot, she changed to Javanese.

'Fetch you? No, no, *Anna-san*, the *colonel-san* told me she is here to *instruct* you. That she will come every day and I must see that she leaves the house at five minutes to five o'clock.' She smiled and attempted to adopt a confident tone. '*Anna-san*, these *okami-san*, they are old women who are trained in formal manners. It is possible that the honourable *Konoe-san* wants you to learn their ways. The *okami-san* are the only ones who can do this in Tjilatjap. I myself cannot do this. I am a humble housewife who cooks and whose hands are raw from washing dishes and scrubbing floors. I have not been taught the noble art of keeping a man well satisfied with my presence.'

'But he has said himself that I could never be a geisha. Not even a beginner, a *maiko*.'

Yasuko shrugged. 'It is perhaps to learn just a few of their traditions? For example, they may show you the manner in which to serve tea. The honourable *colonel-san* is from a very old and famous family who are accustomed to different ways to show one's respect and humility; the geisha, they know these ways.'

The housekeeper's reassurances were comforting to Anna but she nonetheless felt a sense of foreboding as she mounted the stairs. Her room was large and comfortably furnished in the Dutch manner and had formerly been the principal bedroom. It had now been converted to include two easy chairs and a low table. The two chairs, in a room she had believed was exclusively her own, had always disconcerted her. She had been promised complete privacy and this had hitherto been strictly adhered to, with Yasuko being the only one entering to attend to her kimonos, *hadajuban* slips and *tabi* socks. Anna could only conclude that as the chairs were matching, the Japanese sense of order had designated that they be kept together, twins in the art of excessive upholstery. Now as she entered her room she saw that one of the chairs was occupied by a Japanese woman whom she took to be about fifty years old. She wore a *yukata*, a lightweight cotton, black kimono; on her feet were cloth-covered *zori*, and outside footwear with soles of lacquered wood worn without the white *tabi* socks, lest these be splashed in muddy puddles.

Tabi always reminded Anna of the white socks she'd worn to school with shoes that strapped across her instep secured by a single bright black button. Then little schoolgirls had worn regulation twin plaits, each plait tied with a fresh ribbon every morning: white for Monday, green for Tuesday, blue for Wednesday, yellow for Thursday and pink for Friday. *Tabi* were not essential to wear with *geta* sandals, particularly in the summer heat, Yasuko had informed her. Anna on one occasion appeared without them at lunch, only to witness Konoe Akira's temper flare.

'Where are your *tabi*?' he'd barked, pointing to her ankles.

Anna had dropped her eyes. 'I am informed they are not

necessary in this hot weather, *Konoe-san*.'

'Informed? Who informed you?' he'd asked in a peremptory tone.

Anna wasn't going to implicate Yasuko. 'Perhaps I wasn't informed, *Konoe-san*.' She'd looked up at him. 'It was my own decision.'

Konoe Akira was not fooled for a moment. 'Do not ever accept advice from that ignorant peasant in the kitchen! She was born here! She is not a proper Japanese! It is I who will decide what is Japanese custom and what is not! No one else! Do you understand, Second Vase?'

'Yes, *Konoe-san*.'

'You will *never* do this again!' Suddenly consumed with anger he had reached over and grabbed the butterfly ashtray and dashed it to the stone floor, smashing it at his feet. 'Never!'

Anna had screamed, then sobbed, 'Oh! Oh, why did you do that?' The butterfly ashtray had always been her talisman, like the Clipper butterfly I'd given her in Batavia. In her mind, it was yet another connection to me, a constant reminder at lunch each day of our love. After the colonel's departure when lunch was completed she would push the ash and two cigarettes butts aside and touch the glass butterfly and say silently to herself, 'I love you, Nicholas.' Now it lay smashed in six pieces, although strangely it had not shattered in the manner of glass. Unbeknown to Anna it had been made of crystal. One of the largest pieces was about twenty centimetres long, tapered to a point and she observed it contained the thorax of the glass butterfly.

Anna witnessed how the Japanese colonel had winced a moment after he'd dashed the butterfly ashtray to the floor. She knew instantly that he was conscious of having destroyed something beautiful and this increased his fury. 'You will not go about this house like a whore! You will always dress correctly!' he'd stormed.

'I am *not* a whore! I will do as you wish, *Konoe-san*,' Anna had cried, chastened but at the same time defiant. 'It is only a matter of cotton socks!'

The Japanese colonel had appeared to be momentarily taken aback. It had been some time since Anna had defied him. 'You will also modify the tone of your voice,' he'd said coldly. 'You may count yourself fortunate that you are not a whore! Now, return to your room at once and put on *tabi*. You are not correctly dressed!'

On her way back to her room she'd met a frightened Yasuko. 'I should not have told you about the wearing of the *tabi*! Now he will beat me, *Anna-san*!' she had cried, wringing her hands in despair.

'No, he won't. He has destroyed the butterfly ashtray – his tantrum is over. He has destroyed something beautiful and he will now be sad.' Anna had placed her hand on the *mama-san*'s shoulder. '*Yasuko-san*, do not throw the pieces away; it has broken neatly and I wish you to save them. Pick them up carefully, every little bit, and wrap them in a cloth for me to take home.'

The incident of the *tabi* and the ashtray had occurred a week prior to the arrival of her new tutor, or *okami-san*, of the second instruction. Anna had taken the six pieces of crystal home, wrapped in a soft cloth, and had carefully fitted them together. Except for the almost invisible break-lines the butterfly ashtray appeared to be intact. She kept it beside her bed along with the box containing the Clipper specimen I had given her and kissed the box and touched the crystal butterfly last thing every night while pronouncing her love for the butterfly collector she was beginning to despair of ever seeing again.

Now as Anna entered her room, the elderly *okami-san* struggled to get out of the large armchair, her legs too short to reach the carpet. Even by Asian standards she was diminutive, and Anna towered over her. Anna was at once hesitant, not sure of the protocol involved. It was her room and the tiny Japanese woman had been summoned to the house; was she therefore the one to bow second? She decided on the universal custom of respecting age and bowed correctly and low. 'Welcome, I am Anna,' she said softly, her eyes downcast.

The Japanese woman bowed in turn and, in the tradition of saying one thing and meaning quite another, replied, 'I am *okami-san*, my name is Korin, it means little bell.' She bowed again. 'I thank you for inviting me into your home and into this beautiful room. I will do all I can to pay tribute to the warm and gracious welcome you have shown me and I am humbled and greatly privileged to undertake the task you have given me.'

It was pure 'Japan-speak', a term Anna had coined and which frequently sent 2nd Lieutenant Ando into gales of laughter whenever she used it to complain about an obscure sentence that contained at least three possible meanings. Anna was aware that the *okami-san* knew she had not personally invited her, either into the house or into the privacy of her bedroom, and the *okami-san* also understood that Anna possibly had no knowledge why she had come, but only that she was to become a daily visitor.

The Japanese woman had previously occupied the chair Anna usually sat in and now Anna bade her be seated and sat down in the second chair. Anna told herself she was becoming too Japanese, she saw the new ownership of her usual chair as a sign that the little *okami-san* would attempt to be the assertive one in their relationship. She made up her mind that this would not happen. 'Are you *okami-san* at the *okiya*, *Korin-san*?' she asked, trying to make the question about the Nest of the Swallows sound like a casual and unimportant enquiry.

The woman smiled. 'No, I am not one of the *okami-san* who are responsible for running the *okiya*, *Anna-san*. I am the seventh geisha, the seventh *okami-san*.'

Despite the fact that Anna had fleetingly thought she might be subjected to some undesirable geisha instruction in the Nest of the Swallows, she had gratefully latched onto Yasuko's reassurances that it would be a matter of teaching her formal manners. She had expected one of the other *okami-san* and not the seventh, who she knew was responsible for training the young Dutch girls in the various ways of sexually gratifying the Japanese officers.

Even though she and Konoe Akira had grown much closer and to some degree had bonded, she still saw herself in terms of her Dutch and Javanese background. If her heart was Javanese her mindset was decidedly Dutch. While she was required within the Japanese colonel's home to accommodate her captor in the behavioural mannerisms he demanded, her practical Dutch upbringing saw this simply as necessary to his male ego. After all, she'd spent her childhood trying to please her father. Anna regarded Konoe Akira no differently.

Anna now realised she had mistakenly convinced herself that she was doing everything she could to please her captor in return for retaining her chastity. When she thought of the Dutch girls her age who worked in the Nest of the Swallows she was more than a little grateful to him and aware that pleasing him by, among other things, learning Japanese and never appearing without *tabi* was a very small price to pay for the right to retain her maidenhood. However, with the knowledge that the tiny woman seated in the big cushioned armchair in front of her was the seventh *okami-san*, Anna began to visibly tremble.

'What will you . . . what are you going . . . what will you teach me, *Korin-san*?' Anna asked in a hesitant voice.

The Japanese geisha smiled. 'All my life I have been a geisha, a woman who is trained to please a man. It is a task men see as requiring dedication, service, ceremony and submission, but if you listen properly and hear the silent weeping and the muted cry, the unspoken fear in a man's head, then you can also become powerful.' She paused. 'It is a power that cannot be taken away from you because it is *his* submission and not yours that he ultimately requires. What I will teach you, *Anna-san*, is how to gain ultimate power over a Japanese man of noble lineage.'

'But *Korin-san*, the colonel, *Konoe-san*, has *all* the power in Tjilatjap!' Anna protested. 'He has only to snap his fingers and I would be dead – or anyone else if he wishes. He has a savage temper; once I didn't wear *tabi* when I appeared for lunch and I thought he would kill me! His anger was so fierce that he threw a precious and very beautiful ashtray to the floor and smashed it. How can I gain power over such an intemperate man?'

'Ah, he will not beat you. He is of noble lineage, he will always be dangerous, he is samurai, but he will not damage perfection. The ashtray, perhaps it was a small perfection spoilt in a moment of temper? But it was also one that was expendable. But not you – in his mind you are *not* expendable, *Anna-san*. A man such as Colonel *Konoe-san* would not have done what he has for you unless he is besotted. He will not mark you or place an angry hand upon you. Already you have the beginnings of power over him.'

Anna was genuinely confused. 'But *Korin-san*, I do not wish to have power over *Konoe-san*. I only wish to be safe and to maintain my chastity.'

The *okami-san* frowned. 'Ah, your chastity? That is always complicated. But the one cannot be separated from the other. If the pearl is broken the oyster is no longer valuable, and you are no longer safe. You may retain your beauty, but it will no longer be perfection. These matters in a Japanese nobleman's mind are always difficult to understand, and are marked with contradictions. They worship their mothers, who are the great butterflies, but they wish at the same time to keep the chrysalis intact.'

'But I am not a geisha! I have received no training in hearing the silent weeping or the muted cry and I know nothing about pleasing a man in that way.'

Korin-san laughed. 'There are ways to please a man and to keep the pearl intact. This is the power I speak of. In the Nest of the Swallows, the young Dutch girls must learn quickly; they have many patrons – customers,' she corrected herself. 'It is not a nice word, "customers", but not every Japanese officer is a man of a refined nature and he will accept the inept ministrations that are all the young girls are capable of learning quickly. Mostly the things I teach them are not esoteric and lack purity. I must instruct in an hour what should take a week, and in a week what should take a month to refine.' She spread her hands and gave a small shrug. 'But what can I do? I am an old woman and fortunate to be given this task in the *okiya*.'

'But I do not wish to learn these ways of pleasing officers!' Anna cried in an anguished voice. 'Has *Konoe-san* instructed you to teach them to me?'

The Japanese woman looked at Anna, horrified. 'It is not in his nature, *Anna-san*! He is a highly civilised man and has told me of his esoteric desires and ambitions for you. For me it is perhaps the last opportunity I shall get to teach the noble art of *kinbaku*. My hands are not as supple as they once were and they often pain me when I work with the rope, but I have been given the privilege one last time of showing a beautiful woman the true path to power over a civilised and complex man.' She paused and looked directly at Anna. 'If you learn it well, then the pearl will gain great lustre and you will be safe.'

'You mean he will not wish to, does not want to . . . seduce me?' Anna could barely complete the sentence.

The seventh *okami-san* smiled. 'Ah, that is up to you, *Anna-san*. If you do not please him in this art, then he will crush the pearl. The honourable Konoe Akira is a man of unlimited power and his power over life and death requires as its counterbalance an equal arbitrary and capricious submission by him. He has chosen you and *only* you to know this secret, to assuage his guilt. I have been granted the time I need to teach you how this must be done. The honourable Colonel *Konoe-san* requires that you be perfectly trained. If you are diligent and allow me to instruct you in the true art of *kinbaku*, then you will be safe. To keep the pearl growing in lustre within the oyster will become his obsession; in his mind, a sacred task.'

'What is this *kinbaku*, *Korin-san*?'

'It is a wrapping with ropes.'

'I do not understand, *Korin-san*. A wrapping? Ropes tie, they do not wrap. Who does this wrapping?'

'You do, *Anna-san*. Tomorrow I will bring the hemp ropes and we will commence instruction. You will begin to learn to understand the rope, to feel it, as if it were a living thing.'

Anna had never heard of bondage and sadomasochism and while she had tried to imagine what the girls in the Nest of the Swallows were required to do to please the officer customers, she had never thought of anything involving rope or the submission of the male. She had long since recognised the guilt and shame Konoe Akira felt, but thought it was the result of his failure to live up to the expectations of his illustrious family due to the injury to his knee. She had assumed that he saw his appointment to the passive backblocks of Java and Tjilatjap, rather than being in command of a fighting regiment within the Imperial Army, as his ultimate punishment.

'I must learn to wrap rope around *Konoe-san*? But why?' Anna asked, still mystified.

'It is to bring him to submission, to punish him, to assuage his guilt,' the seventh *okami-san* explained. 'To a man such as the honourable *Konoe-san* pain is a cleansing process. This is your power over him, to bring him temporary forgiveness and, for a short time, relief from his terrible feelings of guilt and unworthiness.'

'Pain? I do not wish to bring him pain!' Anna cried, distressed.

The seventh *okami-san* sat silent for a few moments. 'You are not a geisha, you do not understand. It is *his* choice, *his* requirement and it is *your* privilege to serve his needs.'

'But I cannot! I will refuse!' Anna cried in distress.

The diminutive Japanese woman was silent for longer this time. 'There can be no refusal. This is why he chose you in the first instance, *Anna-san*. He believes you have been sent to him. When you fainted at the executions of the Chinese, it was his fate, his destiny, that wished to point you out to him. This is why the pearl remains safely embedded in the oyster and you are not with the others in the Nest of the Swallows.'

'I would rather die!' Anna cried out, jumping to her feet.

'Then that is certainly what will happen to you, *Anna-san*,' *Korin-san* said calmly. 'My advice to you is to take your own life. The alternative is unimaginable.'

Anna sat down again and started to sob but the seventh *okami-san* offered her no comfort; the tiny woman simply waited patiently for nearly an hour, when at last there was a tap on the door, followed by Yasuko informing them that it was almost five minutes to five and it was time for the *okami-san* to leave.

Korin-san rose from the chair. 'I will come again tomorrow, *Anna-san*. If you are not here I will know that I have failed and I will make the preparations necessary for my own death.'

Anna, despite her tears, looked up, startled. 'Why?' she cried. 'You have done nothing wrong!'

The seventh *okami-san* spoke softly. 'It will be because I have destroyed what is perfect. It will be because I have failed in my duty to convince you. In the mind of the honourable *Konoe-san* I will be no longer worthy of my vocation and will have added immeasurably to his guilt.' She paused. 'He will expect me to commit *hara-kari* or he will cause that *kempeitai* brute, Captain Takahashi, to torture and then to kill me.' The tiny woman sighed. 'It is correct that the honourable *colonel-san* should do so. I am old and unworthy and I will have lost my power.' She bowed to Anna and silently left the room, closing the door behind her.

Anna sat stunned for some time before slowly regathering her thoughts. Was the tiny woman's explanation of the consequences of her refusal simply bluff, a case of practised Japanese melodrama, a carefully composed and rehearsed passage brought into play in the event that Anna refused to comply with the colonel's wishes? *Korin-san* might have heard it all before at the Nest of the Swallows, where a recalcitrant Dutch teenager, or perhaps several such, threatened to take their lives rather than submit to a particularly repulsive demand by a Japanese officer.

But Anna quickly dismissed this thought. She had witnessed Konoe Akira's rage over inconsequential matters – the chicken, her *tabi* socks. There were other instances of uncontrollable rage related to her by 2nd Lieutenant Ando that had become legendary among the officers and had resulted often enough in someone's death. Her refusal, her suicide, would not be without consequence and his anger would know no limits.

She knew that he regarded her as a piece of art, the Second Vase, and had worked hard to try to achieve his own idea of perfection. She was, as he had so often explained, the creator and the canvas, the surface on which his every desire and fantasy appeared. If he thought her suicide was caused by the seventh *okami-san*'s inability to persuade her to create this work of art, she didn't have the slightest doubt that he would kill her himself or hand her over to the *kempeitai* to cause her an even more painful end.

Besides, there was another factor working here that, when Anna was relating this story to me, caused her tremendous grief. Although the only way she could refuse to comply with his wishes was to take her own life, she had already bonded almost completely with her captor, Colonel Konoe.

This effect, where the victim comes to completely identify with her captor so that she takes on his cause, has always been known. History is redolent with such instances of victims and villains bonding.

At the very moment the departing seventh *okami-san* closed the bedroom door, Anna knew that she would accede to Konoe Akira's wishes. She would not have been aware of her psychiatric condition at the time. Later the memory of her compliance and cooperation became the cause of an abiding secret shame. Anna was aware not only that her accedence was given in order to save her own life, but also that she did not know how to, or even whether she wished to, refuse him. Having made the decision to learn *kinbaku*, she knew she would take the task seriously and absorb all she could from the instruction received from the retired geisha. The second vase was about to be rearranged. The vibrantly coloured blossoms would soon be displayed in an entirely different interpretation of perfection.

In the four months that followed Anna became an exponent of bondage and various levels of sadomasochism. The learning process was careful and detailed and the wrapping of the hemp rope needed to be done with perfection. As intimate parts of the human body are involved and no knots are used, the smallest mistake could cause the entire effect to come undone and the heightened sensuality and exquisite pain to the submissive male to be alleviated.

She was to learn that the purpose of *kinbaku* is not simply restraint and severe bondage, but the wrapping must be done so as to bring pressure, strain and pain on the genitals without bruising or harming them. The ideal is to heighten the discomfort by the enforced asymmetrical position of the *uke*, the bound one.

This contorted and strange posture when combined with genital pain emphasises the experience. It is with its climax of pain and total submission that the feelings of guilt are assuaged. To the *uke* this is tantamount to perfection, a total expiation in a guiltless, perfect and unchanging world. It signifies his absolute submission to the artistry of the dominatrix, who must in every possible way be perfect, her looks and postures a part of her art, so that the sum of the whole – submission, pain and beauty – becomes the 'Divine Threefold Experience'. The seventh *okami-san* instructed Anna, 'There is with some *uke* the "Sublime Fourth Experience". It is one of gratification and it is performed by himself without your help. You will sometimes be required to be present, but do not need to learn to perform it.'

Anna began by becoming adept at handling the seven-metre lengths of hemp rope, learning the theory of its twists and turns, the feel of its tension on her arms and legs, though the seventh *okami-san* was careful not to bruise her. It was painstaking and often boring work as Anna learned the where, how, what and when of tension and bondage. But the truly painful aspect of the wrapping of the genitals was left for last.

One afternoon toward the end of the second month Anna entered her room to change into a kimono for lunch with the colonel and found to her surprise that a wooden platform, about twenty centimetres in height and about the size of a single bed, stood in one corner of the large bedroom, standing sufficiently far from the wall so that it was possible to move completely around it. Anna knew better than to ask *Konoe-san* why it had been built and placed in her room. That afternoon *Korin-san* arrived to give the second instruction accompanied by a second *okami-san*. The seventh *okami-san* explained that her companion was to be the surrogate *uke*; on her the wrappings and lessons in pain would begin. 'We will work on the platform,' the seventh *okami-san* said, pointing. 'This is not usual, as *kinbaku* is usually practised on a futon on the *tatami*.' She shrugged. 'But those are the honourable *Konoe-san*'s instructions.'

When the other *okami-san* had removed her kimono Anna saw that she wore a tightly fitted cotton vest and shorts that ended at her knees, in appearance not unlike the bathing suits women wore at the start of the twentieth century. She was a woman with very small breasts but these had been tightly strapped to resemble the hardness of the male chest. Konoe Akira was tall and carried no excess weight and his chest would therefore be firm.

Then *Korin-san* produced a triangle of soft leather that had a base eight centimetres wide and straps on either side to create a belt; this was intended to go around the waist and be tied at the small of the back. The triangle, much to the giggling amusement of the two *okami-san* and then eventually Anna, was inverted with the broad side positioned under the navel and the straps from each side tied at her back, so that the apex now hung between the second *okami-san*'s legs. It was pulled tightly down by another strap that hung from the point of the triangle, went between her legs and through the cheeks of her cotton-clad buttocks and was finally attached to the waist belt at the back. The inverted soft leather triangle contained six press-stud halves sewn into a circle at the centre in the exact position a male penis and genitals would hang. It was then that *Korin-san*, to giggles of delight, produced her *pièce de résistance*. Made of flesh-pale suede leather, it was a perfect imitation of male sex organs. *Korin-san* carefully clipped this to the inverted leather triangle.

'The suede leather has almost the same feel as the real thing,' she explained, laughing. Then she stepped back. 'Touch, please,' she commanded. Anna knew the feel of a flaccid penis from her father's drunken need to urinate into a bottle in the cabin of the *Witvogel*. But later, when *Korin-san* produced a second set where the penis was erect, Anna was amazed at the bone-hard rigidity of the erect male appendage. 'When they have been drinking sake it is not always like this,' *Korin-san* laughed.

For the next two months the two *okami-san*, surrogate and instructor, worked with Anna to perfect the genital restraint and the other bondage wrapping until she could do it perfectly while blindfolded. 'Until it can be done as if you are sightless, by feel alone, you will not be perfect,' *Korin-san* insisted. 'Some *uke* wish *kinbaku* to take place in total darkness; it is called "by starlight", and the honourable *Konoe-san* may request this from you, so your fingertips must become your eyes.'

In the process of teaching her, one great difficulty emerged when Anna pointed out that Konoe Akira was unable to bend his right knee and the asymmetrical position *kinbaku* required would need to be compromised. They had worked an additional week on this difficulty and it was Anna who finally solved it with a cleverly devised additional wrapping of the rope. The seventh *okami-san* was impressed. 'To modify but also retain perfection is a great talent, *Anna-san*,' she'd said with genuine admiration.

Anna continued to lunch with Konoe Akira every day during the period of the second instruction, and while he constantly challenged and questioned her on her language lessons, often disputing 2nd Lieutenant Ando's grammar so that the following morning Anna would take back his version to her instructor, he never asked about her progress with the seventh *okami-san*.

Anna, always mischievous, would tease the shy young university lecturer with Konoe Akira's pedantic corrections. Her tutor would invariably shake his head and smile. 'If the Japanese language was the sole province of the intellectuals and the nobility we would be plunged back into the age of the wandering knights of the samurai,' he would say, then hastily add, 'But you must obey him always, *Anna-san*. I am only a 2nd lieutenant and wish to keep my humble head firmly intact upon my shoulders.'

Four months and one week after she had commenced to work with the seventh *okami-san*, finishing lunch with the obligatory cigarette lit and the initial puff sent to the verandah roof, Konoe Akira leaned back and announced in an arbitrary voice, 'Tomorrow, after lunch, there will be no *okami-san*. You must rest in the afternoon in your room, where you will also dine and prepare yourself. I have arranged for a new kimono for you to wear. You will bring green tea with you. *Yasuko-san* will escort you to the door of my room. She will knock twice, then you will send her away. I will respond and open the door thirty seconds later. It will be precisely eight o'clock when I will do so. A car will be ready to return you home at eleven o'clock precisely. Do you have any questions?'

Anna, with her eyes downcast, replied, 'I am honoured to be asked to attend to you, *Konoe-san*.'

The following day Anna made the necessary arrangements for Kiki to come to the police *kampong* to care for her father and told Til that she would not be returning at five o'clock, so it was unnecessary for him to fetch her as the colonel would send her home by motorcar.

Til looked shocked. 'What time will he send you home, Anna?' he asked.

'He is always exact, eleven o'clock,' she replied.

'Then I will be at the gate. I must see that you are safe,' he said in an unequivocal voice. Anna knew better than to argue with him. She knew that he saw himself as her guardian and she loved him for it. Til was sanity in an uncertain world.

After lunch with the colonel Anna went to her room where, hanging in the huge teak Dutch wardrobe, was a new kimono of exquisite yellow silk and a white silk *obi* and *juban*. It was by far the most beautiful of her kimonos and the significance of the yellow and white silk was not lost on her. In Konoe Akira's bedchamber she would become the first vase of flowers, his own arrangement, the art appearing on her canvas, the white 'no colour' of the *obi* to highlight the yellow of singular perfection.

On her dressing table lay a new silver-backed hairbrush with the words 'First Vase' engraved in Japanese. Beside this was placed a tiny eggshell-porcelain bowl containing a single frangipani flower, its petals white descending to purest yellow at its centre. Anna also noted that the raw-cotton bag containing the neatly folded hemp ropes that was usually placed beside the dresser was missing.

Anna spent the long afternoon trying to read an involved text 2nd Lieutenant Ando had given her about correct Japanese conversational form, but was finding it almost impossible to concentrate. She'd washed her hair, then bathed and towelled, she slipped on a light summer satin Chinese dressing gown she'd purchased several months before at the markets. Using the new brush she stroked her shoulder-length hair until it shone like black silk. She had decided to wear the same light-coloured lipstick she had worn on the very first day she had voluntarily given herself up to the Japanese colonel, the day she had surprised him as he returned home for lunch. But then she remembered the incident with the *tabi* socks and his fury about incorrect Japanese dress. The lipstick was Western, not Japanese, and Anna decided she would be better without it.

She tried resting, but after ten minutes her anxiety was such that she jumped from the bed to stand by the window that overlooked the garden and the river beyond. The soldier gardeners were busy as usual, and she wondered if they considered themselves privileged in being excused the routines of guard duty and other soldierly chores to work in the beautiful tropical garden. Each morning after Til had dropped her off she would greet them in Japanese and stop in front of one or another of them for a chat, practising her Japanese. They seemed contented, simple men, happy with their gardener's lot. They also seemed to delight in her progress with their language and three or four of them would come running at the sight of her and gather around. When she answered a question, or asked one with increased confidence and articulation, they would laugh and clap in encouragement.

Watching them from the window Anna thought that the duty she would be asked to perform that night would be about as far from their imagination as it had once been from hers. She would have liked to have a length of hemp rope in her hands, running it time and time again through her fingers, rehearsing her debut, much as a showjumper might warm up a mount prior to entering an event, or a boxer might shadow-box in his dressing-room prior to entering the ring.

For four months she had watched Konoe Akira in a quite different manner, studying his movements, trying to envision his naked form through his carefully cut military dress. Was the tailor who had made it compensating for any aspect of his physique? Was he simply skinny? Did he have any muscle tone, tissue that would resist and assist the wrapping of the hemp rope?

Of course, she wondered about his appendage: was it big or small; how was he hung? She had become so accustomed to the size and the feel of the two suede imitations that she couldn't imagine any different configuration and would grow panicky at the thought that some aberration might present itself and she'd mess up this most important of all the rope wrapping. So carefully had she been prepared for this night that she did not see herself as performing an act leading to sexual gratification, but simply one that met the stringent requirement of the art of *kinbaku*. Her relief would come from his satisfaction in her wrapping performance and if, at the conclusion, she possessed some power over him, this wasn't in the least important to Anna, other than safeguarding the pearl within the oyster.

And so the endless afternoon eventually passed and at six o'clock Yasuko arrived with dinner on a tray.

Anna, by this time, had eaten innumerable Japanese dishes and Yasuko was a skilled cook. Anna had passed the stage when most Western palates pronounce that Japanese food all tastes the same, and had become reasonably sophisticated, able to enjoy the subtle differences in texture and taste.

'I have cooked you *gyoza* and *sukiyaki*.' The mayor's wife put down the tray and pointed to a dish, then clapped her hands happily. 'Also, *chawanmushi*!' she announced proudly. Anna had never tasted this last dish as she had always eaten with Konoe Akira and the steamed egg custard with shrimp was considered a favourite with women.

'Thank you, *Yasuko-san*. I am humbled by your expertise and elevated by your choice of dishes.' Anna was too nervous to be hungry and so ate a little from each dish so that Yasuko wouldn't lose face. *Gyoza* are small fried dumplings made with meat and vegetables; *sukiyaki* is a hotpot containing thinly sliced meat pieces, vegetables, tofu and *shirataki* (noodles), and is eaten after each mouthful has been dipped into raw egg.

At twenty minutes to eight o'clock Anna, assisted by Yasuko, was dressed and ready, and when finally she added the frangipani blossom to her hair, she stood back to look at herself for the first time in the full-length mirror. But what she saw wasn't a beautiful woman dressed in a stunning yellow kimono with white *obi*, but the reflection of a weeping Yasuko with her hands touching her cheeks. 'Oh, oh, *Anna-san*,' the little Japanese woman wept. 'I am looking at the most beautiful woman I have ever seen!'

'Does that include my big Dutch feet in these ridiculous *tabi*?' Anna laughed, then turning, she hugged the mayor's wife. 'Thank you, that is a lovely compliment, Yasuko. Now dry your tears; you have to go and prepare green tea for me to take in to *Konoe-san*.' Anna's eyes widened for emphasis. 'Can you imagine if we are even one minute late?' A look of terror crossed the *mama-san*'s face.

They arrived at the door of Konoe Akira's rooms. It was one minute to eight when the mayor's wife handed the tray containing the pot of green tea and yellow cups to Anna. They waited a further thirty seconds, then Yasuko knocked twice and turned, first touching Anna lightly on the shoulder before she hurried away.

Anna waited and as the big hand of her watch hit the hour the door opened to reveal Konoe Akira. About three metres behind him was a wall composed of light wooden frames with delicate rice-paper panels. The light from the room beyond gave the rice paper a rich and elegant glow.

The Japanese officer was wearing a *yukata*, the lightweight summer robe, and bowed, followed by the usual 'Ho!'

Anna bowed low in the perfect formal manner while holding a tray. 'Thank you for your generous welcome, *Konoe-san*,' she said in Japan-speak.

Konoe Akira turned and indicated that she walk to her left where, at the end of the wall, were two sliding *shoji* screen doors of a wooden grid pattern. Anna was to learn that this was the guest's entrance, while the host's entrance was set into the adjoining wall to her far right, so the host could enter from another part of the house. Sliding back the paper and wooden-framed doors to the guest entrance, he permitted Anna to enter, bowing and then turning to move to the far end of the wall and round the corner so he could enter via the host entrance.

The floor of the room, Anna observed, was made of *tatami* mats set in wooden frames, each a formal area and in Japanese tradition always of the same size. In this room, reserved for the formality of serving tea, the mat configuration denoted where guests were required to sit while the host always occupied a *tatami* mat of their own.

The centre of the room contained a low table of polished dark wood and a single cushion where it was intended Anna would sit. Instead of a cushion for Konoe Akira, placed on the host *tatami*, directly opposite the table where she sat, was a small stool. Anna immediately understood that this was a concession to tradition because of his stiff leg. Seated, as was customary, on a cushion, he would be unable to rise and would require help to lift him to his feet. The Japanese officer, Anna knew, would perish rather than ask for help of any kind. In the corner to the right of the colonel stood a simple polished glass vase containing a single perfect yellow chrysanthemum.

Anna, who had been schooled in a simplified version of the Japanese tea ceremony by the two *okami-san*, proceeded to pour the tea in silence while waiting for her host to speak.

Konoe Akira remained silent for twenty minutes while drinking his tea, then finally placed the cup on the table, pushing it away from Anna to indicate he required no more. 'It will be by starlight,' he said.

'If you wish, *Konoe-san*,' Anna replied, secretly relieved. She was nervous about seeing him naked and now her fingertips would be her eyes. She knew that her ultimate fate would be delivered within the next two hours. She was afraid but didn't panic, trusting that the seventh *okami-san* had trained her well and knowing that if she hadn't, then her own fate would be sealed.

With great difficulty Konoe Akira began the process of rising from his stool. Anna, fearing for his dignity if he should fall, desperately wished to help him to his feet but dared not touch him. In a few minutes her hands would play across his entire naked body as she assessed the requirement of the rope. But now she was forced to remain seated while he struggled, his eyes fierce with determination and his lips pulled tight. She sighed, inwardly relieved when at last he stood. She too rose, ready to bow. Instead her host walked over to the yellow blossom and removed it from the slender vase. 'Now I shall go to my bedchamber, First Vase,' he announced, then indicated the host door. 'Then you must follow in five minutes. I shall place this blossom at the doorway to my bedchamber so that you know where to enter.' He bowed. 'Ho!'

Anna returned his bow. She was to learn that the interior of the entire left wing of the brewer's mansion had been converted into an authentic Japanese house to form the colonel's private quarters. Yasuko would, of course, have known this, but she'd never mentioned it to Anna. Perhaps, she concluded, it was another of his many 'forbiddens'.

After five minutes she left the tea ceremony room and soon enough found the door with the formal yellow chrysanthemum. It had been placed in a duplicate glass vase, the Japanese officer's sense of perfection unable to allow him to simply abandon it on the heavy teak floorboards that extended to the entrance of the rice-paper doorway.

Without knocking, Anna entered into a room that contained no furniture except an inbuilt cupboard with sliding doors that was used to store the futon, padded quilt and bean-filled pillow. Now all of these lay in the required format in the centre of the room. The wooden platform, though more carefully made than the one built in her bedroom, was constructed to exactly the same dimensions. It was, as Anna had previously guessed, another concession to Konoe Akira's stiff leg.

Anna had long ago realised that Konoe Akira, trained from the very beginning of his military career to exercise command, was a man who thought everything out and left nothing to chance. It would have been his idea to have the platform built in her bedroom. She knew now that if she had been trained by the *okami-san* to work on the floor, kneeling in the traditional manner instead of learning to adopt a new and slightly different posture, when suddenly confronted by a platform her technique would have been entirely wrong. Anna now saw that beside the platform lay the cotton bag containing the hemp ropes.

'I will switch off the lights and remove my *yukata*. Then I shall hand it to you so that you may return it to me when it is over.' He pointed to the cotton bag. 'Perhaps you would like to arrange them?'

'That will not be necessary, *Konoe-san*,' Anna said softly. 'With your permission I will first have to explore your whole body with my fingers, you should enjoy the —'

'You may do as you wish, First Vase,' he said, cutting her short. Anna realised for the first time that he too was nervous. She was his work of art and he was about to find out whether he had created in her the perfection of the 'Divine Threefold Experience', his sole reason for bringing her into his complicated emotional life.

Konoe Akira switched off the light, plunging the entire Japanese house into darkness. Moments later Anna received the gown from him and placed it where she could retrieve it again.

This was the moment, the first time she had ever touched the severe and often frightening Japanese colonel. She could hear the words of Korin, the seventh *okami-san*, in her head: '*Anna-san, do not trust your eyes; before you begin, even if it is light, close them, then feel the texture and the tone of the skin, work the whole body with your hands and the tips of your fingers, let the rope find its own path, pull it tight not only with your hands but also with your heart and spirit, respect what you are doing, honour your patron and he will willingly grant you power over him.*'

Anna's hands began to work in the dark, gently massaging and stimulating various parts of his body and discovering its secrets as well as every curve and hollow. Finally, after about twenty minutes, she took up the first length of rope.

She had been trained well and discovered the wrapping was an easier task when performed on a firmer male body. She listened to the pitch of his groans as she moved him into the required asymmetrical position while still accommodating the stiff knee. Sometimes he'd emit a soft moan or sigh of satisfaction as her pliant fingers travelled ahead of the rope, feeling, judging, listening, massaging and finally sensing the agony and ecstasy in his mind.

It took her almost an hour to wrap him before she came to the part the seventh *okami-san* had called the 'Exquisite Pain', the wrapping of the genitals. Anna had only performed this process on the suede imitations and now didn't know what to expect. From this point on she knew she was on her own. If she failed, then the skill that had preceded this moment would be utterly without merit.

Anna worked slowly, carefully judging exactly the right pressure with her fingers until the Japanese officer's erection climaxed at the precise moment she delivered the final wrap to send a shock through his body that, mixed with his ejaculation, created the ultimate moments of perfection, the 'Exquisite Pain'. She allowed the pleasure and the pain to build and build until she had completely drained Konoe Akira's senses and he lay whimpering like a small child in the dark.

It was then, as if from nowhere, she felt complete power over her *uke* surge through her body. Anna knew with absolute certainty that she was safe as long as Colonel Konoe Akira remained alive.

She began to unwrap him, massaging the parts where the ropes had tightened. It took Anna almost fifteen minutes to disentangle him and to return the blood flow to parts of his exhausted body. She then placed the *makura*, a bean-filled pillow, behind his head and the light summer *kakebuton*, the comfort blanket, over him before squatting in the geisha manner on her heels beside the platform to wait.

The seventh *okami-san* had told her that sometimes patrons slept an hour, sometimes eight hours, exhausted; their bodies completely drained. But after only fifteen or so minutes Konoe Akira sat up and called for his *yukata*. Without turning on the light, since his eyes and hers were now adjusted to the dark, he rose from the futon. 'I will bathe and return soon, First Vase. Please wait in the room you entered when you came.'

It was the first time he had ever couched a request with a casually polite 'please' since she'd known him. 'I am at your service, *Konoe-san*,' Anna replied.

'You are everything I had hoped for, First Vase. Yellow highlighted by white – perfection!' She could see the outline of his tall body as he bowed. 'Ho!' he said, then turned abruptly to cross the room.

Anna bowed in the prescribed manner. 'I am glad you are pleased, *Konoe-san*,' she said to his retreating back. In the dark, even if he had faced her, he would not have seen that she was smiling to herself. Anna Van Heerden was no longer afraid.

The lights suddenly came back on and Anna returned to the tea ceremony room, where she placed the pot and cups back on the tray. She took it through the door Yasuko had knocked on that led to the colonel's rooms and placed it at the side to take back to the kitchen when she returned upstairs to change into a sarong prior to going home. Then she went back to the first room, where she sat and waited on the guest cushion provided for her.

Anna was not sure how she felt. She knew she had crossed a line where there was no return and gained a power over her captor that would keep her safe. But she felt as if she wanted to go somewhere very quiet to weep. The four-and-a-bit months of her second instruction had almost been a game; now she knew her innocence was gone, lost in the dark to 'the starlight'. She had been temporarily blessed by the fact that she was no longer in danger, but wondered if she had the right to know what she had come to learn in the second instruction and exploit for the first time tonight. Was it a knowledge that would taint her soul forever?

Konoe Akira, with his hair still wet and combed in the Western manner and wearing a fresh *yukata*, came through the host door. He carried a flat silver box with slightly rounded edges about twice the size of his cigarette case and again twice the depth. He placed it silently on the table and Anna noted that his name had been inscribed in Japanese on the lid. From his gown he withdrew a highly polished, black persimmon chopstick, the same as the ones she remembered were made from the heartwood of the sacred tree. This too he placed beside the box. Then he opened the elegant silver object and she saw that it contained four glass ampoules and two gleaming stainless-steel syringes.

'I would like your cooperation, First Vase,' Konoe Akira said, speaking for the first time.

'Willingly, *Konoe-san*, but I have not received instruction in this. With these syringes,' Anna added lamely.

The Japanese officer smiled. 'Be thankful for that, but the task does not require training.' He withdrew a clean white handkerchief from his gown and wrapped it around his left upper arm, binding it once and holding the ends. 'Place the heartwood where I am about to tie the knot, First Vase,' he instructed.

Anna moved to his side of the table and taking up the chopstick placed its centre across the first bind, holding it steady while Konoe Akira finally secured it in place with the second tie. She realised that it was a task he could, with a little effort, perform himself; that now he simply desired her involvement. Then he reached out and removed an ampoule and syringe from the box, snapped off the glass top and inserted the syringe, drawing the liquid upwards into the thirsty stainless-steel cylinder. 'Now twist the heartwood around so that it tightens. I will tell you when to stop.' Anna did what she was told while Konoe Akira clenched and released his fist. 'Thank you, that is sufficient.'

Anna had on one previous occasion at the headmistress's Red Cross lessons seen a demonstration of how to inject a painkiller into the arm. She had imagined at the time that if ever she was required to do so, she would be wearing a snowy white, starched nurse's uniform and he would be a handsome American airman, shot down and rescued, who was, in appearance, a dead ringer for Errol Flynn. They would naturally fall in love as she nursed him back to health.

Now, dressed in a silk kimono, she was witnessing a senior Japanese officer inject himself to achieve, she suddenly realised, what the seventh *okami-san* had declared the 'Sublime Fourth Experience'.

Konoe Akira inserted the needle into a prominent dark-blue vein and Anna winced as he paused to withdraw a tiny amount of blood and then pushed the plunger home. He placed the syringe on the table and almost tenderly rubbed the small drop of blood that appeared when he loosened the tourniquet.

'First Vase, you must promise me never to do as I have just done. It will spoil your perfection and destroy you,' he said quietly. He glanced at his watch. 'It is half-past ten. Your car will be waiting. You must change and go,' he said.

Anna, venturing to test his will, replied, 'I will instruct the driver to return to his quarters. I have my friend, Til, the *becak* owner, waiting for me at the gate, *Konoe-san*.'

The Japanese colonel rose to his feet with the usual difficulty and bowed. 'As you wish, First Vase.' It was a small triumph, but one she would not have dared to attempt previously.

Anna hurried upstairs to change into her sarong and sandals, helped by a sleepy Yasuko, who nevertheless seemed delighted to see her. '*Anna-san*, it went well?' she asked.

'Yes, I think so,' Anna said, still preoccupied, then stopped. 'Oh, no! I should have taken the tray to the kitchen. I have left it outside the door. Will you forgive me, *Yasuko-san*?' This small forgetfulness now served to focus her mind. 'It is past your bedtime, *Yasuko-san*; but yes, I think the honourable *Konoe-san* is pleased with my humble efforts.' She was learning; the Japan-speak came easily to her lips.

'To please them, that is our sacred task,' Yasuko said, happy for Anna.

Anna dismissed the Japanese driver, who woke with a start and automatically brought his hand up to his cap in a salute when she spoke to him from the darkness. Then she ran to the gate to greet the waiting and ever-faithful Til.

'*Ahee!* Anna, greetings from all – Ratih, Budi, Kiki and even the lieutenant. How has been the day and now this night?'

Anna impulsively hugged the little Javanese man, his presence so normal, real and comforting. 'Oh, Til, I have seen too much tonight.' She climbed into the *becak* and drew the brothel curtain, knowing she was about to weep.

Til started to pedal. 'Allah says, "When the eyes have seen too much they must be closed and as we sleep the eyelids will accept the burdens and when we wake the burdens will tumble out and be lost."'

'That's ridiculous, Til! One of your Allah worsts!' Anna sobbed, laughing at the same time.

'*Ahee!* Anna, do not weep. The Prophet says, "God sees every human experience from every angle and each shows the same thing in a different way. It is what is contained in our hearts that lets us see ourselves."' And Til pedalled into the night.

CHAPTER FOURTEEN

*'The entrance to the pearl is very resilient and not easily
damaged. Soon enough your maidenhood will be taken.
You cannot hold on to it forever.
Perhaps it is time to be practical? To face life as it is?'*
The seventh *okami-san* (*Korin-san*)
The Nest of the Swallows
July 1945

KONOE AKIRA'S DAILY HABITS changed little in the
following three years. He had, however, become so dependent
on Anna that during the dark hours he seemed unable to be
without her until he fell asleep. She was now fluent in Japanese
and spoke it in the refined manner of the educated élite; this
meant he was able to converse with her readily, adding to the
intellectual stimulus and education she had received from 2nd
Lieutenant Ando. It was not in the nature of a Japanese man of
his background to outwardly show affection to a young female,
but Konoe Akira was undoubtedly preoccupied by her presence
in his life.

If it could be said that the Japanese colonel was dependent
on her, then equally it could be said that Anna had bonded with
him. She had come to think of the strange routine as normal. It
was almost as if she had become two separate people; by changing
into a kimono when she arrived she became another, a different
Anna. In fact, in the mind of Konoe Akira she possessed two

separate identities: at lunch and during daylight hours he addressed her as Second Vase, while after dark he referred to her as First Vase. And he had never been guilty of a slip of the tongue and mistakenly used one name at an inappropriate time.

While he had never suggested she live in the brewer's mansion, she was required, with very rare exceptions, to attend lunch daily and again be there at eight o'clock each night, to be present after the colonel had left his study and remain until he was finally able to sleep.

On some nights she would be home by midnight but on others Til, who was now exclusively in the colonel's employ, would pedal her home at dawn. She confessed to me that she looked forward to those nights when he required her to perform both the 'Divine Threefold Experience' and the 'Sublime Fourth Experience'. While the process was enervating, it meant she would be home by eleven-thirty.

The capacity of humans to adapt to almost any situation and see it as normal is the reason we have found ourselves the dominant creatures on earth. For instance, there were some amongst the emaciated near-skeletons that emerged from the Japanese prisoner-of-war camps in Burma who exhibited mixed feelings at the final Allied victory. Many were thrown into a state of confused apathy tinged with anger and a fear of the unknown. This was because survival had become a routine, a skill acquired by those who were strong enough to survive. They had grown highly reluctant to abandon their way of coping in the daily struggle for food. They had acquired a fierce pride in the fact that they were part of an élite, survivors in a hostile environment. It seems a contradiction that this capacity to adapt and adopt also depends on rigid adherence to routine acts, to maintaining regular habits that we have acquired which we believe keep us alive.

It was no different for Anna. She first learned to adapt and then to adopt, learning the language of her captor, his habits, routines, pleasures and predilections, all in order to survive and to maintain her chastity. These became so familiar to her that she no longer thought of them consciously. She had acquired the art of survival. In her own mind, the key was her virginity. She believed that as long as she could hold onto it, she would be safe. She identified it with Konoe Akira's obsession with finding perfection as the antidote to the demons that possessed him. As long as the pearl remained intact she would survive, but if the pearl was to be crushed by some turn of fortune, then she would be placed in an alien and dangerous environment, where the control of her destiny would be taken from her own care and placed in the hands of others.

Perhaps one of the more bizarre instances of Anna's preoccupation with her environment occurred in March 1943 when Piet Van Heerden died of an overdose of morphine.

He had become the size of a beached whale, his legs so swollen he was unable to walk so that he was bedridden. He suffered from shortness of breath, extreme hypertension, renal problems and incontinence. His breath had a peculiar odour not unlike acetone – known as ketonic breath – as well as the distinctive ammonia smell of uraemia. All were the symptoms brought about by what we now know as type 2 diabetes. It was only a question of time before he would die an agonising death caused by kidney failure. The Japanese military doctor gave him no more than a few weeks to live, and told Anna her father would suffer a painful and difficult death. 'If you wish I will do it now. I will give him an overdose of morphine and he will be released without pain,' he volunteered.

'No!' Anna cried. 'No, please, no!' Piet Van Heerden's greatest fear was that he would die at the hands of the Japanese. The doctor was a member of the Japanese military and although he would be performing an act of mercy, it would still mean that her father met his death at the hands of his mortal enemy.

The doctor, aware of Anna's connection with Konoe Akira, bowed. 'As you wish. Perhaps when the time comes you will be sure to administer sufficient morphine?' He was not a cruel man and issued her with six ampoules and a syringe in order that Piet Van Heerden might die less painfully, unnecessarily demonstrating to her how to insert the needle into the upper arm. It was obvious from his expression and tone of voice that he expected her to terminate her father's life when his pain became unbearable.

Anna could not bring herself to end her father's life, despite the fact that he was in great pain. She knew that nobody would ever know what she had done; there would be no enquiry into his death. But she was physically exhausted, trying to spend as much time as possible nursing and caring for him while leading her double life at the brewer's mansion. It was not an imbued sense of morality that prevented her giving the overdose, or even the fact that this was her own father. She had learned how to survive in an environment where life was cheap and taken without conscience. Now, however merciful her action might be, she couldn't bring herself to adopt the mindset of her Japanese captors.

Ratih, hearing from Til about Anna's exhausted state, insisted, despite her protests, that Kiki spend most of her time at the house helping Anna care for Piet Van Heerden. Kiki could do the cooking and, if Anna wasn't present, feed and watch over him, but she lacked the strength to shift his bulk in order to change his wet sheets and she was becoming more and more depressed by Piet Van Heerden's intemperate behaviour towards her. At five o'clock every day she would leave for the evening shift at the *kampong* restaurant in tears.

Anna hadn't discussed the matter of her father's illness with Konoe Akira, other than when she'd first mentioned it and he'd ordered a military doctor to attend to him. She knew if she did, he would simply instruct the doctor to do what was necessary to terminate his life. She also knew that although she was exhausted, if the doctor was correct the passage of a few more weeks wasn't going to make a major difference to her health. However, she had become concerned about Kiki, who would burst into spontaneous tears almost every time Anna looked at her. Kiki's tears were not only causing her to be deeply depressed but also adding to Anna's considerable burden of care. But she knew if she didn't allow Kiki to help with her father, this would have an even worse effect on the little cook.

So Anna decided to talk to Til. 'Kiki cannot endure any more, Til. My father has become irascible and abuses her constantly, calling her a little brown bitch and a piece of you-know-what whenever she enters his bedroom. You must persuade Ratih to say to Kiki that she cannot manage without her in the restaurant kitchen. If I should tell her I don't want her to come to the house, she will lose face and think I do not love or trust her.'

Til listened carefully and, for once, didn't offer one of his Allah or Prophet aphorisms. Instead he said, 'Anna, you are exhausted and I am much worried for you. Your father and the Japan colonel – it is too much caring for one person.' He looked at her fondly, as a father might his daughter. 'How long before your esteemed father will die?' he asked.

Anna told him about the Japanese doctor's prognosis and also about the morphine and syringe. How she had refused to let the doctor give her father an overdose and then his suggestion that she do it herself. Til looked at Anna, amazed, then he shrugged and said, 'But, Anna, you must teach me how I must put in this needle and I will do it for you.'

'But, Til, that would be murder. You would be guilty of murder!' Anna cried in alarm.

Til shrugged. 'The Prophet says, "A wise man will solve three problems with one stroke, but a foolish one will endure all three until they destroy him." If I do this needle thing, then Kiki will not be required to come, you will gain some rest and your father will end his suffering. How can this be a bad thing to do?'

Anna thanked him but then said, 'Til, it will not be long before he dies. I will be alright. Please, will you speak to Ratih about Kiki? She will listen to you.'

'*Ahee!* That one, she only listens to Allah and then not always. Ask the lieutenant, ask Budi – when she has made up her mind she is the mountain that will not come to Mohammed!' He grinned, then continued, 'But I will try.'

A week later an exhausted Anna, despite an early *kinbaku* night, returned home shortly after 11.30 p.m. Piet Van Heerden awoke, heard her coming in and called out in a plaintive voice, 'Anna, *kan jy kom?*'

'*Ja,* Papa,' she sighed. 'I am coming.'

The bedroom stank of urine and Anna had to restrain herself from covering her nose. 'What is it, Papa? Do you want one of your pain tablets?' she asked. She had resumed calling him 'Papa' instead of the more formal 'Father' she'd adopted after reading his last will and testament and after he'd confessed to raping her mother. The resumption of the old familiar term seemed to be a genuine comfort to him, and she saw no point in remaining aloof or showing her disapproval of him in the final days of his life. Now he nodded, and Anna fetched the bottle and a glass of water and gave him a morphine tablet.

Anna then sat in the old chair beside his bed and Piet Van Heerden stretched out a trembling hand to hold her own. His big paw weighed heavy in her tired hands; still holding it, she placed it on her lap. It was such a large hand, yet she knew there was no strength left in it. 'Anna, am I going to die?' he croaked in a querulous voice.

It is a question most people avoid answering, or they reply with a socially accepted rejoinder, such as 'We all have to die at some time, don't we?' But now Anna's answer was forthright. 'Yes, Papa,' she said.

'I don't want to die!' he sniffed, close to sobbing. 'I want to go to New Zealand!' He was still a young man, in his mid-forties, but looked twenty years older. 'Please don't let me die, Anna!' he begged, as if it was within her power to save him.

'Papa, you are *very* sick and in great pain; the doctor says you cannot last much longer,' Anna answered. She did not like herself for being so direct, not knowing if she was doing the right thing. But she felt it was necessary he be given time to come to terms with his imminent death. 'I can ask the doctor to give you an injection. It will take away the pain and you'll simply go to sleep.'

He started to cough violently but eventually managed to croak, 'No! Not that yellow Jap bastard!' Anna had been right about not letting the military doctor administer the lethal dose of morphine.

She was silent for a while. Then drawing a deep breath she asked fearfully, 'Would you like me to do it for you, Papa?'

She expected and hoped for a frightened look and then a panic-stricken refusal. Piet Van Heerden was a coward and his fear of dying she knew was almost absolute. But he didn't react as she had expected, remaining silent for some time. At last he turned to look at Anna, and then slowly nodded his head. Anna saw tears roll from below the thicket of his fiercely tangled eyebrows. '*Ja* – please, *lieveling*, I don't think now I will get to New Zealand.'

Although she could never have taken his life without his permission, now the thought of doing so, of having volunteered and received his permission, shocked her. She left the bedroom and sat silently in the kitchen with three morphine ampoules and the syringe on the table in front of her. Finally she gained the courage to fill the stainless-steel syringe, forcing herself to keep her hands steady and to restrain her tears. She returned to the bedroom hoping he might have changed his mind, but he silently held his arm so that she could apply the tourniquet and responded, albeit weakly, when she asked him to attempt to open and close his large fist. She was fearful that her hands would be trembling and she wouldn't find a vein, even though she had never missed with Konoe Akira. She leaned over and kissed him on the forehead. '*Dank u, skatterbol*,' he said quietly.

'I wish you the Sublime Fourth Experience, Papa,' she said softly as she found the vein and drew up a small amount of blood before pushing the plunger home. Anna waited the short period it took for his breathing to become ragged and cease.

Her entire previous world was now gone. Anna had never felt more completely abandoned and alone. She was very, very tired; much too exhausted to weep for her father or even for herself.

She set the Japanese alarm clock beside her bed for 7 a.m. and collapsed into bed dry-eyed and almost beyond exhaustion. She wakened, seemingly minutes later, to its cheap clattering ring. It was late summer, but the early-morning tropical sun was still sufficiently hot at this time of the year and she knew she ought not keep her father's body in the house for long. She must find Til, give him the money he would need, then ask him to take care of the funeral arrangements. Unlike Katerina, her stepmother, Piet Van Heerden would have a burial site and a tombstone, even though there would be no one but herself to weep at his grave – although Anna wasn't sure she had any tears left.

She didn't know if there was a *dominee* left in Tjilatjap who could conduct a service and burial, but thought she might persuade one of the padres in the internment camps to conduct the funeral. Perhaps it could be a repayment on behalf of the six hundred Dutch women, old men and young children imprisoned in the concentration camp who, one day each week, experienced 'Anna's Day'. This was the name Ratih had given the soup kitchen which she still ran at Anna's expense. Anna had persuaded the Japanese colonel to allow a hundred people from the camp to come to Ratih's *kampong* to be fed each day. It meant that each of the six hundred prisoners received a square meal once a week.

The soup kitchen supplemented the miserable diet deliberately imposed on them out of sheer bastardry by the

Japanese guards, even though food was plentiful locally and available reasonably cheaply. When Anna had attempted to persuade Konoe Akira to allow Ratih to take over the purchase and the preparation of food for the concentration camp at the same cost to the Japanese, he had refused. 'It is not official policy to feed prisoners well,' he had replied, then added, 'You already indulge them once a week, that is enough.'

Anna, despite feeling tired, felt she needed to walk to get away from the house and breathe fresh air, so she started out to cover the one and a half kilometres to Ratih's. She found Til having breakfast with Ratih and he readily agreed to take care of the burial arrangements.

'Anna, I will send Kiki to clean the house afterwards,' Ratih added.

Anna knew that by the time she arrived home from lunch with the colonel, the body of her father would have been removed to a mortuary, the coffin purchased at a bargain price from a friend of Til, a place in the Dutch cemetery would have been secured and the gravediggers already at work turning the clods and digging down into the subsoil. Moreover the sheets would have been boiled and hung out to dry, the mattress on her father's bed disinfected and aired, the house would be spotless and Kiki would be beaming, delighted to be allowed back.

At lunch Anna mentioned her father's death to Konoe Akira, who surprised her by showing concern. 'Where is he to be buried and when?' he asked, then, 'Will you be alone?'

'Til, my friend the *becak* owner, will also attend, *Konoe-san*,' Anna replied.

'Humph!' He thought for a moment. 'I will attend,' he said decisively. 'Let me know when and where it is to take place.'

Anna was horrified. 'But *Konoe-san*, you must not be seen

with me in public!' she protested, then for emphasis added, 'It is against your own rules to be seen fraternising with the local population!' The thought of the Japanese colonel attending Piet Van Heerden's funeral was simply too bizarre to contemplate.

'Ha! We will reveal him as having been our greatest collaborator and bury him with full military honours,' the Japanese officer announced. 'It will account for his not having been incarcerated or sent to Burma, and for your freedom from the Nest of the Swallows.' He smiled. 'A neat solution and one that will ensure you are not alone,' he said, pleased with himself.

Ratih, with Kiki and Budi and, of course, Til, insisted on attending the burial despite Anna's protests that it was not a good idea for them to be seen by the *kempeitai* to be associated with her. The lieutenant also attended, along with the police superintendent and the Mayor of the Squashed Hat and a dozen wearers of the Poached Egg armbands, who represented the local citizenry. The mayor, Onishi Tokuma, wearing full morning dress and his oversized top hat, delivered a hastily composed eulogy to Piet Van Heerden in Javanese. In it he praised the many dangerous exploits (while naming none) performed by the secret agent in the cause of freedom and liberation from the Dutch and named him a man of both conscience and great personal courage, who would always live in the memory of a grateful people.

And so it came about that Piet Van Heerden was given full military honours at his funeral, with a Japanese honour guard in attendance as well as the battalion band playing the Japanese national anthem. The locals henceforth treated Anna with a newfound respect. Furthermore, whereas the women in the concentration camp were forced to bow when a Japanese soldier passed, the soldiers now bowed as Anna passed them. Piet Van

Heerden was regarded as a hero finally.

Anna waited until the brouhaha had died down and two months later placed a tombstone on his grave, carved, of course, by Til's friend, at a special bargain price. On it she had caused to be inscribed:

Pietrus Johannes Van Heerden
1899–1943
Gone to New Zealand

The war continued for another year and a half, and around May 1945, while there were rumours that Germany had surrendered, there was no admission by the Japanese authorities that this was the case. The Japanese high command in Tokyo took great care to keep their troops largely uninformed about the general state of the war in the Pacific region, boasting of the successes while remaining silent about reversals. Japanese propaganda even proclaimed ongoing victories in Java and Sumatra – where there was no action and absolutely no resistance movement. Konoe Akira might have heard one or two rumours, but he would have had no notion that the first defeats for the all-conquering Japanese forces came in May 1942 with the Battle of the Coral Sea, then in June of that same year where, in the Battle of Midway, the Japanese navy lost four aircraft carriers and hundreds of their best and most experienced pilots. From that point on, the Japanese were no longer able to control the Pacific since, despite several tactical successes, their offensive capacity was crippled. In August the Americans landed on Guadalcanal, and the battle against the Australians for the Kokoda Track was reaching its climax. By November the Japanese forces were in retreat. By early 1943 the Japanese were fighting a series of defensive battles on the islands they occupied, Java and Sumatra being the exception. Towards the end of the next year they were under constant attack by air, and the American landings in the Pacific and the Philippines together with that of the Allies in Burma followed in early 1945, leaving the mainland of Japan to face the prospect of invasion.

It must seem improbable, but the command in Java actually knew very little about the true state of the war, and the local people knew even less. One of the first things the Japanese had done when they'd arrived in 1942 was to order that all private radio sets be handed in to the military. It was a severe offence to be in possession of a radio and anyone who was caught with one was accused of being an enemy spy. The punishment for being an enemy collaborator was well known and usually ended with a severed head on a bamboo pole being displayed in the town square.

This ban effectively prevented the locals and the Dutch in the concentration camp from hearing any Allied broadcasts. There was a dawning realisation amongst many of the more thinking locals that the initial promise of their own independence as a nation by the Japanese was very slow in eventuating. Some locals privately admitted to themselves that the Japanese, if anything, were more arbitrary in their authority than ever the Dutch had been, and that the oil reserves in Java, Sumatra and elsewhere in the former Netherlands East Indies were a more immediate priority to the Japanese than the advent of nationalism. Resentment was beginning to percolate among the middle class. If nationhood was ever to come to Java and Sumatra, it seemed increasingly unlikely that it would come about as a recognition of the will of the majority of the people, or as a result of any mandate from the Japanese. There was a growing realisation that their 'liberator' had a different agenda; one that was no less self-serving than that of the Dutch. It began to be acknowledged that if ever the Japanese kept their promise of self-government for the Javanese people, it would be because they no longer saw any advantage in maintaining control of the island. As long as the oil reserves lasted, it appeared to be highly unlikely that the Japanese control would be relinquished.

The Japanese war machine was stretched to its limits. Oil was the lifeblood of its Pacific domination; not to control its source was unthinkable. There were would-be leaders among the local population who, having helped to see off the Dutch, were now beginning to speculate that living under Japanese control might well be a case of 'out of the frying pan, into the fire'.

The leader of the Indonesian Nationalist Party was forty-three-year-old Ahmed Sukarno who, at one stage of his life, had been jailed by the Dutch in 1929 as a threat to public order. At the onset of the 'liberation' he'd cooperated completely with the Japanese and his party members worked with the Nippon forces, considering it a matter of prestige. But Sukarno now began to realise that the hand he'd shaken in welcome had turned into a fist that threatened to keep him down. He began to see clearly that, for as long as the Japanese were in a situation to win the Pacific War, there was very little prospect of nationhood. In July 1945 Sukarno, who was clandestinely listening to secret Allied broadcasts, sat balanced on a very wobbly fence, waiting to see which way to jump.

Budi graduated from high school and Anna gave Ratih sufficient money for him to attend university whenever that institution reopened. Ratih proved to be a good businesswoman and her restaurant prospered. Kiki became a fully qualified cook and opened a second *kampong* restaurant for Ratih in a different *kampong* where Anna purchased a small house for her. The lieutenant was promoted to captain, and Anna persuaded the colonel to allow an army driving instructor to teach Til to drive. She promised Til that whenever a good motorcar became available – a rare occurrence – she would buy it for him as the first taxi in what would assuredly, if it was the will of Allah, become 'Til's Taxi-car Fleet'. As for Anna, life with Konoe Akira changed little, as by her presence and ministrations she continued to attempt to assuage the demons within him.

And then, on a mild tropical winter's day in early July 1945, Anna's life with the Japanese colonel came to an abrupt end.

With lunch completed and after going through the usual motions of lighting his cigarette, Konoe Akira leaned back and announced that he would be returning to Japan to take up a post at the Japanese Military Academy. 'I must do my duty, Second Vase. I am not permitted to disobey this order. As I have been promoted to the rank of Major General it is also a great honour for my family.' He paused and Anna could see that he was struggling with his emotions. 'Nevertheless, this is the saddest day of my life.' It was as close as Konoe Akira had ever come to declaring his love for her.

Anna tried unsuccessfully to control her own emotions. She did not think she was in love with the Japanese colonel in a romantic sense, but she had bonded with him completely. If she had been questioned, she would have readily agreed she cared for him. She knew she would greatly miss him in her life since she was fully aware that, without his presence, her life would change completely. Now she sobbed softly. 'When? When will you go, *Konoe-san*?'

'In three days. I will go by boat to Singapore and then fly by military aeroplane to Tokyo.'

'Has this been our last lunch?' Anna asked tremulously.

'Tomorrow, then the final evening as well. You will please wear the yellow kimono in the evening. Alas, it is the dry season and there are no frangipani blossoms. You wore one on the first day that you came for lunch.' He sighed. 'Ah, Second Vase, these days with you will be good memories to take with me.' Konoe Akira rose in the usual way and Anna stood and waited for him. He bowed. 'Ho!'

Anna bowed formally. 'I am deeply grateful to you, *Konoe-san*.'

To her surprise he didn't turn in his usual abrupt manner and limp off, but seemed to hesitate and then with his expression unchanged, pronounced the Javanese words '*Mugi-mugi diberkati* [My blessings upon you]'. Such was her surprise that Anna's eyebrows shot up and she looked at him open-mouthed. He smiled, almost mischievously, changing back to speaking Japanese. 'When we have taken lunch tomorrow you will stay a further part of the afternoon. I wish to walk in the garden one last time and I have a small gift for you.' He looked directly at Anna. 'Do you remember the second vase I had arranged for the second lunch we had together?'

'Yes, *Konoe-san*, the one with lots of different-coloured dahlias. I am named for it.'

'Yes, that is correct. Do you recall what you said when I asked your opinion of my arrangement?'

'No, *Konoe-san*, it happened three years ago,' Anna confessed.

'You said: "The arrangement is too formal, too perfect. These flowers, they want to dance and you are making them stand to attention. They are not an orchestra, they are a jazz group."' He cleared his throat. 'Tomorrow I would like you to come to lunch in a sarong and sandals. I want to see you as I did the first day you came to me – afraid, but still wild and courageous and . . . wonderful. You were and still are the second vase brought to perfection. At the time, I was too arrogant to understand.' He drew breath. 'Now I think I do.' Then he turned in his usual abrupt manner and limped away.

Anna bowed, as she always did, to his stiffly held departing back. 'Thank you, *Konoe-san*,' she said, smiling.

The following day, Anna arrived a little later as she had no need to change into a kimono. Til, sensing that she was preoccupied, pedalled in silence. He had become accustomed to Anna sharing her concerns with him and when they arrived at the brewer's mansion he asked, 'Anna, is there something wrong?'

'No, Til, something has ended in my life. I am very afraid of the new beginning, that is all.'

Til was sensitive enough not to invent an Allah quote on the spot. 'That is sad, Anna,' he said caringly. Anna informed him that he might have to wait well into the afternoon for her return. Til smiled, and in an attempt to lighten her mood, said, 'I am growing fat and lazy in this job, Anna. There was a time when waiting around cost me money; now I am paid for sleeping in the shade of a poinciana tree.' He shrugged. 'How can I complain? I would wait my whole life for you. *Allah akbar!*

[God is good!]'

Anna realised that while she cared deeply for Konoe Akira, she cared just as deeply for the little barefooted *becak* owner. One man possessed power, the other decency. One was consumed by his personal demons, the other was confident that he was held in the outstretched hand of a benign God. One had a stiff knee above polished jackboots, the other a big toe on a bare foot that turned out at right angles.

Anna wore her prettiest sarong, a deep-blue blouse and in her hair an exotic orchid that she had purchased that morning in the markets. It lacked the simplicity of the frangipani but she saw its several extravagant colours as a metaphor for the second vase.

The lunch session proceeded as usual. Konoe Akira made no mention of Anna's sarong and blouse and simple sandals, except for a gruff 'Humph!' that followed immediately after his initial 'Ho!' Anna took this as a sign, in this particular instance, of his approval. He seated himself and took out his silver cigarette case for his pre-lunch cigarette, but when he opened it Anna noticed that it contained only two cigarettes. This was highly unusual as the case was always meticulously organised, like everything else in his life, with the slim white, tobacco-filled tubes lined up in perfect formation, without a gap in their ranks. It was, she concluded, a small sign that his imminent departure was affecting him.

However, after lunch, when he'd smoked his mandatory second cigarette which was the last in the slim, silver case, he pushed the case across the table towards Anna. 'You will please accept this humble token of my esteem, Second Vase,' he said gruffly.

Anna picked it up and saw that above his name, which was

engraved in Japanese on the lid, was a line in Javanese: *Nyuwun pamit ratu* [Goodbye, Princess]. Anna, close to tears, smiled. 'Thank you, *Konoe-san*. I shall cherish it for the remainder of my life.' Then bringing both hands to her face she wiped her sudden tears away with the tips of her fingers. 'Honourable *Konoe-san*, I too have a gift for you.' With this she reached down to her bag and withdrew a small black box, neatly tied with a narrow blue ribbon. Ribbon was another of the taken-for-granted things that were now no longer available, so Anna had removed a narrow satin ribbon that had been laced through one of the puffed sleeves of a favourite blouse. She removed the orchid from her hair and inserted it under the ribbon tie, then stood and bowed, holding the box in both hands in the Japanese manner. 'It belonged to my grandfather. I would be honoured if you would accept it as a token of my esteem, *Konoe-san*,' Anna said, proffering the gift.

The Japanese officer's expression was a mixture of pleased surprise and amusement as he accepted her gift, thinking it was probably some small keepsake purchased at the markets. Removing the orchid he placed it on the table, weighing the unopened box in his hand. 'It is heavy,' he remarked, smiling at her. Pulling one end of the satin bow he lifted the lid, whereupon a look of astonishment momentarily crossed his face. He didn't look up at the still standing Anna, but instead, as he attempted to recover his composure, reached in and removed the gold pocket watch and chain. Finally he looked up. 'I am not worthy of such a truly valuable gift, Second Vase,' he said quietly. 'I will treasure it and keep it always with me, and each time I wind it I will be reminded that perfection is not simply one colour highlighted by white.' Anna was now seeing an aspect of the colonel she had only glimpsed once or twice before, though at those times she had been unsure that she wasn't simply imagining a softness that might lie behind the hard military exterior.

Later, as they walked silently through the immaculately groomed tropical garden – too fastidious for Anna's liking, although she did not say so – Konoe Akira suddenly remarked, 'I shall miss this garden, this sense of space, its verdancy. Now I must return to a Japanese garden. I wonder if I will henceforth regard that form as perfect? Often such a garden will contain a single bloom, while in this one they are beyond number.'

'Is it not usually a yellow chrysanthemum in a Japanese garden?' Anna asked, remembering what I had told her about Japan.

'Not always, but often,' he replied. 'It is our national flower and the throne from which the Emperor rules is known as the Chrysanthemum Throne. To grow a yellow chrysanthemum is a sign of devotion to the Emperor.'

'I don't suppose anyone will ever rule from a dahlia throne,' Anna laughed.

They had reached a shady corner of the garden when Konoe Akira stopped and pointed to a slender sapling, no more than a metre high. 'This is a persimmon tree, now three years old. With luck it will live to be one hundred years. I have planted one of these wherever I have found myself. I was a small child when instructed to do so by my esteemed and venerable grandmother.'

'The heartwood,' Anna said, remembering the chopsticks and the colonel's description of the persimmon tree at the time.

Konoe Akira looked amused. 'Yesterday I asked if you remembered what you had said to me about the second vase I arranged on your second day to lunch and you replied that you did not. Now you remember the story of the heartwood from your first day?'

Anna blushed. 'It would have been an impertinence to recall my own words, *Konoe-san*. I was honoured that you did so.'

'Your metaphor of orchestral performers and those who play jazz music was a worthy one. For me, the persimmon tree is just such a metaphor for life. It has many metaphors.' Anna remained silent as he explained. 'The outside wood, which is very beautiful, has several characteristics. It is strong, but has the capacity to absorb shock and if it strikes a hard surface it will not splinter. This is the metaphor of resilience. Then, when its trunk is light and smooth it is young, but when it grows older it is veined with purple. This is the metaphor of youth growing into maturity with calm and dignity. In the summer, its leaves are arched and overlap to provide shade for others: animals, birds and humans who labour in the field. This is the metaphor of caring about all creatures and helping others. In the autumn, the leaves drop and the fruit ripens; they are fiery red balls the size of my fist and hang like glorious lanterns from the tree. This is the metaphor of passing on the sweet fruit of life, its joy and tenderness, because, before it is eaten, the fruit must be soft beyond a softness that any other fruit can endure without corruption.'

Konoe Akira paused. 'I have already spoken of the metaphor of the centre, of the heartwood, more resilient than steel, the core that cannot be defeated. These are the metaphors: the core, beyond strength of will; the resilience of the outer wood that will not splinter but always keeps to its resolve; the leaves that, in providing shelter, consider the convenience of others beside themselves; finally, the ripened fulfilment, when the autumn of life comes and with it the soft fruitfulness of wisdom and love to be passed on.' He reached into the pocket of his military tunic and withdrew a tiny envelope. 'In here are eighty seeds of the persimmon tree, Second Vase. Plant one seed every year of your life. May you live to plant the last seed when you reach one hundred. In all things, may your heart be as soft and sweet and generous as the fruit of the sacred persimmon tree, your body as resilient as the outer wood, and your mind as strong as its heartwood.' He turned and bowed. 'Ho! I shall see you tonight at eight o'clock.'

It was the 5th of July 1945 when Anna was the one who was now left, waving a tearful farewell at the dockside as Major General Konoe Akira stood at the rail of a Japanese destroyer and waved. The battalion band started to play, and on a platform in front of the battalion on the docks Captain Takahashi, now Colonel, formerly of the *kempeitai*, called the battalion to attention and then gave the final salute to the departing commander.

Konoe Akira stood rigidly to attention to take the salute, but as the destroyer weighed anchor she watched him lift his left hand above his shoulders. The last thing Anna saw as the Japanese navy ship pulled away from the shore and turned its nose into the river was a string of late-afternoon sunlight as it caught the lid of the gold watch he held up by its chain. Anna knew then that the salute was not only to his former battalion, but was intended for her as well.

She knew also that she had helped to assuage his demons. On the previous night, when she had worn the yellow kimono for the last time, he had instructed her to put away the *kinbaku* ropes. 'It is over, Second Vase, the guilt has lessened, perhaps even gone,' he said quietly. 'Let us drink tea and talk.' It was the first time after nightfall that he had referred to her as Second Vase.

Anna was arrested by the *kempeitai* at dawn the following morning when a detachment of a sergeant and five *kempeitai* soldiers carrying rifles broke down the front door. She was still in bed when she heard the shouts and then the door being smashed. Jumping from her bed she rushed from the bedroom, then screamed as the door, torn from its hinges, crashed to the floor and the *kempeitai* burst in.

The stocky sergeant grinned at the sight of Anna standing in her flimsy nightdress, his smile displaying that one of his front teeth was capped in gold. Then, assuming Anna didn't speak Japanese, he held up both hands to indicate the number ten, then tapped his wristwatch and with a sweep of the arm indicated that she had ten minutes before they would leave with her as their prisoner.

Sobbing softly, she dressed, then took the box that contained the Clipper butterfly, wrapped the six pieces of the butterfly ashtray in a soft cloth and placed them in a large cotton bag along with several sarongs, blouses, undies and a spare pair of sandals. As an afterthought she also packed the three remaining ampoules of morphine and the syringe the Japanese doctor had given her, then finally her few toiletries. She placed the silver hairbrush and cigarette case Konoe Akira had given her in the shoulder bag, then quickly inserted the cartridge case containing the diamonds in the predestined place and hid the two-hundred guilders she had nearby in her bra, leaving the twenty or so and some loose change in her purse.

The *kempeitai* soldiers and the sergeant, apart from his initial lewd gold-toothed leer, had been respectful and had allowed her to pack her things without supervision, but after ten minutes he reappeared at the bedroom door and tapped his watch and, with a jerk of his head toward the verandah, indicated her time was up.

Anna, carrying the cotton bag and with her dishtowel bag slung over her shoulder, walked out of the bedroom onto the *stoep*, where the soldiers waited. Unaware that Anna spoke Japanese, the sergeant instructed them: 'Move the bitch out! Do not harm her or there will be trouble from higher up. Hurry! We must be gone from here before the town wakes!'

In a well-drilled and accustomed manner, four *kempeitai* took positions around Anna. One stood on either side of her, another was in front and yet another directly behind her. The fifth reached out and took the cotton bag, whereupon the sergeant instructed him to go ahead and stow the bag and open the back door of the American car. He pointed to the *kempeitai* soldiers standing on either side of her. 'Sit the She-devil in the back seat in the centre; one of you sit on either side of her and restrain her if she struggles, but do not harm her or mark her or there will be the sort of trouble you wouldn't wish on a money lender.'

'Should she not have handcuffs, Sergeant?' one of the soldiers asked.

'No, they may bruise her wrists! She must be perfect. Those are our orders.'

The soldiers, who were standing at ease with their rifle butts on the floor, were called to attention by the sergeant and made ready to march her off.

Apart from the scream when witnessing the soldiers bursting through the front door and sobbing for the first few minutes as she frantically packed, Anna had remained silent throughout the ordeal. Now the sergeant ordered his men to march and she was effectively taken prisoner in a routine the *kempeitai* detachment was obviously accustomed to performing.

They marched down the brick-edged front path to the gate, and that was when Anna saw it. Spiked to a bamboo pole by the side of the front gate was Til's severed head, his eyes still open and seeming to be looking at her.

Anna screamed and collapsed to her knees so that the *kempeitai* soldier who was marching behind her knocked into her, causing her to sprawl forward onto her face and graze her chin on the gravel, her bag falling from her shoulders. 'You idiot!' she heard the sergeant shout at the soldier a moment before her head filled with a terrible roaring sound that she was unaware came from her own chest and throat. She sprang to her feet and then turning, bodily lifted the *kempeitai* soldier who had inadvertently bumped into her, and threw him into the gate, his rifle clattering on the path at Anna's feet. Anna bent down, picked it up by the barrel and swung it up from the ground to catch the sergeant with the rifle butt on the side of the jaw, knocking him backwards where he crashed to the path unconscious.

The two soldiers on either side of her, taken completely by surprise and with orders not to harm her, hesitated. Anna swung wildly at the soldier on her right so that the rifle butt caught him across the ribs, knocking him from his feet and severely winding him, his rifle flying from his hands. He lay on his back clutching his side and trying to regain his breath.

The second soldier at her side finally came to his wits, dropped his rifle and tackled her to the ground, his body pressing her down, his breath hot against her face. Anna screamed, and raising her head, bit through his earlobe. He jumped to his feet in alarm, clutching at his ear. The fourth soldier now fell upon her, but Anna managed to get her knee up hard into his groin and he howled in sudden pain, clutching his manhood and rolling away.

Then the soldier whom she'd hurled into the gate came running and flung himself upon her, blood streaming down the side of his head and into his eye from the deep gash on his forehead where he'd crashed into the wrought-iron gate. The blood pouring from his eye began to soak Anna's white blouse as he grimly hung on to her struggling form.

The fifth *kempeitai*, the one who'd carried her cotton bag, came running from the car and kicked out at her, his boot planted squarely into her right upper thigh. The soldier she'd kicked in the groin had partly recovered and while two of them held her down the *kempeitai* who had kicked her managed to put her wrists in handcuffs and the two soldiers moved away from her.

Snarling and spitting, Anna refused to stand up and so the soldier with the groin injury and the unhurt kicker took her by the shoulder and dragged her along the path, scraping her knees on the gravel. They finally reached the big American Chevrolet and threw her into the back seat, where she commenced to howl. At last, this was something the *kempeitai* understood – a victim crying. The two soldiers looked relieved as one sat on either side of her in the back seat. One of them, cupping both hands over his groin, groaned, 'The bitch kneed me in the balls!'

The soldier who'd kicked her, still panting from the effort of dragging Anna and the only one among them without an injury, snorted. 'You'll be lucky if that's *all* that happens to you, brother! We are all in deep shit. Colonel *Takahashi-san* wanted the woman delivered to the Nest of the Swallows without a mark on her. The sergeant told me that the *colonel-san* left express orders that if she possessed even a scratch after being apprehended we would all pay dearly.'

'But it was her or us!' the second soldier protested. 'We can explain.'

'Sure! Five of us armed to the teeth with rifles and with a sergeant in command against an unarmed woman. Nice going – wait until the barracks hears about this!'

'What could we do? We couldn't shoot her like we would anyone else resisting arrest,' the second *kempeitai* complained morosely, massaging his gonads.

The uninjured soldier, obviously possessed of slightly more intelligence than the others, glanced out of the window and down the garden path. 'And who is going to drive the automobile?' he asked. 'I can't drive, none of us can, only the sergeant. He's still out like a light. Maybe she killed him? Not a bad thing, he's a bastard. Look at those three others, they're sitting down like wounded soldiers in a battle waiting for the ambulance to arrive.'

'Speak for yourself, they *are* wounded. The bitch is dangerous,' the injured groin answered.

The Japanese sergeant was beginning to come around; still dazed, he held out his hand to be assisted to his feet. The soldier who had taken a blow in the ribs with the second swipe from the rifle butt, grasping his left side and using his right hand, attempted to pull him to his feet. Halfway up, a sudden excruciating stab of pain through his ribs caused him to slacken and then lose his grip, and the sergeant, unable to maintain his balance, fell backwards. He knocked his head on the sharp pitch of an angled brick in the row that lined the garden path, and lay unconscious for the second time in five minutes.

The soldier with the missing earlobe sat on the uncut grass beyond the path with his head between his legs, blood oozing through his fingers.

The *kempeitai* who had been hurled against the gate and who'd bloodied her blouse sat on the opposite side of the pathway. The blood streamed down his neck from the deep gash above his eye and was beginning to form a dark patch on the shoulder of his khaki uniform.

It was only then that a distraught and sobbing Anna found her voice. '*Kisama! Kusokurae! Yarichin! Sensuri koitero! Kusottare!* [Lords of the donkeys who eat shit! Male sluts! Thousand-stroke masturbators! Arseholes!] You killed my friend! You killed my beloved Til! *Teme-konoyaro!* [You dogs!]' she screamed in Japanese to the open-mouthed astonishment of the two men seated on either side of her.

Anna burst into fresh cries of anguish. Her darling, beloved Til had been killed, needlessly, wantonly, and it could only be because of his involvement with her.

As is inevitable, an early-morning crowd began to gather and just as inevitably, one old man, up early in his village to take four trussed chickens to the markets, had seen the whole thing and now, self-importantly, explained to the other onlookers what had occurred. Unexpectedly thrust into the limelight, he told how a young Javanese woman, who would now surely be beheaded, had single-handedly and without a weapon resisted arrest by five *kempeitai* and a sergeant, leaving them injured and sprawling in the dust to lick their wounds.

A woman, seeing Anna seated between the two *kempeitai*

in the big American car, the front of her blouse covered in blood, recognised her. 'She is the daughter of a great liberator, the Dutchman Piet Van Heerden, who risked his life for the Javanese people and for our independence from the Dutch,' she announced, then added, 'My brother, who is a gravedigger, says the Japanese gave him a funeral where the mayor spoke of his brave deeds and the soldier band played and they fired bullets in the air. The Japanese commandant was also there.'

'The daughter has the bravery of the father,' a second woman amongst the onlookers declared, to the serious nods of agreement from the small but growing crowd.

From such beginnings legends are made and myths begun. The local people, from the very start, had hated the arrogant and cruel *kempeitai*, and were growing more and more disenchanted with the Japanese who had promised them independence that, after three years, looked no nearer than when the Dutch occupied their homeland. They were certain that, like Til, Anna would be *bamboo'd* (a local expression), but she had nonetheless given them a great heroic story – here was a mere slip of a girl who, unarmed and furious, had stood up to the hated Japanese *Pak Polisi* and had single-handedly given them a severe beating.

The locals would not soon forget or forgive the brutal beheading of Til. He was a good Muslim, liked and respected in the mosque and town, and especially in the markets, where he had seemed to know everyone. He was also known to be Anna's friend. The terrible and wanton killing of a man who daily, and always wisely, quoted from the Koran and seemed on easy terms with the Prophet and even God Himself was a further tragedy the locals would add to the future telling of the story of 'Anna and the Japanese *Pak Polisi*'.

By this time several of the local police from the *kampong*

had arrived, some still tucking in their shirts. Finally a driver was found amongst them, and the unwounded and wounded *kempeitai*, in various states of physical condition, were transported back to their barracks. There, a *kempeitai* lieutenant, beside himself with fury when he saw the bloodstained and injured Anna, had all the men arrested. Without further ado he ordered the local police driver to vacate the Chevrolet, giving only the briefest acknowledgment for his services, and replaced him with a *kempeitai* driver. With the lieutenant in the front seat beside the driver, Anna, still handcuffed, was summarily transported to the Nest of the Swallows.

It was later discovered that the sergeant had a broken jaw, his four front teeth (including the gold one) were missing, and a severe wound to the back of his head from the point of the sharply angled brick had caused him to become concussed. One soldier had five broken ribs, another now possessed only half an ear and the one with the gash above his eye required twenty-seven stitches and would be left with a purple scar he would wear instead of an eyebrow for the remainder of his life. The soldier with the bruised gonads recovered in a few days without further medication and the unhurt *kempeitai* private was promoted to lance corporal, while the sergeant was demoted to private and sentenced to three months in military detention with hard labour. All the others were beaten and sentenced to two weeks' confinement to barracks.

Anna was bleeding from the side of her face, the skin covering her cheekbone was scraped raw, her left eye was beginning to close, both her knees oozed blood, and her inner thigh, where she had been kicked, ached and later an ugly bruise would form and spread down her thigh and almost to her knee.

The car arrived at a small gatehouse (now used as a

guardhouse) that was situated at a boom gate that must have replaced the original gates. Two guards stood at attention and saluted as the car drew up. Seeing the *kempeitai* officer in the front seat, one of them hurried to raise the boom. The car entered the grounds of a very large mansion that was completely surrounded by a brick wall about three metres high and topped with barbed wire. The Nest of the Swallows was obviously well guarded. They drove up a gravel driveway and Anna briefly wondered if she or any of the working girls would be allowed to walk in the spacious gardens that seemed large enough to be called a park.

At the front of the mansion the young lieutenant, aide-de-camp to Colonel Takahashi and himself *kempeitai*, who hadn't spoken a word during the journey, left the handcuffed Anna in the car under the care of the *kempeitai* driver and hurried up the steps.

He must have specifically demanded to see one of the two *okami-san* who had instructed Anna in *kinbaku* at the brewer's mansion, because the desk clerk went to fetch Izumi, the second *okami-san*, even though she wasn't on duty that day.

Izumi would later relate the conversation Lieutenant Ito had with her in the reception area. She had begun by telling Anna how terrified she'd been when the soldier desk clerk had knocked on her bedroom door, then shouted, 'The *kempeitai* are waiting for you in reception! Come at once!'

Izumi proved to be a clever mimic and, with the trained memory of a geisha, recalled almost exactly the conversation with the *kempeitai* officer from the moment she arrived in reception.

'"What is it we can do for you, honourable *Lieutenant-san?*" I asked him, first bowing low and not looking him in the eye. I was trying to keep my knees from shaking, but was nevertheless relieved to see it was a lone officer without any dreaded *kempeitai* soldiers brought along to arrest me.

'"I have with me a young woman who has been injured. You are instructed to treat her injuries and under no circumstances is she to be made available for the duties of the *okiya*. Disobedience will lead to certain death. Do you understand, *mama-san*?"'

Izumi had laughed. 'That *kempeitai* pig should have known better – an *okami-san* is not a *mama-san*! It is an insult. But I wasn't going to correct him then and there, so I said, "Yes, *Lieutenant-san*, it is very well understood. We will look after her until she is well again." Then I asked, "Will you be sending a doctor?"' Izumi had paused. 'Of course, at that stage I didn't know it was you, Anna.

'The lieutenant replied, "You will call me if she needs one. Her presence must be kept secret and she must be kept away from the *benjo onna*."'

'*Benjo onna*?' Anna had asked.

'It means "toilet girls". In other words, the girl is available to any man to do his business and leave,' Izumi had explained.

'That's horrible!' Anna exclaimed.

Izumi had shrugged. 'It is a nasty term used by people who are not nice, Anna. Then I asked him, "Is she to be prepared for a special purpose?"'

'"She must be without blemish. That is all you need to know, *mama-san*!" he replied. "I will come twice a week to inspect her until I am satisfied she does not have a single mark. Not a single one! You will call me at military headquarters at once if anything goes wrong."

'"Who will I ask for, *Lieutenant-san*?"' Izumi looked at Anna. 'The arrogant shit hadn't bothered to introduce himself so I was forced to ask.

'"My name is Lieutenant Ito. Ask for me and do not speak to anyone else!"

'Then he asked me, "Do you have a room that has a private entrance from outside?"

'"There is one to the side of the house; it leads to a small private garden and can be reached by going around the side of the house from the back," I told him.

'"I will inspect it to see if it is appropriate. She is to be prepared for the highest there is amongst us, someone who does not wish to visit the main *okiya*."

'It wasn't hard to guess who the patron was. That Ito must think we are all stupid!' Izumi exclaimed. 'So I said, "Yes, of course. I will take you to it, *Lieutenant-san*."

'"Do you have the key with you, *mama-san*?"

'"I can fetch it, *Lieutenant-san*. It is kept in the kitchen for the cleaners."' Izumi had paused, taking a deep breath. 'Well, by this time I'd decided I'd had enough of the *mama-san* business, and he was *only* a lieutenant. After all, a geisha must maintain her dignity and her status, even if she has later become an *okami-san*. And so I said to him as sharply as I thought I could, "It is my humble request that you address me as *okami-san*, Lieutenant Ito."

'"Very well," he sniffed, and from the way he looked at me I could see he didn't like my rebuke but had decided to ignore it. "Can we drive an automobile to this private garden?" he asked.

'"No," I replied. "You can bring the motorcar to the back, then it is a short walk to the side of the house."

'"Meet me there. I will wait ten minutes so you can clear the way. I don't want any onlookers. Bring a towel so that we can cover her head."

'I fetched a towel and hurried to the back. The two Korean discipline women were in the laundry, so I sent them to their room.'

'Korean discipline women?' Anna asked.

'They are lesbians. If there are problems with one of the comfort women they are called in. They are not nice, *Anna-san*.'

Anna was not sure she understood. 'Lesbians?'

'They do not love men but make sex with each other instead,' Izumi explained in a disgusted tone.

'Really?' Anna cried out, astonished.

'You don't want to know, *Anna-san*,' Izumi had declared with a dismissive flap of the hand. 'They are brutes.' Then putting the discipline women from her mind, she'd continued: 'Can you imagine my surprise when the car stopped at the back of the house and I saw it was you, *Anna-san*? I wanted to cry out because I could see you were hurt. But then I decided I should pretend not to know you, and to seem indifferent. I didn't, at that stage, know how much the lieutenant knew about our past association. Well, you know what happened after that.'

Indeed, Anna could remember every small detail. When the car drove up Lieutenant Ito jumped out and opened the back door, instructing Anna to remain seated. 'Bring the towel,' he called to the second *okami-san*. As she came up he pointed into the interior. 'Cover her head and face,' he instructed.

Anna could not conceal her surprise as she recognised the *okami-san* as Izumi. It was fortunate that the *okami-san*'s body blocked the lieutenant's view and he didn't see her startled expression. Izumi, in turn, gave no sign that she recognised her, but seeing Anna's bloodstained blouse she gasped. 'But she is badly hurt!' she cried out.

'It is not *her* blood!' the lieutenant snapped. 'Cover her head, then get her out.'

'She is handcuffed,' the second *okami-san* protested. 'With her head covered I must take her by the hand to get her out.'

Lieutenant Ito turned to the driver and instructed him to remove the handcuffs. Anna was immediately concerned it was a bad sign that Izumi had deliberately not recognised her. Not even a flicker of recognition had registered in the second *okami-san*'s eyes. Anna had got to know her well over the three months of her instruction with the ropes. She'd always enjoyed the retired geisha's company, her spontaneous giggle and thoroughly wicked sense of humour. It was she who had taught Anna the profanities Anna had used on the *kempeitai*. Now perhaps she was seeing another side of the woman she'd grown so much to like.

The second *okami-san* placed the towel over her head and face, then taking her by the hand and placing her free hand on the top of her head to prevent Anna bumping it against the edge of the door, helped her from the car.

'You will take care of this woman during the day. At night it will be the seventh *okami-san*, no other. Only you and she must know about this woman whom you already know. I will arrange with the proper authority for this to happen.'

'Yes, *Ito-san*. Myself and the seventh *okami-san* will be the only ones; we will take good care of her,' she said quickly. Anna's heart skipped a beat – was Izumi telling her she was still her friend?

The *kempeitai* officer instructed the driver to remove Anna's cotton bag and her shoulder bag from the car boot; the latter had been retrieved from the garden pathway where it had fallen from her shoulder when she'd dropped to her knees. 'Take me to this room,' the lieutenant demanded. 'I wish to see if it is suitable and secure.' He instructed the driver to bring Anna's things.

The four of them set off. Anna, limping and effectively blindfolded, held onto Izumi's hand. She was as anxious as anyone to keep her identity hidden from the Dutch girls who were forced to work in the Nest of the Swallows. She'd often speculated as to whether they knew about what, to them, might seem her privileged life as Konoe Akira's mistress. If they did, just how would they regard her? Was she in their minds a collaborator or, like them, a victim of their collective circumstance?

A short while later she heard Izumi beside her say, 'This gate is locked, it leads into a walled garden. I have the key.'

'Locked, that is good. Give me the key,' the lieutenant requested. Anna heard him tapping the gate. 'The wood is strong.'

Anna heard the creak of the gate as it was unlocked and opened. Led by Izumi, she felt the scrunch of gravel underfoot as they walked down a path.

'Careful, there are three steps,' Izumi cautioned. Anna was guided up the steps and asked to wait. She heard a door being unlocked and was led inside. 'May I remove the towel, *Ito-san*?' Izumi asked.

'No, I will inspect first,' the lieutenant replied. Then a short while later he said, 'It is suitable. I will take the key to the outside door. You will hear from me, *okami-san*, and you will obey my instructions.'

'Yes, *Lieutenant-san*, I understand. She will be treated with great care. It is an honour for myself and the seventh *okami-san* to be trusted with this task.'

Shortly after, Anna heard Izumi bidding the lieutenant farewell at the door, then came the rattle of the key as the door to the outside was locked and her footsteps as she returned. Then she heard Izumi say, '*Boko no shiri ni kisu siro, Ito! Kieusero!* [Kiss my arse, Ito! Fuck off!]'

Anna, laughing despite herself, removed the towel. '*Izumi-san*, that's rude!'

Izumi giggled and then her expression changed to one of concern. She pointed in turn to Anna's closed and swollen eye, scraped cheek and chin, knees and then to the bloodied blouse. The blood was now dry and had turned a paler colour, more a deep pink than the scarlet of fresh blood. '*Anna-san*, they have hurt you! Did those cruel *ketsu* [arseholes] torture you?'

Anna attempted a lopsided grin. 'No, I fought them, six of the *kisama* [lords of the donkeys] and I won.' She burst into sudden tears. 'They . . . they beheaded Til!' she sobbed.

Izumi, perhaps thinking a Javanese *becak* driver was not of great consequence in the overall scheme of things, waited for Anna to stop crying. 'You are fortunate they didn't kill you as well, *Anna-san*. I will fetch hot water and antiseptic. Except for your eye, which is already turning black, your wounds are superficial, but why do you limp?'

Anna explained her terrible anger and distress at the sight of Til's decapitated head and then the fight that ensued as she best recalled it.

'If you had not been intended for another purpose, they would have assuredly shot you,' Izumi said and then related her conversation with the *kempeitai* lieutenant, whom she referred to as *yarichin* (male slut). 'He has not yet visited the *okiya*, I think he is like 2nd Lieutenant Ando, only one is from a good family and a teacher, the other is a killer – pig swill from the gutters of Tokyo!' she spat. Then she left to fetch the hot water, iodine and ice.

Izumi returned a short while later and commenced to bathe Anna's wounds. She had brought ice and two squares of cotton cloth so that Anna could fold ice cubes into both and hold them against her eye and thigh. She worked carefully and in silence. After a while Anna said, 'I am frightened of Colonel Takahashi, *Izumi-san*. He is different to Colonel *Konoe-san*. I know in my heart he likes to kill. I saw it in his eyes when he decapitated the four Chinese.'

'He is *kempeitai*, he has done many more like that. They are recruited because they are born killers. They like the *katana*, the divine blade, but Takahashi, that is not a name from a samurai family,' Izumi said scornfully, which did little to comfort Anna. But then Izumi added, as if to reassure her, 'We must ask *Korin-san*. She will know what to do. You will recall how she told us there is no man on earth who has not got a secret perversion. All you have to do is find it to give you power over him.' Then, as if the matter was happily settled, she said, 'I will now put on the iodine. You must be brave, this is going to sting.'

The room had been left as it had been for the previous owners and was obviously a study that opened into a small, private walled garden. It contained a large desk and wooden swivel chair, a comfortable leather couch and club chair facing a coffee table. Two Persian carpets covered the floor and, except for two large barred windows looking out into the garden, the walls were lined with shelves filled with books.

'This room hasn't been converted to Japanese style,' Izumi explained. 'It is away from the other rooms and not suitable for entertainment because it must be entered by going through the kitchen or from the outside.'

'Am I to be locked up in this room all the time?' Anna asked fearfully. 'The windows are barred. Am I allowed to open them?'

'All the windows are barred. I think the engineers did it when they came to convert the house to the Nest of the Swallows. But you can slide them up to let in the fresh air.'

'It is the same as being in jail,' Anna protested.

Izumi looked sympathetically at Anna. 'I will ask *Korin-san* to let you use the private garden at night when you cannot be seen.'

'But the door is locked. He – the *kempeitai* – took the key.'

Izumi giggled. 'We have another one. I took the spare one off the ring when I came to the back.' She fished into her pocket and produced the key, then gave Anna a serious look. 'Please, *Anna-san*, do not attempt to escape and never go beyond the little gate. If you are seen in the grounds you will be shot. There is no escape from here. Nobody, except *Korin-san* and I, will know you are here. We will clean and bring you food; there is a toilet and bath.' She pointed to a door. 'It belongs only to this room. I think the person who worked in this study must have been very important to have a toilet and bath only for himself.'

Anna spent the next three weeks reading books and, at night, strolling in the small garden. She thought of the little *becak* owner constantly, and often found herself in tears, for she was certain that she was responsible for his death. But why? Had they tortured him and found out about the box? It seemed the only explanation. Who had beheaded him? The *katana* is an officer's weapon and only the officers are trained in the manner of a beheading. Was it Lieutenant Ito or Colonel Takahashi himself? These questions occupied her mind until she felt she would go insane.

Anna had been encouraged to sleep on a futon by *Korin-san* and was discovering that she much preferred it to the leather couch. Each night she would prepare it and place the Clipper butterfly box, the ashtray and the silver cigarette case beside her. The crystal ashtray, when its six pieces were fitted together, appeared undamaged. If she touched the butterfly at the centre carefully, the ashtray would remain intact. Anna knew it was silly but she saw both these objects as talismans. Each night she'd kiss the Clipper box and touch the butterfly. 'I love you, Nicholas,' she'd say, adding, 'Sleep well wherever you are, my darling.' Then she would touch the silver cigarette case. 'I will be like the heartwood, *Konoe-san*,' she would say.

Anna's healthy young body was healing fast and Lieutenant Ito came twice a week to check her progress. She was growing increasingly concerned over the impending visit of Colonel Takahashi. On the sixth occasion the lieutenant had arrived with the four silk kimonos Konoe Akira had caused the Mayor of the Squashed Hat to make for her. Handing them to Izumi, he'd instructed, 'The first time she must wear the yellow one and must be prepared in the same way as before with the yellow flower in her hair.'

'When will that be, *Ito-san*?' Izumi asked politely.

'When it is going to happen you will be given three hours' notice,' he replied. 'A suitable futon must be placed in the room and you will bring tea, that is all.'

Korin-san had not been able to help her, as Izumi had suggested she might, in preparing for the visit of Colonel Takahashi. '*Anna-san*, if he has a perversion then I don't know about it. He has never come here nor even requested my services at his home.'

'Then he will simply rape me,' Anna replied, frightened.

'He is *kempeitai* and anything is possible, but he is also a senior officer. He will not, I think, want to rape you; that would cause him loss of face. Unless rape is his perversion, he will want your compliance, *Anna-san*.'

'He cannot have it! I will never agree!' Anna cried.

Korin-san smiled. 'I think we have discussed this before, have we not?'

'I will mark myself, cut my face, then he will not have what he wants.'

Korin-san seemed to be thinking. 'If you mark yourself the *kempeitai* will ensure you have a horrible death, *Anna-san*. My advice would be the same as before. Kill yourself now while you may. It will be much the better way. *Izumi-san* and I will share our deaths with you. In Lieutenant Ito's eyes and those of the *colonel-san*, it will mean we have failed to watch over you and we will forfeit our lives. We are both old women and so it doesn't matter; our lives are over and I don't think we will ever see Japan again. But it would be a shame to destroy your young life. The entrance to the pearl is very resilient and not easily damaged. Soon enough your maidenhood will be taken. You cannot hold on to it forever. Perhaps it is time to be practical? To face life as it is?'

'Oh, *Korin-san*, I am pledged to another. It is a gift *only* he must have. I do not want to return to him as damaged goods!' Anna did not want to tell her that, in her mind, she believed she would survive as long as she remained a virgin. She knew that this was an irrational thought but she had become fixated on the idea.

Korin-san sighed. '*Anna-san*, there are thirty comfort women here in the *okiya*; all are beautiful. I am sure they too were pledged to another. If this war ever ends they will be damaged goods, not just a few times to one man, but many times over to many, many men. In the soldier's *okiya* some of the young comfort women who are not blessed with extreme beauty sometimes have to take thirty soldiers a day on their futon. You were fortunate to have had *Konoe-san*, who required other ways. But if *Takahashi-san* is not perverted and you please him, there are worse fates than the taking of the pearl. It will not be difficult for you to satisfy him if you try. The *kinbaku* ropes are only one way and if this way is not his, then I have taught you erotic massage and will show you other ways as well. If you don't please him you will certainly die. This is not a man like *Konoe-san* with a quick temper and a good heart; this one is rotten inside – he is a killer and will not tolerate disobedience.'

'But how can I accept willingly someone who may have killed Til? How can I welcome him to my futon?' Anna asked. 'I do not have the ability to smile and be compliant, to massage his vile body, to have the arms around me that may have gripped the *katana* that beheaded Til! How must I perform some of the other things you have taught me, when I know he has murdered a beautiful man whose only crime was that he knew me – that we were friends?'

'If you wish to live you will find a way. By killing your friend, that is the first lesson *Takahashi-san* is giving you in submission, in making sure you acquiesce to his demands, submit to his will,' *Korin-san* explained. 'The world is a hard place, *Anna-san*. It does not exist for any woman's convenience. The man's will comes first. But to survive is the victory, that is the triumph of the heart. Submission means you keep your life – he keeps his pride and his manhood; your heart remains your own – whereas resistance is inevitable death. Japanese men like the *colonel-san* cannot allow themselves to be defeated by a woman's refusal. He will know that you were *Konoe-san*'s mistress. He will also certainly know that the pearl remains intact. Now that he is the colonel he will want to demonstrate that what *Konoe-san* could not do, he can. In his mind this will make him the superior man.'

'But how would he know about Colonel *Konoe-san* and me?' Anna asked ingenuously.

Korin-san gave Anna a wry smile. 'It was not a relationship that was a very well-kept secret. He is *kempeitai* and they always have spies. No one is safe from them.' She grinned. 'They could have used me, or Izumi, or both as they are doing now, but at the time they may have been afraid we would alert *Konoe-san* as he was the commander and our loyalty was to him.'

'But . . . but how would he know that I remain a virgin? Who would tell him?'

'It's not so hard to work out. It was Yasuko, the mayor's wife! She would tell her husband and that snivelling little rat would go running to Colonel Takahashi in order to ingratiate himself with the new commander.'

'But she was my *friend*!' Anna protested.

'Ah, that is not our way. A Japanese woman's first loyalty is to her husband. He would have asked her and she would have been obliged to tell him everything. Did she not say her husband volunteered her services as housekeeper to *Konoe-san*? What better way to know what's going on in the colonel's private life, eh? I'll say this for the little bastard – he's a survivor. You could take a few lessons from him, *Anna-san*!' She looked sternly at her. 'I mean it. You don't have to snivel and you don't have to beg, but you *must* be compliant.'

'*Korin-san*, I am not a geisha, I have never been with a man!' Anna cried. 'I can't, I simply can't!' She wiped a tear from the corner of her eye with her forefinger.

Korin-san ignored Anna's protests. '*Anna-san*, listen to me, please! Give the *colonel-san* what he wants! I have shown you how this might be done physically. But you must also get into his head. Flatter him. Congratulate him on his appointment to commander. As you massage his body remark that it is a warrior's body, that at another time he would have been a samurai, you are certain of this. Then ask him to turn onto his back. If you have massaged him as you have been taught, he will have a fine stand. Do not put your hand around it but tap it very softly with the tips of your fingers from the top to the bottom and back. "Look how strong the divine sword is, *Takahashi-san*!" you will giggle. Then look suddenly shy and modest and ask in a soft voice if you may confide in him. Then when he says you may, as he most certainly will, then tell him he is a man far above Konoe *Akira-san*, the vile pervert who liked *kinbaku* and was incapable of pleasing a woman like the *real* man in front of you. Tell him that you had always hoped for a real man and not one who on the outside was powerful but on the inside a weakling who couldn't get it up. Tell him how you have waited for a man like him to accept the precious pearl. That you have kept it intact for the very best there is.'

'But *Korin-san*, surely he will not believe all this silly flattery? He is a colonel and a commander and also *kempeitai*. He will know it is all lies!' Anna protested.

The seventh *okami-san* gave Anna a wry grin. 'He is a man. He will believe you. When a man has an erection it is his penis that does most of his thinking.'

CHAPTER FIFTEEN

*'I have always strived to succeed. My family is not descended
from samurai, but how can that count for anything?
That pervert Konoe comes from a noble family
and he is afraid to wield the samurai sword.'*
Kempeitai Colonel Takahashi
The Nest of the Swallows, August 1945

ANNA'S LIFE CONTINUED, EVERY day more
fearful than the last. Each morning she awakened not knowing
whether it would bring a visit from Lieutenant Ito and with it
his decision that she was finally ready. It was the waiting that
created the fearfulness and she had taken to weeping and
shaking involuntarily; her nerves were beginning to affect her
badly. She had fallen into a deep depression.

On July the 27th Lieutenant Ito arrived on a routine visit
and found her in such a state that he was furious and called the
two *okami-san* to task. 'She is now perfect physically, even the
bruises have gone, but he who will be coming will not accept
her the way she is!' he shouted. 'She is a nervous wreck! You
will use the glycerine bullets three times a day for the next
seven days, then I shall return. Then, if she is not of a proper
temperament, you will be made to suffer; your lives and hers will
not be spared. Do you understand?'

On the evening after Lieutenant Ito had visited, the
seventh *okami-san* spoke to Anna. 'The lieutenant is not

pleased, *Anna-san*. Your behaviour is not as he wishes for Colonel *Takahashi-san*. We have been instructed to give you a sedative.'

'What is it?' Anna asked suspiciously.

'It is something we use when a young comfort woman is upset, a little glycerine suppository that goes up your bottom. You won't even feel it.'

'It's not morphine?' Anna asked fearfully.

'No, not morphine, that would not be good; that is for pain and will have a bad result, a stupefying effect. This is simply something to calm you. If you continue the way you are going, you will certainly be killed pointlessly. Izumi and me also. The lieutenant has said so and we believe him. You will have the glycerine for one week and then you will decide if you are calm enough and do not need it any longer.'

'I will decide?' Anna asked, realising that it added another week of protection from Colonel Takahashi, but she was still suspicious. '*Korin-san*, I am not sure,' Anna protested. 'Is it the Sublime Fourth Experience? *Konoe-san* warned me never to partake of it.'

'No, no, there is no needle in the vein. If we did that we would anger Colonel *Takahashi-san* by making marks on your arm. *Anna-san*, please, Izumi and I have agreed we cannot disobey that *yarichin*, that male slut. We do not want to use the two Korean discipline women. We care about you too much to put you through a needless indignity they would greatly enjoy performing. They are dreadful women who take pleasure in inflicting pain. It is, after all, only something that will calm you. You have become too nervous; your temperament has been damaged and we're afraid that *Takahashi-san* will harm you if you are not what he expects.'

'*Korin-san*, I do not think I can ever be what he expects, no matter what!' Anna cried. 'He, *Takahashi-san*, caused my friend's death by decapitation! How can I put this to the back of my mind?'

'*Anna-san*, we have spoken about this before, we have spoken about when there are no choices left, only one action we didn't choose. There is the wisdom of Hongzhi Zhengjue, who lived eight hundred years ago. I will share it with you:

> *Withdraw now from the pounding and weaving of your*
>   *ingrained ideas.*
> *If you want to be rid of this invisible turmoil, you must*
>   *sit through it and let go of everything.*
> *Attain fulfilment and illuminate thoroughly.*
> *Light and shadow altogether forgotten.*
> *Drop off your own skin, and the sense-dusts will be fully*
>   *purified.*
> *The eye then readily discerns the brightness.*

An hour later Anna received her first glycerine suppository that contained heroin mixed with amphetamine. She had no knowledge of heroin, other than administering it by injection into Konoe Akira's arm as the Fourth Sublime Experience, and she didn't know that heroin can be absorbed in the system in several ways – a glycerine suppository was just one way of doing so.

Almost immediately she felt better and soon the full euphoric effect of the two combined drugs began to take hold. Her mind was calmed, her depression non-existent. She felt exuberant, wonderfully calm and, even though she knew she was captive, she felt strangely in control for the first time since she had come to the Nest of the Swallows.

Anna well knew the effect of heroin, and had often observed it as she had waited beside Konoe Akira after injecting him. What follows is a euphoric stupor, a drowsiness that often lasts two hours where the user sits still, feeling contented but incapable of much activity. It was during this time that she would snatch a bit of sleep herself on those occasions when she had been required to stay later than usual. Once this nodding-off stage passed, the colonel used to be in a heightened state of mind and his conversation would be at its sparkling best.

As Anna experienced none of these symptoms – except the last one where she felt wonderful, all her cares forsaken – she believed the suppositories did not contain the drug that Konoe Akira had warned her not to touch. She didn't know that this was because amphetamine combines well with heroin to eliminate the first stage, 'the nods', as it is often described, and takes the user directly to a heightened sense of wellbeing, mental sharpness and enhanced creativity, as well as feeling highly aroused.

'I think this calming glycerine works well,' Anna laughed some time later. 'I feel I have achieved what the honourable writer of the eight-hundred-year-old poem says.' Quoting a part of the last line she still remembered, she said, 'My eye *then readily discerns the brightness*. I thank you, *Korin-san*.'

The retired geisha turned away so that Anna didn't see her sudden tears. But Anna was feeling too good to notice, too high and self-involved. 'Please, *please* take me into the garden,' she cried excitedly. 'Let me see the stars. It is almost August and the dry will soon be over. I'm sure they will be brighter tonight; they always are just before the rains come.'

A week later Lieutenant Ito visited and declared himself

much happier with Anna's temperament and ordered the suppositories to be continued three times each day for at least another week. This was a combination of drugs the *kempeitai* used a great deal to soften up suspects they needed to interrogate but for practical purposes were not in a position to maim, torture or kill. It would almost certainly mean Anna would become a heroin addict.

The seventh *okami-san*, suspecting that Anna was rapidly becoming dependent on the effects of the glycerine suppository, asked her, '*Anna-san*, do you want to continue the glycerine?'

'Yes, *Korin-san*,' she replied quickly. 'I feel sure it helps me to remain calm.'

Late in the afternoon on the 12th of August the call from Lieutenant Ito came that Anna was to receive no heroin for two days. She had already complained to *Korin-san* that she had developed constipation. 'It is the glycerine,' *Korin-san* announced, 'it sometimes has this effect on some of the comfort women. Perhaps we must stop the suppositories?'

'No!' Anna burst out, alarmed. 'No, it is not too bad.' The following morning Izumi explained that Anna would not be receiving glycerine suppositories for the next two days, that she could not be allowed to remain constipated. 'Please, *Izumi-san*, I must have them, I have grown accustomed to being calm. The constipation is nothing,' Anna begged.

'Ah, but it will become a great pain and your stomach will swell up, we cannot allow it. Lieutenant Ito will be angry, *Anna-san*, and, as well, you will suffer greatly from this blockage,' she said in an understanding but firm voice. 'I regret it is the only way.'

Anna began to experience heroin and amphetamine withdrawal within fourteen hours. She endured a sleepless night and the following day (the 14th of August) she found almost unendurable, and she repeatedly begged to be given the glycerine suppositories. Late in the afternoon Lieutenant Ito arrived at the Nest of the Swallows and Izumi was told to prepare Anna for the arrival, at 7 p.m. sharp, of Colonel Takahashi. It was the first time his name had been mentioned, although Lieutenant Ito was aware that the two *okami-san* would have known all the time.

If I appear to be using the tedium of dates in telling Anna's story, you must forgive me. At the time this was happening in the Nest of the Swallows, a great deal was changing in the conduct of the Pacific War. On August the 6th (the 7th in Java), the first atomic bomb was dropped on Hiroshima and while this news may have been picked up by those who could listen to Allied broadcasts (where it was described as 'an atomic device'), the Japanese who were fighting in the Pacific received no mention of the event in their own radio broadcasts which came directly from Tokyo, nor did they receive advice from official sources in Japan.

Colonel Takahashi, if he had been monitoring Allied radio broadcasts, would not have taken them seriously, assuming it was simply propaganda, tit for tat. The American bombings of the cities of Japan had become routine and it was hardly news to someone like Colonel Takahashi to hear of more Allied bombings. The Japanese radio broadcasts were considered to be pure propaganda by the Allies, and there is no reason to suppose that the Japanese colonel did not feel the same about Allied radio broadcasts. The bomb on Nagasaki on the 9th (the 10th in Java) was met with the same lack of official confirmation from Japan, and therefore would have once again been treated with indifference by the commander.

The visit to the Nest of the Swallows on the 14th would have had little, if any, significance to Colonel Takahashi. Such was the propaganda to its own troops – Japanese victory over the Allies was a continuing message in daily news bulletins from Japan – that he would have assumed it was war as usual in the Pacific region.

On the 14th of August at precisely 7 p.m., a large black American car drove through the open boom gate without stopping, the guards having been previously alerted to allow it through. It was dark and they would have been unable to identify the passenger. The car drove to the rear of the Nest of the Swallows to be met there by the seventh *okami-san*.

The driver jumped from the car and opened the back door, saluting as the colonel stepped out. The seventh *okami-san* bowed deeply as the ex-*kempeitai* captain, now colonel and commander of Tjilatjap, returned her greeting with an impatient bow and no more than a jerk of his head, accompanied by '*Hai!*' He stood for a moment and seemed to be thinking, then he removed his *katana* and sidearm and handed the sword and revolver to the driver. 'Lead me to the gate, then leave me. I have the keys. Is everything prepared?'

'Yes, it is how Lieutenant *Ito-san* has instructed, honourable Colonel *Takahashi-san*,' the seventh *okami-san* replied, bowing deeply.

'The woman is ready, no suppositories?' he asked as she led

him around the corner of the large mansion.

'Yes, *Colonel-san*, as was requested.'

'She has been without two days?' he persisted.

'Yes, honourable Colonel *Takahashi-san*, nothing since the day before yesterday.'

The Japanese colonel grunted. They reached the gate moments later. 'You will not be needed again until I depart. You will watch for my car. Do not under any circumstances enter to attend to the woman until I leave,' he instructed.

The seventh *okami-san* bowed again. 'I understand, honourable *Takahashi-san*.'

Anna had been made to wear the yellow kimono, *tabi* socks and sandals. Her face remained without make-up, as Lieutenant Ito had instructed that she was not to be painted in the manner of a geisha but was to appear in precisely the way she had always done for the previous commander.

Waiting alone since late afternoon, Anna was suffering acutely from heroin withdrawal. Her nose wouldn't stop running and that caused her to sniffle. She was also very afraid. It was still sufficiently light for her to see the garden gate open and Colonel Takahashi turn to lock it again and start to walk down the path, his jackboots gleaming in the soft evening light. Shortly afterwards she heard the rattle of the key in the door. Anna waited until it opened, then bowed deeply. 'Welcome, *Colonel-san*,' she said softly, her heart thumping.

The Japanese commander completed the task of locking the door before turning, first putting the key back in his trouser pocket. He bowed by jerking his head in the same cursory and impatient manner he had done with the seventh *okami-san*, and uttered '*Hai!*' His expression remained unchanged as he walked to the left of Anna towards the desk and proceeded to sit in the swivel chair behind it.

Anna turned to face him. 'Shall I pour tea, honourable *Colonel-san*?' she asked.

'No!' he barked. 'There is no tea ceremony yet! Stand there!' He pointed to the opposite side of the desk. Anna moved silently to stand where he indicated. 'Undress!' he commanded.

Anna looked momentarily confused. '*Colonel-san*, now, here?' she asked.

'Take off your kimono, I want you naked!' he barked. 'Then stand to attention in front of me! You will obey!' he snapped again.

Anna proceeded to undress, too frightened and distraught from the drug withdrawal to protest. First she removed her sandals and *tabi* and began to undo her *obi*, a complicated matter as her hands were shaking almost uncontrollably as she unwound the intricately tied high waistband belt. The kimono clung to her body and she tugged at it so that the silk fell loosely away, then pulling her arms free she allowed the yellow garment to fall to her ankles and she stepped out of it. Now wearing only the *hadajuban* and underneath it her cotton drawers, she turned her back on the Japanese colonel and removed the last garments.

'Turn around! Face me!' Takahashi demanded. 'You will never again turn your back on me!' Anna turned with her hands cupped over her groin. 'I said stand to attention!' he ordered. 'Take your hands away. Have you not seen how a soldier stands to attention?'

Anna removed her hands and, blushing deeply, placed them to her side and brought her feet together. She felt totally vulnerable and humiliated but knew if she started to sob it would be what he expected – desired. She started to shake from the craving that mixed with her fear; adrenalin pumped through her system, heightening her misery, but she was determined not to allow him to see the utter sense of shame and degradation he caused her to feel.

The Japanese colonel rose from the desk and walked to where she stood. 'Two steps back!' he snapped. Anna complied and he stood in front of her, peering at her closely, examining her cheekbones, her thigh where she had been bruised, then her knees. He brushed his hand briefly over her pubic hair as if he was testing its quality as well. 'Perfect,' he said at last. Then turning, he went back to his seat behind the desk. 'Two paces forward!' he demanded. Anna stepped the two paces towards him, holding herself rigid, her hands to the side. 'It is correct that the pearl remains intact?' Takahashi asked. Anna made no answer. 'Are you a virgin?' he demanded, raising his voice.

'Yes, *Colonel-san*,' Anna replied, her voice only slightly above a whisper.

'And you are a heroin addict, no?'

'No, *Colonel-san*.'

'Have you not been given suppositories for more than two weeks and are now without them for two days?'

'Yes, *Colonel-san*,' Anna said tremulously.

His voice changed suddenly and took on a conciliatory tone. 'How do you feel, Anna? Now, at this moment?'

'Frightened, *Colonel-san*.'

'And in need of a suppository?'

'Yes, *Colonel-san*,' Anna said in a trembling voice.

'The suppositories contain heroin and amphetamines, pure heroin and methamphetamine crystals. You are now a total addict,' he replied calmly.

Despite her condition, Anna was shocked. 'I did not know this, *Colonel-san*!'

The Japanese colonel reached into the pocket of his military tunic and produced a small, plainly wrapped package Anna recognised instantly. It contained two glycerine suppositories. He placed it on the desk. Then, retaining his sympathetic attitude, he pointed to the package and asked, 'Will you willingly give me the gift of the pearl in return for this?'

Anna could hear her brain screaming. The sensation she felt was as if there was a pair of small, long-nailed hands trapped within her head, desperately scratching and clawing to get out of her skull by crawling through her eyes. *Yes! Yes! Please, yes!* every fibre of her being called out desperately. Relief from her craving was an arm's length away. But somehow she clung on to her sanity. 'No, not *willingly*!' she said. 'You have the power to take it. But I will not give it willingly, *Colonel-san*.'

The Japanese colonel laughed, pointing to the small package. 'Then I regret there will be no more of this. No more, you understand? That is until you agree to willingly give me what you would willingly have given *Konoe-san* if he had not been a rope pervert.'

Anna felt she would break into sobs at any moment, but fought back the need to cry, to beg for the package. 'Colonel *Konoe-san* never asked me and I would not have surrendered to him willingly, *Colonel-san*.'

The colonel rose from behind the desk and walked a few steps to the side of Anna. He seemed to be thinking; his head was bowed and his hands behind his back. Then turning, he said, 'The mixture you have been given in the suppositories is very pure and when you are forced into a prolonged withdrawal, in no more than three weeks you will almost certainly be dead.' He turned to face Anna and shrugged. 'You must make up your own mind, Anna. I am not an animal. I will not rape you. I carry no weapon to threaten you. You may choose to die in agony as a virgin. Or live and be supplied with all the glycerine suppositories your addiction requires.'

Anna remained silent, head bowed, shamed by her nakedness as she looked down over her small breasts and pudenda to her feet. The Japanese officer returned to his former seat, leaning back nonchalantly, his hands folded and resting on his chest. *Korin-san's* words echoed in her head: 'Anna-san, *you cannot hold on to it forever. Perhaps it is time to be practical? To face life as it is?'* Anna took a deep breath, making up her mind, perhaps even saving her life. 'I will be compliant, *Colonel-san,* and come to you willingly and please you greatly if you tell me one thing I need to know.'

'What is it, Anna?' he asked, smiling. 'What is it you wish to know?'

'Why was Til beheaded?'

'Til?'

'The *becak* owner.'

'Oh, him. Well, that is simple enough to answer. I required you to be brought here and to know that you no longer enjoyed the privilege of patronage that that pervert, Konoe Akira, allowed you. It was the simplest and most efficient way to demonstrate that it was all over for you and that you were destined for the Nest of the Swallows.'

'You beheaded a man to tell *me* it was all *over?'* Anna asked, too shocked to add the respectful appendage of *Colonel-san.*

'Konoe made me promise you would be safe and not molested. I am a man of my word, even if he is a pervert and a coward. The *kempeitai* were told that you must not be marked or injured; that they must not lay a finger on you. The beheading was to ensure your cooperation, to intimidate you. It is common practice.' The Japanese colonel chuckled. 'But it didn't work as I had hoped. You attacked and severely wounded four of the five *kempeitai* escorts and one of my best sergeants.' He leaned back even further. 'Very impressive! In my mind you became worthy of my personal attention. The Second Vase, perfect in every respect *and* a virgin, also has the courage of a lioness.' He clapped his hands. 'Admirable! Irresistible!'

Anna realised that Yasuko, the mayor's wife, had been listening to the lunch conversations. 'Did you personally behead him, *Colonel-san?*' she asked, glancing up at him momentarily.

'Who? Oh, the *becak* driver. Yes, of course, it is an honourable and noble function and not a task to be given to a subordinate. I am not like that pervert with the ropes, who would hand this customary and privileged duty of a commanding officer to someone else, as if afraid of a little blood,' he scoffed.

Anna was silent, looking down at her feet, the image of Til's head on a bamboo spike outside the front gate recalled starkly. She had always known that she was the sole cause of Til's death, but now it had been confirmed. Nevertheless, her mind seemed to be screaming *He is dead – you must save your own life!* The package lay so close she could reach out and touch it.

Anna bowed deeply, her eyes downcast. 'Welcome to my futon, *Colonel-san.*' She looked up and into his eyes. 'I have saved the pearl for a *real* man who has courage and honour and is not afraid to use the noble *katana.*' She saw in his expression and the slow nod of his head that *Korin-san* had been right; his ego accepted her compliment and then her compliance, as if she had given the latter willingly.

Takahashi now leaned forward, a simian-like grin spread across his face. 'Excellent!' he exclaimed.

'Perhaps you will allow me to begin with a massage, *Colonel-san?* It will relax and prepare you,' Anna said.

'Then it is willingly done and the pearl is mine?' the commander asked, seeking a final confirmation.

Anna forced herself to smile, remembering *Korin-san*'s advice. 'It is an honour, Colonel *Takahashi-san*,' she said in a low voice, bowing as she spoke.

The Japanese officer leaned further forward and pushed the suppository over to Anna, who forced herself not to snatch at it. 'This will calm you,' he said, smiling in a most benign manner, immensely pleased with himself.

Anna reached out, hoping the colonel would not insist she open the package and insert the suppository in front of him. 'I must go to the bathroom now, please, *Colonel-san*?'

'Of course, I will prepare myself for your massage. I am informed that you are well trained.'

Anna knew that Yasuko had been aware that in order to please Konoe Akira she had received training by the seventh *okami-san* not only in *kinbaku*, but also in erotic massage and other concubinary technique. 'I will do my best for you, *Colonel-san*. I apologise that I do not possess the skills of a geisha,' she said in a self-deprecating manner.

'I will let you know,' Takahashi said, grinning. 'If you do a good job I will give you another suppository packet before I leave; more than one perhaps,' he promised.

Several minutes later Anna returned from the bathroom. Her blue eyes sparkled as she walked with dignity across the room, as if oblivious to her state of nudity, and over to the other end of the large study. There was a specially prepared futon, two cushions and a low table with the tea setting.

Despite her desperation and the pains of withdrawal, she had previously tucked the butterfly ashtray and the Clipper box under the futon in a place where they wouldn't be discovered by a body lying supine. Her life, she knew, had reached an end point. They were talismans, the only source of luck she still possessed; they were all she had left to believe in. While Anna had prepared herself to be raped, she nevertheless thought to have the strange comfort of these two objects with her. She knew that hiding the two most precious things she possessed under the futon was a pointless gesture, even a childish thing to do, but it was one she impulsively felt was representative of a gentler past she would never see again. Kept near her, they would be a part of her until the end came.

The Japanese colonel, completely undressed, sat on the futon, his knees up against his chest and his hands between his legs so they concealed his private parts. Without his uniform he looked suddenly vulnerable; to the line made by his short-sleeved tunic and open collar, his arms and neck were a darker colour from exposure to the tropical sun.

It was the same vulnerability Anna had seen on Konoe Akira's face, and she was surprised to see it again in the eyes of the brute seated in front of her. Other than her drunken, and later ailing, father, this was only the second male she had seen totally naked. The heroin and amphetamine that were now reaching her brain were working wonders. She felt strong and totally in possession of her wits, surprised to find that the naked body of the Japanese commander seated in front of her, his hands cupped about his scrotum, no longer frightened her.

'Will you take refreshment, *Colonel-san*? May I pour tea?' Anna asked, scoring a small silent victory by having him realise that he would need to remove his hands if he accepted.

'No, later, after the massage,' he replied, looking a little foolish, knowing it was a tradition that took place before anything else happened in the *okiya*.

Anna reached for the bottle of massage oil *Izumi-san* had left for her. 'Please, *Takahashi-san*, if you will turn and lie on your stomach?' Anna asked in a soft, pleasant voice.

The Japanese colonel rolled awkwardly onto his side, his hands remaining cupped over his groin until his back faced Anna. It was time, she decided, to once again follow *Korin-san*'s instructions. 'Relax, *Colonel-san*, the sword is still in its scabbard but my hope is that it will soon be drawn,' she said cheekily. She waited for his reaction and by way of reply received what she took to be a complicit grunt. Pouring a few drops of oil onto his back, she began to gently massage his shoulders, removing the tension. After a while she heard him groan, then sigh contentedly as he relaxed totally under her skilled hands.

'You are good, *Anna-san*,' he mumbled with his face buried in the bean pillow. 'Very good.'

'There is better to come, *Colonel-san*. Much better,' she promised, her voice now light and in control. She continued to massage for half an hour, venturing during this time to again test *Korin-san*'s advice. 'You have the shoulders and the back of a warrior; at another time you would have been a famous samurai, I think, *Takahashi-san*.' Then she added for good measure, 'You are already demonstrably the best there can be with the *katana*, the divine blade.'

Anna could sense the erection grow beneath him. 'I have always strived to succeed. My family is not descended from samurai, but how can that count for anything? That pervert Konoe comes from a noble family and he is afraid to wield the samurai sword.'

'Ah, *Colonel-san*, I always hoped for a real man and not one who on the outside was powerful but on the inside a weakling who couldn't get it up,' Anna said, almost exactly duplicating

Korin-san's words.

'I will not have that problem,' the Japanese officer boasted, accepting the outrageous compliment seriously. It was just as the seventh *okami-san* had promised it would be. *He is beginning to think with his penis*, Anna thought to herself, and slapped him lightly on the shoulder. 'It is time to turn onto your back now, *Colonel-san*,' she instructed.

'You know your job, alright!' Takahashi said, all his inhibitions now gone. He turned and Anna observed his erection; it was no bigger than Konoe Akira's but was larger than the pathetic appendage her late father had tragically possessed, although she had never seen it erect.

'A most worthy sword!' Anna giggled. She reached out and tap-danced with the tips of her fingers as she'd been instructed, moving lightly from its exposed head down to the scrotum, massaging his testicles softly and then all the way back again, light, then firm, then light again, teasing, with the ball of her forefinger stroking the pronounced veins that ran its length.

'Careful! Oh, oh, oh! Oh, no!' the Japanese officer groaned, losing control. Anna grabbed him firmly in her oiled left hand, stroking to maximise the coming ejaculation. His eyes were tightly closed as his premature orgasm finally arrived.

'Directly under the sternum, push it in, it doesn't have to go very deep.' Anna, reaching for the shards of the butterfly ashtray, pushed them apart with her fingers and felt for the image of the butterfly's thorax, the dagger-shaped centre section, the biggest part of all the pieces. Lifting it by the blunt end, she plunged the point of the needle-sharp crystal sliver directly under and upward, just below the *kempeitai* officer's sternum.

The Japanese commander's eyes shot open in a momentary look of surprise that turned to sudden terror, exhibiting an emotion he had induced so often in others. '*The victim cannot move as his heart has been shredded. The sudden drop in blood pressure, together with the shock, makes any attempt to retaliate impossible.*'

'That's for Til, you cruel bastard!' Anna screamed down at him, baring her teeth. Her hand, still holding the end of the crystal shard, started to bleed but she held it steady, keeping the point embedded in him, resisting the temptation to withdraw it and plunge it into him again and again in her insane fury. His body quivered in a shuddery paralysis and then he gave a soft grunt, the light departed from his eyes and she saw that he was dead. It happened just as Konoe Akira had told her it would when, during a late-night conversation, he'd explained the many methods in which the *kempeitai* are trained to kill. '*It's the best way with a short blade. You can also do it with a sharpened chopstick.*'

The heroin mixture still completely possessed Anna's sensibilities; it would be four or five hours before she would need another glycerine suppository. She withdrew the crystal dagger and moved in a somnolent daze, her mind detached from her body, towards the bathroom, where she ran the tap and rinsed carefully, the blood from her fingers and the shard disappearing in a pink runnel down the plughole. The blood on her hand seemed to be a mixture of the dead Japanese commander's and her own. Her palm was lacerated where the sharp edges of the crystal had cut into the skin as she'd gripped it. She saw that her cuts were superficial and of little importance. She was going to be dead soon enough anyway. This time there would be no requirement for her to heal so that she was allowed to achieve someone's ideal of perfection.

Anna felt no guilt. She had avenged Til's death and

the price, she knew, would be her own. She smiled softly; Til would be enjoying the seventy-two virgins Allah promised the enlightened. '*Ahee!* Anna, it is too much for an old man! As the Prophet says, an old man who takes a young wife is either a fool or a rich man!' He would laugh and then add, 'But up in paradise, he must also be a very strong one!'

Anna covered the body of the Japanese colonel by drawing the futon completely over his head. Then she returned to the bathroom and, as there was no bathtub in the small private bathroom, she stood under the shower for a long time, washing her hair and allowing the hot water to heal and cleanse her. The soap stung her hand from the cuts, but the bleeding had ceased. It was only when she was towelling herself that she realised that she was still a virgin, that it would be as Takahashi had said – she would die a virgin. 'Oh, Nicholas,' she said aloud. 'I am so sorry. I promised it would be you!' Finally she changed into a sarong and blouse. If she was going to die, she didn't want to do so wearing a kimono.

It was then that Anna began to think more clearly. She searched the Japanese colonel's tunic pockets and found a further half-dozen packets of glycerine suppositories and also a small silver case containing three ampoules of heroin and a syringe similar to the one Konoe Akira had carried. She removed the ampoules so it would appear Takahashi had taken heroin; deliberately but with regret she broke off the top of all of them. She drew the contents of one ampoule up into the syringe, then emptied the syringe and the other two ampoules into the bathroom basin and placed the emptied ampoules and syringe on the table beside the futon. She poured the cold green tea into both cups and emptied them, placing each on the table directly above a floor cushion. Then she placed the packets of suppositories in her shoulder bag, adding the pieces of the butterfly ashtray that were carefully wrapped in a cotton cloth, and the Clipper butterfly box. The silver cigarette case containing the persimmon seeds, together with her silver hairbrush and the morphine ampoules, were padded by her spare underwear. Finally she tucked the guilder notes back into her bra and inserted the wax-sealed revolver cartridge into its designated place.

Anna returned to where the remainder of the dead colonel's uniform lay, neatly folded, passing the leather couch where *The Adventures of Don Quixote* lay open and face down. (How many times had she been told as a child not to treat a book like this?) It was the book she had unsuccessfully tried to read to distract her from her craving. Anna had first studied it while at school and she'd remembered being bored at the hero's silly eccentricity. Now she wasn't so sure – everything around her was consumed by a malignancy and had gone mad. Tilting at windmills seemed a brave and honourable metaphor for opposition to the world's collective insanity.

She found the keys to the study door and to the garden gate in one of Takahashi's trouser pockets. Ready to leave, Anna looked around her, inspecting the study. To anyone entering, it would seem the Japanese colonel was asleep. They'd conclude he'd taken heroin and stayed awake most of the night, finally falling asleep. She knew that *Izumi-san*, warned by the seventh *okami-san*, would wait for his departure before coming into the room. Possibly it would be close to noon the following day before Izumi decided that something must be wrong. Then, when she finally entered, she'd find Anna missing and what appeared to be a sleeping Japanese officer under the futon. She would, of course, be forced to raise the alarm and would probably call Lieutenant Ito, causing even further delay before a search party got under way to recapture her. If Anna was lucky it could be nearly sixteen hours before anyone discovered her escape.

Izumi-san had informed her previously that it was impossible to escape; that the gardens and the grounds were closely patrolled by the Japanese guards, and the walls, topped with barbed wire, were too high to climb. Anna accepted that she might eventually be caught. But it was not in her personality to allow events to overrun her by simply waiting for them to occur. If she was going to die it was far better to do so from a bullet fired from the rifle of a guard than be tortured to death by the *kempeitai*, no doubt with Lieutenant Ito in a supervisory role.

Anna left, quietly unlocking and then relocking the study door to the garden and doing the same when she reached the gate. She was accustomed to big mansions set in large grounds: *Grootehuis* was not all that different from this one and she was aware that they all had elements in common – a large vegetable garden and a small orchard, which usually grew oranges, bananas, grapefruit, papaya, guava, quince and passionfruit. The vegetable garden always faced north and was tucked into a corner where it wouldn't be seen. Furthermore, because vegetables and tropical fruit need full sun, the section of wall enclosing it was always lower, so that the shadow it threw wouldn't be cast over the garden beds.

It took almost an hour for Anna to find her bearings and to locate the orchard in the dark. Once or twice she was forced to hide, her heart pounding like a tom-tom when she heard the footsteps of a Japanese guard patrolling the grounds. On another occasion she almost stumbled into two guards who were sitting together on a garden seat having a quiet smoke.

She finally found herself in the orchard. It was larger than usual, with mature fruit trees. The wall, as she'd hoped, had been lowered by about a metre but, like the rest, was topped with barbed wire. To her surprise, she found a very old quince tree abutting the wall, one slender branch reaching over the barbed wire. Why the Japanese hadn't removed the tree was a mystery. Instead they'd simply trimmed the branches that overhung the wall. But the quince has a rapid and persistent growth, readily responding to heavy pruning. The new branch had grown in the interval since the property had been taken over by the Japanese for use as the Nest of the Swallows, and someone had neglected to remove it. In the moonlight it seemed strong enough to support her. That is, if she could find a way to avoid the barbed wire.

Outside a small garden shed she found a neatly stacked set of boards about two metres long and five centimetres thick. These are commonly used in the wet season by gardeners in the tropics to create pathways through the mud, particularly in a vegetable garden, making it easier to move between the garden beds and preventing a wheelbarrow from becoming bogged in the heavy conditions.

Anna removed one board and carried it over her shoulder to the quince tree. It was probably teak, for it was very heavy. Reaching the tree, she lifted the plank up into the branches with some difficulty, panting from the exertion, but she managed to wedge it over two lower branches. Then, in the bright moonlight she climbed to a branch above and, first resting to regain her breath, pulled the plank higher up the tree, in the process making what seemed to her a fearful racket. With her heart pounding, and breathing heavily again from the renewed exertion, she expected at any moment to hear shouts and footsteps as the Japanese guards ran towards the orchard. Perched even higher up the tree, she raised the plank again, gritting her teeth with the effort. Finally she managed to get it to the same level as the top of the barbed wire. She threaded it through the foliage until the front end rested on top of the wire, allowing a good section of the plank to extend beyond the heavy branch so that if it slipped it would still remain steady. She was vaguely aware that her right hand was bleeding again.

Anna waited until she'd regained her breath from the tremendous effort before she began to crawl the two metres along the plank, stopping several times to adjust her weight as the board proved anything but steady, bouncing and wobbling on the springy wire. She arrived directly above the barbed wire, now held down firmly by the plank and her own weight. Rising carefully to her knees, she reached out for the overhanging branch and flung herself over the wall, gripping the slender branch with all her might. The branch dipped but didn't break and Anna found herself suspended no more than a couple of metres above the ground on the far side of the wall. She released her hold and fell, landing on her feet; then, losing her balance, she sprawled onto the rough ground, landing hard on her bottom. The rush of adrenalin and the effects of the heroin and amphetamine mixture made her oblivious to her bleeding hand, and if she'd injured herself in the fall she wasn't conscious of it. Anna leapt to her feet and ran for her life. The escape had taken her a little under two hours.

It was a few minutes before midnight when an exhausted Anna arrived at Ratih's *kampong* restaurant. The patrons had left and she could hear the clatter as the servants washed up the last of the dishes, pots and woks. Ratih could hardly believe her eyes when she saw her. 'Anna, it is you!' she cried, then ran towards her, holding her tight as Anna collapsed weeping into her arms.

History tells us that the 14th of August in 1945 was the day the Japanese forces officially surrendered in Tokyo. In Java, a day ahead on the International Date Line, the capitulation occurred on the 15th. By midday the local Japanese in Tjilatjap had laid down their arms, opened the gates of the internment camp, those of the Nest of the Swallows and the soldiers' brothel, and allowed the prisoners to walk free. The Japanese troops were ordered to return to their barracks to await the arrival of the Allies.

The war was over. Anna had survived.

The murder of Colonel Takahashi was never officially recognised. Allied records copied from the Japanese enquiry into his death simply stated that he died alone in the officers' bordello, the Nest of the Swallows, on the 15th of August 1945. The report noted that he had taken heroin before stabbing himself under the sternum, a method familiar to the *kempeitai*.

It was presumed that, upon hearing the Emperor's surrender broadcast from Tokyo, he had committed suicide. The weapon used – 'in all probability the short sword worn by Japanese officers with the *katana*' – was never found and likely to have been stolen. The Japanese record noted that his suicide was an honourable death and in the tradition of a defeated hero.

A typewritten note from a British officer was appended to

the short transcript. It noted that Colonel Takahashi had been promoted from the *kempeitai* and that, had he not taken his life, there was more than sufficient evidence to prosecute him for war crimes. The officer had added, in his own handwriting under the typewritten sheet, 'A thoroughly nasty piece of work!'

CHAPTER SIXTEEN

'We've had the traditional sailor's farewell, Nick.
Now I want the traditional woman's farewell.
I want to stand tearfully alone on a railway platform
with a hiss of steam bursting from the engine's wheels,
waving the dearest man in my life goodbye, a small lace
handkerchief crumpled in my trembling hand.'
Chief Petty Officer Marg Hamilton
On the way to Perth from Fremantle, 1942

I CONFESS I WAS shattered when I heard the news that
the *Witvogel* had not arrived in either Darwin or Broome. The
thought that it may have been sunk by the Japanese, that Anna
could be dead, left me depressed and terribly sad. To add to this
I received a letter from my father. It had been handed to one
of the refugees who was leaving New Britain, with the request
that on arrival in Cairns the letter be sent to my godfather, the
Archbishop of Perth.

My dear Nick,

My sincerest hope is that you will receive this letter. If ever
there was a more inopportune time to go butterfly hunting in
Java, then I can't imagine when that might be. But then you
were always a strong-minded child. With the great bastion of
Singapore bound to hold the Japanese forces, the speed of their

advance that caught us all napping in Malaya will soon be halted. Thank God for good old British foresight and initiative.

With every tramp steamer docking in Rabaul I pray that you will be on board. Now that the Japanese invasion of both islands is thought to be a matter of days away, I pray instead that you take ship to Australia. My worst fear is that you are trapped in Java and taken prisoner. What a fearful mess we find ourselves in.

I am sending this letter via Mr Gunnar Petersen, a passenger (or is it refugee?) on the last boat to leave New Britain. Gunnar is a deacon in the Rabaul congregation and a thoroughly decent chap who, I am confident, will make every endeavour to get this letter to Henry in Perth. 'If I have to walk all the way myself, Vicar!' he assured me.

I was, of course, offered passage on the same boat, and my hope is that you will understand why I could not avail myself of the opportunity to escape the island. I am a missionary, not simply for the good times but also for the bad. I have a native flock I feel sure are going to need me in the days and months to come. There are also a number of whites of assorted nationality who are unable to escape, and who will need my spiritual guidance. My hope is that I will not be found wanting.

With a fluency in their language and knowledge of the Japanese mindset, I believe I will be in a position to bring about some amelioration. After all, is this not God's true calling – to bring comfort and restore faith and hope in those around us?

If you receive this letter that will mean you are safe and the Lord God will have answered my ardent prayers for your safe return. These are uncertain times and, with God's will, we will soon be together once again – father and son, priest and sailor, bibliophile and butterfly collector.

I realise that I have not always been the father you may have hoped for. With the premature death of your mother you lacked the maternal care every child is entitled to receive, and I know I should have done better. Yet you have grown to be a splendid man. If I haven't told you as often as I should, I am immensely proud of you. As for my shortcomings as a parent – and I am aware they have been many – I hope and pray that you will forgive me.

I should, perhaps, end with Psalm 23, but choose not to: too much valley, shadow and death and, I fear, very little green pasture is ahead for mankind.

Although, as far as I know, there is not a scintilla of Irish in our family, I prefer to leave you with this simple and traditional secular blessing:

> *May the road rise to meet you*
> *May the wind always be at your back*
> *May the sun shine warm upon your face*
> *The rains fall soft upon your fields*
> *And until we meet again*
> *May God hold you in the hollow of His hand.*

Your loving father,
John Duncan

After reading my father's letter so soon after the news about Anna, I confess I crept away to a quiet corner of the Archbishop's spacious grounds and found a garden seat where I blubbed like a small child. Why is it that we so often reveal our true feelings when the time has passed? I had never once told my father that I loved him and now, possibly too late, I realised how very much I did.

His notion that he could somehow lighten the load of his parishioners by negotiating with the Japanese was naïve but predictable. He didn't have a skerrick of commonsense, and never got it into his Anglican clergyman's head that a good intellect, a dollop of tolerance and a soupçon of God thrown in for good measure isn't the solution to every human problem. Faith, hope and charity – that summed up his attitude perfectly.

I spent the larger part of my so-called 'holiday' (before embarking on the train trip to Melbourne and going on to the HMAS *Cerberus*) lying on the bed feeling sorry for myself. I had found a fleapit to replace Mrs Beswick's establishment with its 'All stations alert – spies are everywhere' and 'One cold shower a day' features.

Two of the three people I cared about most were either dead or imprisoned by the Japanese. Marg Hamilton, of course, was the third. If we ever met again a fourth would be Kevin Judge, telling whoever expects him to face up to the enemy: *I want ya ter unnerstan, I ain't no fuckin' hero!*

Three of these four I now cherished as friends, two as lovers. I hadn't known any of them that long, but when you're a loner you pick your associates very carefully, yet more by luck than good judgment these people had come into my life and I cared about them very much. Perhaps it was because I was finally growing up that I recognised their importance to me. Now two of them might well be dead, and a third would be getting on with his life in the US Navy or back in Chicago. That left only Marg Hamilton, who so wonderfully ended my impatient virginity by guiding me across the post-pubescent threshold into manhood.

Added to my depression was my guilt that I knew I loved

both Anna Van Heerden and Marg Hamilton. Can a man love two women simultaneously? I mean love, like in romance? Marg had invited me into her bed. That was, and still is, one of the truly wonderful events – with bugles blaring – in my life. As importantly, while I didn't recognise it at the time, she gave me the comfort of a woman, the warmth, the closeness, and other outwardly female characteristics I had not experienced as a child. By this I don't mean she was a surrogate mother – nothing of the sort. She belonged to a gender I had instinctively longed to love and, now that I'd been taught to do so, in return she had shown me how to receive love. Does that make any sense?

Anna, on the other hand, made me laugh and want to dance and do somersaults and handstands ahead of her on a green lawn, and feel the sheer joy of being young. She was a lovely mystery to be explored. A butterfly only just emerged from the chrysalis who was testing her beautiful wings in the dewy sunlight.

During my week and a half of being a thorough pain in the arse, Marg took to fetching and feeding me in the evenings and enduring my moods. Then two days before I was due to leave on the three-day journey by train to Melbourne, she'd finally had a gutful of my pathetic self-pity.

'Nick, there is no point in grieving for what *may* have happened. Until you are certain, until the telegram arrives, get on with your life. Even then, you'll mourn them for the remainder of your life, but after the initial tears and heartache we all have to get on with it. We have to find a way to cope.' She paused. 'As I and many others have been required to do.'

See what I mean? That same sentence said by a man would carry an unspoken but underlying criticism: *C'mon,*

ferchrissakes, Nick. Time to get on with it; be a man, will ya!
With Marg, it was loving and kind, wise and understanding
and correct. And all of it was delivered without the underlying
verbal sock in the jaw. It shocked me out of my self-pity.

'Marg, I apologise. You're perfectly right. I'm afraid I've
been a miserable little shit. Thanks for looking after me and
straightening me out, helping me get on top of it all.'

'Well, I rather like the idea of your getting on top of it,'
she laughed. 'Tomorrow night at 6.30 it's sausages, onions and
a volcano of mash with gravy, followed by trifle and custard
and then . . .' She paused. 'I thought the traditional sailor's
farewell.'

'Sailor's farewell?' I asked stupidly, momentarily thinking
it was something to eat, then seeing her mischievous grin. 'Oh!'
I said, blushing.

'When a sailor goes to sea a prudent woman leaves him
with a memory to come home to.' She grinned. 'So her sailor-
boy won't forget her.'

At eighteen, unlike girls, I guess guys are a bit 'um and ah',
resorting more to glottal sounds than to sentence construction.
'Gee, ah, er, ummph, I'm not really, ah, going to sea, but er, ah,
that's wonderful, Marg,' is a rough approximation of my highly
sophisticated reply.

'But you *are* going to sea, Nick. All naval establishments
ashore are treated as ships, and when you leave the front
gate it is called "going ashore". I feel duty-bound to maintain
a tradition that has probably existed since Francis Drake left
England to circumnavigate the globe or to fight the Spanish
Armada.'

I guess it was still on Marg's terms. I lacked the wit or
the experience or whatever it takes to coax a woman into bed,

hers or my own. Not that I had one to coax her into. My bed was an iron army cot on an upstairs verandah that had been converted into fibro cubicles just large enough to contain a narrow bed and a suitcase. I was in no position to conduct the niceties of romance, even if I knew how to do so – which I didn't.

I wasn't expecting Marg's invitation and counted myself dead fortunate that I was being invited to sleep with a beautiful, generous and loving woman. My greatest concern was whether I brought my own frangers this time, or whether Marg (as she had previously done) would equip me with standard naval issue.

I wasn't even certain where one bought French letters. At school, the conventional wisdom was that they were obtained from the barber's shop or the chemist. I wasn't too keen on the chemist shop; they always seemed to have young girls behind the counter who wore a knowing smirk when you asked to see the chemist. Anyway, in my experience chemists are, generally speaking, a scrubbed-up and antiseptic-looking lot who mix potions in back rooms and take themselves fairly seriously: *Take one twice a day after meals; if they cause constipation come back and see me, Mr Duncan.* How can you front up to a bloke like that and say 'I'd like a packet of contraceptives, please, sir', particularly when you don't even know how much they'll cost?

Both chemists in Rabaul were Anglicans and on Sundays they'd arrive at church with their families in big, shiny cars, one a Dodge and the other a Studebaker. They were sort of one notch above the rest of us, except for the doctor and the magistrate and, of course, my dad the vicar. Those four professions, and maybe the headmaster of the local high school, made up the local royalty – oh yes, and the district commissioner, but he was a Catholic. The rest of us were the hoi polloi.

I didn't need a haircut because I'd had one (as a result of Marg's suggestion) when Kevin and I had come ashore. The barber had asked me where I'd been when he saw my hair was practically down to my shoulders. The little bloke had always had a crew cut, but I didn't want to look like a Yank so I'd just had the usual schoolboy short back and sides. Now it looked as if I'd have to get a haircut when I didn't really need one, just so I could casually bring up the subject of French letters.

The following morning I walked into a barber's shop near the wharf, and waited until it was empty. 'Good morning,' I greeted the barber, who looked Italian or maybe Greek – probably Greek, since the Italians had all been rounded up and put in internment camps, even if they'd lived here for fifty years.

'Good morning, sir,' he'd replied, not looking at me, flapping the hair of the previous customer from the barber's cloth to the floor. 'Very good for ze tomato and beans. You want a haircut?'

'Er, yes,' I replied.

He was a little bloke, tummy sticking out, verandah over the toolshed. He looked like he needed a haircut himself and sported a black moustache, waxed and curled up at the ends like a photograph of a German sergeant in the First World War. He turned and looked at me for the first time. 'Why you want haircut?' He jabbed his podgy forefinger at me. 'I cutta your hair two weeks ago! Why you come back? You don't like?'

It was the same barber who'd cut my hair after Kevin and I had come ashore. There'd been so much happening that day and with the excitement of finally making it to Australia, I hadn't noticed the outside of the shop or really taken much notice of the barber. 'No, it's fine, thank you. I just, er . . .'

'You wanna franger? Five bob packet three. You wanna fancy? Tickle pussy?' He bent his arm at the elbow and gripped his left hand with the right, with three fat fingers protruding from the left. He wiggled them. I think this was meant to portray my erection when it was fitted with the fancy condom, the tickle fingers sticking out of the top driving Marg mad with desire. 'Very good, the best! She gonna like *very, very* much. Seven an' six, two packet only fourteen shilling, one bob discount. You want, yes?'

'I'll have the five bob packet, please,' I said, handing him two half-crowns.

He went to the drawer in front of the barber's chair and handed me a small packet. 'Two more week, you come. I give you nice haircut, the best,' he said, then patted me lightly on the shoulder. 'Good luck, you good boy; you don't make baby, leave girl, go to war, get kill, no papa that bambino.'

With the condom issue resolved and the packet safely out of sight in my pocket, I was feeling somewhat more confident. 'What's good for tomatoes and beans?' I asked him, referring to his previous comment.

His podgy hand shot up and he grabbed a tuft of hair on his scalp. 'Hairs. Every night I sweep. Take home dat customer hair, you put in ground for tomato, it grow big like pumpkin, beans, same size zucchini!'

As digging human hair into the vegie patch seemed bizarre enough, I wasn't game to ask him what a zucchini was.

I bought Marg a bunch of carnations, red and white. They cost me more than the condoms. The flower lady wrapped them in butcher's paper. 'It's the war, love,' she sighed in a weary voice. ''Fraid it'll have to be string, brown, no tissue paper, no ribbon neither. For your girlfriend?'

'Yes,' I replied, thinking that Marg was a bit too good to be called a girlfriend, like someone you sometimes took to the movies.

'That's nice. Yer learnin' early. Sure way to a woman's heart. Last time me husband brought home flowers was 1928. He was pissed and stole them from the cemetery after he'd missed the last bus and had ter walk home. It's three o'clock in the mornin' and he's standin' there, holdin' these white arum lilies. "Yer stupid bugger, Perce! Don'tcha know they's bad luck in the home?" I says to him. It's three o'clock in the mornin' and it's garbo collection next day, so I 'as ta go out on the pavement in me nightie and slippers ter throw them in the dustbin. Didn't want no more bad luck in the house, Perce was enough!' She handed me the flowers. 'Good luck, son, hope she's kind ter yer. How come a big, strappin' lad like yiz 'asn't joined up?'

'Next week. Navy,' I said, escaping.

'Good boy!' she called back at me.

So with the barber and the flower lady wishing me luck, I fronted up at Marg's flat at half-past six on the dot. I was wearing my new slacks and shirt and Peter Keeble's jacket, and was feeling in quite a decent mood in a tonight's-the-night sort of way. It's not every day you get this lucky with someone you love. I'd waited at the bus stop for ten minutes so I wouldn't arrive before the appointed hour. I'd been told somewhere that women are never ready on time and that arriving early is considered gauche.

Marg came to the door and I handed her the flowers. 'Nick, how lovely!' she exclaimed, bringing them up to her nose. Carnations have a funny sort of smell, not like roses, but I only found that out after I'd bought them. 'Hmm, beautiful,' she said. 'Come in, dinner won't be long. Starving as usual, I suppose?'

'You look lovely,' I said. She did too: a blue dress that showed off her nice figure, white sort of ballerina-type flatties, suntanned legs and arms, chestnut hair shining, red lipstick and black stuff around her nice green eyes. She looked more glamorous than I'd ever seen her.

'Thank you, Nick. It's nice being out of a uniform. I feel like I'm a proper girl again.'

I needn't tell you what the night that followed was like. Only – just completely – wonderful! We used up my five bob packet and then we had to use naval issue. There's something about nice breasts. You just can't get enough of them, can you? But it was more than that: it was her sweet tenderness, the way she touched me, like I was special. I tried to do the same to her, because she *was* special; I tried sort of stroking her, but my hands are so big it was like a grizzly bear patting a rabbit.

Marg picked me up at the boarding house the following evening in the Austin 7 and drove me all the way to Perth Railway Station. 'I've been saving my petrol coupons. I think we can safely get to the station and there should be just enough in the tank to get me back,' she said. When I'd insisted that I had a travel warrant and could take the bus, she looked at me scornfully. 'We've had the traditional sailor's farewell, Nick. Now I want the traditional woman's farewell. I want to stand tearfully alone on a railway platform with a hiss of steam bursting from the engine's wheels, waving the dearest man in my life goodbye, a small lace handkerchief crumpled in my trembling hand.'

'Oh, Marg, I can't begin to thank you —'

She cut me short. 'Please, no thank yous, Nick. "Thank you" is an ending, not a beginning. Besides, everything we had together was on my own terms.'

'I'll take them rather than enter into negotiations any time of the day,' I said, trying to grin, then almost said 'thank you' again.

On the way to Perth she said, 'Nick, when you've done the course at HMAS *Cerberus* and you're a snotty and they want to send you to a place I can't name or talk about for further training, and you decide you don't want to be in Intelligence or become a coastwatcher, remember, you can always opt out of either – or both. It's not a disgrace, you won't be disadvantaged. The navy will send you to England for further training and you'll emerge a naval officer and I'm sure you'll have a lot of fun. You *will* think about it, won't you?' she urged.

'What's a snotty?' I asked, attempting to avoid answering her.

'A sublieutenant in the navy, the lowest form of officer life,' she answered, a trifle impatiently, immediately recognising my motive for asking.

An idea had begun to form in my head I didn't dare talk about, even to Marg. At first I even rejected it myself, instinctively knowing it was pie in the sky – stupid, irrational. But it wouldn't go away and instead it kept invading my thoughts, nagging at me: as a coastwatcher I could ask to be sent to New Britain, where I could try to discover if my father was still alive.

I guess there was still too much *Boys' Own Annual* or the Saturday movie matinee in me – *Nick sets out to save his father deep in the tropical jungles of New Britain. Will he succeed? Don't miss next week's exciting episode! Etc.* Here I was, just removed from being a virgin, yet still acting like a kid. My mind was filled with too much derring-do and I didn't have enough feet-on-the-ground commonsense.

'I promise I'll think about it,' I said, to ameliorate Marg's concern that I'd be wasting my youth alone in the jungle, that I'd suffer from dengue fever and malaria, and that reporting on the movements of the Japs should best be left to older locals who had been trained for a couple of weeks in the use of a short-wave radio. Marg always saw things clearly. She would have made a good ship's captain.

She was now, quite possibly, the only one left of the people I loved and who were important in my life, and we were about to be separated by the width of Australia. The idea of going to England for further training sounded okay, but judging from the news on the radio, 1942 wasn't exactly party time in Britain.

Nicholas Duncan was back to being a loner, and the prospect of spending time in the jungle didn't overly concern me. It was an environment I understood better than the city and, yeah, I admit, there'd be a chance to catch butterflies. If Anna had been in Australia or Marg closer, then I might have had second thoughts – although I don't know.

However, as things stood, being my own boss in the solitude of the islands sounded a lot better than being a young naval sublieutenant buried in a submarine or aboard HMAS *Something* and being blown out of the water by a Japanese destroyer. I guess all navies are roughly the same, and I'd heard enough about the US Navy from the little bloke to make me wary. Moreover witnessing the slaughter of the shipwrecked sailors from the *Perth* on that lonely beach in Java, then our own lucky escape across the Indian Ocean on *Madam Butterfly*, left me somewhat indifferent to the romance of a career at sea. Sailing is one thing, but surviving at sea or being blown to kingdom come quite another. If I was going to die I wanted to have some say in the matter.

I'd been issued with a travel warrant to be presented to the movement officer at Perth Railway Station, together with my booking slip for second-class travel to Melbourne, all meals included. There were lots of blokes in uniform, air force and army, boarding the train, but no navy. They kept glancing at Marg, probably wondering what a young bloke like me was doing with a terrific sort like her. They probably concluded she was my sister; that is, until they saw the farewell kiss.

When I entered my compartment an air force bloke made room for me at the window. 'Jeez, you don't muck around, do you?' he said admiringly. Then, as the railway guard gave a sharp blast from his whistle and called 'All aboard!', slamming carriage doors as he worked his way down the platform, Marg reached into her handbag. 'This arrived ten minutes before I left the office. Your godfather, the Archbishop, received it in the afternoon mail and phoned. We had it come by naval motorcycle dispatch rider. You'll want to read it on the train,' she said, smiling and handing through the window a fairly large envelope addressed to me with a round printed circle on the left-hand corner that read 'US Army Air Force Command Mail, Colombo, Ceylon'.

I accepted the envelope, looking at it quizzically, but almost before I could comment the guard gave a final blast of his whistle and the train started to pull away. 'Nick, I'm so glad you came into my life, albeit briefly,' Marg said, reaching to touch my outstretched hand and, I could see, trying hard to restrain her tears.

'Marg, I love you!' I called as the train gathered momentum and moved into the darkness where her lovely face was only just visible on the fast-disappearing platform.

It may seem improbable, but I was so upset about leaving Marg that I quite forgot about the envelope I held in my hand. So much had happened; in only a matter of a few weeks my life had changed immeasurably. I guess I'd grown up, in some respects even beyond my years. The air force bloke must have read my thoughts. 'Christ! It isn't easy, is it, mate?' Then he explained. 'I left my wife and two kids all recovering from the measles. God knows if I'll ever see them again. Wife and two little faces looking real crook and sad from the window and me walking down the front path off to war.'

I opened the envelope and withdrew Anna's letter.

Tjilatjap, Java
5th March 1942
My dearest Nicholas – This was struck through and directly below it Anna wrote:

My darling Nicholas,

I do not know if you are alive and have come in the Vleermuis already to Australia. But I think it is so, or I would feel it in mijn heart.

. . . My stepmother commit suicide in the river, she is jumped in the river and Kleine Kiki she cannot rescue her because she cannot swim. They have not found the body. Mijn

father he is also drunk since Batavia.

. . . Nicholas I love you. I am very sorry I did not let you make love to me. Maybe I will die and not know how it would be to make love to you!

I love you, my darling Nicholas. Forever!

Anna – Madam Butterfly X X X X!
P.S. I have always the Clipper butterfly. I will keep it till I die. I love you!
A

I sat stunned, but confess I didn't cry. Anna's letter told me everything we had professed to each other. It told of her love for me and her hopes for the future, but nothing about what would happen to her once she was stuck in Java with the Japanese about to arrive. The suicide of her abusive stepmother must have been very difficult for her, and then having to cope alone with Piet Van Heerden's drunken behaviour. Funny, I'd always thought the big Dutchman was full of shit. Some blokes who seem totally in command of their environment can't hack it when they're removed from their comfort zone.

We'd had a maths master at school, Mr Bruce Batten. We called him 'Bastard Bruce' because in class he was a genuine megalomaniac who delighted in tormenting kids. As vice-principal he was permitted to cane boys. He proceeded to do so on a regular basis and with atavistic delight. He was also one of the two masters in charge of the cadets. When we were on a weekend camp in the bush he'd taken a platoon of first-year students on a map-reading course in the morning and they were due back in time for lunch. By midnight he hadn't turned up and I was sent out with four volunteers to find him. It was a full moon so it was not difficult to see and, as we were not avoiding an enemy, we walked in the open, calling out. We came across their camp in a small dead-end canyon at three in the morning. The juniors had gathered a stack of firewood and made a fire and were sleeping soundly around it. When we woke them, apart from being hungry and devouring the rations we'd brought with us, they were in reasonably good spirits.

However, Bastard Bruce was not amongst them. One of the kids told us he'd seen him heading further up the canyon and he'd seemed pretty frightened. I eventually discovered him about twenty feet up the end wall of the canyon, sitting on a narrow ledge, whimpering. When he was asked to come down he had trouble with his shaking legs. He was exhausted and it took us nearly five hours to get him back to camp, one of our blokes taking the kids ahead. I'd only had to cope with Bastard Bruce for those few hours and I'd found the experience thoroughly distasteful. Poor Anna would have had to deal with her drunken and pathetic father from the moment they'd left Batavia.

As the train chuffed through the night I realised that Kevin and I had been still out to sea, within the range of Japanese warships and aircraft, when Anna had written the letter. Now, anything could be happening to her. One thing was certain: there was likely to be no news, or very little reliable information, out of the island for the duration of the war.

I removed Anna's embroidered handkerchief from my wallet, and when everyone had gone to sleep, I spread it across my knee. Searching for the raised stitching of the embroidered butterfly with the tips of my finger, I placed my hand over it and recited Psalm 23 aloud, though softly. This was the psalm my father had rejected in favour of the Irish blessing when writing his letter. Every schoolboy knows the words off by heart:

> The Lord is my shepherd; I shall not want.
> He maketh me to lie down in green pastures:
> he leadeth me beside the still waters.
> He restoreth my soul: he leadeth me in the paths
> of righteousness for his name's sake.
> Yea, though I walk through the valley of the
> shadow of death, I will fear no evil: for thou art
> with me; thy rod and thy staff they comfort me.
> Thou preparest a table before me in the presence
> of mine enemies: thou anointest my head with oil;
> my cup runneth over.
>
> Surely goodness and mercy shall follow me all the
> days of my life: and I will dwell in the house of the
> Lord for ever.

There I was in the middle of the night, crossing the continent with five other blokes who were sound asleep, reciting the psalm as if by so doing I would keep Anna safe. Even though my father was an Anglican missionary I didn't consider myself particularly religious. But there are occasions when we reach for the comfort of words, and God has created some of the very best. I guess, if He was listening, He may have thought me a bit of a hypocrite. I'd just come from the arms of one woman I loved and here I was asking Him to protect another I also loved. It was what my father might call spiritual bigamy. I was unable to separate the two kinds of loving, and now both of the loved ones were lost to me. I would, of course, write to Marg, but she might as well have been in Timbuktu for all the hope I had of seeing her in the immediate future.

I realised with a shock that, if I ended up in the islands, I might never see her again, or at least not until the war was over, whenever that was. Who knows? I might be dead by that time, although I didn't think I would be. Like most blokes of eighteen, I thought of myself as bullet-proof.

The crossing took three days and nights: first main stop was Kalgoorlie, then across the Nullarbor Plain to Port Pirie, Adelaide and finally Melbourne. The ever practical and thoughtful Marg had sourced two Japanese books for me, explaining that they had been taken from an old Japanese couple who had been interned when the war broke out. 'I can't imagine why they wouldn't allow them to take a book or two with them,' she said at the time. Then she added, 'Intelligence makes some weird decisions. How a couple well into their seventies, having lived in Broome for fifty years, could be considered dangerous enemy aliens beats me.'

'Broome? They probably came over for the pearl diving and stayed on,' I interjected.

'Maybe. Anyway, I found these in the restricted departmental library and, in the name of Naval Intelligence, confiscated them. I thought it might be a good idea to brush up on your Japanese while on the train. I've covered them in brown paper and I suggest you don't let any of the passengers see you reading a Japanese book or they're likely to report you to the conductor.' She laughed. 'You don't want some boofhead police sergeant escorting you off the train at Port Augusta.'

They don't refer to it as the 'outback' for nothing. There's not a great deal other than saltbush to look at from your compartment window. The two volumes were both classical Japanese tales: *The Story of Genji*, which I hadn't read, and *The Forty-seven Ronin*, a tale of honour and great heroism that I'd read as a young boy. My father had urged me to read the first one as a child, but I'd somehow avoided doing so. Inscribed on the flyleaf of both books, rather poignantly, were the names Shimuzi Masa and Shimuzi Korin and the date, 1892. Now the books proved to be a great deal more interesting than the scenery as we crossed the seemingly endless Nullarbor.

We came into Spencer Street Station early on the fourth morning and I said goodbye to my fellow passengers; not a bad mob, although they'd carried on a bit, teasing me about the final kiss on the platform. By the time we'd reached Melbourne, the thirty or so seconds it had taken to kiss Marg goodbye had extended in their imaginations to at least an hour of ardent groping that stopped just short of having sex in public. The last words to me from the air force bloke were, 'Be faithful, Nick. You don't come across a good sort like that every day, mate!' This brought the house down – well, the compartment anyway.

So Nick Duncan, the passionate platform lover, found himself alone in a strange city that was just beginning the workday. My written instructions were that, upon arrival, I was to report to the Naval Recruitment Office in Olderfleet Buildings, 475 Collins Street at 9 a.m. sharp and present the recruitment officer with a sealed envelope that was enclosed herewith. I asked a bloke carrying a briefcase where the office was and he said it was five minutes' walk and pointed up the tram tracks outside the station. I had at least an hour and a half to kill, even if I allowed fifteen minutes to find the recruitment office, so I checked into the railway café and blew some of the travel allowance I'd been given on 'the works': fried eggs, sausage, bacon, tomato and three pieces of toast with a pot of tea that held two cups. I still had time on my hands, so I walked through the city and went and stood on the bridge over the Yarra River, watching the schoolboys sculling on the lazy brown river. Melbourne seemed like a nice place with a park practically in the centre of the city, just across from the station and the railway yards, and stretching beside the river.

I found the recruitment office without difficulty. The ground-floor reception area, more like a small hall, was beginning to fill with young blokes, recruits like me who'd been waiting for the doors to open. We were instructed to queue behind either of two desks, at each of which a female petty officer in uniform sat. Both were quite attractive, and I chose the queue with the prettier of the two, a redhead. Someone in the crowd gave a wolf whistle and, seemingly from nowhere, this big bloke in the naval uniform of a chief petty officer appeared and in a voice that rose above the noise in the crowded hall shouted, 'There'll be none of that! You're in the navy now!' The whole hall went dead silent. Then he added, 'Snotties are entitled to admire silently and that's all, gentlemen!' which caused a roar of laughter. My turn came soon enough and I handed the envelope to the pretty redhead. She opened it, read it briefly, then raised the telephone, dialled, waited a moment, then responded to the voice on the other end, 'Sir, I have Nicholas Duncan, the recruit recommended by the DNI in Fremantle.' She listened for a few moments, then placed the receiver back on the cradle. 'You are to go to the second floor,' she pointed. 'Take the lift. Ask for Commander Rich.' She smiled, then handed me the original letter and wrote my name and the date on a small card that read 'Access permitted'. She stamped it, then signed her initials under the date. 'Hand this to the commander when you get there, Mr Duncan.'

'Nick, Miss,' I replied, thanking her. 'Your name is . . . ?'

Her eyebrows shot up in surprise. 'Cheeky! Definitely officer material,' she grinned, sending me off with a backward wave of her hand.

Yet another important lesson learned. I was simply being polite and now had been inadvertently instructed in yet another of the techniques of approaching a woman. With my sort of loner background, I was taking a bloody long time (despite, thanks to Marg, not being a virgin any longer) to learn how to flirt. The bloke who'd whistled when we'd come in probably knew all the techniques for picking up a sheila while I hadn't a clue.

To my surprise, Commander Rich stood as I entered his office and walked around the side of his desk to shake my hand. 'Rob Rich, nice to meet you, Nick.' He pointed to one of two easy chairs. 'Please, have a seat.'

'Good morning, sir,' I said, somewhat nervously sitting where he indicated. I'd been expecting to be shunted along with all the other recruits and treated like the mishmash we were, and so all this upstairs stuff came as a total surprise.

'Welcome. I will be your commanding officer on HMAS *Cerberus*. I'm just up for the day and thought we might have a chat.'

'Yes, thank you, sir,' I replied. Something was definitely weird. You didn't have to be Einstein to know that a raw recruit to any of the armed forces doesn't get sent into the office of the commander for a friendly powwow. Feeling decidedly awkward, I handed him the letter. He reached over and took it, then placed it on his lap without glancing at it.

'You come to us rather highly recommended, Duncan,' he said.

'Sir?' He could see I was confused and had no idea what he was referring to. 'You mean Lieutenant Commander Rigby?' I asked, surprised.

'Amongst others. I refer to a note from the Archbishop of Perth.'

I could feel myself blushing furiously. 'Sir, please ignore it. He's my godfather!' I begged.

He seemed to be amused. 'Also a two-liner from God Himself.'

I sensed I was in some sort of trouble. 'God, sir?'

'Commander Long – but take no notice of the "commander" tag; in Naval Intelligence he packs a bigger punch than any admiral afloat. I also have a transcript from Lieutenant Commander Rigby telling of your exploits prior to landing in Fremantle. Very impressive. You're the first eighteen-year-old snotty I've come across to have his life marked "Top Secret".'

Now I knew I was definitely in trouble. First the Archbishop's letter, then a note from Commander Rupert Basil Michael Long (as Marg always referred to him). His notes were obviously as clipped and precise as his speech.

I was conscious that Commander Rob Rich was, in a manner of speaking, my new headmaster and I sensed I was about to cop a real serve. 'I'm sorry, sir,' I said lamely, looking him directly in the eye. Surely he must see that I had nothing to do with anything coming out of Perth and Fremantle? If someone was pulling strings, then it wasn't my fault and was in fact the very last thing I would have wanted or expected.

'Right then, let's get on with it. You are not yet officially a snotty so we will consider this conversation off the record. However, there are one or two things I feel I need to straighten out before you join the navy.'

'Yes, sir – thank you.' I was suddenly twelve again and standing up at prep in front of my school boarding house, having arrived late in the first term to boarding school. Grimy Ferret, our housemaster, was asking me questions, a distinctly acerbic tone to his voice. My naïve answers were meeting with howls of orchestrated laughter from the other pupils. Only unlike Grimy Ferret, this guy, Rich, wasn't milking the interview for cheap laughs.

'Commander Long has spoken to you about joining Intelligence.' It was a statement, not a question, and so I remained silent. 'You speak Japanese.' Another statement. 'What did Commander Long say to you, Nick?' A question.

Marg had warned me not to speak to anyone about the coastwatcher thing. I thought she meant not to talk to any member of the public, so I replied, 'He spoke about my joining the coastwatchers, listening to Japanese radio messages, ship to shore, then sending back information by radio code about the movements of the enemy.'

'We'll stop right there. You are already in possession of top-secret information.' He jabbed his forefinger at me. 'You will never, I repeat *never*, say that again! Not a single syllable. Do you understand? What else did he say to you?' he barked, jabbing his finger once again in the direction of my chest.

I found it difficult not to smile. 'I'm not sure I know what you're talking about, sir. Who is Commander Long?'

He leaned back and grinned. 'Well done, Nick. Just remember codebreaking is the most important component of

Intelligence and must never be jeopardised, *never*. If you decide to go in the direction indicated, you will have to become accustomed to leading a double life, a veiled life, even with those closest to you.'

This time I had to smile inwardly. One of those closest to me was on the opposite side of Australia some two thousand miles away. A second, if he was alive, was probably a prisoner of the Japanese in New Britain. The third, if she was alive, was probably in an internment camp in Java. It wasn't as if I'd be spilling the beans in a casual chat with a neighbour across the garden fence. 'I fully understand, sir,' I said.

'Right then, let me fill you in on the next twelve weeks. You'll be one of two hundred recruits at HMAS *Cerberus*. When you graduate the rest of your class will be sent to the UK for further training, choosing their future careers from several specialist naval training options that are available. Because all the others will be discussing their choices, you'll have to pretend to make some sort of decision yourself, perhaps wireless, eh? When the time comes and you're not on the boat going to the UK they'll assume you've failed the course.' He looked up. 'So don't appear to be over-bright during the next twelve weeks. Not a bad idea to start leading a double life right away, eh?'

'Sounds a bit like surviving at boarding school, sir,' I said, relaxing in his presence just a little.

'Not a bad analogy. I see you went to a private school. You're going to find it very similar. I don't expect you'll have any trouble. Cadet captain, eh?'

If only he'd known my greatest hope was that HMAS *Cerberus* would in no way replicate my school career. Commander Rob Rich seemed a decent sort of cove and moreover, though I felt sure it was mentioned more than once in the transcript he'd been sent, he never once mentioned butterflies.

I passed the medical test and the less said about the next twelve weeks the better. I found it difficult to keep silent when I knew the answer to a question with which some of the others were struggling. My years as a kid who kept his mouth shut stood me in good stead. At best, the rest of the class would have taken me for dead average, which was true enough in some ways. It was familiar territory and not unlike my earlier years at boarding school when I'd read most of the books in the school library and was frequently forced to bite my tongue when a schoolmaster made a blatant error of fact or expressed an arguable opinion.

As for the rest, it was twelve shillings and sixpence pay each day. Drill, drill and more drill, with basic seamanship lessons that encompassed navy history, law and etiquette, basic coastal and celestial navigation, small arms practice (where I was allowed to excel; perhaps even show off a bit). Then there was PT, PT, PT! This was followed by unarmed combat, where the average-sized instructor, Wayne Bloggs, nicknamed 'Joe' of course, delighted in taking on the big bloke. I was soon covered in bruises, but I learned a fair bit in the process and decided to take unarmed combat further if I was ever given the opportunity. And there was lots of sport – I was good at cross-country running, despite my size, lousy at boxing and Aussie Rules football, in which I had not the slightest interest.

That was about it, really. In a sense it was much of what I'd done, one way or another, for most of my teenage life, both at boarding school and during the school holidays. That time had been followed by a period when I'd spent a fair amount of time at sea, either on a clumsy, difficult-to-sail missionary boat with an indifferent native crew, or if I got lucky, on a glorious ketch like the inimitable *Madam Butterfly*.

For the passing-out parade we had ourselves measured at the Myer department store in Bourke Street for our uniforms. These were ready two days later and basically fitted where they touched. But we felt grand and very important, each a legitimate snotty at last. All the particular friends I'd made over the course put in to hire a hotel room at the London Hotel in Elizabeth Street and we had a party. A lot of the blokes were from Melbourne and so they brought their sweethearts. Mary Kelly, the pretty redhead petty officer who'd been behind the desk when I'd registered as a naval recruit, accompanied me. When I'd left Commander Rich's office and come back down again in the lift to the reception hall she'd risen from her desk and walked over to me; without saying a word, she'd pushed a small piece of paper that had her name and contact number into my shirt pocket and returned to her desk.

I'd taken her out on the four occasions when we'd been granted shore leave, not counting this graduation party. She was an excellent kisser, with a tongue that was a better explorer than David Livingstone. But anything below the chin was strictly off limits. She was a Catholic and pronounced that anything else was 'for the marriage bed'. Or, as she once replied to my urgent pleading, 'That sort of malarky is for between the sheets and they're folded in cellophane paper in my glory box, Nick!'

Still, she was fun, with a quick Irish–Australian wit. I always enjoyed her company, even though after spending my shore leave with her I'd invariably return in the train to HMAS

Cerberus nursing a severe attack of lover's balls. I was learning that when in the company of a pretty woman my brains seemed invariably to migrate and take up residence roughly eight inches below my navel. But afterwards, when the ache finally wore off, knowing that I'd been faithful to Marg I felt terrifically noble.

I guess all young blokes are hypocrites. I secretly knew that if Petty Officer Mary Kelly, for whatever unlikely reason, decided to metaphorically rip the cellophane from a couple of double-bed sheets in her glory box, I'd be down to the barber's shop in a flash, or I'd put in for a packet or two of standard naval issue.

No such luck. On our night ashore at the London Hotel most of the blokes got pretty pissed and so did some of the girls. One or two couples even paid for a room for a short time, something the London Hotel seemed to accept as standard practice. But, as usual, I didn't get past Mary's chin, even though she'd managed to down eight brandy crustas and needed a fair bit of physical support at 5 a.m. when I finally escorted her home to Fitzroy on the early tram. She slept with my arm around her and her head cushioned against my shoulder for most of the trip, which was really nice. It felt good, taking your bird home at dawn after a big night. Then, when we got off the tram and walked the short distance to her home, she'd kissed me at the front gate and said, pointing to a lighted window in the small house, 'Dad will be getting up to go to work at the docks. Better make yourself scarce, darlin'. Thanks for a t'riffic night.'

Two more lessons learned – never step out with a girl who lives at home, and a good Irish Catholic girl is a peak too high to scale, even with a pocket full of naval issue condoms. In the tram going back to Flinders Street Station I recited 'Sweet

Mary O'Rourke', the ballad the broken-down jockey, Tony Crosby, the cadge-a-drink guitarist in the pub at Rabaul, used to sing. This met with laughter and applause from the early-morning passengers and a demand for an encore. I guess I must have been a bit more pissed than I'd thought.

The day before our passing-out parade Commander Rich summoned me to his office. This time I entered and stood at rigid attention and saluted. 'Sit down, Sublieutenant Duncan,' he invited. When I was seated he took the chair beside me. 'Well done, Nick. Your written material is of a very high standard and thanks for keeping your presence in class low-key.'

'I'm not so sure if it was always deliberate, sir,' I grinned.

'Enjoy the course?'

'Yes, sir.'

'You'll never make a footballer or a boxer but your small arms results are as good as any I've seen.'

I grinned, rubbing my chin. 'I guess I'll have to learn more about martial arts, sir.'

He laughed. 'Yes, you seem to have taken a tumble or two from Petty Officer Bloggs, who reports you have lots of guts. That's good. The navy, as you will have come to know, is obsessed with the subject of guts.' He paused, then said, 'Guts isn't always a physical thing; sometimes it takes considerable guts to change one's mind.'

'Yes, sir,' I replied, not entirely certain what was coming next.

'Nick, you will make an excellent officer and, if you decided to stay in the navy, I feel quite sure you would have the ability to excel. Wars are very good for rapid promotion, Nick. I believe you have the ability to reach Lieutenant Commander before this war looks like finishing. I don't say this sort of thing too often; some of our brightest have been known to disappoint. I think you should know that if you change your mind about reporting to Airlie after you've had your post-graduation break, the navy would think no less of you. You would go with the other graduate lieutenants to the UK. What do you think? Have you made up your mind to stick with Intelligence?'

'Thank you for your confidence in me, sir. Yes, I think I —'

Before I could add another word he said quickly, 'Nick, you're only eighteen and the task they want you to undertake is a highly dangerous one. I feel compelled to tell you that were it not for your fluency in Japanese I am sure DNI would not have entertained the idea of recruiting you. It's a job for old hands – men who have been in the islands a long time and know their way around.'

'Yes, sir, I understand what you're saying.'

'But do you? Do you really?' he urged. I was aware that I was forcing him to be more persistent and persuasive than he might have preferred to be in the presence of a snotty. Naval commanders don't generally ask for cooperation. They simply demand compliance.

I felt certain that if I hadn't been expressly sent to HMAS *Cerberus* for training by the Department of Naval Intelligence, Rob Rich would not have permitted me to choose the task Commander Rupert Basil Michael Long (as I'd come to think of him) had persuaded me to undertake. Moreover if it hadn't been for my father's presence in New Britain – though no doubt he was already, or very soon was likely to be, a prisoner of the Japanese – I might have changed my mind. I had enjoyed the basic course and felt sure I would have liked to undertake further study in Britain.

I felt I owed Rich an explanation. 'Sir, in a manner of speaking, except for my age, I feel I have the qualifications needed. I speak pidgin and several, though certainly not all, of the many coastal native languages. I know the coastline of both New Britain and New Guinea, and all Pacific islands are similar in topography. I can handle a rifle, sail a boat and understand how to survive in the jungle. As you yourself indicated, a thorough knowledge of Japanese is a very useful component, although I would doubt if any of the old-timers speak or understand it. I would, of course, just as they would, be required to learn those other skills you cautioned me never to mention.' Anticipating that he might raise the matter, I added, 'My father is a missionary. I am well accustomed to being alone, sir.'

He sighed. 'Yes, well I don't suppose butterfly collecting in the field encourages group activity.' It was the first mention he'd ever made of butterflies, though he hadn't spoken in a manner that suggested he thought butterfly collecting an arcane pursuit.

He spread his palms. 'Well, Nick, while I personally think you're making the wrong decision, you have guts and you're obviously stubborn. Both characteristics will stand you in good stead. As for your other qualifications and prior experience, I can't argue, they're first-rate in every respect. Those additional technical skills you'll need you'll acquire easily enough.' He grinned and stuck out his hand. 'It's a damned shame, Commander Long wins and the navy loses. I wish you luck.'

We shook hands and I stood to attention and saluted. 'Thank you, sir. Thank you for the talk. I appreciate the advice.'

Commander Rich rose from his chair with a half-smile on

his face. 'Go on, piss off, Duncan, you're dismissed.' He wasn't a man who liked to lose at anything and especially not to someone like Commander Rupert Basil Michael Long. I couldn't help feeling that he was a little surprised that he'd failed to persuade me, but he'd nevertheless accepted my decision with more or less good grace.

I'd been invited to spend the two weeks' leave on a property on the Mornington Peninsula that belonged to the parents of a fellow snotty, Bill MacKenzie, but, of course, I was forced to refuse. Bill was a thoroughly decent bloke and, knowing I was alone (travelling to Perth to see Marg was out of the question and I couldn't get a railway travel pass anyway), suggested that I stay with his family until the boat sailed. His parents would see us sail off to what he claimed his second-generation Australian father referred to as 'Going home'. Telling lies is never pleasant, especially to people who are kind and generous. And, of course, I wasn't sailing to England with the rest of the blokes.

Instead, I took a room Mary Kelly's mum found for me in a boarding house in Fitzroy where she worked as a day cook. I spent the days studying Japanese and walking around Melbourne, a city I immediately warmed to. That is, as much as one can enjoy a city environment. At night we went dancing – Mary training my two left feet into some kind of coordination – or to the movies, or we just wandered around the city.

Sailing day approached and I was beginning to panic. How was I going to tell Mary not to come to the docks to see me off? Her dad had already organised for her to stand on a special spot where I would be able to see her as virtually the last hand waving when we (that's supposedly me) drew away from the shore.

Two days before the boat was to sail, a tearful Mary informed me that she'd put in for leave on sailing day but permission had been refused; she'd tried every ruse she could think of to no avail. 'It's not as though we're doing anything special, Nick,' she protested. 'I even got Erica Kransky to agree to stand in for me, but they got quite cross. "You'll be at your desk at 9 a.m. as usual, Petty Officer Kelly," the Chief Petty Officer said. "Why, Ken? Erica says she'll stand in for me," I begged him. He's usually pretty good; I mean, if someone has a wedding to attend or something. As long as the recruitment desk is manned he doesn't really care.'

'It's the command mentality. Even if it's your grandma's funeral, dying isn't the excuse it used to be – it's what you're supposed to do in a war,' I replied, trying to comfort Mary while, at the same time, saying a silent thank you to Commander Rich.

'I tried the grandma thing, even though the old chook died ten years ago – she'd be well out of purgatory by now. The chief just said, "Mary, it comes from above, 'fraid there's nothing I can do." Bloody navy! I told them why I wanted the morning off. You'd think they'd bloody well understand seeing off your sweetheart was important, wouldn't you?'

'It doesn't matter, we'll have the last night together. There'll be a big crowd at the wharf. It's not much of a way to say goodbye anyway.' I was remembering Anna on the *Witvogel*. How quickly she'd become a blur in the late afternoon light and how afterwards I'd walked back to the yacht, lonely and confused, wondering what was going to happen to us. I'd found somebody I *really* loved and then lost her almost as quickly in a crowded, tearful farewell amongst cranes and *godowns*, ships' horns and yelling, waving people.

I was almost out of money but I took Mary to a swell restaurant in St Kilda Road: white damask tablecloths, serviettes made into chef's caps, waiters in uniform, *bombe* Alaska on a separate dessert menu (which made me think the owner must have had black-market connections) and a booze licence to sell liquor on the premises beyond six o'clock.

Afterwards, we'd found a concealed seat under a Moreton Bay fig tree in the Domain Gardens. Mary had downed a couple of brandy crustas at the restaurant and I'd had a beer or two. We were doing the usual above-the-chin snogging when Mary suddenly pulled away. 'Nick, you know how I said nothing below the chin and about the sheets in my glory box wrapped in cellophane?'

'Yeah,' I said manfully. 'I've suffered terribly as a consequence. It's going to happen again tonight,' I lamented. I'd previously mentioned the advent of lover's balls to her and how it could be prevented, but she'd remained steadfastly unsympathetic.

'Well, what I meant was under *my* chin. Not under yours,' Mary said, grinning. Whereupon she slid down to her knees on the grass and proceeded to carefully unbutton the fly on my trousers.

'What's this?' I asked, astonished and delighted.

'Shush! I have to concentrate. I have to remember what Erica said to do.'

Either it comes instinctively to a woman or Erica Kransky should have been a chief petty officer, because her instructions were so explicit. Mary Kelly's farewell on the night before Nick Duncan's supposed departure to England was spectacular, to say the least. If the chin may be considered to be north, then this was mouth-to-south resuscitation.

The following morning I checked out of the boarding house and said a fond farewell to Mrs Kelly, who smelled of fried onion and fatty bacon. She hugged me and gave me a sweaty, powdery kiss. 'Nick, we loves yer. Yer come home to Mary when yer get back from England, yer hear? Mary says you're an Anglican, high church – that's almost the same as us, so you've got our blessin', providin' you bring up the kids Catholic. But don' ya leave it too long, mate. She's not the sort to become a nun, nor to wither on the vine.'

From the boarding house I took the tram to South Yarra to report as instructed to Airlie, the headquarters of the Allied Intelligence Bureau on the corner of Punt and Domain roads. It was a large Victorian house on the top of a small hill that rose steeply from the slow-flowing Yarra River. One of four military guards at the gate stopped me to examine my papers, made a phone call and told me to report to a dark-green door on the side entrance, to press the bell and wait until somebody came for me. 'Private Rawlings here will escort you, sir,' the guard said.

I was ushered into the office of an overweight army colonel with a bristling moustache who required me to stand, though admittedly at ease, while he interviewed me. He asked, on three separate occasions, 'Do you have guts?' Fortunately he didn't wait for a reply before putting up his hand to indicate silence as he continued reading my dossier. 'Ferchrissake! Butterflies!' He looked up at me in some bewilderment. 'You collect butterflies?'

'Yes, sir.'

'Those things with wings that land on flowers?'

'Yes, sir.'

'Did you say you had guts?'

'Well, no, sir. I mean I didn't say, sir.'

'Well, do you? Speak up, Duncan!'

'Yes, I think so, sir.'

'Navy, eh? Butterflies! Do you have accommodation for tonight, Sublieutenant?'

'No, sir. I checked out of my boarding house this morning.'

'Sergeant!' he yelled. 'Give the butterfly collector from the navy an accommodation slip for a bunk in the hut tonight. He can eat in the officers' mess.'

The following morning I was given a priority movement order to Hervey Bay. This involved a trip from Essendon by Dakota for the seven hour flight to Sydney, where I stayed in the nearby airport accommodation overnight. Late the next morning I flew to Brisbane, another five and a half hours, stayed overnight there and then flew on to Hervey Bay, where I arrived in the midafternoon. In all, the trip took the best part of three days. From Hervey Bay I was taken by launch to Fraser Island, where I was to receive further training.

Fitness, fitness, fitness, until I felt I was jumping out of my skin.

No letters allowed to Marg or Mary. No letters to be received. I had simply disappeared from the planet. Unarmed combat followed, especially the use of knives, then the required training in wireless, map work, basic coding of messages, morse code, security, malaria treatment: all the standard skills required for small élite forces being trained to act independently behind enemy lines in tropical jungle conditions. Some of the training was exciting, although most of it consisted of tedious repetition. In the months that followed the tedious bits were to prove the most important.

Finally, when I was about two weeks short of completing my training, after lunch one day Sergeant Major Wainwright, who'd become my mentor on Fraser, turned up. 'CO wants to see you, Duncan, in his office at 1500 hours. I'll escort you myself.'

'What's it about, Sergeant Major?' I asked him.

'Can't say, Sublieutenant,' he replied.

'Can't or won't?'

'Not for me to comment,' he said, closing the conversation. He was our chief weapons instructor, tough as old boots. He'd been in Malaya and Singapore for more than a year before the war started, and had been a member of one of the first commando units that was formed in England in 1940. He'd been sent to Singapore to train small stay-behind units to work as guerrillas if the Japanese should attack. He was an expert in harassment and survival in the jungle. You don't find too many blokes like him, even in the army, and I admired him greatly.

Fortunately, he'd been sent back to Australia before Singapore collapsed. His speciality was the Owen submachine-gun, but there was nothing he couldn't do when it came to dirty fighting. He trained us in the use of an Owen, amongst other things, and

I took to the weapon like a duck to water.

Colonel Voight was a laid-back Queenslander, formally a grazier, popular with just about everyone but nevertheless a pretty forthright sort of cove, the quiet-voice-with-big-stick type. 'You're still a couple of weeks short in your training, Sublieutenant Duncan, but I'm afraid you're needed elsewhere. You're being seconded to the Yanks,' he said, straight off.

'Americans, sir?' I replied, surprised.

'I don't know if you've drawn the lucky or unlucky straw, but they're desperately short of people who are trained as coastwatchers and can speak Japanese – in fact you're it. You're off to the New Hebrides, to Luganville, to be precise.'

I'd heard that the small town of Luganville on the southern coast of the island of Espiritu Santo was where the US forces had established their major Pacific base. They'd turned a sleepy Anglo-French coastal village into a virtual city that stretched for five miles along the magnificent natural harbour. It could house a hundred thousand American troops and their support personnel, possessed six telephone exchanges, hospitals, cinemas, several dozen mess halls that could feed a thousand men at a time, and major ordnance repair facilities. I wasn't exactly excited about the prospect of being a translator in a makeshift city that was a long way from the war zone.

'Luganville, sir? It's not exactly what I was trained for,' I said, openly showing my disappointment.

He shrugged. 'Ours is not to reason why but to do as we're told. The message to get you to Luganville brooked no contradiction. Oh, and by the way, congratulations – the order included a promotion to lieutenant. Somebody in HQ Intelligence understands that the Yanks respect a bit of extra braid. Cheer up, Duncan, you'll be the youngest lieutenant in

THE PERSIMMON TREE   617

the Australian Navy.'

'Sir, I'd much prefer to stay a snotty and do the job I was trained to do.'

'Well, in that case you've drawn the short straw.' He glanced down at my training reports. 'Hmm, I see you've excelled in unarmed combat and close-quarter knife fighting.' He grinned. 'You may get to use a paper knife to open envelopes. Bad luck, son – afraid it happens to the best of us. Now get your arse into gear, pack your kit; you're catching the two o'clock launch to Hervey Bay and taking a night flight in a B-17 to New Caledonia. They'll fix you up with your extra braid in Hervey Bay.'

'Sir?'

His hand shot up to deny me. 'Don't ask me any more questions, that's all I know, Lieutenant.'

I saluted. 'Yes, thank you, sir,' then left his office. 'Shit! Shit! Shit!' I yelled once I was outside. I could see it all. I'd be stuck in an office in Luganville, translating Japanese radio broadcasts for the Yanks for the duration of the fucking war. So much for the intrepid boy coastwatcher rescuing his dad from the clutches of the evil Japanese invader! That's the trouble with the Saturday matinee, you still have to go home and mow the lawn.

CHAPTER SEVENTEEN

'Yes! Goddamn, yes! Tjilatjap airport!
What was her name?
Anna, that's right, Anna!
The most beautiful young creature
I've ever seen.
Violet blue eyes, remarkable!'
Colonel Greg Woon
US Army Air Force Command
Guadalcanal, August 1942

I PACKED MY KIT: three white shirts and shorts, socks, white tropical shoes, underpants and toiletries. All kept to a minimum so that I could stow the unassembled parts of an Owen submachine-gun, some spare magazines and three hundred rounds of ammunition. I admit that taking an Owen with me must seem like a pretty stupid thing to do but I was trained to be very efficient in its use. It was an Australian invention, not a weapon the Americans used in combat, hence the ammunition. The Owen submachine-gun competed with the Austen, the Australian-made British Sten gun, as the utility weapon in both armies, but there was a big difference between them. The Sten gun, while light, was essentially a piece of water pipe with a butt, crude magazine and trigger, a hastily welded-together piece of crap that was prone to jam and overheat, often failed to work in muddy conditions or after being submerged, and couldn't be effectively aimed at anything beyond fifteen yards. You could almost spit more accurately. On the other hand, the Owen was reliable, seldom if ever jammed, didn't overheat, worked in all combat conditions and in well-trained hands was reasonably accurate up to fifty yards. But it was heavier – and this was often the reason why troops preferred the Sten gun, reasoning that they were unlikely to find themselves in close combat conditions and resenting every bit of weight they had to lug around. The bureaucrats in Defence Headquarters in Melbourne, who counted numbers, not bodies, saw the Sten gun as cheaper and quicker to manufacture and therefore easier on the war budget.

I told myself that if ever I went to work behind enemy lines as a coastwatcher, I wanted a weapon with which I was thoroughly familiar and, more importantly, one that was reliable and wouldn't let me down in a crisis. I had won this particular Owen at Fraser Island in a shooting competition. The butt had been varnished and carried a small polished brass plate that read:

Sublieutenant
Nick Duncan
'Mr. 98%'
Fraser Is. 1942

The 98 per cent was the score I'd achieved in the comp. While this may seem remarkable by ordinary army marksman standards, I was being trained by Z Force and 90 per cent was the required competence, and that with a double tap – the ability to hit the enemy at around twenty-five yards in the chest and above the bridge of the nose in two single, near-simultaneous shots.

On the afternoon the CO told me to pack up, Sergeant Major Wainwright appeared with a standard skeleton wire buttstock he'd personally painted in camouflage colours. 'Leave the nice one with me, boyo, this one is lighter. Take the brass plate for luck, keep it in your breast pocket over your heart. Legend has it a pocket Bible once saved some Christian git in the Boer War – never know when your luck might run out, boyo.'

On the 26th of August 1942, lugging an overweight kitbag, with my naval uniform carrying more rank than the person wearing it was entitled to, I climbed into a B-17 for the night flight to New Caledonia.

I couldn't help wondering what the Yanks would think of an eighteen-year-old naval lieutenant. I knew that, unlike us Australians, they admired success and didn't set about cutting down tall poppies, but even so, I felt they'd be more than entitled to question my navy credentials – a young snotty does not easily earn the right to wear a lieutenant's braid in any man's navy. The path from midshipman to full lieutenant is often said to be the hardest in a navy career. Someone at Naval Intelligence HQ obviously hadn't looked at my date of birth. They'd been thinking protocol, not wishing their man (who would be working alongside our Allied friends) to be disadvantaged by the lowest officer rank in the navy.

Fortunately, at six feet three inches and fourteen stone (or, as the Americans would have it, one hundred and ninety-six pounds), I looked a bit older, maybe twenty-two, even if I only had to shave twice a week. Even twenty-two is a bit young for that sort of rapid promotion. I decided if anyone asked, apart from those who could check my official documents, I'd claim to be twenty-five and that I was slow to mature. Lying about your age is a long-established military and naval tradition. The youngest soldier who fought at Lone Pine in Gallipoli turned out to be fourteen years old and eleven-year-old boys fought with Nelson at Trafalgar.

Still sulking somewhat, I reached New Caledonia just after sunrise. After refuelling and a change of aircrew, a cup of coffee and a cold croissant, we resumed our flight to Luganville, where I was met on the tarmac by a US lieutenant, whom I immediately saluted, momentarily forgetting I'd been gratuitously promoted. He saluted in turn, but looked a bit confused, thinking no doubt it must be something we do in the Australian Navy. I could feel myself colouring, the prickly heat spreading up my neck and into my face with embarrassment. If only he knew how undeserved my new rank was, he might have understood. He introduced himself as Marty Kellard of the US Army Air Force.

'Nick Duncan,' I said. 'Australian Navy. Sorry about the salute – I've just been made lieutenant, a thoroughly undeserved promotion, and I forgot I was no longer a snotty.'

He laughed. 'It's a long trip, Nick.' Then he said, 'Afraid there's a bit more to come, we're pushing you straight through. We have to get you to Guadalcanal and we only fly there while there's sunlight; Henderson Field doesn't have night-landing equipment.'

'Guadalcanal?' I repeated, just to be sure, my heart suddenly beating faster.

'Yes, Lieutenant. They urgently need your Japanese language skills. You are trained in radio, morse code, are you not?' he asked.

'Yes,' I replied, then couldn't help myself. 'Whacko!' I reckon my smile would have covered half the runway.

'I can't even offer you a cup of java – the next B-17 leaves in fifteen minutes.' He pointed at an aircraft some way away.

'They're already warming up the engines, so we'll need to hurry.'

I slung my kitbag over my left shoulder and we began to move at a fairly rapid pace towards the waiting B-17. 'Guadalcanal, hey? Fancy that! I thought I'd drawn the short straw and was going to be consigned to a translator's job here in Luganville.'

'We're learning fast.' He was beginning to shout as we approached the plane and the noise of the engines made it difficult to hear. 'If it hadn't been for one of your coastwatcher guys, Martin Clemens, sending in one of his men to warn us of the Japanese attack at the Alligator River four days ago, we'd have been unprepared. Most remarkable story! A Jap patrol captured the messenger, Sergeant Major Vouza . . .' Marty Kellard couldn't continue above the noise of the props. He smiled and deliberately came to attention and saluted and I laughed and gave a wave before entering the plane. Nice bloke.

After another four hours' flight we came over the island of Guadalcanal. I knew enough about this kind of Pacific island to know that fighting on it would be a bloody nightmare for soldiers, though it was almost perfect for a coastwatcher. The island is bordered by a narrow coastline plain that varies from a few hundred yards wide west of the Matanikau River to a width of several miles. The flat land is covered in kunai grass that cuts the flesh when you brush past it, whereas the peaks, up to six thousand feet, are densely covered with brooding, dark green jungle.

The best way to describe the landscape that was below us is to imagine a giant hand reaching down and grabbing the island as if it were a swatch of fabric, then pulling it to a point and letting it fall again to create a series of incredibly steep ridges and valleys. It was the type of country I knew and, strangely, one

I loved. I could anticipate the fetid jungle smell brought about by everything seeming to drip and rot as you watched. This was where the perpetually dark, wet, twisted labyrinths of vines seemed to eventually choke everything, and where the most dangerous element is one of the smallest – the malaria-carrying *anopheles* mosquito.

I was completely whacked when we finally made a quick and dirty landing on the metal airstrip. I'd been in the air, or waiting to reboard, for the best part of twenty hours. During the flights I'd been cramped into what was little more than a few canvas straps that pass for a passenger seat on a B-17. Apart from a cold croissant and a tepid cup of coffee in a paper cup, I hadn't eaten since the lunch on Fraser Island.

But the Americans, as ever, were friendly and hospitable. The marine sergeant sent to meet me saluted and introduced himself as Joe Polanski. He had a jeep waiting at the edge of the runway. When I remarked on the strange construction of the runway he explained it was made with marsden matting. This was an interlinked, metal-strip system made from high-tensile steel; hundreds of thousands of small sections were clipped together to make a firm, safe surface for the heaviest of loads, spreading the weight of an aircraft landing or taking off evenly throughout its surface. This unique landing strip or runway was an unsung American innovation that made all-weather flying possible in the rain-sodden Pacific.

On the way to the marine base, upon hearing I hadn't eaten in a while, Sergeant Polanski immediately suggested he take me to the sergeants' mess when we arrived. 'I can take you to da officers' mess, sir, but da grub it's better at ours. The ingredient, dey da same, but we has got us a better chef who, by da way, work at da Waldorf Astoria in Noo York before he joined up after Pearl Harbor.'

'Sergeant, you don't happen to come from Chicago, do you?' I asked.

He looked surprised. 'How you know dat, sir? Dat's me, sirree, Chicago born an' bred.' I was being escorted by a Polish version of the little bloke, except that Polanski was a big bloke – maybe not quite my size, but Kevin Judge would have almost fitted under his armpit.

Arriving at the base I saw that Guadalcanal was no Luganville. It comprised a few scattered quonset huts, together with hundreds of tents and hastily thrown-together shacks, each with a dugout or slit trench beside it. The whole lot was built on a large copra plantation so that the tops of the coconut palms, together with the camouflaged material of the tents, would have effectively concealed it from Japanese aircraft.

The sergeants' mess was a large tent that was open at the sides to let the breeze through (what breeze?), with the kitchen in another similar tent abutting it. Food smells pervaded the air and I could feel my mouth beginning to salivate. That's one thing about the Yanks, they look after their men in the field. Sergeant Polanski was right – the food was excellent. He waited until I'd had a second cup of coffee before saying, 'Colonel Woon, he be waitin' ta see you, sir.'

'Shit! I'm sorry,' I apologised, rising quickly from my chair. Then glancing at my watch I saw it was five o'clock. 'Sergeant, why didn't you mention it before? We could have gone directly to see him.'

'Sir, it jes' ain't right to send a man inta combat wid a empty belly.' He grinned. 'Besides, planes comin' in all da time; Colonel Woon, he only Intelligence, he ain't gonna know what B-17 you gonna be arrivin' in.'

'But it's 1700 hours, knock-off time. He isn't going to be happy.'

'Knock-off time?' he asked, then realised my meaning. 'He ain't going home 'til he's seen you, sir. Dere's a war on, donchaknow.'

What did he mean by combat? I thought, as I hastily tried to tidy my crumpled blue serge naval uniform that was completely inappropriate for the tropical conditions. I remembered thinking that it would be crushed to buggery if I stuffed it in my kitbag with the Owen submachine-gun, and that since I would probably have to front up in Luganville and report to Intelligence HQ I'd better try to look like an officer instead of an oversized schoolboy in the standard tropical Australian Navy uniform.

Big, big mistake, Nicholas Duncan! Now I was sweating like the proverbial pig and the collar of my white shirt was rimmed with dirt. I was making a pathetic job of being a smartly turned out navy lieutenant.

I tried to brush the creases from my jacket, pulling at the hems below the pockets and smoothing the lapels. I should have removed it when I'd entered the aeroplane but it was bloody cold at altitude and I'd kept it on. I must have looked like a derro who'd salvaged a tired-looking naval uniform from a rubbish bin. I dusted off my cap, only to see that somewhere along the line I'd picked up a grease mark on the crown that was half the size of my fist. So much for the trappings of my new unentitled rank.

Sergeant Polanski must have sensed my nervousness, and in an attempt to comfort me increased my anxiety by saying, 'Colonel Woon, he a good guy, sir. Only sometimes you get on da wrong side o' him, he got him a fine temper dat go off like one o' dem Chinese firecracker.'

That must have been what he meant by my going into combat with a full belly. I was about to meet an irascible American colonel. Equipped with this warning and hoping he wasn't a stickler for dress code, I followed the marine sergeant to the colonel's office, came to attention at the open door and saluted, then announced, 'Lieutenant Nick Duncan, sir. Royal Australian Navy!'

'Come in, Nick,' the colonel said, in a pleasant enough voice.

I fronted, bringing myself to rigid attention, hoping that my smart salute might make up for my untidy turn out, and said again, 'Nicholas Duncan reporting for duty, sir.'

'Well, hello there, son. It's real good to have you with us.' He smiled, indicating a chair with a sweep of the hand. He had an open face and a nice smile; a big man, not that tall, but built, as they say, like the proverbial brick shithouse. 'Please sit, you've had a long flight, never easy. I was in your country, in Bris-bane, a month back, real nice folk. Getting back to Luganville was bad enough, now you've added another four hours. How you feeling, son?'

'Not too bad, sir.'

'That's good. We're mighty pleased to see you. I've read your dossier. You've packed a fair bit into a short life. How fluent are you in Japanese? Could you, for instance, translate a radio broadcast?'

'Yes, sir. Japanese radio operators are selected for their clear diction.'

'What? In the field of battle?'

'Yes, sir, they are specifically trained. It's the Japanese way. For example, the mechanic that works on the engine doesn't know anything about the gearbox or the diff. They do one thing and do it very well. Personal initiative is not a prized component in their society.' I was mouthing off, being a smart-arse, but was too nervous to keep my answers short and crisp. 'There aren't too many Japanese who are jacks-of-all-trades,' I said, gilding the lily further.

'And you learned all this by the age of eleven?' he asked with a half smile, his eyes amused.

He'd obviously read my dossier. 'No, sir. My father is an academic who took a First at Oxford in Japanese studies. He worked for thirteen years as a teacher in Tokyo. I guess I picked all this up from listening to him. He is also somewhat of an anthropologist who has made a life study of the Japanese.' *Shut up ferchrissake, Nick*, I said inside my head. My replies were becoming much too garrulous.

'Interesting,' Colonel Woon remarked, then stretched back in his chair. 'Well, son, we can certainly use your talents.' He suddenly changed the subject and, leaning slightly forward, said, 'You know, Nick, I feel sure I know you. That we've met before and, if not, that your name has cropped up somewhere over something . . .' His voice trailed off.

'I wouldn't think that likely, sir. Though, of course, both Nick and Duncan are fairly common Scottish names, a bit like John Brown with the Brits. Someone else with the same name, perhaps?' *Dammit! Still too many words!*

He seemed to be thinking. 'Yes, possibly.' Then he suddenly lunged forward and slammed his fist down onto the surface of his desk. 'Yes! Goddamn, yes! Tjilatjap airport! What was her name? Anna, that's right, Anna! The most beautiful young creature I've ever seen. Violet blue eyes, remarkable!' He pointed at me. 'She gave me a letter for a Nicholas Duncan, care of the Archbishop of Perth! I promised I'd see it got to him. That you?' He could see by my expression that he'd hit the jackpot. 'Goddamn yes, it is.'

'Anna? You met Anna – in Java, sir?' I stammered, overcome by surprise.

'You get the letter? I sent it in a top Army Air Force priority bag from Colombo.'

'Yes, sir. Thank you very much. It . . . it was astonishing. I mean, er . . . unexpected, wonderful!' I had lost it completely, overwhelmed by the coincidence.

'Anna? She your sweetheart?' he asked, smiling.

'Yes, sir, very much so. I was expecting her to arrive in Australia by boat even before I got there myself.'

'You mean in the yacht you renamed *Madam Butterfly*?' The colonel was proving once again that he'd read my dossier thoroughly.

'Yes, sir, when she didn't . . . well, I've been terribly worried ever since. The letter . . . at least she's . . . she's alive,' I stammered, suddenly close to tears, hating myself for showing my emotions in front of the American colonel.

'We don't have much news coming out of Java, Nick. With the natives cooperating with the Japanese there's no resistance movement to tell us what's happening. But the little we have suggests that the Dutch women and children are only now being rounded up and placed in concentration camps. With no resistance, I guess the Japs saved themselves from having to feed them for the first six months after their invasion. Chances are, if she got through those, she'll be okay. That's a little girl with one hell of a lot of initiative,' he said, attempting to comfort me.

'Sir, if you hear anything – *anything* coming out of Java, could you, would you please let me know?' I said, using influence I didn't possess.

'Of course, Nick. It isn't my theatre any more, but I'll make a point of finding out what I can for you.'

'Thank you, sir.'

'The yacht, *Madam Butterfly*, did you name it after her, or because you're a butterfly collector?' he asked.

'Well, yes, sir – after Anna. The "Madam" was sort of . . . in anticipation,' I grinned.

He laughed. 'Well, let's hope for the best, eh, Nick? War and loved ones – never a good combination.' He'd been sitting forward with his elbows on the desk, or rather folding table, and now he straightened up and leaned backwards again. 'Well, I suppose you'd like to know why you're here, son?' he asked.

'Well, yes, sir. Actually it's a tremendously nice surprise. I thought I was going to be stuck in a translator's office in Luganville.'

'Well, I don't know how much you know, but stop me if you do. We landed here on the 7th of this month with very little fuss. There were just a few Japanese engineers and a labour force of about two thousand Koreans building a large airstrip at Lungga Point. They offered almost no resistance and we were most grateful for the airfield, which we named Henderson Field. Later we put down the marsden matting. Your Mr Martin Clemens had informed us in July that it was almost operational, one of the major reasons we sent the marines ashore at Guadalcanal.'

I should just mention here that while he referred to Martin Clemens, the famous coastwatcher, as one of us (meaning an Australian), Clemens was in fact a Brit, and had been a district officer who had elected to stay behind to support intelligence operations using native police to spy on the Japanese.

Colonel Greg Woon continued. 'When the US 1st Marines arrived under the command of Major General Vandegrift and we took the airstrip, Mr Clemens came out of the jungle the following day and briefed me, giving us a comprehensive picture of the Japanese troop build-up here. It became immediately apparent to me that intelligence sent from your men out there, the coastwatchers behind enemy lines, was going to be invaluable to us. When Clemens again sent Sergeant Major Vouza, one of his native policemen, to warn us of the impending attack from the Alligator River that occurred five days ago, we realised that information from the coastwatchers was going to be an essential aspect of winning the war in these islands, in fact, in the whole of the south Pacific.'

'Sergeant Major Vouza, sir? Lieutenant Marty Kellard, who met my plane at Luganville, mentioned him; said it was, or he was, remarkable. But then the noise from the B-17 prevented him saying anything further.'

'Well, yes, if I had my way, he'd get the Medal of Honor. Let's hope the Pentagon responds well to my report. Sergeant Major Vouza was on his way to bring us the message about the impending attack when he ran into a Japanese patrol. They tied him to a tree and bayoneted him, leaving him for dead. He chewed through his bindings and staggered through the jungle to alert us that the Japs were going to mount a major attack at the crossing at the Alligator River.

'Well, we had time to position ourselves and set up our machine-gun posts and when they crossed the river we cut them to pieces with heavy machine-gun fire. God knows what might have happened if he hadn't reached us.

'The Japanese were led in the attack by Colonel Kyono Ichiki, a name that may not mean too much to you, but the sonofabitch goes back a long way, to the incident at the Marco Polo Bridge that started the Japanese war with China in 1937.'

He looked up. 'You are right about their single-minded attitude, Nick. In a last desperate attempt to get to us, despite the fact that they were being cut to ribbons by our machine-guns, Kyono drew his samurai sword and, waving it above his head, led his battalion in a series of frenzied *banzai* charges against our position. When we found him he had more holes in him than Huck Finn's eel bucket.'

The colonel spread his hands and jerked his shoulders. 'So you see, we've quickly learned to take you guys seriously and that's where you come in, Nick. I want you to monitor the radio network, bringing in all your guys on the various islands on a regular basis, in particular the coastwatcher reports from Bougainville and New Georgia. Given even half an hour's warning of an impending Japanese air attack, we can get our fighters to take off and gain height to attack their aircraft from above and west of Henderson Field. If you could intercept and interpret Japanese unit radio traffic, that would be immeasurably valuable to us. It seems crazy that the internment camps in the US are full of young Japanese–Americans who are loyal to the Stars and Stripes, and we go to war in the Pacific with hardly any radio operators who can speak Japanese! You've got to wonder about the cockamamie brains that run the Pentagon.'

'Sir, you do understand? I'm trained as a coastwatcher, who speaks and understands Japanese; I know how to use a field radio, of course, but I'm not a radio technician.'

'Yes, understood. Corporal Belgiovani is to be your offsider. I'm told what he doesn't know about setting up a radio transmitter and receiver isn't worth broadcasting.'

'Thank you, sir. I guess that means I stay here on base, no field work?'

He looked regretful. 'Afraid we need you here, son. Later

I'll see what I can do. Get your set-up working efficiently. That's our number one priority.'

'Yes, thank you, sir. I'll do my best.'

Colonel Woon looked directly at me. 'Yes, Nick, I think you will.' He nodded slowly. 'I think you will, son.' If this bloke had a quick temper then he was bloody good at hiding it; he'd managed to assuage my disappointment and give me confidence at the same time. He glanced at his watch. 'Can I buy you a beer, Nick? Bud is all we've got at the moment but it will be cold. When we arrived we inherited a newly built iceworks from the Japs, an excellent unit that is now under new management!' He suddenly slapped the top of his head. 'Jesus Christ, son, I guess you haven't eaten in a while?'

What could I say? I wasn't going to start my career with the Americans by dobbing in Sergeant Joe Polanski. And so I grinned. 'I'm an Australian, sir. The beer always has priority.'

He laughed. 'Well said, but we'll get you something to eat anyway. You look hot in that uniform, would you mind if I suggested you use our jungle fatigues? I'll get someone to sew your naval rank onto your shoulder tabs.'

'I'd be enormously grateful for the fatigues, sir. Don't worry about the rank insignia.'

'No, son, anyone who's made a naval lieutenant at your tender age is worthy of recognition.'

'Well, yes, maybe, but in my case it's not strictly true, sir.' I proceeded to tell him about my dubious promotion from snotty to lieutenant, the sole reason being not to diminish my position with his mob.

'It will be a pleasure to watch the marines salute you, Nick. Anyhow, I have a hunch you're going to more than earn your rank.'

The officers' mess was an identical set-up to the sergeants', although I wondered if Colonel Woon knew the sergeants and not the officers had the fancy chef from the Waldorf Astoria. He ordered two Budweiser and when they came he opened them both and handed one to me. 'Butterflies, eh? I find that interesting. Tell me about it,' he said, taking a slug directly from his can.

I had begun to relax a little in his company, so I grinned. 'Are you sure you want to hear, sir? In my experience it's a subject few people outside of small children find enchanting.'

'My father was an entomologist, a professor at Yale,' he replied. 'Before I could recite "Little Bo-peep" I knew the Latin names of at least two hundred insects. In me you have a kindred soul, Nick. But first let's order something to eat; you must be starving.'

I guess at eighteen there's always a hole to be found that remains unfilled. I ordered a hamburger that turned out to be the usual shit on a shingle, chopped beef on a bun, and served with mashed potatoes. I proceeded to tell the colonel about my boyhood hunting butterflies in the jungles of New Britain and New Guinea.

'Some childhood – from the streets of Tokyo to the depths of the jungle, Japanese to pidgin English! Not too hard to see why you want to get back into the field,' he said, when I eventually, and not too tediously I hoped, came to the end. 'Do a good job for us here and I'll see what I can do.' Then he asked, 'With all that time spent in the jungle, do you suffer from malaria, Nick?'

'Everyone does, sir, it's only a matter of time. The dreaded *anopheles* mosquito leaves no vein untouched. However, I'm fortunate; some people fare better than others. When I go down with a bout it's not too bad and only lasts two or three days, then I'm right as rain again.'

'Yah, the first casualties are beginning to come in. Nasty business, *culicidae*,' he said, perhaps showing off a bit with the Latin name for the mosquito family.

'I guess the enemy has the same problem,' I ventured.

'Quinine, disgusting taste, lingers for hours,' he spat.

The existing radio set-up was a tribute to Corporal Belgiovani, and inside a week we had the coastwatchers on Bougainville, New Ireland and the Solomon Islands coordinated and making regular incoming calls and, in turn, receiving our messages. The reception was in morse code, or by voice spoken in English or pidgin English. The brilliant, over-chatty Belgiovani soon had us receiving Japanese field unit transmissions, many of them uncoded. Most of the traffic wasn't very helpful, but every now and again there was a real gem. When I got something good I reckon I made Colonel Woon's day; he would take it to the general wearing a smile on his face like a Cheshire cat.

It didn't happen immediately, but after a few days I began to translate the meaning of unspoken Japanese. Allow me to explain. The Japanese language is built on extreme politeness: what is said is seldom what is meant; it is the unspoken meaning that often counts the most, the underlying interpretation being overlaid with a pattern of words that appear harmless. It is how the words are put together that counts. Now, suppose you've spent your entire lifetime (as has every Japanese person) speaking this silent language. You develop your own pattern of pauses, inflections, glottal sounds or whatever, but the unspoken language is still perfectly understood by everyone. The patterns are known. Emotion, excitement, panic, anxiety, important information, even the deliberate attempt to be obscure, lies in the silent gaps, the unspoken syntax, if that isn't an oxymoron. I understood this aspect of the Japanese language and so I believed I came to read, in a sense, what was really going on in the Japanese radio operator's mind. I began to be able to pick a deliberate piece of false information or obscuration that was meant to lead us away from what was *really* happening. I even believed that we could put together the bits of 'unstatement', if that's a word, so that we could become aware of the true situation.

For instance, the knowledge that the Japanese were running hopelessly short of supplies was reported through listening to 'silent' language long before it became known by our high command. With our aircraft controlling the beaches during daylight hours, the Japanese could only bring their supply ships in to unload at night and they simply couldn't resupply their troops at a rate that was fast enough.

But, of course, this is not the kind of thing that causes you to rush into the colonel's office yelling 'From the land of the silent language, Eureka!' So I would add it as a paragraph, an addendum at the end of a report. Naturally, at first nobody took any notice of what must have seemed to be pure speculation on my part. Even I was somewhat hesitant when writing such information, a little negative voice in me would be saying, *What if this is all bullshit?* But when, more often than not, we, the deadly combination of Corporal Belgiovani and over-promoted Duncan, began to be proved right, they started to take the extra paragraphs very seriously and these addenda became known as 'Nick's Knacks', often becoming the subject of some rather serious meetings between Intelligence and the top brass.

Even after the excitement of the first week of establishment, I began to think about some way to get into the field. I literally longed for the jungle, to be alone or with a small tightly knit group of natives whom I trusted, and operating behind enemy lines.

I was surrounded by several thousand marines, some of whom were beginning to carry battle scars, unshaven faces and a certain look I hadn't seen in the faces of young blokes before now. More often, they wore the plum-bruised and hollow-eyed look of malaria recovery, or exhibited the sniff and over-bright eyes that warned malaria or dengue fever was about to strike them down. I wanted some of their action – not as a sitting duck in a dugout, but on my own terms in the jungle.

But secretly I wondered – that is, when I had the chance to question myself, lying on a stretcher at night in my tent – whether being a coastwatcher was really what I wanted. The reports over the radio coming in from behind enemy lines clearly showed that these were mature men, steady, enduring and diligent, who knew who they were, and while observing the enemy's movements, would go to extraordinary lengths not to confront him. It was not the excited chase of a boy after a butterfly, but a nerve-racking vigil by patient men, spent in a wet jungle that you could watch rotting while you boiled a billy. They worked in an environment where everything happens slowly, methodically; great sentinel trees are slowly strangled by vines restricting their supply of rising sap, finally choking them to death. Jungles are much more about slow death than urgent life. It takes patience and extreme caution to reach the canopy.

When Commander Eric Feldt set up the coastwatchers network he adopted the cartoon of Ferdinand the Bull, the mild-mannered young bull who hated violence and would sit under a tree while all the other bulls fought each other for, well, you know what bulls fight for. Then when they'd battled themselves to a standstill and collapsed in a heap, Ferdinand would get up, stretch, yawn and saunter over to Daisy, the object of every bull's desire, accepting the prize with a sense of dignity and entitlement, brains triumphing over brawn. What this patently meant was that coastwatchers don't get involved at the sharp end. They had inverted the traditional soldiers' motto to read 'Ours is not to do or die, but to reason why'. I didn't want to be like Clemens and Kennedy (the coastwatcher on New Georgia) and the others, valiant and praiseworthy as they undoubtedly were. In my mind the jungle was the ideal place to *fight* the enemy – I didn't see it as simply somewhere to hide, as did these older, wiser coastwatchers.

While I would never have spoken or, God forbid, bragged about my capabilities, nevertheless I would review them in my mind while lying in bed under a mosquito net. Although I appeared to be sufficiently competent at the radio task I'd been given, and my knowledge of Japanese was a bonus, I would tell myself this was only one small part of what I'd learned to do in life and merely a component of the training I'd received. I'd tick off my supposedly wasted credentials in my head. I could sail just about anything that carried canvas, from a beautiful ketch like *Madam Butterfly* to the clumsy, wallowing and totally uncooperative mission boat. I knew how to work and survive in the jungle. I spoke pidgin and several of the coastal native languages. I had practically gained the status of a sniper with a rifle. I could use an Owen submachine-gun better than anyone in the course. I had a sound knowledge of martial arts and unarmed combat that allowed me to defend myself more than adequately. I knew how to use a knife at close quarters. My reactions had been tested and shown to be well above average. I was big and strong and not too clumsy.

All these things I knew about myself with the exception of one: my courage had never been tested in combat. During the months since the slaughter of the sailors from HMAS *Perth* on the beach in Java, I'd brooded on the fact that I had never buried them properly, that I'd been terrified that the natives who had murdered them would return and find me. I had lacked the courage to do the right thing. In my mind's eye I could see the crows and the gulls pecking, lifting out entrails with their sharp black and pink beaks, and the crabs crawling up the beach at night to feast on rotting flesh. I even tried to invent a king tide that rose high enough up the beach to wash them out to sea again so that they received a belated and honourable sailor's grave.

When I recalled the scene I could now clearly see them as skeletons – white bones on yellow sand, rib cages with the sharp ends buried in the sand, grinning skulls, scalloped hip bones, spines like empty cotton reels strung together – intact skeletons neatly laid out side by side, with the skull of the headless sailor still separated by several inches from his neck and shoulderblades. All because I had been consumed by fear and had lacked the courage to give them a decent burial.

We fight dragons in our imaginations and win, always win. But now I longed, yearned, my subconscious screamed out to me, that I must be tested, that I must resolve whether I had courage or remained the coward who had snivelled on the beach. I needed to find out whether I had the balls, the raw guts it takes a thinking man to go into combat.

Marg Hamilton had been correct. Coastwatching was an

old man's game. The Japs had Anna. God knows what they'd do with her. She was much too pretty to remain safe and undefiled. I can't tell you what I imagined was happening to her: horrible, terrible stuff. I was angry and I wanted to have a crack at the slant-eyed yellow bastards, to test my courage against theirs, to avenge whatever Anna was enduring.

What I didn't want to do was to sit out the remainder of the war with a pair of earphones clamped to my head, listening to bucktoothed Jap radio operators jabbering at each other, and attempting to read their supposedly inscrutable minds. Or, for that matter, to find myself sitting on a rock with a pair of binoculars spotting enemy planes and doing a Ferdinand the Bull – avoiding contact with the enemy at any cost.

But all this was pie in the sky, lying on my camp stretcher staring at the dark canopy of coconut palms from the open tent flaps, the Owen machine-gun, oiled and clean, lying uselessly at my side. It was fairly clear that Colonel Greg Woon thought I was the ant's pants, the cat's pyjamas. I was stuck for the duration, seconded to the American Army Air Force Intelligence, and they had no plans to turn me into either a hero or a body bag. I was to remain Nick Duncan, writer of addenda, Nick's Knacks, clever young sod with fat little Corporal Belgiovani at my side chewing gum and 'dis-and-datting' in Brooklynese.

And then, completely out of the blue, an opportunity arrived. We'd received reports that the Japanese were planning an assault on Henderson Field. I'd first picked up something on their field network and though it was in code I'd Nick Knacked it, and then Martin Clemens had confirmed it, warning us of a major attack coming somewhere around the second week in September. Colonel Woon had called me in. 'Nick, we're pretty certain the Japs are going to be coming at us in a few days and our headquarters in Luganville have been pestering me for a battle piece intended for American radio, something that brings home the fighting on a Pacific island. Do you think you could do a running commentary on the assault? Stay away from the fighting but be close enough to see the action? You'll have to do both, listen in to the Japanese field radio and report what you hear, as well as attempt in the quieter moments of battle to mount a commentary. Listening in and reporting on their field radio is obviously the more important.'

The warmth of my smile would have raised the temperature in the hut he used as his office. 'Yes, sir!' I said, my voice making no attempt to conceal my excitement.

'Lieutenant, I said *observe*. You're not to get involved other than in the commentary and listening in to the Japs. Do not use that popgun you brought with you! Those are my specific instructions. Observe, comment, listen to the enemy field radio and stay out of the fight! Colonel Edson will be in charge of the defence and you'll accompany me on a briefing with Major General Vandegrift tomorrow at 1500 hours at HQ. Be here just before then and we'll go together.' He leaned back – Woon was a great one for leaning back. 'If Colonel Edson or the general ask you a question, answer it specifically, then throw it back to me as soon as possible. The general doesn't much care for the press. He doesn't want some would-be Ed Murrow with an elevated rank in the Army Entertainment Unit flying in from the States in a tailor-made set of fatigues, with a Cuban cigar jammed into the corner of his mouth. Do you think you can do both tasks?'

I wasn't going to miss out on such a great opportunity,

even if I mucked it up and they sent me back to Australia in disgrace. At least I'd have been in a fair dinkum stoush. 'Yes, sir. Shall I do it in an American accent or my own Australian?' I volunteered. *Smart-arse!*

'You can do an American accent, Nick?' he asked, surprised.

'Only Chicago, New York or your own, Boston,' I replied.

Listening and mimicking is a talent most loners perfect from childhood. You do a lot of standing aside and listening, and tonality can often define a person. In principle, it's not very different from listening to the silent language of the Japanese. How people colour their words to express meaning is our equivalent in English. I was fairly sure I could capture the American accent, even if I missed out on one or two of the more subtle nuances.

He leaned back in his chair and folded his arms across his chest, then, smiling, said, 'Do the Lord's Prayer in all three accents.'

I grinned. 'You've lucked in, sir. Being the son of a clergyman, I may just be one of the very few Australians who know all the words.' I proceeded to do the little bloke's Chicago accent. Then Gus Belgiovani, in Brooklynese, followed by the colonel himself in Boston English.

Halfway through my mimic of his own accent, the colonel chuckled and put up his hand, indicating I should stop. 'Goddamn! You could have fooled me, Nick. You may do the commentary in my accent. That will make it easier for me to overlay your field commentary with a lead-in and conclusion.' He continued, 'Don't worry, if it all works out you'll have a credit at the beginning and end. '

'That won't be necessary, sir. I only hope I can pull it off.'

'We'll know soon enough; the general will have to give the final approval,' he said, adding, 'You're still young, Nick, so don't get too worried if we don't get it right first time; it's essentially an experiment in recording events on the battlefield, then broadcasting that to people in their lounge rooms in America. We're not even certain yet if it's a very good idea and it's going to need the ultimate approval by some asshole colonel in the Pentagon.'

Colonel Edson chose the highest ridge, directly overlooking Henderson Field on its far side, to dig in using his own Marine Raider Battalion supported by elements of the Marine Parachute Battalion, all of them élite soldiers. The corporal and I found a place where we could see the battlefield but be more or less out of the way, and we too dug in.

Gus Belgiovani was not a marine and had joined Army Air Force Intelligence with much the same attitude as the little bloke had; that is, to avoid confronting the enemy at any cost. We'd climbed into our dugout on the late afternoon of the 12th of September knowing the Japanese attack could come at any time, that night or the following one. He'd arrived with our radio equipment, his ample waist circled with hand grenades and extra ammunition for his Springfield rifle. Apart from boot camp he hadn't used either since leaving the States and I reckoned I was probably in more danger of getting killed by him than by the enemy.

'Beljo, mate, we're here as observers!' I protested. 'The colonel will have our guts for garters if he hears you've lobbed one of those, or fired a shot in anger. We're commentary, not combat.' That's not to say that I hadn't done a little daydreaming of my own. 'Take that grenade belt off, Corporal Belgiovani,' I said. 'I'm confiscating it in the name of my personal safety.'

He pointed accusingly to my Owen. 'Say, buddy, who own dat cockamamie popgun?'

'It's only here for the outing,' I said. 'I want it to become familiar with the sounds of a battle.'

'Dat de same for dat dere ammo?' he asked, pointing to the three hundred nine-millimetre rounds and the half-dozen loaded magazines I'd lugged laboriously into our dugout.

'Yup, they only fly true when they've been in a blue,' I quipped, to a look of incomprehension. In idle moments we'd swap slang, Australian for Brooklynese, but I'd obviously not yet translated the meaning of 'a blue' for him.

In retrospect, perhaps I'd acted like a bit of a mug lair in the uniform department. I was wearing my Australian jungle greens that had come about in a peculiar way. I'd written to Sergeant Major Wainwright on Fraser Island soon after I'd arrived, just to let him know how things were going with the Yanks. I'd told him the story of my lamentable navy uniform and how grateful I'd been to get issued with two sets of US Marine fatigues, boots, etc. A few days later a huge parcel had arrived with a stamp that read 'Australian Army HQ Brisbane – Confidential' to lend it an air of importance. This was something only Wainwright and the Allied Intelligence Bureau could have brought about. The parcel (it looked more like a small bale) had contained three complete sets of Australian jungle greens – three long-sleeved shirts and trousers in the new, deep shadow green, the webbing and gaiters in a slightly lighter green. There were half a dozen pairs of socks and two pairs of high-topped rubber-soled boots with canvas tops that made them light and comfortable to wear.

Tucked in the pocket of one of the shirts was a hastily scribbled note: 'Time you wore the correct bloody uniform, boyo.' It was signed simply 'Wainwright'. Then came a postscript that was longer than the note: 'Remember, if you are moving in the jungle then you are vulnerable. The soldier who stays still gets the kill. W'

Apart from his immediate generosity, I was aware that I owed the wiry little Englishman a great deal. He spoke with a soft Somerset burr, and he referred to it as 'Zoommerzet'. I'd never once heard him raise his voice. Although I quietly fancied myself in the jungle, he had raised my skills to yet another level. When I'd won our group's shooting competition and the CO had presented me with the Owen submachine-gun with the brass plate bearing my name, he'd called me to the sergeants' mess that evening, bought me a beer and drawn me aside. 'Guns, laddie, to be sure we need them, but what we need most as a jungle fighter is the right personal equipment.'

'Yeah, I suppose, Sergeant Major,' I'd replied to what seemed like an obvious piece of commonsense, though I knew better than to think that was all it was.

'Nay, boyo, you've not got my meaning, the right *extra*, your own personal addition.' He'd paused, then said, 'I've trained you how to use a knife and even if I am forced reluctantly to say so, you're not too bad.'

'Thank you, Sergeant Major,' I'd replied, somewhat surprised, since 'not too bad' was the ultimate praise, about as good as it ever got. He had spent weeks instructing us in silent killing, training us in the first rule of using a knife in order to kill – if you stab you're as good as dead; knife fighting is all about slashing. He'd taught us that when armed with a sharp knife anyone coming at you with a bayonet was, to put it into his own words, 'fookin' dead'. If the hapless, bayonet-carrying rifleman is facing a well-trained, knife-wielding opponent, he's going to be dead before the bayonet blade comes within six inches of the intended gut.

Then he'd handed me an object wrapped in a chamois. 'Open it,' he'd urged.

I'd unfolded the chamois to see it was a commando dagger, a plain, rather narrow knife with a tapered double-sided blade about nine inches long. He'd handed me the canvas sheath separately. Such a dagger was originally intended to go on your belt, but he'd trained us differently and we all knew it rested inside the left or right gaiter, depending on your knife hand.

I confess, I was overcome. 'Thank you, Sergeant Major,' I'd stammered.

'You'll use it every morning to shave. If you have a bad shave then it's not sharp enough, boyo,' he'd said gruffly. 'Stay sharp in everything: fitness, attitude, awareness, caution, circumspection, respect, brains, but above all these, keep your blade sharp and ever at the ready. Half of one second of carelessness may be the difference between dying and staying alive. The whetstone is your dagger's best friend.' He'd reached over and patted me on the shoulder, smiling. I'd never seen him smile. 'The knife is yours for the duration of the war. Then I want it back. I want you to personally hand it back to me. Righto, Duncan, it's your shout, boyo.'

And so I found myself in the radio dugout with my Owen submachine-gun and wearing my Australian jungle greens, with the little brass plate resting in the pocket above my heart. I can't say the fatigues hadn't attracted attention in the week I'd been wearing them since Wainwright's parcel arrived. 'Thou shalt be fit, fitter than anyone else in the army, navy or air force' was the first mantra of our training on Fraser Island. I had promised my instructors that I'd keep up what we'd come to know as the 'morning death bash'; that is, running five miles in army marching gear carrying an Owen with a light pack containing two hundred rounds of ammunition and four thirty-three-round magazines. I'd do this in the cool of every morning, resting on Sundays. At first there were a good few wolf whistles and chiacking from the marines, but eventually they got accustomed to seeing me jogging through the plantation, around the airfield and back along the beach from Lungga Point. Young blokes like me react to the standards set by men they respect, blokes who are better than them in every department. I felt, despite the sedentary radio job I'd been given, that I wanted to stay combat fit and razor sharp, the way we'd been conditioned on Fraser. One or two marines had come along with me a couple of times and I guess I'd earned their respect. They stopped calling out 'Robin Hood', 'Joe Palooka', 'Charles Atlas' or even once 'Hey, Tarzan, where's Jane? I needa get laid bad, buddy!'

The Japanese assault arrived that night led by Major General Kiyotaki Kamaguchi. The first attack seemed tentative and I quickly picked up on their radio that elements of their force had been delayed; they were having trouble getting troops into position for a coordinated attack. I couldn't believe it when I heard the Japanese general screaming abuse at his officers directly, without using code. This inability to mass his troops would clearly prevent a major assault that night.

However, this didn't mean the Japs were a pushover,

far from it. My first taste of combat, even if only as a witness from the relative safety of our dugout, was horrendous, beyond anything I'd imagined. All night the Japs attacked the perimeter of our positions in small groups. The noise was unbelievable and reporting back to base during the night was almost impossible. I took to jotting down notes within a time frame for later use. Any commentary I would make would have to be done by using recall. The almost continuous cracking of rifles and streams of tracer bullets from our machine-guns, together with the 'crump-crump' of grenades exploding, seemed to make the air fizz with sound. But most of all, the concussion of shells landing left us virtually deaf. Yet through all this hellish cacophony, amazingly, you could hear the screams of dying and wounded men.

Some Japs managed to penetrate in between our foxholes where desperate hand-to-hand fighting took place. But by dawn the marines had held firm and the enemy had all but withdrawn. I handed Beljo his grenade belt. 'Go on, mate, throw one so you can say you fought at Guadalcanal.'

'Jesus, thanks, Nick,' he said, taking the grenade, pulling the pin and hastily hurling the grenade into the battlefield. 'Take dat, ya dirty yellow slant-eyed sonofabitches! *Banzai* and fuck ya too!' he yelled.

As none of the enemy had come within fifty yards of the radio dugout the grenade landed harmlessly. Belgiovani had just boosted his eventual grandpa-to-grandchildren 'How I won the war in the Pacific' bullshit factor by 100 per cent.

The slopes of the ridge back to the edge of the jungle two hundred yards away were strewn with bodies, many more Japanese than ours, but we'd copped more than our fair share and several of the officers I'd got to know and like lay dead. One of them was Brutus Brokenhorse, an American Indian who'd jumped the colour divide and been made lieutenant: 'Hey, buddy, I'm coming over to ride a big old kangaroo in your mesa desert when this goddamn war is finished!' He was the only bloke who'd managed to stay with me on a morning run and we'd become good buddies. I was pretty choked but was about to learn that grief has to be reserved for a private moment.

All morning a stream of the wounded left the ridge for the forward hospital at Henderson Field. Burial details removed the bodies of the dead marines from the ridge and placed them in white cotton shrouds, loading them carefully into trucks, then the bodies of the Japs were manhandled and piled in heaps at the bottom of the slope to discourage the enemy if they thought to come back for another go at us – as we expected they would. By early afternoon they had begun to smell in the heat. Dog tired, I spent the morning and half the afternoon collating and translating documents taken from dead Japanese officers for our tactical intelligence report.

Despite the fact that I'd managed almost no on-the-spot commentary, Colonel Woon – who'd come to our dugout in the mid-morning and had a bit of a listen to the wire recording – reckoned the experiment to get radio commentary recorded on the battlefield into the homes of America had the potential to be a big success.

Our early report that Major General Kiyotaki Kamaguchi wasn't able to mount a full-scale attack was, as Colonel Woon put it, 'A fucking triumph, Nick!' This accolade was delivered despite the fact that we could probably have picked up the broadcast by the Japanese field radio and made the same report while remaining at the base. He probably knew this, but it was possible Colonel Edson didn't. On the ridge we were technically under the same orders as the marines, who were told to clean their weapons and remain in position for the night to come. While I would have given anything for a shower and a clean uniform, Beljo and I were obliged to do the same.

We spent the late afternoon checking our equipment and went through the usual routines. I'd taken the precaution of again forbidding Belgiovani to touch his grenades. 'Stick to your Springfield if we need to go into action,' I advised, 'but for fuck's sake, Beljo, remember why we're here: commentary, not combat.'

We were both pretty whacked. Between us we'd edited the sounds of the previous night's battle and dubbed in my voice, using the time-frame notes I'd made, and the results seemed plausible. Anyway, with Greg Woon top-and-tailing it, I reckoned we probably had a goer. After this, I'd managed about an hour's sleep in the dugout.

Although we'd kept the faith and (except for Beljo's bullshit-factor early-morning hand grenade) we hadn't personally been involved in the fighting, nevertheless, I felt, despite a night with only an hour's sleep, a huge sense of relief that I'd survived. I can tell you for a start, Nicholas Duncan was beginning to seriously modify his previous gung-ho, let me at 'em, *Boys' Own Annual* attitude. War was shit and I'd already had a gutful without having fired a shot.

The marines were looking pretty tattered around the edges; they too had had almost no sleep, a great many of their officers were dead, there were no reinforcements and they were outnumbered by Japanese on a ratio of at least two or three to one. If anyone ever decries the Yanks' ability in battle in front of me they're likely to get an unexplained punch on the nose. The American marines, after I'd observed just one night of fighting, would always have my utmost admiration. These blokes were as good as you can get on a battlefield.

However, the battle was far from over. With a depleted force and many of the foxholes on the ridge unmanned, the shit really hit the fan on this night, the 13th of September 1942, in a battle that would become known as 'Bloody Ridge'.

There is a half-light in the tropics, a short period between dusk and dark, when the eyes have to adjust, and it was precisely at this time that the Japanese attack began. Screaming, blowing whistles and banging gongs, they came out of the jungle into the small valley beyond it and started to climb the ridge. The first part of the battle was much the same as we'd recorded on the first night so I let it pass, but by ten o'clock with no moon, the tempo started to change. Wave after wave of Japs came screaming across the open valley and storming up the ridge, and in a matter of minutes they were all over our front positions. The hellish noise accompanied by the horrific sight of men locked in battle seen in the white glow of flares and star-shells, of men dying, the glint of bayonets seen in the flash of the heavy shells being fired from Henderson Field and landing in amongst the Japs, was like looking through the gates to hell.

There were more Japanese than ever there'd been in the previous attack and they just kept coming, like ants around an ant heap before a storm. While the previous fighting was perhaps one hundred and fifty yards away from our dugout, it was now much closer and coming towards us. Then, illuminated by a burst of star-shells, a group of six, led by an officer who was brandishing a sword, broke through into our perimeter and came directly towards us. 'Sorry about this, Colonel,' I said into the noise, tapping Belgiovani on the shoulder and pointing to his Springfield. In moments he was crouched over his rifle firing blindly into the air with his eyes closed. In my mind I heard the little bloke's voice: *'I want yer ta unnerstan'*,

I ain't no fuckin' hero.'

A single blue–white parachute flare hung in the sky and amongst the flashes of shells landing I saw that the six Japs and the bloke with the sword were still coming at us. I stepped out of the dugout to get a clear shot. I could hear Wainwright saying, *'Now listen, boyo, this may be a submachine-gun, but it's best used as a semi-automatic, one shot at a time. It's an extension of your arm, laddie. Wait until the enemy is at around twenty-five yards, then it's one in the chest and one just above the bridge of the nose – accuracy is life. We don't want the enemy to suffer, do we? Don't think, just let your body and your eyes do the work.'*

I guess I fell into some sort of neutral trance. I felt nothing and seemed unaware of what I was doing. Twenty to thirty or so yards in front of me each Jap in turn seemed to be acting as if they were puppets in slow motion with the strings suddenly loosened above them – there'd be a slight check as the first Owen bullet hit them in the chest, then almost instantly a sharp snapping back of the head as the nine-millimetre slug tore into their brain, whereupon they simply collapsed. In twenty seconds all seven were dead, the whole violent few seconds punctuated by the bucking of the Owen. Some popgun!

'Holy shit! Did I see that?' I heard Belgiovani shout.

Our position was at the base of the last knoll. Quite how the battle had skewed toward us I can't say, but now the marines fell back and took up new positions, jumping into empty foxholes around us. I don't know how you know these things, you simply do; perhaps it's because you sense you have only moments to live, but I instinctively knew that this was close to being the last stand. There were no officers amongst the marines – they were probably all dead – and with one lousy pip I held the senior rank in that part of the battlefield.

I emptied my magazine at a group of Japs, breaking up their charge. One of them got through and I didn't see him coming at me in a furious bayonet charge until almost too late. My magazine being empty, I dropped the Owen in great haste and reached down to my ankle and slid my dagger out of its sheath. What happened next was a story that was to grow out of all proportion in the next few days. But Wainwright had been correct – the way the Jap was charging at me, he was as good as 'fookin' dead'. The whetstone had done its work. Pivoting sideways and using my left hand, I grabbed his Arisaka rifle behind the long bayonet and pulled him off balance and towards me. The commando dagger sliced into him just above the belt, a rounded lightning slash, and then I pushed slightly upwards so that his entrails would spill onto the ground; using his momentum as he started to pivot over my hip, I withdrew the blade a fraction and then ripped it up under his sternum to shred his heart. The only sound from the Jap was a small surprised gasp. He was dead before he hit the ground. Jumping back into the dugout I realised that I was shaking. At the time I couldn't have explained how I felt precisely, but I later realised it was a mixture of adrenalin, fear and disgust. But I have to be honest and confess that I also felt a fierce exhilaration. There is something very personal about killing a man with a knife and I was to learn that one never quite gets over it – those four seconds would haunt me all my life. I would also always remember the peculiar coppery smell, mixed with cordite, where the Japanese soldier's blood had soaked my jungle greens.

'Jesus, Harry H. Truman! Did I *also* see that?' Belgiovani cried. Later several marines claimed to have witnessed the incident and swore they hadn't seen a knife and that I'd ripped out the Jap's entrails with my bare hands.

But there was no time to dwell on anything except the battle. The next group of what was to seem like a never-ending wave of Japanese was coming at us, illuminated by the flares that festooned the ridge. Changing magazines on the Owen, I joined the stygian chorus of deafening small-arms fire that was cutting down the Japs. But still they came. During the remainder of the night I fired nearly all of the three hundred rounds I'd lugged into our dugout. As the pale light of dawn (a hackneyed phrase, I know!) finally arrived we realised that the Japs were retreating, although by no means in an orderly manner. They'd turned their backs on us and were running down the slope, many dropping their weapons on the way. The marines surged out of their foxholes and chased after them. I'm ashamed to say I was amongst them. What followed was a frenzy of killing, but we were halted short of the valley fronting the jungle by the snarl, the roar, of aero engines as our fighters swept low over the ridge, strafing the frantically retreating enemy. They were closely followed by bombers who dropped high explosives on the periphery of the jungle and beyond. We would later learn that a further six hundred enemy had been killed as they attempted to flee and hide in the jungle.

It was sunrise on the 14th of September and the ridge was still ours and so was Henderson Field. Belgiovani had declined to join us in the mayhem and slaughter that ensued, but I was later to learn that he had instead grabbed the microphone and yelled into the wire recorder his own version of my personal battle with the 'popgun' and a knife.

All around me marines lay dead, slumped over their Springfield rifles. I couldn't help wondering how many of them might be alive if they'd been trained by Sergeant Major Wainwright in the use of the Owen submachine-gun together with 'the right *extra*, your own personal addition' resting snug within a canvas sheath inside a high-top boot.

We were young. We had survived. We had held our ground. We were warriors. The Battle of Bloody Ridge was over. It would take its place in the code of valour, be writ large in the annals of the mighty American marines: 'Semper Fidelis – Always Faithful'.

I was filthy, drop-dead weary, but unscathed and, better still, alive. The enemy had finally been broken; those who hadn't been killed by the air attack died of their wounds or starvation in the jungle. The Japanese were only able to land on the beaches by night and had barely sufficient food for the healthy and the courageous, and they weren't going to waste it on the wounded or cowardly.

Bloody Ridge had been a near thing – sometimes only a handful of yards and a few minutes of hand-to-hand fighting around the last knoll and several other points along the ridge separated defeat from victory. Once they'd got over the ridge it would have been virtually impossible to stop the Japs reaching and regaining Henderson Field. No force can adequately mount an offensive running backwards. If Henderson had fallen and returned to Japanese control, it would have had disastrous results for the Americans and their allies in the Pacific. With this airfield and the others they'd built, the Japanese could effectively block supplies coming by ship from the west coast of America and Australia. Henderson was the key to the master lock. They had to have it under their control.

I was frantically writing. I'd done zero commentary notes and I was trying to catch up and make sense of the night while enjoying a brew-up, in this instance a cup of java, when Belgiovani, who'd barely had his helmet above ground level throughout both nights, suddenly stood and snapped to attention. 'Brass, Nick,' he called out of the corner of his mouth. I looked up to see Colonel Edson and a group of officers about ten yards in front of the dugout with a marine captain pointing to one of the dead Japs who littered the slope in front of us and then at another and a third until they all began inspecting the corpses. I slung my Owen in the required fashion over my shoulder and stood beside Humpy Dumpty and saluted. Time passed, maybe a minute or so, with the two of us standing to rigid attention saluting and not being noticed. It must have been a funny sight, Belgiovani no more than five feet five inches and almost as wide as he was high, the walls of the dugout coming to the middle of his chest, and me at six foot three. Both of us were filthy, my face black from cordite and the mud and shit the shells had thrown up at us. Edson finally looked up and replied to our salute. 'Easy,' he said, then gestured for us to come closer.

The same captain who'd originally pointed at a dead Jap came up to Colonel Edson. 'Twenty-eight, sir. There may be more, all have a third eye.'

Edson looked up at me. 'Lieutenant, how do you explain that all the dead Japanese have a bullet hole in the forehead just above the nose?'

Before I could open my mouth to answer, the battle-hardened midget from Brooklyn blurted out, 'Nick here, sir – I mean, Lieutenant Duncan, sir, he just stood outside the dugout and hit 'em wid his popgun – Owen, sir. He bagged seven in unner twenty seconds.' Still not letting up, he pointed to the Jap who'd lost his guts. 'He done dat wid a knife, right up close. Jes' before I was about to be bayoneted, sir,' he announced, giving me the gratuitous credit for saving his fat little life.

Colonel Edson eyed my Owen gun. 'Give me a look at that, son.' I unslung the Owen, handing it to him. He opened the breech, then looked up. 'You've cleaned this already this morning,' he noted.

'Yes, sir, they'd have my guts for garters if I hadn't – er, I mean, that's the way we're trained, sir.'

The officers all laughed. 'Guts for garters, eh? Nice way of putting it, Lieutenant,' Edson said. 'Your name?'

'Duncan, sir.'

'That's not a marine uniform you're wearing?'

'No, sir – Australian.'

'Yes, of course, Intelligence radio, you're with Colonel Woon.' He indicated the Owen. 'Does he know about this? Did you have his authority to use it?'

I was in the deep do-do. 'Sir, your marines regrouped around us; they had no officer, sir.' I gave an almost imperceptible shrug.

Edson smiled. 'Well done, son. You wouldn't like to join the marines, would you? We can arrange for American citizenship.'

He'd said it *sotto voce* and while I thought he was joking, I couldn't be absolutely sure. 'Thank you, sir, an honour, but I feel obliged to remain Australian, sir.'

This got an all-round laugh. 'Pack up and get back to base, Lieutenant. Report to Colonel Woon and tell him I'd be most obliged if he'd accompany you and come to the HQ tent at 1600 hours.'

I snapped off a salute as they turned away and I heard one officer say, 'There wasn't a half inch of difference in any of the head shots and all within a range of about twenty-five yards.' While being given permission to leave the ridge, which meant a shower and some hot chow, once again my impetuosity and clear disobedience of Greg Woon's clear-as-crystal orders had drawn unwelcome attention and I only hoped Edson wasn't going to dob the boss in with the major general. *Surely a bloke can't get into that much trouble killing Nips – isn't that what we're supposed to be doing, killing Japanese?* I tried to convince myself. But I already knew enough about the army, or in my case, the navy, to know that taking matters into your own hands is the antithesis of what your training is all about.

A short time later a jeep arrived and we loaded our radio gear and the wire recorder I'd barely used all night. We ground our way slowly along the muddy track to Henderson. On the way we passed weary marines, slouched, head down, too tired to march on their way back from the killing ridge to Henderson base. All the way down I became aware of grins and thumbs up and calls of 'Hiya, Killer!', 'Great work, Popgun Pete!', 'Will you marry my sister, Lootenant?' The bullshit was spreading and we'd soon be sloshing around up to our knees in it.

Shit, shave and shower – the combat soldier's glorious three 'Ss'. A change of jungle greens, a hot breakfast and then a kip. I'd reported to Woon and explained that we'd had a pretty hairy night and that I hadn't managed to do very much of the commentary – in fact none. I told him about Colonel Edson's request to see him and to take me along at 1600 hours.

'Did Colonel Edson indicate what this is all about, Nick?' he asked, looking far from chuffed, I can tell you. I guess one colonel doesn't like being ordered to front up by another.

'I'm not sure, sir. I think it's about some dead Japanese,' I replied.

He looked at me, leaning forward. 'Nick, you haven't been using your popgun, have you?'

'Just a little bit, sir – but strictly in the defence of the radio intelligence unit, sir.'

'I see – you were defending the contents of the commentary you didn't manage to make,' he said. Then with a wave of the hand he added, 'Go on, get some sleep. You're talking bullshit, Nick.'

After breakfast I collapsed onto my stretcher in the tent. I awoke with a start because someone was shaking me. I grabbed for the Owen at my side. 'Hold it! It's me, buddy,' Sergeant Polanski shouted. 'You're late, sir – better get movin'. Colonel Woon ain't in a real happy dis-po-sition.' It was half-past three; I'd been asleep since half-past nine.

We arrived at the boss's office to find him pacing, hands behind his back, grim-faced. I saluted. 'You're late, Lieutenant. Let's go!' he snapped in a peremptory voice. He hadn't ever called me 'Lieutenant' in private, not even on the first day. I was clearly in the deepest shit imaginable.

We walked the five minutes to Colonel Edson's HQ, arriving exactly on time. We entered a large tent and I was immediately tempted to creep out again. Major General Vandegrift, Colonel Edson and a bunch of senior staff officers were standing around a map table. I just about snapped in half with the rigidity of my salute. But instead of the grim faces of an impending censure, we were met by smiles all round. The boss cursorily touched his cap, not giving an inch in Edson's tent. Then the general said, 'Be at ease, gentlemen, you are amongst friends, fellow officers.'

Yeah, real chummy, I thought. *The lowest rank in this bloody tent, apart from me, is a full colonel!*

The general came over and shook the boss by the hand, then did the same to me. *Christ, what was happening?* I'd just shaken the hand of a general in the American Marines!

'Well, what can I say, Colonel? You pick your men well,' the general said. 'I wish all our boys would show his kind of initiative in moments of crisis on the battlefield.' He turned to me. 'If ever there was a young officer we'd like to have in the marines, he's you, son. How old are you?'

I hesitated for a moment, but you can't tell a lie to a general when you've just shaken his hand, can you? 'Eighteen, sir – I can explain, sir,' I added hastily. 'I was jumped up in rank from midshipman to come here. It wasn't deserved, sir.'

'If you were in the marines I'd promote you to Captain, son. Well done.' He turned back to the boss. 'Colonel Woon, have you told Lieutenant Duncan what we propose to do?'

The boss grinned. 'No, sir, I thought Nick would rather hear it from you.'

'We're putting you in for the Navy Cross, son.' He paused. 'I have the greatest respect for your King, but we know in advance the Brits won't allow you to wear it. The rule is strictly no foreign decorations for His Majesty's army, navy or air force. Nevertheless I want what you did for the American marines put on record. There will be a parade at 1100 hours, day after tomorrow. Colonel Woon will inform you when and where it will take place.'

Gob-smacked isn't the word! I'd been convinced I was on my way home or, worse still, about to be court-martialled. 'Yes, sir – thank you, sir – I'm honoured, sir,' I said, like an idiot. I mean, what else is there to say when you've been completely floored, flummoxed and find yourself totally bemused? Me? Navy Cross? Even if I wasn't allowed to wear it. What can a man say? I could almost hear Sergeant Major Wainwright laughing. *'Your shout, boyo! Half of that fookin' Navy Cross you can't wear belongs to me!'*

Colonel Edson walked up and stood beside the boss, who'd obviously feigned anger at our being late so as not to let the cat out of the bag. 'Frankly, we thought we had a serious problem, Greg. I was called to inspect a number of corpses that appeared to have been murdered. You know, wounded enemy deliberately shot between the eyes. Not the marine way, serious implications, court martial . . . Your man was the closest to the dead enemy and, for a moment, it didn't look too good for him. But upon closer inspection we observed that the shots couldn't possibly have been fired at point-blank range, barrel held against the head: there were no powder burns and the entry was neat.' Colonel Edson looked at me. 'Where did you learn to shoot like that, Nick?'

'Sergeant Major Wainwright, Fraser Island, Queensland, sir. You don't leave his basic weapons training until you can use an Owen submachine-gun with your eyes closed.'

'Sergeant Major Wainwright?' He turned to his offsider. 'Get the details. May get him over to talk to our staff sergeants. Maybe do a weapons course for us, eh?'

'Good idea,' General Vandegrift said, then he turned to the boss. 'Can't you get a man transferred from the States who can speak Japanese and train him in radio intelligence, Greg? This young officer is wasted in the rear.' He called over to a staff captain. 'Captain St George, how many of the enemy had the chest and head shots?'

'We counted twenty-eight, sir,' he replied.

CHAPTER EIGHTEEN

'You try a bit of everything,
insects and plants,
if they don't make you sick
then you can eat them.
It is like life, trial and error with
occasionally a little good fortune.'
Lieutenant Gojo Mura
Electrical Communications Unit
Ministry of Colonisation, Rabaul
Seconded to Mount Austen
Guadalcanal Island, 1942

BATHED, BRUSHED AND BUSHY-TAILED, wearing the full blue serge never intended to be worn in the tropical heat, I arrived at the medal presentation parade. Because I was in the parade, Belgiovani had been put in charge of both the recording and the commentary for the final episode of a four-part Radio America report we'd prepared for the boss. Episode one of the first night on the ridge had been flown to Washington and a report had come back that the Pentagon was impressed and wanted more of the same.

Colonel Woon was rather pleased with himself. Mums and dads all over America were getting an appreciation of what their sons were going through to keep the Land of the Free . . . well, I guess, free. But in this final episode they wouldn't be hearing the blow-by-blow link man in the educated voice of my imitation of Colonel Woon, but the narrative would go into the homes of America in pure Brooklynese. I could almost hear Belgiovani: he'd be adopting a confidential tone just above a whisper: *'Now folks, da General is geddin' ready. His pudden on 'is glasses t'make da speech t'da marines all assembled heuh taday. Dis a historic occasion for one an' all and it is a great priviluge ta be standin' heuh 'mong da wounded an' da brave.'*

It was decoration time for a lot of men who had fought valiantly. The parade began with a speech from Major General Vandegrift, the usual sort of thing: annals of marine history, pride in the flag, pride in the marines, in the name of freedom, naming the battle officially as 'Bloody Ridge', praise from the President and congratulations all round. Then a staff officer called the names of the wounded; all would receive the Purple Heart. Those marines who hadn't been evacuated to Noumea (the more seriously injured went to Brisbane) and were able to get to the presentation, many bandaged, others limping, came forward to be pinned by the general with Colonel Edson standing beside him to shake each one by the hand.

After the wounded came the Bronze and Silver Stars for gallantry on the field of battle, some of these also being awarded to absent wounded. The recipients who were present were pinned and congratulated, whereupon the general announced that Colonel Edson had been awarded the Medal of Honor, the equivalent of our VC and every bit as hard to earn. Spontaneous cheering followed the announcement as it was seen as recognition of the battle of Bloody Ridge and its importance to the war effort in the Pacific.

While not being allowed to wear the navy medal I had been awarded, I nevertheless felt it was an honour being allowed to participate in the parade and to stand alongside the lieutenant in the platoon that was nearest the rostrum. I can't say I wasn't disappointed, because I was a bit. But I was comforted by knowing that I'd proved to myself that I had the courage to fight in a fair dinkum battle, which helped quite a lot to assuage my guilt at my lack of courage with the Java beach burials. But honour or not, I was sweating like a pig in my navy blue serge and after an hour standing in the tropical sun I couldn't wait for the parade to finish so that I could shower and get back into jungle greens. With the general awarding the big gong to Colonel Edson, I reckoned that must be about it, time to pack up and go home.

Colonel Edson stepped up to the microphone and announced that there was one more duty to perform, that a special citation and award of the Navy Cross was to be made to Lieutenant Nicholas Duncan of the Royal Australian Navy. He then read a (thankfully) brief outline of my part in the battle to hold the ridge: conspicuous gallantry in the face of – blah, blah, blah.

To my astonishment the battalion was brought to attention. I confess I was physically shaking and wanted to make a run for it. I could feel a flush of heat rising up my neck and to my face. Then the lieutenant beside me came to sudden attention and said quietly out of the corner of his mouth, 'I'm your escort. Let's go, Popgun Pete.' He used the playful nickname the marines had given me after Bloody Ridge.

As we marched forward the band struck up 'God Save the King'. It was a huge gesture and I shall never forget it. It was undoubtedly the most singular honour and tribute I have ever received.

General Vandegrift pinned me, knowing I couldn't wear the

medal officially, then shook my hand and said, 'Well, Lieutenant Duncan. I want you to know the United States Marine Corps happen to think your promotion to naval lieutenant was both fortuitous and thoroughly justified. Well done, son.'

The following morning I was called from the radio tent to see the boss who, after I'd duly saluted, bade me be seated. He'd congratulated me the previous afternoon and now it was business as usual, or almost.

'We've asked the States to find a Japanese–American soldier to be trained in radio intelligence and although Major General Vandegrift has asked me to release you for intelligence operations in the field, I'd like you to remain long enough to train the new man. How long do you anticipate that will take, Nick?'

I thought for a few moments, knowing that it wasn't about training but about having the courage to follow a hunch, to create your own version of a 'Nick Knack' while thinking not in your own language, but in Japanese. 'Well, sir, if he's been brought up with Japanese spoken in the home he'll probably pick things up fairly quickly. The hard yakka is all done by Corporal Belgiovani.'

'Yakka? Talk American, Nick.'

'Hard work, sir – the technical aspect. But it's more than that. Belgiovani seems to have a genius for sifting out the voices of the various Japanese field radio operators. They have all been given nicknames and we've created a character profile on each and the way they like to operate. After a while it's like reading their minds, you can almost tell if they haven't had breakfast.'

'Nicknames?'

'Yes, sir. "Motor-Mouth", "Spitfire", "Misery Guts", "Goat", "Greta Garbo" —'

'Greta Garbo?'

'Doesn't say much and likes to be alone,' I explained.

Greg Woon laughed. 'We will miss you, Nick. You certainly have developed a knack.'

But I was quick to protest. 'No, sir, it isn't really that hard. It's like being familiar with how a friend expresses himself and then judging his mood. The new bloke – er, guy, will soon enough get the hang of it. "Goat", for instance, has a fist that transmits morse code smooth as silk, "Misery Guts" thumps it out like he's using a three-pound hammer. It's not hard.'

'I sincerely hope it's not, for everyone's sake,' the boss said.

I hesitated, then said, 'Sir, I know it's none of my business. But do you think you could promote Corporal Belgiovani to sergeant?'

The boss's expression changed to one of alarm. 'What did I *think* I just heard you say, Nick?'

'Belgiovani to sergeant, sir.'

'Yes, that was what I thought you said. I've always considered it a minor miracle that he managed to claw his way up to the dizzy heights of corporal. What are you saying? That he's earned the extra stripe because he was on the ridge and saw combat?'

I grinned. 'No, sir, I don't think he saw very much from his position at the bottom of our dugout. There has to be a worse soldier in the American army but Belgiovani, without question, would qualify for the grand finals.' In my mind I was comparing him with the little bloke, but I reckon Kevin was half a nick on a rifle butt above him. Then I added, 'There also has to be a best field radio operator in the United States Army Air Force Intelligence – and he has to be somewhere near the top. He has a genius for sifting out the voices and isolating the unique morse fist of every Japanese operator. The wizards as well as the brave should be recognised; in my mind he has earned the promotion, sir.'

'That's pretty full-on. I'll think about it, Nick. What's a morse fist? You mentioned the term before.'

'Well, sir, every operator using morse possesses a series of rhythms, speed and pauses that is referred to as his "fist". It's like his signature if you have an ear for it. I can't recognise each one very well, but Corporal Belgiovani is a whiz.'

Colonel Woon grinned. 'What the hell! With the acceptance of our broadcasts to the States we're expanding the section and we'll need a sergeant anyway. I guess Belgiovani won't ever have to lead a squad of men into battle, so the American armed forces are not placed in any immediate danger. I'll have my clerk draft the paperwork. Sergeant Polanski will be thoroughly disgusted and that's not an altogether bad thing.'

'Thank you, sir.' I knew that I'd instantly added to the Battle-Hardened Brute from Brooklyn's bullshit quotient. I could almost hear it now: '*After da Battle o' Bloody Ridge dey made me a sergeant. I ain't saying so myself, but Colonel Woon, he said – I is only quoting him now, yer unnerstand – "Belgiovani, we is elevatin' you to da rank of sergeant for your leadership, courage and competence at Bloody Ridge."*' But of even greater importance, with his new rank he'd be allowed to eat in the sergeants' mess where the chef from the Waldorf Astoria ran the kitchen. Belgiovani would think he'd died and gone to heaven.

The new Japanese–American translator, Private Lee Roy Yamamoto, finally arrived. He was the eldest son in a third-generation Japanese–American family. This lengthy American background had exempted them from being interned as enemy aliens. Yamamoto had volunteered even before Pearl Harbor, but in the paranoid climate that then prevailed this could have been seen as deeply suspicious – enemy infiltration into the army. He'd finally been vetted by the FBI and given a high security clearance. Belgiovani expanded like a puffer frog when he realised he was now the senior rank in the radio unit.

Fortunately, Private Yamamoto possessed a phlegmatic disposition and a good sense of humour and accepted the situation as fact. He appeared to be an archetypal Japanese, with the lenses in his glasses seemingly made from the bottom of Coke bottles. He had slightly protruding teeth and one of the front ones was chipped as a result of a pick-up game of football at college. Belgiovani promptly nicknamed him 'Da Nip widda Chip'. He was short, although an inch taller than the Brooklyn Brute, bandy-legged and yellow-skinned, and the appearance of a nude Japanese in the shower block nearly caused a riot amongst the marines.

By the end of September Lee Roy Yamamoto's training was completed. At last I was free to leave the radio tent with a clear conscience and the blessing of Colonel Woon who, as it turned out, would remain my boss. I was to be known as 'Field Intelligence' and was required to receive some additional training in patrol work, leaving Yamamoto and Belgiovani to go it alone.

It was in early November that the new boy on the block and the Brute from Brooklyn proved they'd come of age as a · combination. They'd been listening in to an unimportant Japanese field transmission when, unbelievably fortuitously, they picked up a conversation in the background which, when translated by Private Yamamoto, indicated that a large detachment of troops that had been expected from Rabaul, together with their equipment, had been sunk by marauding

American fighters and bombers, christened the 'Cactus Air Force' by the marines.

In addition to this lack of fresh troops, what was coming through in the messages was the Japs' ongoing inability to land sufficient supplies of both food and equipment. Supplies could only be brought in at night by small craft that ferried them from the supply ships to the beach, and from there the provisions had to be manhandled by sick and malnourished soldiers into the cover of the copra plantations. But with the dawn patrol by the Cactus Air Force, many a night's supply was left to lie useless, strafed and burning on the beaches or floating out to sea.

It seemed unlikely that under these circumstances the Japanese possessed the capacity to mount regular major offensives. After Bloody Ridge, where I'd seen about as much fighting as I required for one man's war, I wasn't looking forward to more of the same, even if the Intelligence radio unit was meant to do nothing except observe. I was happy to settle down to the daily routine of sending and receiving messages for the coastwatcher network and trying to make sense of the Japanese field radio operators.

But that's not the Japanese way. They simply kept landing more and more troops, allowing those who were dying of malaria, dysentery, dengue fever and – most of all – starvation, to perish. The fresh troops fighting for the Emperor would then take their turn to die in one of these several ways; dying in combat was the least likely event of them all.

Determined to oust the Americans, the Japanese High Command thought of their men as totally expendable. For a Japanese soldier, to land on Guadalcanal was tantamount to being handed a death sentence. A wounded Japanese colonel who was captured (a rare occurrence as members of the officer corps invariably suicided), upon being questioned by Colonel Woon, with me acting as interpreter, was asked why senior officers had such a callous disregard for the lives and welfare of the soldiers under their command. The Japanese officer showed no indignation at this suggestion and replied by saying, 'When you fire a rifle you don't expect to get the bullet back'.

The Japanese succeeded in mounting two more serious assaults. The first was on the 13th and 14th of October, exactly one month after Bloody Ridge, when the Japanese battleships *Kongo* and *Haruna* bombarded Henderson Field and base with their fourteen-inch guns. After enduring a very long night of explosions and imagining every shell had my name on it, I decided that if I had to die I wanted it to happen when I could see my enemy's face. I can tell you the anonymity of shells exploding in my vicinity left me a very scared puppy.

The second assault was a major attempt by the enemy to cross the Mantanikau River to the west of Henderson. But by this time, while they had ample men who they were prepared to sacrifice at any cost, they were badly hamstrung by the difficult tropical terrain. A lack of supply prevented them from massing enough well-equipped, well-fed and healthy troops backed with artillery and air support. Moreover the furious retaliation of fighter planes operating from nearby Henderson led to what amounted to a virtual massacre.

Malaria was becoming the major factor to cause weakness, not only in the ranks of the Japanese but also amongst the marines, with over six hundred cases a week, many needing evacuation to Luganville and Noumea. From early August to December, 2879 men were flown out and a further one thousand left by sea, while untreated malaria coupled with malnutrition, or more correctly starvation, killed the Japanese in their thousands.

Over twenty-three thousand Japanese died at Guadalcanal, most from sickness and starvation. When they left in February 1943, using destroyers at night anchored on the western side of the island, they evacuated just over eleven thousand men, of whom the vast majority were sick and starving.

In effect, with the failure of the arrival of fresh troops, those that remained at the disposal of the Japanese command after Mantanikau River were simply unfit for use in major combat. Although theoretically the Japanese forces still outnumbered the Americans and had thirty-five thousand combat soldiers on the island, you can't expect a soldier who is suffering from malarial fever and dysentery, shaking uncontrollably while at the same time spraying shit like a hose at the firemen's picnic, to fire a gun or throw a grenade or even to advance at a trot with fixed bayonet.

However, although the Japs may have lacked the capacity to mount a major assault, they made up for it with very effective small-scale skirmishes and suicidally stubborn defence. At night they kept the marines virtually confined to the immediate area of Henderson Field. While the Americans owned the day, the Japanese controlled the night. If a marine patrol couldn't get back to Henderson by nightfall the patrol members didn't get a lot of sleep over the next ten or twelve hours.

The Japs also controlled Mount Austen, the highest point in the area, which lay to the immediate south of Henderson; its northern face looked directly down onto the airfield. There is little doubt that, despite everything they suffered, the Japs were a tenacious and determined enemy. Lugging heavy field artillery up a mountain that was covered to the summit in almost impenetrable jungle, and had precipitous ravines and slippery slopes, was a remarkable achievement and one that the Marine

Field Artillery Unit had previously considered impossible.

Having achieved this astonishing feat, the enemy was determined to defend its mountain artillery positions. US fighter planes made regular sorties to oust the Japs, but the enemy was well concealed and protected by huge rocky outcrops on the slopes and near the summit, and the raids met with very little success. The Japs were using the mountain not only to fire down on Henderson but also to send reports of US aircraft taking off to attack their ships in the area.

More and more it was looking as if the marines would have to go up the mountain to silence them. It was a task only the foolhardy or the very well trained dared to attempt and the marine field command was reluctant to authorise it, knowing there was only one known path up Mount Austen and it was in Japanese hands.

However, eventually it was decided the enemy had to be dislodged from the mountain and I was to be included as the field intelligence officer in the battalion chosen for the task. The marines, having fought on the more or less flat coastal area where Bloody Ridge was the highest point in what essentially passed for rolling hills, were not familiar with jungle warfare and we were required to undergo extra training. To my surprise we were advised in our training and objectives by J.V. Mather, who was an Australian seconded for duty with the 1st Marines.

Our objectives were first to locate and explore a suspected trail leading around and behind Mount Austen that seemed to be used by the Japanese to move troops and supplies from west to east of Henderson, and second, to seek out and destroy enemy artillery and observation posts overlooking Henderson from the slopes. Finally, we were to locate the field radio that was alerting the enemy navy of the impending arrival of our aircraft. This last objective was my own particular responsibility and I was to be given a squad of marines to help me achieve it.

While Mather didn't minimise the Japanese presence on the mountain, he was careful to point out that the first enemy we would face was the mountain itself.

'It's a bugger,' he announced. 'The mountain is covered, as you can see, by thick jungle. I won't say it's impenetrable because the canopy is so thick that in many places the sun doesn't get down to the floor and so there is very little undergrowth. But it's the deep gorges that have been scored out of the underlying limestone by the many streams originating on the mountain that make access difficult. These are often so deep and vertical in nature that it is tantamount to walking in the semi-dark or deepening dusk. When it rains, which can be several times during each day, the streams become raging torrents in a matter of minutes. The only way to get up the mountain is to follow the streams and traverse these gorges.' He looked around. 'This takes both ingenuity and courage. If you're not drowned by a rush of water from a sudden downfall emanating from the top of the mountain, you could be stuck in the bottom of a gorge like ducks in a shooting gallery with the enemy firing down at you. This is not a recommended procedure.'

This understatement drew a scared laugh from us all as he went on to say, 'However, the two native constables accompanying us are excellent forward scouts and I have every confidence in them.' He then proceeded to brief us further. 'A downpour blots out visibility and this, if anything, is to our advantage as the enemy cannot see or hear you until you are on top of him. Of course, it also works the other way around as well.

'Moreover after each downpour the surface you move across

turns to mud that, due to the peculiar nature of the soil type, also feels and behaves like grease.' He concluded by saying, 'Mount Austen will not be an experience you will easily forget, gentlemen. Of the two enemies, count the mountain as a close second.'

It was just the kind of briefing that made me almost regret the decision by Intelligence to send me along with the marine battalion. When giving me the initial orders Colonel Woon had said, 'Just your type of thing, Nick: plenty of jungle and sloshing about in the rain and then the glory of capturing the Japanese radio operator. But do be careful, son, we don't like casualties in Intelligence, all that bothersome retraining to go through.'

Coming to the end of this briefing on the mountain and the jungle Mather said, 'I take it the untidy bloke in the Australian jungle greens is Lieutenant Nicholas Duncan from Army Air Force Intelligence?'

'Yes, sir,' I replied, laughing.

'Well, Nick, I'm told that you have reason to suppose that only one Japanese field radio is operating from the mountain?'

'Yes, sir, we have only identified one voice, and one fist when sending morse.' In the radio unit we'd named the Mount Austen operator 'Goat' – for obvious reasons. Looking up to the mountain from the base, you could imagine him located in the rocky outcrop near the summit. It would be an ideal position from which to contact ships and even Rabaul, but, because of the constant bad weather and other ground level interference, we seldom received him clearly and we really knew, or rather guessed, very little about him. The best the direction finders had been able to give us was a 'cocked hat'; that is, a triangle on the map giving a general area of the mountain as his location. While it narrowed things down a bit it was nonetheless like trying to find a needle in a haystack.

'Well, Nick,' Mather said, 'my suggestion is that if you are going to be successful wheedling him out it's going to have to be a one-man operation. He's probably sending from a limestone cave, of which there are hundreds. If any more than one person attempts to catch him unawares it is likely to spook him well before you get near enough to find him or his equipment.' Then he added, 'Have you had jungle training, Lieutenant?'

All about me faces turned to hear my reply. 'Yes, sir, in New Britain and New Guinea as well as in Australia, on Fraser Island.'

He looked at me doubtfully. 'New Britain and New Guinea; in what military capacity?'

'None, sir, as a butterfly collector.'

A roar of laughter followed from the assembled marines, but because of my navy medal, it was of a good-natured kind. Mather was not the chuckling type, but nevertheless couldn't resist milking a laugh. 'Well, there are certainly lots of butterflies on the mountain, but I don't recommend you take your butterfly net along.' Another big laugh followed.

I knew J.V. Mather was correct when he suggested I locate 'Goat' on my own. This wasn't a job for a squad. I'd be back in the jungle on my own and, despite his advice, I felt Mather, even though we were fellow Australians, wasn't all that impressed with the butterfly collector's chances of finding the Japanese radio operator. Mind you, I confess I wasn't that confident myself.

The reconnaissance of the mountain began on the 24th of November with a battalion of marines led by Lieutenant Colonel Carlson and accompanied and advised by Mather.

With us was a scout from Malaita who was a member of the native constabulary, and also the famous Sergeant Major Vouza. Their task was to guide us through the initial phases of the operation.

Because I spoke pidgin and Solomon Islanders speak a similar version to that spoken in New Britain, I struck up a friendship with the two guides. Sergeant Major Vouza was the more gregarious and I was not surprised to learn that he was still pretty cranky at the way he'd been treated by the Japs and was aching for payback, a long tradition on the islands. While he laughed a good deal about this, I could sense he wasn't going to be happy until he'd avenged the bayoneting he'd received at the hands of the Japanese patrol that had left him for dead, tied to a tree. He wanted to accompany me to the summit to find 'Goat' but it was outside his brief. I requested permission from J.V. Mather, who said he'd discuss it with Lieutenant Colonel Carlson. In any event, permission was refused.

I admit I would have felt a lot safer with Sergeant Major Vouza at my side. But he said to me on parting, laughing uproariously as he spoke, 'Time yufella come back long mountain yumi lookim man Japon, mifela like takim stakka head long em for putim long haus blo mifela.' Roughly translated, this means 'When you return from the mountain, we'll go out hunting Japanese so that we can take their heads and place their skulls in my house.'

On the 28th of November we located a trail on the north side of the mountain leading up into the slope and the real toil and trouble began. Even climbing the lower slope was sheer brutish effort.

For me, being in the jungle was not the unfamiliar experience it was for the marines. I was accustomed to the

dull, dark light, even to the limestone gorges, where the effect
is of being in a huge Gothic cathedral. But on Mount Austen
the gorges were more numerous, some of them very deep, with
almost vertical sides where we'd be defenceless against a hail
of enemy bullets if we were ambushed from above. This made
almost every step a scary experience. You can't move a battalion
of men carrying fifty-pound packs over a rocky surface such as
those found in a gorge without making a hell of a clatter.

Then, as an added factor, there was the rain. If you are
familiar with the jungle you know when it's about to rain – there
is a silence and then a thickening of the atmosphere, as if
the air is swollen. Invariably, minutes later comes the roar of
heavy drops tearing at the canopy a hundred feet above you.
To someone who has spent time in the jungle there is no
mistaking when a drenching is coming. Lieutenant Colonel
Carlson wasn't prepared to believe me until it was confirmed
several times by the two scouts and their advice was promptly
followed by a heavy downpour. We would get the hell out of
a gorge before the explosion of rushing water could sweep us
away. Or, alternatively, we wouldn't enter a gorge if a cloudburst
seemed imminent.

Having proved my jungle credentials I was permitted to
become a forward scout. I felt a great deal safer on my own than
amongst the reverberatory clatter of a battalion trying to make
ground with the elements and the terrain constantly against
them.

With each downpour of blinding rain, during which you
could see no more than ten yards ahead, I comforted myself that
this distance was perfect for the Owen. But J.V. Mather had
been correct. The slopes were so slippery that it was often two
steps up and three or thirty down for the marines. It was like a

three-dimensional game of snakes and ladders where a missed step, like an unlucky throw, sends you, accompanied by a hail of curses, into the file of men behind you.

With me acting as a scout with the two native constables, we managed to stay out of trouble and avoid Japanese forward patrols. We didn't want them to know we were on the mountain and thus be ready and waiting for us in their artillery positions on the slopes and near the summit. But the noise of our advance was difficult to muffle, and after three days we happened upon a small ammunition and weapons dump that we promptly destroyed. Encouraged by this find, Company F was sent out on patrol to search the area thoroughly, with the constable from Malaita as their guide. One of these patrols, of single squad strength, stumbled across an enemy force of around a hundred men in a bivouac on a rocky slope during a rainstorm. Because of the noise of the tropical downpour and the impossibility of seeing for any distance, both sides were caught by surprise. The Japanese had their weapons stacked and the marines used their automatic small arms to all but wipe them out. Seventy-five Japanese lay dead after the brief and violent encounter, the blood from their wounds carried away in the runnels formed in the mud by the pounding rain.

There were no marine casualties, but the following day a marine was killed by an enemy sniper and I was given the task of eliminating the Jap. I borrowed a Springfield, sighting it first. I enjoyed the patient stalk, listening to sound and movement that you sense are alien in the jungle, often not moving for minutes at a time. It took me an hour to cover the fifty yards needed for a clear shot.

If you are required to kill an enemy your most earnest hope is that you will take him by surprise with a clean shot so that he's dead before he can react to the threat. That's the way I'd like to meet death, dished out to me quickly and impersonally, one moment here and half a breath later, gone. But I have to say, it is important to me that I see my enemy face to face. In the split second before I die I'd like to see the face of the bloke who pulls the trigger. For me it is a matter of mutual respect. To creep up behind a bloke and shoot him in the back, while required in war, is slaughter at other times.

There had been some suggestion at Fraser Island that I might like to leave Naval Intelligence to train as a sniper. While it was considered a compliment to my ability with a rifle, I was secretly aghast at the idea. A sniper fires in cold blood and should never get close enough to face the enemy. In retrospect, the thought of my being trained to be a killing machine horrifies me. I had never thought of myself as belonging to those men who have a naturally aggressive attitude. Always a loner, I wished nobody harm and at school and elsewhere would go to considerable pains to avoid a fight. I am by nature a poor hater, reasoning that a mean spirit only injures itself. I considered myself a reasonable and reasoning bloke. I recall Sergeant Major Wainwright, a soft-spoken, calm and reasoning man if ever there was one, saying, 'Nick, hotheads, haters and trigger-happy morons can't be relied on to do this job. It takes calmness and reasoning, aptitude and some real intelligence. Hate clouds judgment and stupidity confuses the issues involved. We only kill because we are forced under the prevailing circumstances to do so.'

Nonetheless while I would never again experience it, I cannot deny that I'd felt a real sense of exhilaration when I'd killed the seven men coming at me on Bloody Ridge and during the fight that had followed beside the marines. I deeply regret that this innate ability to kill is contained within me. The affinity with killing is a primordial force you hope will never surface. When I eventually heard Anna's story, I could feel a deep, dark stirring of the force within me, but thankfully this was drowned in the tears I shed at her suffering.

I eventually found the Japanese sniper behind an outcrop of rock on the edge of a jungle clearing and initially he was unaware of my presence. There is an unwritten code all fighting men obey – that a sniper is never captured alive. My orders from Lieutenant Colonel Carlson were 'to eliminate this present danger'. That's Geneva Convention language, but as an order, it's specific enough. So I stepped into the small area so that he could see my face and he was dead before he could even register a look of surprise. When I set about searching the poor bastard to verify his identity, he was virtually reduced to skin and bone. If he was any indication, the Japanese on the mountain were doing it *really* tough.

This episode in hunting the Japanese sniper gave me a little added confidence for finding 'Goat' on my own. It also, incidentally, earned the respect of J.V. Mather, who thereafter refrained from referring to me as 'Lieutenant Butterfly' – a little joke that had earned him a chuckle each time and one he'd felt he could get away with in company, as I was a fellow Australian.

He wasn't a bad bloke and was damned good at his job. I guess he didn't want it to look as if he was favouring a countryman. When I was ready to leave the battalion to hunt for 'Goat' he came up and patted me on the shoulder and said, 'I've bet Lieutenant Colonel Carlson a pound you'll find the Japanese radio operator, Nick. Go to it, son, don't let me down.' He'd grinned. 'A quid, especially if it comes out of my pocket, is a bloody fortune.'

'Thanks, sir,' I'd replied, also grinning. 'I would have hoped I was worth at least a fiver!'

You will recall how I described the island of Guadalcanal as being like a piece of fabric that had been picked up at the centre and dropped to the floor, to leave ridges and valleys and a more or less flat coastline. Mount Austen was typical of this formation and we had arrived at a point later described by Lieutenant Colonel Carlson as 'the hub of a spiderweb of ridges'. This was an ideal place for the enemy to mount their artillery and it was while we were approaching it that we were met by a strong Japanese combat patrol.

The fierce fight that ensued lasted just over two hours, both sides using automatic weapons and mortars. The enemy attempted to surround us by executing a double envelopment but we fought them off, then through the quick thinking of Lieutenant Colonel Carlson we managed to surround them and the fight was eventually won. We had killed twenty-five of the enemy while we suffered four marines wounded. I would later hear that one of them died the following day.

The time had come to venture alone into the jungle, then scour the limestone crags in search of 'Goat'. I had decided that as a fellow radio intelligence operator, albeit on the other side, I didn't want to kill him unless my own life was threatened. Mather had urged me to take along an American Springfield rifle but I was reluctant to do so – it's a very good rifle, but I reckoned the terrain would ensure any confrontation would be at short range, and I'd have a good chance of taking him prisoner.

I packed a week's rations, although if I was successful I could be off the mountain in two days or, depending on the weather and avoiding any stray Japanese patrols, three days at the most. But if I was fortunate in my search and took 'Goat' prisoner, he would also need to eat. I wondered how he'd go with GI rations after subsisting on a handful of rice and anything else he might have scavenged in the jungle. If you knew what you were doing you could always find a meal of sorts, sometimes quite a good one – worms, grubs and insects were excellent protein, and several types of edible mushroom grew in the boles of giant trees. Often, where a large tree had fallen and created a clearing for the sun to get through, the almost instant undergrowth this created was the home of several edible plants.

I had been taught all this by my childhood native companions or by experimenting while chasing butterflies in New Britain and New Guinea. A single fallen tree that is rotting can often render a more than adequate meal from those things that live under the bark or grow in the clearing that it creates. Now I wondered if the Japanese had received any instruction on how to forage for a meal in the jungle. From the emaciated condition of the sniper I very much doubted it. I didn't mind going it alone, in fact I was secretly glad since guiding a bunch of marines (who had not received specialist training and were therefore 'clumsy in the jungle') silently to the whereabouts of 'Goat' would have been virtually impossible.

I set out at daybreak, knowing the Japanese radio operator would be transmitting the information about the early fighter and bomber flights as they left Henderson before the cloud came up and obscured his view of the airfield. By midmorning I'd gone about two hundred yards, travelling up steeply through the jungle. It has always astonished me that trees two hundred feet high, veritable forest giants, can tenaciously dig their roots into the limestone cracks and fissures so they anchor themselves on such precipitous slopes.

Two hundred yards in five hours when you're stalking isn't too bad as I wanted to arrive at the base of the limestone cliffs that rose out of the jungle well before nightfall. I could then attempt to climb the cliffs the following day while 'Goat' was busy transmitting the information about the morning flights from Henderson. I stopped for breakfast (a Hershey bar and water from a mountain stream) and stopped again for lunch (this time a cold can of pork 'n' beans, as there was no question of lighting a fire). It rained early and midmorning and again in the afternoon. This was good; although the rain reduced my vision down to a few yards, the tremendous noise as the virtual curtains of water hit the canopy allowed me to move a little faster, despite the slippery conditions. Also, it meant it wasn't necessary to cover my footprints as the rain washed them away almost immediately.

I'd reached the base of the cliff face by midafternoon and moved to the edge of the jungle where I could see the surface of the whole of the north-facing cliff. I settled down to watch and to study it closely. Men always choose the easiest way to climb up any object. Using my binoculars I soon spotted a likely way up the face though it meant passing dozens of fairly large fissures, each of which could have housed a cave. So I looked for fissures that had some sort of rock platform directly outside, as it would be patently impossible to step out of a cave into thin air. Twenty or so appeared to be candidates, but there were only two that appeared to have a ledge leading to a rudimentary pathway, often no more than eight inches wide. The path ran more or less diagonally down the face of the cliff into the jungle canopy that grew right up to the edge of the cliff. This meant the caves were about two hundred and seventy-five feet above ground level, an impressive eyrie or eagle's nest and an ideal place from which to transmit a radio signal.

Studying this rough path, which was virtually a crack in the surface of the limestone that had occurred possibly at some Pre-Cambrian time, I observed that small parts of the face had been recently broken away to slightly widen it almost directly in front of one of the caves, the work of army sappers or someone with a rock chisel and a heavy blunt-nosed hammer.

I knew immediately I had found a habitable cave, though not necessarily the one that housed 'Goat' – or anyone else for that matter. Like many of the artillery positions we'd found, it might have been vacated. We'd killed over a hundred Japanese since coming onto the mountain. This would have been sufficient to man the light artillery the Japs had installed on the slopes. The Japanese command, because of the shortage of fit troops, would have left the barest minimum number of combat soldiers on the mountain. The difficulty of supplying a large body of men in such terrain, coupled with the unlikely event of an American assault, would have meant their officers would see this as a logical decision. A small force, sufficient to stave off American patrols, would be enough, just sufficient to man the artillery and supply 'Goat's' need for batteries to run his transceiver and to bring him food.

We hadn't been harassed in the gorges and had only been attacked by a not very large patrol. This suggested that the mountain summit was relatively free of enemy troops and that we'd accounted for most of them. When all of these factors were taken into consideration, this particular cave, seventy-five feet above the canopy, appeared to be my best bet for finding 'Goat', who would almost certainly be left behind in any retreat the Japs made from the mountain. His messages to Japanese ships out to sea would be deemed too important.

I settled down for a cold, wet wait until morning, in the process enduring a five o'clock downpour. Walking in a jungle rainstorm is never pleasant, and sitting through one is bloody miserable. But just before nightfall, when the rain had stopped and the last of the sun broke through the clouds, I was unexpectedly rewarded. A Japanese soldier came out of the mouth of the cave and stood on the edge of the small platform and prepared to urinate. I watched as the bright stream of urine caught the last rays of sunshine as it arched into the canopy below. I was glad I hadn't brought a Springfield as I might have been tempted to make an easy rifle shot, almost certainly killing him. No man deserves to die when taking a wonderful piss like that.

It became quite clear to me that I couldn't go up the cliff to get him out. In the process I would make far too much noise and, if he had an automatic weapon, he had merely to stand within the cave and when I appeared at the entrance blast me to kingdom come. I would have to wait until he came down into the jungle. Sooner or later he would have to do so, to forage for food, take a crap or simply to stretch his legs.

If he was indeed the 'Goat' then I knew his broadcast routine. He would work the dawn schedule, when visibility for aircraft was better and the flying conditions were more favourable and most of the offensive operations were mounted out of Henderson. The dawn flights went looking for Japanese food and supply dumps that had been landed on the beaches by enemy destroyers overnight. Then he'd watch for the second morning flights that were going out to seek and destroy enemy shipping. The cloud cover started to thicken over the land by late morning and as the day progressed afternoon rain squalls sweeping over the island would cause visibility to decline. That was when I expected he'd come down.

No night spent in the jungle is ever pleasant – everything with a mouth that creeps and crawls seems to find you – but, thank God, near the summit I was above the mosquito line and so by morning, nursing a bite or two, I remained relatively unscathed. I endured yet another cold breakfast and a long wait, my only pleasure being to watch the butterflies in the clearing. They were plentiful and of several different varieties; all, with the exception of one, contained within my collection at the mission. That is, of course, in the unlikely event that it still existed intact.

The one exception, a large butterfly that alighted near me, made my heart skip a beat. I knew it from pictures in a book – John McGillivray, a British naturalist who visited the island in 1885, had discovered it. It was peculiar to Guadalcanal and adjacent islands, and its generic name was *Aetheoptera victoriae*. If I'd had a net with me, I'm sure I would have been quite unable to resist giving chase, abandoning my hunt for 'Goat', not even caring if the entire Japanese army heard me as I blundered through the jungle after this magnificent specimen. With the rare species you often only get one chance in a lifetime – it might take months, even years, to come across one this size again. I'd known of its existence since a child and now, for the first time, I'd seen a perfectly splendid male alight on a shrub no more than three feet from where I sat and I couldn't move a finger to catch him.

On the dot of eleven when the cloud cover began, the soldier appeared, urinated in the same spectacular and satisfying way and returned to the interior of the cave, then twenty minutes later he reappeared. I watched him through the binoculars and saw that he carried what appeared to be a flat, medium-sized book under his arm together with a bamboo rod, although I couldn't be sure. He made his way down the narrow path and while it was obviously dangerous he seemed to traverse it with a sure-footed nimbleness. If he was indeed 'Goat', then we'd named him well. He was a small, very slight man, and to my astonishment he evidently carried no weapon.

I moved silently to the point where I calculated the natural progression of the diagonal path on the cliff face would reach the floor of the jungle and waited. Ten, then fifteen minutes passed, but he didn't appear, nor could I hear any sound of his progress. I felt sure as he drew closer I would hear the clatter of a small rock falling or the crunch of his footsteps on the narrow path or, if he'd come to its end and entered the jungle, the snap of a twig – something that would give him away. Unless you are prepared to move no more than fifty yards in an hour, planting each footprint with infinite care, the jungle will reward a pair of alert ears to another's presence within thirty or forty yards almost every time.

I studied the cliff carefully once again, focusing my glasses at the point where the so-called path entered the canopy. I decided the path must suddenly run parallel once it entered the trees, gradually descending to the very end of the cliff face, possibly a hundred yards from where I stood. So I made my way carefully to where I could see a part of the cliff wall existing below the line made by the canopy. No path continued in an area that fell some seventy yards short of the end of the huge rocky outcrop that formed the summit.

'Goat' – or whoever it was – had simply disappeared, vanished into the dark green canopy. Once again I focused on the point where the path entered the trees abutting the cliff. My father had once told me, 'Nicholas, there are no mysteries to a patient man.' The tree line beneath the cliff was almost straight but then I noticed that, at the point where the diagonal cliff path entered the canopy, a forest giant rose perhaps eight feet above the rest of the trees. *Holy shit, it's the tree! He's come down the tree!*

It took me nearly an hour, hugging the cliff face, to traverse the sixty yards to where I thought the tree might be and then, quite suddenly, I came upon it. Metal spikes had been driven into the trunk; they protruded about nine inches, making it relatively easy to climb or ascend. The giant tree had become a ladder growing up against the face of the cliff to the point where the path virtually petered out.

The Japanese soldier hadn't made any attempt to conceal his footsteps and the first thing I noticed was the smell of faeces where he'd defecated and covered the result with a pile of dead leaves. Using a twig I scraped them clear and examined what was a very small bowel movement. He'd been eating insects and perhaps a little rice and some forest greens. It was at best a subsistence diet, but not an entirely unintelligent one. I pushed the leaves back in place and then proceeded to pick up his trail, not a difficult task, although I continued to move very quietly.

I finally reached a clearing beside a small stream, the babble of water running over limestone caused sufficient noise to cover any tiny sound I might have made with my approach. I stood about ten feet behind him and slightly to his left and watched. A large tree had fallen to create the clearing, allowing the sunlight to penetrate. It must have come down fairly recently, for the bark showed no decay and the undergrowth, feeding on the sun, had not yet overwhelmed the area to form a wildness of scrubs scrapping for the available space.

The Japanese soldier was seated on a wide branch of the fallen tree. Resting on his knees was a small sketchbook and beside him on the branch, a box of watercolours and a tin mug containing water. I noticed with detached interest that the squares of colour within the box were all but used up. On the ground in front of him was a large green leaf and on the leaf, with its wings arranged in the open position, was a butterfly.

I could hardly believe my eyes! It was a Clipper, the very same species I had boxed as Anna's keepsake! Later I was to tell myself that it wasn't such an amazing coincidence – the Clipper is found throughout the islands, and though it is not common it could not be called scarce. But it was spooky and at the time I thought of it as an omen, though whether a good or bad one, I couldn't yet say.

On the ground beside him lay the net made from mosquito netting, a twist of wire and the bamboo stick I had seen him carry. It was basic, but perfectly adequate for the task. The little enemy soldier, I hoped it was 'Goat', was humming what I took to be a Japanese tune, every once in a while singing a snatch of words, then returning to humming, meanwhile painting the lovely butterfly whose wing pattern was reminiscent of a sailing ship.

It was a situation beyond my wildest imagining; even if he wasn't 'Goat', this man's life was as good as spared. His uniform was in tatters but clean, his hair, which fell down to his shoulders, was also clean, and more surprisingly, his cheeks and chin were shaved. I glanced over to the stream to see resting on a rock a cut-throat razor placed on a ragged scrap of towelling. This was a man who, despite his isolation, was trying to keep himself together.

It was ten minutes past noon. 'Good afternoon,' I said, greeting him in Japanese. '*Hajimemashite* [I am pleased to make your acquaintance].'

The sketchbook went flying from his lap and he leapt to his feet to stand to attention without turning to look at me. I could see he was shaking, obviously terrified. 'I can explain, sir. The cloud cover – I cannot use the radio – I am not neglecting my duty, sir,' he stammered.

He was standing with one boot planted on the big leaf with one of the Clipper's wings protruding from its toecap. He had mistaken me for a Japanese, a tribute to all the listening I had done over the months. I felt a shock as I witnessed the crushed butterfly under his boot. Was it a bad omen, telling me that Anna was dead, crushed like an insect under an Imperial Japanese boot?

'You may turn around. I am *gaikokujin* and you are my prisoner,' I replied, informing him I was not Japanese.

He turned slowly to face me, lifting his arms above his head in the universal gesture of surrender, his expression showing astonishment – perhaps it was at my size as he couldn't have come to more than halfway up my chest. 'Ah-meri-can, sir?' he asked in a trembling voice.

'No, Aus-tra-lian,' I pronounced carefully. He didn't reply, merely nodded his head and so I said, pointing to the crushed butterfly, 'I am sorry to have caused you to crush *Parthenos sylvia*.'

He glanced down at his boot, withdrawing it in horror at what he'd inadvertently done. Then he asked, 'This is its name, sir?'

'Latin name. In my language it is called a Clipper.'

'Clip – clip – Clip-purr,' he finally managed. 'You are

konchugakusha? [You study insects?]' he asked.

'No, I am a butterfly collector,' I answered, realising that if he knew the word for 'entomologist', he probably wasn't a peasant. 'Please, bring your hands down and relax. I am not going to kill a man who carries no weapon.'

'Oh, but I have one, sir.' He glanced in the direction of the cliff face, then added somewhat ingenuously, 'I think it is rusted.' Visibly relaxing, he brought his hands to his side. 'What will you do now?' he asked.

'You are the radio operator who monitors the aeroplanes leaving? The only one?'

'Yes, sir, there is only me.'

I grinned. 'You are very good, your morse fist is fast and smooth.'

'Thank you, sir. I was trained in the Telegraph Department of the College of Engineering in Tokyo.'

In retrospect this sounds like a ridiculous conversation to have with a just-captured Japanese soldier – gruff-voiced instructions, a bit of assertive manhandling and prodding with the barrel of the Owen was the recommended method. But unless he was a very cool-headed master of kung-fu or jujitsu and was trying to lure me to come closer, he was physically incapable of harming me. Nevertheless I remained standing to one side of him and out of reach of either his feet or his arms. 'After that you joined the army?' I enquired.

He looked horrified. 'No, sir, *watashi wa minkanjin desu.* [I am a civilian.] I was required to attend *Takunan-juku*, the school run by the Ministry of Colonisation. I was *kaigun rijisei* [a cadet attached to the navy].'

I looked surprised. 'Navy? I am also in the navy.'

'It is only technical, sir. I was given the token title of Naval

Commissioned Officer Trained in Radio Communication.' It seemed somewhat amazing that he too felt he was not entitled to his rank. Then he added, 'I have never been in the navy, sir. I was sent to Rabaul to work for the *Minseibu*, the civil administration. I worked in the Electrical Communications Unit.'

'Then how did you get here?' I asked.

'In the cave?'

'No, to Guadalcanal.'

'I was seconded, sir. Malaria caused too many casualties amongst the field radio operators. I was sent to train others.'

I glanced up, indicating the cliff face with a jerk of my head. 'And now you are up there?'

'Yes, sir. It is demanding work requiring the use of ciphers and long-distance transmissions. Most field operators would not have these skills. I was happy when it was agreed I should go.'

'Happy to be so isolated?'

He smiled, looking down at his boots and shaking his head slowly. 'I am not a fighting man, sir.'

'No? A painter of butterflies then?'

'*Shirouto* [amateur], sir. There are so many in the jungle and they are interesting, fascinating to me.'

I laughed. 'What – to eat or collect?'

'Some to eat,' he said, taking my little joke seriously. 'It is shameful, all are beautiful.'

'You are *shirouto no konchugakusha* [an amateur entomologist]?' I asked.

'I am not worthy of even the amateur title. I have no reference books. These are not insects I have seen in Japan, I simply try to paint them without knowing their Latin names. My painting too, it is unworthy, *shirouto no gaka*,' he said shyly, stating his amateur status once again, then looking in the direction of the fallen sketchbook.

It was time to introduce myself, though I still kept my distance – if he was an expert in unarmed combat my own knowledge might not be sufficient to compete and I really didn't want to have to shoot him. 'My name is Duncan Nick,' I said, reversing the order and stating my surname first in the Japanese manner.

'My name is Gojo Mura. D – Da —.' 'Duncan' is a difficult name to pronounce in Japanese, and he was having trouble getting his mouth around it.

'Nick, call me Nick,' I allowed quickly.

'Yes, thank you, sir – ah, *Nick-san*,' he said, chuckling at his own clumsiness. It was the first time he had laughed aloud.

'You do not need to call me "sir", *Gojo-san*. We have the same rank in the navy. Would you like something to eat?'

'I thank you for the honour, *Nick-san*, but I have eaten – a little rice this morning.'

'Rice with insects and weeds,' I replied. 'It is probably better for you than my C rations – my soldier's food,' I corrected myself. 'Some insects I have eaten myself, they can be good protein.' Then I pointed to a plant growing close to me. 'When boiled this tastes a little like seaweed. Maybe later you will be hungry?'

I realised that, with the exception of the crackers, there was not a single food item in my rations with which he could possibly be familiar; the bread portion maybe, though bread made from wheat is not part of the Japanese diet which is based on rice, fish with seaweed and various green vegies. Fish and rice were both absent from any C rations and canned carrots and peas were the only vegetables. Moreover if he was starving (and his appearance gave that impression), I would have to give him very small amounts of whatever he could stomach of my Western food.

He grinned. 'You try a bit of everything, insects and plants, if they don't make you sick then you can eat them. It is like life, trial and error with occasionally a little good fortune.' We were silent for a while, then he said, 'When will you shoot me, Nick-san?'

I smiled. 'Gojo-san, I can tell from your family name that you are well-born, and we are both officers in the navy. It is not in my nature to kill a man who goes into the jungle without a weapon to paint butterflies.'

'I am not worthy of such generous treatment, Nick-san. It is not what we were led to expect from the enemy.'

'We butterfly people have to stick together,' I replied, somewhat embarrassed. Then I admitted, 'I confess, I have killed some of your soldiers in combat, but it was in the heat of battle – them or me. I am not a cold-blooded killer.'

He nodded sympathetically. 'What will happen now?' he asked.

'Well, if we agree as officers and men of honour that you are my prisoner, and you give me your word that you will not attempt to escape, I will take you to safety.'

'I will not be tortured? I am ashamed to admit I have no courage, no fighting spirit. I am a civilian. That is why I am here, so I cannot fight the Ah-meri-cans.'

I had just met the Japanese version of the little bloke from Chicago and the fat one from Brooklyn, the duo who shared the one mantra: '*I want ya ta unnerstan*', *I ain't no fuckin' hero!*' Hero or not, it takes a fair amount of character to starve slowly on a diet of insects and weeds as Gojo Mura was doing alone on the mountain.

'No, *Gojo-san*, you will not be tortured. But you will be interrogated. I will probably be the interpreter. You may have information we need.'

'Then will I be shot?' he asked.

'No,' I replied once more. 'You will be sent to Australia or America, where you will be interned as a prisoner of war.' I wasn't sure about the destination, though as a prisoner of the Americans it would probably be the States. '*Gojo-san*, I will need to go up to your cave. I am sure you have some small personal things you want to take with you?'

'I would be most grateful, *Nick-san*. There are two sketchbooks and a photograph of my family.' He smiled sheepishly. 'Where you will take me I do not think I will need the butterfly net.'

I pointed to the sketchbook lying on the ground. 'May I take a look?' I asked, knowing I could do so if I wished, but wanting to ask anyway.

He looked at me shyly, stooping to pick up the sketchbook and handing it to me, in the Japanese manner using both hands. 'It is not worthy, *Nick-san*, I am *shirouto* [amateur],' he protested again.

I moved away a safe distance from him and slung the Owen. Opening the sketchbook I was astonished to find that he had painted at least twenty varieties of butterflies, and every insect big and small I could ever remember seeing in the jungle. Not only were they expertly done, they were exquisitely detailed and the colours were remarkably accurate. Every page was filled with a dozen or so drawings of creepy-crawlies and butterflies. I wasn't an expert on watercolours, but I *was* one on butterflies and I had never seen more accurate depictions. Gojo Mura was both an acute observer and a delightful painter.

'They are wonderful, *Gojo-san*!' I exclaimed.

He shrugged, dismissing the paintings, but I could see he was secretly pleased. I handed the sketchbook back to him. 'It is not worthy but I would be honoured if you would accept it, *Nick-san*.'

I thanked him. It was a wonderful gift. By this time, I would have bet London to a brick that *Gojo-san* was harmless and well-meaning, almost grateful to have been taken prisoner. Nonetheless the Japanese see things differently to us. I could hear Wainwright's voice in my head: '*Never take anything for granted, boyo. Never relax your guard and when on bivouac, stay cautious, even in your dreams.*' There had been several cases during the campaign where a wounded Jap soldier had waited until a marine medic was sufficiently close whereupon he'd pulled the pin on a concealed grenade, killing himself and one more of the enemy.

I followed Gojo Mura up the tree, staying well back so that if he decided to commit suicide his falling body wouldn't take me with him. I did the same on the narrow cliff path, though I'd decided that if he wanted to take his life by throwing himself over the edge, there wasn't a whole lot I could do about it.

The smallish cave, neat as a new pin, had a fairly wide entrance that allowed the natural light about halfway in so it created a twilight effect towards the cave's end. To the left stood the dull grey metal casings of a sophisticated high-frequency receiver and transmitter, with the capacity for long-distance transmission and reception – probably capable of reaching Rabaul as well as the local command. How they managed to get it up to the cave was another example of sheer Japanese tenacity. As a unit it was far more elaborate than the Mark 6 sets I had trained on. Belgiovani would have lusted after it.

I found Gojo's rifle and he was right – the magazine was rusted in places and I had no doubt the barrel was also blocked with rust.

'This rifle is a disgrace, *Gojo-san*,' I laughed.

'I have not got the courage to use it, *Nick-san*,' he replied.

I walked from the cave and hurled the useless weapon over the cliff.

'Any hand grenades?' I asked.

He shook his head, horrified at the idea. 'Did you know, *Nick-san*, they have just this one little pin and then, if it falls out, bang!'

There was yet another test for Gojo Mura to pass. '*Gojo-san*, if I give you a frequency, will you set the transmitter for me?' I asked.

The Japanese radio expert nodded and I gave him the frequency belonging to Marine Command. If he already knew it, then he didn't let on. It took a while for the set to warm up, but then I got through to Henderson immediately and asked them to patch me through to our Intelligence radio unit. To my relief Lee Roy Yamamoto answered, which allowed me to speak in Japanese in case any of the enemy operators had heard me speaking to Marine Command. Keeping my message suitably ambivalent I said, 'Nick calling Yamamoto. I have got "Goat". Will be back two days.' I used the Japanese method of terminating a radio message. Private Yamamoto, I knew, would take the information directly to Colonel Woon.

I smashed the transceiver and remembered Belgiovani's last words to me, 'Don't cha forget da fuckin' accumulators – da batter-ies, Nick.'

Gojo watched dolefully as I dragged his precious radio

unit to the edge of the cliff and pushed it over, followed by the batteries. 'Gojo-san, do you have any code books?' I asked. It was yet another test. I had seen them neatly stacked on a rock ledge.

The series of code books Gojo Mura handed to me were, in fact, infinitely more valuable to us than ever his own capture might be. No field operator in the normal course of duty would have been trusted with them by the Japanese High Command. Gojo explained to me that it was only because he was in daily touch with Rabaul and several other centres that he had been permitted to possess them. The information concerning the fighters and bombers taking off from Henderson was thought to be critical to Japanese operations in the entire Pacific region. His instructions had been that if it seemed he might be captured he was to destroy the books and then kill himself. As for their importance to us, they allowed our Marine Command to gain access to Japanese encoded signals, enabling us to decipher their communication with Rabaul and possibly other Japanese war zones in the Pacific.

Going down the mountain was as hard as going up, though with the constant slipping and sliding the descent was considerably faster. On the way back to Henderson base we shared four meals together using my C rations. Gojo Mura ate very little – the food was totally unfamiliar to him and besides, his stomach had shrunk – but he loved the sugary tinned pears. On one occasion when I'd foolishly given him a Hershey bar I heard him vomiting up the chocolate violently during the night, although he said nothing to me the next morning.

I guess that if he'd wanted to he could have bolted; apart from my having to sleep, there were several occasions when we became separated and he could have attempted to escape.

I wasn't overly concerned. I knew I'd track him down soon enough. When I slept I took the precaution of removing the Owen magazine and kept it in my pack, on which my head rested. However, I would have been very surprised if Gojo Mura knew how to fire it. Despite having survived in the cave by gleaning some daily nourishment from his environment, he knew very little about the jungle. To any half-decent tracker who was following him it would be bull-in-a-china-shop easy. Whenever we were separated he always appeared soon afterwards, and on one occasion he must have thought he'd lost me because he started yelling out, 'Nick-san! Nick-san! Where are you?' This was a very different Japanese prisoner from the blokes who blew you up.

Coming in to Henderson in the late afternoon we were met by quite a committee. I'd taken the radio man off the mountain where he'd been making a nuisance of himself for several months and the brass, including an army air force colonel, seemed well pleased. Lieutenant Colonel Carlson was present and came over to congratulate me. I was to learn that he'd been back since the morning with half the battalion, and while he'd changed, showered, fed and possibly snatched some sleep, he still looked pretty whacked. The other half of the battalion had returned the previous day. Together the two sections had effectively removed the Japanese from the northern slopes of Mount Austen.

'I've lost one pound to Mather. How much is that in American dollars?' Carlson asked, grinning.

'About two, sir.'

'I want you to know it was worth it, Nick. Well done, glad you came along with us.'

When the provost staff sergeant arrived to collect Gojo Mura, he was more than a little surprised. 'He's not constrained, sir?' he said, bemused.

'Constrained?'

'Manacled, sir.'

I explained to the provost staff sergeant that it hadn't been necessary; that I had captured possibly the least dangerous Japanese in the entire Pacific War.

'Did you not take manacles?' he asked, in an obviously disapproving voice.

'Yes, they're in my pack. I told you, they were unnecessary, staff sergeant.'

He shook his head, still not understanding. 'Sorry, sir, I'll have to do it now.' He handcuffed poor little Gojo Mura while I explained that he was to be fed only a little rice and tinned fish. 'Goddamn, sir, I ain't seen nuttin' that looks or tastes like a fish since we left San Diego.'

'Rice and vegetables then,' I repeated. 'He'll die if you put him on our diet.'

'This would be a tragedy?' he queried.

'Staff sergeant, be careful. This prisoner is a major intelligence asset. Colonel Woon will fall on you like a ton of bricks if anything happens to him,' I warned, using the boss's name without a prickle of conscience.

The following morning, after a glorious night's sleep and back in Colonel Woon's office for a debriefing, he said, 'I'm not at all sure that J.V. Mather's advice to go it alone was such a good idea, Nick. Are all Australians determined to get their own way?'

'I beg your pardon, sir?'

'Working your way into field work and risking your life?'

'No, sir, but Mather was correct, it *was* a one-man operation.'

'Private Yamamoto acted as interpreter when I questioned the prisoner last night. As I understand it, his cave was nearly three hundred feet up a sheer rock face and you got him out?'

The rumours were already beginning. Popgun Pete was back in the marine gossip columns. 'No, no, sir,' I hastily corrected him. 'I waited at the bottom in the jungle until he came down for a shit.'

The boss laughed. 'What? Caught him with his pants down?'

'Not quite, sir, but the rest was fairly easy. Lieutenant Gojo is not a very willing soldier; in fact he makes Sergeant Belgiovani seem practically gung-ho.' I then told the boss the story, including the presence of the rusted rifle. 'So, anyone could have captured him, sir,' I concluded – which was perfectly true, although it would have helped if the 'anyone' spoke Japanese and liked butterflies.

'That's bullshit, son,' Greg Woon said. 'The code books alone are a major breakthrough in Intelligence. We're putting you in for a commendation.'

'Thank you, sir, but, I promise, it is misplaced and unnecessary. It was, like I said, a very easy operation.'

I didn't want to diminish the honour but, as with being made a lieutenant, it was another totally undeserved recognition.

'Could I ask a favour instead, sir?' I asked clumsily. 'Could you insist that Lieutenant Gojo gets only rice and tinned fish with a few steamed vegetables? Oh, and tinned pears! He has taken to our tinned pears. It's the sugar, I think. But all to be given in very small quantities for the next few days. He's very malnourished, having lived off insects and weeds and a spoonful of rice every day. He could die if he is subjected to a high-protein Western diet.'

'And you'd care if that happened, Nick?'

'Oh, yes, sir, very much. Gojo Mura is a remarkable artist.'

'Artist? What's he paint?'

'Butterflies, sir.'

'Jesus H. Christ!'

CHAPTER NINETEEN

'I hope you don't want your uniform or boots returned
because they went into the incinerator.
A rubber-glove job if ever there was one –
never know what could be lurking in the seams.'
Dr Ross Hayes
Heidelberg Military Hospital,
December 1942

GOJO MURA WAS HELPFUL with information, recalling for us what Japanese shipping was operating in the immediate area. He was polite and answered our questions and, quite correctly, volunteered no information he had not been asked for specifically.

Colonel Woon was impressed when I showed him the sketchbook he'd given me. 'My dad would have loved someone like this as an assistant. He was a lousy photographer, never happy with the specimens he recorded. You're right, Nick, they're good.'

'Sir, I realise the prisoner was captured, so to speak, under the American flag, but do you think you could pull some strings and have him sent to Australia?' I added, 'That way I can keep in touch. I'd like to get to know him better after the war.'

The boss gave me a quizzical look. 'Nick, you're a bit of an enigma, aren't you?'

'Enigma, sir?' It would have been the last way I would have described myself.

'Well, son, take your actions on Bloody Ridge. Now you want to be bosom pals with the Japanese?'

'One individual Japanese, sir – this bloke would apologise if he killed a fly.'

'I'll see what I can do, son.'

'Thank you, sir. That way I can get someone to, you know, keep an eye on him; send him sketchbooks and painting materials.'

'What, so he can paint all the Australian bugs?'

I laughed. 'It will have to be a very long war – we've got more than our fair share of those, sir.'

Almost from the time I had brought Gojo Mura down from the mountain things had begun to change. The Japanese were now clearly on the back foot and the 1st Division marines were beginning to leave the island. US regular army units had started to arrive by mid-November and there was a general sense of happiness as preparations for the major exodus began to take place. Of course, for security reasons, nobody (that is, nobody outside of headquarters) knew the precise date when the handover would occur.

Three days after I'd arrived back from the mountain Colonel Woon began his usual short, morning briefing session with 'Nick, while it's not yet general knowledge, the marines are moving out on the 9th and 10th. As you are aware, we're all in pretty bad shape and the 1st Marine Division needs a rest. You may not know the full extent of the damage but while we've already sent well over three thousand men off for medical attention elsewhere, we've got at least another three thousand who need some sort of hospital attention, mostly for malaria, but quite a lot have other tropical diseases that come from being pitched into hell. We're starting to kick the Japs in the butt here in the Pacific and the balance has shifted, but not without cost. It's now the job of the US Army to do the search and destroy, the cleaning up here on the island.'

'Sir, do you know where the marines are going and are we staying here?' I asked.

'Affirmative and negative – that's what I wanted to tell you. The 1st Division marines are going to Australia for rest and retraining, to Mel-bourne. Our orders have not come through, but I anticipate our unit may well be required to stay with the US Army.' He shrugged. 'The men coming in are fairly green and know nothing about fighting the Japanese. I guess it's fair to speculate that our Intelligence unit will be needed more than ever. You will – we all will – be required to conduct training classes for the new field radio operators and eventually our own replacement personnel. These guys are really civilians with a few weeks in boot camp.' He paused and looked directly at me. 'Are you disappointed, son?'

'No, sir; I guess we still have a job to do here,' I replied, but of course I was secretly disappointed. Although I didn't want to leave without the colonel, Beljo and Da Nip widda Chip, like everyone else I'd had a gutful of the island. I have neglected to mention that I'd had two bouts of malaria – nothing too bad, three or four days feeling crook, then back on my feet again. On each occasion Colonel Woon had volunteered to send me home to Australia. But I knew how it was with me and malaria, and that I'd soon come good again. Well, to 'come good' is the knowledge that you can get through the day but, in the process, still feel pretty crook.

Colonel Woon had come down with a bout, but he'd

refused to be evacuated. Lee Roy Yamamoto had a bout as well. The exception was Sergeant Belgiovani who, despite being unequivocally the least fit soldier on Guadalcanal, had, with the exception of an upset stomach for three days (no doubt from overeating), remained unaffected. The theory was that the local mozzies couldn't penetrate the blubber.

The original Army Air Force Intelligence unit was a team and we liked to think that each of us, in his own way, was indispensable to the others. This was nonsense, of course. With the arrival of the regular army I knew we'd probably lose the closeness of being a small but unique intelligence force. The unit had been expanded and we now had twelve operators, most of them in training, with the sergeant from Brooklyn, the survivor of Bloody Ridge, being the senior non-commissioned officer and strutting about with a sense of happy and harmless self-importance. His war memoirs were being expanded: *'Wid duh marines gone, I hadda train duh whole goddamn U-nited States Army who don't know nuttin' 'bout radio in duh jungle!'* In the meantime the idea of letting down your mates because of a touch of malaria, and lying between soft clean sheets in a hospital in Melbourne with pretty nurses in attendance, was unthinkable. *What am I saying?!*

On the morning of the 9th of December the boss came into the radio tent. We all jumped up to salute him and he responded with a casual half wave, his fingers not even close to touching the brim of his cap. 'Come with me please, Lieutenant,' he instructed.

Together we strolled towards the beach where the revving of trucks, jeeps and landing craft reached us and made it obvious the big move was under way. Then emerging onto the beach we saw the marines lounging around, happy as sandboys, waiting for the signal to board the waiting ships. They looked like kids going on an excursion – and then it struck that, like me, they were in their late teens or early twenties, and in peacetime they'd still be regarded more or less as kids. 'Lookee here!' one of them shouted. 'It's Popgun Pete! Hiya, Lootenant! Hiya, Colonel!' they called happily, knowing they would be allowed some slack on this of all mornings.

Several of their officers broke away and came to greet us, exchanging the usual pleasantries. The Americans are invariably polite as a race. General Vandegrift had left by plane but his senior colonel came over and greeted us. I snapped a salute just in case the prevailing *laissez-faire* attitude on the beach didn't extend to headquarters staff. He looked at me, grinned, and gave a return salute so casual it would have made the colonel's earlier one in the radio tent seem presidential. 'Nick, your name came up at dinner several nights ago when we were discussing the capture of the Japanese radio man on the mountain. Well done, by the way.'

'Thank you, sir,' I answered, having grown weary of explaining how Gojo Mura had practically captured himself.

'Well, the general asked me to pass on his comment to you via Colonel Woon here, but now I can do so myself. He said, "You tell Nick Duncan as long as there's a 1st Division marine around, he'll always have a buddy".' He smiled and extended his hand. 'Thanks, buddy,' he said quietly. It was one of those moments when you feel a lump in your throat and you know you dare not speak.

As we watched, a long line of marines began to file onto the landing craft and for the first time it struck me how beaten up and tired they looked. While the mob on the beach had seemed cheerful enough, chiacking with us, it was a last attempt at keeping their good humour. These blokes who were embarking were really down. I guess they were loading the sick first. Their uniforms were ragged and they walked with a weary gait, heads hanging, chins almost touching their chests. They were well and truly stuffed. Once a mighty division, seven thousand men had been lost – either killed, wounded or sick; the enemy probably had lost four times that number. These ragged heroes had withstood everything a fanatical and determined Japanese force could throw at them for four months without respite. They'd spent a lot of this time living in stinking, mosquito-infested mud holes and rain-lashed tents, with air raids and bombardment from the Japanese navy almost daily occurrences. They'd repulsed the enemy in several major assaults, and the way they'd fought on Bloody Ridge would be remembered forever in the history of the United States Marines. If, as Napoleon said, a soldier marches on his stomach, then somehow they'd done all this while living on C rations or alternatively, a monotonous diet that (if Belgiovani's latest complaints were to be taken seriously) even the chef from the Waldorf Astoria failed to improve. I would have willingly killed for a steak with a spot of rich brown gravy, a fresh green salad and new potatoes. I'd dreamed once of bread and butter pudding and woke up just as the spoon was about to enter my mouth.

I turned to Colonel Woon and without thinking commented, 'These blokes are done like a dinner, Colonel. This mob is totally whacked!'

'I *think* I get your meaning, Nick. I'm going to miss your colloquialisms. It had never occurred to me that the Australian vernacular only belongs tangentially to the English language. By the way, have you looked at yourself lately? You're a big guy, but I guess you've lost thirty pounds, maybe more.'

I glanced down at my faded and torn jungle greens. The knees, long since out of my trousers, had been mended by whiz needle man Belgiovani, who'd patched them from scraps of an olive-green marine uniform he'd found somewhere. '*My grandpa was a tailor in duh Depression, he taught me. He'd say, "Lissen, kid, if you c'n sew neat den you gonna eat sweet."*' The jungle-green trousers were always a baggy fit – the idea was to keep you cool and make it comfortable and easy to move – but now they hung off me as if they were a couple of sizes too big. The loss of weight was probably due to the two bouts of malaria and what the marine medico who was treating me termed 'a nasty gut infection'. My spare pair of boots (the first pair had long gone to boot heaven) were in the process of giving up, the canvas uppers beginning to peel away from the rubber sole.

It's curious how you don't see these things when they happen gradually. I guess it must be a bit the same as ageing; it happens so slowly that the mind adjusts. Furthermore, I hadn't seen myself in a mirror for three months at least – wouldn't have known where to find one. I looked at Colonel Woon, who I knew was thirty-five, and realised that he appeared closer to fifty. His hair had turned salt and pepper (more salt than pepper), there were deep lines etched from the corners of his mouth and the creases around his eyes were permanent and deeper.

'I guess we've all taken a bit of a hiding, sir.'

'Nick, you're out of here, son,' he said suddenly.

With the revving of the landing craft engines I wasn't sure I'd heard him correctly. 'I beg your pardon, sir?'

'You're going back home.' He must have seen my surprised look. 'The order came from higher up. Your commendation's come through and there's a bit of something going to happen in Australia. It's not the marine way to wear down a good man needlessly. You've done enough. In fact, more than enough, and it's time for a rest. Not my orders, but I wouldn't countermand them even if I could. I've also received a medical report; you've got a severe intestinal infection.' He chuckled. 'You're whacked – done like a dinner.'

'When, sir?' I asked, completely taken aback at the news.

'Before Christmas. You'll probably have to spend it in hospital in Mel-bourne.'

I thought for a moment. 'Sir, would you allow me to send a letter in the priority bag? There is someone in Australia I must notify.'

'Sure, we'll send it out first flight tomorrow. Give it to Sergeant Polanski, he handles the bag.'

Marg Hamilton had dropped me a line once a fortnight and I'd replied promptly. My letters were of necessity circumspect – 'we did this and then we did that' – purely routine stuff. I wrote a fair bit about Belgiovani and Yamamoto, throwing in Sergeant Polanski for a bit of variety, trying to be amusing, but there wasn't a lot I was permitted to say. She'd been sent to Melbourne for a three-month training course that would culminate in her becoming an officer: Naval Lieutenant Marg Hamilton. How about that? Unlike my own elevation I knew she thoroughly deserved it.

Her letters, by contrast, were chatty and personal, though not exactly lovey-dovey. I told myself that she wasn't the sentimental type and, besides, she'd always insisted our relationship was strictly on her terms. At first she didn't seem to like Melbourne much, missing Timmy (her dog) and especially Her Royal Highness Princess Cardamon (her Burmese cat). Her Aunt Celia had come all the way from Albany to care for them while Marg was away. Anyway, I felt I couldn't exactly land on her doorstep in Melbourne, arms spread wide, greeting her with, 'It's me, Nick, your lover!'

In a state of some excitement, I wrote, telling her I'd be in Melbourne for Christmas. I was disappointed to be leaving my mates in the radio unit, but the thought of sharing Christmas Day with lovely Marg was more than a little compensation. Now that I was leaving the island, I realised how bloody tired and unwell I felt. I was building up to another bout of malaria and the gut thing caused me to have waves of nausea followed by a longing for a good meal.

A week later, on the 17th of December (I'd been told I was flying out on the 19th), a letter arrived with Marg's familiar handwriting on the envelope. I tore it open with huge anticipation but also some apprehension – my dread was that she was writing to tell me she was going home to Perth for Christmas. Humans who love their animals passionately don't always put other people first.

Melbourne
12th December 1942

Darling Nick,
You must know how very dear you are to me. My most earnest hope is that we will remain friends forever. I shall always cherish the time we spent together, and standing on the platform watching you leave Perth was a moment of infinite sadness I shall never forget.

But there is also the joy I felt that first night we made love and the times we were together. You are a very special and beautiful man, Nick. As I told you that first night, whatever subsequently happened between us was to be on my terms. I am eight years older than you and, at the time, felt that it would be unfair, knowing you had a sweetheart on her way from Java to Australia, not to allow you to take your leave from me graciously when the time came.

I admit, you were such a beautiful young man that I simply couldn't resist the temptation – the joy of initially having you to myself for one night and thereafter for a short while.

That I allowed myself such a glorious indulgence is one of the nicest things life has ever permitted me to enjoy. There are memories we all store in a special compartment in our hearts and this is one that is securely locked away for safekeeping. Some day, when I am an old woman, I will unlock it and recall the gorgeous young man that, as a young woman, I had the privilege to know and love.

By now you will have guessed the tenor of this letter. It is to tell you that I have met someone else here in Melbourne and we will be spending Christmas together at his family's cottage on the Mornington Peninsula where we hope to announce our engagement.

By a curious circumstance, or perhaps not so curious, you know him: Commander Rob Rich. He speaks enormously well of you and shares my anxiety about your whereabouts and secondment. Thank God you are coming home.

Rob and I met at Cerberus during the course I came over to do and, well, the rest you can guess – thirty-five-year-old bachelor meets twenty-six-year-old spinster . . .

By the time I'd reached this part of Marg's letter I could feel the tears running down my cheeks. I guess I was emotionally vulnerable due to the gut thing. No! That's bullshit! I felt as if my heart had been ripped out and jumped on. I was utterly miserable. I had lost the last of the three anchors in my life, the tide was going out and I had become a boat without a rudder floating out to sea. (What a lousy metaphor!) I was also, I am ashamed to say, hurt and filled with self-pity and even, for a short while, angry. But deep down I knew I had no right to be any of these things, for Marg had unfailingly played with a straight bat. She'd always been honest with me and had given me more, much more, than ever she'd received from me, a gangling boy with too much testosterone and a longing for the comfort of her beautiful breasts. The heart is a lonely hunter and I had found the joy of a beautiful woman who took my loneliness and turned it into loving.

I was flown out in a B-17 to Luganville and then to Brisbane – a short stop, where I went to the toilet and threw up (green slime). Then we went on to Melbourne where I arrived about eight o'clock at night and found, to my chagrin, that a marine ambulance waited on the tarmac to take me to Heidelberg Military Hospital. I'd left Fraser Island just four months previously, fitter than I'd been in my entire life. No way was some well-meaning bastard going to strap me into a stretcher on my return.

'We have specific orders, sir,' the marine NCO medic insisted.

'Bugger the orders! I'm not lying down on that thing. I'm not dead yet!' I said, damn near collapsing with a sudden gut spasm.

'Please, sir?' he urged.

I turned to the other man. 'Corporal, help me up to sit in

the front. I'm an officer and this is *also* a specific order.' It was intended to be a bellow but it came out somehow differently, more as a croak.

The corporal, with a five o'clock shadow, who reminded me a bit of Belgiovani (though a slightly thinner version), and the medic lifted me into the front of the ambulance. I don't remember a great deal about the trip to hospital. Somewhere close to our destination, or as we arrived, I must have collapsed, hitting my head against the dashboard, which resulted in a black eye the next day.

It's strange how, when you let things relax because you're close to relinquishing responsibility for yourself, everything suddenly falls apart. I must have come to fairly quickly, because I still insisted I wouldn't be strapped down. Wheeled into a hospital emergency department on a stretcher wasn't quite how I had envisaged my triumphant return to my homeland. I was later told I walked into the hospital carrying my kitbag, shrugging off the help of the two medicos. A bloody stupid thing to do, but I don't remember a thing.

I knew that what lay ahead was something different; a new turn in my short life. My secondment to the Americans was coming to an end. I was home, wherever that was – initially it had to be a hospital bed in Victoria. While I had always thought of myself as a loner – but had never felt lonely – I was experiencing the most complete sense of being alone, and with it a loneliness such as I had never felt before or since.

Apart from Marg Hamilton, there were two people I thought about every day of my life, Anna and my father, and I knew they might well be dead. I wondered how I could wangle a coastwatcher's job in New Britain, where at least I'd be able to learn the truth about my father. In both cases, with Anna and the Reverend John Duncan, it was the not knowing that was the worst part. My father had always said 'Superstition is what keeps humans ignorant', but Gojo's boot on the wing of the Clipper butterfly had really shaken me. The symbolism was so strong – the Imperial Japanese boot crushing the wings of Anna, the beautiful butterfly. I tried to tell myself that Gojo Mura was hardly a symbol of Imperial Japan. But you know how it is with an image; it gets stuck in your head and won't go away.

I'd often fantasise about sailing *Madam Butterfly* to Java after the war and finding Anna and bringing her home with me. She'd be skin and bone but I'd pack the yacht with good things to eat and by the time we got back to Australia Anna would be her old self again. Of course, in my fantasy I didn't take into account what being crushed under the Imperial Japanese boot might have done to her head.

Now that I had returned to Australia, it all became confusing. That's the whole point about being in the forces. You don't have to think about the next step, the next move. It's 'Bang!' and you're dead or broken. Or you wake up each morning and follow orders and the routine.

I didn't know quite what I was going to be asked to do, or what my next destination would be. I didn't mind being the leader, providing there was a purpose, such as the little bloke and me escaping in *Madam Butterfly* from Java. My life had changed so completely that I'd forgotten in just a few months how to be a civilian. In fact, come to think about it, I'd had very little practice at leading a normal existence. As a teenage boy I'd either been institutionalised at boarding school or I'd been in the jungle hunting butterflies. I'd had a short stint of six months working in Moresby with W. R. Carpenter, but that was only to get enough money to go butterfly hunting in Java.

I didn't really know who Nick Duncan was. When I'd gone to Java it had been a bit of an adventure; the excuse was the search to find the Magpie Crow butterfly, an escapade straight out of *Boys' Own Annual*. I'd also found Anna and that had been a wonderful bonus. The murder of the men on the beach was the first time I'd been tested and, alas, I'd been found wanting. Maybe that was a turning point? Sailing *Madam Butterfly* across the Indian Ocean with the little bloke in tow had allowed me to bury the incident, and the guilt. The entire time at sea my mind was occupied with the business of getting us back to the safety of Australia. But it had always been there: the feeling that I wasn't the decent bloke, the intrepid young fellow I pretended to be; that the burial incident on the beach had shown me to be a coward.

Marg Hamilton had led me gently and gloriously into manhood and had urged me not to become a coastwatcher. I might have listened to her pleas, but for my father's foolish decision to remain behind in New Britain. At the time, that news seemed to open a way to make up for my failure at the beach. I would rescue him and prove to myself that I wasn't who I hoped I wasn't.

Then came the secondment to the marines, and Bloody Ridge where I suppose I proved I wasn't a coward. But, in turn, the fighting revealed a new aspect of my personality: the ability to kill calmly in the heat of battle and, while it was happening, to feel a peculiar exhilaration.

Who the hell are you, Nick Duncan? This was becoming a recurring question I kept asking myself in hospital. I don't suppose calm analysis and introspection is a good idea when you're going through the shakes and sweats brought about by *falciparum* malaria. But there you go. I was feeling like shit, both outside as well as within my heart and my head.

I had been placed in a large malaria ward with twenty other officers, all from the army and air force. I don't suppose too many navy blokes are exposed to the *anopheles* mosquito. In addition to malaria I was diagnosed with jaundice, which accounted for my constant feeling of nausea, the vomiting, headaches and a whole set of aches and pains. My skin had turned yellow and now the very idea of food was abhorrent.

The doctor, a young lieutenant, was a cheerful bloke named Ross Hayes. Unlike most civilian medicos I'd met in the past, he didn't adopt a superior 'I know best' manner and after we'd been introduced suggested I call him Ross. I responded with 'Nick's the name, doctor.'

'Nick, you're pretty damned unwell; not just *falciparum* malaria, which, under normal circumstances, would be enough to lay you low, but you also have a hepatic infection of some kind. Frankly, we're seeing all sorts of bugs in blokes coming in from New Guinea, ones we've never encountered before. Tropical medicine is undergoing a fast learning curve. Your symptoms are fairly typical of jaundice. We'll run some liver tests but if it's viral, as usual we'll have to hazard an educated guess and call it jaundice. You are going to feel pretty off-colour with the quinine drip for your malaria, and the only treatment for jaundice is lots of rest and avoidance of fatty foods.' He paused. 'Oh, and *absolutely* no alcohol for three months. That, I'm afraid, puts the kybosh on a Christmas beer or two. While I'm at it, you also have a nasty worm infection. We've found hookworm and threadworm, but fortunately we can clean them up fairly quickly.' He pointed at my face. 'And how did you get the black eye? It's a beauty!'

'Dizzy spell coming in from the airport. I must have knocked it.'

He looked amused. 'Very careless getting a black eye while strapped to a stretcher . . . Never heard of that particular injury before.'

I laughed, well, sort of laughed, as I was too crook to make a good job of it. 'I hit it on the dash of the ambulance coming here.'

'Yes, I heard you weren't very cooperative at the airport or when you walked into emergency. My boss, Dr Light, your admitting doctor, nearly had a conniption when you pulled your Owen gun from your kitbag and shouted "Anyone who puts me on a stretcher dies!" Fortunately there was no magazine in the weapon and, equally fortuitously, that was the moment you chose to black out.'

'Oh, God! Can you bring him to the ward so that I can apologise to him?'

'Don't worry, he's a digger from the Great War, served at Gallipoli, then later in France; it won't go any further. By the way, what's your unit? It's not marked on your admitting papers.'

'I'm just an unattached navy lieutenant at the moment, Ross,' I said, trying to sound matter-of-fact.

He laughed suddenly. 'Bloody stupid of me. I should have realised you were with the funnies. Not too many naval lieutenants arrive here in patched-at-the-knees jungle greens and with the uppers coming away from their boots. I hope you don't want your uniform or boots returned because they went into the incinerator. A rubber-glove job if ever there was one – never know what could be lurking in the seams.'

'How long will I be here, Ross?'

'How long is a piece of string? I can't give you a time. It will be largely up to you, Nick. You look pretty strong and before the tropics got their claws into your body you must have been very fit, otherwise you would have been here weeks ago. I'm going to hit you with a heavy course of intravenous quinine and you're going to feel pretty sick for a few days. I'll try to judge the dose so you'll be with us on Christmas Day. Thereafter you'll need to recuperate for a month, perhaps a little more. You're an officer and with a clearance from me, after two weeks you can technically sign yourself out, as long as you report for morning rounds.' He paused and smiled ironically. 'But for that to happen, you'd have to be superman.'

You wouldn't want to wish an intravenous course of quinine via a drip on your worst enemy. It's a toss-up whether the cure is worse than the malaria. For five days I experienced an almost suicidal headache; I would undergo bouts of shivering interspersed with burning fever; the bed sheets were drenched with sweat and had to be changed several times a day. A constant and maddening ringing occurred in my ears, like the clanging of church bells right next door. I kept on drifting off and the subsequent dreams were snippets of everything: the sudden flight of a butterfly; the severed head of the sailor on the beach; the face of the young Japanese soldier I'd killed with a knife at Bloody Ridge; Gojo Mura's boot on the Clipper butterfly; the look of surprise on the face of the sniper I'd taken out; my father reading in his study with his horn-rimmed glasses positioned on the end of his nose; Kevin crouched in the cabin of *Madam Butterfly* after the storm at sea. Perhaps most curiously, a Japanese woman beating me as a child and shouting that I was a non-person, an 'it'. They went on and on, flashes that went past me almost too fast to see, a blink on a silver screen, while others were detailed. All of them were dreadfully stressful, so that I would often come out of these hallucinatory moments – dreams, imaginings, whatever – weeping softly.

Five days passed including Christmas Day. I seem to remember hearing snatches of carols and once imagined a choir had entered the ward and a pretty nurse had kissed me on the forehead, but I couldn't be sure. On Boxing Day morning I woke to find the nightmare was over. I felt weak but completely rational; the headache and the ringing in my ears had gone. It was like being born again, getting a brand-new start in life. I wondered if I'd been given something to make me feel so good. A nurse seeing me attempt to sit up came over to arrange my pillows and asked me how I was feeling.

'Great!' I said. 'But you look tired, nurse.'

She giggled. 'Hangover. Our Christmas party after coming off afternoon shift, it lasted most of the night. Matron is going to be pleased you've come around. She was worried you wouldn't be right for when your visitors come.'

'Visitors? What visitors?'

'I'm not allowed to say.' She giggled again and despite her hangover she was pretty; nice pretty, like a friend's sister.

Moments later the matron came in, a little woman with sharp blue eyes, and wearing a smudge of red lipstick. Her greying hair was pulled sharply back into her white, starched triangular veil that looked rather too big for her head, like a huge gull's wing fluttering on top of her body. 'Good morning, Lieutenant, you're only just in time,' she said in a prim voice.

'In time for what, matron?'

'Why, General MacArthur, of course! Nurse Parkes – shirt,

tie, jacket, brush and comb. Quickly, we haven't got all day. I hope you weren't amongst the nurses partying all night; the wards this morning are a disgrace.'

For a moment I thought I was back hallucinating. 'General MacArthur? *The* General MacArthur?' I asked.

'There's only one,' she said, impatiently looking around. 'Where *is* that silly girl?' Nurse Parkes arrived with what I took to be one of my white shirts, washed and ironed, a tie and my naval uniform cleaned and pressed. 'Nurse Parkes, I said *only* the jacket! The patient won't be needing his trousers,' Matron snapped. 'Lieutenant Duncan is not to leave his bed under any circumstances. Wash and dress him from the waist up, change his sheets and bring an extra pillow. We want him sitting to attention. Hurry up, girl! I don't know what's happened to you lot this morning. Cap? Cap? Where is our patient's cap?'

Ten minutes later I was dressed from the waist up, the bottom half hidden under a clean sheet, with my naval cap resting on the bed. The matron had gone walkabout while Nurse Parkes was getting me ready. 'Bit of an old dragon, what?' I said as soon as she'd departed.

'The worst part of it all is that she's my aunty,' Nurse Parkes said *sotto voce*, glancing over her shoulder to make sure the matron hadn't suddenly appeared behind her.

'Every family has its crosses to bear,' I said, comforting her.

'Oh, God, here they come. What'll I do?' Nurse Parkes said fearfully.

'Hold my hand, I'm scared witless,' I whispered in a pathetic way. She grinned and took my hand. 'Look Florence Nightingale-ish,' I whispered.

'Stoppit! I'm petrified. You'll make me laugh,' she giggled.

In fact, sitting rigidly to attention, I was fairly nervous

when the famous general entered the ward, accompanied by the matron who seemed to come to no higher than his waist, Dr Light with grizzly ginger eyebrows and a weary expression, a dozen photographers all wearing hats, and an equal number of army top brass above the rank of major. Their combined footsteps on the polished cement floor made enough noise to wake the dead.

As MacArthur approached he cocked his head towards the whispering aide beside him, nodded, then having been given my rank and name extended his hand, palm upwards, into which the aide, with a practised deftness, placed a medal at the exact moment the general reached my bedside. It was military precision of the highest order.

I sat so rigid that if you'd slammed my torso with an axe handle it wouldn't have budged. 'Congratulations, Lieutenant Duncan, well done,' the general said, and pinned the medal with an expertise that indicated he'd done it a thousand times before. I hadn't ever thought about it, but I guess being a general and pinning medals is synonymous. General MacArthur saluted me, flashbulbs exploded, whereupon he turned abruptly on his heel and walked towards the doorway, followed by aides, sycophants and the press. His expression hadn't changed a wink throughout the entire procedure that had taken no more than twenty seconds.

Overwhelmed as I was, I heard myself mutter, 'That bloke's got about as much charm as a goanna in a chookhouse.'

Nurse Parkes laughed, withdrawing her hand and shaking her wrist. 'Lieutenant, I think you've broken every bone in my hand.'

'Nick,' I protested. 'We've been holding hands in front of a general, we're practically intimate.'

'Is that intimate or invalid?' she asked, rubbing her hand.

I apologised and then added, 'I'm sure I'm not the first guy to get a medal presented to me by a general when not wearing any trousers, but it felt pretty strange.'

'Caught with your pants down!' she laughed.

The box in which the medal resided had been left on my bed, together with the citation that was very short on detail: 'For valour when facing the enemy'. In truth, I wasn't at all sure why I was being honoured with the DSC (Distinguished Service Cross), the medal they usually gave to coastwatchers. It was the 'bit of something going to happen in Australia' Colonel Woon had mentioned. I could only surmise it might have to do with the commendation for the non-eventful capture of Gojo Mura. But two weeks later the quite separate commendation from the marines came through.

I don't want to belittle the honour, because a lot of brave and good men earned this particular medal the hard way – coastwatchers who had risked their lives almost daily and put in the thankless, grinding years alone in the jungles with sickness and hardship and very little backup. It was just that I felt I didn't deserve it.

I was about to learn that what I grew to think of as my 'goanna medal' had very little, if anything, to do with me. The very next day I was to begin to get an insight into the nature of war and of politics.

The following morning both the *Argus* and the Melbourne *Herald* ran a photo of General MacArthur presenting me with the medal and under it a story of my 'conspicuous bravery' while serving as an adviser with the American marines in the Pacific. Both papers, but for a few pars, carried much the same story. They mentioned Bloody Ridge, the Navy Cross, and how later

I'd taken out a sniper in the jungle at great personal risk. Added to this was my single-handed capture of a vital and heavily defended radio post set three hundred feet up a cliff face that had been alerting the enemy to the movement of American aircraft in the Pacific.

It was a story, vague in actual details, but at the same time vastly exaggerated, suggesting great courage by a local boy who made good in the field of battle. There was no mention of malaria, and the caption to the picture in the *Argus* of Nurse Parkes and me read 'Lieutenant Duncan, repatriated to Australia, requires a nurse constantly at his bedside'. That gave the strong impression that I'd been severely wounded. There was also a nice sentimental bit that told how, unable to rise from my bed, I had nevertheless insisted on wearing my naval uniform for the medal ceremony.

Finally, having been honoured by the Americans with the Navy Cross, I was being awarded the DSC by my own people in recognition of the contribution our own brave sons were making in the Pacific War. It ended with a bit about allies working together in the spirit of mutual cooperation, hands across the sea, blah, blah, blah. If not exactly a beat-up, the heavy hand of a government propaganda machinist wasn't hard to spot and I couldn't help thinking how many of the really brave bastards at Milne Bay and Kokoda had gone largely unrecognised.

Nurse Parkes was delighted to be in the papers and I must say, despite her hangover, it was a very nice picture of her. Later that day she came over to my bed, very excited, to say that a lady reporter named Esmé Fenton from the *Women's Weekly* wanted to do a story on her and did I mind?

Over the Christmas period I was informed by a letter from Naval Intelligence that, despite my secondment to the SRD

(Services Reconnaissance Department), naval officers would come to the hospital to conduct a formal debriefing covering my time with the 1st Division marines on Guadalcanal. The first session would take place at 1000 hours on the 2nd of January. The debriefing was to begin with an unexpected visit.

After all the brouhaha of the general's visit, where every visitor entering the ward seemed to come over to congratulate me, I had been moved to an alcove that contained a single bed; it was a space usually reserved for officers above the rank of major. Nurse Parkes henceforth referred to it as 'Naval Headquarters'. A heavy curtain separated me from the remainder of the ward and a large bay window looked out onto the hospital garden. After the endless coconut palms and the damp, fetid jungle, the well-tended garden was reassuringly normal with its mowed lawn and a box hedge, clipped to within an inch of its life, surrounding a circular bed of roses.

You may imagine my surprise when, at exactly ten in the morning of my debriefing, a nurse parted the curtain to the alcove and announced, 'You have a visitor, Lieutenant,' whereupon Commander Rob Rich entered the alcove.

I guess he saw my surprise, followed almost immediately by my acute embarrassment as I proceeded to blush violently – crimson blush against a yellow skin is not a good look. He brought his hand up as if to prevent me from talking. 'Nick, let me speak first,' he said, not smiling. I nodded my head, quite incapable of saying anything.

'May I sit down?' he asked, indicating the chair beside my bed. I nodded again. I knew I should have been more in possession of my wits, but I simply wasn't. I mean, what the hell do you do when your superior officer is about to inform you he's taken your girlfriend for himself and intends to marry her?

Especially when you know you really love her.

'Nick, Marg has told me everything. When she informed me she'd written to you in Guadalcanal, she burst into tears. I know how tough it must seem, how unfair – you copping all the shit in the islands and me back here with a cushy desk job in Intelligence. I respect and honour you and only hope I can prove myself a worthy contender.'

I was beginning to regain a bit of composure. 'Thank you, sir. It . . . it came as a bit of a surprise, that's all,' I stammered, uttering one of the great understatements of my life. I continued, 'I had no right to expect —'

Rob Rich cut me short. 'No, no, Nick, you had every right to assume you and she were together. Marg explained that to me very carefully. As you know, she does things on her own terms.'

'You too,' I said, trying to cheer up a bit.

'You'd better believe it!' he grinned and extended his hand. For a split second I thought about not accepting it. He may have been my superior officer but, in this instance, I felt I had the right to refuse. But that would mean I was spitting the dummy and I guess I was too proud to let him see me sulking like a child. 'It's okay, sir.' I know I should have gone on to congratulate him, but there are limits. We shook hands.

Commander Rich then got down to business. 'Nick, Commander Long, in fact all of us, are tremendously pleased at the way you've conducted yourself with the Americans, the marines. Not an easy call.'

'No, sir, that's not correct. In fact the 1st Marine Division was very generous and my job under Colonel Woon, as Japanese translator in their radio unit, was not dangerous. It's not as though I've been a coastwatcher and doing the hard yakka.'

'Well, I'm not so sure about that. Mather put in a very

good report on your work in the field, as did Colonel Woon, and there was another very complimentary one, at a very high level, from Marine Headquarters concerning your bravery at Bloody Ridge. Congratulations on the Navy Cross – it's not a medal the Americans hand out gratuitously. Our division has benefited from all this. Recruiting you in Perth is being seen as a masterstroke by the old man.'

I thought maybe he was laying it on a bit thick because of Marg. I guess we should all learn the difficult art of accepting compliments, but I felt compelled to add, 'Thank you, sir, but all I did was what I was trained to do here in Melbourne and by Sergeant Major Wainwright of Z Force on Fraser Island.'

Commander Rich ignored this further protest. 'Let me explain something to you, Nick. The war in the Pacific is in its second phase and, whether we like it or not, the Americans are in charge. MacArthur and his people call the shots, every single one of them. The more we can involve ourselves with the Americans, the more indirect influence we will have with them. It doesn't have to be at the top-brass level for it to work. Your contribution is a perfect example.'

'A-ha! That accounts for my goanna medal.'

'Goanna medal?'

I explained the general's presentation methodology and the subsequent simile. He laughed. 'I guess you're pretty close to the mark, but the DSC is no cheap brass badge with a ribbon. Wear it with pride, son. Even if it was an opportunity for a spot of good public relations with the Yanks, that doesn't demean it. You've earned it fair and square.'

'Sir, what they said in the newspapers was a load of bulldust!'

'Nick, it was very likely based on a PR release prepared by

SDR and followed the protocol of the three reports received. You can't stop the newspapers adding their own spin. The *Argus*, in particular, is always going to beat it up. Commander Long, and those above him who are responsible for policy, are already looking ahead to when the Japs are finally defeated. If the Pacific War has shown us anything, it is that we can't rely on the Brits to come to our aid in a crisis. After Singapore, Churchill decided to abandon Australia. He had his hands full in Europe and the Mediterranean and decided we were expendable. As Pacific nations, America and Australia are far more logical allies.'

I was growing up fast. Being described in impersonal terms as an asset, a tiny cog in the machinery of diplomacy, made me realise that whatever happened to the Nick Duncans of this world, the Commander Longs would still be spinning their webs and using whatever they could find to feed the system. I accepted this, realising that with the advent of the Japanese entering the war, as a nation we were fighting for our very lives. Whatever the machinations, Commander Rupert Basil Michael Long was, in a sense, responsible to the nation first and foremost; my own life came far down in his charter – if it appeared in the small print at all.

'Over the next few days various members of Intelligence will arrive to debrief you, Nick,' Commander Rich instructed. 'There'll be a navy stenographer accompanying them. We'll return the transcripts for you to read so we get it exactly right. We are going to need a fair bit of privacy, hence your move into this alcove. I hope you don't mind.'

'No, sir, I'm grateful for the peace and quiet. The stenographer? It won't be Petty Officer Hamilton?' I said, grinning, but my heart was suddenly ka-pounding.

'No, she'll be made a lieutenant in two weeks.' He paused

and seemed to be thinking. 'Nick, Marg's asked if she can come in.' Then he added quickly, 'She'll understand if you'd rather not. But she'd really like to see you.'

'May I think about it, sir?' I didn't know if I was sufficiently grown-up to cope with a visit from Marg.

'Of course.'

Changing the subject, which was still a pretty tender part of my consciousness, I asked, 'Where will I be going after I leave hospital, sir?'

'Nick, you're entitled to leave and we want you to take it; get a good rest. Then there are several options. But if you stay with the SRD, or whatever they're calling themselves this week, they've already indicated they want you back with the Americans. It's an easy match.'

'The marines?'

'Yes, they've already told us they'd like you back when you've recovered. Like I said before, we're in no position to argue. Of course, you can always choose to go into the regular navy; that would get you off the hook.'

Over the following two and a half days the debriefing took place. Every tiny detail of my time with the marines was teased out and the notes returned to me to sign as accurate. On the second day I was questioned about the Mount Austen Operation, the sniper and the capture of Gojo Mura and the code books, which I related in exactly the way they'd occurred.

Early next morning a motorcycle dispatch rider delivered an envelope stamped 'Top Secret' for which I had to sign. Opening it I saw it was the transcript of the stuff we'd discussed the previous day. Underlined in red ink was the sniper and radio operator incident with margin notes that read: 'Due modesty and the attempt at humour has no place in this report. This version contradicts all the official reports we have received. PLEASE RECTIFY.' It was initialled 'RBML'. I was learning that the propaganda machine takes precedence over accuracy. Shortly after the delivery a navy stenographer arrived and, despite the request to rectify by Rupert Basil Michael Long, I dictated a note saying I regretted I couldn't, in all conscience, alter the document; the facts were given as I had understood them. I apologised in effect for not lying. I was unlikely to get a further promotion in the navy anyway, but this response would certainly put the kybosh on any chance I might have had.

That afternoon I received yet another visitor – this one less contentious. It was the lovely redhead, Petty Officer Mary Kelly, who, while being insistent that the sheets in her glory box would keep their cellophane wrapping until her marriage night, had rewarded me with a wonderful session of mouth-to-south resuscitation on the last night of my so-called departure to Britain.

She parted the curtains and entered, her red head aflame and her eyes sparkling. 'Hello, Nick. My gawd, ya look ten years older! 'Owyagoin', mate? Jesus, what have they done to you?' Mary, while being a good Catholic, mentioned the Son of God frequently in her conversation.

I was grinning like an ape. 'Nice to see you, Mary. How'd you know I was here?'

'Talk about a mug lair! You're all over the papers like a rash. Mum says I've got to ditch the Yank and get back with a real hero!' She laughed. 'But I can't, Nick, he's lovely. He comes from Brooklyn, "Eye-talian".' She extended her right hand to show me an engagement ring.

I covered my eyes. 'I'm blinded!' I cried, not meaning to be sarcastic.

'Bastard!'

'No, really, it's lovely. Congratulations, Mary. His name doesn't happen to be Belgiovani, does it?'

'No? Fiorelli. Why?'

'Nothing.'

'You didn't go to England? You knew all the time, didn't you?' she accused, smiling. 'That's why I couldn't go to the ship to say goodbye. My dad had even organised a place by a crane for me to sit. I waited for a letter from England but you were off bashing around in the jungle somewhere.'

'I couldn't tell you, Mary. I was seconded to the Americans.'

'Me too!' she said happily, glancing at her engagement ring.

I laughed. Mary Kelly hadn't lost any of her wit. 'It was all rather hush-hush, Mary – you know, confiden—'

'Yeah, that's what my dad said when we saw you in the *Herald*. We all thought you were a bit of a Proddy bastard. You know, not writing and all, like I'd been clean forgotten. But when we saw your picture in the paper and General MacArthur giving you a medal, well, then my dad said, "See, I told ya. Nick was fair dinkum all the time. He's in the bloody secret service, no bloody wonder." And mum said, "I always liked that boy, nice manners and always real polite."'

'Mary, I couldn't write, you know, tell you where I was. I apologise for deceiving you. Being a Proddy, a Protestant, had nothing to do with it.'

'Course yer couldn't, Nick. Secret service! All is forgiven.' She cocked her head and smiled. 'Sorry about Fiorelli, Nick.'

I grinned. 'Story of my life.'

She leaned over and kissed me on the forehead. 'You've

taken a right hiding, haven't ya, mate?'

'Nah, just a spot of malaria, soon be right as rain,' I protested and then, in an attempt to get the subject away from me, I asked, 'Sheets still in the glory box?'

Her eyebrows shot up. 'Of course!' She laughed, recalling. 'You know how you use'ta complain, I mean going back to HMAS *Cerberus*,' she grimaced, 'feeling, like, real sore?'

'Yeah – lover's balls,' I grinned.

She giggled. 'Well, Fiorelli said that when he went back to camp the other night his, you know, what you've just mentioned, were hanging so low that he tripped over them by mistake!'

'Ouch!' I laughed. 'Don't you ever show any mercy, Mary?'

'I told ya, Nick, that sort of malarky is for between the marriage sheets and they're still folded in their cellophane paper.'

I must have been feeling a lot better because there was a severe stirring under my own sheet. We were silent for a moment, probably because I was distracted. 'Mary, I'm so glad for you. After the war will you live in America?'

'Oh yes, Fiorelli's father is in the trucking business; he seems to be a bigwig in the Eye-talian community and also in their union. It's called the Teamsters.'

'I feel sure you'll be well protected, Mary,' I said, not explaining that I'd heard the Teamsters was a notoriously violent and corrupt union organisation with links to the Mafia.

'Fiorelli says Eye-talians look after their women,' Mary said. 'Not like here.'

'That's good,' I said. 'I wish you luck, Mary.'

She looked serious for a moment. 'I came to say goodbye, Nick. I'm proud you're a hero. I thought you might need a little hero worship.' She grinned and slipped her hand under the sheet, finding what she was looking for with ease. 'My, my, it's nice to know something hasn't changed.'

'Oh, God!' I said, closing my eyes and throwing my head back into the pillow.

'Anyone likely to come in?' she asked.

'Only the tea trolley in half an hour,' I gasped.

'Good. You're still getting bugger all from my chin down, Nick Duncan.' She grinned. 'I've promised Fiorelli he can sleep with the Virgin Mary on his wedding night.' She knelt beside the bed and pulled the top sheet aside. The rest, as they say in the classics, took place mellifluously, deliciously and wonderfully. I will not soon forget the loveliness of Mary Kelly.

Seeing Mary seemed to somewhat ameliorate the hurt of Marg. They were not to be compared and I don't mean that in a derogatory way. They were simply different women. Marg Hamilton turned me into a man, first gently, then wonderfully and stridently, demanding as much as she gave. The Virgin Mary was full of the contradictions of her working-class background and her Catholic faith, giving selflessly as much as she could without tearing the cellophane from the sheets in her glory box.

In fact I had lost both of them, one to my superior officer and the other to the Mafia. There wasn't a whole heap of my immediate past left, come to think of it; not much of my distant past was there either. But, as always happens, no sooner do you think the past is gone forever when it returns to bite you in the bum.

The note delivered to the hospital by a military dispatch

rider, who didn't leave his name, simply read:

> *Hiya, Hero! Call me urgent! Bris. 9287. Ask for Petty Officer*
> *Kevin Judge. If yer cain't call, write to Navy Procurement*
> *Office, Turbot St, Brisbane.*
>   *Your best buddy,*
>   *Kevin*
> *P.S. Brisbane is in Queensland but I ain't seen the fuckin'*
> *queen yet.*

Making a phone call from the hospital wasn't easy. The phones, only two of them, were in the corridors, there was always a queue of patients lined up and you had to have the exact amount of money to put in the slot. Frankly, it was a pain in the arse. I figured the little bloke, whose petty officer title seemed to me about as jumped up as my promotion to lieutenant had been, probably worked in a warehouse at the US procurement depot. They'd have to find him and then I'd run out of change and there'd be the usual tongue clucking and 'Shake a leg, mate' going on, with the queue growing longer by the minute. So I decided to write. The big mystery was how Kevin's note to me came to be delivered in Melbourne by a military dispatch motorcyclist, whereas mine would probably be opened by the censor and take ten days to arrive. That's the strange thing about wartime. In the attempt to speed everything up, everything slows down.

In the ten days that passed before I heard from the little bloke again I received a note from Marg Hamilton asking if she could visit. I'd recovered a little emotionally and didn't want to appear churlish, so I swallowed hard and wrote back to say I'd be glad to see her. I told myself once again that I had absolutely no right to feel aggrieved. Marg had handled everything, as usual, with complete decorum. I was the sulky bugger with the chip on my shoulder.

Nurse Parkes had arranged for two lounge chairs (heaven knows where she found them) to be brought into the alcove and I sat in pyjamas and dressing-gown, reading. There wasn't a great deal of choice in the hospital library, which consisted largely of books left behind by previous patients. I'd selected a Raymond Chandler novel. I forget its title, but I recall I'd just read a sentence that brought me back to reality in the context of Marg's visit: 'Dead men are heavier than broken hearts.' I was still alive and kicking, my heart was still pumping and I was about to turn nineteen. I guess my life wasn't entirely over. *For Christ's sake, pull yourself together, Nick,* I silently urged.

She came in wearing her WRANS uniform with her lovely chestnut hair shining. At work she usually wore it tightly swept up to accommodate her hat – cap? – I could never decide quite what it was. I instinctively knew she'd let her hair down, worn it loose for me. She knew how much I loved the shine, the colour and thickness. She was even prettier than I remembered.

'Nick, how lovely.' She looked genuinely pleased to see me and her eyes sparkled. I started to rise from my seat, but before I could do so she'd bent down, placed her hands on the points of my shoulders and planted a generous kiss squarely on my lips. Then, drawing back, 'I've been dying to see you, darling,' she declared happily.

I grinned stupidly, nervous, licking my lips, tasting her lipstick. 'I've been dreading this moment and, as usual, you've handled it with aplomb,' I declared.

'And that's another thing! I've missed the only eighteen-year-old man in Australia who can string a sentence together using a natural and extensive vocabulary. I like "aplomb"; it sounds like an expensive pudding.' She turned and settled herself in the chair opposite me, arranging her long legs.

'Too many grown-up books as a kid, and a bibliophile Anglican missionary father who thinks every truly noteworthy word has at least three syllables or doesn't get used too often,' I replied, grinning. In a matter of moments Marg had, as usual, settled things down. I wondered to myself if there was any situation, no matter how fraught, that Lieutenant Marg Hamilton couldn't handle. She could, I felt sure, turn a major metropolitan earthquake into an orderly evacuation. With her at his side, Rob Rich was almost certain to reach the rank of admiral.

'You look perfectly ghastly, darling. What have they done to you? I hear you've had malaria, amongst several other nasty things. We're terribly proud of you, Nick. Rob told me about the twenty-second MacArthur thing and your "goanna medal". That's naughty. It really is *no* such thing. He says you've earned it twice over and that the Americans love you.'

She'd slipped his name in so naturally that I hardly felt the jolt in my chest, although I noted she was speaking a tad too fast in an attempt to conceal her own anxiety. 'Marg, he's a great bloke,' I said. 'Congratulations.' The six words came out like regurgitated razor blades.

'Thank you, Nick,' she said in a quieter, slower voice. Then she looked me directly in the eyes. 'Nick Duncan, don't you *ever* think for one moment that I didn't and don't still love you,' she scolded. Then she threw back her head, her lovely chestnut hair momentarily covering her face, then curtaining to swing back into place just above her shoulders. 'I loved you with aplomb!

You were simply the most delicious pudding!'

Marg rose from her chair and came to kneel in front of me, taking my hands in her own and looking directly at me. 'Nick, I shall be terribly sad if we can't remain loving friends for the rest of our lives. I shall never trivialise the special time we had together. What I said in my letter about locking the memory of you in my heart, I meant. When I'm an old woman I shall remember a beautiful young man I once had the privilege to love.'

I felt ashamed at the sudden tears that ran down my cheeks. Aren't women the ones who are supposed to cry? I have no idea where the tears came from. They just came out of nowhere.

'I'd like that – I'd like that very much,' I heard myself saying.

Loneliness can be a bugger of a thing.

CHAPTER TWENTY

'Yoh can say dat again, buddy! Opportunity only
knock once. When da good Lord place it in ya way,
it ain't logical yoh gonna refuse it. Matter of fact,
where I come from, it a downright sin.'
Kevin Judge, aka 'Da Judge'
Brisbane, 1943

I HAD WRITTEN TO the little bloke saying that when I
got out of hospital I was entitled to a month's leave, and I'd like
to come up and see him. I asked if he knew of a boarding house
where I could stay and take it easy. I explained that I had just
my kitbag but I wanted a bit of luxury after Guadalcanal and
the hospital – somewhere clean where I could have a decent
mattress and a hot shower (if necessary more than once a day).
Also, as my appetite was slowly returning, I wanted a place that
served a decent hot breakfast.

I had four months' pay plus allowances in my pocket:
nearly sixty pounds. By soldier standards at twelve shillings
and sixpence a day, it was a veritable fortune and I would be
able to treat myself and pay my own way with the little bloke
and his friends. That kind of money isn't left under your
and I decided I'd put it in the bank when I got to Brisb
father had an account at the Bank of New South W
originally been used to pay my school fees and
he wanted brought home on school holida

still open with one or two quid sitting in it.

The priority telegram read: EXPECT YOU STOP ALL TAKEN CARE OF STOP LOTSA ACTION WAITING STOP KEVIN.

Then a day later a dispatch rider delivered an envelope to the hospital that contained a priority movement order made out in my name, with the date yet to be filled in. It entitled me to fly to Brisbane from Essendon Airport. The trip was getting more and more bizarre.

I guess if Belgiovani could make sergeant then Kevin could make petty officer, but Beljo had a remarkable skill, while Kevin's only demonstrable accomplishments appeared to be his ability to climb through toilet windows into supermarkets and to sell numbers tickets and black-market cigarettes. These didn't seem to me to be the kinds of talents that led to promotion in any of the armed forces, except perhaps for our own underhanded bunch – and they were as far removed from Kevin Judge as it was possible to get and still be on planet earth.

As Ross Hayes (the doctor) had indicated, my recovery wasn't quite as fast as I'd hoped. By the end of January I was up and about, although two trips into the city, one with Marg and the other with Nurse Parkes, left me pretty whacked on each occasion. Marg visited several times and I must say it made a big difference. I can't pretend I didn't still lust after her, because I did. But there you go, she was proving to be a great friend and I can honestly say I think she enjoyed visiting and wasn't just doing it to cheer me up.

Towards the end of January, Mary Kelly arrived unexpectedly with Fiorelli in tow. I had imagined a version of Belgiovani, whereas the bloke who came in with a serious-looking Mary was almost my size, trim and hard as a jarrah log, with the looks of what in the twenties used to be known as a 'matinee idol'. He stabbed his forefinger at me and then turned to Mary, balling his fists, his expression fierce. 'Dis duh guy been messin' wid ya, baby?' he asked. They must have seen the look of bewilderment on my face because they both burst into laughter. Fiorelli extended his hand. 'Nice tuh know ya, Nick. Mary tell me you a regular guy and a hero, got yoself a medal from duh big guy.'

'Fat lot of good it did me,' I grinned, pointing. 'That little bitch left me in the cold and went and took up with a Yank!'

Much laughter ensued and Mary, grabbing Fiorelli's arm and looking up at him, said, 'See? I told ya, mate!' – although what she'd told him I shall never know.

They stayed a while and when they left Fiorelli preceded Mary and, parting the curtains, turned and pointed a finger at me again. 'You come Stateside – Noo York, you hear, you our guest, buddy.' He looked over at Mary. 'You say solong ta Nick nice, babe,' he said, drawing the curtains behind him.

Mary, left alone with me for a moment, kissed me . . . if not passionately, the contact was more than perfunctory. 'Cheerio, Nick, luv ya!'

'I hope Fiorelli's getting a little hero worship, kid!' I whispered.

'Nick! What kind of girl do you take me for?' she retorted with a pretend look of shock on her pretty Irish face. 'Goodbye, sweetheart,' she said softly, kissing me again. I was left with the memory of a flame of red hair as the Virgin Mary parted the curtains and exited my life.

By mid-February I had received advice of my next posting and was sufficiently recovered to leave for Brisbane; Nurse Parkes, using the office phone when matron was doing her rounds, made all the arrangements. We'd grown rather friendly but she had a boyfriend who was practically her fiancé; he was in the air force and you don't go there. The article in the *Women's Weekly* had been published and it was such a success that in the following issue a full photograph of her face had appeared on the front cover with the caption 'Nurse Suzanna Parkes – The Compassionate Face of War'.

Matron was not pleased. Overnight one of her nurses had become known nationwide. She'd called her niece into her office and afterwards Nurse Parkes came into the alcove looking upset and repeated what Matron had said to her, mimicking her clipped voice. 'The old cow said to me, "A nurse's vocation is a selfless and silent one. We do not splash our faces over the covers of magazines! You come from a very respectable country family, Nurse Parkes. I simply cannot think what my sister, your mother, will think."'

However, her mum was delighted and wrote to both Nurse Parkes and her sister, to say how proud they felt in Suzanna's home town of Bairnsdale. So the matron gave tight-lipped permission when Nurse Parkes insisted on coming with me to Essendon, where I would get a flight to Sydney before going on to Brisbane. We hitched a ride into the city in the back of one of the hospital ambulances. It was on its way to Spencer Street Railway Station to pick up casualties who were arriving.We were dropped off near Collins Street and made our way to the Block Arcade for a quick cup of tea. Nurse Parkes had arranged for us to be taken to the airport by the Army transport shuttle service that left from the Olderfleet Building.

Because I'd lost so much weight, Marg had organised for

me to go to Myer and have a new uniform made up – the tropics and more than a spot of mildew hadn't been too kind to the old one. The fitting had been done on one of the city excursions after which I'd returned to the hospital totally whacked. When Marg visited and I tried to arrange payment she simply said, 'The navy owes you, darling.' I decided to wear my new uniform to the airport just in case the travel movement order wasn't fair dinkum – at least they'd see I wasn't an impostor.

When they announced the plane to Sydney Nurse Parkes, standing on tiptoe, kissed me. 'I'm going to miss you terribly, Nick. But make sure you don't come back,' she said, close to tears.

'Thanks, Suzanna, you've been a brick. I won't forget you. Tell your bloke in the air force that the infamous winner of the goanna medal says he's a bloody lucky bloke to have you. I mean it!' I said with emphasis. It was the first time I had used her Christian name and Nurse Parkes started to weep softly, knuckling her tears, then waving me goodbye.

By the time the plane landed in Sydney I was feeling exhausted – even thinking longingly of the crisp white sheets at the hospital. The accommodation at Mascot for officers in transit was noisy and not conducive to a good night's sleep. I was glad to get out of there and take my seat on the dawn flight to Brisbane.

Arriving at Eagle Farm Airport I took a bus to Brisbane Railway Station and then sought directions to Turbot Street on the edge of the city. The US Navy Procurement Office had taken over a large four-storey building. At the gates I was accosted by two navy shore patrol personnel who, though not quite as tall as me, appeared a damn sight wider around the shoulders now that I'd lost forty pounds of weight. They were the kind of blokes with whom you decide not to argue even when they're still approaching from some distance. The fact that I was wearing naval uniform and, these days, a bit of fruit salad on my chest, didn't seem to impress them and they failed to salute.

'Sorry, Lootenant, this a restricted area,' one of them said before I'd even opened my mouth to speak.

'I'd like to see Petty Officer Judge,' I replied, looking him in the eye. I was the officer and they were the enlisted men, and while I don't care much about these things, there is a respect for rank, even between Allies. I had been taught you are saluting the rank, not the man.

He glanced at the second gorilla and smiled. 'That just about every-body in Bris-bane, sir.'

'Petty Officer Judge?' I asked, not sure he understood. Then I added with a touch of acerbity, 'I'm not asking to see your commander in chief.'

'That just about who you *is* asking to see,' the second big ape chortled.

The Americans were very unpopular in Brisbane. The infamous Battle of Brisbane had taken place early the previous year when a goon like one of the two standing in front of me from the US Military Police had shot an Australian soldier named Edward Webster. It was the culmination of weeks of brawling, initially aggravated by resentment that the better-paid American troops, with their access to the PX, nylons, chocolates and other goodies, were pulling all the prettiest local girls, leaving the scrubbers for our blokes. It had resulted in two nights of pitched battle involving a couple of thousand soldiers from both sides. After the incident, not only the troops but also the locals, with the exception of the girls who were the original cause of the fracas, thought the Yanks were somewhat on the nose. Now I sensed a bit of reciprocated feeling coming from the two naval patrol guys barring my way.

I attempted to smile, though not over-successfully. 'No, you don't understand. My name is Nick Duncan and Petty Officer Judge and I are friends, old war buddies.' Then I added as further explanation, 'We sailed together in a yacht across the Indian Ocean escaping from the Japs.' No sooner had I said this than I realised how absurd it must sound.

A look of incredulity appeared on their faces and they started to laugh. Then one of them stopped suddenly. 'Hey, wait on, that happen to him. He got himself a medal for doin' that.' He looked up and asked, 'Wha' cha say the name was, sir?'

'Duncan, Lieutenant Nick Duncan. Why don't you call Petty Officer Judge? That will clear this matter up,' I assured him.

'I can try, sir, but Da Judge, he don't *take* calls. He only *make* them.'

'The Judge?'

'Yeah, that him,' he said, not explaining. 'Wait on, sir, I'll try.' He walked over to the guardhouse situated within the main building, returning a minute or two later shaking his head as in disbelief. 'Sorry, sir, no disrespek intended. It just that every day lots o' people try to see Da Judge.' He grinned. 'I'll get my fat ass kicked if I let somebody in who ain't legit. Follow me, please, Lootenant.'

We climbed the stairs to the first floor, which seemed entirely occupied by women in naval uniform working at comptometer machines. They were known as WAVES and I assumed they were somewhat similar to our WRANS, although they didn't seem to be subject to the same naval discipline. Marg once claimed that she'd met dozens of them in the course of her work and she'd never yet found one who knew what the acronym stood for. Then she'd told me: Women Accepted for Volunteer Emergency Service.

We climbed yet another set of stairs to the third floor. The vast space had been divided down the centre, forming a long corridor, and a series of small cubicles had been built to house clerical staff either side of its entire length, except for the very end where I could see doors to two much larger offices, the walls enclosed to the ceiling. Along one wall of the corridor there were twenty or so chairs, and the eight nearest the two large offices were occupied by six male civilians, an army colonel and a naval officer with the rank of captain. The civilians were of various ages and sizes, all of them with their brown or grey felt hats placed on briefcases that, in turn, rested on their knees. All sat very still, including the army and navy bloke, and nobody smoked. Then I noticed there were no ashtrays to be seen anywhere. Lesson one of day one of Intelligence training had taught us that temporary nicotine withdrawal was the first act in setting up an interrogation. Offering a cigarette when the interrogation got under way was the second lesson. *Let them sweat, then let them think you're friendly.* Judging from their haircuts and suits I could see all the civilians were Australians.

I was ushered to the end seat, number nine, whereupon the naval patrol guard who'd escorted me saluted smartly, then turned and continued to the end cubicle directly outside the two large offices and informed whoever was inside of my presence. Somewhat bemused, I sat down to wait.

A minute or so later the door of one of the large offices swung open to reveal the little bloke with a cigar stuck in the corner of his mouth. 'Jesus H. Christ! Am I seein' ya, Nick? Lookin' at ya? Or is dis a hallucination? Like the visit from the

Virgin below decks?' He laughed, the cigar wobbling. Ignoring
the seated men, he came hurrying towards me with his arms held
wide. He'd put on at least ten pounds, maybe a little more, and
there was a definite paunch showing above his belt. I stood as
he approached and he embraced me unashamedly, his head no
higher than the top of my chest. Then he turned to the seated
men. 'Gennelmen, I apologise, but we cain't see you today.
Please see da secretary, she gonna make another appointment.'
He smiled, the essence of charm. 'Be patient, gennelmen,
believe me dis inconvenience, it gonna be worthwhile when yer
come back same time, same place, same chair, tomorrow. Adios,
thank you for ya cooperation.'

'You're looking a million dollars, Kevin,' I said, grinning.
He was too – immaculate uniform, splashed with fruit salad and
well groomed, the little bloke had come a long way from where
I'd left him waving to me from a US Navy car, blistered from
the sun, the parts that weren't peeling looking sore and refusing
to tan.

'You look like shit, Nick. Where da fuck yer been? I don't
mean da cockamamie hospital. Da newspaper say you wid da
marines in Guadalcanal? Dat true? You're a hero, Navy Cross?
Dat serious shit, buddy! Yer out o' yer fuckin' mind! Lissen,
sonnyboy —'

I held up my hand. 'We don't say that – remember?'

He laughed uproariously. 'I want yer to unnerstan', I ain't
no fuckin' hero! Come, Nick, come meet da chief.'

He'd managed to say all of this without losing the cigar.
Walking into his office I remarked, 'Hey, what's with the cigar?'

He propped, removing the cigar from his mouth for the first
time and looking at it as if surprised that it had been stuck in
the corner of his mouth all along. 'Buddy, this ain't no ceegar!

Dis a Cuban ceegar! Dat a big, big difference.'

'Kevin, if I didn't love you, I'd think you were an opportunist.'

'Hey, Nick, whaddya mean? I'm American! It da same thing, ain't it?' he said, spreading his arms. 'Dis da land of the fee.'

I thought he had simply mispronounced the word, but I was soon to be enlightened. It was strangely comfortable to be back with the little bloke.

The office was big and plush: patterned carpet on the floor, big desk, fancy drinks cabinet with ball-and-claw legs, two easy leather club chairs and a coffee table upon which rested a silver tray containing a big square cutglass bottle with a glass stopper and surrounded by six little glasses to match.

He indicated one of the leather chairs. 'Sit, buddy, make yourself comfortable.' He sat in another, facing me across the coffee table.

'Irish whiskey?' I asked, pointing to the decanter and glasses on the little tray.

'Yeah, da best there is,' he said, not without a touch of pride. 'Wanna nip?'

I shook my head. 'Father Geraghty?' I asked. 'The priest at the orphanage, he's still got you by the short and curlies, Kevin.'

'Yeah,' he said, not denying it. 'When da bastard was whacking the livin' crap outta me wit his big leather belt, me touchin' me ankles wit my shirt tails round me ears, I'd look at dat bottle on his desk. *One day I gonna have me one like dat*, I said to myself.' He pointed to the whiskey decanter. 'Because dat cut bottle wit da glass stopper, dem little glasses, dat silver tray – dat got da power!'

'Ah, the verity of Geraghty,' I said, laughing.

'Don't yoh evah forget nuttin', Nick?' he asked.

'We spent a lot of time talking on *Madam Butterfly*; there weren't too many distractions,' I replied.

The little bloke suddenly grew quiet, then looked up at me, his face serious. 'I also ain't forgot. I owe you big time, Nick. We gonna have us a good time.' He jumped to his feet. 'C'mon, I wan' cha to meet da chief. How ya like da office?' he said, sweeping a proprietary hand in the air.

'Very nice – you must have done something very bad to deserve this,' I grinned.

He pointed to a door on the right wall that presumably led into the second office. 'You ain't seen nuttin' yet, buddy,' he boasted. 'Wait 'til yoh see the set-up next door.'

'What does it all mean, Kevin? You're a petty officer. I don't want to be rude, mate, but even that is a minor miracle.' I indicated the surroundings. 'This is – well, what can I say?'

He laughed. 'Yoh can say dat again, buddy! Opportunity only knock once. When da good Lord place it in ya way, it ain't logical ya gonna refuse it. Matter of fact, where I come from, it a downright sin – the verity of Geraghty. When I got back to San Diego dey done a big story on me in da newspaper. Next thing I got me a Purple Heart.'

'But you weren't wounded!'

'Wha' cha sayin', buddy? Lyin' under dem bushes wit me head wound, unconscious, concussed? Wha' cha mean? Dat ain't wounded?'

I laughed. 'Yeah, okay, sort of.'

'Then I got me a Bronze Star.'

'What for?' I asked, amazed.

'Da battleship sinkin', the raft, me covered in fuckin' black oil, lone American helping dem Australians to get ashore, lyin' under dem bushes wounded, escapin' from duh murderers on the beach. Den dere's the boat I sailed across the Indian Ocean,' he laughed, adding, 'almost single-handed. Navigatin' by da fuckin' stars, using dat rope wit da knots. Comin' through dat storm where I's at da helm forty-two hours wid no sleep. Jap fighters like fuckin' bees in da sky above. Livin' on a handful of weevil rice and rainwater. Sun burnin' down remorseless, like it the fires o' hell, peelin' me skin like a tomato when dey dump it in boilin' water. Opportunism, buddy! It the American way! When ya got material like dat, if'n yoh don't use it, it a crime against humanity! This is numbuh one prime bullshit yoh got at ya disposal, buddy! Da best yoh can get! Yoh ain't nevah gonna find better.'

He patted the ribbons on his chest. 'Not too many heroes come outta the US Navy Quartermaster's Department.' He grinned, recalling, 'Dey was fallin' over each other to promote me to petty officer, gimme these ribbons.' He chuckled. 'I should'a asked for chief, but by the time I realised it was too late, 'n so I was forced to run outa bullshit.'

'And how did I feature in all of this?' I asked with a grin.

Kevin threw back his head and laughed uproariously, 'Who?'

We crossed the room, Kevin knocked at the inside door and, not waiting for an answer, opened it. He was right. The next office was even grander: carpet deeper, four leather club chairs, bigger coffee table and drinks cabinet. There was a large vase of gladioli on the coffee table but no cutglass decanter. The huge desk was covered in photographs in elaborate silver frames. They seemed to be mostly of family, the usual happy snaps at home or groups of navy personnel. Four telephones and a teletype machine rested on the desk behind which, seated on a leather swivel chair, sat a big bloke I judged to be about fifty. The upper sleeve of his uniform was covered with chevrons (known as 'hash marks') and badges denoting his rank and years of service. He was the navy equivalent of the master gunner sergeants at Guadalcanal, the blokes who knew everything, controlled everything and had to be respected regardless of rank.

On the wall behind the desk were three large framed photographs: one of President Roosevelt, another of Admiral Ernest J. King, Commander in Chief of the US Fleet, and the third, which was just as large and important-looking, was also an admiral but one I didn't recognise. Later Kevin told me it was the Quartermaster General, 'from where all bounty flow,' he'd said at the time.

'Meet da chief,' Kevin said, smiling broadly. 'Nick, dis is Chief Petty Officer Bud Lewinski. Bud, dis my buddy, Nick Duncan, who saved my life twice.'

Bud Lewinski rose and extended his hand, coming from behind the desk. 'We meet at last, Nick,' he said, shaking my hand. 'For Da Judge here, there's the Virgin Mary, Jesus and Nick Duncan.' He laughed. 'And not necessarily in that order.' Drawing away he stopped and stabbed a blunt finger in the direction of my chest. 'Hey, Nick. I hear you got the US Navy Cross – how come you not wearing it?' he asked, just a tinge of belligerence to his voice.

'I regret I'm not officially allowed to wear it when in uniform,' I said.

'What kind o' cockamamie bullshit is that?'

'The King. Some rule. He's the only one allowed to award medals. Oh, and General MacArthur,' I replied, 'but I suspect only our own. The Navy Cross was much more than I deserved,' I added, so that he wouldn't think I'd dismissed the American honour lightly.

'Them limeys are a regular pain in the ass,' he snorted. I was to learn that Chief Lewinski was a pretty forthright kind of bloke. He was big-boned, carrying a little too much weight, but like Colonel Woon, built solid as a brick shithouse, with a ruddy complexion, hazel eyes, crew-cut hair with thick black Groucho Marx eyebrows. He was what Marg Hamilton would have termed 'a man of striking presence', meaning that it had nothing to do with his looks. Rupert Basil Michael Long fell into that category even though he and the grizzled, bearlike man seated at the desk were quite different physical types.

'This is nice,' I said, taking in the office. 'What's the admiral's office like?'

Both men laughed. 'Admirals don't run the navy, Nick,' Chief Lewinski replied. Instead of taking a seat with us he was now half sitting on a corner of his big desk.

'Oh? I thought that was their job.'

'No way, José!' Kevin retorted. With his 'adios' to the seated men outside and now this expression, he'd obviously picked up a bit of Mexican slang while in San Diego.

'It don't work like that,' Chief Lewinski explained. 'Startin' tomorrow mornin', take away the admirals, generals in the army and air force, the war go on as usual. Take away the petty officers, the chiefs, the sergeants, all the NCOs – and the fuckin' war stops. Nuttin' is goin' nowhere from that moment on. We got admirals on the other three corners this building. If they don't show up tomorrow nobody will notice; in a month, maybe a few questions, but still no alarm bells are clangin'. On the other hand, if we don't get here eight hunnert hours pronto, the US Navy in the Pacific gonna miss a heartbeat.' He pointed to the teletype machine. 'Every day by o-nine hunnert that thing's smokin' and the phones 'r jumpin' offa the desk.'

'How do yoh suppose t'irty t'ousand mosquito nets get made and delivered to the wharf to arrive on the 26th at Cape Gloucester – where you goin' next, Nick,' the little bloke chimed in.

I was stunned. Kevin couldn't possibly know this. It was classified information. Like any planned movement, it was a closely guarded secret. My Intelligence training let me pass his comment without remark – it could wait for a private moment with him. I laughed. 'Looks like I've got the wrong rank and I'm in the wrong branch of the navy, gentlemen,' I quipped.

Chief Lewinski tapped a cigarette out of a Camel soft-pack, threw the box down onto his desk, lit the cigarette, inhaled and exhaled, then squinting at me through the smoke, said, 'That's what we do; we make it happen, son. Your little buddy here is my right-hand man and half the left one as well. He can find anythin' and the little prick has a memory like an addin' machine.'

'No admirals, no generals, no war: now that's a thought,' I said, musing.

'Them bums wouldn't know how to pour piss out o' a boot, even if we put the instructions on the heel,' Chief Lewinski retorted.

'Piss in boots,' I said as a throwaway line, unable to resist the rather obvious pun. 'Would I be right in thinking you don't have an especially high regard for the officer class?'

'Hey, dat clever, Nick. Piss in boots – but it's true, we supply da boots, da laces, da instructions, da only thing da brass gotta do is supply da piss and even den dey don't always aim accurate or pour it out wit'out spillin' it over der big clumsy feet,' Chief Lewinski said.

'The civilians outside when I arrived? I take it they're suppliers?'

'Hope to be, bend over backwards to be, crawl-on-their-knees-over-hot-coals and piss-in-every-pocket-I-got-on-me-uniform to be. They'd sell their mothers, sisters and daughters to be Uncle Sam's suppliers in the Pacific. But we have to first remind them that America is the land of the brave and the fee.'

There it was again, this time from Chief Lewinski. I was beginning to realise that the business of supplying the requisites for the Pacific War was probably the biggest completely safe commercial bonanza Australian businessmen had hitherto encountered. They'd be falling over themselves to get to Chief Lewinski and, now apparently, the little bloke. I guess I'd been naïve, but it had never occurred to me (not that I'd ever thought about it) that all this business opportunity might involve a bit taken, so to speak, off the top.

In a way, I suppose it was navy tradition. Captain Cook was expected to profit from his ship's supplies. Lord Nelson did the same at Trafalgar, although he didn't live to spend it. The barrel of brandy in which they pickled his body to prevent it decaying in the summer heat on the way back from Spain to Portsmouth had probably had a nip or two skimmed off the top to find its way into the admiral's stores before going into the ship's hold. You may be sure the bosuns at the time had a grubby hand in all of it.

I guess this sort of thing has always been going on, and it explained the anxious-looking bunch in the passageway. Nor did I doubt, now that I thought about it, that the briefcase-and-hat brigade, once they knew the percentages involved, would simply add the gratuity to the cost of their goods so that Uncle Sam was the only ultimate loser.

'What about the two senior officers?' I asked. I'd noted to myself that they seemed to have the demeanour of two errant schoolboys waiting outside the principal's office.

Chief Lewinski grinned, stubbing his cigarette in an ashtray. 'The colonel wants to see if we can get his ass out of a crack. He's lost three truckloads of Bud – trucks, beer, the lot, all disappeared.'

'And you can find them for him?'

'Not me,' he turned to the little bloke. 'Finding things, that's Da Judge's speciality.'

'Jeez, thank you. Nick, I almost forgot. I gotta check dey've off-loaded half the cargo off o' one of dem trucks.' Kevin walked over to the telephone, dialled and spoke to someone named Naval Rating Wilson. 'Da colonel can easy explain half a load missin' and all his trucks and da rest of his beer got back safe,' he said generously, after returning from making the call.

'And the navy captain?' I asked.

'Hams. Needs a cover up. He sold fifty to his girlfriend's father who sold dem on da Christmas black market.'

'But you won't get those back! It's already February,' I said ingenuously.

'Nick, Nick, you gotta be educated!' Kevin cried, almost despairing. 'Next week we send out a t'ousand o' dem hams to the fleet. Five short here, another five dere, who's countin'? F'chrissakes, it ain't difficult ta lose fifty goddamned hams. Dat not da problem here, see. If dat captain bin on a ship, den his crew, bad luck dey'd just be short of a bit o' ham to go wit der eggs in the mornin'. But he ain't at sea. He's in charge of one of our biggest depots – de sonofabitch been depot dippin'. We can't have officers doin' somethin' dishonest like dat. It just ain't decent!'

'It's a disgrace!' Lewinski said cheerily. 'Tut, tut, life's tough, one US Navy captain just got himself busted. He's just a greedy small-time crook, but worse than that, stoopid!' He reached for the pack of Camels on his desk, then glancing at his watch said, 'Nick, why don't you go with Da Judge, take a deck at how we work? He'll show you around, fill you in. I'll see you both at t'irteen hunnert in the lounge at the Bellevue.'

It was easy to see the little bloke had landed on his feet. The key to everything was that they never dealt in actual goods as the naval captain had done. 'Goods is evidence,' Kevin said. 'Cash ain't.'

'So your mob didn't heist the beer?'

'No way!' Kevin said in a hurt voice. 'We ain't common thieves, Nick.'

We'd reached the outside of the building where I expected to catch the bus to the hotel. But one of the naval patrol guys, not the one who'd taken me upstairs, ushered us to a huge Packard sedan with two stars on the fender pennant. He opened the back door for me and the little bloke went around to the other side of the olive-green car and climbed in. Behind the wheel sat a big black guy.

'Meet Joe "Hammer-man" Popkin,' Kevin said.

'Howdy,' the black bloke said, glancing back. 'Nice meetin' yoh at las', Nick.'

'You're kidding!' I pointed towards him, not believing my ears. 'The Joe "Hammer-man" Popkin from Illinois State Reformatory?'

'One an' da same,' Joe Popkin laughed, drawing away in the Packard.

The little bloke was grinning like a chimpanzee. 'Joe and me, we got ourselves together again.'

'A coincidence?' I asked, knowing it was probably no such thing. I was learning fast.

'Dis war not long enough for coincidence, buddy; yoh wait for coincidence, ya gonna be an old man.'

'Opportunist?'

'Yoh got it.'

Joe Popkin, steering expertly through the lunchtime traffic, glanced quickly backwards. 'I's glad you've come, Nick. Since we seen you in da noospaper I ain't heared nothin' else. My head got so many Nicks in it, it bleedin' internal, man. My friend heah, he owes you big time, but he sure don't stop talkin' 'bout it.' He paused. 'Like I owes him big time. One day I'm workin' in da blacksmith shop in San Diego wid dah Seabees, de navy construcshun crowd, an' da next I's comin' here.' He laughed. 'I ain't even evah heard o' dis place, Australia, man!'

The big Packard parked outside the Bellevue Hotel and we got out. 'You want me to wait?' Joe Popkin asked.

'Nah, go back to Turbot Street. I'll call yoh, buddy,' Kevin said.

'Joe's not coming to lunch?' I asked.

'Nah, this fuckin' navy, army, air force – black guys wash da dishes, dig da ditches, pick dat cotton, tote dat bale . . . even dah chief ain't got enough influence to change dat,' Kevin replied.

It accounted for the fact that there were no black marines at Guadalcanal, something I'd been curious about but hadn't dared to ask why. 'It's the same with our Aborigines,' I said. 'Although many of them fought with distinction in the First

World War they still have to deny they're Aboriginal when they enlist. They say they're Maoris or Islanders to get in, or pass themselves off as dark-complexioned whites. Once they're in the ranks they mysteriously turn back into Aborigines, by which time, of course, nobody gives a stuff; they're totally accepted for what they are – mainly bloody good soldiers. Make no mistake about it, we're also a racist society, mate.'

Kevin stopped at the entrance to the hotel and turning to me said, 'Da blacks is not accepted wit us, buddy. If dem Southern recruitment sergeants say ya black, den yoh is black. Den it's diggin' ditches or kitchen dooty for you in a labour battalion. Wit'out Joe, I'd 'a been a dead kid up-State in dat reformatory. Like you, buddy, he is my brudder. Fuckin' brass pissin' in der boots again! Most o' dem from da fuckin' South.'

We walked into the Bellevue Hotel – a posh-looking hostelry and certainly not likely to be mistaken as the corner pub. It wasn't hard to see the little bloke was well known, with greetings flying around like bats at twilight. The clientele was essentially businessmen and officers, American and Australian, who seemed to have less of an antipathy towards each other than did the enlisted men. I guess at the officer level access to the good sorts evened out a bit.

The little bloke, with me not far behind, was probably the lowest rank in the room, yet seemed to command a great amount of respect. Prosperous-looking business types called out greetings and one or two came over, but Kevin gave them the brush-off. 'I ain't doin' business today,' he said, smiling. 'Call me in da office, day after tomorrer.' He withdrew a card from his shirt pocket and handed out one; I noticed it was blank except for a number. 'Say dis number when you call,' he instructed. They nodded, grateful to have been granted an audience.

'You still in the numbers racket?' I joked.

'Wit'out a number dey don't get no appointment. No names until dey sittin' in da chief's office and dey bin checked out.'

One bloke, well dressed, with a rather pretentious air force moustache, a gold wristwatch and starched cuffs showing under an expensive suit, approached. 'I can explain, Mr Judge, it was a —' Kevin put up his hand to silence him. 'Not here, not now!' The bloke with the moustache quickly backed away. 'Asshole! He tried to substitute blade f'r sirloin in a beef contract to the officers' mess at naval headquarters. Big mistake. Stoopid!' I was quickly learning that the facts of life involved more than knowing where babies came from.

A waiter, his dark hair combed straight back and plastered with Brylcreem so that it shone and looked like a lacquered shell closely fitted to his head, and wearing a white apron that hung from his waist to his ankles, came over. 'Your table is ready whenever you are, sir,' he announced, his manner polite, bordering on obsequious.

'Thank you, Fernando, we'll have a drink at the bar while we wait for Chief Lewinski to get here.' Two bar stools mysteriously appeared and a truly terrific-looking barmaid with breasts as nice as Marg Hamilton's came over. She had a great open smile and gave me a quiet up-and-down appraisal, so that I reckoned it might be well worth returning at a later date to check out its meaning.

'Afternoon, Mr Judge,' she said, giving what she had upfront just the tiniest nudge forward. 'Same as usual?'

'Thanks, Sally,' Kevin replied.

She turned to me, her eyes widening slightly – or perhaps I imagined that bit. 'Coke, please, miss,' I said politely. She was an absolute knock-out.

'Coke? Wha' cha mean, Coke!' Kevin cried out, horrified.

'Jaundice – can't drink for another six weeks. It's a bitch – er, bugger,' I said colouring, realising the nice-looking barmaid was still present.

'Irish over ice and a Coke,' Sally said as she moved away, giving me a look that seemed to suggest she'd prefer me sober. Oh God! Her breasts were lovely.

'She likes you, buddy; half this cockamamie town is tryin' to get into her pants.'

'What about you, then?' I teased.

The little bloke shook his head. 'Nah, she's outa my class, buddy. Money don't buy her sort.' Then he added, 'Beside, she gets all the chocolates and nylons and whatever she wants free. She don't have ta put out for nuttin' to nobody.' He paused. 'I got an arrangement wit a young widda, her husband was killed in North Africa.' He didn't explain any further.

I hadn't brought up the subject of accommodation. The bus from the airport had taken me to Brisbane Railway Station where I'd left my kit in the luggage room before walking to Turbot Street. 'You didn't happen to find a boarding house where I could kip?' I now asked.

'Sure, you staying right here, buddy.'

'Here?' I laughed. 'Mate, I'm on a naval lieutenant's pay.'

'On da house,' he smiled. 'Matter o' fact, da owner's suite. Da publican gives it to us for nuttin'. He owes us big time, dis de only hotel in Bris-bane dat never runs outa Scotch.'

'I thought you said you don't deal in goods.'

'We don't. Not like dem hams. We buy it ourselves from ourselves. It's all fair and square on the books. It's what Chief Lewinski calls "kosher".'

'Thanks, Kevin. I could use a bit of luxury, but what I had

in mind was a firm mattress, clean sheets changed once a week, a hot shower and a good breakfast.'

'Dey got all dat here upstairs, Nick.' He chuckled. 'And Sally downstairs.'

'I should be so lucky,' I said, grinning.

'Well, dat your only problem, Nick. You gotta work out how to bring her from downstairs, up da stairs. Other dan dat, I pick up da tab while you're here.'

'I can't allow that, mate,' I protested. 'Let me pay for drinks and meals.'

The little bloke sighed. 'Nick, it ain't a big deal, buddy. We don't pay for nuttin' in dis establishment.'

'A little Scotch goes a long, long way,' I said.

'It ain't such a little,' Kevin replied. 'Give me da luggage ticket. Joe will go fetch your kitbag an' bring it here.'

The drinks arrived, carried by the magnificent eyeful. Not long afterwards Chief Lewinski joined us. We finished our drinks and the waiter with the lacquered head led us to a table in a private alcove. 'I'll send the drinks waiter right away, sir,' he said.

One or two minutes passed and Sally arrived. She looked at me and grinned, eyes twinkling. 'The drinks waiter was busy, sir, I hope you don't mind?' she explained in a mischievous voice.

I laughed. 'I want to make an official complaint to the management, miss,' I replied. Then I added, 'Please, call me Nick.' I was trying not to look at her breasts, fixing my eyes on her very pretty face, freckles around her nose.

'Thank you, Nick. Same again?'

I nodded. 'The Coca-Cola kid.'

'Don't take no notice I'm here,' Kevin grinningly complained.

'Irish over ice?' Sally asked, throwing him a gorgeous smile and then turning to Lewinski. 'Scotch on the rocks?'

'You've got me in one, young lady,' the chief replied. 'Mr Johnny Walker.'

We watched as she left – tall, nice legs, and the way she swung her hips wasn't at all painful to the eye. Thinking about her later created a definite stirring elsewhere. I was recovering from hospital fast.

The owner's suite was more luxury than any one man needed: big bedroom, lounge and its own bathroom. I'd never been in a place as posh as this. Kevin explained that sometimes they needed to use the lounge for meetings they couldn't hold in the office, but he'd let me know well in advance.

On the second night, Sally agreed to go to the movies with me and then dancing later at the Trocadero. She was a terrific dancer and undertook to teach me, picking up where Mary Kelly had left off, and managing my clumsy big feet with expert ease. The Yanks had brought jitterbug and jive to Brisbane; Sally already had the hang of both and I had a go, though I wasn't very good. Holding her and swinging her around, we laughed a lot and by the end of the evening I hoped I was getting better at them. I took her home in a taxi. She lived in a block of red-brick flats and shared with three girlfriends. I said goodnight at the front door, and although I'd flung her around all night like a rag doll, I didn't attempt to kiss her despite multiple stirrings.

The following night I met Kevin's widow lady, Brenda. She was a plumpish, pretty girl in her early twenties and the three of us went to dinner together. She appeared to be quiet and loving, and although nothing was said (how could there be with her still in mourning?), it wasn't too hard to see she liked the little bloke a whole lot and, while he was acting a bit tough, it was obvious he felt the same about her. She was even tinier than he was and he referred to her as 'Bren Gun', a weapon I didn't know he knew about. 'She get mad at yoh, it rapid fire, she don't take no shit,' he explained in her presence at dinner.

Brenda's eyebrows shot up. 'Kevin! I beg your pardon? Mind your language! Wash your mouth! You're not with your navy friends now, Kevin Judge. Apologise at once!' I must say her chastisement came out spontaneously without too much pausing for breath.

'See what I mean?' the little bloke said happily, not apologising. I guess, like Father Geraghty, the cruel cut of a nun's tongue at the orphanage had left a mark on the little bloke. We never quite recover from our childhood, him with this and me seeking the comfort of a woman's breasts.

After we'd dropped Brenda and Kevin at her flat in Ipswich and Joe Popkin was driving me back to the hotel, he casually enquired, 'How ya going wid da barmaid, Nick?'

I laughed, and asked, 'How do you know about that? Is nothing sacred around here?'

Joe threw back his head and laughed. 'Da Judge, he tell me she a mind blow an' she like you, man!'

I explained that I'd taken Sally to a movie and then dancing, but that was all there was to it. We were going out again in two nights' time, I told him, that was providing her mother didn't come into town from Toowoomba.

'Yeah, man, da mudder factor, dat ain't easy,' Joe said, consoling me. 'But nevah yoh mind, yoh take it nice easy, slow action, dat always da best way. Some chicks, dey see a uniform, dey cain't wait. But, my experience, yoh take it easy, play da game smart, slow, polite, keep ya tongue in ya own mouth, wid ya hands doin' a little bitty more movin' evertime yoh gonna touch her. Dat way dey gonna come to da party nice and natural and wake up in ya bed like it der own.'

'How long should this slow process take, Joe?' I asked, thinking I had just over three weeks of my leave left.

Joe Popkin appeared to be giving this some serious thought. 'Well now, I reckon about fordy-eight hours,' he said finally. When we arrived at the Bellevue we shook hands and I thanked him. He handed me a box. 'Da Judge, he says you cain't keep a mudder an' chil' on a lootenant pay. Dere two dozen US naval issue in dere; yoh wan' more, jes ask, yoh heah now?' I thanked him and secretly appreciated his optimism that I'd be fortunate enough to use twenty-four and then request more! 'Now remember, Nick, slow action! Wid a woman evert'in' gotta be reeeaaal slow – evert'in',' he advised. He pushed the Packard into gear and pulled away. I could hear him chuckling as he steered the big car through the browned-out streets.

The following day at lunch with the little bloke and the chief, Sally was in attendance looking good enough to eat with a spoon. When she'd left to fetch our drinks, Chief Lewinski asked, 'How're you going with the pretty broad, son?'

'Does everyone know everything around here?' I protested. 'I've taken her to the movies, then dancing, just the once. We're going out tonight again, touch wood. She's agreed, but thinks her mum may be coming from Toowoomba.'

'Joe told me,' Kevin said. 'Her mom got herself a nice bunch o' roses and all three girls in da apartment dey gonna take her to da movies and den dinner. Sally gonna be available. It's all set up, buddy. She's comin' and she's wearing her best gown.'

'Huh? What's all that mean?'

'Joe says, one o' da most certain moves in slow action is ta show da object o' your desire dat yoh a real classy guy.' He spread his hands. 'So yoh gotta take her to a real classy joint.'

'What, Lennons?' Lennons Hotel was where General MacArthur was billeted.

'Nah, any two-bit officer can do dat – too many guys promisin' der girlfriend dey gonna see da cockamamie general.'

'Where then?'

Chief Lewinski then said, 'Wear ya uniform wit all da ribbons and take your Navy Cross ribbon. When ya get dere, take my advice, son, pin it on – ain't going to be no fuckin' limeys dere.'

'But where's "there"?' I asked again.

'It's wait and see time, buddy. Joe will pick you up nineteen-hunnert hours outside, den to Sally. Your table's booked for twenny-hunnert hours. No tips to da waiters – ya keep ya money in ya pocket.'

Promptly at seven Joe Popkin arrived in the Packard wearing his dress uniform. I jumped in the front. 'C'mon, Joe, play fair, where are we going?'

He grinned. 'Nick, I get mah black ass kicked iffen I tell yoh, man!' He handed me a small box and I opened it to see it contained a large white orchid with a pinkish throat. 'She wearin' a nice blue dress, like da sky, dat orchid go nicely wid it,' Joe said, smiling in a proprietorial manner.

'Does everyone except me know everything around here?' I asked.

'Dis da best slow move, Nick, patient is da virtue. Forty-eight hour it nearly passed, man. Soon yoh got yohself more chick love dan I sincerely hope yoh can handle.'

'Oh,' I said, 'it's all settled then?'

'It's da slow movin' guy dat catch da fly,' he said mysteriously.

Arriving outside the block of flats, I climbed the stairs and knocked on the door, a bit nervous at the idea of meeting Sally's mother and the three flatmates who might not approve of me. A lady opened the door and, holding it open, stood back and looked at me.

'Good evening, Mrs Forsythe,' I said.

'Well!' she said. 'Oh yes, I do approve.' It wasn't hard to see where Sally's looks came from.

Sally came to the door. 'Hello, Nick,' she said. Then twirling around to show off her dress she asked, 'Do you like it?'

She looked stunning: her blonde hair and deep-blue eyes matched the blue silk taffeta gown, which had a bodice that was cut low and off the shoulder. It clung to her body so that her every movement was accentuated. Before the war, the evening dresses I remembered seeing had wide extravagant skirts, but wartime austerity demanded the use of minimal material (if any could be found), and I must say, austerity had one good thing going for it – the result was drop-dead sexy. She also wore silver sequined high-heeled shoes (I mean, they were *really* high!) and pearl earrings which she later told me she'd borrowed from her mum. She'd done something to her eyes that was marvellous and her lips were painted Rita Hayworth-red. I stood there like a dimwit with my mouth half open. She'd simply blown me away.

'Well, come on, handsome. How do I look?' she urged, her head held slightly to the side, smiling.

I swallowed hard. 'Wonderful,' I said; my voice suddenly grown hoarse came out almost as a croak.

'I think he approves, darling,' her mum said, laughing. 'Come in, Nick.'

I handed Sally the box and she squealed with delight when she opened it. She ran to the bathroom and appeared a minute or so later wearing the orchid, not on her dress as I'd assumed, but in her hair. 'Wow!' was all I could think to say; I was honestly and truly bowled over.

Her three flatmates emerged from their bedrooms and we all said hello. Moments after we'd left the flat I couldn't have told you if they were collectively brunettes, redheads or blondes, pretty or plain. I simply couldn't take my eyes off Sally Forsythe.

Joe Popkin was waiting for us next to the Packard and I introduced Sally to him. 'Evenin', ma'am,' he said politely, not extending his hand.

'Mr Popkin! I've heard all about you. You're the hammerman! Saved Da Judge in the reformatory!' Sally exclaimed, genuinely excited to meet him. 'Da Judge often talks about you.'

'Yeah, I got dat message, ma'am,' Joe said, smiling, although I think a little embarrassed. 'Da Judge, he got a big mouth,' he chuckled, shaking his head.

Then, impulsively, Sally stood on tiptoe and kissed him. I thought for a moment that the big black bloke was going to collapse on the spot. Then he smiled, touching his cheek. In one spontaneous gesture Sally had won his heart forever.

We climbed into the back of the car, Joe holding the door open. Once inside and settled Sally said, 'I'm so excited, Nick – where are we going?'

'Ask Joe,' I said. 'I haven't a clue.'

'Hospital, ma'am.'

There was a second of silence as we took this in. 'Hospital?' we both exclaimed.

'Yes, ma'am,' Joe replied politely.

'Is this some sort of practical joke, Joe?' I asked. 'Because if it is —'

'No, Nick, patient da virtue, wait on. Dis a hospital even Da Judge and da chief, dey cain't get in.'

I turned and looked at Sally; we were both mystified. 'Why would they want to?' I enquired.

'Cos everbody want to! Nearly dere,' Joe said enigmatically.

We hadn't gone much further when we turned into a road with a sign that read 'US Navy Mobile Hospital No. 9. Camp Hill'.

'Jesus, what now?' I whispered.

'We nearly arrive, Nick.' He braked the big Packard and turned to me. 'Da chief, he say, yoh gotta pin dat Navy Cross ribbon.'

I think by this time Sally was close to tears. I fished the ribbon from my outside jacket pocket and pinned it beside the DSC. Then Joe Popkin accelerated and we proceeded down the road. Moments later we heard the strains of a Glenn Miller tune coming from what sounded like a swing band. We drove into a gravelled circular driveway and halted outside a building that was ablaze with light. 'If this is a hospital, then the patients are having a whale of a time,' I said in an effort to cheer Sally.

'Dis hospital got two t'ousan' patient, Nick.' Then Joe started to chuckle. 'It also got da navy senior officers' club, da best in da land. Admiral Ben J. Horn office, dey make da arrangements. Da Admiral 'pologises he cain't be wid yoh all tonight, but he want yoh to have a good time and evert'in' took care of; no money change hands.'

'Shit!' I exclaimed, temporarily forgetting there was a lady in the car.

Sally giggled. 'Nick, come to think of it, I've heard it mentioned in hushed tones at the Bellevue, but I never dreamed . . . Oh, are we posh enough?' she suddenly exclaimed.

'Don' cha worry, ma'am, yoh gonna be da prettiest dere. All dem doctor, admiral, dey gonna want to dance wid yoh. Nick, dat der Navy Cross, dey gonna be fallin' over demself. I be back here t'enty-tree hunnert hours but yoh c'n stay long as yoh want. Be happy, enjoy, I'll be waitin'.' He grinned as he let us out of the back of the big two-star car.

It turned out to be one of the most enjoyable going-out-somewhere nights of my life so far. Lots of top brass (there weren't any other kind), one of them a captain, came up to our table to congratulate me on my award, though it wasn't too difficult to see that the captain's primary motive was to get a closer squiz at Sally. He couldn't take his eyes off her, and sent a bottle of French champagne over to our table. He was fairly young for his rank, no more than forty I'd say, so he must have been a bright bloke. For the first time we both tasted caviar, Sally with champagne, me with Coca-Cola – not quite the same experience. We ate and danced and it was easy to see Sally was having a great time. She went to the powder room around ten o'clock to freshen up and came back smiling. 'All the women want to know where I found you, Nick. I could see they didn't believe me when I said, "I served him a Coke from behind the bar at the Bellevue Hotel."' She laughed. 'One of them, an older woman, turned to the others and said, "Not only stunning, but she's also got a great sense of humour!"'

We danced until we nearly dropped and it was one o'clock when we came out of the club to find Joe waiting, asleep behind the wheel. We took Sally home, the mother factor preventing anything else. But on the way she snuggled into me in the back of the Packard, and Sally's kissing had the same David Livingstone intrepid-explorer touch the Virgin Mary had perfected in Melbourne.

I was bushed beyond belief and when I got back to the Bellevue and thanked Joe he said, 'Nevah yoh mine, Nick. Ain't no man evah gonna beat da mudder factor. I reckon yoh was right on time to catch dat fly. Da contrack herewith cancelled. I reckon we gonna renegotiate. Yoh got yourself 'nother forty-eight hours extension, yoh heah?' I laughed, thanking him for the night. 'Yoh heah me now, boy!' he said, pulling away and, as usual, chuckling to himself.

I realised I wasn't quite as far into my recovery from the malaria and jaundice as I'd supposed. I slept until twelve the next day and only woke when Sally phoned to say the little bloke and the chief were expecting to have lunch with me in half an hour. She greeted me at the bar, looking like magic. 'Mum's going home this afternoon,' she announced. 'She said to say goodbye,' she laughed. 'You've got the royal seal of approval.'

At seven that evening, after the cocktail hour, when Sally finished work and I'd arranged to pick her up, she handed me a small canvas bag. 'Can you take this upstairs? Keep it for me 'til later. I just want to freshen my make-up. See you in the foyer in five minutes,' she said in a perfectly natural voice.

I guess I should have cottoned on, but I still wasn't sparking on all eight cylinders from the night before. I went upstairs, dumped the little bag and came back down again to find Sally waiting. Halfway through dinner at a local café, Sally said to me with a mischievous grin, 'Did you peek into the bag?'

'Of course not!' I said, genuinely shocked.

'Someone help me!' she sighed. 'Nick Duncan, what am I going to do with you?' she asked in apparent despair.

'What?' I asked. 'I wouldn't do a thing like that. Look into a lady's bag?'

'I should have guessed,' she sighed. 'Navy Cross, Distinguished Service Cross, commendation from the marines – you'd think with a record like that you'd be capable of just a little, I mean a teensy-weensy bit of personal initiative.'

'Sally, what the hell are you talking about?' I asked, completely mystified.

'What happens if the cap comes off the toothpaste and squeezes all over my fresh bra and panties for the morning?' she giggled.

I'd made it with time to spare on Joe 'Hammer-man' Popkin's renegotiated 'patient is da virtue' slow-move contract. He'd allowed me forty-eight hours but I'd made it in thirty-one, not counting the time it took to finish dinner, get back to the hotel, climb the stairs and check the toothpaste tube.

CHAPTER TWENTY-ONE

'Darling Nick,
I'm seeing the surgeon.
Will never forget you,
Love
Sally XXX

P.S. Mum sends her love.'

Sally Forsythe
Brisbane, 1943

SALLY FORSYTHE AND I spent a glorious three weeks together – she only had to descend the stairs to start work with the lunchtime crowd at noon and her shift ended after the cocktail hour at seven in the evening. As that lovely saying goes, they were 'days of wine and roses'.

The little bloke was more than kind, extremely generous and a great deal more grown-up. His lady, the quick-firing but loving Bren Gun, had all but eliminated the 'f' word from his vocabulary, reducing his use of it to occasions of real agitation. Although it was early times and Brenda, fortunately also a Catholic, was the kind of girl who would dutifully and willingly respect a mourning period for her soldier husband, their relationship nevertheless had a permanent, comfortable feel about it.

In Joe 'Hammer-man' Popkin I had made another friend I hoped never to lose, although in a time of war, permanent friendship is always a dangerous pursuit. I had written to Colonel Woon to ascertain the whereabouts of Gojo Mura. He'd replied to say that Gojo had been placed in a prisoner of war holding camp in Luganville, but he'd emphasised that Gojo was technically a Japanese civilian and he'd requested that he be sent to Australia. At this stage Marg got involved and, through the Services Reconnaissance Department, pushed through the official paperwork requesting the Americans to transfer him to our new facility for civilian Japanese prisoners of war at Hay in New South Wales. She may only have been a newly promoted naval lieutenant but I was constantly made aware that Marg Hamilton was a great deal more than she appeared to be. She also sent Gojo Mura two new sketchpads and a professional set of 'quite impossible to find' watercolours that, of course, she'd duly procured somewhere.

I was headed back to the marines who were recovering in Melbourne and would be rested until October. While this might seem a long time to be out of a combat zone, it was, in fact, only just sufficient to bring the battered, the weary and the sick back to health and fighting fitness and to re-equip them. After taking the leave owed to me I was to return to Fraser Island for much the same period and reasons. In the Machiavellian mind of Commander Long, I was a legitimate combat hero with the Americans and therefore regarded as a tiny cog in the wheels of mutual cooperation. Or that's how Marg Hamilton put it, in a letter where she once again urged me to resign from Intelligence and the clutches of the SRD. 'You've more than done your bit, Nick,' she'd urged. 'You have your whole life ahead of you and you're entitled to sit out the rest of the war in a job that keeps you interested, occupied and safe. I'm sure the navy can find just the right billet.' This was, of course, shorthand for: 'I've talked to Rob Rich and he'll arrange something away from the machinations of the SRD, Naval Intelligence and Rupert Basil Michael Long.'

However, the original obsession to find my father remained. There had been no news out of Japanese-occupied Rabaul and he might well have been dead, but I couldn't in all conscience rest until I knew his fate. Though our own troops were in New Guinea, some of the marines were probably going to be based at Goodenough Island in the D'Entrecasteaux Group to the east of New Guinea, and this seemed to offer the better option of eventually getting me into New Britain.

The paradox, of course, is that I had arrived in Guadalcanal fighting fit: probably in a better physical state than Joe Louis would have been when he defended his world heavyweight title against the German heavyweight Max Schmeling in 1938. Within four months the islands had chewed me up and spat me out, carrying the scars of the work of battle, stress, malaria, jaundice and a whole heap of unknown intestinal bugs and infections.

I'd been restored to health in Australia; now I was to be trained even more specifically, my fitness regained and I would be returned to the islands so the whole process would begin again. In my case I was a willing participant, but this was not so for many others. Tens of thousands of Allied soldiers, including my own 1st Division marines, were patched up in hospital, rested, re-equipped, then sent back to combat under the same previous conditions. This back-you-go-again routine was fair enough in the European theatre of war, where a rest and repair job might get a soldier back to being fighting fit, but malaria was something you couldn't cure with a pill or a week in hospital.

The disease usually lingers on for years and you can quickly become reinfected.

The majority of casualties sustained in the war conducted in the south-west Pacific could be attributed to the sting of the *anopheles* mosquito rather than to being wounded from a bullet, mortar, hand grenade or enemy artillery fire. God knows how many of the enemy were struck down in the same way, but it eventually transpired that the Japanese lost ninety per cent of all the troops they sent to the islands.

When Naval Intelligence had informed me that I was returning to the marines I had hoped it might be to Colonel Woon's mob, but Japanese–American translators such as Lee Roy Yamamoto (Da Nip widda Chip) had proved so successful that I wasn't required in my capacity as a translator and interrogator. Instead, there was more interest in my local coastal knowledge and the fact that I could liaise with the natives using pidgin English and a few local languages with which I was familiar. In effect I was finally to become, in part anyway, a coastwatcher – and this required me to get fit and undertake a refresher course on Fraser Island.

As I mentioned previously, my stay in Brisbane had been wonderful and Sally Forsythe had given me a tearful farewell and we'd promised to write to each other. She'd been loving and perfectly wonderful, and probably, with the exception of Anna, the best-looking of the women I'd known. But with the loss of Marg Hamilton I'd grown up a fair bit and realised that in affairs of the heart the warrior going off to war can't, or shouldn't, make permanent plans. On the morning of my last day in Brisbane, after we'd made love, Sally, sitting astride me, suddenly cried out, 'Oh, Nick, I'm going to miss you awfully! Whatever will I do without you?'

I still blush when I think about it, but I gave her a serious look and then launched into a totally pompous speech about not waiting for the soldier boy to return; that times were uncertain; that I was eventually going back to the islands; anything could happen and that I'd be upset, I think I said 'saddened', if she (this is the pompous prick bit) remained celibate when I was gone. Ouch! Marg Hamilton would not have talked to me for a week if she'd known I was capable of spouting such arrant and presumptuous juvenile crap.

Sally cried a bit but then sniffed and dried her tears on the edge of the sheet and said, 'Do you remember the American naval captain who sent us the champagne at the officers' club?' I nodded. 'Well, he's from Boston and a senior surgeon at the hospital and he's been downstairs at the bar at least eight times since then.'

'Yeah?' I said, taken by surprise, but then fortunately recovered sufficiently to cover it up by saying, 'I ought to go downstairs and punch him on the nose.'

Sally looked shocked. 'You will do no such thing, Nick Duncan! He's a very nice man and hasn't made a single advance!' She grinned down at me. 'Yet.'

How's that for a classy rebuttal? She was four years older than me and it showed in the sophistication of her reply and the arrogance of mine. Later I would comfort myself with the thought that at least she'd climbed up the promotional ladder while remaining with the navy. I also feel sure her mum would have approved – even if the surgeon captain was old enough to be *her* husband. Young naval lieutenants are not the world's greatest catch.

The little bloke and I had lunch together on my last day in Brisbane, again in the private alcove where we could talk unheard and undisturbed. Kevin had changed, not only because of the influence of the Bren Gun, but also because of his quartermaster responsibilities and by being exposed to Chief Lewinski, a permanent navy man who had become almost a surrogate father. Kevin was savvy, but I was about to find out just how much he had learned. After a dozen oysters Kilpatrick he leaned over the table. 'What yoh gonna do after da war, buddy?' he asked in a confidential voice, even though nobody could hear us.

'Huh?' I was taken aback. After the pompous little talk I'd given Sally that very morning, 'after the war' was an impossible thought. Of course, the fantasy of sailing to Java and rescuing Anna had always been present. But that was Duncan dreaming; I was smart enough to know stuff like that didn't lie within the context of the little bloke's question.

'Nick, this gonna all be over inna next three years, maybe a little longer. After da war everybody gonna go home and celebrate peace and goodwill, dey ain't gonna want to ever come back to da islands – da hula-hula in da South Seas ain't no attraction no more. Home and family, apple pie and picket fence, automobiles, Chevy, Ford, Chrysler, dat's da American way. So what's gonna be left behind? Answer me dat, buddy?'

I looked at him, mystified. 'Stuffed if I know, Kevin. The local people picking up the pieces?'

'Hey, dat ain't so stupid!' He laughed. 'Pickin' up da pieces! Do yoh know what ya sayin', buddy?'

I continued to look at him, completely bewildered. 'I'm not sure I understand what you mean, mate.'

'Scrap!' he said, just the one word. Moments later he added, 'Metal.'

'Scrap metal?' I asked.

'Connection! Nick, da Pacific, it littered wit war junk. Non-ferrous metals, copper, brass, lead, bronze. It a gold mine, buddy, 'cept we don't have ter dig for it. Joe and me, we partners and you, Nick, we want you to climb aboard. You da thurd, we da three musketeer.'

'And D'Artagnan,' I said, being a smart arse. He was the inspiration for the fictional adventures of the little gang that was dedicated to justice and the French way.

'Who? Wha' cha talkin' 'bout, Nick?'

'The man whose life was the basis for the adventures of the three musketeers.'

'Nick, yoh gotta stop readin' all dem cockamamie books, it de-fin-ately affectin' ya brains.'

'Well, thank you, Kevin.'

'Maybe dere gonna be four,' he said impatiently, 'but we da three, buddy. Maybe Chief Lewinski, when he retire from da navy, he can be da number four. Da miners everywhere, dey been so greedy dey pickin' da rim around der ass and sellin' it to da US Government at da top price. Dey over-capitalised. Come da end of da war, manufacturers ain't gonna pay da mining companies da money dey bin gettin' from da US Government. Dey gonna go broke. Dere's gonna be shortages o' everthin'. Da manufacturers gonna be lookin' for cheap foundry metal and it ain't gonna be dere.' His excitement was palpable. ''Cept, halleluja! Dere enough scrap lying around da islands to feed da post-war furnaces in da US of A, England, Europe, everywhere!'

Getting a lecture on post-war economics, about which, incidentally, I knew nothing, was the last thing I expected from the little bloke.

'So? Partners help each other, make a contribution, how the hell do I fit in?' I asked, mystified. The sheer absurdity of the idea overwhelmed me, then moments later, the possible genius of the concept hit – not that I was sufficiently knowledgeable in such matters to be able to judge which of the two it was. In the end all I knew was that it was a concept, nothing more. Supplying cheap metal to the foundry furnaces of the world was about as far removed as you could get from the experience of an Anglican missionary's son who hunted butterflies.

Kevin, starting with Guadalcanal, commenced to elaborate on the grand plan. While in the islands I was to map out every dump, every ship's prow sticking out of a bay, every wreck (ours or Japanese) found on the beaches, every artillery cache or abandoned airfield I came across. 'If we get a start on da competition, den dat all we gonna need,' Kevin assured me.

'Hey, wait on; this isn't the Klondike gold rush, you can't just stake a claim. How do we move the stuff we find?' I might have known nothing, but at least I knew to ask that particular question. Finding something weighing several hundred tons was one thing, getting it somewhere else quite another.

'Dat Joe's job,' Kevin assured me.

'No, that's not what I mean. Chartering ships, that takes money.'

'Hey, buddy, already ya startin' ter think,' the little bloke said, smiling. 'Goddamn right it takes money!'

'Well, yeah?' I said, thinking we'd reached some sort of impasse. 'Where's it coming from?' It seemed a reasonable question.

'Dat da second part of dis meetin' – er, lunch, Nick.'

At that moment the waiter arrived with the main course: steak, mashed potato and green beans. We'd both ordered the same meal but Kevin's was covered in a pepper gravy, the speciality of the house, while mine was the tried and true, mum's-Sunday-lunch-after-church variety. While the waiter fussed about, the little bloke took out his cigar case and selected a Cuban cigar, carefully cut the end and lit it with his black Zippo lighter. It seemed a strange time to be lighting up, but there you go. The waiter departed after asking if everything was to our satisfaction. 'Yeah, yeah, thank you, Fernando,' Kevin said impatiently, waving him away with his cigar.

When the waiter had gone, the little bloke reached down and picked up a small Globite suitcase of the kind a kid would take to school. It was made of some sort of reconstituted cardboard. He placed the case on the table, turned it to face me and, reaching over, used the ball of his thumbs to click it open, pulling the lid back under his chin. 'Five t'ousand pounds,' he said calmly.

'Fuck!' I exclaimed. I'd never seen anything remotely like that amount of money in one place, let alone in a kid's school suitcase.

'We gonna buy three o' dem wooden vessels built here in Australia and used for harbour and coastal defence work. Dey da best. Eighty feet long, forward hold, two-ton derrick cargo, 8LW Gardner diesel, deckhouse and cabin at rear. You know dem, Nick?'

'Yes, of course,' I said. 'They're a good, sturdy vessel, ideal for that kind of job.' I had to admit, the little bloke's grasp of detail was beginning to impress me. If this was a pie-in-the-sky scheme, the money in front of me on the table and the fact that he'd got the shipping requirements correct left me bewildered; these were real meaty chunks in the sky pie.

'After da war dey gonna got too many dem boats. Maybe we pay a t'ousand pounds, maybe less; it up to you, Nick.' He paused. I'd long since started tucking into my meal but Kevin hadn't touched his; the pepper steak sauce was turning grey and growing a skin. The little bloke pulled on his cigar and exhaled, the sweet-smelling smoke clouding the alcove. 'But now we got us a big problem, Nick,' he said finally.

'What's that, mate?' I asked.

He waved the cigar at the suitcase. 'If I take dat back Stateside, dey gonna lock me up in San Quentin twenny years! You mention before you got a bank account wit your father, Nick?'

'Sure, Bank of New South Wales. Right now it has forty-two pounds, ten shillings and sixpence in it.' I laughed. 'It's probably never carried more than a hundred pounds.'

'Look like it gonna grow big all a sudden,' Kevin grinned.

'Christ, what if the bank manager asks?'

'Chief Lewinski says dey don't never gonna ask,' he chuckled, 'but if he do, ya gonna tell him yoh robbed a bank.' He looked at me seriously. 'If da manager ask just say "mine your own business". Dat Chief Lewinski's good advice. Den if dere no bank heist in da noospaper next mornin', you ain't never gonna hear a peep from dat bank manager again. He gonna be smilin', waitin' for his next promotion.' Kevin suddenly looked down at his plate. 'Dis fuckin' food is cold!' he exclaimed.

Chief Lewinski's advice had been correct. The bank manager had stared pop-eyed at the contents of the Globite suitcase but remained silent. Kevin was made co-signatory on our account. Before we left, the little bloke stabbed his cigar towards the manager. 'Dis only da beginnin'; we's gonna be puttin' more in time ta time. Nex' time I come we gonna maybe talk 'bout an interest increase earnin' rate, Mister Bank Manager?'

Kevin insisted Joe Popkin drive me to Maryborough, the staging point for Fraser Island. 'Yoh gonna take good care o' yourself, Nick, we got business.' He paused and grinned. 'Put ya hand over ya heart.' I hesitated, not sure what he meant. 'Go on, do it, buddy.' I placed my hand over my heart. 'Now repeat after me, "I want yer to unnerstan', I ain't no fuckin' hero!"'

We arrived at the landing pier in Maryborough just as the sun was setting. I guess the conducting officer would have been expecting me to arrive on the army truck that was coming from Brisbane, bringing the other men who were recovering from New Guinea or embarking on a Z Force course. A weedy-looking lieutenant approached as we arrived and seeing my rank stared at me with puckered mouth. You could see at a glance he was officious and full of his own importance. He didn't look a bit impressed when I stepped out of the big olive Packard staff car.

Joe Popkin, jumping from the car, saluted him as he stood glaring at me. 'Excuse me, iffen you don' min' mah sayin', sah? Lootenant Duncan, as yoh can see, is in da navy. Dat mean he got superior rank to yoh. Dat mean yoh gotta salute him, sah.'

'That's all right, Joe, the lieutenant is in the army, he doesn't know any better,' I suggested. The suddenly indignant lieutenant, colouring furiously, might not have known that a navy lieutenant is equivalent in rank to an army captain. Joe was a very big guy and I wasn't too small myself, and so I got a reluctant salute, which I promptly returned. 'Nick Duncan. Nice to meet you, Lieutenant.' Then I asked *sotto voce*, 'Your name?' I was playing games, forcing him to call me 'sir'.

'Neville Turkiton, sir. The barge is due in. Make your way down please, Lieutenant,' he instructed, avoiding a second 'sir'.

'I'll tell da admiral yoh arrived safely, sah?' Joe suddenly said to me. 'He gonna be real glad to heah dat.'

Lieutenant Turkiton turned abruptly and walked towards the landing pier.

'Dat lootenant, he named good,' Joe Popkin chuckled as we watched the officer's retreating back. 'Dat guy a real turkey.'

The canvas-covered army truck with the remainder of the contingent for Fraser bumped into view and shortly afterwards, just as it was growing dark, the barge pulled in to take us on the two-hour trip across the bay to the island.

Arriving on Fraser the barge pulled up to the beach and we walked down the ramp to be met by a waiting Sergeant Major Wainwright and the other instructors standing under a row of gas lamps They had hurricane lamps rigged on poles and a barbecue going, for the smell of roasted meat reached me, wafting in the clean evening air. When it came my turn to shake hands with Wainwright he looked me up and down. 'Bastard islands.' He pronounced it 'basstid'. 'You've been through the mangle, haven't you, boyo?'

I laughed. 'Nothing you didn't tell me to expect, Sergeant Major.'

'Well, Nick, you're no use to me or anyone else until you're fit again. You wouldn't last two days the way you are. We're growing accustomed to your lot coming in from New Guinea and the other islands looking like walking cadavers. You're here for several months, so there's plenty of time to get you back into fighting condition. In the meantime we've set up a holiday camp for the desperate and the shagged.' (*If only he'd known about the generosity of Sally*, I thought.) Then he said softly, out of earshot of the others, 'I'm bloody proud of you, son.' It hadn't taken more than five seconds to say, but coming from him, it meant a great deal more to me than the twenty seconds the goanna pinning had taken from the general. What's more, this time I was wearing trousers.

'Thanks, Sergeant Major. Just lucky, I guess. Wrong place at the right time.'

He pointed to my kitbag. 'Did you bring your popgun, boyo?'

'How'd you know about that?' I asked, amazed.

'We like to keep an eye on our favourite sons,' he replied, not explaining further.

'Yeah. It's a tad worse for wear: needs a new paint job; I don't have any cartridges left and I dumped all but one of the magazines.' I grinned. 'But the Owen gun is clean and oiled, Sergeant Major.'

A group of us, all worn-out warriors, mostly from New Guinea and the other islands, were taken to a small beach where they'd set up the so-called holiday camp tents. We were expected to start getting fit at our own pace. Given an edict like that was not an excuse to take things easy, as Wainwright knew that we were keener even than he was to see us get back into shape. But malaria, jaundice and assorted intestinal bugs take a fair recovery time, the jaundice in particular, and compared to some of the other blokes, I wasn't in such bad shape. In two weeks I was running again, no more than three miles and at a pathetic pace, but nevertheless it felt good and I knew I was on the mend. I received two nice chatty letters from Sally and then a third, this one only a two-liner with a P.S. added:

Darling Nick,
I'm seeing the surgeon.
Will never forget you,
Love
Sally XXX

P.S. Mum sends her love.

How could I possibly feel sorry for myself? But I did.

After I'd recovered my fitness sufficiently to get stuck into the hard yakka under the stern and sometimes paternal guidance of Sergeant Major Wainwright, the days became long and had to be taken in deadly earnest. It was much the same training as on the previous occasion but with more unarmed combat, instruction on the new up-to-date radio equipment, some fairly delicate high explosives work and the setting and avoidance of booby-traps. Then there were lessons on the use of folboats – folding rubberised canvas kayaks, great for infiltration purposes. I loved these dearly and couldn't think of a better way to exercise early in the morning and again at dusk, paddling through the surf, with fish and dolphins jumping around the little craft. Most of our training was onerous, but this part was magic. I was also sent off to Richmond Air Base to undergo a parachute training course. I wasn't much looking forward to it. I understood and loved the sea, but falling out of the sky wasn't, I imagined, what a navy man should be expected to do. However, I was quite wrong and hugely enjoyed the entire experience. The months passed quickly. In this type of training there isn't any time to be bored. October came, the month when I was due to rejoin the marines who were heading back to the islands. I was my old self again. I'd regained the weight I'd lost and as the saying goes, I wasn't carrying an ounce of fat.

I didn't travel with the marines but went separately by an American B-17 to Goodenough Island, over the strait to the north of New Guinea. A great deal had happened in the ten months since leaving Guadalcanal and the pace of activity was speeding up as, increasingly, the Japanese were being forced onto the back foot.

Elements of the 1st Division marines began arriving on the island by ship on the 24th of October. Unfortunately it had been decided that Colonel Greg Woon, Belgiovani and Da Nip widda Chip (Lee Roy Yamamoto), heading a vastly expanded radio intelligence unit, were to be stationed at Milne Bay.

It was good being back with the Americans, who were fit and re-equipped with M1 Garand semi-automatic rifles and an enormous range of amphibious craft. The news seemed to get around that 'Popgun Pete' was back and within days I was getting the usual banter on my morning runs. Sergeant Major Wainwright had personally repainted the camouflage on my Owen and handed it back to me on my day of departure. 'Goodbye, boyo. I don't want to see you coming back with anything but a good conduct award. Take my advice and stay out of the rough stuff this time – we're beginning to get the Japs on the run, but that doesn't mean you've got to be out in front chasing them.'

While the marines engaged in their final re-invasion training we undertook a series of reconnaissance missions at night. Landing from PT boats, we paddled ashore in rubber inflatables. The idea was to seek out the best landing beaches for the invasion and to establish the whereabouts of Japanese defensive positions. It was rather hairy stuff, particularly when the moon was full. If the Japs had spotted us landing there wasn't a lot we could have done to defend ourselves.

The first of the major amphibious assaults took place at and around Cape Gloucester in the south-west on the 26th of December 1943 and, despite the difficult terrain, the Japanese were routed. The job of chasing them all the way back to Rabaul was taken over by American army units who were later relieved by Australian troops.

It was around this time that I found myself once again at the pointy end of the war. The 1st Division marines had departed but I had requested to remain behind in New Britain for obvious reasons. For the first time in combat conditions I was placed under Australian command: with Major Peter McVitty from the ANGAU, the Australian New Guinea Administration Unit. The Japanese were now restricted to Rabaul and the Gazelle Peninsula; they couldn't break out and couldn't supply themselves by air or sea. In strategic terms they had nowhere to go. Despite this, they had to be contained as the presence of such a large, well-equipped force behind our advance posed a serious local threat.

I was on New Britain soil at last and it was now that my personal and private war began in earnest. We – twenty-nine coastwatchers commanding four hundred armed native troops – were put at the front end of the invasion. Our task was to ambush any Japanese patrols who attempted to venture beyond the immediate area of Rabaul or the Peninsula.

I selected ten men. You can move fast and silently with ten good natives, whereas any more tends to slow you down. I chose Tolai warriors for two reasons: the first being that I had a working knowledge of their language, and the second being that they had a reason to hate the Japanese.

The Tolai are a clever and sophisticated people with an age-old tradition as coastal traders. I'd learned their language while moving around the island in the mission boat and, besides, knew that they had their wits about them. Furthermore, because of their trading tradition, they could speak a number of the other tribal languages. This was particularly useful when we came upon native villages where the inhabitants didn't speak pidgin.

However, perhaps most importantly, the Tolai had a particular axe to grind against the Japanese. Many of their women had been systematically raped and their men and children murdered by enemy soldiers. In numerous cases, family members had starved to death when the Japs had plundered their village food gardens.

For them, as for me, it was payback time. I hadn't told anyone of my plan to attempt to locate my father or, should I discover that he was dead, that I wanted to find out how his death had occurred. Intelligence organisations in particular hate that sort of personal crusade, vendetta, assignation, whatever, as it invariably leads to an operator in the field taking unnecessary risks. Had the powers-that-be known of my intention (in fact, my sole reason for going to the New Britain area), they would have withdrawn me from that particular combat zone. Marg Hamilton was the only one who knew and I trusted her to keep it to herself.

The action soon became fairly rugged. 'Merciless' might be a better word, as we conducted a guerrilla war against Japanese patrols attempting to venture beyond Rabaul. It took almost a year but we gradually confined them to within thirty miles of their completely encircled base. The final squeeze was on. We were dealing with a starving and desperate enemy who were reduced to starting their own vegetable gardens to stay alive. Desperate men do desperate things, and when we encountered a Jap patrol it was on for one and all.

The Tolai had led us to the mass grave of one hundred and thirty Australian troops who had been massacred at a place known as Tol Plantation. Their hands had been tied behind their backs with wire and they had been shot or butchered using bayonets; some had had their heads removed. When you witness this kind of thing all thought of mercy disappears, and I did nothing to stop the obvious pleasure my Tolai warriors took in killing every man in the Japanese patrols we ambushed. Taking prisoners was out of the question, anyway – we were a fast-moving, small fighting unit and it became simply a matter of kill or be killed.

I was beginning to fear that my war experiences were turning me into a man without compassion. For month after month we hunted enemy patrols; it was dark, dispassionate and remorseless work and my conscience played no part in the proceedings. Killing became routine, payback was my excuse if I needed one. We knew that if we were captured alive we would be tortured and then executed in a ruthless manner by the enemy.

We were patrolling in the mountains to the south-west of Rabaul where the Japanese were contained. We'd been making contact with the villages in the heart of the jungle to re-establish the

Australian presence on the island, and were close to the end
of our field trip. We'd been fortunate not to meet any Japanese
patrols and I was looking forward to returning to our base near
Wide Bay on the Gazelle Peninsula, a hot shower, a square meal
and a decent sleep. We'd stopped in a clearing outside a village
and as was customary, Ellison, my sergeant, entered to check it
out. We were having our evening meal – bully beef and cold
boiled yam – when he returned with a local in tow who now
stood in the shadows of the tall trees.

'One fella boy long hia, hem like lookim yu. This fella hemi
say hem nao savvy you long time befo.' What Ellison was saying
was that he'd brought along a villager who claimed he knew
me. I called for the man to step out of the dark. He emerged
hesitantly and I was overjoyed to see it was Peter Paul, one of
the crewmen off the mission schooner. We shook hands in the
native manner, holding hands as he told me the joyous news.

'Daddy belong yu stap long village closeap long hia. Emi
sick tumas and mifella wait long time for yufella long army for
come back long hia. Man Japon closup spoilem hem finish but
mifella takim out long town back long place blo mifella.' ('Your
dad is in a village close to here. The Japanese tortured him and
left him for dead, but we took him from Rabaul to my village to
recover.')

We left at first light and six hours later, just after 1300
hours, we arrived at a typical Melanesian village set in a clearing.
These places always reminded me of what a hopeless battle man
fought against nature. The giant trees towering impossibly high
formed a wall that was seemingly impenetrable, yet the sunlight
glared down on the clearing to bring growth to small subsistence
gardens on which the villagers depended. The huts, built on
piles roughly three feet from the bare earth, were arranged in an

irregular triangle. I watched as a ubiquitous black sow snuffled under one of the thatched huts; the tips of her pink teats where her piglets had been suckling were the only clean parts of her hairy, black, mud-encrusted body. Seven piglets quarrelled and squealed around her. Village curs with their ribs showing and their tails between their skinny back legs sniffed lethargically at the things all dogs seem to check out with their noses, while others lay in the shade cast by a banana tree, panting with their tongues lolling, sides heaving in the torpid heat. Chickens did what chickens do, scratching and bathing in the dust, fussing as they sorted out the pecking order amongst themselves and shying away with an exclamatory squawk as the barnyard ranking adjusted itself. In the early afternoon the day had grown weary.

The village was exactly where we shouldn't have been – deep inside Japanese-held territory. It occurred to me that I'd accepted Peter Paul's information at face value and on the basis of trust earned in years past. This was a very naïve and careless assumption, and just the kind of thing Intelligence training taught one never to do. There was always the possibility that we were being led into a Japanese ambush. We approached very carefully so that the sleeping dogs failed to bark and raise the alarm.

And then I saw him. Or at least I saw a white man dozing under a paw-paw tree, seated in a crude bamboo chair. He was very thin and as brown as a nut, grey-bearded with his hair down to his shoulders. He wore a once red, faded to pink, cotton shirt with the sleeves ripped out and open at the front to reveal his scrawny chest and stomach. Below the waist he wore a *lap-lap*, the local name for a cotton sarong.

My ten warriors moved so silently that we soon fronted

him, with me standing in my customary position at the far left of the line. It was at this stage that two of the mangy mongrels decided to bark and the sleeping man woke up with a start. I still wasn't certain that this skin-and-bone individual with a beard, matted hair and deep, bruised eye sockets in his skull was indeed my father.

Bare-breasted women started to come in from the gardens with small naked children clinging to their thighs. The man rubbed his eyes, not sure he wasn't dreaming, confronted suddenly by natives in dark-green uniforms; their shirts saturated from sweat seemed to make them look even darker. Curiously, he didn't seem afraid. Instead he gave out a soft sigh of resignation as if he was trying to gather his thoughts sufficiently to make sense of the scene that confronted him in the harsh afternoon sunlight. He slowly pushed himself up from the chair and it was then that I saw the deep purple scar that ran from the centre of his chest and in a soft curve down to his stomach. Perhaps it had been made by a bayonet, or more likely an officer's sword. I could feel myself growing furious. This quiet, intellectual man of God, who'd stayed behind because he believed he understood the enemy's culture and would be able to reason with them, had been brutally assaulted, left to die, a lump of meat rotting in the tropical sun. At that moment I was willing to accept that he'd lost his senses, that my father – because I now knew it was him – had gone mad. That he'd become insane with the disappointment that the human intellect and peace and goodwill to all men couldn't be sustained. That barbarism and rapacity prevailed as the stronger force in the affairs of mankind.

His eyes travelled slowly across the faces of my Tolai soldiers and eventually reached me at the end of the line. I was wearing a slouch hat with the brim down so that my face was in shadow and now, very close to tears, I removed it.

'Nick?' he asked, uncertain, not believing. Then, 'Nick, lad – it's you?'

I moved towards him, blinded by the tears streaming down my cheeks. 'Dad – Dad, I've found you. I've bloody found you!' He stretched out a trembling hand and I steadied him gently on his feet. He placed his arms about me and rested his head on my shoulder and we both wept, his tall, skinny frame pressing against me, his frail chest heaving. It was the first time my father had ever embraced me. It was also one of the most cherished moments of my life, as I realised how very much I loved him.

My Tolai were laughing and crying at the same time, overjoyed for me. I guess the reactions to a happy ending are universal. Finally, sniffing then knuckling the tears from his eyes, my father drew back and attempted to smile. I noticed that several of his teeth had been knocked out and his nose had been broken and had mended with a bump in the centre. He'd been a good-looking bloke in his time, but now it was hard to see. 'What is the date, Nick?' was his first question.

'It's the 19th of February 1945,' I replied.

'Ah! The anniversary of the Peace of Westminster, 1674, when the English took possession of New York from the Dutch. My war is also finally over, how very appropriate.' There was bugger all wrong with the old man's mind. 'Dear boy, I do hope you've remembered to bring along something for me to read?'

I grinned. I happened to be carrying a copy of T.S. Eliot's 'The Waste Land' which I'd found in a second-hand bookshop in Brisbane. 'Hmm, how about my diary?' I teased. Unslinging my pack, I placed it on the ground in front of me and rummaging through it I produced the book containing the masterful poem. Then I handed him his spectacles. He had been notorious for losing or neglecting to bring his reading spectacles on the various occasions he'd travelled to Brisbane to attend a synod meeting, and so he'd taken to keeping a pair at the bank. Almost as a talisman I'd retrieved them from the bank manager and had packed them in my bag.

He hugged the book to his emaciated chest. 'Food, food, food at last!' he exclaimed, then spontaneously quoted:

> *'I have heard the key*
> *Turn in the door once and turn once only*
> *We think of the key, each in his prison*
> *Thinking of the key, each confirms a prison*
> *Only at nightfall, aethereal rumours*
> *Revive for a moment a broken Coriolanus.'*

Then, still not looking at the small book, he said, 'Thomas Stearns Eliot. How very apt. Thank you, my dear boy.' I guess some people are never going to change.

We carried the Reverend John Duncan on a litter back to Wide Bay, a task that took several days. Moving with ten Tolai warriors over enemy territory is a fast, silent process, but carrying a litter is a slow and sometimes noisy one as we moved through patches of dense scrub. During the time it took to get out of reach of the Japanese patrols I was in a constant state of panic. To lose my father now that I'd found him was unimaginable.

But we made it, late on the fifth day. I had sent Sergeant Ellison ahead with a note torn from my diary, requesting a launch to take my father to Cape Gloucester Airfield for evacuation to Brisbane. For the first time I went public with the search to find my dad. In the note I related the story of his torture at the hands of the Japanese, their attempt to kill him by disembowelment, leaving his body lying in the mission compound for Peter Paul to find and take to his village, and finally my discovery of him. I certainly lacked the authority to get him quickly to Brisbane, but I asked that the contents of the note be transmitted to Colonel Woon on Cape Gloucester. The 1st Division marines had departed in March '44, but his Intelligence Unit had remained behind to work with the US Army and latterly the Australian Army. The unit had moved from Milne Bay to be closer to the Australian base. I knew that he'd do everything he could to authorise the evacuation and would try to get a launch to Wide Bay.

On the track an hour out from Wide Bay we found Sergeant Ellison waiting for us. 'Mifella come back for lookim yu bakagen. Olgeta long ples blong yumi hemi lookout long yufella and daddy blong yu. Mifella go lookim olgeta nao for tellim em yufella close up come.' ('I've told them you are coming with your father and they're looking forward to your arrival. I must go back and tell them you will be there in one hour.')

We arrived at Wide Bay to find the whole base lined up to welcome us with Colonel Woon, Belgiovani and Lee Roy Yamamoto (Da Nip widda Chip) standing three paces forward in the middle of the welcoming line of Australians. Colonel Woon was in the centre and above his head, secured to two poles held aloft by the radio operators on either side, was a large white canvas banner that read:

> *Popgun Pete*
> *Arrives with*
> *Pop!*

The three Americans stood to attention and saluted me as

I arrived, Sergeant Belgiovani using his left hand to do so. It was good to see that the Brute from Brooklyn was as inept as ever. (*Whaddya mean I cain't salute wid da left hand? Da udder one was holding da goddamn banner!*) Then Major Peter McVitty from ANGAU called for three cheers from the Australians.

The launch that had brought Colonel Woon, Beljo and Yamamoto stood ready to take my father. After he'd had a shower, I'd roughly trimmed his hair using a large pair of scissors, leaving his beard intact for more competent hands than mine, and finally I'd clad him in a pair of jungle greens that hung from his emaciated frame like the drapes of a theatre curtain. From Cape Gloucester Airfield, in a series of air hops, he finally arrived in Brisbane. There he was hospitalised and visited (God knows how she managed it) by Marg Hamilton, who subsequently also organised a travel pass for him to Perth, where he could recuperate at the Archbishop's palace.

The next few months went by in what had become routine jungle work – if it can be said that there is such a thing. The jungle never disappoints in the process of making things difficult. Thankfully, the Japanese became even less interested in venturing out of their fortress, Rabaul.

The Australian High Command drew up plans to invade the capital, Rabaul. But when they were submitted to General MacArthur he quickly scuppered them, denying them the necessary landing craft and air support. The head of the Australian Armed Forces, General Blamey – fat, loathsome and deeply unpopular with his men – who had helped to devise the plans for the invasion, went into a sulk and was heard in

Canberra to have 'spat the dummy'.

MacArthur refused to budge, allowing the surrounded Japanese simply to wither on the vine. He hadn't forgotten his earlier costly victory at Buna on mainland New Guinea, and wasn't going to repeat that experience.

Just as well. The planned Australian invasion was based on the fact that there were twenty thousand Japanese troops in Rabaul. When Japan surrendered, this calculation of the enemy's strength proved to be wildly inaccurate. In fact, there were one hundred thousand Japanese. Their front-line troops might have been weakened from sickness and starvation, but Rabaul was the main garrison and the troops there were reasonably well fed and in good health. If we'd invaded it would have been an absolute bloodbath. For all his manifest faults, there ought to be a shrine to MacArthur in Australia for saving our soldiers' lives by vetoing the unnecessary actions proposed by the pompous and vainglorious Blamey and his cohorts, and denying them the ordnance to invade.

Late in July 1945 Major Peter McVitty called all the coastwatchers together and said he'd received a somewhat puzzling and elliptical signal discouraging any unnecessary offensive activity over the next fortnight.

We were as stunned as the Japanese to hear the announcement that America had dropped an atomic bomb on the Japanese city of Hiroshima, followed shortly after by another on Nagasaki. Then came the surrender on the 15th of August 1945.

I felt greatly honoured to be invited, along with all the other coastwatchers, to be present in Rabaul on the 6th of September when the Australian Lieutenant General Vernon Sturdee (thank Christ it wasn't Blamey!) formally accepted the surrender of the Japanese forces in the region from Lieutenant General Imamura on board the British aircraft carrier *Glory*. It was all over bar the victory marches, the ticker-tape parades and the joyous dancing and cheering in the streets of our cities and towns.

It was the start of the salvage company Judge, Popkin & Duncan Pty Ltd, Island Trading and Salvage Merchants. It was also time to find Anna.

CHAPTER TWENTY-TWO

*'Inside is your butterfly handkerchief and also eighty
persimmon seeds. You must sow five immediately,
because I am five years behind now.
Then, you must sow one seed each year on my birthday.
You must promise me, Nicholas.'*
Anna Til
Beautiful Bay, Port Vila,
New Hebrides, 1950

WITH THE WAR OVER I had one final task ahead
of me, and that was to find Anna. While I counted myself
extraordinarily fortunate with the women who had graced my
young life, the most special of them being Marg Hamilton, I had
never forgotten Anna. I would be fibbing if I said that every
day I read the letter she'd sent to me from Tjilatjap via Colonel
Woon, but I certainly did so at least once a week. My fear, of
course, was that she'd perished at the hands of the Japanese.

In any eastern or western society Anna would have been
seen as a beautiful young woman and my hope was that this
factor had saved her life. The stories of the Japanese use of
comfort women were beginning to circulate in the first weeks
after the Japanese surrender, told by Dutch refugees coming to
Australia from Java. It wasn't difficult to speculate that Anna
may have been forced to act in that capacity. I wasn't at all

sure how I would react to this possibility. My hope was that it
wouldn't matter – that she'd still love me and I would feel the
same about her. I certainly wasn't concerned about her virginity,
but rather about how she may have been affected, and how she
might regard me.

There was a constant niggling thought that I'd only known
her for a few weeks and that people change, particularly under
difficult circumstances. I knew I'd changed, changed enormously.
I'd grown up to discover that within me there was a killer and
a lover. I hated this dichotomy but was forced to accept that
Nick Duncan was no longer the ingenuous butterfly collector to
whom Anna had professed her love.

If I had changed, then how much more would she have
changed? I even asked myself the question: *Why don't you just
remember her fondly as a teenage fling, your first love, one that
was never consummated? Remember Anna as a beautiful girl you
met when you were both young and innocent and the world was a
different place, before hate and violence and killing had become the
paramount occupation of most of the so-called civilised world?*

Lying in a sleeping bag in the jungle, I would think: How
could I possibly expect to resume our relationship from the
time of her tearful farewell when she stood on the deck of
the *Witvogel*, clutching the little box containing the Clipper
butterfly?

After hours of silent argument, I'd all but convince myself
that it was pointless trying to find her. When this happened, I'd
pat the breast pocket of my jungle greens where the butterfly
handkerchief she'd embroidered for me rested in a flat oilskin
wallet I'd devised so that the thin cotton material didn't
disintegrate and stain from the sweat of a jungle patrol.

The handkerchief had been my talisman throughout the

periods of active combat. It was with me at Bloody Ridge, at Mount Austen where I'd killed the sniper and captured Gojo Mura, and at the subsequent ambushes of Japanese patrols in New Britain. It had been in my breast pocket when I'd found my father. I would often take it out in the dark and run my fingers gently across the butterfly embroidery and then I'd hear myself saying, 'Don't give up, Anna, I'm coming to get you. Nick's coming, darling.'

I'd never addressed Anna as 'darling'. It was a word I'd not had occasion to use and one I would not have fully understood at the time. Marg Hamilton had been the one to first introduce me to its intimate as well as its casual, throwaway meaning. But in my mind messages to Anna I found myself attaching 'darling' as an adjunct, almost as a prerequisite to the development of our invisible and imaginary relationship. It was as if the ambiguity of the word more deeply enhanced and established what now seemed, after so much time, a tenuous 'ships passing in the night' relationship. Thus the little cotton butterfly handkerchief served as a constant reminder that continued to stoke the embers of my memory of Anna and kept the flickering flame alive.

I began the process of finding Anna in an obvious manner. I called Marg. Who else? 'Marg, who do I contact in Canberra to see if Anna Van Heerden came into Australia?'

'Department of Immigration and Customs,' she replied, then laughed. 'You will remember Bert Henry, the first day we met? Thank God he's long retired.'

'Yeah, but do you know someone I can – or you can – call, so I don't have to go through all the red tape?'

She phoned back several days later. 'No luck, Nick. No one of that name has ever entered Australia.'

It was a dead end, another disappointment. Perhaps Madam

Butterfly was purposely avoiding me. How could that be? I was certain she'd try to come to Australia; after all, we'd promised each other that we would meet here and she knew how to contact me through the Archbishop of Perth.

The little bloke, anxious to get under way with the salvage operation, was less than impressed when I told him I had to go to Java and expected to be away at least a month. The account in the bank had reached an astounding twenty-five thousand pounds and he was panicking that what he called the 'Eternal Revenue' would somehow come looking for what he also referred to as the 'stash'.

I had located most of the big salvage sites in the Pacific, using my own observation and getting Belgiovani to ask on the Intelligence network, posing the question as if some official plan existed. The main Japanese source of non-ferrous scrap metal was Rabaul where, after the peace treaty had been signed on the decks of the *Glory*, I'd done the survey myself.

We also possessed an important asset in the form of ex-Major Peter McVitty, who had been my senior officer during my time in New Britain as an erstwhile member of the coastwatchers' detachment. As a civilian he was still heavily involved at a senior level in ANGAU, the Australian New Guinea Administration Unit. This organisation was busy re-establishing Australia's post-war colonial administration in the islands.

Peter was in an ideal position to 'facilitate' and to influence the outcome of a great many things and, at my suggestion, had taken an interest in scrap metal. Not many people had woken up to the potential bonanza offered by the wreckage of war. Even fewer had the necessary resources, skills and equipment to handle the task. With Peter scrutinising the tenders and making use of all the bureaucratic and legal quibbles available to a skilled lawyer, many of our competitors' tenders were rejected.

Peter McVitty, once a lawyer and now turned post-war bureaucrat, had agreed to help under two conditions: that he benefit personally from the result of our salvage operation, and that we use his brother Stan for our legal work. Stan was the head of the well-known, respected and somewhat silvertail Melbourne law firm McVitty, Swan & Allison, which had been established by their father in the early 1920s.

This sort of jiggery-pokery wasn't my area of expertise and I referred it to the little bloke, who was fairly busy milking the last of the quartermaster advantages to be had in Brisbane before repatriation to the States. Stan McVitty proved reluctant to come to Brisbane, claiming that he was much too busy with important clients and couldn't spare the time. The little bloke wasn't accustomed to being treated in an offhand manner and took a fair bit of umbrage as baggage down to Melbourne with him, hitching a ride in a military plane. He would later recall the experience.

'He fat, he bald, he got dis long nose and one o' dem crocodile smiles like Father Geraghty. When I tell him what we want to do he ask, "Scrap metal? Are you sure you know what you're doing?"' Kevin mimicked. 'Den he says again, "Scrap metal! It's hardly the kind of thing a senior partner would handle." Den he look at me an' he shrug an' sigh, "Oh well, as my brother Peter is involved, I daresay we'll have to take you on." So den I ask him where he fight in da war? I'm trying ta be sociable, ya know, nice, smiling, 'cos I don't want dis guy ta see I think he's a fuckin' asshole. "Flat feet, old chap," he says wit dat crocodile smile. "Some of us had to stay back to mind the farm." Nick! Dis ain't right! We dealin' here wit a fuckin' draft dodger!' Which, coming from the little bloke of 'I want ya ter unnerstan' —' fame, was perhaps just a tad hypocritical. If the judge hadn't given him the choice of joining the US Navy or going to prison, there is absolutely no doubt the little bloke would have ended up as a very artful dodger.

'Mate, we're stuck with him; we're going to need his brother, Peter. You're going to have to let the crocodile continue to smile.' In fact, Kevin's 'Crocodile' – as we all came to term Stan McVitty – promptly handed the legal ramifications of our business to a junior, one of the few female lawyers in the country. Miss Janine de Sax called Kevin and asked if she could fly up to Brisbane to get a proper brief. Kevin agreed and asked me to sit in on the meeting together with Joe Popkin.

It was a frantic period for my two American partners, as neither knew when they'd be repatriated. I was proving my worth as the third musketeer by buying essential equipment. Before I was demobbed and when still in New Britain I'd purchased two eighty-foot wooden coastal boats and a landing craft, mooring them in Rabaul. All three were virtually brand-new and I bought them for a song since the local American ordnance officer, a nice bloke, Captain John Tulius, seemed happy to get rid of them. A day later I met him in the officers' mess and bought him a beer. 'I hear you were with the 1st marines on Guadalcanal?' he asked. 'Won the Navy Cross at Bloody Ridge?'

I laughed and replied with my by-now practised rejoinder: 'Wrong place at the right time.'

'Can't let that go unrewarded. What say we make it two landing craft with spare engines, same price.' You can say what you like about Americans, but in Nick Duncan's war I never met a bad one. As it turned out we'd underestimated the amount of stuff lying around and the extra landing craft eventually proved a godsend.

Based on this single piece of sheer good fortune I was appointed the purchasing officer for the company, but not without a lesson in the art of buying from Chief Lewinski. Our needs ranged from a couple of bulldozers, welding equipment, spare parts, generators and a small crane for lifting heavier items right down to other items such as clothing for our crews and workers. Heavy construction was Joe's department and expertise, but a black American sailor couldn't be seen bidding at an American army disposal auction. So he'd do the spotting and the pricing and I'd do the fronting up at the auction. Da Chief called me, together with Joe Popkin, into his office and began by congratulating me on the purchase of the two boats and landing craft, especially the spares. 'Joe here will tell ya, spare parts are everythin', Nick. Always see ya get spare parts. Jeeps break down in the jungle – ya wanna know ya got the parts to fix 'em. Same wid a boat at sea. But first ya gotta know the auction system, son.'

'Yes, thank you, Chief. I haven't a clue. I've never attended an auction in my life,' I admitted.

'It ain't the auction, it's what happens before that's important, Nick.'

'Ah, there's a process before?' I asked naïvely.

'Well, it ain't official, son.' He turned to Joe. 'Ya pack six dozen cold Bud and a small tin wash tub wid ice in the Packard, Joe. When ya get to the depot find a nice place to stand where the potential buyers pass by. Joe, ya standin' in ya navy uniform and ya yellin' out, big grin, nice polite, "The US Navy wud like to buy ya a beer, gennelmen." Soon ya got yourself the main crowd, all wid a Bud in their hand. Then ya establish the ground rules.'

'Ground rules, isn't that what the auctioneer does?' I asked.

Chief Lewinski smiled. 'These're the non-official ground rules, son, known in the purchasin' and procurement business as "the prior arrangement". Ya decide amongst yourselves who wants what and how much each wants to pay. After that, it's just a matter of mutual respect.' Joe grinned and I looked concerned. The Reverend John Duncan's son was getting into collusion, an area I knew nothing about and in which I wasn't over-keen to advance my knowledge. Sensing my reluctance Chief Lewinski continued, 'Nick, there's enough for everybody. Ya don't want some cockamamie auctioneer to get himself a big bonus for exceeding the estimates. Uncle Sam don't need the cash, ya do.'

I must say there has to be a dishonest streak in everyone. It worked like a charm as we bidders arranged amongst ourselves who would get what and what the chosen one was prepared to pay. I guess it was collusion, but in a good cause: ordinary blokes, some battlers, guys recently demobbed and doing a little planning for their future. Few of us had very much disposable income, and we were benefiting from Uncle Sam's largesse. 'Ain't nobody got hisself hurt 'cept da man wid da white beard and da big hat decorate wid da stars 'n' stripes,' Joe said happily each time we returned from a successful auction.

But if we were learning fast in the area of procurement, what the three of us didn't know about the law and the rigmarole involved in setting up a company was practically encyclopaedic. The meeting with Janine de Sax was to change everything. She proved to be smart as a whip and nice to boot, but more importantly she was totally discreet. Her immediate advice was to use a tax haven. She outlined a scheme to set up a holding company in Port Vila, the capital of New Hebrides, which was now administered jointly by the British and the French as a condominium. 'No tax of any kind and well away from the prying eyes of the Australian Government,' she advised, then added, 'I hope you don't mind, but I've incurred some expense on your behalf by consulting with a top young barrister named John Kerr with whom I was at university. We sought a second opinion with a Sydney colleague, Garfield Barwick. Both are agreed that if domiciled there your company will be immune from Australian law and therefore taxes.' She looked up, a trifle concerned. 'I hope you don't mind; it seemed money well spent on lawyers' fees.'

Joe drove her back to the airport in the Packard and Kevin and I had a beer at the Bellevue. Sally, by the way, had long since left, sailing as a war bride, married to an ex-US Navy doctor who was to set up a practice as a neurosurgeon in Boston. The funny part was that while I'd been introduced to him the night we'd attended the dinner dance at the officers' club and he'd sent over a bottle of French champagne, I couldn't for the life of me remember his surname. Whatever the married Sally Forsythe now called herself, I hoped she'd be very happy.

'Now dat what I call a lawyer,' Kevin said, fixing himself a cigar. 'I'm tellin' yoh, Nick, dat one smart lady. Dat Crocodile smilin' asshole, he gone done us a big, big favour.'

It was then that I told him I'd be away for a month at least and was going to Java to find Anna.

'Wassa matta wit you, Nick? Yoh got broads fallin' all over demselves ter get to yoh.' He pointed at the bar. 'Nobody could get inta Sally's pants and yoh done it widout buyin' her a drink, nylons or chocolates – sweet fanny! Bren Gun says ya a born natural magnet fer womankind. Now ya gonna go to Java to find yerself some li'l girl yoh only know'd three weeks when yer catchin' fuckin' butterflies, who been under da Japanese occupation fer years and – who da fuck knows what happen to her in da meantime? Maybe she ain't even wit us no more. You crazy or somet'in', buddy?'

'Kevin, I've got to go. I made myself a promise.'

'Den *un*-promise yerself, fer fuck's sake! Yoh hear what I'm sayin', buddy?'

Naturally I went straight to Marg Hamilton. I took the plane down to Melbourne, where I stayed at the same boarding house where the Virgin Mary's mother worked as a day cook. She welcomed me like a lost son and still smelled the same – of fried onions and Johnson's baby powder. Mary was already in New York. 'Her family, the whole mob, they live in a compound. It seems the father is someone real important and doesn't want his kids to leave him. Ain't that nice, Nick?' she informed me proudly.

I'd previously booked a table for two upstairs at Florentino's, and was already waiting and rose to greet Marg when she was ushered to my table. She kissed me. 'My goodness, Nick, fancy "Flory's". You *have* come up in the world.'

I blushed. 'I wanted to take you somewhere good, Marg, so I phoned our lawyer and she suggested here.' I looked around at the murals. 'I've never been in a place as nice as this before.'

'You must have a *bombe* Alaska for dessert, it's their specialty.' She looked up at me. 'Lawyer, and a "she"?' Her eyebrow just slightly arched with her query.

I told her about the salvage idea and about Janine de Sax. 'She would have been a partner in the firm by now, but she has two children, two girls, and refuses to work eighteen hours a day every day of the week,' I said to impress on Marg that she wasn't some two-bit shyster lawyer.

The waiter came and we ordered, steak for me and fish for

her – no accounting for people's taste, even that of the beloved Marg. I'd eaten enough fish sailing the mission boat as a kid to last me a lifetime. 'Marg, I want you to help me get to Java. To find Anna,' I said as soon as the waiter had departed.

There was silence. Some silences are just silences. But this one was heavy and hung in the air like a dark cloud. Her red lips were drawn in a pucker and her eyes downcast. I could see she was upset and shaking with anger. 'No!' she exploded – just the one word, loud and hard so that people at other tables turned to look.

'Why?' I asked. She was going to marry Rob Rich, I still adored her, but our relationship was long over.

Then it came out slowly, carefully. 'Nick, I fell in love with you within minutes of entering the office when that ridiculous old man from Customs, Bert Henry, was interviewing you as if you were a dangerous alien. You were brown as a berry and where your tangled mass of hair parted at the back of your neck your skin was tender and vulnerably white. You were an astonishingly beautiful young boy in faded shirt and shorts, both virtually in rags – but clean rags. You'd sailed halfway across the Indian Ocean in a tiny boat, avoiding the Japanese and caring for a wounded American sailor. Your innocence was palpable. I loved you almost from the first moment. When you said, with a shy smile, that you were a butterfly collector, I nearly wept. Then I watched the beautiful boy be hijacked by Rupert Basil Michael Long, who quickly and expertly exploited the fact that you were obsessed with finding your father. I witnessed your sadness when Anna, your first love, failed to arrive in Darwin. Then I watched my beautiful boy go to Guadalcanal and when he came back he wore medals for bravery but his soul was corrupted and his beautiful young body was broken. He went back and he found his father. It was the same brave heart and determination that had sailed across the ocean, but it was a different man. The butterfly man had lost his innocence. I didn't care, you were alive, Nick. You'd made it through to the end. My beloved boy was safe. Yes, you were still my beloved boy, even though by then I'd found my true partner. But the young, improbable love of that part of my life was back, battered, hard-eyed, but back.'

She stopped and looked at me and I thought she was on the point of weeping. 'No, Nick, there is civil war in Java. The Dutch who ran with their tails between their legs from the Netherlands East Indies now self-righteously want to claim it back. It's a nasty, brutal little war where white men are the enemy. The Indonesians, as they're calling themselves, have a right to their independence, but that is not a matter for you or me. Anna, if she is still alive, will make her own way out. There is an active refugee program. If she isn't there then you are just as likely to be caught in the crossfire.' She suddenly looked furious. 'No, no, no! I will do nothing to help you! In fact I will do quite the opposite. I will do everything I can, everything Rob can, to prevent you going!'

'Marg, please; I didn't mean to upset you. I'm truly sorry that I asked you.'

'And what the hell does that mean in Nick-speak? That you'll find another way to get there? Like finding your father? Nick, grow up! Your Anna is probably dead. If she isn't, she's permanently and psychologically damaged. Even if you found her, you're not the same Nick and she's not the same Anna. War changes everything, everybody. Anna's particular war under Japanese domination may have scarred her forever, destroyed her life. For God's sake! This isn't a pair of lovers running into each other's arms in slow motion against a backdrop of the setting sun.'

'Is that your last word?' I asked, not happy at her chastisement.

'No! My last word is "No!"'

The waiter arrived and put down our plates in that manner waiters have when they sense a quarrel – perhaps they're trained to be invisible and obtrusive at the same time. Marg Hamilton rose and threw her napkin onto the table. 'I don't feel like fish!' she declared, then stooped to pick up her bag and gloves and walked out of Florentino's, past the murals and down the stairs.

The steak looked delicious, but I didn't eat it. I sent it back. When the waiter looked concerned, fussing and protesting and offering to replace it even though it was obvious I hadn't touched it, I glared at him. 'Bring me a bloody *bombe* Alaska,' I growled.

'I'm sorry, sir, we do not serve *bombe* Alaska on Monday. It's the dessert chef's day off.' He reminded me of Fernando at the Bellevue. 'May I suggest crème caramel?'

'No, you may not! Bring me the bill,' I demanded in a more mollified voice. Being back in civilisation wasn't all it was cracked up to be.

I found a café in Bourke Street just down from Florentino's and ordered a toasted egg and bacon sandwich and a milkshake. Still upset, I asked the little sheila with rat's-tail hair and acne who was serving me, 'What's crème caramel?'

She shrugged. 'Never 'eard of it.' She turned and yelled to the bloke behind the counter, 'Hey, Tony, what's cream caramel?'

Tony shook his head and called into the back of the café, 'Hey, Mama!' Seconds later a stout lady arrived and stood at the door, wiping her hands on her apron. 'What's cream caramel,

Mama?' Tony asked.

'Crème cara-mel'a?' She said the words as if they were poetry. 'Da brown sugar – da raw one – wid butter inna dish. Den bit cream, three egg, milk, bit honey, bit vanilla, mix all up, pour inna da bowl an' put in slow oven one hour, it set'a just like'a jelly. Why you ask'a me, Tony – you want crème cara-mel'a?'

The next most likely person who could help was Peter McVitty. I guess I could have gone to see the dreaded Rupert Basil Michael Long, but he had one agenda too many in his nefarious mind and I thought it wise to stay out of his clutches. Peter had a fair bit of clout in Canberra; he'd been (and for all I knew, still was) on the committee of the Directorate of Research and Civil Affairs. The title covered almost everything and nothing. It was a somewhat shadowy group that had a large influence over ANGAU which, in turn, was largely responsible for shaping the policies designed to bring New Guinea and the other islands back into the Australian colonial fold. This group had been brought together by Alf Conlon and was said to include some of the brightest in legal, academic and government circles. The members were being groomed to be the movers and shakers of post-war Australia. I called Peter in Canberra and made an appointment to see him.

When I asked Peter if he could find a way for me to get to Java, his eyebrows shot up. 'Java? There's a civil war going on, Nick. Nasty business. Under Japanese occupation they missed out on fighting in the big stoush, now they've created a war of independence of their own. Very messy. We've decided to back the Indonesians in the United Nations and the Dutch are not real happy with us. They point to the fact that we're going back into New Guinea and why can't they do the same in what they insist on calling the Netherlands East Indies? Arrogant bunch, three hundred and thirty years of colonial rule and they want more.'

'They've got a point, though – I mean us and New Guinea, the islands,' I said.

Peter McVitty smiled. 'Selective perception, old chap, it's redolent in all governments. What's good for the goose in this instance is not good for the gander. The conscience we took to the United Nations in San Francisco got lost somewhere in the air over the Pacific. You've heard it all before: "We're different, our indigenous population are still head-hunters, a hundred years away from self-rule, can't possibly be left to manage on their own."'

'Seems wrong though, doesn't it?'

Peter McVitty looked at me sternly. 'Nick, for Christ's sake, don't venture that opinion to the blokes from External Affairs. They'll immediately conclude you want to go to Java to stir up trouble. We're not neutral but we won't interfere with the outcome.'

'No, of course not,' I assured him. 'I simply want to get to Tjilatjap and have no intention of getting involved other than to try and find a friend,' I said.

'Friend? Let me guess. Female. Dutch or Javanese?'

'Half and half, Javanese mother; someone I met before the war.'

'You sure that's wise, Nick? There's been a lot of water under the bridge, mate. Young Dutch women had a rough time under the Japanese.' He didn't need to elaborate. 'My personal advice is to stay well away.' He smiled. 'But I've worked with you long enough to know your determination. By the way, how is your father?'

'Recovering slowly. He's been ordained a bishop.'

'Nice, do we get him?'

'You mean the islands?' He nodded. 'Yes, New Guinea, New Britain,' I laughed. 'Anywhere there's malaria.'

'Nick, I can't promise; right now Java and Sumatra are officially "no go" diplomatic zones, but that may change. I'll see what I can do.'

'Do I hang around or go back to Brisbane?' I asked.

'No, no, hang around. It will be "Yes" or "No" pretty damn quickly. Where are you staying?'

'I'll find somewhere.' I rose and, reaching over, shook his hand. 'Thanks, Peter. Whatever the outcome, I appreciate your help.'

'Wait a mo', Nick.' He picked up the phone. 'I'll book you into the Hotel Canberra. Parliament's in session and they're announcing the interim budget tomorrow. Canberra's booked out, but they have to keep a couple of rooms vacant in case someone important to the government unexpectedly arrives in town.'

After checking into the hotel I went out for a walk and I must say, for a national capital, Canberra was less than spectacular. Back at the hotel I found a message waiting for me: 'See you for drinks, your hotel, 1800. Peter'.

Over a whiskey and soda (beer for me) he said, 'The notorious Nick Duncan luck is still holding. There's a delegation going to Batavia, or as the leader of the proposed Republic of Indonesia, Sukarno, refers to it, Jakarta. You will be attached as an observer.' He grinned. 'That's a word that covers a multitude of sins.' He paused, sipping at his scotch. 'Only catch is, they're leaving from Perth in two weeks. You'll have to make your own way overland; the rest is taken care of.'

'I owe you, Peter, thank you.'

'Yes, you do, Nick.' He grinned. 'Just make bloody sure that salvage business of yours is a huge success.' Then he added modestly, 'By the way, it wasn't all that difficult to swing. When you joined Naval Intelligence you signed on forever. You're still on the reserve list, so it's time you got something back. All the committee did was to call Commander Long in Melbourne to check on your past performance and I'm told he simply said, "Give him anything he wants."' Peter grinned. 'As they say in the islands, "Yu numba one fella."'

I returned to Brisbane where the little bloke, very reluctantly I must say, and after I'd picked up the dummy he spat out and placed it back in his mouth, arranged for me to hitch a ride to Perth on a military transport plane. I arrived two days later, having stopped overnight in Adelaide. I was three days early and it gave me a chance to see Bishop John Duncan at the Archbishop's Palace where I stayed. The old man had put on a little weight, but his personal war had knocked the stuffing out of him; he looked ten years older than a man of fifty-one, although his intellect remained as sharp as ever. When I told him where and why I was going, all he said was, 'Ah, the foolish affairs of the heart; do be careful, dear boy.'

I made arrangements the next day to have lunch with Lieutenant Commander (now Captain) Rigby at the Perth Yacht Club and arrived an hour early so I could inspect *Madam Butterfly*. Nothing appeared to have changed – even the yard foreman, whose name I couldn't recall, was the same and recognised me immediately. 'Come back to visit the *Madam*, mate?' he asked with a grin, then stuck out his hand. 'Ray Davis.'

'Nick Duncan – yeah, how is she?' I replied, shaking his hand.

'Good as new, mate. She's still a bloody beautiful cutter. That's the good thing about boats – the women yer love grow old and ugly, the boats stay beautiful.'

He removed the canvas that covered *Madam Butterfly* and I climbed aboard. It was at once obvious that the lovely yacht had been well cared for. 'She's in good nick, Ray, thanks, mate.'

'Commodore'd have me balls for ping-pong practice if she weren't,' Ray replied.

Lunch with Captain Rigby was pleasant and we talked of old times, the war and, of course, Marg Hamilton. I didn't tell him of our contretemps. Roger Rigby grinned and at one stage said, 'Nick, I guess you've realised by now that Marg was very much more than the sum of what you saw?'

'Certainly was – is,' I replied. A sudden thought occurred to me. 'You mean – professionally?'

'Yes, petty officer was simply a cover; technically she was my superior.'

'A spy?' I asked, completely gob-smacked.

'Not in so many words – someone who could listen in, take notes in high places, in meetings when we were dealing with the Americans. "Observer" is perhaps a better word.' It was the word Peter McVitty had said covered a multitude of sins. I was beginning to think there was no end to the talents of Marg Hamilton. 'She's resigning from Naval Intelligence to marry Rob Rich, have children – the full domestic tragedy. Pity, there aren't too many like her. If she'd been a male she'd – well, God knows where she would have ended up.'

'She's going to make Rob Rich a wonderful wife,' I ventured.

'She's going to make Rob Rich an admiral,' Roger Rigby replied, laughing.

The delegation to what everyone now referred to as Indonesia was to make the journey over three days in three hops: to Broome where we were to stay overnight, then to Tjilatjap, on the west coast of Java, and then to Jakarta or, as it was previously known, Batavia. The delegation was conducting local talks in Tjilatjap before flying to the capital. I'd previously arranged – or, to put it more precisely, it had been arranged – with the Department of External Affairs that I would remain in Tjilatjap and catch the plane later when the delegation passed through as it returned to Australia. I had four days in which to find Anna and hadn't a clue where to begin. The central police station was my guess. For a start, I was pleased I was carrying an Australian passport with diplomatic immunity, just in case some overzealous policeman, thinking I was Dutch, apprehended me.

I stepped out of the old Dutch colonial-style hotel where the delegation talks were to be held that afternoon before it left for Jakarta, and into a large square. It was dominated by a huge bronze statue of a man on a tall stone plinth who, judging from his attire, was some Dutch historical figure. I could only guess this, because his head was missing. The decapitation was a good indication that the natives would not be over-friendly to someone, like me, who could be mistaken for a large Dutchman.

I walked into the central police station and in an enquiring tone addressed a single word to the policeman behind the desk: 'Captain?' He looked at me, not comprehending. 'Captain?' I asked again. I figured it was a word that translates into most languages, as most military titles tend to do. I remembered a few Dutch words from my time with Anna, words such as 'please' and 'thank you', but this was neither the time nor the place to use them.

He stared at me quizzically and then seemed to catch on. '*Kapitein?*' he asked.

'*Ja, ja!*' I said, pleased. '*Kapitein!*' I repeated, nodding my head vigorously. '*Ja*' was another near-universal word. He indicated that I should sit and disappeared into a room to the side of the charge desk. A minute or so later he returned and with a wave of his hand gestured for me to enter the office, standing aside to let me pass.

Seated behind an elaborately carved teak desk in the Javanese tradition was, by local standards, a fairly big and certainly well-fed bloke. He didn't get up as I entered and merely took my hand, barely touching it as I attempted a handshake. His expression was non-committal and he took the passport I proffered and opened it without apparent interest, glancing at me and then at the photograph within it. Then his face lit up. 'Ah, *Australien?*' he said, suddenly smiling.

He rose and offered his hand, this time allowing a very much firmer grip. 'Lieutenant Nick Duncan,' I said. External Affairs had advised me to use my previous navy ranking since all foreign civilians were suspect visitors.

'*Kapitein* Khamdani,' he replied. He turned and called to the policeman, motioning me to wait. He spoke at some length and the policeman nodded and left. The captain smiled and indicated the chair in front of the desk. I sat and we remained silent for twenty minutes, frequently smiling at each other, at which time he'd repeat '*Engels kom*,' which, even with my limited Dutch, I knew meant 'English come'. The police captain had sent out for a translator.

Finally a young bloke of about seventeen entered. 'Good – morning – sir,' he said haltingly, as if practising each word on his tongue, not expecting it to emerge correctly.

I stood. 'Good morning, and your name is?' I enquired, helping him along.

'Budi. I learn English in my school.'

'You speak well,' I complimented him.

'No, not so good,' he replied, smiling.

'Budi, can you tell the *kapitein* I'm here to look for someone?' I asked.

Budi translated quickly then turned back to me. 'Name, please.'

'A Miss Anna Van Heerden.'

There was no mistaking the look of surprise. 'Anna?' he questioned, plainly astonished.

'You know her?' I said, excitedly.

He turned to Captain Khamdani who had also recognised Anna's name. 'Anna?' he said, then his face clouded. He went deadpan and turned and said something to Budi.

'He want to know, why you want Anna? Why you come, Tjilatjap?'

'Anna Van Heerden was my friend. Her boat broke down here in Tjilatjap.' I produced Anna's letter and handed it to him. He read it slowly, his lips moving. Then he looked up. 'Nicholas! She has tell me – told me —' he corrected, not completing the sentence. Then turning to the police captain, and waving the letter excitedly, he talked rapidly to him. Captain Khamdani kept nodding his head and smiling.

'Do you know where she is?' I asked, glancing at both men, my own excitement palpable.

There was a moment's silence and then Budi shook his head slowly. 'No, we don't know. She has gone. We are very sad for this.'

That evening I met Ratih and Kiki and learned the full extent of Anna's stay in Tjilatjap, or as much of it as an exhausted Budi with his limited English could translate.

It was obvious that they thought of Anna as some sort of saint and I learned how she'd paid for Ratih's restaurants, Kiki's house, Budi's high-school education and had also left behind money for his university tuition when the university reopened in Jakarta or Batavia – the name of the capital depending on which side won the struggle that was going on. They told me about the tragic death of Til, and how Anna had loved him as her friend and confidant. They also hinted at something dark in Anna's past. Nothing was actually said, but my Intelligence-trained antenna immediately went into full alert.

I stayed the four days and after the second, when they'd come to trust me, I learned that Budi was a young freedom fighter, home for a week's leave from his unit in the jungle. I spent the next two days talking to him, teaching him how to set up effective ambushes, showing him a few tricks of the jungle fighter's trade. We rapidly became good friends.

'Maybe for me you can be my brother, Nick?' he'd asked in a serious voice when it came time to part.

'Yeah, Budi, I'd like that. I never had a brother.'

'Me too never had,' he said. 'Now I am got for me,' he said happily. I left him my address in Brisbane and our accountant's address in New Hebrides.

'Get in touch if you need anything, Budi. If you hear anything – I mean *anything* – about Anna, please let me know!' I paused and placed my hand on his shoulder. 'Don't ever forget what I told you about fighting in the jungle.'

Budi looked at me, his young face earnest. '*Ja*, I always remember, Nick. He who stays still gets the kill,' he repeated, quoting Sergeant Major Wainwright's axiom.

The delegation flew in from Jakarta and we returned to Broome, then to Perth. I was sad not to have found Anna but, at the same time, the knowledge that she had not perished at the hands of the Japanese was encouraging. I told myself if she could live through what Ratih, Budi and Captain Khamdani had told me about the Japanese occupation, there was a good chance she'd survived. I knew I'd keep looking, that I'd never give up. The same obsession that made me a butterfly collector was still intact. As long as she was alive I was more determined than ever to find her – Anna, the most beautiful butterfly of them all.

I called Marg Hamilton to tell her I'd returned safely. We hadn't spoken since she'd stormed out of Florentino's. 'Marg, I'm back, unhurt,' I said quickly when she answered the phone.

'In that case you are forgiven, Nick,' she answered. 'Seeing that you're still alive, would you mind giving me away at my wedding?'

'That's a tough call!' I laughed, agreeing happily. She was getting a really good bloke and it would have been pointless to sulk. I asked her what she wanted for a wedding gift.

'A puppy, please! Poor darling Timmy died peacefully of

old age and Cardamon is lonely.' Cardamon was, of course, her beloved Burmese cat.

Setting up all the details and getting the heavy equipment we'd bought at US surplus auctions took a fair bit of time. The little bloke and Joe had been repatriated to San Diego, but by the middle of 1946 Kevin had returned to Brisbane. He promptly proposed to Bren Gun, whose period of mourning was finally over, and they planned to marry in the cathedral with myself and Joe Popkin as best man and chief groomsman. It turned out that Bren Gun had family coming out of the woodwork, and eight bridesmaids between the ages of four and eleven materialised.

Kevin, at great expense (probably not personal), bought sufficient parachute silk for Bren Gun and her bridesmaids to have the full catastrophe, dressed in the latest fashion with matching bridesmaids' outfits.

Somehow, using Marg Hamilton (who wasn't even a Catholic), we got James Duhig, the Archbishop of Queensland, to conduct the nuptial mass in St Stephen's Cathedral and gained permission for Protestant Nick and Joe to be present. There were more flowers in the cathedral than in the Brisbane Botanical Gardens and two hundred and nineteen members of Bren Gun's family attended, some coming down from Cairns and Darwin and across from Adelaide and Melbourne.

The wedding reception at the Bellevue Hotel lasted until breakfast the following morning, with half the male guests and several of the females snoring in a drunken sleep under the tables. Every room was booked out plus those in all the surrounding hotels. The little bloke, who'd never had a family of his own, was now a member of a family of two hundred and fifty-six, if one included the great-aunties and uncles who were too old to travel to the wedding. Most of them seemed to be good Catholics who, judging from the size of their families, didn't believe in contraception.

The only blight on the joyous occasion was a pre-wedding hitch when Joe Popkin was, in effect, apprehended at the airport under the White Australia Policy. It was good enough for him as an American to be stationed here during the war, but now, barely nine months after, he was back to being a nigger and not allowed to come into Australia without a return ticket and an endorsement from someone who was prepared to guarantee his return to the States.

If there was one thing that made me dead ashamed of my country, it was this heinous policy. I received a call from the airport, where they referred to Joe as 'American Negro, Popkin' and asked me to come out and vouch for him. Some war, hey? We'd just fought against tyranny and supposedly for the values of freedom and justice, and I was on my way out to Brisbane airport as a character witness for a man whose only crime was the colour of his skin! It made me want to puke. When I apologised to him, Joe said, 'Nevah yoh min', Nick. Dey bin doin' dis to Negro folks since I is a piccaninny.' I sensed he'd chosen the last word deliberately as it was often used when referring to black children.

Even Marg Hamilton couldn't get a permit for Joe to remain in Australia but, fortuitously, he was needed in Rabaul to run the salvage operation. Joe was a natural leader who didn't tolerate bullshit; at six feet four inches he also possessed a fairly impressive presence, though he seldom needed to exert it. He soon became loved amongst the men who worked for us.

I'd been over to Rabaul, flying in a Catalina, prior to Joe's arrival to take over and I'd appointed ex-Sergeant Ellison as foreman and his *wantoks* from my group as nucleus labour. When Joe arrived he continued the tradition and the Tolai formed the basis of what was to become a very large labour force.

Having a dark-skinned bloke in charge seemed to make the men happy. I never heard Joe shout, but he would sometimes bodily pick up a worker, grabbing him by the shirtfront and lifting him with one hand to the level of his face and then telling him, nose to nose, in pidgin (which he'd picked up rapidly), to get on with it. I don't think Joe ever fired a man. On the other hand, with Ellison as recruitment officer it was probably never necessary, for Ellison could detect a real shirker at three paces.

The greatest bonus of all was what the Japanese left behind at Rabaul. We began collecting the thousands of tons of munitions needed to sustain a large garrison. I began to realise that the waste inherent in war was simply astonishing and, in our case, to the victor went the spoils. I'd often wince when equipment that would have cost a fortune was broken up and turned into scrap metal. Magnificent precision rangefinders, fuse-setting machines, radio equipment that in the earlier days would have caused Belgiovani to have an orgasm on the spot, generators, switchboards, entire aircraft, artillery parts: all were chopped into easy-to-handle pieces. Equipment that was the best the world could produce was reduced to junk by sweating kanakas, some of whom had never heard a radio broadcast.

By November, Bren Gun was pregnant with child number ninety-two in her family's fecund pipeline. You'd have thought it was the first child in the next generation of what appeared to me to be the most sexually active family in Australia. The birth date was expected to be two weeks after the arrival in

Rabaul of the first ship the little bloke had chartered. I had arranged to fly back to Brisbane to be there to hold the little bloke's hand. Eight thousand tons of ready-to-use non-ferrous metal was waiting to be loaded and I'd booked a phone call to Kevin to tell him when the task was completed. The line was crackling and pinging, but when he answered I shouted, 'Kevin, we just loaded —'

'Nick, where are yoh, buddy? Come quick, da fuckin' baby is premature! Bren Gun, she in da hospital and they ain't lettin' me come in. Can yoh get here, buddy?' he implored. 'Please, yoh always know what ter do!'

'Kevin, I'm in Rabaul!' I shouted.

'What's dat? I cain't hear yoh, buddy, dis cockamamie phone! Come quick, da Marta Hospital, Brisbane. Take a taxi! I be waitin' outside!'

Kevin and Bren Gun's baby, although two weeks premature, proved to be a healthy girl who was none the worse for her early arrival. When I managed to get a call through the next day he said, 'Yoh wouldn't believe it, Nick. She just like my mom. Da spittin' image. I swear, buddy, it like a goddamn thro' back.'

'I hope not,' I laughed. 'Congratulations to you both. Well done!'

I could almost hear Kevin's pride swelling over the telephone. 'It weren't nuttin' I couldn't handle, buddy. Yoh tell Joe we was gonna call it Joe Nicholas Judge,' he cackled happily. 'But it turn out to be a liddle gorl. Now we gonna call her Nicola Josephine Judge. Yoh like dat, buddy?'

Every day in business, once you're organised and get into the swing of things, is pretty much the same. Each salvage dump presented us with one or two new logistical problems, but nothing we couldn't resolve. Our teams might be dismantling a wreck on the beach or in a shallow bay, disarming an ammunition dump, cutting, crushing, loading – and all this in places the departed armies had long since forgotten.

Of the bigger, well-known dumps, other jackals who'd begun to realise the potential were beginning to prowl. Peter McVitty's perspicacious handling of major contracts kept us gainfully employed. We didn't get everything going, but he saw to it that we got the cream. In return we did the hard yards, smaller and more difficult dumps, clearing wrecks in deep bays that nobody wanted to know about. There were even places where the local colonial administration, fearing an ammunition dump might explode spontaneously, were pathetically grateful that Canberra had organised someone to make the area safe. In fact, usually the dumps were fairly safe anyway. Under Joe's guidance we became the most skilful, quickest and most economical outfit in the island by a country mile and, after a short time, Peter McVitty was almost acting with a clear conscience when he pushed a contract our way.

We were working around the clock, seven days a week, until the local bishop, the Right Reverend John Duncan, interfered and insisted that if we kept employing mission boys amongst our labour force we must give them Sunday off. The Seventh Day Adventists tried for Saturday as well, but Joe gave them a generous sum of money to build eight schoolhouses in villages and told them to shove it or there'd be no more donations. And so, having arranged things so there were no taxes to pay, we became very rich by immediate post-war standards.

Janine de Sax remained in charge of our affairs, but the

man with the crocodile smile, fat, unctuous Stan McVitty, was now all over us like a bad rash, sycophantic to the point of making you want to throw up. If it hadn't been for his brother Peter in Canberra I feel sure the little bloke would have taken out a contract on him. 'Dat cocksucker ain't to be trusted,' he'd declare after every meeting.

'Keep the crocodile smiling, mate, we need his brother,' I'd always reply.

'One day – one day,' the little bloke would say in a threatening tone, though what he meant by that, Joe and I had no idea.

During all this time I hadn't given up on finding Anna. Every three months I placed an advertisement in the personal columns of Amsterdam's *Algemeen Dagblat* and *de Volkskrant*, London's *The Times*, *Daily Mail* and *Daily Telegraph*, the *Manchester Guardian*, America's *New York Times* and *L.A. Times*, as well as, from time to time, in various other newspapers throughout Europe. The message never changed:

> *Interested party wishes to know*
> *the whereabouts of Anna Van H.*
> *of Tjilatjap 1942–45 over matter to*
> *great advantage. Write: Nicholas,*
> *P.O. Box 68, Port Vila, New Hebrides.*

I suppose over the next five years I must have spent a veritable fortune running the ad without success; several confidence tricksters contacted me and said they knew how to find her but needed a sum of money, hinting that the process was a tricky one. Checking them out by using a local private detective wasn't difficult. Anna had simply disappeared. Either that or she was dead, or, as I'd previously thought, she didn't wish me to find her. In 1949 the United Nations Commission for Refugees was established and Peter McVitty got its staff on the job; they even checked the marriage certificates of all the Dutch refugees in case Anna had married, but again without success.

But then, at last there came a break. It came out of the blue from the ever-discreet Janine de Sax, who was aware of our antipathy – in particular, Kevin's – to Stan McVitty, but had never once reacted when the little bloke had given us all the pleasure of his singular opinion concerning the unctuous lawyer.

I had built a house close to the water on a small bay in Port Vila, in order to satisfy the residential requirements needed to maintain our tax-free status. I was spending a lot of my time in the islands and decided to make the house a fairly grand affair, with wide verandahs looking over the bay. It offered a sheltered mooring and after a trip to Australia I took the opportunity of sailing *Madam Butterfly* back to her new home. I also wanted a place I could keep my butterfly collection, which had by now become, I suppose, a major world collection. The house I named simply 'Beautiful Bay'.

From time to time Janine, who was having marriage problems, would come to stay with her two little girls. I adored Chloe and Jessica, who sometimes came along if a business matter arose during school holidays. Janine and I had become good friends; nothing more than that, just really good mates.

The little bloke couldn't believe I wasn't sleeping with her and constantly urged me to marry her. 'Buddy, you're stuppin' her. Why not slip on da gold ring, make it legal, den we got ourselves a lawyer in da family and no more fuckin' crocodile.'

In fact, I was doing no such thing. Our relationship was a purely platonic one. She was an attractive woman, but she was married – even if unhappily – and besides, was the company's lawyer. I didn't lead a celibate life – in the islands that's like asking it not to rain – and I was never immune to the charms of a beautiful woman.

Then one night I received a crackling phone call at Beautiful Bay. 'Nick, I'd like to come up.' It was Janine.

'Of course, you know you're always welcome,' I assured her, adding, 'Bring the kids.'

'No, Nick, it's not business. I'll pay my own way.'

'Janine, don't be bloody silly, put it on the tab.'

'No, Nick. That would be indiscreet.' After a few minutes when I'd managed to verify the time and date of her plane through the static, she hung up. I thought her visit must have something to do with her marriage and was gratified that she'd think to confide in me. Janine was the most discreet person I'd ever known – except for my father, who only spoke about personal matters to God.

Janine arrived on the afternoon plane from Brisbane two days later. She'd taken the opportunity to see Kevin before flying to Port Vila. Driving back to Beautiful Bay from the airport when she mentioned she'd seen the little bloke, I naturally said, 'We'll pay for your trip, Janine.'

'Nick, I can't accept, it wouldn't be right.'

I knew better than to ask any further, knowing she would pick her time and place to talk.

Port Vila is outside the malaria belt and we dined on the

verandah, watching a full moon coming up over the bay. After a pleasant meal and while waiting for the maid to bring in the coffee and the brandy decanter, Janine finally said, 'Nick, I've come across something that may be of interest. Our company is involved with police corruption in Melbourne. As you know it's endemic; there can't be a top-flight law firm in Collins Street that isn't representing a corrupt police officer of one sort or another. Most of the accused cops are involved with the SP bookmakers, brothels or pub owners selling sly grog after the six o'clock swill. I sometimes wonder if there's a straight policeman in Victoria! You may not know this, but the police control the cocaine trade, and heroin and amphetamines are as easy to buy in the lower end of Spring Street as lollies. Stan McVitty will occasionally get his hands dirty, but the crime work is usually handled by the other two senior partners. As you know, I work with Stan, and several days ago he was with a notorious property developer client and wanted me to send over a file that he kept in his personal safe. He told me where to find the key behind a legal book.' She glanced up. 'There are literally hundreds of these case law books in the firm and all he would have to do is to place the key behind a different one when he returned, write the title in a note to himself and stick it in his wallet. Nobody except him could find it. Anyway, this must have been a pretty urgent matter, so he told me the title of the book and the file he wanted.'

Janine paused, then continued. 'I suppose I'm as inquisitive as the next lawyer, but it isn't my style to go sniffing about.' She laughed. 'It's probably why I'm not a criminal lawyer. But looking for the contract Stan wanted I came across one called "Madam Butterfly Pty Ltd". I don't know why I was curious.' She pointed to *Madam Butterfly* in the moonlight at its mooring on the bay. 'Most probably because you'd told me about the boat and why you'd named it. Anyway, I pulled at the tape and opened it. It wasn't too involved and quite short. The company articles established that it operated mainly in the entertainment and property industry. I wasn't all that interested, but it was a nice title for that kind of business; *Madam Butterfly*, the Puccini opera, seemed fairly apt. But reading other documents in the file I realised the company was operating a brothel – or brothels – at the top end of the trade. The address of the property was at the upper end, that's the expensive end, of Spring Street. Then I looked at the shareholders; one of them was the wife of a police superintendent with a ten per cent holding, another was Stan McVitty with fifty-one per cent, and the third was a woman named Anna Til, who had the remainder.'

'Anna Til? It doesn't mean too much, Janine,' I said, perhaps a little dismissively. 'As for the Madam Butterfly – as you said, it's a good name for a brothel,' I laughed. 'Come to think of it, a bloody wonderful name, in fact.'

'Nick, there's more to it. I made a note of the address and retied the file, found the one Stan McVitty wanted and sent it off with one of the firm's messengers. As you know, most legal firms have several private detectives on their books, usually retired police officers who were formerly attached to the CIB or the vice squad. We use them mostly in divorce cases, getting photographs of errant husbands in bed with the wrong partner. It's a profitable part of every law firm's business. I also handle divorce and have got to know one of our "privates", as we call them.' Janine grinned. 'This one is named – appropriately for an ex-police officer in the vice squad – Rusty Weatherall.' She pronounced it 'weather all'. 'Anyway, Mr Weatherall was in for a briefing concerning a Toorak client who suspected her husband had found a girlfriend. I asked him, quite casually, whether he knew about a brothel named Madam Butterfly in Spring Street. He laughed. "Oh yes," he said. "Very classy. Not exactly a brothel; they deal in *kinbaku*."'

Janine cast me a quizzical look, then continued. 'I'd never heard the term. "*Kinbaku?*" I asked Weatherall.

'"Japanese bondage, sexual torture, a sort of Asian twist on what we used to call bondage and discipline," he explained. "Very bloody popular among the silvertails, the judges, lawyers, you know – the high end of town. Why are you asking?" His left eyebrow shot up and he nodded his head towards Stan McVitty's office. "Bit close to home isn't it?" Well, I ignored his implication. "What more do you know about it, Mr Weatherall?" I asked.

'"Not much, its very discreet; whoever's protecting the operators is fairly high up in the force. It's never been raided, never appeared in the papers, not even in the *Truth*. It's run by this woman, Eurasian, tall, an absolute cracker to look at – she's got these amazing violet eyes. They say she's as cold as a nun's tit."

'"Spare me the intimate details, Mr Weatherall," I told him. Then I asked, "Do you know her name?"

'"Yeah, Anna – Anna Til."'

It was the repetition of the name that sparked recognition. I looked open-mouthed at Janine. I admit I was trembling. 'I need a stiff brandy,' I exclaimed. It had suddenly clicked and I could have backhanded myself at my sheer stupidity. Of course. Anna would have lost her papers, or had them confiscated. Coming out of Java as a refugee she could have been anyone she wanted to be. She'd decided to take the name of her old confidant, the *becak* driver, and use it as her own surname as a tribute to her murdered friend. Hence, Anna Til.

I arrived in Melbourne three days later, booking into the Hotel Windsor on Spring Street, opposite Parliament House. I'd arrived in the late afternoon and although the room was comfortable, I confess I endured a near sleepless night. So much was tumbling on the endless conveyor belt that ran through my head.

It had been five years since the end of the war, nearly nine years since I'd watched Anna's tearful farewell as the *Witvogel* pulled away from the shore. I was twenty-six, nearly twenty-seven years old, and about the only thing that resembled the previous Nick – or Nicholas, as she'd insisted on calling me – was that I remained a passionate butterfly collector.

My war had certainly had its occasional hairy moments, but from what I'd heard from Ratih and Kiki, these paled into insignificance compared to hers. Did I have any right to interfere? Renew our teenage relationship? Wasn't I presuming far too much? 'Cold as a nun's tit' kept reverberating through my head.

At dawn I rose and walked to the river and watched the sun rise. Silly with lack of sleep, I found myself silently asking why the Yarra was always brown; it was just one of the crazy thoughts that wouldn't stop racing through my mind. I was almost within a stone's throw of Anna, yet I felt more terrified than I had been at Bloody Ridge.

After breakfast I wrote her a note, several notes, all eventually scrunched then thrown in the wire wastepaper basket. Finally I settled for:

Dearest Anna,
I'd love to see you. May I suggest morning tea tomorrow, say
11 o'clock, in the lounge at the Hotel Windsor?
Sincerely,
Nicholas Duncan

It may seem like a simple enough note, but it had taken an hour to compose. Each word carried a purpose: *Dearest Anna* (friendly), *I'd love to see you* (implies for old time's sake), *May I suggest morning tea tomorrow* (no disaster if you refuse, a tentative and casual arrangement), *say 11 o'clock* (not too firm), *in the lounge at the Hotel Windsor* (sophisticated, worldly, urbane, non-threatening), *Sincerely* (relaxed, non-committal), *Nicholas* (nostalgia), *Duncan* (recall).

I sent the note in an unsealed envelope together with the butterfly handkerchief, handing the goggle-eyed pageboy a pound. 'See that it is received by Miss Til at the address on the envelope and *nobody* else! Wait if you have to,' I instructed somewhat forcibly. With a week's wages in his claw he could only nod, stupefied.

The 20th of September 1950, a beautiful early spring day in Melbourne, brought probably the longest morning of my life. Anna entered the lounge at the Hotel Windsor at one minute to eleven. I had expected her to be late. She was so stunningly beautiful I wanted to cry, to burst into sudden tears.

I jumped to my feet like a schoolboy. 'Anna!' I exclaimed.

'It is you, Nicholas,' she replied, a tiny smile at the corners of her mouth, her violet eyes looking me up and down, inspecting me. 'You are still beautiful,' she said, suddenly laughing.

She reached into her bag and pulled out the Clipper

butterfly in its teak box and placed it in front of me. 'You see, Nicholas?' she said. 'I have never forgotten you.'

In an hour, over a pot of Darjeeling tea, I fell head over heels in love with her again.

I spent the next fortnight in Melbourne, not attending to business needs that should have found me in Canberra and then back in the islands. I kept on receiving frenetic calls from the little bloke, all much the same. 'Wassamatta, Nick, ferchrissakes wha' cha doin' down dere? So yoh found Anna? What we suppose ter do? Wait til ya ain't lovesick no more? We got two contracts, dey both bigger dan da secon' comin'! Yoh gotta get ya sweet ass ter Canberra. Fuckin' place's goin' crazy widout ya.'

Joe called from Honiara, the town built in the Solomon Islands by the American forces. 'Nick, wot cha doin', mah man? Pussy like baked sweet potato, dere ain't never one dat don't taste good. Yoh crazy 'bout dat doll, yoh bring her home, yoh heah?'

During those two weeks I'd make a time to see Anna and she wouldn't turn up, or someone would call (never her) and apologise, saying she was indisposed. But whenever we did get together you could see she loved it. We'd have dinner or lunch and she'd leave obviously feeling great – either that, or she'd become the world's greatest actress.

But she wouldn't allow any intimacy between us. Her greetings and farewell kisses were chaste, to say the least. She physically drew away if I reached out and touched her arm. Anna had lost something important from deep within her. Her beautiful eyes would still sparkle, but if you caught them at an unsuspecting moment they showed a sadness, even sometimes a blankness. The trouble was that at such moments, when she looked vulnerable, she was even more beautiful.

Then Janine de Sax came to see me. 'Nick, Kevin's calling me every day, sometimes twice a day. You know how he is, full of bombast and bluff. But he's genuinely worried about you.'

'Janine, just give me a bit of space, a little more time,' I begged.

'Nick, I have some bad news,' she said suddenly.

'What?' I asked defensively and a little angrily, even rudely I suppose.

'Rusty Weatherall has been making enquiries. Anna is a heroin addict. It's a long-time addiction; she's used the one supplier since she arrived in Melbourne.'

'Oh, Jesus!' I clenched my hands around the broad armrests of the lounge chair. It explained so much of her recent behaviour. 'What will I do? What the fuck will I do now?' I wailed pathetically.

'See the doctor. Get something to calm your nerves,' Janine said quietly.

It had become obvious Anna enjoyed being with me and now I understood why she sometimes cancelled our assignations. I spent another sleepless night and in the morning called Janine. 'Can you find out if there is a specialist who knows something about heroin? One who treats it regularly?' I asked. The missionary in my father was showing in me. He'd always said to me as a child, 'Nicholas, read and inwardly digest; knowledge is power. First find out and understand what is known and only then have you a right to question it. The world is full of ill-informed people making the wrong decisions based on speculative and impulsive information.'

Janine found a professor at the University of Melbourne who had been a biochemist and had then turned to psychiatry, the newest of the medical areas of human study. Surprisingly for a high-ranking academic, she was a female.

Professor Sue Wilson ('Chemicals have a great deal to do with everything, Mr Duncan') was busy, but she agreed to see me. She was tall, slim, blonde and not at all professorial looking, although her manner was politely abrupt. 'What is it you wish to know, Mr Duncan?' she asked moments after I was seated in her office.

'How does one withdraw from heroin addiction?' I replied.

'You, or someone else?'

'Well, yes, someone else,' I said.

'Does he, she, wish to give it up?'

'I'm not sure. Maybe?' I ventured.

'And the cow jumped over the moon! Nonsense!'

'I beg your pardon, Professor?'

'Nonsense!' she repeated. 'He, she, must want to withdraw.'

'I think she does, she just doesn't know how,' I suggested.

'You think she does, or she does?' she asked pointedly.

'I think she does,' I said, guessing.

She sighed and I knew she'd caught me out. 'Mr Duncan, every heroin user I have ever encountered wants to give it up. But there is a peculiar aberration in the brain that is difficult, if not well-nigh impossible to overcome: every heroin addict believes that they need only one more shot to stop the torment and thereafter they'll commence on the road to a certain cure. "Just one more shot" is the mantra of this drug.'

'Well, presuming she does, what's involved; how do I go about helping her?'

'How long has she been addicted?'

'Five years, maybe more.'

'Is she sick?'

'No, I don't think so, just unreliable.'

'Is she injecting?'

'What, into her arms? No, there are no needle marks, or none that I could see, anyway.'

'Is she on the street?'

'No.'

'Has she got the money to buy drugs?'

'Yes.'

'Then she's probably chasing the dragon.'

'Chasing the dragon?' I was beginning to feel very ignorant.

'Smoking heroin, that way she avoids the illnesses associated with injecting the drug.'

'Well possibly, but will she die if she is suddenly withdrawn?'

'No, of course not! And in case you were about to ask, Mr Duncan, unlike alcohol rehabilitation, she won't even need medical supervision.'

'How long before she's free of the drug, Professor?' I sensed she was growing impatient with me.

'There are two answers to that question. The major symptoms that reflect the drug in her body should be over in seven to ten days.' She paused. 'But she's not out of the woods then, a protracted abstinence syndrome will persist, often up to thirty-one weeks.'

'You mean psychologically? Psychological addiction?'

'It's a little more complicated than that, but, yes, the mind is the most powerful factor.'

'Will she, I mean, with the withdrawal symptoms, will she, you know, suffer a lot?'

'What do you think, Mr Duncan? If the cure was a simple matter, then every heroin addict would be clean. Let me list the symptoms of withdrawal for you.'

I was beginning to think she was secretly enjoying answering my questions, putting me in my place. But I could hear my father saying 'Persistence, sheer persistence, will eventually prevail. Knowledge is only gained by curiosity and curiosity is fuelled by persistence.'

'Yes please, Professor, I need to know what to expect.' Why do doctors always assume you're a couple of intellectual levels below them?

She seemed amused. 'I hope you're a strong man, Mr Duncan. Let me begin with what you can see.' She started to count on her left hand, using her forefinger to tap the pad of each finger in turn, then flicking the fingers and thumb on her right hand to continue: 'Dilated pupils, piloerection —'

'Piloerection?' I interrupted.

'Goose bumps,' she said impatiently, then continued, 'watery eyes, runny nose, frequent yawning, tremors, vomiting.' She paused and repeated, 'Vomiting! Nausea, this is the big one, here is where you'll need to be strong.' She continued, 'Shaking, chills, followed by profuse sweating. Those are the symptoms you can *see*,' she concluded.

'And the ones you can't see?' I asked.

'Ah, muscle cramps, stomach cramps, insomnia, panic, diarrhoea, irritability. That's about it,' she said, smiling. 'But once you're over the primary symptoms, you have to battle depression and, more importantly, what I previously mentioned, the certainty in the addict's mind that feeling better is just a single dose away. That is why so many addicts relapse, they know the drug can make them feel better than their present state of mind.'

Whew! It was quite a list.

I tackled Anna the following day about her addiction. At first there was denial, then anger, then tears. 'Nick, you don't understand, I didn't do this on purpose, become an addict.'

'Anna, you can tell me about all that later. What's important now is getting better. Darling, I love you. I always have.'

She was suddenly furious. 'Love? What are you talking about, Nicholas? Where is there love? Show me?'

'Well, for a start, in me, for you.'

'Nicholas, you talk bullshit.' I forgot to mention that Anna now spoke English perfectly and obviously idiomatically, with only the slightest trace of an accent.

'No, Anna, it's not bullshit.'

'Nicholas, you know nothing. You don't know the Japanese. What they did!'

'Well, no, but I killed a few and saved one. Even the Japanese understand love.' I was thinking of Gojo Mura.

'Jesus! Where have you been?' she yelled. 'For fuck's sake!'

'Anna, do you want to get off the shit?'

'I don't know! Yes, yes, yes!' It was then that she started to sob. I held her in my arms for ages, kissing her forehead, her hair, her neck. But all she did was sob against my chest. When she'd recovered a little I put her in a taxi. It was a short ride, we could easily have walked there in ten minutes, but I gave the taxi driver a quid for a two-bob fare. 'See she gets home safely,' I urged.

The following morning I wrote her a note giving her my telegraphic address in Port Vila: 'If you want to try and get clean, come and stay. I love you, Anna.' There didn't seem to be any more I could do or say. I've never felt more miserable or helpless in my life.

A month passed and then one afternoon a telegram arrived: NICHOLAS STOP I BE ON THE AFTERNOON PLANE TUESDAY STOP ANNA. It was a lapse in grammar, the first I'd seen her make.

Tuesday was three days away. I was aware she might change her mind, but I provisioned *Madam Butterfly* for six weeks, then called the little bloke. 'Mate, I haven't taken a holiday for five years, I'm taking six weeks off, going sailing, no way you can reach me, see ya!'

'What about da time yoh spent wit da broad in Melbourne?' he protested.

'Get stuffed, Kevin.'

'Hey, Nick, don't hang up, buddy, I got good news.'

'Yeah?'

'We got dat asshole, da crocodile! Anytime he step outta line we skin him alive an' put da skin on my wall! Dat bondage brothel story – if da newspapers get dat, he's finito. Dat Janine, she tol' me 'bout dat. Now da special good news, buddy – Bren Gun, she pregnant again. Joe Nicholas, he on da way – only seven months ta go!'

I met the plane and to my enormous joy Anna was on it. Her suitcase was about half the size of the tray of my utility. In those days there was no customs inspection and the case was carried to my truck by a sweating porter. Anna waited until she was seated in the cabin before she kissed me. 'Thank you for inviting me to your home, Nicholas,' she said.

I laughed, unable to hide my joy. 'Delighted you could come, Anna.'

Anna dug into her handbag and produced a small box tied with a white ribbon. 'Inside is your butterfly handkerchief and also eighty persimmon seeds. You must sow five immediately, because I am five years behind now. Then, you must sow one seed each year on my birthday. You must promise me, Nicholas.'

I smiled. 'I promise, Anna, but why persimmon seeds?'

'I will tell you some day, not now,' she said quietly.

We arrived at the gates of Beautiful Bay and as we went down the long driveway I suggested, 'Shall we plant one persimmon each year along this driveway? What do you think, Anna?'

She clapped her hands and clasped them to her breast in the same way the old Anna had always done when she was excited. 'Oh, Nicholas, I would like that! I would like that very much.'

'Then it shall be done,' I said, grinning. 'Seventy-five as well as five immediately.'

The cook and the two maids, the three gardeners and the boatman had all been lined up by Ellison on the front steps and were grinning their welcome. 'Oh, what a beautiful house!' Anna exclaimed, getting out as Ellison stepped forward to open the ute door. She walked over and plucked a frangipani blossom and pushed it into her hair.

Ellison lifted the suitcase from the back of the truck and carried it up the steps, placing it on the verandah.

'Anna, I thought you might want to rest for a while and then we might go for a sail at sunset. Do you think you're up to it?'

'Oh yes, I would love that, Nicholas,' she exclaimed.

'Ellison will take your suitcase and Mary, our housemaid, will unpack for you.' I watched Anna's eyes as they darted over to the large suitcase. 'No, no, thank you, that is not necessary, I will do it myself.' I could sense the urgency in her voice.

Ellison knew what to do later after we'd sailed away on

Madam Butterfly. He'd been told, should it prove necessary, to strip the lining of the suitcase to find the heroin I was certain Anna would have brought with her.

Each of the servants, smiling shyly, came up and shook Anna's hand. 'Welcome, madam,' they said. After they departed I instructed Ellison to take the suitcase and place it in Anna's room. Then we climbed the steps onto the front verandah, and Anna turned and looked over the bay to where the cutter was moored. '*Madam Butterfly!*' she screamed, again clapping her hands and clasping them to her bosom in the old familiar Anna way. Then she turned to me, her beautiful eyes serious. 'Oh, Nicholas, I really want to try to give up, you know that, don't you?'

'Yes,' I said quietly. 'Yes, I know. I'll be with you, Anna – every step of the way.'

Anna moved forward and I took her in my arms and kissed her. Then she drew away. 'Nicholas, I have kept my promise. You will be the first,' she said.

At five o'clock we had afternoon tea with a sponge cake the cook had baked. Anna had slept for a couple of hours, showered and was wearing shorts and a blue shirt, a white sweater hung over the back of her chair, as I'd previously warned her that a south-westerly blew in about seven and it could be quite chilly out on the bay. The boatman had brought *Madam Butterfly* up to the landing pier at the bottom of the garden. It was nearing the end of a beautiful day. 'Come,' I instructed. 'The gardeners have prepared the soil, you have five persimmon seeds to plant. They must be approximately ten feet apart. I looked it up in the *Encyclopaedia Britannica*. We've put a small wooden stake at each location.'

Anna planted the persimmon seeds, carefully smoothing

the soil with her palm. She was sobbing softly. They were private tears and so I left to fetch a watering can. Her persimmon seeds would receive their first blessing of water from her hand.

In my mind I went over the inventory. Water tanks full, six weeks' food and drink, spare clothes for Anna (I'd guessed at her size), spare sails, diesel for the engine I'd installed, bedding, headache tablets, anti-nausea tablets (though I'd been told they wouldn't help her), pills to stop diarrhoea (same advice), extra towels, sponges, hand cream, face cream, suntan lotion, toothpaste (six tubes) and toothbrushes. I couldn't think of anything else.

'Oh, Nicholas, I have waited so long to do this!' Anna cried out, still sobbing. I handed her the can and she walked down the driveway, pausing at each wooden marker she held the nozzle over it, baptising the planted seeds. When she'd completed the last she said softly, '*Sayonara, Konoe-san.*'

At six o'clock we walked down to the pier where the beautiful cutter was waiting. I took Anna's hand, saying, 'Here, let me help you aboard.' Anna stepped from the pier onto the scrubbed deck of *Madam Butterfly*. 'Welcome to *Madam Butterfly*, Madam Butterfly,' I said softly, to Anna's scream of delight.

I felt a real bastard. I was lying to her, but I could think of no other way. Anna was my first love – not my only love, but my first. She had taken a shy young butterfly collector and given me the joy of loving a woman, a sense of belonging, of being wanted; she had helped the loner to find that being alone was not the only way. I remembered the first time I'd seen her when she'd come to my door in the *kampong* near *De Kost Kamer*.

I'd seen then a slim, fine-boned girl who was quite tall. She'd worn a simple, light-blue cotton dress, worn off the shoulders, the sleeves slightly puffed and covering the top of her arms, which were the colour of honey in sunlight. Her hair fell just short of her shoulders, was jet black and framed a heart-shaped face. Her lips were full and generous and her cheekbones high; together with her arched eyebrows they seemed to emphasise her incredible eyes that were only slightly almond-shaped and framed in rich dark lashes. Even in the prevailing lamplight they appeared to be a remarkable deep violet colour. When she smiled, my heart had skipped a beat.

Now, on *Madam Butterfly* with the sun beginning to set on Beautiful Bay, my heart was still pounding. *Nicholas, whatever it takes*, I thought to myself. A sudden breeze sprang up, not unexpected but also not necessarily dependable. I'd take a chance and not use the engine. '*Anna, forgive me, darling*', I whispered to myself as I went forward to hoist the mainsail for what I knew would not be six weeks of plain sailing.

POSTSCRIPT

THERE ARE FIFTY-FIVE PERSIMMON trees that line the driveway to Beautiful Bay. Some are grand old trees and when the leaves drop in the dry season and they come to fruit, their golden lanterns shine through the years, a symbol of sweet fecundity. The newest seedling has just popped its head up above the soil. Each year on Anna's birthday, when it's time to plant a new seed, I thank God for her and for having had such a fortunate life.

Nick Duncan, November 2000

Bibliography

Sources
Headquarters, US Marine Corps
United States Marine Corps Historical Monographs,
     Division of Public Information, US Army Historical
     Series
Australian War Memorial, Canberra, Australia–Japan
     Research Project
Australian War Memorial, Canberra, Monographs on the
     Pacific War
Australian War Memorial, Canberra, Collections Database

Books and other publications
Australian Dictionary of Biography, John Ritchie (gen.
     ed.) Vol. 16, 1940–80, Melbourne University Press,
     Carlton, 2002
Campbell, Lloyd, *Z-Special*, Australian Military History
     Publications, Sydney, 2006
Chapman, F. Spencer, *The Jungle is Neutral*, Times Books
     International, Singapore, 1997
Courtney, G. B., *Silent Feet, The History of 'Z' Special
     Operations 1942–1945*, Slouch Hat Publications,
     Melbourne, 2002
Evans, Bernard, *Japan's Blitzkrieg: The Allied Collapse in the
     East*, Pen and Sword Books, London, 2006

Feuer, A. B. (ed.), *Coast Watching in World War 2*, Stackpole Books, Penn., US, 2006

Forrester, Stanform M., 'An introduction to the Poetry of Taneda Santoka', *Simply Haiku*, vol. 3, no. 3, Autumn 2005

Gullett, Henry, *Not as a Duty Only*, Melbourne University Press, Carlton, 1976

McKie, Ronald, *The Heroes*, Angus & Robertson, Sydney, 1960

McKie, Ronald, *Proud Echo*, Angus & Robertson, Sydney, 1953

Parkin, Ray, *Wartime Trilogy*, Melbourne University Publishing, Parkville, 2003

Pfennigwerth, Ian, *The Australian Cruiser* Perth, *1939–42*, Rosenberg Publishing, Sydney, 2007

Russell, Sharman Apt, *An Obsession with Butterflies*, William Heinemann, London, 2003

van der Graaff, Nell, *We Survived*, University of Queensland Press, St Lucia, 1989

Acknowledgements

Increasingly I hear and read that old-fashioned generosity of spirit has largely disappeared. This may well be true in the wider world but, it seems to me, it hasn't yet reached the world of books and writing.

Every novel I write requires a great deal of hard knowledge: facts, dates, people, places, natural phenomena, background, foreground, speculation and intelligent guesswork. No author, least of all this one, can pretend to possess the intimate and specific knowledge required to write a large, wide-ranging story.

In effect, I launch into every new book with my begging cap extended, knowing that without the intellectual donation of others it isn't going to be possible to complete the work.

I am constantly surprised at the generosity of friends and strangers who impart hard-gained knowledge without payment and quite often offer me their further involvement by giving their time and energy.
I thank you all for your help and for sharing what you know with me.
In some small or large part, *The Persimmon Tree* belongs to you as much as it does to me.

I would like to thank John Adamson for his guidance as a grammarian, for his erudition and unfailing dedication. Thanks also to Jessica Wynands for her good scholarship and a clear point of view.

I am grateful to Syria Angina, Yasuko Ando, Tony Crosby, John Forsyth, Tony Freeman, Michael Harrison (Gardner Marine Diesels, UK), Alex Hamill, Marg Hamilton, Celia Jarvis, Christine Lenton, Irwin Light, William McKenzie, Don Thomas, Susan Thomas, Connie Wang and Greg Woon.

Then there are those who played a pivotal role in bringing the novel to fruition and to whom I owe a special thank you. My partner, Christine Gee, worked so hard as my chief co-ordinator as well as performing a hundred other tasks, and kept the flow of information (as well as delicious meals) and encouragement going at all times. Like all authors' partners, she endured months of loneliness downstairs when I frequently worked all day and deep into the night. Her spirit, passion and intelligence are always an inspiration.

Bruce Gee, who acted as my major researcher, constantly astonished me with his depth of knowledge and ability to check and counter-check information. He often worked more hours than I did and always delivered on time. His suggestions on narrative were always sound and frequently inspired. If a book may be said to bear the stamp of good research, then this one should have his name embossed on the front cover. Bruce made every direction I decided to take a possibility, and this novel should bear his imprimatur.

Lee White was my editor and without good editors bad things happen in books. Lee worked under

extraordinarily difficult circumstances connected with
this book and did so uncompromisingly, with both the big
picture and the minutiae always in mind. She is what all
editors should be but seldom are: constantly questioning,
somewhat didactic, usually right, uncompromising,
dedicated to the truth, intolerant of hyperbole and with
the ability to maintain and enhance the author's own
'voice' without intruding on his narrative style. I thank
her for the long hours, consistency of viewpoint and her
patience.

Publishers tend to stay in the background, often
doing the hard yards and expected to perform the
ambiguous roles of headmistress and cheerleader, issue the
rap over the knuckles and soothe the damaged
ego – or to put it into the Australian vernacular, give
the pat on the back and the kick up the arse, both
accompanied by a serene smile. In this regard and in many
others, Rachel Scully is your number-one woman. If she
doesn't deliver, then it's trouble for everyone concerned
with the book, but she always does.

Then there are the workers in the field of dreams,
those numerous people who make a book possible. At
the top of the Penguin pyramid sit Gabrielle Coyne, Bob
Sessions ('Uncle Bob') and Julie Gibbs, who encourage,
reprove, decide and remit. Then there are Alan Jacobs,
who guards the brand name, and Dan Ruffino and Sally
Bateman, who take each new book to market afterwards.
Then, Nicole Brown, Tony Palmer, Deb Brash, Anne
Rogan, Saskia Adams, Jessica Crouch, Ian Sibley,
Lia Kelleners, Fumie Ode-Smith, Carmen de la Rue,

Peter Blake, Louise Ryan and Peg McColl – I thank you all for your hard work, tolerance, persistence, patience and good humour.